# SUCCEEDING at SEX and SCOTLAND
## Or the Case of Louis Morel

# SUCCEEDING at SEX and SCOTLAND
## Or the Case of Louis Morel

*A Tale of Two or More Mysteries*
*Not Excluding the Novelist's Labyrinth*

# Hunter Steele

BLACK ACE BOOKS

First published in 1997 by
Black Ace Books, PO Box 6557, Forfar
DD8 2YS, Scotland

© Hunter Steele 1997

Typeset in Scotland by Black Ace Editorial

Printed in Great Britain by Antony Rowe Ltd
Bumper's Farm, Chippenham, SN14 6QA

A CIP catalogue record for this book
is available from the British Library

ISBN    1–872988–81–4 (Hardback)

ISBN    1–872988–86–5 (Paperback)

The publishers gratefully acknowledge
subsidy from the Scottish Arts Council
towards the production of this book

# ACKNOWLEDGEMENTS

Considerable trouble has been taken to give due credit within the text for short clips and quotes from other works still in copyright. Any remaining omissions or errors which are brought to the publishers' attention will be specifically apologized for and rectified in subsequent editions of the present work.

Translations from the French have been taken, so far as possible, from published versions by professional translators. For quotations from French Immortals such as Rabelais, Stendhal and Maupassant we are indebted to the excellent English translations available in Penguin Classics. Only where no more competent versions were or are available will the reader be doomed to take the present authors' own renderings more or less on trust.

We are grateful to a number of friends and colleagues for reading and commenting on this book at proof stage, and for saving it from an even greater degree of corruption than is inevitable in any published work containing nearly two million bytes of 'information'. Hearty thanks in this regard are particularly due to: Mercedes Clarasó, John and Val Craig, Hannah Crow, Nigel Dennis, Julian and Jane McCormack, and Michael Minden. All typos, anachronisms, stylistic excrescences and other carbuncle boo-boos still seeming to survive are either entirely our own fault or else are absolutely deliberate.

And finally most boundless gratitude is eternally due to that stalwart band of very real contributors so nearly named within the tale, and still undead, and who have not contacted their solicitors yet. Or until they do.

H.S., et al, Angus, May 1997

# SEX CLIPS

One evening [*as the plague raged all around*] one of my associates happened to bring home to supper a Bolognese prostitute called Faustina. The woman was very beautiful, but she was about thirty. However she had with her a little maid of about thirteen or fourteen. As Faustina belonged to my friend I would not have touched her for all the gold in the world. Although she declared that she was madly in love with me I never betrayed my friend's trust. But when they went to bed I had the little maid, who was as fresh as fresh; and it would have been worse for her if her mistress had known it. I had a wonderful time that night and was much more satisfied than I would have been with Faustina.[1]

*Unaffectedness* is extremely important. It is the only coquetry permissible in something as serious as a love like that of *Werther*, when all sense of direction is lost. At the same time, by a happy coincidence, it is the best tactic. All unsuspectingly, a man who is really in love says the most delightful things, and speaks in a language unknown to him.[2]

Chimpanzee testicles are six times larger than those of a gorilla, even though their bodies are only one-third the size . . .

It is interesting that, while chimps can mount, thrust, ejaculate and dismount in about seven seconds, gorillas are much more leisurely, and may take up to twenty minutes to do the same. By the time copulation takes place, the dominant adult male gorilla has already succeeded in eliminating the competition. He did so when he originally gained control of the group — and its females.[3]

---

[1] Early 16th century. Italy. From Benvenuto Cellini's *Autobiography*. Penguin translation by George Bull.

[2] Early 19th century. France. From *De l'Amour* by Stendhal. Penguin translation by Gilbert and Suzanne Sale.

[3] Late 20th century. U.S.A. From *Sociobiology: The Whisperings Within* by David Barash.

# SCOTLAND EPICGRAPHS

So long as a hundred of us are left alive, we will yield in no least way to English dominion. We fight not for glory nor for wealth nor honours; but only and alone we fight for freedom, which no good man surrenders but with his life . . . *[And so]* We pray you to admonish the King of England (to whom his own possessions may well suffice, since England of old was enough for seven Kings or more) that he should leave us in peace in our little Scotland, since we desire no more than is our own, and have no dwelling-place beyond our borders; and we on our part, for the sake of peace, are willing to do all within our power . . .

*[Be warned, however, that]*

If too readily, or insincerely, you put your faith in what the English have told you, and continue to favour them, to our confounding, then indeed shall slaying of bodies, yea and of souls, and all those evils which they shall do to us, or we to them, be charged to your account.

(*From the Declaration of Arbroath, 1320, translation by Agnes Mure Mackenzie, God and the Pope abandoned by ourselves.*)

Corruption is so entirely disowned by all men, that I may be allowed to say, when I name it, that I name the blackest of crimes; and when I name any guilty of it, I name a very odious criminal. But corruption is more or less dangerous in proportion to the stations in which corrupt men are placed. When a private man receives any advantage to betray a trust, one or a few persons may suffer; if a judge be corrupted, the oppression is extended to greater numbers; but when legislators are bribed, or (which is all one) are under any particular engagement, that may influence them in their legislative capacity, much more when an entire state of parliament is brought under those circumstances, then it is that we must expect injustice to be established by a law, and all those consequences which will inevitably follow the subversion of a constitution, I mean, standing armies, oppressive taxes, slavery; whilst the outward form only of the ancient government remains to give them authority. (*Andrew Fletcher of Saltoun, 'The First Discourse . . . ', 1698, ed. David Daiches 1979.*)

The Scots and English are different races, according to an industrial tribunal which has decided that a senior police officer's claim of racial discrimination can be considered. (*The Scotsman, 27 March 1997.*)

# NOVEL IDEAS

Among other good uses for which I have thought proper to institute these several introductory chapters, I have considered them as a kind of mark or stamp, which may hereafter enable a very indifferent reader to distinguish, what is true and genuine in this historical kind of writing, from what is false and counterfeit. Indeed it seems likely that some such mark may shortly become necessary, since the favourable reception which two or three authors have lately procured for their works of this nature from the public, will probably serve as an encouragement to many others to undertake the like. Thus a swarm of foolish novels, and monstrous romances will be produced, either to the great impoverishing of booksellers, or to the great loss of time, and depravation of morals in the reader; nay, often to the spreading of scandal and calumny, and to the prejudice of the characters of many worthy and honest people. (*Tom Jones*, Book IX, Chapter 1.)

When bad weather began to confine me to my house, I tried to resume my indoor occupations; I found it impossible. I saw nothing anywhere but the two charming girl friends, their man, their surroundings, and the country they lived in, nothing but objects created or embellished for them by my imagination. I was no longer master of myself even for a moment, the delirium never left me. After many vain efforts to banish all these fictions from my mind I was in the end altogether seduced by them, and my only occupation was to try and impose some order and sequence upon them, to turn them into a sort of novel. (Rousseau's *Confessions*, Book Nine – 1757. Penguin translation by J.M. Cohen. The sort-of novel was *Julie*.)

It is the duty of any novelist worth the salt on his porridge to publish at least once in his career a novel which critics might wish to retitle *The Ultimate Unfilmable Novel*. (Wringhim Knox, in his 'Chief Work', forthcoming.)

'I hope,' the Golux said, 'that this is true. I make things up, you know.' (From *The Thirteen Clocks* by James Thurber.)

11

# Contents

## Part IV – Succeeding at Sex Itself

# Contents

*This book is dedicated to*

The memory of my mother, Katharine Steele
Who would have detested much of it
And supported all of it

And the celebration of my father, Mungo Steele
Who has not doggedly devoured many other
768-page works of densely packed 'fiction'
In recent years, let alone endorsed them

And the moral enrichment and perfection
Of my goddaughters, Hannah and Rachel—
May they dip and paddle a little herein
Before stampeding to breed

*Part I*

# Let's break the rules

# *1*

# Trailers

George Payne Rainsford James is no longer a name to conjure with. Recently we examined a lunchtime gathering of English lecturers at StrathKelvin University on their familiarity with lesser-known nineteenth century novelists. All the academics had read something by, or at least knew a little about, such writers as Charles Lever and Harrison Ainsworth; but none had heard of James.

'Don't you mean Henry?' was one response.

Yet G.P.R. James was one of the most prolific authors in a most prolific century – surely one of the few whose publishers regularly begged him to write less.

'Why is it', the young lion complained in a letter to his literary friend Allan Cunningham, in 1833, 'that I write too fast for that slow beast the Public? Is it because I rise earlier? or because I do it every day and cannot do without it? There are four and twenty hours in the day, are there not? Seven for sleep, four for dressing and feeding, four for reading, five for exercise and pleasure, and four for writing. I cannot write less than five pages in an hour, which gives at the above calculation six thousand pages in a year of three hundred days; and let me tell you, if either you or I were to publish half as much the world would cry Hoo! hoo!'

So severe were the embarrassments occasioned by his productivity that he regularly attempted, in public, to play down his own output. But the record speaks for itself. 1847, for example, witnessed the publication of *The Castle of Ehrenstein*; *Russell, a Tale of the Reign of Charles II*; *The Convict*; *A Whim and its Consequences*; and *The Life of Henry the Fourth of France* – each a three-volume work.

And then a relaxing year off?

On the contrary:

In 1848 James produced *Gowrie, or the King's Plot*; *Camaralzaman: a Fairy Drama*; *Margaret Graham, a Tale Founded on Facts*; *The Last of the Fairies*; and *Sir Theodore Broughton* (a novel based on the murder of Sir Theodosius Boughton by John Donellan, in Warwickshire, in 1781).

How to explain this phenomenal industry? In an autobiographical preface, James admits:

'I am an early riser [often at 5 a.m.]; and any one who has that habit must know that it is a grand secret for getting through twice as much as lazier men can perform . . . Then, again, the habit of dictating instead of writing with my own hand, which I first attempted at the suggestion of Sir Walter Scott, relieves me of the manual labour which many authors have to undergo, leaves the mind clear and free to act, and affords facilities inconceivable to those who have not tried it . . . I think all these circumstances may account for my being able to produce more than many others, without the works themselves being either better or worse on that account. However that may be, the public, which judges for itself, has judged favourably of my productions.'

That was true.

For many years James was one of Britain's top-selling novelists, and when his vogue at home began to wane he removed to the United States and achieved similar success there. When Thackeray visited the New York sanctum of James Harper, and asked him to name the best-selling author in the United States, the famous publisher replied:

'George Payne Rainsford James heads the list, far ahead of any other author . . . He turns out a novel every six months, and the success is always the same and tremendous.'

When Thackeray sought the secret of James's magic, Harper promptly opined:

'The main reason is that his romances can always be safely placed upon the family table, with the certainty that no page will sully, or call the blush to, the cheek of any member of the household.'

Here, in our opinion, is the first clue as to why James is now unread – the most recent British edition of any of his works, according to the Scottish National Library computer, being *The Smuggler*, reissued by Nelson Classics in 1914. It is not just that James's romances are inoffensive (where, after all, is the offence in Dickens?), but rather the sententiously prunelike desire to edify and uplift, *without regard to either historical or moral truth*, that – though the mores of the day lapped him up – has helped tip James into oblivion.

His attitude was honestly confessed – that he looked:

'More to the benefits to be produced to society by combining amusement with moral instruction . . . to improve and elevate the human mind, and to purify and ennoble the heart.'

Even worse, in his preface to *The Ancient Régime*:

'I judged it impracticable to remove the period of the story into any other reign than that of Louis XV, although the insane debaucheries of his latter years rendered the monarch's court the last which one would willingly depict. I trust, however, that in those passages where the scene is laid in Paris or Versailles, nothing will be found which can offend the most delicate mind; and I am certain that not a word can be discovered which has a tendency, directly or indirectly, to encourage vice, or which has for its object any thing but the promotion of that high and holy philosophy which came from God, and leads man to him.'

And what could be more sanctimoniously despicable than that?

James, in a word, was a novelist for the Thatchers and the Whitehouses, and that is one good reason why posterity has abandoned him. Another is his appalling prose – inundated with mannerism, cliché, prolixity, tautology and repetition – for which the sharper critics of his own day had abandoned him already. One such, in *The Athenaeum*, wrote:

'The first and most obvious contrivance for the attainment of quantity is, of course, dilution; but this recourse has practically its limit, and Mr James had reached it long ago. Commonplace in its best day, anything more feeble, vapid – *sloppy*, in fact (for we know not how to characterize this writer's style but by some of its own elegancies) – than Mr James's manner has become, it were difficult to imagine. Every literary grace has been swamped in the spreading marasmus of his style.'

We are not always great lovers of critics ourselves, but here we have to concur. And if we trawl for the roots of James's terminal logorrhoea, we cannot ignore the means of production of which he was so innocently proud: the practice of dictating to a secretary, of which Maunsell B. Field recalls:

'When James was dictating he always kept a paper of snuff upon the table on which his secretary wrote, and he would stride up and down the room, stopping every few minutes for a fresh supply of the titillating powder. He never looked at the manuscript, or made any correction except on the proof sheets . . . '

This arrogant dereliction of self-scrutiny, combined with the cheery lack of wit often found in early risers of Protestant-Ethic persuasion, was largely responsible for there being never a virtuous maiden in James's romances that is not 'sweet and fair'; never a cavalier hero who is not

gallant,[1] honourable, and given to falling into long solitary spells of
deep thought on the back of some solitary game steed, in some solitary
wilderness valley. So that the prospect of a morally complex protagonist
allowing his rising excitement to press (albeit, decently, through his hose
and her chemise) upon the heroine he has rescued from ravishers, and a
heroine with physical appetites of her own, to boot – for James it was
literally unthinkable.

So why mention James at all?

One reason is that he doesn't on all counts deserve the obscurity he
has achieved. In character – apart from a natural resentment of malicious
reviewers, especially anonymous ones – James was unusually warm,
generous, loyal, courageous, and given to wishing nothing but good
fortune and success on his brother novelists. This latter quality seems
to us sufficiently unique to merit a PhD thesis all by itself.

James's life, too, was more colourful and eventful than many: from his
boyhood acquaintance with Byron; through his enlistment in the army
at the age of barely fourteen; his arrival at Waterloo a day too late to
be killed in battle; extensive early wanderings in Europe – particularly
France, which he loved, and whose language he spoke and read like a
native; friendship with Sir Walter Scott, whose encouragement launched
James's literary career; conspicuous success, fame and fortune; valuable
contributions towards the Copyright Act of 1842; adventures in America,
of which he wrote, 'This is a very wonderful country, and no Englishman that I know of has done justice to it'; intercourse with writers
such as Washington Irving, Longfellow and Nathaniel Hawthorne; and
admirable forbearance in his later years, when reduced popularity and
affluence decided him to become British Consul in Virginia, and, finally,
Venice, where he died in 1860.

The only biography of James known to us (*The Solitary Horseman*,
by Stewart Marsh Ellis) was published in 1927. Though it is valuable
as a compendium of information (and we gratefully acknowledge that
many of the present facts are drawn from it), it is rather dated, unbalanced
and downright weak as a biography; lapsing, latterly, into protracted
quotations from a manuscript autobiography by one of James's sons.
Isn't there, then, a critical biographer, perhaps at some university in
Britain or America today, who could do James juster justice?

---

[1] In the English sense. Never the French.

As a historian, too, James is worth a reassessment.

In recognition of his *History of the Life of Edward the Black Prince* (1836, dedicated to the Princess Victoria) James was appointed Historiographer Royal to William IV. This status was evidently continued after William's death, for the title page of James's *Life and Times of Louis the Fourteenth* (1838) describes the author as 'Historiographer in Ordinary to Her Majesty'. James was a voracious reader, he had a phenomenal memory, and his serious historical works are much better written than his novels. An indication of his conscientiousness as historian is that publication of his *Life of Henry the Fourth of France* (1847) was postponed to enable the author to compare his work with *Les Lettres Missives* due to be published by the French government. In James's life of Henri IV, when we personally were researching a novel of our own set in sixteenth-century France,[2] we found much invaluable material, some of it not related by any of the other British or French authorities we consulted.

But perhaps the best reason for giving G.P.R. James a posthumous plug today is that, but for him, you would not be reading this book now.

Having already, in factoidal fashion, dealt with France during the fifty years to 1618, and toying with the possibility of a sequel, I became fascinated by the character and behaviour of Cardinal Richelieu, and especially his relationship with Louis XIII. This interest in due course brought me to James's romance *De l'Orme*, and within minutes I knew I was on the trail of something extraordinary.[3] I already knew James's novels are invariably based on some dramatic episode in history (preferably set in France), with the steamy bits excised, a formula superstructure of callow romance plugged on, and a naff larding throughout of priggish do-goodery. So the interest, for me, was that James knew his history so well that some of his stories remain exciting even despite his dismal telling. I doubt if I shall engage him again myself, and so am happy to recommend his services to any other novelists, screenwriters, etc, keen to explore what a period costume-drama can be made to say about today.

Anyway, *De l'Orme*, I was quickly convinced, belonged in a class

---

[2] *The Counts of Mount Venus*. Contaminated by less untruth than most novels.

[3] 'Surely sharp-eyed Hispanists will claim to be whiffing Cide Hamete Benegeli already – ?' [P.C.]

of its own. Many of the James trademarks, mannerisms and clichés were present, but not in the same way, and not in the same concentration. Whereas the standard James mode is a classic (or hackneyed) pontification by an omniscient narrator (Novels by The Top Monad, as Leibnitz might have put it), here was a more intimate telling, told by a first-person voice.

Or voices?

Within moments of reaching the action set in Sedan, I strongly suspected that what James had done in *De l'Orme* was bolt together a number of original documents and memoirs, and give them, so to speak, a thin finishing coat of voice-over – like margarine on fresh granary bread, it was enough to spoil the original flavour, but not disguise it entirely. First corroboration of this theory came from James's characterization of the Count of Soissons, which is lifted wholesale out of the memoirs of the Cardinal de Retz, who writes:

'The Count had not one grain of this discerning faculty [judgement], which is but seldom to be met with in the sublimest genius. His character was mean to a degree, and consequently susceptible of unreasonable jealousies and distrusts . . . '

But how many other voices?

And how to identify the speakers?

My next step was to scan the entire text of *De l'Orme* on to my computer, correct it with a number of purification utilities developed for more commercial purposes, and then subject it to Style Analysis. Precise results varied, but their general tenor was the same: *De l'Orme* was an amalgam of several styles, but with one distinct voice dominating the first twenty-three chapters, then breaking off, then resuming towards the end.

Was James himself the dominant voice?

To test this I now scanned two of his English romances, and ran a detailed comparative analysis. Here my three programs were unanimous. *The King's Highway* and *Forest Days*, they assured me, were by the same writer. *De l'Orme*, in its grammatical and semantic handwriting, was so different that it must have been written by at least three other writers.

And yet it hadn't!

It had been written, or at least published, by James.

So what kind of evidence were the analysis programs focusing upon?

One of James's signature tunes is a fondness for repeating exclamatory dialogue. Thus, '"We will watch him; we will watch him!" exclaimed Guy de Margan', in *Forest Days*. Compare with '"Bring her along! bring her along!" cried another voice', in *The King's Highway*. Yet of this bad habit *De l'Orme* is . . . not entirely free, but almost. Similarly with 'a thousand'. James, in full flood, would never allow a character to say 'Thank you'. 'Thank you very much' was also inadequate, and real gratitude had to be expressed as 'A thousand thanks!' or even, not infrequently:

'A thousand thousand thanks, kind sir!'

Again, though not untouched by such epidemic waffle, *De l'Orme* was thus blemished *so much less* than the other texts I examined that I soon began to wonder:

Could it be an effect of translation?

That the accents and overtones of James in *De l'Orme* were the result of some original French memoir having been processed through James's rapidly pacing, freely translating, guffing-up and bowdlerizing-down, and furiously snuff-sniffing brain?

Almost in the same instant, though, I was assailed by doubts:

How far might my computer results, and the hypotheses based upon them, be distorted by input bias born of my undeniable overriding preference: that here be the basis of something genuinely remarkable, hence ripe for conversion into a publishable faction?

Hoping to counter any such warping tendency of my own enthusiasm, I next pass the disks of the three scanned romances to a friend of a friend in the computer science department at StrathKelvin – an expert on the establishment and interpretation of textual clusters.[4]

All I say, so as not to prejudice the outcome, is:

'I'm particularly interested in one of these texts. Please give all three a good grilling, from as many angles as you have time for, and let me know what comes up.'

The chapter files are then siphoned off my disks, on to the university's mainframe, and interrogated by a relentless concordance program written specially for the pursuit of Shakespeare.

Three weeks later the postman delivers a fat printout of the results. Yes, *De l'Orme* is different: almost certainly a nineteenth-century English translation from seventeenth-century French. Yes, even through

---

[4] And a world authority on whether or not Shakespeare really did not write *Titus Andronicus*.

the clothing of the translation, a number of distinct voices can be distinguished. Yes, there is one dominant voice. No, that voice is not consistent throughout; possibly the same voice, in the earlier and later chapters, belongs to the same speaker at different stages, or perhaps in significantly different circumstances, of 'his or her' life.

Bingo.

But whither now?

Who was De l'Orme, and where were the original documents?

The week before Easter I flew off to Paris, tingling with sunny optimism, and spent the next three days flat out in the Bibliothèque Nationale.

Zilch.

The only remotely relevant De l'Orme (variously spelt) I could unearth was one Marion, who cropped up in a surprising number of beds, and who is typically described in Cardinal de Retz's account of Cardinal Richelieu's love-life:

'Marion de Lorme, one of his mistresses, was little better than a common prostitute. Another of his concubines was Madame de Frugues, that old gentlewoman who was so often seen sauntering in the enclosure. The first used to come to his apartment in the daytime, and he went by night to visit the other, who was but the pitiful cast-off of Buckingham . . . '[5]

As the doors of the Bibliothèque Nationale closed behind me for Easter, I even ventured to wonder, in my frustration, whether James might have hoodwinked his public with a rather fiendish hoax: transposing the sex of the strumpet Marion, and cooking her into a palatable cavalier whom even Victorian maidens might admire with nary a blush?

But no, I concluded, sitting gloomily outside a Boulevard café, watching all the girls go by, and gingerly sipping possibly the most expensive Carlsberg in the world. James would never attempt any-

---

[5] George Villiers, 1592–1628. First Duke of Buckingham. Gaveston to James I of England, who lovingly called him 'my Steenie'. Cf Alexendre Dumas (père), several musketeers, Richard Lester, Faye Dunaway, etc. Did Buckingham actually get to tup Anne of Austria (Mrs Louis XIII) or not? This is a crucial question, so please bear it in mind throughout the present work.

thing so risqué, and, though thoroughly amiable, he simply hadn't the wit.

Exit Marion de Lorme.

'Where is the story set?' my hostess, at dinner that night, sympathetically inquired.

'All over France, and northern Spain, but it kicks off in the Pyrenees.'

'In Béarn?'

'Why, yes.'

'Near Pau?'

'Not far. Just a few miles from Lourdes, in fact.'

'Have you done your location research?' asked my old friend from Edinburgh, who now runs a translation bureau in Paris.

'Not yet.'

'Well . . . '

Now, over cheese and a vintage Bordeaux, it all begins to jell. Michael and Laura know the area intimately, as her parents have a holiday home south of Pau. When I explain the background, and spell out 'De l'Orme', they with one voice exclaim:

'Morel!'

And that was it.

Even James was capable of an anagram, and – when the libraries reopened the following week – two hours of further beavering in the Bibliothèque Nationale gave me a reference which led to the Cabinet des Grandes Tromperies Historiques, and there, later that afternoon, in a basement vault the KGB could have been proud of, closely supervised by two nicotinely moustachioed and disturbingly muscular members of the Cabinet's security staff, I was presented with a trolley piled high with leather-bound old volumes, the third of which contained the two books – limited editions published privately in Geneva in 1704 – of Louis Morel's memoir fragments, and the complete text of his death-cell confession.

My next problem was how to capture this elusive text, since the Cabinet des Tromperies' security, combined with traditionally French suspicion of foreigners, was so stringent that, not only were photocopying and microfilming clear nonstarters, but even my notes were officiously scrutinized at the end of every day, to ensure no verbatim copying of the works consulted. Fortunately this flunkey paranoia did not extend to the frisking of my person, and my eventual solution, undignified but effective, was to dictate the texts sotto voce, under cover of random notes clattered out in the privacy of a typing cell, on to a microcassette-recorder smuggled in my under-wear.[6]

So, back to Scotland with the recorded texts to transcribe and edit, and with the additional challenge of where to get the information not provided by the Morel memoirs – incurably turgid at worst; bittily staccato at best – and not covered by his death-cell confession. In particular, how best to portray the run-up to the battle of La Marfée and the killing of the Count of Soissons?

---

[6] This procedure, so far as we are aware, involves no legal breach of rights, and, though we apologize to the bureaucrats at the Cabinet for having to some extent deceived them, we would also hope that the interest of the outcome – the book you are presently reading – may argue for a more liberal attitude to alien scholars attempting research in Paris in the future. Meanwhile the true identity of this most officious satellite of the Bibliothèque Nationale has been discreetly masked. This is partly for the protracted avoidance of irreverent retributions, but also for the sake of spayning you literary supersheep sleuths from those out-and-out rampant goats.

# 2

# A Welcome Birth?

Morel's memoir fragments are most informative concerning his childhood, and increasingly peppered with lacunae as his life grows more mysterious – and the morality of his own behaviour more questionable. As a prose writer he was pedestrian at best, and a protracted literal translation of his relatively detailed early pages might expose the narrator to accusations of having told the story in a somewhat humourlessly fustian style reminiscent of the later Sir Walter Scott – not to mention his umpteen inferior imitators.

Thus:

'I was born in 1619,' Morel records, 'in the mountainous principality of Béarn, which, stretching along the northern Pyrenees, interposes between France and Spain a gigantic bulwark, scarcely broken but by narrow and difficult passes.

'On the French side, the dwelling of my father, Roger, Count Morel, was perched high upon a hill, about two leagues from Lourdes, and looked far over a most fantastic scene below.

'The wide valley, with its rich carpet of verdure in summer, the river smashing in a spray of white diamonds through the rocks in winter, the long far windings of the deep purple mountains, filling my young mind with vague but grand imaginings; the majestic shadows of dark forests like black mantles round the shoulders of the peaks; the intricate disappearing perspective of the passes towards Cauteratz; and the Pont d'Espagne, with the Vigne Malle towering icily beyond . . . '

And so he goes on at considerable length.

Much undelightful descriptive detail dilates – possibly of some service to casual browsers who have never yet visited Lourdes but already give credence to its miracles.

Of more interest to the serious reader will be the extent to which Louis Morel appears ahead of his age in the heartfelt (if undoubtedly cumbersome) appreciation of Nature to which he gives voice. The response of sixteenth- and even seventeenth-century intelligences (as it took no less a twentieth-century intelligence than Ernest Tuveson's to point out) to impressions of the great and wild in Nature was typically revulsion and terror.[1] Despite the enraptured confusion of a few seventeenth-century English divines such as Thomas Burnet – whose delirium derived much from a somewhat hazy grasp of the Newtonian cosmology and its implications for metaphysics – there is little doubt that aesthetic veneration for the Mighty and Awesome in Nature was never theoretically systematic, or even casually commonplace, before Addison's comfortable encapsulations in his *Spectator* essays on 'The Pleasures of the Imagination' – in the early eighteenth century. Consider, for instance, *Spectator* No. 413, in which it emerges that for Addison the *Beautiful* corresponds to enormously less important aspects of the moral world than does the *Immense*. This is because:

'When we look at the vastness of the heavens or at the expanse of the sea, we look upon no mere "supernumerary ornaments," but upon the very image, so far as we can comprehend it, of God Himself, in His extended omnipresence.'

And though it may savour of old hat to us, it is characteristically maverick of the man that, in the nostalgic delectation of sensibility with which Louis Morel recalls the 'fantastic scene below', the 'river smashing in a spray of white diamonds . . . ', and so forth, he is in his implicit theory nearly one century, and in his impulsive emotive romanticism perhaps more like two centuries, in advance of his contemporaries' aesthetics. Could not Mary Shelley, indeed, have penned those very words?

Not even when at last he homes in on the particulars of his family situation can a faithful rendering lend Morel the semblances of vigilant self-snipering irony and linguistic pyrotechnomania which are taken as *de rigueur* in a fashionable novel of the 1990s.

Thus:

'The château in which my eyes first opened was little smaller than the castle of Lourdes, yet vastly too large for the few retainers that my

---

[1] Cf Tuveson's 'Space, Deity, and the "Natural Sublime"', *Modern Languages Quarterly*, Vol. 12, 1951. See also R.W. Hepburn, 'Aesthetic Appreciation of Nature', *British Journal of Aesthetics*, Vol. 3, No. 3, 1963.

father's reduced finances could support. Our diminished household must have seemed, within such immense mediaeval walls, like a shrunken old miser, clad still in the broad and lavish garments of his youth; and yet my fond parent insisted upon as much pomp and ceremony as his own father had kept up with a hundred servants.

'Still the trumpet blew for dinner, though the broken-lunged maître d'hôtel could squeeze but a hollow croak from the brass. Still all the domestics – five in all, including the gardener and the cook – must assemble by the staircase, in unstarched ruffs and tarnished liveries of green and gold, while my father, slow and solemn, escorted my mother down to dinner. Still would Father talk of his seigneurial rights, though his domain scarce covered one thousand hectares of mountainside, and of his vassals – of whom hardly any remained. However, the banners still hung in the hall; and it was impossible to gaze upon the turrets, pinnacles and battlements of our old castle, without some attendant image of the power and influence that the lord of such a fortress must possess. Thus, even Father himself was able to forget the decay of his house, and fancy himself great as his ancestors.'

On the surface, you could say, it's like *Gormen* without the *ghast*. A sense of decline and decay abounds, there's a plentiful subtext of mildew and cobwebs, and yet . . . the more one wrestles with the ponderous woodenness of Morel's phrases – a stodginess really quite hard to achieve in seventeenth-century French – the more convinced one inevitably becomes of an extra dimension of meaning lying concealed, not so much between the lines as between the very words. Of Roger Morel, for example, he writes, and still we translate literally:

> In character my father was liberal to a fault, physically courageous, kind, humanely sympathetic, and yet – at the same time he was invincibly lazy, and could endure nothing that gave him trouble. The wars of the League,[2] in my grandfather's time, had gradually lopped branch after branch off our estates, and hewn deeply into the trunk. My father, alas, was not the man, either by active enterprise or

---

[2] Ie the tripartite struggle for domination which ruined France in the later sixteenth century: between the Crown, the Catholic League, and the Huguenots. Cf *The Counts of Mount Venus*, chapters 1–32.

by court intrigue, to mend the failing fortunes of his family. On the contrary, after two campaigns, and having distinguished himself in several battles, out of pure lassitude he retired to Château Morel, there to spend the rest of his days, never undertaking a longer journey than to Pau; and forming in his solitude a multitude of glorious schemes, which all fell to nothing in a moment, like the castles of cards that children build, which the least new breeze must topple down.

As to his mother:

> The only failings her young son perceived were a strong streak of family pride – which made her, at times, sharply sensitive to our straitened circumstances – and occasional passionate bouts of impatience with my indolent father. For the rest she was goodness and generosity incarnate, as many a poor begging soul could testify, who had received lavish alms from her hands.

Now call us cynics if you will, but I rapidly became convinced – and this was on the basis of Morel's testimony alone, before I had uncovered evidence adducible from other documents – that what, at some level of consciousness, he was attempting to portray was his father as a terminally impotent wimp, and his mother as a chronically frustrated go-getter with a seething passion for life, attention and bonking, which her husband could never satisfy.

And what could be more corroborative of such lustful suspicion than the purely cosmetic whitewash of the following three paragraphs?

'A willing aid to my mother's benevolence was Father Francis, our chaplain. For many years he had tended the souls of the little village of Allurdi, in the Val d'Ossau, but his sight and strength both failing, he had made way for a younger curé, and brought as gentle a heart, and as pure a spirit, as ever tenanted mortal frame, albeit a superstitious one, to dwell within Château Morel.

'Such, then, was the household awaiting my birth, which was unmarked by any peculiarity save that my mother had till then remained childless throughout eight full years of marriage. The joy and devout thanksgiving which attended so late a birth, of a longed-for heir, and a son besides, were profound and prolonged, and meanwhile more corporeal and bibulous celebrations than for many a year echoed loud in the great hall, and even louder in the servants' parlour.

'My father declared I should infallibly retrieve the fortunes of my house; Father Francis, glad tears in his eyes, proclaimed me a blessing from Heaven; and my mother, weak but radiant, was beside herself with bliss.'

'*Baldertish!*' murmured I.

For *why* had his mother remained childless during those eight years?

Was his father really his father?

And if not, who was?

# 3

# First Brush with Death

One of the puzzles to challenge any student of Louis Morel is: who did he intend his memoirs to be read by? There is about them, in the early pages, a sense of self-conscious literary endeavour – a constrained striving to impress the reader with felicities of style – which is singularly at odds with what we intuit of Morel's personal character, and which hence suggests that, whoever his target audience was, he was bent (certainly on some level of awareness) on deceiving it. Nowhere is this more manifest than in his narration of the following events.

I was an only child [*he records*]. My father spoiled me, and my education suffered in consequence. From Father Francis I grudgingly acquired, in approximately equal measure, a rudimentary knowledge of Latin and Greek, the basics of mathematics, and a hundred antiquated fancies which he expounded with infinite reverence, under the name of Philosophy.

My corporeal instruction, however, Father took upon himself, and as his laziness was of mind rather than body, he taught me thoroughly, from my very infancy, all the skills he deemed essential to the perfect cavalier. I could ride, shoot, fence and wrestle before I was twelve years old, and these martial lessons were quick to strengthen a frame and muscles already robust by natural endowment, and a constitution resistant to disease. Only in my inability to swim was I left, as it were, with a heel like the young Achilles, as my father had a horror of water.

The springy vigour of my body, combined with a fiery imagination, invested my youth with a mad passion for adventure, and appetite for danger. To scale the steepest rocks, explore the deepest caverns, to gaze from a dizzy precipice to the spuming cataract below, till my eyes watered over and my ears were numbed as by thunder – such were the solitary enjoyments of my youth, which doubtless rendered my every absence from our home a quiet torture for my mother.

I will pass over a host of the minor mishaps which befall every grow-ing boy, save for one which occurred when I was not long twelve, and whose consequences would catastrophically alter the envisaged pattern of my life.

One fine clear morning, strangely pensive on so summery a day, I went strolling along a deep ravine, that wound up far into the mountains. I knew the walk well, and proceeded almost unconsciously, with scarcely a glance at the profusion of wild flowers, and trees of every hue, that flourished among the rocks.

The path followed a high ridge in the cliff overhanging the river, on a level with the glistening knuckles of a substantial cascade, which fell to a deep black pool, by the side of which was an old stone mill, constructed to be driven by the falling water's power. Now the clacking of the mill-wheel, its staccato rhythm beneath the roar of the river falling, all mingling with the mountainous grandeur of the scenery above and beyond, appeared, I cannot say why, to have intoxicated my romantic young senses, with such a potency of vertiginous reverie, that before I could regain control of myself I had swooned, hit the back of my head on a sharp projection from the rocky ledge, and was pitched headlong into mid-air, thence to plummet like a discarded doll the height of many men to the mill-pool below.

The winding shock as I hit the water, the rasping desperation as the ripples closed over my head, the agony of regret at this consequence of my own reckless folly – I relive them all as vividly now as if the event itself happened but yesterday. Plunged by the height of my fall to the very floor of the pool, I managed once to kick upward enough for my head to surface for one piercing yell. My only hope was that the miller might hear me, but in an instant I realized that my shout, no matter how loud, could never carry past the mill-wheel's constant clatter, and the waterfall's roar above. Thus, struggle and thrash as I might, yet, my father never having taught me to swim, I felt utterly abandoned, and, as my flailing arms weakened, and my gasps for breath gave way to gulps of water, I felt surely doomed to drown, and how well I remember wondering, in an instant of feeble indignation: when would the fabled story of my life parade, in images like dreams, before my dying eyes?

Instead I experienced a suffocation as if my chest must burst, a violent hammering in my ears, and a flashing of fire like battle gunnery in my brain. Yet this quickly faded, and now a detached but not unpleasant sensation came over me, as one might feel if strolling wearily, but still contentedly, through green pastures in autumn twilight. The fear and the struggle were over, and my consciousness vanished.

My next awareness was of a painful burning throughout my body, most of all in my heart, accompanied by a feeling of floating, I knew not where, and the certainty that I was blind. In the background was an indistinct buzzing, like wild bees in a distant wood, and when my eyes suddenly opened of their own accord I found myself lying in a sparsely furnished room in the mill, with a circle of anxious faces gazing down at me; including, I slowly recognized, the wide pocked nose of our old maître d'hôtel, and the smooth kind countenance of Father Francis.

My father too was there, as I realized when, perceiving that I should live, he sank to his knees with a groan, and addressed tearful thanks to Heaven. Vaguely reassured as to my own continued existence on this earth, I felt myself yielding to an irresistible lassitude, and a minute after I had awoken from the verge of death, I fell into a curative slumber . . .

A further problem here is that we know (as you may learn) that, by the time he wrote the paragraphs you have just read, Louis Morel at least had strong grounds for suspicion that his fall from the cliffside path was caused (not by his romantically bumbling against a rocky projection, but) by a malefactor who had followed the route of his walk, crept up behind him, tapped him on the head, and pushed him into the millpool below.

Who, then, was Morel's written record supposed to deceive?

And why?

# 4

# Dutiful Thanks

For whatever reason, the expedition described in the present chapter is the last episode for some years which Morel's memoirs depict in prose that has clearly been revised and polished – almost laundered, one can't help suspecting – and in paragraphs impeccably connected. One possible explanation is that, having introduced the ravishing Hélène, he was too burdened with embarrassment, over many of his thoughts, fantasies and actions thereafter, to countenance the depth and intensity of confession which a coherently unbroken narrative would require.

Here, in any case, is his account of how they met:

Much rejoicing attended my recovery. My father celebrated; my mother wept for joy, prayed intensely, and lovingly scolded by my bedside; and the servants caroused so liberally that – as I later learned – the maître d'hôtel lost a rare front tooth, due to falling forward on a flask of spirits.

The day she felt my strength was restored, my mother told me that, having expressed abundant gratitude to God, it was now our duty also to thank God's agent in my rescue. This was a lad little older than myself, son of the Procureur at Lourdes, who had been fishing some way upstream, chanced to glimpse my fall, and rushed down the rocks to save me. Regardless of the danger to himself, he had dived into the pool, wrestled my limp weight to the water's edge, and dragged me to the mill. There, curiously, he remained only long enough to see me in safe hands, and receive assurance from the miller that I should probably recover, before hurrying away – for fear, he made out, of incurring his father's anger, by such a long absence.

As to what token of gratitude we should offer, my father left it entirely to my mother, and accordingly we set out early the next day for Lourdes – my mother on a docile mare, and I by her side on a small but fleet Limousin stallion which my father had given me for Christmas.

This was not, to be sure, the equipage with which the Countess of

Morel should have visited a town once under the dominion of her husband's ancestors, but what was to be done? My father, a little sheepishly, perhaps almost resentfully, merely remarked, as we mounted to depart, before he retreated into his library, that he hoped my mother had commanded adequate retainers to accompany her.

My mother, ever pragmatic, replied that she had ample, and so we set out — with a single groom to hold our horses, and a local lad to show us the way, to the dwelling of the Procureur.

Now the father of the youth who had saved my life — and who, like him, was named Jean-Baptiste Arnault — had only recently settled in Lourdes, and much to the initial consternation of the inhabitants. He had formerly, it was said, been intendant, or steward, to some nobleman in Poitou, and having, by means best known to himself, obtained the title of Procureur in Béarn, he had briefly practised in Pau, and thence removed to Lourdes.

The prospect of an attorney had at first terrified the good people of that town, but they soon discovered Maître Arnault to be eminently approachable. Very short, with an enormous head, he was hardly handsome; but as he soon displayed more useful qualities, the citizens gradually made him their confidant, and before long their paid adviser.

In all his dealings Maître Arnault remained mild and deferential, and yet, somehow, it seemed that the people of Lourdes turned insensibly quarrelsome and litigious, filling the lawyer's office with clamouring clients, with discord — that faithful jackal of attorneys, like a sentry on his steps.

Such were the rumours that drifted up to Château Morel. Our maître d'hôtel, when he repeated them, laid a forefinger astride his florid proboscis, and winked hugely to imply:

'Maître Arnault is a dastardly fox.'

However, my mother being slow to think ill of anyone, we arrived in Lourdes still convinced that the father of my deliverer must be an honest and worthy man.

After a short prayer of thanksgiving and lighting candles at the shrine of Notre Dame du Bon Secours, we proceeded to the lawyer's *étude*. It was a miserable chamber, with one low table and four hard chairs, three of which were littered with books of law, and with papers greasy and brown as the coarse-handed peasants in whose interests they were written.

To our surprise, Maître Arnault himself was nowhere to be seen, but at his table sat an entirely different gentleman suited in dusty black, and riding boots with immense funnel-shaped tops, which were even dustier. The dust, and the disarray of his long wavy hair, suggested he had ridden far; while a large Sombrero hat, and the slender Toledo sword which lay beside him, bespoke him a native of Spain.

By his dress one might have judged him a merchant of middling fortunes, but his features and bearing told a different tale: pale, even sallow, in complexion; a high broad forehead rising steeply from a quizzical brow; floating curls of dark hair flecked with grey; the long but straight nose; the mouth on the brink of a gently cynical smile, seemingly dwarfed by a wide moustache; and above all the noble speed of concentration with which he was writing, at that table opposite the door.

'Maître Arnault?' my mother inquired diffidently – indeed, for her, almost timidly, and with a most becoming blush.

The stranger broke off his writing, momentarily looked stunned, recovered swiftly from his distraction, leaped up, bowed politely, and said:

'If Madame will please be seated, the Procureur shall attend her directly.' With that he scooped up his papers, and hurried out of the chamber.

Moments later Maître Arnault entered the room – a tiny man with a head like a prize-winning pumpkin,[1] and with peculiarly small black eyes, like boats adrift in a sea of oily countenance. How well I recollect my laughter at his appearance, in spite of my mother's agitated reproof; and my asking him, with the insolent frankness of the spoiled only son, if he was not the ugliest man in the world.

Maître Arnault affected to take my cheek in good spirit, and called me a frank young gentleman, but there was a glint in his black boat eyes which belied his words, and I since have had reason to believe that he never forgave my childish affront. He was vain in proportion to his hideousness, and his conceit, I would later learn, had been nourished not a little by succeeding in persuading a very handsome woman to be his wife.

Once my mother had apologized profusely for my immature rudeness, the conversation turned to the service his son had rendered me. In token

---

[1] The perfect reader must compassionately forgive, if hos will not positively applaud, our painstaking attempts to render Louis's laboured tropes in such a guise as never to distract hom. Okay?

of our appreciation, she proposed that the young Jean-Baptiste should be received into Château Morel, and educated with its heir – which she considered the highest honour we could offer.

'Secondly,' she said, 'we wish two hundred livres per annum to be settled upon him for life.' A sum of no small importance in those days, and in that part of France.

Maître Arnault's astonishment is hard to express. Spontaneous liberality was so alien to his bosom that his first thought was clearly that some sinister motive must underlie my mother's proposals. But he speedily recovered himself, and accepted the monetary pension with great effusion. As to boarding young Jean-Baptiste at Château Morel, the father nigh wrung his hands in affected joy at the honour my mother did him, but his son, he regretted, was training to be his clerk, and he could not manage without him.

This refusal offended my mother's pride, and she was rising abruptly to take her leave, when, as if suddenly inspired, the Procureur implored her to stay one moment longer, and, as her bounty had already been so great:

'My son', he said, 'is absolutely necessary to my business. But I have also a daughter, who – her mother being long dead – I have no means of educating as I would wish. If the Countess will transfer the benefit she intended for my son, to his sister, she will lay my entire family under an everlasting obligation.'

My mother cleared her throat doubtfully, but Maître Arnault jumped up nodding his great head to himself, and hurried from the room to fetch his children.

Before I could quiz my mother on the wisdom of burdening our household with the daughter of such a hideous father, Maître Arnault reappeared with the lad who had saved my life and a little girl of some ten years old. Jean-Baptiste was about fifteen, totally unlike his father in stature and personality, but with recognizable vestiges of the Procureur in his features.

Little Hélène was so different, and so beautiful, that my mother and I were amazed. Though her hair was silky blonde, her brows were dark; her skin was fair to the point of pale, yet her cheeks glowed delicately pink with a rare vitality; and her eyes – such eyes – a blue like milky marble, habitually cool with self-possession, but with a twinkle of mischief ever waiting in the wings.

Though I was but twelve I was smitten at first glance, and my apprehensions did such a somersault that now my heart fairly galloped with fear. Fear that my mother, slighted by the lawyer's refusing her his son, would be revenged by declining his daughter instead. But Hélène's manners were naturally as charming as her face was pretty, and her answers to my mother's questions were so quick and intelligent, and at the same time engagingly shy, that in a minute my mother was won over, and all the details were quickly agreed.

Jean-Baptiste was then thanked personally, with warm courtesy by my mother, and with clumsy condescension by myself, all of which he received in an affable and at once strangely sheepish manner, as if he were simultaneously gratified and distressed by the commendations showered upon him – almost, somehow, *ashamed* of having dared to manhandle a social superior to safety.

Finally, before Mother and I took our leave of Lourdes, she established that Father Francis would call by at next day noon, to escort to Château Morel, with her necessary belongings and playthings, the little girl, who would become the young woman, who was to wholly obsess my life.

# 5

# Methodology

Since Louis Morel's own coverage of his early teens now peters into abrupt and scattered notes, often elisive and sometimes downright elusive, we had best make necessity virtuous, as follows.

Faithful to the memoir fragments (except where these are internally inconsistent or incontestably contradicted by external and objectively authenticated evidence) and bound by that knowledge of the rules of human character which licenses the novelist, to a modest degree, to flesh three dimensions out of two, but strictly on the basis of suggestive data established (a little as the paleobiologist will presume to reconstruct the whole dinosaur out of fossil remains), we[1] will henceforth, in respect of those teen years regarding which Morel's own testimony survives, incorporate his freshly translated words into a rounded account of that period which not only best fits all the facts your present narrators have been able to uncover, but also seem to them the way Morel himself might have written it, had he too been alive to retrospect – with the hindsight benefits of psychoanalysis, post-counter-deconstructionism; and, above all, the safer sex of the 1990s.[2]

---

[1] 'This voice is presumably not meant to be the same as the "I" of Chapter 1. Or is it?' [P.C.]

[2] 'Don't ask me why, but short chapters in long novels always strike me as a bit fishy.' [J.R.]

44

## 6

# Flirting with Manhood

As Louis Morel enters into young manhood he is tormented to distraction by Hélène Arnault's inaccessible perfect beauty expanding into maturity. Meanwhile a new neighbour takes up residence nearby. This is the Chevalier of Montenero,[1] the tall Spanish-hatted gentleman whom Louis and his mother met in Maître Arnault's office at Lourdes. The Chevalier becomes an uncle surrogate for Louis; frequently visiting the Morels.

Now for some time the punitive excesses of the salt tax – the *gabelle* – have led to booming business for certain Spanish smugglers. French abettors of Spanish smugglers are thought to use the mill as a contraband dump, though the French customs officers have never yet caught them. Louis has childhood memories of overflowing good things in the region of the mill – Alicante wine, dates, pomegranates – and of dusky smugglers telling hair-raising tales of their adventures. The smugglers would even come up to the Château to sell certain items, and Louis's father would buy from them despite Countess Morel's remonstrances. The Morel family has thus acquired a reputation for benefacting smugglers. Louis particularly remembers closeted audiences between his father and one Pere Garcés – a tall, burly personification of Robin Hood in Catalan Spain.

During this time Louis also has some contact with Jean-Baptiste, who

---

[1] For reasons immensely inscrutable to us, and possibly even more so to you, both Louis and occasionally the Chevalier himself are inconsistent between 'Montenero' and 'Montenegro'. 'Montenero', strictly nitpicking in late-twentieth-century terms, is not a proper Spanish name or vice versa at all. 'Montenegro' might best please present-day Castilians, while Catalans would rather 'Montnegre'. However, for the sake of not burdening the reader with too many tiresome distinctions and petty justifications, and also for the sake of conserving unknowable pints of printer's ink, we have opted to regularize on 'Montenero'.

calls to visit his sister, Hélène. His father, Maître Arnault, seems not to care much about his daughter, but Jean-Baptiste seems an unusually attentive brother. Louis's maturing gratitude, and tokens of it, in favour of Jean-Baptiste, end up with Jean-Baptiste seeming to feel more obliged to Louis than Louis is to him. In the course of their awkward companionship Jean-Baptiste teaches Louis to swim.

Louis Morel, at fourteen, is sent to college at Pau.

Three years glide by during which, presumably, Louis came home periodically for holidays from his studies — though this period is virtually a vacuum in terms of reliable information on his life.

When, at seventeen, Louis is due to return home from college for good, he is bristling on the threshold of manhood: slim, tall and vigorous; handsome. When the great day comes, even according to his own confession, he is all a-tremble with thoughts of Hélène Arnault uppermost in his mind — having saved himself for her. Eagerly he gallops out of Pau, leaving the astonished Old Hussaye, his family retainer, to plod along behind.

Having passed the small, dreamy, slate-roofed Château of Coarasse, in which Henri IV was reared,[2] Louis stops at the Lestelle post-house to requisition their best fresh horse. In the post-house kitchen he gulps back some wine and fidgets impatiently till his new horse is ready.

But out in the courtyard an arrogant stranger arrives, with five servants, and commandeers Louis Morel's new horse. Louis strides out and orders the newcomer to leave the horse saddled:

'It is taken.'

The newcomer turns and, seeing no martial beard, backhands Louis Morel's nose, which bleeds. Louis's fiery soul explodes in a reflex drawing of his sword, which he lunges at the stranger's heart. Saved only by Louis's slightly blurred vision following the backhander, the stranger desperately draws himself, and a furious duel ensues. The stranger, wounded in the arm, loses his temper and control. Louis disarms him and knocks him flat, while the stranger's lackeys gape.

Louis, raging with the heat of insult and combat, is poised to finish off the arrogant stranger, but now the Chevalier of Montenero intervenes. How he came to be in the vicinity is never explained, but in any case he trotted into the courtyard some moments ago, from a different

---

[2] See *The Counts of Mount Venus*, Chapter 4.

direction – with a scarlet-diamonded bandana bibbed across his face below his eyes, like a Mexican ranchero garbed against the desert dust – and has been looking on with avuncular interest since.

Louis, restored to his senses by the Chevalier's cool counsel, commands the vanquished stranger to rise up, take his sword, and be gone.

The stranger departs with sinister nods and threats.

The Chevalier of Montenero and Louis Morel embrace, then ride together for Lourdes. On the way the Chevalier warns Louis to beware. The arrogant stranger, the Marquis of Roquefort, is an influential and highly dangerous man – and he tells Louis two tales of the Marquis's rivals in love being murdered:

The first rival was lulled into lunch with the Marquis of Roquefort then expired in writhing agony some hours after riding home. The second rival, says the Chevalier, is believed to have been murdered by the Marquis of Roquefort's henchmen after visiting his lover/wife whom the Marquis himself had failed to woo and marry; and the widowed loved-one to have given up her ghost in a convent six months later.

Louis falls into brooding silent sympathy for the wronged young lovers, whom he identifies with himself and Hélène, then confesses that he wishes he had dispatched their tormentor after all.

The Chevalier rebukes Louis, counsels him never to regret a generous action, and warns him that killing the Marquis of Roquefort would have entailed certain ruin for Louis. Furthermore, the Marquis has immensely powerful friends, has never been known to forgive, and hence the Chevalier advises Louis Morel to flee for a while to Spain: till the Marquis quits the vicinity.

In Lourdes the Chevalier goes off to visit Maître Arnault, and Louis proceeds on his way home, pausing to admire the spectacular scenery of the Argelès basin:

' . . . dazzling misty sunshine, symbolizing' – the older memoir writer now perceives – 'the fancied delights of youth, which never can be attained.'

Arrived at Château Morel, he rushes to greet his mother in the embroidery room; but finds only Hélène Arnault. Hélène starts up; blushes. Her tomboy days over, her lips quiver; her knees shake.

Louis bounds forward, kisses one flushed cheek then . . . cannot bypass her lush but trembling lips.

Hélène recoils and sinks into a chair, weak with astonished distress. Without pausing to apologize, Louis hastes away to kiss his mother. His parents he finds walking affectionately together in the trapezoidal-walled garden. He learns his mother is weak from a recent illness, which banishes from his short-term memory the vexed encounter with the Marquis of Roquefort. However, now Old Hussaye wheezes in with his distorted account of the fracas, gathered from hostlers at Lestelle.

To counter Old Hussaye's hyperbole, Louis Morel takes up the narrative himself. His father indignantly applauds, and his mother nearly faints.

Louis, seeing his mother's weakness, postpones relating the Chevalier of Montenero's caution. Louis and his father support the ailing Countess Morel to her apartments. There, seeing Countess Morel's tears, Hélène rushes forward to embrace her. This causes the Countess to burst into maternal sobs. She despairingly recounts to Hélène the now much embroidered incident involving the Marquis of Roquefort.

Hélène's full snowy bosom, just panting into womanhood, now heaves with emotion until suddenly she swoons back, overcome. When she revives she attributes her swoon to bending too long over a miniature she is painting for the Countess. Consequently, the anxious Countess insists that Hélène take a walk every morning in the mountains, before bending down to her painting.

Louis reflects ominously on how those lone mountain walks of Hélène's were to 'set the seal on my fate'.

At dinner that night Louis relays the Chevalier of Montenero's counsel. At length it is agreed that the Chevalier's advice must be followed. Louis's father scoffs, but hand-wringing suasions from Countess Morel and Father Francis prevail: they too are convinced of the relentless vengefulness of the Marquis of Roquefort. So Louis is doomed by his parents to set off for Spain: accompanied by Old Hussaye and Father Francis, to join the Chevalier of Montenero at Zaragoza, where the Chevalier has business interests and estates.

Next day, his last before banishment to Zaragoza, Louis bounds up fresh and off to the mountains to shoot a few izards. Proudly he reflects that yesterday was the first day of his manhood: he had held his own, and shed his enemy's blood. Then he plunges into morose brooding that Hélène might have taken his kiss as insulting; debasing, even. Impulsively he romantically debates whether to polish clean his own slate and gratify what he feels must be her natural feminine expectation: that he should propose to her the decent thing – marriage when he returns from Zaragoza.

Mentally battling furiously with himself on the rocky ridge over-hanging the valley of the Gave, Louis espies a figure strolling by the river: Hélène. So he begins a scampering descent down the rocks to join her.

Louis finds Hélène seated on a flat rock beneath an old oak: in the arousingly perfect spring of her nubile virginity.[3] He greets her with callow bravado. She flushes, then pales. Both are confused; tongue-tied.

After halting smalltalk with unbearable silences Hélène makes out she must return to the Château, to get on with her painting for the Countess. Louis begs her to stay, to listen to what he has to say, especially since he may never have a chance to say it again.

With gladly reluctant timidity she allows herself to be detained. Louis now announces a secret which he must share before he departs for Zaragoza, so that the keeper of the secret can divulge it – in the supremely unlikely event of Louis's untimely death in Spain.

Hélène is conned into bright-eyed curiosity, blonde ringlets being brushed back from her finely pencilled brow.[4]

Louis asks her to promise never to reveal the secret while yet he lives.

She inquires whether he would not do better to entrust the secret to someone more mature than a young and inexperienced maiden like herself. Father Francis, perhaps?

Louis counters that Father Francis is not adequate. And anyway: the prelate is going to Spain too.

Now Hélène vows she *will* keep his secret.

Louis professes his absolute love for *one special girl*, and offers any penance if any kiss he stole offended *her*. He snakes his arm round Hélène's waist, as her head falls against his shoulder, and she weeps uncontrollably. He would be worried that she found his declaration obnoxious except that she leaves her captive hand in his and murmurs, between her tears:

'Oh, Louis.'

At length, during which time he takes advantage of their intertwine-ment on the riverside rock to caress her with noble subtility, she

---

[3] Etc, etc.

[4] Regrettably, Louis Morel really does linger thus, his cliché of smitten rapture exceptional, on the pulchritudes of Mademoiselle Arnault.

collects herself and accuses him of making her at once 'both happy and miserable'.

But why?

Because his parents would never allow him to wed a lowly bourgeoise like herself, even one whom they themselves have befriended.

Louis tries but fails to persuade Hélène that his parents *would* in time consent, but Hélène is adamant: as her thoughts re-assemble she becomes anxious to quit his present company. And she begs him, as he loves her, never again to try to meet her thus, alone, as she would only feel doubly guilty on having to face his dear mother later. Further, she insists, weeping once more, but controllably now, that, as they mutually promise secret-keeping, he will try to forget her, and marry some lady of his own rank, who may love him remotely as much . . .

But now the control breaks down.

Louis passionately badgers her to reconsider.

Hélène sobbingly refuses, since she could never become his wife without the consent of his parents.

Louis now rants and raves, and threatens dire consequences not ruling out suicide by any means, whereupon Hélène offers to promise instead that she too will never, never *consent to wed another*.

On that note she withdraws her hand, and retreats towards the Château.

Louis, delighted to find himself beloved, but desperately vexed by Hélène's resolution, bounds back up into the rocky heights to blast the izards into justifying his absence.

The following day he sets off for Spain – with a heavy heart, plus Old Hussaye on a nag and Father Francis on a mule.

At Luz they prepare to pass the night at a seedy cabaret – so seedy, Louis recollects, that he instantly hoped for no better fare 'than pumpkin soup and goose thighs'. In the cabaret parlour they encounter a fat greasy monk with a thin black companion who looks like a mourning sword in a tatty black scabbard.

Father Francis instantly takes against the fat monk and his thin fellow. Exhausted, Father Francis, before he retires to bed, whispers to Louis that he should retire likewise the moment he has finished his supper. However, seeing the surprisingly tasty dishes being served to Fat Monk and Thin Accomplice, Louis elects to join them.

Alas, the wine is sour.

Louis asks Fat Monk if no better wine can be had.

Fat Monk explains that the aubergiste will not produce his fine Cahors till he sees some suitable silver.

Louis grandiosely flourishes a crown from his purse; Fat Monk calls for good wine to rejoice a poor Capuchin.

An hour passes with Fat Monk telling tall stories, guaranteeing their truth, and drinking deep to his own veracity.

Thin Accomplice affects to disbelieve Fat Monk; Fat Monk says order more wine . . . Thin Accomplice says:

No. Let's play for who pays for the wine.

Cards and wine are produced, windows shut and candles lit; wine flows and Thin Accomplice loses to chuckling Fat Monk.

Louis enjoys looking on as Fat Monk continues to seem to thrash Thin Accomplice at cards. Then Fat Monk challenges Louis to join the game, swearing even such a young novice such as he could beat Thin Accomplice.

Louis beats Thin Accomplice, who appears even more irate . . . soon Louis is cajoled into playing one last game for higher stakes: he loses.

Louis is angered into vengefully insisting on his right to win back his loss. Thirsty, he drinks while playing. Now, staring into his wine, Louis deduces from changing reflections on the glass that Fat Monk is cuing his Thin Accomplice with information re Louis's cards. Louis, perplexed, determines to nudge Old Hussaye, but is relieved to discover Hussaye has been awake all the time, spying on the fraud through heavy-hooded eyes while affecting to slumber on a trestle.

Louis lets the fraud proceed then jumps up and seizes Fat Monk's hand in the act of signalling. Old Hussaye jumps up too and floors Thin Accomplice, out of whose sleeves two aces flutter.

Fat Monk seems flummoxed for a moment then bursts into jovial laughter and congratulates Louis on rumbling them, and asks if he isn't grateful for this invaluable lesson learned.

Louis promises he always kicks sharpers down the stairs.

This is the ground floor, jibes Fat Monk.

Then I'll throw you out of the window, threatens Louis.

I weigh two hundred pounds, counters Fat Monk.

Louis scowlingly lets them go, having recouped his stolen money, and Fat Monk and Thin Accomplice roll away, leering.

Old Hussaye cackles with glee at how heartily Louis's father would laugh. Louis says for heaven's sake never mention it to his parents, and especially not to Father Francis. And now, on reflection, Louis flushes crimson with shame at having nearly gambled away all the money Count

Roger had given him, out of such limited means, to fund his sojourn in Zaragoza.

To rid himself of such scolding thoughts he swigs back a last glass of wine, hurries to bed, meets Fat Monk on the stairs, and athletically kicks him down them.

Next morning the Luz landlord warns Louis Morel quietly that Fat Monk is no monk really but a great rogue, in league with Thin Accomplice, and with sinister connexions. Louis rebukes the landlord for not imparting this information at the outset, and punishes him by only paying half his bill. Then he rides on to Zaragoza, there to tryst with the Chevalier of Montenero.

The Chevalier takes them to search for suitable apartments. In due course Louis is billeted with a disapproving old crone who runs a tall house in a narrow street, in a modestly priced but not disreputable quarter. Louis, determined to see all Spain as soon as possible, takes an upper front room with a view of the windows opposite.

Insightfully the Chevalier quietly warns Louis about dangers of Spanish towns, and women.

Louis affects not to know what the Chevalier is on about.

Father Francis now distraughtly confesses to the Chevalier that a certain packet of papers entrusted to him by Maître Arnault, for delivery to the Chevalier, appears to have been stolen.

The Chevalier, normally imperturbable, is greatly agitated by the disappearance of this packet, so Louis suspects its contents must somehow have been vital to the Chevalier's affairs. But in what way?

The Chevalier, ever considerate, tries to ease Father Francis's distress, but still fishes to deduce how the packet could have vanished.

Father Francis recalls that he stashed the packet at the bottom of his valise, together with a modest cache of saved-up alms money, at the sleazy cabernet in Luz.

The Chevalier mutters, evidently trying to console himself, that destiny seems to demand that he will *never get hold of these papers*, after searching for so many years.

Father Francis gently reproves the Chevalier's fatalism.

A warm debate ensues between the Chevalier and Father Francis on: predetermination, free will, divinity . . .

Louis, politely bored, excuses himself and retires to bed to dream about women, and what it would feel like to physically possess one.

For the next few days Louis is rather left to his own devices, as the Chevalier spends time on his business affairs. The talkative landlady tells Louis how the Chevalier had acquired high honours in the New World, both as statesman and warrior. To escape the landlady's conversation, Louis spends much time in his room, hoping to learn all about life in Spain by peeping from his window. However, he is disappointed to discover that the windows opposite belong mainly to servants' quarters at the back of grander houses.

One night, desperate for intelligent company, Louis goes to call on the Chevalier but discovers him absent. Returning to his lodgings, Louis throws himself down in a chair by the open window. Thinking merely to stargaze, he now gasps at a tableau suddenly visible in a top-storey chamber opposite:

A young Spanish woman in aristocratic dress is gazing down at the street below, her dark eyes intently glittering. Over her shoulder Louis sees the chamber door open to admit a brown-robed priest. The Spanish damsel pulls the jalousies shut, and an hour later the priest – the lady's father-confessor, Louis presumes – exits quietly through a narrow door at street level.

Louis now discovers that, despite his ongoing spiritual devotion to Hélène, he is head-high in lust for the dusky maja across the way, and all that night his sleep is crucified by searing images of what it would feel like to physically possess her.

Two days follow of Louis watching intently at his window.

Though the priest visits each evening he sees nothing more of the lady. On the third day, following the departure of the priest, she appears at the window looking drawn and angry, glittering eyes smouldering.

Louis tries waving to her engagingly but she looks daggers at him and slams her jalousies. However, the following evening, at the same time, she reappears, looking ravishingly forlorn, her eyes bright with tears.

Louis salutes gallantly.

She makes as if to retreat from his view.

On an adolescent impulse, histrionically he blows her a kiss.

She can't suppress a weak smile.

In quixotic sign language he asks if he can be of service.

She shakes her head emphatically, and reaches to close the jalousies. Then a thought strikes her, and she calls across the street in a subdued husky voice:

If he wishes to alleviate her distress he should go instantly to the theatre, and wait in Box G.

At that moment Father Francis bursts in, tuts at the gloom in Louis's room, and proposes a bedtime session of reading Seneca together.

Louis blushes madly as he says he is going out to the theatre.

Father Francis hopes this juvenile love of 'bad places' will soon pass.

In the foyer Louis is embarrassed to discover that G is the curtained box of the Chief Justice of Zaragoza. Still, he bribes the old-woman key-holder to let him use the Corregidor's box. This she allows, so long as Louis undertakes to keep the curtains well drawn – as the Corregidor is known to be out of town for several days.

Louis takes a seat in the box. His breath is bated for the approach of the glittering maja. Gradually, though, he is seduced by dramatic cunning into empathetic sharing of the passions portrayed on stage, and soon he is wrapt in the exquisite dialogue between Henry VIII and Anne Boleyn when lo:

A lady glides into the box enveloped in a black mantilla, and a blacker velvet mask.

She drops the mantilla, revealing a tautly bodiced body, but keeps up the mask.

Louis makes to kiss her hand.

She asks in a low voice if the box to the left is occupied.

He says no and presses her to relax: in the discreet company of such an adorer as himself.

She allows her waist to be encircled as Louis lards her in formal Spanish with the gallant guff he has read about in romances, and even presumes to caress her breast and kiss the neck beneath her mask.

Now she unties a ribbon to let fall the mask, and Louis is aghast at the savage heat, so close, of her fiery dark beauty, especially when she begins to reciprocate his ardour, in ways he would never have suspected of a lady.

As they cuddle and fondle, all above dress for the moment, she tells Louis she is the Corregidor's daughter. Her mother is dead, her father loves her to distraction, she would never leave him *even to marry a king*, but nevertheless she rhapsodizes about passion, love, and jealousy.

Infatuated, Louis is deaf to all dangerous overtones.

The maja explains that, most unusually for a young woman of her class,[5] she is allowed unlimited freedom by her autonomy-respecting and virtue-trusting father, and that tomorrow night Louis may visit her in her own house. Come, he is told, to the small door beneath the window of her dressing room; at midnight it will be open.

Louis Morel's memoir voice admits at this point that, even in those moments of romantic madness he heard whispers of his conscience protest. And he proclaims that though he 'chose to ignore those whispers', there was yet some desperate frontier at which he intended *to stop dead short of Vice*:

'Alas. And let it be remarked that the steps I now took in Wrong, by an extraordinary chain of circumstances, caused all the misery of my existence.'

All the following day Louis spends irritably champing, upsetting Father Francis, killing time before the assignation which he prays but cannot quite believe will result in the physical consummation he so burningly covets.

At ten o'clock he feigns fatigue, dismisses Old Hussaye, and retires as though to bed. More intense waiting, then midnight chimes, and with a deafening heart he descends his lodging stairs.

Then he darts across the street, pushes open the narrow door and gasps to be grasped by the maja's waiting hand: fever-hot. He attempts to kiss her on the lips but she pushes him away and in silence leads him up two flights of stairs to a small, elegant, lamp-lit dressing room.

Louis sees she is deathly pale and attempts to reassure her with effusive vows, tender caresses, and implications of sexual chivalry.

For a moment she allows him to embrace her but then pushes him away, distractedly, and scolds him for coming to visit a lady with a sword. She unbuckles his sword, leads him into a splendid room beyond and tells him now is the time when he must prove to her his love is really real.

Louis half hopes and half fears she is intimating that he should forthwith undress and prove his manhood, but he is at the same time unnerved by the maja's terrible pallor, her tense behaviour, and the

---

5 Another superficial anomaly is that we wouldn't normally expect a Corregidor's daughter to be described, or to describe herself, as a 'maja'. But this one may simply be due to a mistranslation by Louis himself.

unnatural hotness of her hands.

She asks if he has a stout heart.

He gulps; says yes.

She leads him to what seems like a heap of cushions, pulls off a sheet and reveals a naked corpse, weltering in its own congealing gore.

Louis gazes in fascinated horror on the lust-visaged corpse of the brown-robe priest.

With eerie calmness the maja confesses:

She killed the priest for having used confessional secrets as blackmail to seduce her, then forsaking her for another, then daring to return to debauch her again, and clinchingly for threatening her with betrayal if she would not yield.

'So you did yield?' Louis murmurs, embracing her with wonder.

'I had to,' the maja replies distantly. 'But then . . . I *killed him* – with *this:*'

And she produces a bloodstained dagger from her bosom.

Louis gently asks the maja what she proposes doing with the body.

She replies that Louis must without delay cart the corpse away and dump it in the great fosse, beyond the city wall—

If truly he loves her.

# 7

# The Chevalier's Warning

It being essential that the reader appreciate the strength of the Chevalier of Montenero's determination to stress the sinister significance of the Marquis of Roquefort, already so instrumental in precipitating Louis Morel's flight into Spain, let us now peruse in full the Chevalier's own account of the caution he urged upon Louis,[1] following the latter's precocious humiliation of the Marquis outside the post-house at Lestelle.

I then informed him [*the Chevalier confirms*] that his opponent was the infamous Marquis of Roquefort, who had been strongly suspected in two instances of having used foul means to be rid of a successful rival.

'In the first case, he at length prevailed on the Chevalier of Valenais to break bread with him,' I informed your son. 'The repast was excellent, the wine incomparable; the Marquis . . . fascinating in his conversation, and impeccably the perfect host. Poor Valenais returned home believing he had lost an enemy and gained a friend. Alas. Ere he had been half an hour in bed, he called his valet in great agony, and before morning he had lost all his enemies together, and gone to join his friends in Heaven. The physician shook his head; but after an hour's conversation with the Marquis, he became convinced the poor youth had died of an abdominal inflammation.'

The other tale is not of itself so conclusive, but from this man's general character, I have no doubt of the Marquis of Roquefort's designing criminality. He some years ago proposed to marry the beautiful Henriette de Vergne, and offered himself to her father. The old man, finding that the Marquis had property worth rents of some three hundred thousand livres per annum, felt instantly convinced that Roquefort was the most honourable, sweet-tempered, and amiable man in the world; precisely

---

[1] In a letter to Countess Morel, which survives in the Carpentras Documents. See Chapter 81.

thrice more so than the Count of Bagnols, to whom he had already promised his daughter, and who had but *one* hundred thousand livres per annum.[2]

'Sending for the young Count,' I told your son, 'Mademoiselle de Vergne's father informed him forthwith that he was not near so eligible as the Marquis of Roquefort, enumerated several weak reasons, and without further ado broke formally his commitment to the Count. Immediately Bagnols sent his cartel to the Marquis of Roquefort, who accepted it, but named a distant day. Before that day arrived,

---

[2] It is in the acutest consciousness of numismatical deficiency, vanquished only narrowly by a uniquely post-Kleistian strength of resolution that no reader must be unduly bamboozled without good cause, that the following list of coinage equivalents is proffered:

One sou (or sol, or shilling) equals five centimes. One crown ('*couronne*') equals five sous (or sols, or shillings), and therefore twenty-five centimes. One livre (or franc) equals twenty sous (etc), hence one hundred centimes or four crowns. One louis-d'or equals twenty livres (or francs), hence eighty crowns (and so on). According to *Britannica*, 'French writers would speak without distinction of so many livres or so many francs, so long as the sum mentioned was an even sum; otherwise livre was the correct term, thus "*trois francs*" but "*trois livres cinq sols*".' Fascinatingly, however, 'In 1795 the livre was converted into the franc at the rate of 81 livres to 80 francs, the silver franc being made to weigh five grammes.'

But for the sake of not being completely confused (as the French have always wished us foreigners to be, with regard to the their currency, culture, language, *et n'importe quoi*), we shall stick in the present history (wherever not impossible) with the *louis-d'or*, which is *worth twenty livres*, the *livre* being *worth four crowns*, the *crown* being *worth five sous*, the *sou* being *worth five centimes*, with the miserable *centime*, at the veriliest arsehole end of the debasage chain, *worth virtually bugger all*. Unlike the Count of Bagnols, who, even if thrice as poor as the Marquis of Roquefort (and we have only the Chevalier's word for this) was nonetheless stinking rich by any decent-minimum-wage standard, if only we could get one.

the young Count was mysteriously accused of aiding the Huguenots at La Rochelle,[3] and for that he was arrested.

'Before his trial – no-one knows how – he contrived to escape, and to transfer a great part of his wealth into Spain; but now comes the more obscure part of the tale. The marriage of the Marquis to Mademoiselle de Vergne approached, and great preparations were made at her father's château; but a man was seen lurking about the park, whom many of the servants later claimed to have recognised as the Count of Bagnols. They, for whatever reason, said nothing; though it was generally rumoured amongst them that the Count had in a secret ceremony been wed to their young lady some weeks before his arrest. The night, however, on which the Marquis of Roquefort arrived (and which was to precede his marriage by one week), an uneasy conscience having rendered him restless, he by chance beheld a man descend from the window of Mademoiselle de Vergne's apartment. Not unnaturally the Marquis gave the alarm, and with much fury declared he had been cheated, deceived; betrayed.

'It then appeared, they say, that the fair Henriette *had* really married her lover, the Count of Bagnols. He was now, however, a wanderer in exile. Henriette's father declared he would have the clandestine marriage annulled if the Marquis of Roquefort would but do him the honour to stay and wed his daughter as previously contracted. But the Marquis sternly refused, and that very night departed – to take up a lodging at the village hard by.

'And reflect well on this, my dear Louis,' I cautioned your son. 'That the Count of Bagnols was never heard of more. Two mornings after the removal of the Marquis to the village there was found in the park of M. de Vergne a broken sword, near the spot where it was supposed the lover used to leap the wall. The ground round about was dented with the struggling of many feet, and daubed with much gore. Part of a torn cloak, too, was found, and a long train of bloody drops from that place to the river's edge. Later a local peasant furthermore deposed to having seen two men fling a weighty burden into the fast-flowing water at just that spot. He could not be persuaded to *swear* it was a dead body, but he presumed it must have been.'

'And what became of Mademoiselle de Vergne?' demanded Louis, with all the ardour of his youth.

'The Countess of Bagnols,' I replied, 'for no doubt remained as to her

---

[3] See Chapter 8.

marriage, removed – or was removed, I know not precisely which – to a convent of her father's choosing . . . where she died within a year.'

For several minutes we rode on in silence. Then your son confessed, in a voice not wholly steady, that he felt he could have wept for the fate of the beautiful young woman and her true lover; that his heart burned like a baker's fire to think such devilish wrongs should go unpunished; that all his sympathy for the lovers translated into rage against him [the Marquis] whom he [Louis] looked upon as the cause of the death of both [the lovers].

'How I regret', he exclaimed in remorse, 'that I my sword did not thrust through their murderer's foul black heart, when he lay prostrate before me. Thus to speed the vile assassin to another world, there to answer swiftly for his dastardly crimes in this.'

Such was the righteous vengefulness of your son's emotion, dear Madame, and so notoriously long is the arm of M. Roquefort's malice, that I deem it necessary to add the force of this written testimony to my spoken counsel of yesterday: that your son take refuge awhile in Spain, where I myself may the better watch over him.

Begging you, Madame, to rest assured of your humble servant's salutations the most salubrious [&c., &c.],

Montenero.

# *8*

# Love and Death in Zaragoza

In the previous chapter the two accounts of the Marquis of Roquefort's villainy, and the tragic sundering of the mutual passion of the Count of Bagnols and Henriette de Vergne, relate to other momentous events in the 1620s, when the Huguenots (the French Protestants) were driven yet again into their traditional last stronghold of La Rochelle, a strongly fortified seaport on France's Atlantic coast. Cardinal Richelieu, years later, looking back on the achievements of his administration, would record:

'When your Majesty [Louis XIII] called me to your councils, I can truly say that the Huguenots divided the State with you; the nobles conducted themselves as if they were not subjects, and the governors of provinces as if they were independent sovereigns. Foreign alliances were despised, private interests preferred to public, and the dignity of your Majesty so abased it could hardly be recognized. I promised your Majesty to use all my industry and power to ruin the Huguenot party, lower the pride of the nobles, lead all subjects to their duty, and restore the country's name among foreign nations.'

By 1628 Richelieu had for four years been pursuing his policy of destroying the Huguenots, and his triumph was consummated in late October of that year when, after yet another siege immortalized by the scarcely credible heroism of the besieged inhabitants, even La Rochelle was eventually obliged to surrender. The relevance of all this to the case of Louis Morel is that any gentleman suspected between 1624 and 1628 of actively aiding the beleaguered Huguenots – as per the poison-pen accusation against the Count of Bagnols – would have attracted the relentless persecution of Richelieu on grounds of treason against both French King and French State (ie Richelieu himself). If, then, as the Chevalier of Montenero's telling implies, it was indeed the Marquis of Roquefort who wielded the poison pen behind the back of the Count of Bagnols, then certainly this was a disgracefully vindictive but also undeniably effective curb on the liberty, happiness and breeding prospects of a better man in love.

For more background on the history of the Huguenots, and French

Catholic and other campaigns against them, the reader is welcome to repair to any large library. We, meanwhile, must bounce forward again to Zaragoza in the late summer of 1639, where and when, a few pages ago, we left Louis Morel: in the bedroom of the bloodstained maja.

Louis, not to put too fine a point on it, already has an erection. With this in mind we can safely say that really only now is the true character of Louis Morel, the man, beginning to manifest itself. Though not daunted for a moment by fear of being apprehended in custody of a murdered priest, he is both inflamed with adolescent craving to physically possess the maja, and nearly demented by the vibrations emanating from her pounding bosom to the effect that she would much rather Louis bundled up and removed the dead priest's body now, immediately, without further delay.

Sensing his reluctance, she fiercely threatens to kill both of them with the dagger she has not ceased to brandish since plucking it out of her cleavage.

Louis tries to reason lovingly with her – cajoles, murmurs, caresses, takes her in his arms, and kisses her with gauche heat.

Melting, it seems, the maja sobs, drops the dagger, goes limp in his embrace, and apparently in a welter of remorse she begs him to go, repents ever having asked him to help her in such a criminal way, swears she must have been mad, and sighs to think how now she must remain alone to face her fate. Then she weeps at the thought of the dishonour and misery that will ruin her father's old age.

Louis heroically consoles her and vows he most certainly will carry away the evidence of her guilt but pleads with her first to gratify his passion, lest his mission to ditch the corpse should founder in arrest, or direr misadventures, which might frustrate their union ever after.

With fiery Aragonese impulsiveness the maja acquiesces with a shrug, throws off her clothes and lies down on the bed where she was effectively raped by the priest such a short while since. Clumsy with frenzied haste Louis too undresses, joins her on the bed, and within moments his virginity is lost. Minutes later he jumps up to dress again, pugnaciously resolved to carry out his pledge to save the maja's honour. Strangely fearful now on his behalf, she makes to hold him back but he says 'no, no', hoists the priest/corpse across his shoulders, kisses the maja a tersely fond farewell, then proceeds to bear the awkward dead-weight down the narrow stairs, along several dark backstreets to the fountain, thence to the rampart which looks over the olive groves beyond.

There, furtively confident he has not been seen, he heaves the corpse from the rampart down into the great fosse that skirts the city. Next, relieved yet uncontrollably agitated, he weaves home by a roundabout route. Nearing his landlady's house, he pauses for several minutes in a side alley to be doubly sure of not being followed. At length, seeing no-one, hearing no sounds of human wakefulness, he creeps across the street and darts towards the door of his lodgings.

But just in that same moment a tall figure rounds a corner coming the other way, on the far side of the street.

It is the Chevalier of Montenero. Strangely though, as in a dream, despite Louis Morel's trembling certainty that he sees the Chevalier seeing him, the Chevalier passes on without remark.

In his bedroom Louis sinks into a panic of anxiety as to what the Chevalier may be thinking of him. Also neurosis regarding his own virility, and hankering to prove it properly as soon as possible. Then he notices, and spends the next two hours trying to wash away, three small dark bloodstains on his outer garments. By the time he pours the last small bowl of bloodsponged water from his window he is thoroughly exhausted and collapses on his bed. But even now he cannot sleep, and keeps coming to with nasty jolts at recurring dreadful images every time he drifts off toward the shores of nightmare.

At last a deep sleep grips him tightly – but almost instantly, it seems, he is shaken rudely awake by an unkind fist, only to find his room fatly packed with various officers of the Spanish law. Convinced he is about to be arraigned for the maja's crime, Louis gathers his wits with cool speed tempered by a sense of righteousness deriving from his resolution, as a French gentleman, to protect the lady's name and uphold her honour at no matter what cost to himself.

Now a leering alguacil (the arresting officer, plump and slimy) starts with ponderous cunning to interrogate Louis as to his reasons in general for being in Spain at all. Louis defends himself by pre-emptive allegation: accusing the alguacil of coming to extort money, which he assures him he won't get.

The alguacil retorts with sneering venom that Louis is under arrest for the murder of Father Avecido, whose oft-stabbed body has been discovered in the fosse. Louis scoffs high-handedly and orders the alguacil not to bother him with such nonsense until the return to Zaragoza of the Corregidor (chief magistrate, and also the maja's father), whose good sense and probity, he predicts with confidence, will swiftly see through the alguacil's manipulative fabrications. All this is to gain time to think and learn on what precise grounds he is accused, and these tactics for the moment seem to work, especially since the pasty Spanish police begin to quail at the thought of being kicked down stairs by the burly Old Hussaye, who now has joined the throng with curdling threats and gestures to caution any fool who would dream of harming a single hair on his young master's innocent head.

Now Father Francis too bustles in and earnestly urges Louis to clear himself by answering the alguacil's questions, as the police downstairs have a witness who claims to have seen the murderer entering this house.

Louis continues his high-handed tone: only to the Zaragoza Corregidor will he answer. While Louis dresses, the police witness, officer of the *real hacienda*, is called in and instantly identifies Louis as The Man. Moreover, the hacienda officer answers Louis so fully and truthfully, about having seen him dump the priest's body in the fosse, and then tracking his roundabout route home, that Louis is unable to prevent an angry flush from embarrassing his features.

This causes the alguacil to exult with loathsome glee.

Louis attempts to bluster the congregation into perceiving his flush as the rightful expression of his outrage at wild injustice. Nevertheless he is jostled downstairs and out into the sunbright street, where a roar of ugly emotions rises up from a crocodile crowd of bystanders. Fleetingly, before he is marched away, he glimpses two hooked female fingers pulling the maja's jalousies to.

In a waiting-room in the Zaragoza Corregidor's house, layers of lackeys peel away till only the alguacil himself is left, and he asks Louis what he'd give to get away.

Louis contemptuously dismisses such a typically base proposal.

Soon the Corregidor arrives and Louis is taken before him. The Corregidor, a noble-featured gentleman of sixty, politely informs Louis of his situation, and explains that, since no-one has yet adduced any reason to doubt the hacienda officer's testimony, detention of Louis himself, between now and his time of trial, looks inevitable.

Louis requests permission to speak. Granted. He denies murdering anyone, then asks rhetorically why he should have killed a priest he never knew?

The Corregidor suavely acknowledges the superficial plausibility of the defendant's rhetoric, but now the audience chamber doors are opened and a gulp of persons belches in: the alguacil, other officers, the witness, and sundry onlookers. The hacienda officer is examined and tells his tale with the ring of simple truth.

Rumblings and scufflings at the back of the audience chamber begin to sound ominous, and things are looking grim for Louis when the Chevalier of Montenero arrives upon the scene, tight-lipped and severe. Courteously the Chevalier requests permission to question the witness. Such are the Chevalier's standing and reputation locally that the Corregidor consents without demur, and, by stitching together portions from both the Zaragoza court records and a second letter from the Chevalier to Countess Morel, we obtain the following exchange.

'You own, sir,' begins the Chevalier, 'that you never once perceived the figure of the murderer – granted for the moment that the bearer of the body and the taker of its life were one identical person, which of course is a monumental assumption . . . that you never once perceived the figure of the murderer *except in shadow*?'

'That is correct, your worship,' the *real hacienda* officer replies.

'So he never for a moment emerged even into the moonlight?'

'Not fully, your worship.'

'And by your own evidence, if it has been reported to me aright, when at length you arrived *at the end* of the street where the accused young gentleman is lodging, you were so far behind the personage you were following as, in your own words, "only to catch a glimpse" of that figure entering the house. Is that a fair summary?'

The witness cannot deny it.

'So you dare not swear, on your oath before God, that you *certainly* saw Monsieur *Morel* entering a house. Only that you saw *some person* entering a house? A person, who, it seems, from all you report, could just as well have been a tallish woman as a man?'

'Yes, but—'

'And the house. *Which* house? As you were far behind, the street is long, the doors were plunged in shadow – shall you then swear *the house* which *some person* entered was *the same house* in which Monsieur Morel is lodging?'

'Yes, your worship.'

'Before Almighty God?'

'Well, no, your worship.'

'I thank you, sir, for your candid admission,' says the Chevalier kindly. 'And confess that *even I*', he stresses, in tones pregnant with meaning, 'have on occasion been greatly deceived, in thinking I recognised a dear and long-known friend, when circumstances have afterwards indicated that it *could not* have been him.' Here the Chevalier flashes

Louis a private glance of stern contempt which Louis, in his incommunicable determination to protect the maja, clearly registers with resentment stronger than his gratitude for the Chevalier's intervention on his behalf.

In any case, though he has yielded on the identity of the house, the hacienda officer refuses to relinquish his conviction that the corpse-dumping fugitive *was* Louis. Hot on the tail of this, the leering alguacil now points out that Louis's pourpoint is still damp from recent washing: not all over, but in patches, wherein are perceivable faint stains as of blood oozed out of a corpse.

Loud murmurs, and out-of-order anonymous comments fill the air.

The Chevalier grits his teeth furiously as Louis unconvincingly protests that the stains were merely from wine. The Zaragoza Corregidor frowns grimly and has already begun issuing orders for Louis Morel's detention when a servant rushes into the audience chamber and whispers urgently in the presiding ear. 'Not now,' says the Corregidor dismissively – whereupon, reluctantly, the distraught servant presses a note into the Corregidor's hand.

Impatiently the Corregidor looks at the note. Moments later he pales, goggles, looks about to vomit, rises, and weakly orders all present to remain as-is till his return.

Following the Corregidor's bizarre transformation and removal from the chamber, the noise level mushrooms. The Chevalier of Montenero stares sternly from a window down to the street, without a glance at Louis. Meanwhile his landlady inveighs raucously in favour of Louis's flawless character, courtesy, gentleness, handsomeness and generosity – all of which, by incessant iteration, begins to sway the sympathies of the rabble.

A long hour later the Zaragoza Corregidor returns. He looks two decades older, and so desperately ill and close to death that all present groan with horror. In a pathetic croaking voice the Corregidor instructs his secretary now to take the evidence of Louis's proposed witnesses.

Father Francis and Old Hussaye testify for Louis – honestly, and blithely dishonestly, respectively. Next, their landlady proudly lies through her teeth re her front door and locks, and the impossibility of Louis egressing late at night without her knowledge. She also reviles the accusing *hacienda* witness, luridly adducing past instances of that officer's transgressions and corruptions of justice. This enthusiastic attack on the principal witness for the prosecution swings public opinion so far in Louis Morel's favour that the Zaragoza Corregidor is enabled credibly to conclude that Louis is so clearly innocent of the murder and dumping of the priest, Father Avecido, that there are insufficient grounds for formal proceedings against him.

So he is now free to go.

Then with an awful sob the Corregidor breaks down, weeps uncontrollably, and announces through his tears that his only daughter is dead.

This tragic disclosure is greeted by a silence of deep shock; then respectful dispersal from the audience chamber of all persons bar two: Louis being requested to remain for a private word with the Corregidor himself.

No account survives of the conflicting violence of Louis Morel's emotions at this juncture, but they naturally would have included:

*Doubt.* Is the maja really dead? Or is the present development a ruse devised by her, to sway her father into pardoning Louis? *Dread.* Whether or not she is dead, how much has she told her father, and what will be the consequences for Louis? And how much lower will he fall in the Chevalier's esteem? *Self-disgust.* If she is dead, to what extent has Louis helped to kill her? *Frustration.* Some very feminine readers may find this thought disturbing, but we must record a suspicion, which will be reinforced by his subsequent behaviour, that any nobler emotions experienced by Louis are compromised by an underlying panic of irritation at not knowing with whom he will get to prove his manhood for the second time – if, that is, the maja is truly dead.

And alas: she truly is.

The Zaragoza Corregidor's despair is beyond the power of a Garrick or Kean to feign. At length, drying his eyes, he motions Louis to follow him upstairs to a small private room overlooking an internal courtyard rife with ornamental vines. There he wordlessly points to a table on which lies Louis Morel's forgotten sword, which he left in the maja's bedroom when he carted the dead priest away. At the sight of his sword Louis bursts into tears, and the Corregidor too now abandons himself to shameless weeping. At length, regaining some measure of self-control, he informs Louis wearily that his daughter had told him all – before she finally died of the poison she had taken.

*All?*

In a surge of relief combined with shame at the realization that the maja, even in the poisoned agony of her last moments of life, has not spilled the beans to her father regarding her more carnal relations with himself, Louis breaks down again in a fit of Latin tears.

Now it is the bereaved old father who consoles the young French lover, at the same time begging that Louis, out of respect for the dead girl's memory, will *swear never to tell a living soul in all Spain* that the maja's death was by her own hand, or how the depraved priest had driven her to it.

Louis swears.

The Corregidor thanks Louis with pathetic profusion and proceeds to blame himself for his daughter's death: having spoiled her . . .

No, no: such tragedies are no-one's fault, says Louis, who then is advised by the Corregidor to quit Spain without delay lest the Inquisition gets in on the act, due to the murdered man having been a priest.

Louis returns to his lodgings in unbelievable turmoil and irately shrugs off the embraces of his exulting landlady, who claims all the credit for having got him off the hook. Father Francis greets Louis with great joy and news that here is a letter from his father, summoning him home – but first the Chevalier of Montenero is waiting to speak with him upstairs, much troubled.

Louis finds the Chevalier forbiddingly grave and stern. Fear of *appearing* guilty, double-bound by his pledge to the Corregidor to maintain absolute secrecy, sends rebellious hot flushes pumping up the young blood's cheeks. Consequent anger at his inexcusable embarrassment makes Louis bitter in manner: he answers Chevalier of Montenero's direct questions with sarcasm.

The Chevalier of Montenero says *I saw you*, and invites Louis to admit it. Louis scolds the Chevalier for doubting him, agrees it *was* him the Chevalier saw in the street at dead of night, but categorically denies the crime of which he was accused.

The Chevalier responds with a supremely scathing:

'Tcha!' Then he clatters away, leaving Louis fuming with resentful indignation.

Father Francis, finding Louis beside himself with pent-up vehemence, tries to cheer him with the letter from his father: in which Count Morel gladly informs Louis that since, following a recent visit to Château Morel by the Marquis of Roquefort, it is clear the Marquis bears Louis no such grudge as was forecast by the Chevalier, the father now instructs the son to return to the bosom of his family without delay.

That evening, as Louis prepares to begin his homeward journey the following morning, he broods over potentially more effective ways to convince the Chevalier of his innocence, without breaking his promise to the Corregidor. By ten o' clock, having had more than a little wine with his supper, Louis is resolved to seek the Chevalier out for a final frank face-to-face before returning to France, but this is pre-empted by a hand-delivered roasting farewell letter from the Chevalier to Louis, as follows:

> I leave you, and for ever. You have done me the greatest injury any man can inflict upon another. You have shown me what human nature really is, and have made me a misanthrope. I, having watched you from your childhood, had fancied that, amongst the many failings from which youth is never exempt, I perceived the germs of great and shining qualities, both of mind and of heart. I pledged myself to aid in the cultivation of such promise, and bitter now in proportion to my efforts is the atonement which you this day have forced upon me.
>
> Adieu, monsieur. Seek me not, henceforth. Know me not if we meet. Be to me as a stranger, as I to you. Though for the sake of your unhappy mother I rejoice in your escape from the punishment your crimes deserve, my interest in your future is over, and I pray to God that time will rase you from my memory.
>
> Adieu.

Heart-swollen by the scalding injustice of the Chevalier's accusations, Louis by degrees finds himself questioning the integrity and motivations of the Chevalier himself. Surely any impartial judge would have given him a fairer and more patient hearing than this. Whence, then, the Chevalier's impetuous prejudice? And does this not reflect a different light on the Chevalier's impassioned denunciation of the Marquis of Roquefort – who, to judge by his father's letter from Morel, sounds less of a vicious villain than the Chevalier was at pains to make out?

As for long hours he fails to sleep that night, it is only the scant comfort of seeing the Chevalier waning in his own estimation, and the autumnal relief of plans for his imminent Pyrenean trek, that save Louis from even deeper depression.

# 9

# Discussion with Janet

Now by the close of the previous chapter your narrators felt famished for feedback. The public's appetite for literate literature has seldom been more jaded – too many yahoos watching flaccid porn all night on satellite TV,[1] not to mention the ongoing miseries of Thatcherism. So, as few professional writers today can afford to spend a year[2] writing a book which no-one will want to buy, some market research at an early stage is increasingly indispensable.

For those reasons, and because Koo was away on a selling trip that week, I asked our dear friend Janet, with whom we sometimes doss in Muswell Hill whenever a trip to London can no longer be postponed, if she would comment on these pages so far.

'Delighted,' said Janet, whose diacritical severity was amply demonstrated ten years previously, when, as reader for BirdDog Books, she recommended that my first novel should not be reissued as a paperback – on grounds of insufficient moral earnestness.[3] The extent to which this has not ruined my life, and the comradeship which Janet and I have since achieved, may be attributed largely to the advent, proliferation and benevolent advantages of the personal computer – brands of, and cunning software for which, have even displaced

---

[1] Now that we have satellite television ourselves (English terrestrial reception in the Greenadder valley being so abysmal) we note that the porn appears with greatest flaccidity on Wednesday and Saturday nights. Rather as if the broadcasting authorities have been quietly advised that Mr and Mrs Europe do (or should) wish to be aroused into their paroxysm of potentially procreative congress on average twice a week. This, if true, would go hand in glove, you might say, with nuclear family culture.

[2] 'Or five years, as the case may be!' [P.C.]

[3] This of an author who for two stolid years had wrestled with Kant's ethics under the late great H.B. Acton.

money from its long-held number-one preoccupation position in many writers' minds.

In the world of the PC, we may say, there are no real experts; only the ignorant and the less ignorant. This has had the admirable consequence that millions of users all over the world, diverse persons who only a decade before would have had little or nothing to say to one another, are now sharing problems, solutions and (particularly) billions of dollars' worth of other people's copyright software. The gains already made are colossal, and the future potential for increased international communication, co-operation, understanding and harmonious key-tapping peace in the world must surely be estimated to be incalculable when you remember that even a grumpy novelist and the publisher's reader who sabotaged him can be lured by computing exigencies into a relationship of mutual endeavour and subsequent niggleless amity.

All that might very well issue in a different tale, and likely it will soon enough. Its relevance to this story is simply that, were it not for the silicon factor, you would not be about to read the following conversation: transcribed from a tape made last night on the Greenadder Farmhouse answerphone.

'Don't tell me it's no good,' I began. 'I don't want to know.'

'Calm down,' said Janet, 'and let's begin at the beginning, with your "Trailers", which I was surprised to find quite fascinating.'

'But?'

'I do have a few queries.'

'How you amaze me.'

'Shall I go on?'

'Yes, yes. Please do.'

'Well, this James character?'

'George Payne Rainsford?'

'Is he real? I mean, did he really exist?'

'Of course he did, Janet. You'll find him in *Britannica*, if you want – twenty sketchy lines or so, but still a lot more than Godfrey Blobbs'll get a century hence – sandwiched between "James, David," English actor, real name Belasco, and "James, Henry", Anglo-American novelist, brother of William. I know you seldom believe me, but really I've said it so often—'

'Said what?'

'That my novels are less fiction than most people realize, and that I never make things up if the facts are already adequate.'

'Ah, yes. I was forgetting. Anyway, you say here that you already knew James's novels were invariably based on some dramatic episode in history, preferably set in France, with the steamy bits excised, plus — and I'm quoting now — "a formula superstructure of callow romance plugged on, and a naff larding throughout of priggish do-goodery".'

'That certainly rings a bell.'

'Sounds to me as if they're tailor-made for Mills & Boon. Why don't you revamp some of them, and make a fortune that way?'

'If I could, I very well might. But I can't.'

'Why not?'

'Most of these people are already working at the ceiling of their ability. If they weren't, Mills & Boon would see through them. Both editors and readers. In these terms, my ceiling may be no higher, but at least it's in a different building.'

'How modest you are.'

'Thanks.'

'Getting back to James, it seems to me you've let him rather peter out at the end of "Trailers".'

'And?'

'That seems a shame.'

'Why?'

'Because you begin with him, he wins your reader's initial curiosity. So couldn't he be stitched in again later?'

'How?'

'Maybe your narrator could find the De l'Orme-cum-Morel original character elsewhere in James's oeuvre.'

'Actually, your author — as opposed to his narrator — already has!'

'But you haven't told us this.'

'Not yet. Or at least, I hadn't.'

'When will you? In detail, that is?'

'Not sure I'm going to.'

'Why ever not?'

'If all the information in the universe were simultaneously present to one intelligence, that intelligence could never fall in love, except conceivably with itself. Nor could it derive any pleasure from reading novels.'

'So what?'

'Satisfying the reader is a function of reducing hor ignorance. But if by the end of the story you reduce hor ignorance to zero, you deprive hom of the option of metapleasures associated with spirited debate, deconstructive dismemberment, and even occasionally reading the same book again. Who ever read *The Day of the Jackal* twice?'

'What do you mean by "hor"?'

'It's a gimmick – to needle you! Seriously, I get so fed up with "his or her". It's ruining the language. You feminists, I mean.'

'Now look here. If you're not going to take my comments seriously, we might as well pack it in. This is costing me a fortune, you know.'

'Yes, yes. Only kidding. But let me phone you back – this should be on my bill, and anyway I need to put a fresh tape in the machine.'

Half an hour and two cups of coffee later, Janet went on:

'Then, right at the end of "Trailers", you say: blah, blah . . . reader will be, quote, "now enabled to judge for yourself whether Louis Morel killed his father after all."[4] But why "after all"? This is our first hint of possible patricide, and I'm not sure we shouldn't have had a clue rather earlier? Your digressions are . . . mmm, competently executed—'

'But?'

'I would worry that some readers may need a sense of something stranger happening sooner. After all, you've got two mysteries going at once, haven't you?'

'What are they?'

'One, the story itself. Two, the narrator's tracking. And I feel you need to consider whether an impatient reader – and so many readers are *unbearably* impatient these days – '

'Alas, poor Yorick! Fast forward, fast forward!'

'Whether he or she—'

'Hos!'

'I beg your pardon?'

'*He* or *s*he – *hos*. English as she ain't yet spoke.'

'Whether he or she may not expect to be sopped rather earlier with the promise of something more exciting about to unfold.'

'What could be more exciting than the possibility of killing your father, especially when you focus on the *sub*possibilities?'

'Meaning?'

'Deliberately you can kill a man whom you believe to be your father. Biologically he may in fact be your father, or he may not. Again,

---

[4] 'This sequence has evidently since been spirited forward to what is now Chapter 81. Yes?' [P.C.]

deliberately you can kill a man whom you believe *not* to be your father – but what if you are mistaken, like Oedipus? Add *witting but accidental* killing, and that multiplies patricide scenarios again. And again, when you consider that the accidental killer *may not realize* he has killed anyone.

'On top of which, as light relief, are all the situations in which the protagonist may believe, with or without guilt and remorse, that he has killed a man – who may or may not have been his father, no matter what he in fact believed regarding his paternity – when, fortunately (or unfortunately, as the case may be – if, say, the target is a megalomaniac torturing tyrant) the truth of the matter is that no-one has actually died or is going to die. That probably bumps the eventualities up to at least thirty-six, though to be precise one would need to sit down quietly and work it out with a pencil.

'But the point here is that (unlike Shakespeare, who was a dab hand at *making up* and (more often) upgrading stolen crafty plots which turn on the consequences of X believing Y has died – usually when Y hasn't, not yet anyway, as in *Romeo And Juliet* and *Measure For Measure*, say) what we've got here is a rather good story – which we can say without blushing, since the goodness is almost entirely in the historical facts, rather than our invention – off from which the unbearably impatient reader is welcome to peel at any point!'

'You talk too much,' said Janet. 'Now let's push on to characterization, shall we? Otherwise you'll soon be paying British Telecom far more than you'll ever make out of royalties from this novel.'

'It's *not* a novel. Besides, what's wrong with my characterization?'

'Louis himself . . . '

'What about him?'

'As yet I don't *see* him. I mean, no – I do see him, but not in colour. Too many details missing. As if he were a puppet with a blank where his face should be.'

'Don't you think some readers – especially in this age of boobtubes, when soaps, cinema and twenty-four-hour television news shove every last wrinkle, wart and earlobe down your throat for you – prefer the meat of their characters in faction a little leaner? Some space remaining for imaginative DIY?'

'Quite possibly. But even so, Louis Morel to this point, for my money, remains several degrees underdone. Didn't you, in your researching, come across any contemporary portraits of him?'

'There's a deathmask profile in the Cabinet des Grandes Tromperies.

No inscription, hence no proof, but a strong circumstantial presumption that it is of Louis Morel.'

'What does he look like?'

'His own testimony tells us he was tall and strongly built, and this is corroborated by various feats of athleticism and martial-arts-type derring-do which he definitely accomplished. The deathmask portrays no colours, naturally, but the bone structure agrees well with my own prior impressions of Louis. Head large, brow high, cheekbones high, chin strong to pugnacious, nose rather too long and sensual for classical balance – but then some women like that, don't they?'

'How do you see his colouring?'

'Eyes, dark brown. I'd stake a case of wine on that. Hair, I'm not so sure. Probably in – as it were – Mediterranean keeping with his eyes, but possibly lighter. Any shade up to the flawed blonde of wet straw would be credible. As a young cavalier, he would have worn it long, in wavy ringlets to his shoulders, and complemented by a narrow moustache in the form of Cupid's bow pointing upward. Very likely, also, a small ornamental beard like the tip of an ice-cream cone stuck on the point of his chin – but otherwise cleanshaven. How's that?'

'*Moral* character?'

'Very imperfect, as has already been revealed. And yet otherwise: where should we get our drama?'

'I find it hard to believe that even a man could behave with such hideous selfishness.'

'In which episode?'

'Forcing that poor girl to submit to his lust, beside the dead body of the priest who had raped her.'

'Ah. Several points here. First, let's not forget that the Zaragoza maja was manifestly no shrinking virgin. Second, we have only her word for it, as conveyed to and reported by Louis, that the hapless Father Avecido was blackmailing and abusing her. There is no proof, in other words, that the truth was not vice versa.'

'Meaning?'

'That the maja herself, in a black Spanish frenzy of vengeful resentment, did not murder the priest for having virtuously spurned her own advances.'

'But his body was naked.'

'She could have stripped him off after killing him, to strengthen the yarn she was spinning for Louis.'

'You really think a woman would behave like that?'

'I'm not saying she did. Only that she *might* have. And there's another important point here: that transactions which in real life may be vanishingly rare between cool English gentlefolk in the Cotswolds, hence implausible in fictions set there, may be common as crickets in hot Zaragoza. The same goes for your query about Louis having sex with the maja on the bed beside the corpse. A young English nobleman, educated at Eton, probably wouldn't have. Louis wasn't, and he did. Don't forget, however, that we have no reason to believe that Louis Morel's surrendering his virginity to the maja in any way constituted rape, or even that – aside from her impatience to be rid of the corpse – the maja herself was anything but avid. She might even still have been in the throes of an arousal which the priest had refused to satisfy.'

'That's a disgusting suggestion.'

'Terribly sorry.'

'And why do you think she killed herself?'

'I don't know. I haven't uncovered any telling clues, and I suspect that no-one ever will. It may have been on the spur of altruistic desire to get Louis off the hook without compromising her father's honour, or equally to bury for ever her own shame at being pregnant by the priest, or even conceivably a spitefully Pyrrhic attempt to torture Louis with remorse at the thought that his rapacious importunity had precipitated her into suicide. Most likely it was the catastrophic resultant of several such motives. Maybe even combined with the knowledge, or at least belief, that she herself was on borrowed time from incurable cancer – like the beloved of Raimon Lull. Stranger things have happened.'

'I feel you have a serious problem there. The tip of a major iceberg.'

'A K A?'

'The way men writers depict women.'

'Some of us do our best.'

'Well, it isn't good enough. I object also to your saying, for example, in Chapter Six, that Hélène's quote "full snowy bosom, just panting into womanhood, now heaves with emotion until suddenly she swoons back, overcome". Unquote.'

'What's wrong with that?'

'You complain at the outset about James's pale vapid paragons of virginal virtue, so surely you should be developing Hélène into something much more natural yourself.'

'Chapter Six, given the elliptic compression of its note-form style, should surely be granted the licence of a leaven of caricature. In any case you'll find—'

'Really,' interrupted Janet, with steamrolling indignation, 'there is no excuse at all for turning Hélène into yet another of those sexless two-dimensional female wimps with which English literature, traditionally the preserve of men – "men of letters", eh? telling phrase! – has been diluted and debased until all too recently.'

'Until the dawn of Fay Weldon, would you say? In any case you'll find—'

'Women, for God's sake,' fumed Janet, '*do not swoon!*'

'Yes, they do.'

'No, they don't.'

'I've known some that have. By which I don't mean for a moment to suggest . . . on top of which my elder goddaughter has swooned several times in the last few months. Hormones powering up, and all that.'

'How old is she?'

'Thirteen. And physically very close to the stage of development attained by Hélène in Chapter Six. Yum, yum. In addition to which, it surely is widely acknowledged that women of breeding and refinement have, in various periods of history, cultivated The Helpless Swoon as a technique for terminating unwelcome situations, and the attentions of repulsive men. In any case you'll find—'

'I'm not convinced,' said Janet. 'And that brings me to my last point, under the "any constructive suggestions" you requested so eagerly.'

'Yes, yes?'

'Now you say in your synopsis that later on you're going to have this Holmes/Watson-style dialogue with one Dr Macpherson, a historian.'

'Yes.'

'A woman?'

'Very much so.'

'Then how about this? I would think you'd have to have this sort of dialogue far more than once. So couldn't this Dr Macpherson—'

'Audrey to you. She's younger than us. Well, a bit.'

'Couldn't you make her into a kind of anti-heroine—'

'A *real woman*, you mean?'

'To counterbalance la belle Hélène?'

'In what way?'

'Perhaps have your narrator fall for the lady historian, without wanting to. And as a result having to kill off his fictional "son", Louis, as that "son" does his father?'

'Or doesn't.'

'If you say so.'

'So you would have me – that is to say, my narrator – sha–bonking Audrey Macpherson?'[5]

'If you must.'

I must have subliminally paused or sucked my teeth at this point, because Janet immediately chortled:

'You have, haven't you?'

'Mentally I have,' I conceded. 'Though not with indecent frequency.'

'God!' she pounced triumphantly. 'You men are all the same.'

'I would agree, in that regard, that some eighty-five per cent of us are all the same. A fact of ineradicable nature which most of your contemporary lady novelists industriously deplore with a deeply naive although – I grant you – occasionally fetching sort of eureka abhorrence, as though bonking an attractive woman in your mind were merely an uncurbed bad habit like picking one's nose. Interpersonally ingenuous, that, and intellectually profoundly gauche. No doubt good for sales, though, in the pulper corners of the market.'

'You talk too much,' said Janet.

'*That*'s like picking your nose,' I agreed. And so, to the strident sounds of her daughters returning from music practice, we adjourned.

---

[5] As the later greater Lord Clark so aptly remarked, intellectual intercourse with the fairer gender is almost wholly civilizing.

# 10

# Reaction from Charlton

What we didn't mention to Janet, lest it sully her zeal, was that we had simultaneously sent the same batch of chapters to Charlton Palser. Charlton and I became friends a few years ago, when I had the Arts Commission Writing Fellowship at StrathKelvin University. At that time a diligent academic, but unpublished as a novelist, he was panting into the final three thousand laps of his monumental saga *The Quintain*, which has since made quite a splash. As we were then able to offer Charlton some invaluable advice, both creative and contractual, and also to lend a modest hand in persuading Cowgate Press that they would be crazy not to publish *The Quintain*,[1] so he was now graciously overjoyed to inject a little stimulus into Louis Morel. As some readers may savour the gender differences between Charlton's comments and Janet's, we now present Charlton's letter in full.

Dear H.,

I trust you both had a marvellous time on Skye. And I hope the disk of ******** arrived safely and is working okay. Your style analysis techniques sound most intriguing and I wonder if perhaps you shouldn't do them to Godfrey Blobbs and see if he really writes all that stuff himself. I'm off to Spain myself for a fortnight on Thursday so these are just some hasty thoughts slapped into the computer after reading your TS. I wrote some of these notes before I saw your synopsis of the remainder and so found out how far I was wrong but I leave them to stand anyway since they are my fresh impressions while reading, which is what is important.

I take it that though James certainly existed and may have written *De l'Orme* Louis Morel's *Memoirs* are in fact invented by yourself? Your 'Trailers' chapter works quite well though your prose is a little

---

[1] Incidentally, Tiphanie, what ever happened to our bottle of Glenmorangie?

long-winded here and we don't need to know so much about James. Get more quickly to your strange adventures in Lourdes and those delicious meals in the sunlight of Provence! And could you think of a way of cross-cutting back to the present at intervals throughout the text as you sleuth your way towards further discoveries?

In the first pages of the story proper you have many good narrative possibilities – romance, rivalry, danger – but so far you don't have enough mystery. (Except of course regarding the paternity of Louis and the business of whether someone tried to murder him when he was a child.) But though plentiful, the narrative possibilities seemed to me too obvious: Louis loves Hélène; his relationship with her brother will be one of rivalry and suspicion but will probably turn out well; he has made a dangerous enemy in Roquefort (the local big cheese?) but he has a faithful supporter in his Spanish friend Montenero. Would you think about making these possibilities less straightforward and introducing more enigmas, or stressing more strongly the mystery elements you've already got?

The note I wrote at the end of your chapter on 'Methodology' is as follows:

'I hope you're going to interact as the narrator character all through the text. What would be interesting would be a double trail. First, the murder/love interest of the story story. Second, the quest of the narrator to find out the truth. I'm not sure you shouldn't pretend to discover papers that don't exist, to make the reader uncertain what is invention and what based on real hard-fact evidence. I think it might be good if the modern character had a sort of shadow story unfolding. If you are wanting to draw parallels with contemporary people and events this might be done by juxtaposition. I.e., since not all readers are clever enough (or sufficiently awake, when they read fiction) to think this sort of thing through without clear pointers. The Marquis of Roquefort, for example, at least until the doubts raised at the end of Chapter 8, seems morally on a par with a malignant narcissist such as S—— H———. Do you really mean him to be that bad?'

I liked the sequence of the beautiful Spanish girl and the cliff-hanger involving the priest's corpse that Louis has to dispose of though I must say that if this were a novel by me the sequel in Chapter 8 would be very different. In the presence of such danger and death how far is any virility at all to be credited? Louis is of course French and we are invited to believe Maupassant could have done it but we sometimes have to remember, do we not, that not everything that happens in reality will be easily swallowed in a story?

As regards characterization, in my terms there is perhaps not enough inner/mental life in Louis so far. I appreciate that this is entirely deliberate and in keeping with your opinion of Wittgenstein but I mention it all the same. And what about Hélène? Is she going to remain a pure virginal girl all her life or is she soon to blossom into conflicting desires, impulses, and initiatives of her own?

I take it, by the way, that your denouement will reveal (whatever else) that Louis Morel's physical father is indeed the Marquis of Roquefort.

Or is it the Chevalier?

Anyway, I hope we're all still on for the first Saturday of next month.

Best wishes,

C.

# 11

# Pyrenean Whiteout

Though undoubtedly imperfect, considered as pure story, the narrative which follows is nonetheless of polyvalent significance. There are, for example, fresh perspectives to be gleaned on the attitudes to nature and to animals – recalcitrant mules especially – of a youthful French Catholic aristocrat in the middle years of the seventeenth century.

How different from the hardhearted vegetarian Animal Defence Terrorists we know today – and why?

And what instruction, in the refreshingly naive particularism[1] of Louis Morel's raconteering?

Whereas your average Hampstead novelist and literary critic might suffer great pains to milk much symbolism from such paragraphs as you are shortly to savour, to write into them and then (as it were) read out of them certain subconscious objective correlations with Louis's *fall* from grace with the Chevalier, and his *loss* of virginity to/with the maja, plus the construable *bullish* sexism implicit in the *cowlike* mule's being *female*, and so forth, we may with confidence wager two cases of our favourite Rhône wine that even the most analistalytic apparatus would be hard put to discover any such thoughts in the head of Louis Morel when he later described these traumata, let alone during the hectic hours of his undergoing them.

Thus for us the principal values of this chapter are:

(a) a closer contact, through the bending medium of his own translated words, with the *character* of Louis Morel – this being one of the most sustained and vividly recollected of his early fragments.

*And:*

(b) the bitter-sweet goad to puzzling dreams (like a can of chilled

---

[1] Compare and contrast, if you will, with arguments and examples presented by R.W. Hepburn in 'Particularity And Some Related Concepts In Aesthetics', *Proceedings Of The Aristotelian Society*, 1958–9.

strong lager on a blistering beach) of the cliffhanger upon which, with such innocence, he concludes.

Since our arrival [*writes Louis*] three months had cooled the fierce lion of the Zaragoza summer, and cold autumn winds saluted us rudely the moment we got beyond the sheltering walls of the city, piercing to our bones. I would have given ten pistoles[2] for an hour of the hot-breathing siroc, to warm the air till we could heat ourselves by exercise. As we approached the mountains, however, it grew steadily colder, and the prospects of those high snowy passes fell chill and cheerless upon our anticipations.

Though I rode along in melancholy, Father Francis was well acquainted with the many changes of my mood, and consequently, attributing my silent seriousness to the recent events at Zaragoza, he wisely kept his counsel to himself, hoping the rancour of my parting with the Chevalier would fade from my memory soon.

Towards evening on the second day we arrived at a little village consisting of some six shepherds' huts, situated at the very foot of the mountains. Here we learned that the Port de Gavarnie, by which we had intended to enter France, was completely blocked up with snow; but that

---

[2] Very sorry about this, especially in the light of the simplage undertaking so rashly paraded in the second note of the seventh chapter. It's Louis's fault, though, as his numismatics appear to have been temporarily inflected by his Zaragoza sojourn. As to the equivalent value of one of these ten pistoles he would or might have given, it was, according to Chambers, an old Spanish gold coin ' = about' seventeen shillings. But the *Britannica* entry was evidently contributed by more of an old-style enthusiast, for it tells us:

'PISTOLE. The French name given to a Spanish gold coin in use from 1537; it was a double *escudo*, the gold unit, and was worth 16s. 11 ¼ d. sterling. The name was also given to the *louis d'or* of Louis XIII of France and to other European gold coins of about the value of the Spanish coin.'

Given the generous vagueness in relation to other European currencies, the missing three farthings from the *Britannica* sterling value was presumably due to having changed your pistoles in an English 'high street' bank.

less had fallen near Gabas. Thither, then, we directed our steps the next morning, having procured a guide amongst the shepherds, who agreed to conduct us to Laruns, though often he looked at the snow-laden clouds above and shook his head, muttering:

'All speed. We go too slow.'

Soon, as we ascended, the scene all around began to shiver beneath the cold robe of winter. The higher mountains seemed but one mass of snow, and every precipice under which we passed looked crowned with an impending avalanche, which nothing but the black limbs of gigantic pines, which flourish in that region, held back from an instantaneous descent upon our heads.

No frost, however, had yet plumbed the ravines up which we travelled. Our path was rather damp and slippy, and the streams rushed down over the rocks beside us unslowed by the ice of winter. Father Francis' mule, which had delayed our former journey, now proved more sure-footed than the horses ridden by we three others, and the good priest, feeling himself secure, dilated with zeal on the grandeur of the scenery surrounding us, and the magnificence of Nature in general, in even her rudest forms.

'No misanthrope am I,' enthused he, 'and yet I find in the works of God a charm that man and all his arts shall never communicate. When I look upon the mighty productions of Creation, I feel them to be all *true*. All *genuine*. Unchangeable effects of Universal Beneficence in concord with Almighty Power.'

'But of course,' I humoured him pleasantly.

'Alas,' he continued, 'when I consider the deeds of *man*, even the most splendid, I must wonder: for what bad ends were they designed? How much injustice may their execution have cost? And how much vice and misery will attend their consequences? In all man does, you see, there is that germ of *evil*, while the works of God are ever *beauteous in themselves*, and Excellent in their Purpose.'

'And yet, my good father,' said I, glad enough to warm our chill way with some controversy, 'though you pronounce the flashes of worldly glory to be but misguided meteors, and power a perilous precipice, and love a volcano of hot disaster, are not there yet *some* mortal deeds which *even you* can behold with delight? Protecting the weak? Assuaging grief, dispensing joy; the leading unto virtue? And salvation?'

'How very true!' Father Francis replied. 'But though all these *actions* are admirable, how many of all the *motives* which prompted them are good? Only, I believe, when we look deeply into *our own breast*' – here he tapped his – 'then and there do we find how many faults, weaknesses, follies . . . *crimes—*'

That last pregnant word Father Francis pronounced almost as a sob, but before I could inquire what particular images of wickedness assailed his holy mind, he went on:

'Whereas here, in the wilderness, all is so magnificent, abundant; perfect. All without striving. Proceeding from Him who is All Wise. Reminding us, dear Louis, that even death itself, the worst earthly evil to befall this frail body, is also to be welcomed.'

'You go too far!' I protested with all the passion for life of my youth, but then was silenced by an eerie glimpse of painful serenity on Father Francis' face, as he trotted close beside me on his mule.

'No, no, Louis,' he insisted breathlessly. 'For death too is the work of that Great Creator who made both the body *and the soul—*'

The culmination of the good father's wisdom was now drowned out by a vast muffled rushing noise, that caused us all to look up to the cloud overhead, which like a thick veil screened the mountain peaks from our view. In a moment the cloud itself became agitated as by a strong wind, while a roar more awful than thunder filled our ears with a dreadful oppression.

'*Valancha, valancha!*' cried the guide.

In that same instant I seized Father Francis' bridle and spurred my own mount urgently forward. To my surprise, the obstinate mule, far from resisting my effort to pull her on, was only too eager to gallop. Hussaye and the guide followed hard on our heels and within a minute we reached a sharp corner of solid cliff which – the valley forking abruptly east – afforded a certain shelter. Glancing back we saw, cascading down the mountain to obliterate the path where we were just moments ago, a devastating shapeless mass of a dim blue hue, which raised a misty atmosphere like a growing snowball all around itself as it fell.

The mountain, even to where we stood, shook violently with the shock.

The valleys, precipices and caverns echoed back the tremendous roar of its fall. Immense masses of rock rolled down before the irresistible avalanche, and long ere it reached them the tall pines swayed and teetered as if writhing in certainty of their impending destruction. Moments later they all fell crashing and were uprooted like flowers as down, down, down the avalanche rolled on – dazzling the eye, deafening the ear, and sweeping all before it until, striking the valley floor like a thousand cannon discharged at once, it blocked up the entire pass, dispersed the stream in a cloud of mist, and by the sheer concussion of its echo shook a multitude of crags and rocks down from the summits on either side.

Father Francis raised his hands to heaven. Though few men can ever have been better prepared to leave this earth, yet with that instinctive love of corporeal life, which neither stoical philosophy nor devout religion can ever wholly banish, he thanked God most fervently for our preservation from the calamity just past. We had, indeed, to be grateful not only for our deliverance from the avalanche itself, but also for having accomplished our passage before its fall cut off our route.

The shepherd guide, however, seemed less overjoyed. Such a massive *valancha*, he said, was uncommon in this season. When they did happen, they were always indicative of some great commotion forthcoming in the atmosphere. Neither did he love those heavy clouds that rested half-way down the sides of the mountains, nor the dead stillness of the upper air; both of which phenomena seemed to him to forbode a snow-storm, the most certain agent of the traveller's destruction in winter.

Nothing remained, however, but to press forward as fast as possible. Yet now Father Francis' mule resumed with a vengeance her hereditary obstinacy, and neither fair words nor vigorous blows would induce her to move one step faster than suited her, thus hobbling all our hopes of reaching Laruns before darkness fell.

After a further vain campaign to woo the impassible animal, we were obliged to yield, and journey onward as slowly as she chose, while occasionally a distant howling in the gorges of the mountains gave warning that the apprehensions of our guide were well founded. A large eagle, too, sailed long before us, breaking, with its ill-omening voice, the profound and deathlike silence of the air. Over all the scene was a dark and inexpressible gloom, which penetrated heavily to our hearts.

Gradually the howling up the mountains grew more loudly incessant, and soon the wind broke upon us in quick sharp gusts that almost threw us from our horses, while a shower of small fine sleet drove sorely in our faces. The guide now grumbled loudly at the slowness of Father Francis' mule, and declared he would not linger to risk his life for any mule in Spain.

We were now upon the French side of the mountains, and, as the road seemed reasonably defined, I doubted not that we should find our way without his assistance. As his insolence waxed louder, therefore, I told him that, if he were a coward, and afraid to stay by those persons he had undertaken to guide, then he should canter ahead forthwith and deliver us from his whingeing tongue.

He answered with surly dignity:

That he was no coward; but that, having his wife and children to provide for, his life was not without value; that if we would go faster he would guide us on; but that, if we would not – on our own heads be it.

Seeing him thus determined I thought it best to send Hussaye forward with him: to return with some local mountain men, lest Father Francis and I should by then have missed our way, or been overwhelmed by snow. Hussaye was too much the old soldier to oppose an order, and so reluctantly rowelled his horse to follow the guide down to Laruns.

An hour later, so sharp was the wind in our faces that we could hardly distinguish our way, being nearly blinded by a mingle of snow and extremely fine hail. So dim and obscure was the atmosphere that we could not see twenty clear paces before us, while through the opaquing air loomed fantastic shapes of giants, castles, and monsters of the peaks. Even to our mounts these transformations appeared, and once my horse shied violently from a promontory rock which appeared, to me also, in the guise of a white-shrouded ghoul. Soon after that we were many minutes more than we could afford in whipping the mule past an old pine which the tempest had hurled down the mountain, and which, leaning over a mass of stone, looked like an immense serpent, stretching out its neck to devour any creature that passed beneath.

Meanwhile the ground was piling thick with snow, and every footfall of my horse sank deeper. Both mule and horse soon lost their vigour with fatigue, and we now had much difficulty in making them proceed. As darkness gathered it was with feelings I have seldom felt that I observed all vestige of a path being rapidly effaced, till soon the only means of following our road was by the murmuring of a rockside stream below, on which the snow drifted like great broken lilies, rushing on. Even the black patches where some salient crag had defied the drift were now swallowed up by white, and it became evident that much more snow had already fallen on the French side than we had been led to expect in Spain.

So every step became more perilous, none of the holes and crevices in the path being visible, while the dashing snow in our eyes combined with the oncoming night to render us effectively blind. Thus far I had led myself, but Father Francis now insisted upon going first, on account of the surer feet of his mule, which never once had faltered – whereas my own larger gelding twice had stumbled, on slippery rocks concealed by snow. After some opposition I consented, gripped by the guilt of fatigue, and by a growing despair of doubt that we could ever disentangle ourselves from this terrible knot of cold, darkness, flailing wind, the yawning abyss to our left, and the melancholy howling of the pine-wooded mountains all around.

For some minutes, however, the mule plodded on with the methodical caution peculiar to these animals, and my horse followed meekly. Still the snow blew, and the wind roared round the mountains with escalating violence, till suddenly the mule stopped dead and expressed her implacable determination to venture no further. Fearful of some snow-covered danger which she alone sensed, I dismounted and went forward some paces, trying the ground carefully at each step. But all seemed firm enough, there was road width for two carriage horses to advance abreast, and I therefore concluded that Father Francis' mule had merely been actuated by a fresh fit of her obstinacy. So I mounted again, and made to lead the way, to try whether the mule would now at least follow.

Alas, as I urged my horse past her the vicious brute struck out with her hind hooves full in my gelding's chest. He reared, plunged, reared again, and in that moment I felt his haunches sliding over the precipice behind. With the instinctive speed of self-preservation I abandoned the bridle, rolled sideways forward from the saddle, and, catching hold of a wiry bush protruding from the brink, found myself swinging in the snowy air with my toes scraping helplessly against perpendicular rock.

My brain, already giddy, was agonized by a fearful sound – something between a neigh and a human scream – from the depths below, which told me dreadfully the fate of my horse, that I myself had so narrowly escaped. Slowly, with desperate caution, fearing every moment that the roots of the pliant bush to which I clung would give way, and plunge me down into the horrid abyss beside my horse, I contrived to ease my body back over the edge to safety – where, a few panting moments later, I replied to the anxious calls of Father Francis, who dimly had seen the horse slide over, and heard his cry below, but knew not if I had fallen with him.

My heart still beat too madly, and my brain revolved too dizzily, to permit of our proceeding for some minutes. The loss of my horse, also, was a serious extra burden on my own fatigue, and hence to our corporate peril. Remedy, however, there was none; and so, after pausing to recover our breath, we attempted to resume our journey. To lead her on, I laid my hand upon the mule's bridle – but . . .

Nothing would make her move.

The moment I tried to *pull* her forward, and Father Francis touched her with his whip, she shied back towards the edge of the precipice till one further step would have toppled her over.

Nothing now remained but for the elderly priest to descend and press forward also on foot. As soon as he was safely off the back of this contrary she-devil which had caused us so much distress, I essayed to *force* her to oblige us; resolving, in my anger, that if she again approached the edge I would bundle her over with nary a qualm. But with cunning equal to her obstinacy she divined my intent, and calmly lay down on her side in the snow, leaving us bound to continue without her.

Now began the most painful part of our journey.

Every step was fraught with danger; horrific gloom enveloped us; and death lay beckoning all around in a hundred unknown shapes. Wherever we ascended we had to struggle against the full force of the overpowering blast, and then, when the path verged into a descent, we needs must pick our way with redoubled caution: on a road so thick with snow that it was hardly possible to keep one's feet, and with the precipice just inches away.

For perhaps an hour we continued thus, sometimes falling, frequently knocked back by the wind, drenched in consequence of the driven snow melting within our clothes, while the cold of the atmosphere increased as the night matured. At length, in blizzard conditions compounded by absolute darkness, Father Francis, who hitherto had struggled on with a vigour that belied his age, now fell beside me in a heap, and protested his incapacity to continue.

'My days are over, Louis,' he murmured weakly as I knelt beside him. 'Leave me, and go forward as best you can. If I mistake not, we are near the pass above Laruns. Speed on, my dear boy.'

Immediately I protested:

'But, Father—'

'Would that I had strength to battle on a little longer, Louis. But I have not. I have done my utmost, and now . . . I must surrender.'

He spoke so feebly that I knew there was no hope of him rising, but to leave the good old man in that situation was of course unthinkable, and consequently I expressed my determination to wait there also for the return of Hussaye, who, I forecast with a confidence I did not feel, could not be long in returning with assistance to aid our rescue.

'No, Louis, no!' poor Father Francis wheezed. 'The wind, the snow, the cold . . . all hazards grow worse. You *must* go on. If you do not, *you* will perish also. But first a message . . . for your mother. Most vital . . . '

'What is it, Father?' I encouraged him sorrowfully. His voice was so faint that I pressed my ear to his lips.

Painfully he croaked:

' . . . confided to me . . . but as I now cannot, *you* must tell her . . . '

'Tell her *what*, Father?'

Though he mouthed a few more broken words, the howling of the storm was so dreadful that I could not make out what he said. Thinking, in a mad moment, to carry Father Francis to safety in my own arms, I flogged my dwindling strength to lift his weighty body from the snow. Alas, before I had taken three steps with my limp and sightless burden, a blast of gale whirled us round like a top and threw our bodies sprawling into what must have been the jaws of a pot-hole, deeply drifted. Down, down into the dark yielding drift we sank until our bodies must have utterly disappeared from level view, if light there had been.

A minute later, gasping from the panic of suffocation, I contrived to scrape aside the wall of snow between myself and Father Francis, of whose sleeve I still had hold.

'Father, Father?' I called as in a dream, as I rolled myself beside him, thinking to cocoon our bodies together, to share our warmth till the storm should wane, and daylight come. 'Speak to me, Father. Father? What must I tell my mother?'

He made no reply.

I raised his head, but respond he could not. I forced my hand within his robe, upon his heart, and found it had ceased to beat.

# 12

# Après Whiteout

The cliffhanger effect at the close of the previous chapter appears to have less to do with any narrative deviousness on the part of Louis Morel than with the fact that, not long after the death of Father Francis, Louis himself lost consciousness in the snow. His memory of the next few weeks is garbled at best, and the motif which recurs most frequently in his notes is a cycle of horrible haunting dreams, 'the vilest that ever I dreamt', which torment him with guilt at being solely responsible – so he cannot but feel – for Father Francis' death.

'The principal of the party was *me*,' he repeats several times, 'and *I* gave the order to travel.'

Curiously, there is no speculation on the vital message which Father Francis was prevented by death from conveying to the Countess. Nor is there any evidence of further remorse, or even brooding, over his tiff with the Chevalier. Likewise his fornication with the maja, and the possibility that this may have contributed to her suicide – these matters are simply not mentioned.

What is most on his conscious mind, during this period, is his relationship with Hélène Arnault. When, after three weeks of bed-bound debilitation and delirium, his powers of reason revive sufficiently to service his long-term memory, he finds himself lying in bed in his mother's dressing chamber. Before his eyes open he hears his mother's voice request that Hélène will continue to watch over the slumbering patient for the rest of the night, as she, the Countess, is knackered.

As Louis's faculties collect, he feigns continued sleep. Hélène sits down by his bedside, and a minute later he feels her warm sweet breath fan his cheek. All in the same instant, his eyes open, his arm encircles her startled neck, and he kisses her full on the lips.

'Oh, Louis!' cries Hélène, in a turmoil of fright and delight.

Louis is of course too delicate to take further advantage of Hélène at this juncture. The effort of embracing her has exhausted him, and now he is too weak to manage more than merely to swear how terribly much he loves her, while Hélène rushes away beside herself to tell the Countess the glad news of Louis's awakening.

Now ensue massive maternal joy, weeping; remonstrative kisses.

Then two months of convalescence, which one can't help suspecting Louis deliberately protracts. Through his weakness he is licensed to have Hélène with him, and to get closer to her than ever before in their maturity, and yet it seems Hélène is still tantalizingly adept at avoiding any advances beyond the bounds of decorum, and at cutting short or flitting away from all declarations and propositions of devotion, marriage, sexual intercourse, and whathaveyou. Before his parents she enacts the solicitous sister, yet in their moments alone, though she is bright-eyed, affectionate, attentive, and all, and though despite teasing him over his various residual frailties she manifestly rejoices in his recovery, she invariably shies away and quits his room several seconds before any truly irreversible proposition parts his lips — 'like a butterfly fleeing a shadow'.

As Louis's exceptional natural vitality revives he becomes increasingly irritated by Hélène's elusive behaviour, and is close to resolving to teach her a lesson by leaping up unexpectedly and pinning her into the sort of corner from which not even a butterfly can flit, when one morning — this is in early December — the Countess, while bedbathing Louis, is alarmed to notice that her son has a stupendous erection.[1] Of course, being a well-bred aristocratic lady of discreet years,[2] she makes no comment to Louis himself. But from that moment, as though a portcullis had been dropped between them, he conspicuously ceases to be nursed in alternating shifts by Hélène, and is assigned Old Hussaye instead.

In consequence, Louis's return to full physical health is accelerated as

---

[1]  In its own terms — ie, presumably.

[2]  Sadly, Countess Morel does not have long to live. In December 1640, however, she is still, to all external intents and purposes, a zestful and extremely handsome woman of forty-four. Her relationship with Louis shares a number of instructive correspondences with that between Gertrude and Hamlet. See, for example, our own *Prince Hamlet, HypoStar*, Chapter 17, and possibly also Apollinaire's *Les exploits d'un jeune Don Juan*, Chapter 1, which we've also thought would be enormous fun to film.*

    * **'What are these irrelevancies FOR?' [J.R.]**

by magic, but all to no avail so far as his access to Hélène is concerned. She is busy sewing samplers for his mother. Or she is indisposed, as young ladies are. Or she has gone to Lourdes to visit her father and brother. Or anything, just so long as she is never where Louis can get her alone to himself. Feeling conspired against, he turns morose, fidgety; irascible. Piqued by his mother's evident lack of confidence that he would not debauch Hélène, given half a chance, Louis punishes her – his mother – by protracting his silence regarding the lost vital message from Father Francis.

Thinking again of Father Francis, Louis now quizzes Old Hussaye more closely as to the manner of his rescue from the snow. Reluctantly Hussaye confesses that the first person he approached for help was the Lourdes lawyer's son, Jean-Baptiste. Although Jean-Baptiste himself was all set to kit up and follow Old Hussaye back into the mountains, his father, Maître Arnault, would not allow it.

'In fact, Master Louis . . . ' Hussaye admits uncomfortably.

'Yes, Hussaye? Hold nothing back. Tell me all.'

Now it emerges that Hussaye's straining ears overheard Maître Arnault tersely mutter to Jean-Baptiste that:

'"Indeed it will be the better for you, Jean-Baptiste, if young Morel dies, because then . . . "'

'Because then *what*, Hussaye?'

'I'm sorry, Master Louis. The rest I could not catch.' Hussaye proceeds to relate how he then effected the rescue with the aid of several sturdy mountaineers prised from a local tavern and armed with inextinguishable resin torches.

'So Jean-Baptiste was not with you when you found me?'

'No, Master Louis. He wanted to be, despite all what his father had said, but the Maître absolutely forbade it.'

'Hmn.' Half of Louis's brain thinks Old Hussaye is making some of it up, this stuff against Maître Arnault, since why should a lawyer – even a lawyer as hideous, and with such black-boat-mean eyes, as Maître Arnault – have an interest in Louis Morel's death? Surely no adult's resentment of a child's careless insult could fester so long. Could it?

During the Christmas festivities Maître Arnault comes to Morel bearing gifts for Hélène. To the Count and Countess, and even to Louis, the lawyer acts humble and fawning. But Louis is disturbed to note that Jean-Baptiste, habitually somewhat sheepish and awkward, has now turned thoroughly tongue-tied and surly with the hostility of embarrassment, if not full-blown shame. But why is this?

Hélène too seems affected by this Christmas visitation, and by a New Year pilgrimage to her old family situation in Lourdes. Though hormonal maturity has brought out in her an unexpected streak of demurely vivacious cheek, verging occasionally on the delicately waspish, these year-end contacts with Maître Arnault and Jean-Baptiste seem to regress her into a withdrawn phase of moody sadness, in consequence of which she becomes more difficult than ever for Louis to get hold of alone.

Tortured by indignation and doubt as to the causes underlying Hélène's melancholy unattainability, Louis embarks on his most extravagant bout of speculation and fantasy to date. In romantic moments he determines to elope with Hélène at midnight tonight and marry her at noon tomorrow. In lustful interludes he images creeping upon her sleeping virginity in the smaller hours and mounting her with loving tenderness before she has a chance to wake up and protest. In conservative moments he projects marrying her before mounting her. Never once – so staunchly the French gentleman is he – does it occur to him that perhaps Hélène is being quietly withered by impossible passion for *another man*, after whom she hankers much more than ever for Louis.

By mid January, deprivation of Hélène's company, attention and admiration, combined with his restoration to robust full strength, have whipped Louis into a cycle of ill humour, short temper and severe impairment of manners. Perceiving this as normal in a young gallant deprived of society, Count Roger floats the notion that perhaps the time is high for Louis to sample the excitements of city and courtly life – if not yet regiments and battles – and within a week the Countess agrees. Meanwhile Louis learns of the visit to Château Morel, paid during the later stages of his own sojourn in Zaragoza, of the Marquis of Roquefort . . . whose polished elegance and frank character have apparently banished from Count Roger's mind any suspicion that the Marquis is anything other than a benevolent wellwisher, whom the Chevalier of Montenero, it seems, has rather unfairly and excessively traduced.

Countess Morel is less obviously sold on the Marquis of Roquefort's unctuous blandishments, but she does not veto his coming – when, in late January, he offers to call again: to kiss and make up with Louis, and discuss how a modest marquis's influence might be harnessed into service of Louis's career.

On the afternoon of the last Saturday in January the Marquis of Roquefort turns up at Château Morel, all charming and effusive, with only two servants to attend him. In his description of the subsequent reception Louis admits that though smouldering pique against the Chevalier of Montenero may have made him more disposed to form favourable impressions of Roquefort, he would nevertheless – 'as would any impressionable young gentleman, as yet unblooded in wars' – have found the Marquis thoroughly fascinating:

Profoundly knowledgeable; widely travelled; honourably battle-hardened; sensitively discriminating in his aesthetical tastes; urbane; witty . . . the complete catalogue of laudatory adjectivals would be wearisome to reproduce.

Now over the past few years, it appears, Countess Morel has, by spartan frugalities, or other means best known to herself, repaired to some extent the Morel family fortunes, and hence four new youthful attendants are present to make up eight liveried lackeys altogether to grace the hall on the evening of the Marquis of Roquefort's arrival. Louis's own explanation of this extravagance is that his mother is determined her only son shall not suffer the burden of a great name combined with inferior fortune. Then comes an amusing but essentially immaterial comic dispute between Old Hussaye and the maître d'hôtel as to who should sound the dinner trumpet, followed by a more acutely observed account of how, while Count Roger hands the Countess down the grand stair to dinner, the radiant Hélène is smoothly snaffled by the Marquis of Roquefort before Louis even realizes he has missed his chance.

'What a breathtakingly beautiful daughter you have, madame,' beams the Marquis, as they settle down to their hot fish soup.

Hélène blushes redder than the peppers that float in the soup, and the Countess diplomatically explains that Hélène Arnault is not her *real* daughter, then introduces Hélène formally to Monsieur de Roquefort as Mademoiselle Arnault. Hélène's discomfiture and Louis's indignation at being ignored are for some courses patched by a conversation between the two senior gentlemen, transparently insincere on the Marquis's part, on the morality of eating meat. The Marquis, affecting to gracefully consume his venison casserole out of courtesy to his hosts, simultaneously parades a languid vegetarianism in principle.

To this Count Roger replies with some warmth:

'It is a philosophy I can never accept, sir. The simple act of eating is surely not in itself degrading, and gains dignity by the noble objects to which it tends – the preservation of life, invigoration of the

body, and, consequently, the liberation of the mind from all thralls
of corporeal weakness. To these ends, what holier means could the
Good Lord have provided us with, than fresh red meat cooked with
love?'

Smiling in polite acknowledgement of the energy with which Count
Roger rides his hobbyhorse, the Marquis of Roquefort replies:

'Each to his own preferred poison, sir. Absolutely. Myself I conceive
no dignity in eating flesh off the mangled limbs of other animals slain
for our use.'

Keen to abort such a germ of acrimony in her dinner-table atmosphere,
the Countess, leaning towards the Marquis and touching his elbow with
what Louis records as 'a strange air of admiration tinged with distrust',
switches subjects as follows:

'You look not so cynically, sir, we can but hope, on all other failings
of humanity?'

'Other failings, madame?'

The Countess meets the Marquis's cynical twinkle squarely with her
own hot-blooded gaze, and, as Louis puts it, leaps 'to a topic on
which all French women theorize incessantly, and entertain innumerable
opinions':

'*Love*, for instance?' she challenges him.

In the same breath: Count Roger frowns, Hélène gasps in horrified
delight and stares down at her plate, and Louis watches guardedly to see
how the Marquis will respond.

First, he raises his glass to the Countess, and blows her a debonair
kiss. Second, he toasts the incomparable beauty of Hélène, who blushes
deeply to her bosom. Then he announces:

'No-one, madame, but no-one, could be more devoted to the love-
lier part of creation than am I – and yet . . . ' he ponders provocatively.

'Qualifications, sir?' the Countess reprovingly inquires.

'And yet, I cannot but applaud the ancients who portrayed our
archetypal Venus as emerging from the *foam* of the sea.'

'Her nakedness emblematic', rejoins Count Roger, 'of the *lightness* of
her nature, and *fickle* as her parent waves?'

'Often as *cold* and *cruel* too,' blurts Louis, as inadvertently he
ogles the furiously flushing Hélène. Pre-empting parental reprimands,
he rushes on to observe in more educated tones:

'But you forget, Monsieur de Roquefort – or rather, being so adroit
an antagonist – you decline to remind us – that the foam of the sea, to

engender the great goddess Venus, was impregnated with the blood of Coelus,[3] which we translate *drops from heaven.*'

'Happily turned!' claps the Marquis, with a smile full of barbs. 'But I wonder, young friend, if your classical sapience is equally aware that the *queen of love* is only ever to be *won outright*, as our peerlessly tumid Racan[4] would put it, by the victorious *god of arms*. And therefore whether you yet have subscribed to the field in which – as I know to my cost! – you were born to achieve highest honours? I mean the military service of your King.'

'Not yet,' the seething Louis has to admit.

'Fie, fie!' cries the Marquis. 'Be informed, sir, that *every* gentleman, whatever his ultimate projects, must serve his nation in at least one campaign. Well! It is rumoured all over at present that our wars in Italy will infallibly soon be renewed. In that event I shall of course resume command of my regiment, and if your venerable father shall permit you to serve under me, we shall turn our two sharp swords, that once crossed in frivolous quarrelling, against the serious enemies of France. What say you?'

Louis, sorely stung in his machismo, is on the verge of accepting, but Countess Morel interposes that she already has reserved a soldierly place for Louis, via her old friend the Countess of Soissons, in the camp of that lady's great son. A harsh twitch of lips betrays that the Marquis of Roquefort seems fleetingly displeased to hear of this liaison with the house of Soissons, but he recovers immediately and with courtly adroitness steers the conversation along innocuous tacks.

Dinner concludes without further incident or controversy, and Louis later recalls with considerable exasperation his wholesale captivation by

---

[3] We cannot imagine where Louis got this mis-spelling (of, we take it, the Roman 'Caelus') or his bowdleprettied version of the story – except perhaps out of some tender concern not to cause blushing virgins to swoon. Otherwise, surely, he would have frankly reminded the dinner party that Venus (Aphrodite) in fact emerges from a foaming sea previously impregnated (a little over nine months ago?) by the severed genitals of Uranus, these having been hacked off him by his son Cronus.

[4] Racan, Honoré. Soldier and poet. Died in 1670 aged seventy-one. An original member of the French Academy. 'Overpoweringly sedative.'

the mesmeric charm of the Marquis of Roquefort, despite the naked malignity of their prior encounter at Lestelle.

On the second day of the Marquis of Roquefort's stay at Morel, the winter weather is brightly fine, and an izard[5] shoot is proposed. Louis, having penned unquenchable love songs into the small hours, and therefore slept in, gets a little behind in his preparations for the hunt. As he flusters across the hall with his gun he is urgently intercepted by Hélène, whose flushed cheeks and slightly dishevelled mien seem to Louis more unbearably lovely than ever. As Hélène pulls him aside, Louis, scarcely believing his luck, encircles her waist, hugs her close, and starts burbling his candlelight verse.

Hélène, encouragingly, does not break free from his embrace, but rather presses her finger to his lips and orders him in a whisper to shut up and listen.

'To what more heavenly music?' trills Louis, nuzzling her neck in ecstasy.

'Stop that, Louis,' she rebukes him. 'This is serious.'

'What is?'

'The Marquis of Roquefort—'

'What about him?'

'I have reason to believe . . . '

'Yes, yes – oh, Hélène!'

'The Marquis is no gentleman, but rather the arrantest villain.'

'None arranter!'

'Oh, *Louis*.' Now she tries fearful tears. 'This is serious. You must be careful.'

'Upon what ground?'

Hélène averts her gaze and mutters that she has not time to tell him now, but she fears for his safety in the Marquis's company, and begs him to stay home from the hunt. Louis, outraged by such a cowardly prospect, draws breath to examine her further, but now irate clattering sounds are heard of Count Roger chasing up Louis, at which point Hélène seizes her

---

[5] Your izard being the Pyrenean chamois, rather redder and smaller than his or her Alpine cousin. That anyone could dream of shooting such an exquisite creature surely highlights, does it not, the gulfs between then and now, evil and less evil, them and us – who only ever shoot the droves of ravenous flea-riddled rabbits that devour our organic green beans?

opportunity to break free and glide away.

By midday, in the snowdusted heights above the valley of Argelès, the three hunting guns are spread out. After an hour of no luck, suddenly a prime buck izard bounds up in front of Louis, and he follows. Angling for a shot between baffling rocks, Louis hurries towards where the desperate izard is trapped in a sheer dead-end, when sharply a loud bang rings round the slopes and a bullet from above passes through the crown of Louis's cap. Whirling in rage, he sees the Marquis of Roquefort, on a ledge higher up, kneeling to reload while jovially cursing having missed the izard with his opening shot.

'Shoot now, Monsieur Morel,' the Marquis calls generously to Louis. 'As I have failed, do you shoot now, and the kill is yours.'

Louis duly turns, takes careful aim, and in a moment the izard is dead. Later there is no overt allusion to the Marquis of Roquefort's dangerous shot, but Louis can't help brooding privately over whether the Marquis's failure was really to kill the izard, or . . . himself? Partly despite and partly because of this tingling suspicion, at dinner that night he accepts the Marquis's cordial invitation to accompany him back on the morrow, for a bout of better hunting in the hills round his own shooting lodge at Gagnères.

'I acknowledge', Louis later reflected, 'that my motives were a curious motley. Aside from cavalier revulsion against my own apprehension, that Monsieur de Roquefort had attempted to take my life, and might again, and with more facility in his own domain, I was driven still by a yearning to discover the Marquis less heinous than the Chevalier had portrayed him.' All of which was multiplied, on the night, by annoyance with Hélène (who was 'indisposed', and would not see him) and reaction against his mother, who most strenuously attempted to scotch this hunting expedition to Gagnères.

But:

'Let the lad follow his nose,' decides the easy-going Count Roger. 'He'll be all right with Hussaye.'

So the following morning, furious with Hélène for not coming down to his sending-off, Louis departs with the Marquis, accompanied only by Old Hussaye and the Marquis's own two burly armed attendants.

# 13

# Who Kills Whom?

The chivalrous reason for inflicting a chapter break between there and here is to forearm feminists against a little passage coming up shortly which might make their pulses quicken. We're sorry for any inconvenience and offence this may cause, but there are some responsibilities we simply will not shirk. For insight into the background, consider H.S. Eveling's seminal discussion in 'Composition and Criticism'.[1] We might add that in our view Stanley Eveling is one of the most accomplished British playwrights of the past forty years, and the fact that his work has not received acclaim of the order enjoyed by the likes of Tom Stoppard seems to us thoroughly symptomatic of the attitude in general of London to Scotland – an attitude in turn disturbingly similar to the manner in which the United States relates to the rest of the world as a hole.

But where were we?

The day was dry and crisp and the ride delightful [*Louis recalls*], and yet he [the Marquis] contrived to withdraw my attention from the scenery by the fascination of his conversation. The first subject he discoursed upon was my proposed apprenticeship with the Count of Soissons, and in this regard he dashed off a flurry of bold yet telling sketches of some of the principal courtiers of the day.

'You must be a keen observer,' said I politely, 'of those particular characters you know, and of human life at large.'

'Life,' Monsieur de Roquefort surprised me by replying, as we trotted a riverside road, 'as life, is little worth considering. It is a stream that flows by us without our knowing how. Its turbulence or its tranquillity depend little upon ourselves. If there be rain in the mountains, then life shall be torrential. In drought? A thin trickle. Any way, it will flow as it will for each one of us, till we have naught left to do but die.'

---

[1] *Proceedings of the Aristotelian Society*, 1959.

* * *

Though Louis courteously declines to share in the Marquis's cynical fatalism, he is troubled by the strength of its logic. His bones and muscles and brain, each morning still waking to feel themselves more puissant than yesterday, revolt against any notion that the will that drives them may not be free, but what good arguments can they adduce?

Louis's solution, so typical of philosophical immaturity, is to jettison all the *thoughts* thought, on grounds of the thinker's turpitudinous *conduct*. This emerges when he deplores the Marquis's reasons for commending 'moderation' as the most golden word any language possesses.

But why?

'His advocacy was certainly upon no principle of virtue,' Louis records a trifle pompously, 'either moral or religious. Rather was his counsel of restraint for the sake of *pleasure alone* – that it should be more durable in the savouring, and unsoured by the bitter interest so often payable, on excessive borrowings from health. This coldly calculating hedonism, expressed by Monsieur de Roquefort, naturally turned my conscience back uneasily to improving conversations, in days gone by, with the Chevalier of Montenero. For the moment, however, I contented myself with replying to the Marquis, that if men had no stronger motives to moderation than the expectation of avoiding unpleasant effects in the future, they would seldom put much restraint upon their passions.'

'"Nor do they!" he agreed in triumph. "Not often."

'Soon after that we arrived at his *pavillon de chasse*, and I must own that never before had a more sumptuously luxurious dwelling regaled my eye. It was not a large building, by château criteria, but all was perfectly geared to comfort and pleasure. Piles of cushions, rich carpets, easy chairs, Persian sofas, oriental tapestries . . . every chamber was a hive of ease. Books, too, and pictures were there in abundance, but all of a certain class. Catullus, Ovid and Petronius lined the shelves, while the walls were adorned with many a nymph and satyr, in antic tableaux never dreamed of at Château Morel.'

Now Louis, like many other men of action, is notable for disparities between certain spontaneously billygoatish bouts of his behaviour, and a marked vein of stilted prudery in his dialogue and writings. Thus, all he actually tells us, concerning the next two days in the Marquis of Roquefort's *pavillon* at Gagnères, is that the moments sped by like musket balls, that each hour was stuffed with new enjoyments, but that to his taste it all quickly palled into a gel of sweetness cloying, in response to which:

'One felt it to be overly luscious. Like the decadent Romans, Monsieur de Roquefort spliced his wine with honey, and the draught for me was too rich.'

To counterpoint Louis's reticence it may be instructive to mix in here a short memoir by a diarist whose life was tame by comparison, but who wrote with exemplary candour. Here, in other words, comes the debatably obnoxious passage advertised at the top of this chapter.

So if you don't wish to know, close your eyes now.

After dinner [*writes Vicomte Turenne*, of a phase in his youth during the year 1637], the Marquis, having proposed the wager, led we three, his youngest guests, to a small private chamber festooned with scarlet drapes. [This was in another of the Marquis of Roquefort's hunting lodges, a stunning sixteenth-century building by Clément Métezau, near Dreux to the south-west of Paris.]

On a floor thick with Persian splendour reclined six opulent doxies, all unclad and nibbling sweetmeats. At a word from the Marquis, soft spinet music began to play behind the drapes and the sprawling women gathered their bodies in the form of a Star of David, with their heads at its centre, where they continued to confer, in low giggling tones, and to pick at their sweetmeat dish, while their rumps pointed outwards invitingly, like points of the Star somewhat blunted.

Now the wager was, to the value of one hundred livres each, whether, beginning as it were with doxy Number One at two of the clock, we blades could manage twenty strokes each, at each woman's crupper, and continue thus all the way round. [Ie, up to and including twenty thrusts for Mademoiselle Number Six at midnight.] Any man who succeeded would pocket his hundred livres, but he who failed must pay the Marquis. Alas, despite all our youth and considerable virility, not one of us, nay not even I myself, but failed to come adrift in the region of Four or Five. The Marquis had disciplined his doxies with great cunning, having learned such techniques in the East, and thus we lost our money.

Concerning Louis Morel's sojourn at Gagnères, there is no proof that he was subjected to identical entertainment, but evidence will be presented shortly which indicates that Louis certainly has managed somehow to become drastically less sexually inexperienced than he was with the maja in Zaragoza. In addition, we know from his own testimony that on the third morning of his stay *chez* Roquefort he woke up torn between (a) revulsion at his own weakness, verging on 'depravity' (in his own self-castigating estimation), in wallowing so long in the mallow delights abounding at Gagnères, and (b) rebellious reluctance to forsake them.

In that mood he sets off early on a solitary walk along the river bank, and on his return he is astounded to overhear, through the thickness of a twenty-foot yew hedge, the Marquis of Roquefort's persuasive drawl instructing some unseen other as to the most efficacious procedure for slitting some third party's throat – but whose?

'"Hold him down," the Marquis was saying, "just so. When you have him secure upon the ground, arc your blade just under his jaw. Just so. Then he shall not struggle again, and in a moment he is dead – ah! Monsieur Morel. Good day, sir . . . "'

So the Marquis greets Louis as he and his companion turn through an arched tunnel in the yew hedge too suddenly for Louis to hide.

'Are you well, sir?' the Marquis goes on smoothly. 'Your appetite honed for a tasty breakfast, on such a breathtaking day? This is . . . '

Louis next describes the Marquis of Roquefort's companion, who is introduced as Monsieur Saint Simon:

'He was about my own height, which is not inconsiderable, but at the same time remarkably stout, with a face in which the merriment of fatness cohabited with a leering slyness, that gave a sinister twist to his mouth. Instead of the broad, low-crowned, plumèd hat then in fashion, Monsieur Saint Simon had his huge head protected from the heavens by an interminable beaver, whose high-pointed crown resembled the steeple-tower of a church. We have since seen many similar [hats] amongst the English and the Swiss, but at that time such a headpiece was so uncommon in France, and appeared so ridiculous, that I could scarce refrain from laughing – though my blood was somewhat chilled by the remarks I had just overheard.

'From under this extraordinary bonnet rolled down over Monsieur Saint Simon's shoulders a profusion of black wavy hair, and his short moustachios were of bristly black, as was his small pointed beard. Just as singular was the rest of his dress, which consisted of a coarse brown pourpoint, laced with tarnished gold, and a slashed *haut de chausse* tied with black ribands; while a huge sword and long dagger dangled at his either mountainous side.

'"Monsieur Saint Simon is the wiliest fisherman in France," the Marquis assured me with a nod. "We were speaking just now about the surest means to kill a carp, which fish, you must know, is the most prodigiously tenacious of life. Are you a fisherman at all yourself, Monsieur Morel?"

'Not in the least,' replies Louis guardedly, and the Marquis monologues on, unperturbed, for some minutes about a vast foxy carp known affectionately as the Countess of Soissons, which lurks in the dammed pool to the south of the *pavillon*, and which for years has defied all anglers' efforts, and which Monsieur Saint Simon is here to attempt. This is Monsieur Saint Simon's cue to depart, which he does with a roguish twinkle, as he says:

'Be assured, most noble Marquis, I shall take you at your word. Not only the Countess of Soissons shall have her throat slit this day.'

For Louis this disrespectful abuse of the name of the Countess of Soissons, his mother's oldest and closest friend, is the last straw, and he formally advises the Marquis of his intention to depart forthwith.

'What?' protests the Marquis. 'But surely you will at least stay for breakfast?'

Thank you, but no – is Louis's response.

'As you will, Monsieur Morel,' says the Marquis without concern. 'But do remember, that whether I myself am in residence or no, you shall always be most welcome to fish my waters, here, where we have not only the Countess of Soissons, you know, but umpteen gullible gudgeon besides.'

Louis thanks the Marquis coolly, bows, and rushes off to prepare to depart. Five minutes later he is furious to discover Old Hussaye apparently still so drunk from carousals the previous night that he looks incapable of mounting a horse. In urbanely helpful voice, the Marquis of Roquefort suggests that either Louis should moderate his impatience to depart, or else, at the least, Old Hussaye should be allowed to wait behind till he sobers up. Hussaye himself, however, will hear nothing of this, rolls on to his horse off a mounting block, spouting brain-damaged gibberish all the while, and charges away at a gallop. This obliges Louis to bid the Marquis an even curter farewell than he had intended, in order to be catching up when Hussaye comes a cropper, which he inevitably does some four miles south of Gagnères.

Conquering his rage at finding Hussaye lying comatose and horseless by the roadside, Louis decides there is nothing to be done but leave him in the care of some cottagers from the nearest village. This he arranges with the aid of some silver, cursing all the while at the daylight travelling time he is losing, and fretting at the prospect of failing to reach home by nightfall, since he has now got it into his head that Hélène will be worried sick about him, in view of her suspecting the Marquis of Roquefort of evil designs. So when Hussaye is taken care of, Louis gallops south hard and without a break until, as the afternoon light is fading, he crosses a ford, enters a thick broadleaf wood some five miles from Château Morel, and is knocked from his saddle to the ground by a huge heavy body swooping down from an overhead bough.

Severely winded by his fall and dazed by a violent blow to his head, Louis nonetheless rallies to fight for his life when he realizes his assailant has an arm raised to slash at his throat with a double-edged dagger. Grabbing the deadly wrist with all his might Louis succeeds five times in forcing the dagger point up and away from his throat, but then with a bellow of murder his attacker breaks free and stabs down at Louis's windpipe, which certainly seems to spell curtains for the victim until in the last split instant he contrives to parry the stab with his upturned left palm, through which the dagger point passes and sticks.

As Louis roars in vengeful pain and bucks madly to dislodge the assassin a drumming of hooves comes down through the wood and moments later an aristocratic voice commands the aggressor to stand up and be still. In response to this the would-be killer redoubles his frenzy of efforts to yank his dagger free from Louis's hand and slash at his throat again. For this insolence he is rewarded by a short sharp shot to the head from a smoking pistol in the newcome horseman's right hand.

Mercifully for Louis the villain is now deceased, and this is hardly surprising when you learn that most of the left side of his face has disappeared into strawberry jam. His massive body, however, collapses as dead weight on Louis's chest. As Louis struggles to roll free he hears the commanding voice order another party to lend a helping hand. Moments later Louis finds himself blinking up through the bosky dusk at the Chevalier of Montenero, who, fuming with cold contempt, loses no time in berating Louis's crassness in having trusted a dangerous enemy after repeated cogent warnings.

Disadvantaged by proneness, weakness and shock, Louis nevertheless manages to retort that if Chevalier of Montenero could wrong Louis Morel he could also wrong the Marquis of Roquefort.

Icily the Chevalier replies:

'If a *man* has the *means* of restoring *honour* to his name, he must utilize those means — or else remain under presumption of *guilt*.'

Dizzily Louis begins to prate about the moral complexities of conflicting obligations but the Chevalier interrupts him with a cutting *Tcha!* and departs at a canter, having ordered Jean-Baptiste to assist Louis home.

The lawyer's son, for he it was who helped heave the corpse off Louis's chest, can't make up his mind what to do, so Louis, his head clearing, instructs Jean-Baptiste to leave Louis one of his pistols (Louis's own pistols having vanished with his horse), and make his way to the nearest dwellings, to fetch help, a horse, and some torches.

By the rising moonlight Louis wincingly prises the dagger from his hand, and attempts to stanch his bleeding with a kerchief wrapped round it and gripped tight. Then as he waits, and the moonlight waxes, he turns his attention to the dead assassin. It is of course the carp man from Gagnères, Monsieur Saint Simon – but lo besides. As Louis gingerly inspects the horrific wound where the left side of the carp man's face used to be, he feels an immense black wig slide loose in his hand to reveal enough tonsured head and reminiscent features to identify Monsieur Saint Simon as also the Capuchinesque Fat Monk who, with his Thin Accomplice, had attempted to cheat him at cards in the sleazy cabaret at Luz, and whom he kicked down the stairs for his pains.

Bewildered by secondary waves of shock, by loss of the blood which his kerchief is failing to keep in his left hand, and stunned by the accumulating evidence of the Marquis of Roquefort's intricate treachery, Louis gropingly searches Monsieur Fat Simon's garments with his right hand, and in due course locates an inner pocket containing a packet of papers in an oilskin wallet. This he stuffs into his breeches, on the ground that these are the last garment likely to be removed from his unconscious body if soon he passes out from the appalling pumping pain creeping up his left arm from his wound. Then it occurs to him that perhaps the Thin Accomplice is insufficiently far elsewhere, and with this in mind he wriggles backwards to prop his pounding head against a large knuckly root of the tree out of which his attacker dropped, and with Jean-Baptiste's pistol wedged warily between his knees he pleads with his faculties to not desert him till help arrives.

Half an hour later it does, in the form of Jean-Baptiste, several other citizens of Lourdes, and a bizarre short-arsed declamatory Thespian who introduces himself as:

**'Achilles Lefranc!'**

Now in the hinterland of hallucination from the severity of his pain, coupled with slumping relief at being rescued, Louis shakily waves the flapping little player away, and simply gasps to Jean-Baptiste:

'Take me home.'

But the histrionic Achilles, apparently with Jean-Baptiste's endorsement, asserts in guff so flowery as absolutely to defy translation into twenty-first-century English, that before being called to tread the boards he served his apprenticeship as an apothecary — hence is the best qualified person present to properly bandage Louis's wound, before he dies from loss of blood.

Louis commands Achilles to confine himself to plain language, to hurry up with the bandaging, and to present himself tomorrow at Château Morel: for a suitably handsome reward.

Then he passes out.

As might be expected, a terrific flapping fuss attends Louis's wounded arrival back home. As he is hoisted into the Château he recovers enough consciousness to note with pique that Hélène is not present. This, a streaming-eyed Countess Morel explains, is because Hélène has swooned at the news of the attack on Louis, and has had to be put to bed. In his own chamber Louis fights to remain *compos* long enough to smuggle the packet of papers from his breeches to under his mattress.

Then he passes out again.

The following morning he is delirious with fever, caused by poison in his wound. That the toxin has not already killed him is deemed to be thanks to its being less a malicious lethal potion than the residue of rancid fish guts on Monsieur Fat Simon's dagger point. In any event by lunch the patient is lucid enough to sit up in bed, send his attendant mother to lavish her ministrations on Hélène, and peruse the packet of papers from beneath the mattress.

'To my amazement these documents contained nothing relating directly to Monsieur de Roquefort. They consisted principally of a number of letters, plus the certificate of marriage, between the Count of Bagnols and his sweetheart Henriette de Vergne, whose tragic tale had been told me by the Chevalier. The letters, from citizens prominent in La Rochelle, appeared to prove that Monsieur de Bagnols, though sympathetic in a correctly passive manner, had never materially aided the Rochellois as per the denunciation by the Marquis of Roquefort, as that had been portrayed to me by the Chevalier of Montenero. There was, however, not a word in the papers to implicate the Marquis, as indicted by the Chevalier.'

Yet the Marquis had commissioned Fat Simon to kill him, and the Chevalier had once again saved his bacon. But why should the Chevalier have bothered, especially when he was still being so unreasonably hostile over Louis's honourable secrecy regarding the nasty business in Zaragoza? And why, moreover, had the Chevalier been close by when Fat Simon fell upon Louis from the oak?

Keen to solve these riddles, Louis also has to be careful what he says to whom in the Château, since he knows that, if Count Morel suspected for a moment that the Marquis of Roquefort had hired a hitman to kill his son, the Count would go gunning for the Marquis forthwith, and would most likely be killed himself. So on the second morning of his present invalidship, having given out to his family that really he had no idea who could have wished to assassinate him, 'probably a case of mistaken identity', he summons Jean-Baptiste to a bedside interview.

'Did you find the villain's horse?'

'Yes, Master Louis.'

'And?'

'In his bags, Master Louis, we found the gown of a Capuchin brother.'

'Ah. What about his person?'

'Nothing, Master Louis.'

'So no-one knows who he was, or what he was after?'

'It seems not, Master Louis.'

'You seem very fidgety today, Jean-Baptiste. Distracted, even. What's the matter?'

'I'm, em, worried about Hélène, Master Louis.'

'Why? Is she still unwell? Surely she's been told I'm recovering.'

'I don't know, Master Louis. Your mother will not let me see her.'

'Well, in a moment I shall entrust you with a message for Hélène, from me personally, to be conveyed only by you personally. That should do the trick. Now tell me . . . '

Louis goes on to ask Jean-Baptiste how long the Chevalier of Montenero has been home from Spain.

Jean-Baptiste, after some hesitant humming, explains that the Chevalier had arrived in Lourdes around noon on the day of the attack on Louis.

'Why was he riding north, later that afternoon?'

'When he learned from my father, Master Louis, whom it was you had gone to visit, he declared you was in great danger, and must be rescued.'

'Did he tell my parents anything of this?'

'No, Master Louis?'

'Good. Then neither must we. Promise?'

'As you will, Master Louis.'

'*Promise?*'

'I promise, Master Louis.'

'Excellent. Now, please tell Hélène . . . '

That Louis salutes her with eternal affection; that she must not worry about him; that though his wound still throbs, the swelling is ebbing; that his strength and spirits are reviving by the minute; and that she is welcome by his bedside at any time.

But by mid afternoon there is still no glimpse of Hélène and for this Louis blames his mother.

'Of course not,' agrees the Countess. 'If the poor girl were to see your arm like that, all puffed out like a pumpkin, she would certainly swoon again.'

Louis does not spell it out, but it is patently obvious he would much sooner be bedbathed by Hélène, and not by his mother. In the course of quizzing the Countess further, ferreting for any other benevolent measures not to his liking, he learns that the shortarsed loquacious Thespian, Achilles Lefranc, has twice turned up at the Château gates, and twice been turned away.

'But why?' he protests. 'It was *I* who told him to come.'

'The man is intolerable,' observes the Countess matter-of-factly. 'His declamations would wear you out.'

'Has he been rewarded?'

'What for, Louis?' asks the Countess as she wrings out the sponge.

'For helping me, of course. For bandaging my wound. God, Maman, the man has medical training, for all his faults. He could be helping me now – speeding my recovery.'

'If he turns up again,' the Countess promises, 'he'll certainly be given some money. In the meantime—'

But at that point a servant knocks and enters with the news that Achilles Lefranc is again at the gates. So this time he is summoned up and, as the Countess looks on guardingly, the ex-apprentice-apothecary-cum-out-of-work-actor, lubricating his exertions with torrents of his own deathless hyperbole, lances pus from Louis's palm and leaves it wrapped in a moist herbal poultice. This treatment is so effective that by midnight the swelling and throbbing have all but subsided, leaving Louis with energy and attention enough to lie churning with bitter gloom at having lost the Chevalier of Montenero's regard so unjustly, yet feeling unable to do anything about it.

Before at last he falls asleep, more exhausted by mental torment than by the draining effects of his injury, Louis resolves to rise early in the morning, before the Countess has a chance to forestall him, and to ride over to Lourdes, where the Chevalier is lodging *chez* Maître Arnault. There, Louis determines, he will thrash matters out with the Chevalier once and for all, if necessary confessing everything pertaining to the maja, and her murder of the naked priest – on the casuistic ground that his precise promise to the Zaragoza Corregidor was 'never to tell a living soul *in all Spain*'.

So after a short fitful sleep Louis rises early, and rides down to Lourdes to seek out the Chevalier. Alas, Maître Arnault informs him, his black eyes bright with triumph, in the study where the child Louis insulted him so grandly years before, Monsieur Morel has missed the Chevalier by nearly an hour.

When will he back?

Maître Arnault shrugs with gleeful ignorance, and makes out he doesn't know where Chevalier of Montenero has gone, only that he will be absent for at least three months.

Louis treats the lawyer with forced civility, as he is the father of Hélène, but cannot entirely conceal his suspicious disgruntlement. As he descends the lawyer's front steps he hears what sounds like a snigger as Maître Arnault shuts the door behind him. Later he will learn that the Chevalier was in Maître Arnault's house all the time, asleep upstairs after a late-night business meeting – so why should the lawyer have lied?

Back at Château Morel the household is stirring, and Louis bumps into Old Hussaye, who has reappeared following his comatose disgrace. Louis warns Hussaye to keep his mouth shut about the Marquis of Roquefort's villainy, if he doesn't want to be soundly thrashed for drunken dereliction of duty.

Hussaye protests:

'Just two cups, Master Louis. Nothing really, for a man with a head like mine. So I reckons the wine was *drugged*, oh yes. No doubt about it.'

Louis doesn't dismiss the idea, and he is about to question Hussaye further, when he is summoned by his father to breakfast, which has been held back for his benefit. Here, for the first time since the fishgut stabbing, he sees Hélène, and is delighted by the warmth of eager concern in her cheek, and the joy in her eye when he demonstrates to the table at large that his left arm has deflated to nearly normal, and that the poison has been vanquished.

After breakfast Louis's mother retires for a nap – being a little worn out, she says, by the worry of Louis's malaise. Count Morel withdraws to his library, and when from a first-floor window Louis sees Hélène walking out alone towards the park, he rushes to seize his hunting musket for a manly excuse to follow her. But before he gets to the foot of the stairs he is thwarted by Count Roger's voice: booming round the walls a summons to the library.

'We have here, Louis,' his father taps a letter, 'kind confirmation from her ladyship the Countess of Soissons.'

'Confirmation of what, Papa?'

'That you are welcome – indeed, warmly pressed – to serve under the Count, her son.'

Itching rather to get his hands on Hélène, Louis tells his father politely that he isn't enormously interested in serving under the Count of Soissons, unless and until there is a campaign with the promise of bloody battles to fight and win glory in.

'Soon there will be, Louis, and I have decided that you must go. Read this.' Bemused by visions of family grandeur regained by a conquering son, Count Morel hands Louis the letter from Soissons and instructs him to say at dinner when he will be ready to depart.

Bemused by altogether different visions, Louis reels away from the library and hastens out into the warmly precocious spring noon to catch up with Hélène. By a cool fresh tributary of the Gave he finds her: hugging her knees, she has her head turned up to the sky, eyes closed, drinking in the promises of spring the sun showers down.

Evidently Hélène is not avoiding him. Louis thanks her for this, and asks her why. She opens her eyes in no alarm, as if she were expecting him. Drawing him down to the bank beside her, Hélène shyly inquires whether he recalls their previous streamside heart-to-heart, so long ago – and what he then proposed?

'Why, of course I do!' exclaims Louis, his excitement rising. 'But what of it? Have you . . . '

Tremulously Hélène confides that since then certain circumstances have changed, such that now she no longer sees such absolute no hope of ever becoming his wife.

'What circumstances?' demands Louis suspiciously.

'I beg you not to press me, Louis,' Hélène entreats him. 'For it is a matter concerning which I am bound to remain silent, until such time as it may be necessary to persuade your parents in our favour.'

'That time is now!' protests Louis. 'We shall tell them today. And so first you must tell me.'

Hélène looks away from him, closes her eyes, and turns her head up to the sky once more.

'No, Louis,' she murmurs. 'I cannot.'

'But *why*?' he insists, embracing her, and subtly presuming to soothe her breast as on the first occasion.

'For the moment we are too young,' sighs Hélène. 'Your parents would never agree, *even if* I were to inform them . . . '

'Inform them *of what?*'

'Besides,' she reflects, lying back on the yielding turf in response to his suasions, and gazing up at him without fear. 'As a gentleman you yet have to tour the world, and discover by comparison if it is my poor self you truly desire.'

'Oh, Hélène, do not mock me.'

'I am serious, Louis,' she insists. 'How could I believe you loved me as a husband should, if you had known no other women?'

Louis records that at this point he seriously considered confessing to Hélène his episode with the maja, but for some reason he decided against it. Instead he ejaculates passionately that as, on the previous occasion, Hélène swore by all she held sacred to wed no other, and he did too, so now with tenfold ardour he reaffirms his pledge.

'I will not hold you to it, Louis,' she assures him, though with less angelic altruism than before. 'For there are many temptations in the world, very hard for a young man to resist, are there not?' She smiles at him bravely, but the drives of untold species are starting to burn in her eyes.

And Louis's hands are beneath her garments as he says:

'Oh, Hélène, how long must we wait? Perhaps for ever, I suppose.'

'What do you mean, Louis?'

'That I am bound to depart in the morning, to enlist with the Count of Soissons.'

For a moment Hélène suspects him of teasing her, maybe fishing for more generous favours. But Louis dispels her doubts:

'It is true, Hélène. My father has decided. And you know how it is with him. Once bent, he will not be budged. And so I must be gone, my love, and may be killed ere I return.'

This has the calculated effect of causing Hélène to pulsate with mature emotion, wrap her arms around Louis's neck, and hug him close to her bosom. In his record:

'Knowing now', Louis admits revealingly, 'how warmly women desire a measure of kisses, caresses and pleasure, before the cardinal act . . . '[2] But then, infuriatingly, he fudges over just how close to the cardinal brink he has brought Hélène when their commerce is interrupted by a scream from the trees followed by an echoing report and the plop of a musket ball in the stream beside them.

'Run, Hélène. *Run,*' roars Louis as he scrambles to his feet adjusting his hose and grabbing for his gun all at once. 'RUN.'

As Hélène obediently flees down the bank wrapping flaps of clothing about her, Louis whirls to face the menacing figure of a man bursting forth from the encircling copse with his gun butt brandished high like the head of a woodman's axe, and screaming:

'Rape my Hélène, you would, rape my Hélène, you bastard you—'

'Be calm, Jean-Baptiste,' Louis cautions the madly advancing lawyer's son. Let me explain—'

'*Bastard, bastard, bast—*'

'You don't understand, Jean-Baptiste,' Louis warns more forcefully, his right hand cradling his musket muzzle towards the oncoming aggressor's belly. 'Hélène and I – aaargh . . . ' Louis breaks off in agony as of an abscessed tooth when Jean-Baptiste's gun butt hammers down on his protectively raised left forearm. As the vestiges of fishgut poison in his blood seize their chance to reconvene, Louis nearly faints. Jean-Baptiste, his moon face purple with fury, pushes forward to follow up his advantage by swiping at Louis's weak arm again. Raising his weapon like a club twice as high as the midday sun he gibbers all the while a slimelike trail of blasphemic oaths and threats of eternal torment for the seducer of Hélène.

Once more, stepping unevenly backwards down the bank of the stream, Louis begs Jean-Baptiste to *listen.*

Jean-Baptiste braces himself for a rush.

Louis has no alternative but to raise his musket deterringly.

Jean-Baptiste spurns the danger. His own spent weapon now tossed aside, he hurls himself forward as though to strangle the handicapped Louis. As the muzzle of Louis's gun swings up, hinged only by his right wrist at its stock, it is seized hold of by Jean-Baptiste. Either supremely confident of not being shot by the young noble who owes him life, or perhaps just berserk with cackling rage, or whatever, the lawyer's son handles Louis's gun barrel like a pitchfork, its haft

---

[2] See now, Dearest Bright Eyes, how gratuitous the Star of David interlude was not?

against his midriff, to heave his quarry back, back, back to the edge of the bank.

'No, no!' cries Louis. 'Jean-Baptiste, noooo . . . ' And Louis topples backwards into the stream in the same moment that his weapon fires and Jean-Baptiste collapses on the bank with blood gushing out of his jerkin.

# Part II

# Mainly Spain

# 14

# Writers, Alcohol & Hypocrisy

We had hoped to kick off Part II with an interim response from one of Scotland's louder literary lions, Wringhim Knox,[1] to the adventures of Louis Morel so far. This was at Wringhim's own suggestion, since he had been chatting to Charlton Palser at an Arts Commission knees-up, and could not bear the thought of not being included in an interactive faction if Charlton was.

So here, instead, is an extract from the clutch of smudged photocopies that, accompanied by a passionate apology in Wringhim's inimitable calligraphy, hit our breakfast table on Saturday morning.

Moreover on the matter of wriggling furtively in the face of anticipated gloating denouncement, it is certainly the custom for certain genres of literary depredation (such as the 'critical commentary') to stoop to the most sickening lengths to defuse in advance the rain of hostile reviews which due to the prevalence of envious spite in academe is in any case bound to fall. In the present less specialized instance I think everyone will agree that such nauseating sop-throwing is doubly not worth the bother, thanks largely to the sadly not-yet-extinct species of littery gent (I deploy the phrase bisexually) whose grandest achievement it is to write sourly in the newspapers (sourest of all when a *Scottish* littery gent writes for an *English* newspaper) about better writers' books. Integral to this brand of rancorous impotence (itself too often an incestuous cohabiter with what is oft euphemistically glorified as 'a drink problem') is the deep-rooted though never honestly paraded conviction that:

Whatever is *not solemn*, is *not serious*.

On particularly imbecilic Saturday or Sunday mornings, not impossibly thanks to fifteen-round bouts from which the 'drink problem' emerged victorious yet again, we are by desperate extension exposed to the even wilder fallacy that: whatever *is* solemn, *must* be serious.

---

[1] After whose fiction style our own early efforts, some of them, were, to a modest extent, humbly modelled.

('"Not *q*" entails "not *p*"', if you like a smattering of logic with your reviewers, would not imply '*q* entails *p*' *even if* the former proposition were remotely true in the first place.) But so what?

So this:

That it is precisely the above-rubbished breed of cadaverous misery-gutsery which, if it were not vigorously stealthbombed up the Mumbo[2] from time to time, would soon deprive us of Shakespeare's *Comedy of Errors*, Graham Greene's 'entertainments', Clint Eastwood's *Bronco Billy*, and Kingsley Amis altogether. (Hmmm!) And then how long before we were also robbed of Rambo, Rocky, Robocop, and even Arnold Schwarzenegger?

Nails to hammer here:

*Not solemn* does not imply *not serious*;

*Serious* does not imply *solemn*;

*Serious* implies *not solemn*;

*Serious* and *solemn* are non-composable (to borrow Bertrand Russell's slogan ripped off Leibnitz).

To complete the spectrum here being bandied, we might go from *solemn*, through *serious* to *deadpan*, then *whimsical*, and finally *hilarious*. (Purists will instantly appreciate how much this quincunxial taxonomy owes to the dearly departed F.R. Leavis.) In any event the apparatus of qualitative distinctions just elaborated is appropriate only to the artist/writer's *attitude* to and *treatment* of his/her/its (not to discriminate against computer paintings and poems) productions.

But quite apart from vilifying his author's attitude and treatment, the solemnly well-meaning critic whose drink problem permits it will also wish to advance some traducement of the work in question's Literary Importance. To this end a qualitatively different architectonic for waffle is required, and one could do worse, couldn't one, than the second quincunxial series which descends from *great*, through *considerable* and *slight*, to *negligible* and, finally, *pernicious* (since in literature what is bad is worse than useless)?

Now Mr Rankles . . .

The remainder of Wringhim's tirade waxes downright abusive, obscene,

---

[2] Mumbo Rankles. Once wrote minor novels. Long ago turned reviewer. Contributes to English newspapers. 'Pseudo-menopausally vindictive.'

blasphemous, and arguably libellous too, so we'd better cut him short just there, and admit that of course the above passage is from Wringhim's latest letter to the editor of *The Crimes*, complaining in no uncertain terms about an unkind review, by Mumbo Rankles, of Wringhim's latest novel. The first reason for its being relayed to me, hence to you, is that *The Crimes* declined to publish it — and Wringhim quite understandably always refuses to take no audience at all for an answer. The second reason is that, incensed by this just typical new proof of English 'cultural' imperialism, Wringhim elected to mollify his mortification with a couple of cool pints in McEwan's,[3] while he skimmed through the laser proofs I had sent him, of all our chapters to date.

Unfortunately, as tends to happen, Wringhim encountered several other Scottish writing cronies in the tavern,[4] and by midnight they were all so high on righteous nationalism, and similarly plastered, that my pages were left abandoned in a murky alcove, and have never been seen again since. Now whether, as Wringhim pleads, I shall forgive him enough to let him loose on a second batch of chapters, at a later stage, remains to be seen. In the meantime let us resurrect a virtue out of Wringhim's lapse, by dilating a moment longer on what is a very serious problem: the relationship between 'western civilization' (as totemized by its writers) and alcohol, and the hypocrisy enshrouding the lot.

Take Hemingway. In his case, latterly, 'heavy drinking' was said to mean two bottles of gin before lunch. Or Scott Fitzgerald. How come he didn't crack up long before? Then Malcolm Lowry. What a miracle that he even completed *Under The Volcano*, let alone that it is so magnificent. Not that anyone seriously expects fine writing to flow all the afternoon that follows two bottles of gin before lunch, and there is scant doubt that Hemingway was by this stage already a burnt-out case. Yet where is the evidence that such writers were titanically tee-total in their early twenties, when their best work had yet to be written?

And what follows?

Does the lavish drinking, up to a point, actually *cause* the great writing?

Certainly not infallibly, Wringhim would say, otherwise most critics

---

[3] Inviting large bar in the University ghetto of Glasgow. Not noted for undue sobriety. Said by some to have inspired the limerick that begins: 'There was a duff pub at Hillhead . . . '

[4] Some of them published.

and reviewers would be great writers too.

So should we reverse the logic, and inquire whether the pinnacles of literature would not be even higher, the summits yet more sublime, if their authors were teethed on the wagon, and never later allowed to jump off it?

But if that were so, we ought already to be stocked with examples – authors who – for reasons of health, preference, or simply poverty – had never touched a drop before their masterpieces were penned. And who can we nominate? Chaucer? Hardly likely. Marlowe? Certainly not. Shakespeare, Fielding, Poe, Kingsley Amis; Wringhim Knox? This case is not strong.

Then may not *moderation* be the cornerstone? As discernible in some of the Top Ten poetic geniuses of all time – such as Goethe, whose 'relation to the divine gift of the vine', as lovingly portrayed in Thomas Mann's *Lotte in Weimar*, 'had always been one of blithe and grateful acceptance'. But now, in the dialogue of 'moderation', we approach the third panel of our triptych today: hypocrisy. For even Goethe was not above a glass of cheering madeira after breakfast, and what could be less moderate than that, in the eyes of a government resolutely committed to better health for all, fewer deaths on our roads, and who would go bankrupt tomorrow if we all stopped drinking alcohol?

In Britain, of course, the pivot of governmental hypocrisy on the matter is the British Medical Association (in whose ranks exemplary abstinence is hardly absolute), whose recommended maximum intake of alcohol is $3n$ units per week for men, and $2n$ for women. When we discover also that in exchange for our $3n$-unit ration we get precisely hardly any pints per day of a beer so watery that only a sheepshearer in the midday sun would want to drink it, we are hardly surprised to learn a week later that – not only Wringhim Knox and his henchmen in Glasgow, but – three out of four men across the nation drink more than the officially recommended maximum.

And what percentage of politicians and doctors, we wonder, is in the remaining most obedient quarter?

Certainly few educated persons are now in doubt that *too much* alcohol is bad for you – bad for your liver, your brain, heart; rots your bowel, droops your sex-life . . . and that hence Goethe should have been more concerned than he apparently was to discover his eleven-year-old son, August, drinking seventeen glasses of champagne that day. But the crunch we inevitably loop back to is:

*How much* is too much?

'*Et alors?*' the grape-growing paysans in Provence will scoff. '*Poof!*'
And afresh they will chant their triumphal refrain:

> *Un verre*
> *Ouvre la voie.*
> *Trois verres*
> *Donnent la joie!*

which earlier this century we might safely have translated as:

> *One glass*
> *Opens the way.*
> *Three glasses*
> *Make you gay!*

and in its day, in marketing terms, was a runaway rout of the slogan with
which the hypocritical French government (few of them conspicuous
abstainers) had attempted to sop the health lobby:

> *Un verre,*
> *C'est assez déjà.*
> *Trois verres,*
> *Bonjour dégâts.* [5]

Times change, though. Fresh perceptions have a mutating effect
on average behaviours, and new knowledge (like nuclear bombs) is
relatively difficult to unknow. Hence, for example, even Wringhim Knox
drinks appreciably less than Hemingway at the same age. And whereas,
say, Louis Morel would only have expected Old Hussaye to be sober
enough to function – ride his horse, drive the carriage; whatever – we,
his inheritors, rather prefer our taxi-drivers to stick to tea till they knock
off, our airline pilots to be rigidly abstemious always, and so forth.

For all that, we can't help hoping that, even if the dread day comes
when the wowsers win, to the point where train drivers, dentists, doctors,
pork-pie assembly-line workers, traffic wardens, and valued public
servants in all walks, are forbidden on pain of prolonged imprisonment

---

5 'One glass is already quite enough. Three glasses will bugger your
health.'

to touch a solitary drop of alcohol, ever, the same drastic strictures shall never, in all eternity, be imposed on the practising novelist. We say that very sincerely, since we honestly believe that in a world deprived of alcohol no great novel will ever be written.

It may be, unfortunately, that for other reasons (such as satellite television and the World Wide Wank) great novels will never again be written anyway, but that is surely no reason to legislate against the attempt. And to pre-empt the unlikely event that some critic of the utmost solemnity, to phrase it in Wringhim's taxonomy, should level a charge of subcutaneous hypocrisy against the previous paragraph itself, let us rush to confess:

'But of course!'

To be a writer of fiction is to be human, and to be human is to be a hypocrite. Among the short definitions of 'hypocrisy' in Chambers's we get 'concealment of true character or belief (not necessarily conscious)'. Well! Who doesn't? And consider the novelist closely. Proudly he parades before the browsing consumer his hard-wrought package of related statements, many if not all of which are transparently downright false. 'Mr Leopold Bloom ate relish with the inner organs of beasts and fowls.'

Lies, lies; *lies!*

And look at you. Without a blush you purchase your package of falsehoods,[6] settle down with a cool gin and tonic, or a loathsome WhatRail? coffee, and wittingly, on a good day, you swallow it all wholesale. Yet at the back of your mind (if that far) you *know* you're gobbling lies.

*LIES!*

Why do we do it, you and I? Is it for the sake of a Profounder Truth underlying the froth – like the dribble of real Guinness you sometimes get beneath the head, in a W1-postcode pub? Or merely to pass the time? Or to be comfortably diverted from our worser selves until, at last, with luck, the intershitty train gets to London before the underground goes to bed? If so, what a further perfect instance of the benefits of hypocrisy!

Hypocrisy also means that next time Wringhim Knox encounters Mumbo Rankles at an Arts Commission knees-up, it is just possible

---

[6] At least, we hope you do. Public Lending Right income in these countries is pitiful.

he won't smash him over the nose with a half-full bottle of Australian Cabernet Sauvignon, and what could be more civilized than that? So much so that hypocrisy may be declared to be the single overriding meta-theme underpinning all fiction. This is to say that surrounding, informing and suffusing all birth, copulation (especially) and death (most of all) is millions of tons of the hypocrisy that makes us so human – writers, readers, and alcoholics alike.

Hypocrisy, in a word, is the deceitfulness we approve, if it is conscious, and the self-deception of which we disapprove, if it be unconscious. Few of us will think Wringhim a nobler soul if he does hit Mumbo with the bottle, yet everyone knows he would love to. Hip-hip for hypocritical restraint. And yet it is with a frown that we contemplate Mumbo's earnest lamentations over Wringhim's sozzled benders, and the harmful effects on his writing, when we all know full well that Mumbo is a chronic dipsomaniac himself.

Yes, the writers-alcohol-hypocrisy triumvirate is humanly indissoluble, in additional proof of which I am now going to tell you a true short story from my own personal autobiography.

When in the autumn of 1986 I returned from sowing wild oats in Provence, to resume a graver existence in Scotland, I thought it wise to strike up with, and obtain a free once-over from, the National Health quacks in the local village – in case any of the damage done to my health by two years of seldom adulterated sunshine, bon-bon rouge, garlic sausage and full-fat cheese, was still not irreversible.

'Let's kick off with your blood pressure,' suggested Dr Carruthers.

How could I lie?

'That's grand,' the doctor nodded, to my exhaling relief, as he packed his pump away. 'Tobacco?'

Smugly I undraped the absolute truth:

'One cheroot per day, with morning coffee. Very occasionally a second in the evening, but only in tribute to an exceptionally splendid dinner.'

'Alcohol?'

'It would be dishonest', I announced, staring him steadily in the eye, 'to pretend that I do not exceed the British Medical Association and Their Majesty's Government's recommended maximum intake.'

'How much?'

'Oh, I suppose I drink about the equivalent of about two pints of sheepshearer beer per day. Possibly two and a half.'

That was where I ceased to believe what I was hearing myself say, so spontaneously, and with self-congratulatory forthrightitude. For the truth of the matter, never before broadcast to the public, would have been closer to:

'Two pints of emphatically *not*-sheepshearer beer, plus half a bottle of wine, plus a moderate malt whisky for a nightcap whenever possible.'[7]

*Me!* Lying. Lying to my doctor? Undeniably. But why? To obtain which benefit? In the hope of what admiration? *Crazy!* Futile too, as I discovered in a moment when Dr Carruthers (himself more florid of complexion, and greatly more overweight for his age than I) was called out to reception, to placate a hysterical lady of eighty, who was accusing her nurse's syringe – used to take a blood sample from her arm – of infecting her with AIDS. Under cover of this fracas I nipped round the doctor's desk, and on his notepad, under my name, I read:

*Drinks too much and lies about it.*

Now if I, who am appreciably more honest than most novelists, can be hypocritical in that despicable way about my relationship with alcohol, what can you expect from the likes of Wringhim? You could say, in Wringhim's defence, that he drinks so much that he cannot fairly be expected to remember how much he drinks. But that won't wash, since there are always enough less stotious hangers-on, and empty bottles the morning after, to give him an approximate idea. Don't imagine, though, that I'm saying all this to do Wringhim down, or that I'm resentful about him losing my chapters in McEwan's Bar. Indeed not. Rather are we nearing a terribly important general point about the alcoholic hypocrisy of writers.

And it is this.

That though we all realize two bottles of gin before lunch must be

---

[7] Even this average could be proved to be false, if you counted in Christmas dinner, entertaining unexpected guests, Arts Commission knees-ups, vanishingly rare long lunches with old-style publishers, hours cooped in delayed WhatRail? express trains with nothing better to do, and secondary self-deception. However, even if you totted all that up, then doubled it, we'd still be lagging gallons behind Wringhim & Co in Hillhead.

*bad* for us, as it was for Hemingway too, so many of us experience an irrepressibly resurgent intuition that the daily dosage of alcohol that is positively *good* for us, or at least for our writing, is vastly more than should be permitted an airline pilot, and in many cases more than double the maximum recommended by the British Medical Association in conspiracy with Their Majesty's Government.

And like everything else, it's all got to do with consciousness.

Whereas we trust the pilot of our jumbo to maintain his faculties in peak survival trim, reflexes super-sharp, etc, the novelist may gain much from the occasional jovial dulling of his upper inhibitions. In a bustling bar athrong with fascinating characters, yet another pint may legitimately lubricate the acquisition of what Fielding so aptly termed 'knowledge by conversation' – an art in which some of our fellow Scots are particularly adept, although most of them are confined to Glasgow.

Again, the pilot's job is to look outwards. We don't want him scrutinizing his conscience in mid-air, or searching within for his soul, but would just as soon he kept his eyes on the sky ahead, his ears tuned to the weather report, and so on. We novelists, by contrast, and the best of you readers too, have an obligation to observe both objectively (with which finger, of which hand, is the prime creep's nose picked?) and subjectively – how do we honestly feel about being passed over for the Nobel Prize again this year, and what do these feelings prove? And in the latter enterprise, a little drink may come in handy once more. While in the cold sober morning we may, like Anthony Burgess, have written off the unwon Prize as a pitiful bauble, a ten-pint session in the pub that night might reduce us to tears of despair.

So where, between those poles, lies the truth?

But perhaps the greatest contribution of alcohol to literature is its catalysing the fissuring of forms, the flouting of hidebound rules, the pickling of conservative intentions, a temporary boggling of tyranical causality, and thus the fantastic irruption of the unexpected – which on feast days strikes a blow for progress. Just as the lager lout who heaves a brick through the butcher's window may liberate some offal he wasn't expecting, so the lurching novelist on a streak of luck may suddenly see, as it were through a new hole in hor own brain, a shortcut forwards which practically parallels a transcending of the speed of light, at least in its inscaped preferability to the pedestrian plan it surpasses.

And this brings us to the crunch of the present apologia: that thanks to Wringhim's mislaying my chapters in McEwan's, and my hence not receiving his opinions on Louis Morel as scheduled on Saturday morning, I rebelliously powered down the computer, began my weekend two hours early, and by midnight was – not 'pissed as a raving newt', as a callous chauffeur put it, but – incontestably in excess of the British Medical Association's and Her English Majesty's Government's recommended maximum intake. In consequence I slept like an agitated log for several hours, and by five o'clock on Sunday morning my head was luridly bobbing between weird waves of dreams, whereon, as his head bobbed likewise, in some moments close as a whisper, though in others further off than a shout, I conducted the following ☞ 8

---

8 'If you can wheedle or bully any Cervantes scholars into wading out this far I think you may find they accuse you here of attempting imitative "narrative dynamism" by which if my own understanding isn't even further out to sea they will mean "dirty tricks of the crudest sort".' [P.C.]

# 15

# Conversation with Louis[1]

'Now when you come to your senses again, after toppling backwards into the stream, you feel remorse beyond description, do you not, over having slain the brother of Hélène, and indeed your own saviour from drowning?'

'Very much so. However, once I have struggled to the bank, and am kneeling to bend over poor Jean-Baptiste, I feel a heavy hand grip my shoulder from behind.'

'The hand of whom?'

'It is Pere Garcés.'

'The notorious Herculean smuggler, who on occasion would visit your father with contraband goodies, for sale at favourable rates?'

'The same.'

'And what does he say?'

'He asks me sternly what has happened. I tell him. He informs me coldly, with the moralistic disapproval so typical of some Spanish outlaws, that I should not have seduced the sister of Jean-Baptiste.'

'How do you take that?'

'I vehemently deny having seduced Hélène. She is still a virgin, I assure him.'

'She wouldn't have been much longer though, would she? If Jean-Baptiste hadn't interrupted you?'

'That is our affair. We are lovers. It is a private matter.'

'Does Pere Garcés believe you?'

'Why should he not? Knowing now that Jean-Baptiste accused me wrongly, Pere proclaims that Jean-Baptiste deserved to die, and has only himself to blame.'

'Do you agree?'

---

[1] Recorded on a snug Sony Talkman as it hirpled up the heather-hazed heath to the wind-rippled Greenadder Reservoir; with only a few trace elements of Freudian Slopoutiness excised.

'No. I feel pity for Jean-Baptiste. I blame myself, and I cannot forget that but for him I would have drowned years ago. In great distress, and weeping, I propose carrying Jean-Baptiste's body back to Château Morel.'

'But Pere Garcés has different ideas?'

'Completely. Reminding me that the dead are dead, and that the dead youth's father is a vindictive attorney, Pere leaves Jean-Baptiste's remains where they are, and hurries me up to the mill, where I can hide till we see how the land is going to lie, and take further action accordingly.'

'The mill by the pool, from which Jean-Baptiste lifesaved you?'

'Yes. It is a staging post for the smugglers, and has a large and concealed vaulted cellar, where a man might take refuge for weeks.'

'It never occurs to you to simply return to the Château as if nothing had happened, and later make out that Jean-Baptiste must have been shot by a passing smuggler?'

'Later, at the mill, it does occur to me. I put the idea to Pere. But he immediately objects that since Hélène had fled, believing *me* to be the victim of an attack, we must expect that she will have summoned aid to my assistance.'

'So that when *your* rescuers found *his* dead body, that would immediately point their fingers at *you*?'

'Naturally.'

'But couldn't you then simply have claimed reasonable self-defence? After all, it *was* Jean-Baptiste who attacked *you* in the first place.'

'That's true. However, as Pere pointed out, to do so would have led to questions being asked about my involvement with Hélène, which might well have compromised her honour, and put in jeopardy our future together. We had, moreover, to bear in mind the Cardinal's campaign against the aristocracy, and his tendency to encourage the execution of gentleman caught killing their peasants, which Maître Arnault would no doubt have made much of.'

'All this wisdom you got from Pere Garcés?'

'I was bewildered. Shocked. Without Pere to advise me, I don't know what I would have done.'

'This takes us to the mill. What now?'

'Pere and the miller decide between them that my only safe option is to repair again to Spain until a written pardon can be arranged.'

'And you go along with that?'

'I have no reason not to. For the moment I am utterly passive. I wish

I could die myself.'

'Surely not. Why?'

'It is bad enough that, albeit accidentally, I should have killed her brother. But now in my mind's eye I contemplate my dear Hélène's accusing gaze. It is too much, and I cannot bear it.'

'But you know Jean-Baptiste was trying to kill you, and you know that Hélène knows that too! What's the problem?'

'In his own terms Jean-Baptiste was quite justified. I was lying on top of his sister, kissing her, caressing her, and so forth. I am sure he sincerely believed I had mounted her—'

'Which you hadn't? Not—'

'So at bottom the blame is mine. Had I not been making love to Hélène, Jean-Baptiste would not have lost control of himself. Even crueller is the thought that, but for the poison still in my arm, from the wound I received of Monsieur Saint Simon, I should have overcome Jean-Baptiste with my hands – no need of my gun – for I am much stronger of frame than he. Thus the tragedy would have been averted.'

'It seems to me, Louis, that you're being a little hard on yourself here. Almost maudlin, in fact.'

'I do not deny it. Besides, there is also the effect of the brandy which the miller makes me drink, while Pere returns to the scene, to deal with Jean-Baptiste's body.'

'Ah, yes. Brandy! How much?'

'No doubt, in my daze, I have already drunk more than a sober gentleman should. In any case, when Pere returns with the news that Jean-Baptiste's body has already been removed, I desist.'

'Fetched back to the Château?'

'He cannot say.'

'Louis, you're weeping.'

'I'm sorry, but I cannot help it. In my mind's eye I see Hélène. Her reaction to the sight of Jean-Baptiste: bloody, inert; lifeless. I know she knows that he attacked me. But I do not know if she believes my killing of him was an accident. Perhaps she suspects me of slaying him vengefully, after overpowering him first. For doubtless her father, who hates me, will put such thoughts in her mind. So as I imagine her now she is weeping too. Kneeling in attempted prayer. Tears course down her cheeks. Her eyes are awash with grief, suspicion; distrust. All is confusion.'

'Surely Señor Garcés will not allow you to remain long in this mawkish condition?'

'How right you are. Once Pere has done telling us how the body has disappeared, he urges me not to be womanish, consoles me cheerfully with a story of one of his own justified murders, and tells the miller to pour me more brandy.'

'Which you accept?'

'For the moment I have no will of my own. I am a pawn in Pere's hand.'

'What happens next?'

'Sedated by plentiful brandy, I become drowsy. As Pere and the miller secrete sacks of salt, I lie down on a cot in the cellar. Moments later, it seems, I am hammered into wakefulness once more by a tremendous knocking on the main mill door above.

'"Who is it?" I hear Pere hiss.

'"Customs," replies the miller softly.

'"How many?"

'"Just one officer that I can see, but he has a crowbar raised to the door."

'Now I hear Pere call a warning:

'"Go away, customs pig. You have no business here. Go away."

'"Open the door!" replies the customs officer, in a high shrill voice. "In the King's name, open the door."

'"You have no warrant," guesses Pere. "No authority. Go away. Be warned."

'In response to that, the foolish customs agent sets about the door with his crowbar . . . '

'And then?'

'By this time I have risen from the cot, and am mounting the cellar stairs. As my head emerges through the ground-floor trap I am just in time to see Pere pull open the door. In falls the customs officer. He is grabbing at a pistol in his belt. Before he has his weapon free his head has been crushed by a tremendous blow from the back of a hatchet in Pere's hand.

'"What have you done?" cry I, aghast. "What have you *done*?"

'"Merely punished a villain," replies Pere coolly, "for entering another's dwelling without authority. Go back to bed, Monsieur Morel. You are weary, and must rest."

'As I lie in the cellar again, sleep eluding me, my mind is a maze of strange reflections caused by Pere's cool approach. For some time I try but fail to take comfort from the thought that Pere's slaying of a government officer is greatly more heinous than my own accidental killing of Jean-Baptiste.'

'What happens to the customs man's body?'

'I learn later that Pere has carried it to a crag three hundred feet above a crop of rocks by the river's edge.'

'So the fall will disguise the hatchet wound on the victim's head?'

'Just so. As the corpse rolls away into the river, Pere throws the officer's crowbar after him, but not before working the cliff edge to look as if here the ground had given way, beneath the officer's espying feet.'

'Quite a practised killer, your Pere. Doesn't this worry you?'

'He has his own standards. In his terms he is a resistance fighter, and a patriot. I have no apprehensions in his company – as one would with a common criminal, or a paid assassin like Monsieur Saint Simon.'

'But does he really betray no compunction, for the life he has snuffed away?'

'In his own fashion, yes he does. When he returns from dealing with the body, and he and the miller continue with the caching of sacks of salt, they work in a sort of silence that to me suggests inner remorse. And when that work is done, and Pere calls for a horn of aguardiente, he tosses it back – and then another, and another – as though in need to dull his conscience.'

'Yet by morning, when he leads you off to Spain, he is already matter-off-fact once more? Indeed, cheerful!'

'Yes. Sensing from my silence how overcome I am, with feelings of regret and loss, as with each mile through the heights of Argelès we ride further from my home, and from the lady I love, who now must hate me, Pere takes pains to distract me with practical thoughts of the future. Suggesting, for example, that for the sake of remaining incognito I must embrace a more lowly role, and disguise, than is merited by my rank.'

'To which you agree?'

'How could I not?'

'Now we know from your memoirs, Louis, that refreshingly soon you cheer up enough to have a whale of a time with Pere Garcés' Aragonese henchmen in the mountains – red wine and aguardiente, singing and dancing round camp fires, and so on. And, seeing you have the protection of their leader, you are embraced like a brother by the Spaniards, who confer upon you the honour of a place near the horses – hence more sheltered – for your bed. And that though you passionately fancy Garcés' own wife – or woman, at least – herself, perhaps because, with her black hair, glittering eyes and hot blood, she reminds you so much of the maja—'

'Never do I say—'

'You don't. I agree. But it shines through nonetheless. Anyway, wisely not rocking the boat with Garcés, you have a fling instead with his wife's younger cousin, Maria-Carmen.'

'I do.'

'A girl three years younger than Hélène?'

'In her body, her emotions, her sexuality, she is fully a woman.'

'You could be put in prison for that, you know. In England today.'

'That is of no concern to me.'

'And what about Hélène?'

'What about her?'

'How is she going to feel, about your cavorting with Maria-Carmen?'

'You forget that I have no notion whether I shall ever see Hélène again, or how she might receive me. Besides, Hélène is the love of my life.'

'Whereas?'

'My affair with Maria-Carmen is a mere fluke of youth, and passion.'

'So you would defend a viable distinction between lowlier passion and loftier love?'

'No gentleman in France would not—'

'You're in Spain, don't forget!'

'And anyway: why do you ask me such questions?'

'I'm fascinated by your attitude to women.'

'Fascinated? Maybe. Prurient too, perhaps. And envious.'

'What do you mean?'

'I mean that I suspect you of wishing that you too were as actively successful with women – in cases where you yourself would flirt and tease with abandon, then timorously shy short of the carnal contact women crave.'

'There you are!'

'Where am I?'

'How do you know they all crave it?'

'Most of them do.'

'Actually I don't disagree with you. However, not all carnal contacts are isomorphic with the compulsive vaginal bruising you give Maria-Carmen. As to my being timorous, don't forget that everyone has to husband his resources, and that I am twice your age.

Which corresponds roughly with the difference between thrice a night and thrice a week (once on Wednesday, twice on Saturday night stroke Sunday morning, if you're blessed with satellite television), or "once a month if your lucky", as Mumbo Rankles' wife muttered savagely over her vindaloo, in a Glasgow curry house the other week.[2] Also – another difference between you and me – I have AIDS to bear in mind.'

'What of AIDS?'

'It's like an elephant in your sitting-room, as Bernard MacLaverty said of the Ulster Problem, or a dinner guest who lays a loaded revolver on the table. Either way, ignore it at your peril.'

'You have your AIDS. We have several varieties of pox.'

'Yes, but you don't understand etiology as well as we do, so your behaviour is not so influenced. For my own part, if I were your age again, today, I would be much more celibate than I was then – or than you are now.'

'I think that proves my point, doesn't it?'

'Which point?'

'That your obsession with my sex-life is prurient, envious, hypo-critical—'

'What else!'

'And probably morbid too.'

'Why is that?'

'On the one hand you castigate me, for seeking solace with Maria-Carmen, when I am parted from Hélène. But on the other you brazenly admit that were it not for your advancing decrepitude, not to mention impotence, and your horror of contracting AIDS, you would do just the same yourself.'

'Oh, I don't think I see any serious contradiction there.'

'Why ever not?'

'Because, Louis, it wasn't me who leaped to defend a viable distinction between lofty passion and lowlier love. Nor am I now, nor shall I ever be, a French gentleman like you. Okay? Now I'd like to hurry you on, if I may, to the morning when you and the band of smugglers are preparing to depart southwards, further into Spain, when suddenly sounds of an

---

[2] In fact Mumbo is (or certainly looks) several years older than you and me put together, but Mrs Rankles was thinking back to a time when he wasn't (or didn't).

altercation are heard, followed by a muscly lookout smuggler marching round a bush the flustered and squeaking person, in an armlock, of the shortarsed Achilles Lefranc.'

'What about Achilles?'

'The Spaniards are about to slit his throat, when Achilles, seeing you and understanding not a word of Spanish, throws himself on your mercy?'

'Yes.'

'And you speak for him?'

'I say I believe him to be harmless, but admit I have no knowledge of his background.'

'Pere Garcés then questions Achilles Lefranc in French, Achilles Lefranc replies with involuntary hysteriorionic bombast, whereupon Pere Garcés warns him on pain of strangling to cut the cackle and stick to the point. Achilles describes having returned to Château Morel, to inquire after young Monsieur Morel – that's you – and see if you were in need of any further moist herbal poultices. But when he got to the Château he found all in bedlam, mounted men everywhere, all heavily armed, and got a belt round the ear when he mentioned your name?'

'That's right, and next he describes his solitary progress to Argelès, and thither into Spain, where, here and now, by accident, he has stumbled upon our camp.'

'What's he doing in Spain?'

'He claims that, having found no employment in France, as either apothecary or tragedian, he has determined to apply for the post of French Buffoon to the Barcelona Repertory Company.'

'Does Pere Garcés believe him?'

'He believes Achilles, but feels he cannot let him go free, lest with his irrepressible mouth he give away the location of the camp.'

'What about keeping him within the band, and making him pay his way – as, say, a cook?'

'Pere sees no use for Achilles of that sort, and he is reluctant to keep him at all, since he suspects he will eat a lot, and annoy the others with his prattle.'

'So what's the solution?'

'Pere considers slitting his throat anyway. But, being a freedom fighter rather than a hired assassin, as I mentioned before, he has a revulsion against butchering the innocent.'

'So what *does* Pere do with Achilles?'

'Nothing. This is where I step in. As a favour to Pere, and as a kindness to Achilles – to whom I remain grateful for his poultices – I offer to accept responsibility for him, and take him on as my man.'

'Your personal valet, factotum, and dog's-body?'

'I expect so.'

'Good. That brings us up to date on how Achilles Lefranc comes to be with you in Spain. And I wonder if you'd mind if I were now to paraphrase the rather long-winded section of your memoirs where you relate what Achilles tells you, as you continue south toward Barcelona, of the story of his life?'

'Anything you say.'

'My mother's husband', Achilles informs you, to your not inconsiderable amazement, 'was intendant to the Count of Bagnols. What a woman she was, my mother!'

'In what way?' you reply.

'Good, kind, loving – and beautiful beyond compare, Master Louis. Oooh, la! How oft do I wish I had been sired by the Count of Bagnols upon my mother, and not by my father at all.'

'Why do you wish that?'

'Because then I should be tall, handsome and courageous too. Instead of being merely good-natured, charming, and witty. But the Count of Bagnols, the dear man, had eyes for no lady in the world, save Mademoiselle de Vergne. God rest her heavenly soul.'

'You do not honour your father, then, whom you term your mother's husband?'

'Out of duty and respect, Master Louis, and ignorance, we are all of us obliged to assume, are we not, that our father is indeed our father, until we are traumatized to the contrary? But in France these days, you know, no man can be sure he can be sure of his paternity, as he may be confident of his mother. Certainly, if I had been my mother, I would have slept with other men—'

'Why do you say that?' you halt Achilles sharply, in tones of admonition.

'Why, Master Louis, because she was so beautiful and giving – and he so ugly and mean. And besides, a beautiful woman in her prime of life is never so easily satisfied, you know, as no matter what handsome man . . . never mind a begrudging dwarf.'

'Why did she marry him then, if he was so unattractive?'

Achilles Lefranc windmills his arms in a shrug of ignorance so expressive that he nearly slides off his pony.

'Lord, Lord, Master Louis!' he wails. 'Who knows for a moment why almost all women submit to almost all men? The Good Lord must wisely have fashioned them nine tenths blind, that way, else procreation would long since have petrified, and the world would be peopled by bears. Poor, dear mother . . . ' And for several moments he lapses into a rare and reverential silence.

Having considerately allowed time for this echo of Achilles' filial grief to fade away, you now invite him to rehearse from his own point of view the history of the Marquis of Roquefort's successful sabotaging of the betrothal of Henriette de Vergne and the Count of Bagnols.

Achilles obliges.

After repeating what Louis has already learned from the Chevalier, Achilles further relates how from his confinement in the beastly Bastille—

'I never knew he was in the Bastille!' you interject.

'Three months and a day, Master Louis,' Achilles nods vehemently. 'In the summer of twenty-five, if memory serves. Yet somehow he managed to write secretly to his intendant, with orders to locate certain papers—'

'What sort of papers?'

'Papers, Master Louis, what would prove the Count clean innocent of the charges against him.'

'Charges of actively aiding the Huguenots?'

'Just so, Master Louis.'

'Brought against him by the Cardinal, as incited by the Marquis of Roquefort?'

Achilles spits expressively, between his pony's ears.

'And did the intendant find these — those papers?'

'Never tried, Master Louis. So far as I know. Suited him better, I reckon, for the Count to remain in the Bastille.'

'Which he did, presumably.'

'Well, no. There's the mystery of it. On the second day of the fourth month, the Count of Bagnols disappears.'

'Murdered?'

'Not yet.'

'How do we know?'

'Why, because within a week the Count is secretly back at Bagnols, to interrogate his intendant.'

'Whom he then punishes severely?'

'On the contrary, Master Louis. Somehow the intendant persuades the Count he has done everything in his power to further his interests. In consequence, the Count takes the intendant even privier into his confidence. In consequence, knowledge of the Count's whereabouts in hiding soon reaches the Marquis of Roquefort.'

'As a result of which the unfortunate Monsieur Bagnols is assassinated?'

'Fresh from his lady-love's window,' sighs Achilles. 'Lord, what a world.'

'And Mademoiselle de Vergne? She dies some months later – in a convent, I believe.'

'In a convent, yes, Master Louis. But in childbirth, too – Lord comfort her.'

'*In childbirth!*' you expostulate. 'The Chevalier said nothing about childbirth!'

'Comes to all women, Master Louis,' says Achilles breezily. 'Well, most what are not nuns, that is, and even some what are. As to your Chevalier's discretion, well, there's the difference between a well-bred gentleman and lowly me.'

'What sex was the child?'

'No-one knows, Master Louis. Leastways, not me.'

'What happened to him or her?'

'No-one knows, Master Louis.'

'The inheritance? I mean, the Count of Bagnols' estate?'

'Would have been seized by the Cardinal, no doubt, if most of it hadn't already disappeared.'

'Where to?'

'Can't say, Master Louis. That's the sense of "disappeared", ain't it not? Then again, there was them what noticed, not long after, that the intendant had suddenly, as by a miracle, discovered himself well enough found to set up as notary – independent, like – and buy a new house in the same town as his dear old friend Monsieur Lefranc, the apothecary.'

'Look here, Achilles,' you now remark sternly. 'Ever since we passed by the water-shed you have been talking, in a very impersonal manner, about the Count of Bagnols' "intendant".'

'That's very true, Master Louis. What an acutely attentive young gentleman you be.'

'But the intendant was your father, Achilles. Is it because you disapprove so severely, of his evidently shady dealings, that you decline to describe him as your sire?'

'Not exactly, Master Louis.'

'Well?'

Here there is a break for lunch on a hillside to the north of the river Segre. As the Catalan bandits eat and drink, discuss their next contraband load, and crack black jokes about the Spanish overlords they can't wait to overthrow, and before you all begin the hot, dry, dusty descent towards Lérida, Achilles – with a gushing frankness that at first you find hard to stomach – confides details, some of them luridly intimate, of his beautiful mother's many *affaires*, and her several children of diverse appearance.

'But wait a minute, Achilles,' you object. 'Surely a while back you told me that, if you had been your mother – given the ugliness of your father – you would have slept with other men.'

'That I did, Master Louis.'

'But that implies that your ravishing mother in deed [*sic*] remained faithful to your hideous father, does it not? Whereas now you're telling me that, not only did she distribute her favours with commendable generosity, but that she had several children by other men besides. This is very confusing.'

'What I meant, Master Louis, was that *if I too* were as vivacious, desirable, and lavish of life as my mother, *then I too* would have slept with other men. As my mother, with untold delight, so frequently did.'

'So the nub of your drift, whose nuance eluded me at the time,[3] is that you *do not blame* your mother, for her . . . warmly sociable nature?'

'If I did, Master Louis, I should be wishing my own life away.'

'Ah. You mean you suspect your father, or the Count of Bagnols' intendant, is *not* your father?'

Achilles, by way of explication, describes in graphic detail his mother's tragic illness, and the deathbed scene where she summons all her lovers to her bedside, obliges her husband to swear he forgives and to embrace all the neighbours, friends and relations who have

---

[3] Stress patterns in spoken French have always been more open to misconstruction than in English.

cuckolded him. Then, in the final hour of her life, she allocates care of her five children to the various implicated fathers, with – curiously enough – only the youngest son being assigned to the intendant himself, while Achilles is entrusted to the care of Monsieur Lefranc, the apothecary.

For some strange reason, confected, we take it, before the apothecary becomes alienated from the intendant, over tupping his wife and siring Achilles upon her, the apothecary has custody of the lost/secret Bagnols papers – which he keeps in a drawer with his dirty syringes.

'What happened to the Bagnols papers?' you, with poorly disguised excitement, demand of Achilles Lefranc.

'Couldn't make much sense of them myself,' admits Achilles. 'Left them where they were. By now, however, my conscience – which always has been troublesome sensitive – was hurting at the horrors of my profession, and the number of innocent folk we killed. With my warm, generous and outgoing nature, and my passion for communication – and applause, I cannot deny it – I had long had a fancy to try on the buskin. Thus far, however, alas, Monsieur Lefranc had invariably walloped me round the ear whenever the topic rose up.'

'But now?'

'One day when my gaffer is away on the far side of town, to kill off an old gent with quack potions, for the sake of his much younger wife, there comes to our door an enormous fat Capuchin monk.'

'What does he want?'

'After beating about the bush with innumerable haws, and various other lies, he confesses he is sent to purchase back the Bagnols papers, for which he offers me ten coins—'

'Ten measly livres! For a package—'

'Ten *louis d'or*,[4] Master Louis!'

'Which offer, of course, you dismiss with contempt?'

'Which offer, Master Louis, I accept with boundless gratitude, and glee, and am fled the premises before the gaffer returns – now to seek my fortune on the boards.'

'So now, having failed to locate the said fortune in France, and having – which it is commendably candid of you, Achilles, not to conceal from me – been laughed off the stage in Paris, you are here

---

[4] Worth twenty times as much, if you remember. And if you don't, perhaps cast quickly back to Chapter 7, Note 2.

today, and riding with me, in the fond belief that your personal pot of gold may lie lurking in Barcelona?'

'I surely will be almost as happy serving you, Master Louis,' replies Achilles, with a beam of irresistible loyalty.

By now you are entering the outskirts of a village some ten miles north-west of Lérida. Excited by the perspective cast by Achilles' tale, on the recent events in your own life, your thoughts flutter constantly back to the Bagnols papers, which are still in your own possession, and the ramifications surrounding them:

Would the Count of Bagnols' life have been saved, if those papers had not been withheld by the wicked intendant and passed on to the grasping apothecary?

If so, would the Count of Bagnols and Mademoiselle de Vergne — or rather, the Countess of Bagnols, as it seems she secretly became — have lived happily ever after? Ie, instead of being assassinated at the time, and dying miserably in childbirth, respectively?

If so, who and what would Henriette de Vergne's baby have grown up to be?

Did the child in any case survive, and if so: who and where is he or she?

And so on.

'Is that a fair summary?'

'The story you tell is true,' concedes Louis sulkily. 'But these words are not mine.'

'Oh, come off it, Louis!' your contemporary commentator scoffs airily — for the reservoir is far behind him now, the farmhouse is looming up, his hangover is yielding, and he is aglow with visions of an imminent light restorative lunch consisting principally of a half litre of chilled Stella Artois (the real stuff, brewed in Belgium), followed by roast lamb, roast potatoes, baked onions, and organic green beans in a fluffy white sauce, all gratefully washed down by a bottle of Vacqueyras rouge — 'come off it, Louis! Some of your words are a little bit wooden, let's face it. If we used all of them, and only all of them, we would be risking committing the only ultimate crime!'

'Which is what?'

'Convulsing our readers with yawns!'

'So why do you bother with me,' Louis snarls back, to my surprise, like a child resenting bedtime. 'If I'm so wooden, why don't you forget about me, and instead write a moral exposé of the evils of social deprivation and rickets in Gartcosh,[5] like you promised the Arts Commission you would?'

'I promised them no such thing, Louis. All I said was that I would *consider* making such a promise *if* they made Gartcosh a non-negotiable precondition of my banking their bursary. Happily, in their superior insight, or else because someone on the Awards Board forgot, they made no such stipulation. Just as well for you too, Louis!'

'Excuse me?'

'I mean that otherwise you'd still be festering in the Cabinet des Grandes Tromperies, like Dracula in his box. Besides, don't get me wrong. It's not *you* I find wooden at all. It's how you express yourself in writing that needs attention. *You personally*, on the contrary, I find fascinating. Why else would I labour so long and hard to present you to the public? There is no contradiction, you know, between *being* very interesting and *writing* very boringly. And vice versa, more's the pity. It's a bit like film stars and film directors. Most of us are well advised to stick to what we do best. Look at Michael Caine.'

'And what do I do best?'

'Fight duels, seduce young Spanish girls, kill——'

'You mock me.'

'Only gently!'

'Well, I can't help wondering what motivates you. I mean, to go to such lengths. Other than your morbid obsession, of course, with my greater success with women.'

'Success is a relative concept, Louis. Moreover, if you press me to be serious for one last moment before lunch, I will confess to being intrigued by the mechanisms of, and popular responses to, all forms of tyranny.'

'Calling me a tyrant?'

'No, no! I'm thinking of the events you're about to get caught up in: the Catalan uprising against the Spanish oppressor. Compare and contrast with the momentous events we have witnessed in Eastern Europe since this decade began. How much has changed? Has anything improved? Then your flirtation with Richelieu; his fawning domination of Louis XIII; the bizarre sexuality of the King, and its consequences;

---

5 Node of Greater Glasgow renowned for its dearth of fresh fruit and vegetables – hence rich in heart attacks, lung cancer, and rickets. Twinned off the motorway with Uddingston. All tourists should visit such places at least once before they die.

Richelieu's dictatorial government of France. Imagine him in bed with Lady Thatcher. If the Cardinal too had been so stupid as to self-petard himself up the arse with the Poll Tax, would he likewise have been toppled before his death? On a personal and private level, there is food for sober thought also in your relationship with your mother—'

'What about my mother?'

'She hasn't died up to now, but she is doomed to soon. How will you respond? I was in my late thirties when my mother died – and yet, like a snowball on a bottomless slope, the aftermath rolls on. But then I am Scottish; you are French. I was present; you will not be. How will you respond, and what divergences will thereby be revealed, between your character and mine? Finally, before we break for lunch, there is the matter of *your* father.'

'What about *my* father?'

'Wait and see!'

# 16

# On to Barcelona

By the beginning of this chapter Louis Morel is again fantasizing seeking out the Marquis of Roquefort and avenging both himself and the unfortunate Count of Bagnols—

When suddenly round a corner the smuggler band he is travelling with enters a small village four miles up the valley from Lérida, on the river Segre.

The day is dry and hot, the colours light, bright, and dusty upon the eye.

The village itself is like a primitive still landscape until Louis Morel's breath is stalled in his throat by the fragile lissom beauty of a teenage girl who rushes forward from a doorway to be swept up and hugged by Pere Garcés.

This, Garcés explains, is Isabella, his wife's elder brother's only daughter.

To Isabella he introduces Louis as a gallant French gentleman, meanwhile frowning sideways to warn Louis that Isabella, sexually speaking – and as opposed to Maria-Carmen, who everyone accepts was dying for it – is fruit so forbidden that to be caught attempting to pluck her would spell suicide on the spot.

'Oh, Uncle Pere!' wails Isabella, after the first flush of greeting, when the huge Catalan restores her to the ground.

'What is the matter, Isabella?' he inquires sternly.

She confesses her fears for her father, Francisco, who should have returned from Lérida for dinner the previous evening.

As Pere questions her further about conditions prevailing in Lérida, a galloping horseman arrives claiming to be in possession of dramatic news of Francisco.

'Where is he?' snaps Pere Garcés.

'He is in the Lérida donjon dungeon,' explains Juan the horseman, 'and things look mighty black.'

'He won't stay there long,' vows Garcés grimly.

'In any case, of what is he accused?' asks Louis, whose Catalan is somewhat stilted.

Ignoring Louis, Juan launches into an impassioned lament on the rottenly unjust and insecure state of Catalonia since the tyrant Count-Duke[1] puppeteering the Central Government in Madrid has overrun the province with the most callous, undisciplined and lawless soldiers in all Spain.

'And that's saying something,' Juan viciously concludes.

'But what is Francisco supposed to have *done?*' insists Pere Garcés.

It emerges that Francisco's crime was to interrupt a drunken Central Government soldier in the process of groping a local woman, whereupon the soldier fumbled for a pistol with which to shoot Francisco, whereupon Francisco stabbed the soldier in the stomach.

'Did the soldier die?' wonders Louis coolly.

'Not yet.'

'What happens if he does?' asks Pere Garcés, again following the logic initiated by Louis.

'This morning it was proclaimed', says Juan, his dark eyes moist with tears, 'that if the soldier dies, then Francisco will be fired live from the great cannon on the donjon battlements.'

After pausing for Pere Garcés to reflect, Louis continues:

'And if the soldier doesn't die?'

'Then Francisco is sentenced to life service in the galleys.'

'In the Mediterranean?' supposes Louis. 'To row Central Government boats against the Turk?'

Juan can't say. His mental map of the world beyond Catalonia is not precise. Pere Garcés, meanwhile, has become sidetracked comforting the nubile Isabella, who responds to the news of her father's predicament by weeping hysterically, and seems likely soon to swoon.

The next few hours are taken up with entrusting care of Isabella to dependable matrons, billeting the men and women of the smuggler band with village residents, and dining broodily in an atmosphere of long silences broken only by isolated interjections, inevitable eating noises, and emotive promises of retribution to be visited on the Central Government and all its agents.

After dinner, on the orders of Pere Garcés, all the villagers and the visiting smugglers retire to bed early, to be fresh to face trauma

---

[1] Olivares. See Chapter 18.

tomorrow. While his attendant-cum-valet, as Achilles Lefranc now is, gets lodged with a number of younger smugglers in a loft above a stable, Louis himself is billeted with Garcés, and the horseman Juan, in the adobe dwelling belonging to Francisco. No mention is made of Mrs Francisco, so Louis quietly concludes that Isabella is already an orphan on her mother's side, which will compound her loneliness horribly if Francisco, her only parent, is indeed blasted live to his death from the mouth of a battlement cannon.

At first Louis's mind is so vivid with images of Isabella – how slender, vulnerable and virginal her beauty; so much more like a brunette Hélène than the ardent voluptuousness of Maria-Carmen, which he has had to make do with of late – and what it would feel like to physically possess her, that he fears he will never sleep. His body, though, is doggedly weary from long riding over rough terrain, so it is only moments after the first surge of his newestfound cerebral romance is spent that he falls fast into a sleep from which he is only woken with stinging vigour at just gone midnight: by Pere Garcés, armed to the teeth.

'Where are you going?' mumbles Louis.

'Lérida,' mutters the Catalan darkly.

'I'll come with you.'

'No. I go alone.'

'But why?'

After swearing Louis to eternal secrecy, Pere Garcés briefly outlines his short-term plans. Then he counsels Louis, in politely general terms, that he absolutely must not tup the local girls before his departure from this vicinity – which, in his own interests, should be as soon as possible.

'But where shall I go from here?' protests Louis, who, since his revelationary conversation with Achilles, has been so engrossed with complexities of personal relationships, and speculative analyses of possible past worlds, that he had entirely forgotten his own current status as fugitive outlaw, and the need to somehow reassemble the scattered fragments of his life.

Pere Garcés now sketches a number of options to Louis and offers him a letter of introduction to the new Corregidor at Zaragoza:

'A secret but loyal supporter of our cause. With my blessing, he will give you shelter, and perhaps some occupation with his papers, until your troubles blow over.'

'No, no!' blurts Louis. 'Not Zaragoza. In any case, whatever has happened to the old Corregidor? I knew him once. Himself and . . . '

'He died last month of grief, we hear. Having lost his only child.'

Louis bites his lip but makes no comment.

By now he is up and dressing by the moonlight that beams through the open adobe window. As he buckles up, Pere Garcés tells him, in effect: okay if you don't fancy Zaragoza you can come with me towards Lérida, then make for Barcelona and get a ship for Paris, where you can conceal yourself as well as in Spain, and perhaps be better situated to angle for your pardon.

Louis assents to this plan, hoping through the intercession of the Count of Soissons – son of his mother's best friend, and a prince of the royal blood – to be saved from the ignominy of execution as a common felon, which is the fate he knows the agents of Cardinal Richelieu would endeavour to procure for him if he were convicted of the murder of Jean-Baptiste. These thoughts restore him to tormenting himself with the reflection that it is Hélène Arnault's brother he has slain, and hence she *never* could be his, *even if* he succeeds in wangling a pardon, or otherwise evading apprehension.

And so, quintessentially young, French and romantic, he curses the life he clings to. Nevertheless, even more quintessentially young, French and human, he keeps right on clinging, and half an hour later, in the fading moonlight of almost dawn, he sets off in the direction of Lérida, with Pere Garcés, Juan the horseman, and four other villagers, plus Achilles Lefranc at sea on a borrowed cart-horse, much too large. Louis remains silent for the first few miles but gathers from fag-ends of dialogue between Garcés and the village men that all of Catalonia is currently ripe for revolt, needing only one signal match to set the tinder exploding.

'Surely shall the hand that ignites it be *mine*,' mutters Pere Garcés, 'if they have plucked one single hair from poor Francisco's beard.'

At a crossroads within sight of Lérida, Pere Garcés shows Louis Morel the way to Barcelona, due east into the brightening day, and presses him to take his present borrowed horse as gift, and a token of the smuggler's esteem. Louis accepts graciously and hopes to reciprocate such handsome generosity at a later date.

'What about mine?' gasps Achilles Lefranc, as his cart-horse catches up with the crossroads.

'Yours too,' chuckles Pere Garcés, and on that note the two Frenchmen take leave of the Catalans.

The morning rises clear and warm, with a slight westerly wind which pursues the motley rider pair with ominous sounds of drums beating in Lérida, then cannonfire and musketry, and later a trumpet retreat. Louis, determined not to be mistaken for one of the French government provocateurs who have been fomenting revolt amongst the Catalan peasantry, now resolves to get to Barcelona and quit Spain asap. To this end he gees Achilles up into a sort of canter, but unfortunately the cart-horse soon proves to be jaded as well as vast, so they are obliged to proceed at an equine dawdle until they come to some habitation harbouring horses to exchange. Alas, Catalonia in the seventeenth century being even more sparsely populated than France, it is two hours before they come to any village at all, and even then it is too small and poor to possess any swappable horses other than cart-horses even older and more knackered than the one Achilles is already on.

So Louis is obliged to temper his impatience and cool his heels while their present mounts feed and doze restfully in the midday shade. After a lunch of stale bread, ripe goat's cheese and coarse red wine, Louis himself is nodding drowsily on the shady side of the red-roofed village well when suddenly from the east a heavily armed and armoured Castilian trooper gallops in at great speed on a bloodily wounded horse, which he now clambers off. Glowering round him suspiciously – for it is the rapacious alien Castilians, imposed by and symbolic of Olivares, and all Central Government repression, whom the Catalan nationalists abhor – the trooper espies Achilles Lefranc in the act of tempting Louis Morel's smuggler mare to a nourishing leftover crust.

With predictable arrogant brutality the Castilian trooper shoulders Achilles aside and begins to commandeer the mare. Louis himself, roused by squeals of rage from Achilles, bounds to his feet and in polite formal Spanish tells the interloping Castilian trooper to fuck off.[2]

Now the impetuous trooper, failing to perceive the fearless brawny aristocrat within the cottar's garb, raises a foolish gauntleted fist to

---

[2] If on the day he left school Louis was able to thwart the Marquis of Roquefort's attempt to steal his horse, it is perhaps hardly surprising that now it never occurs to him to think twice about refusing to take this sort of shit from a common soldier.

knock Louis aside. The aggressor's wrist is arrested in mid swipe as by a flying vice, he is lifted bodily from the ground, armour and all, by Louis forearming his crutch, and he is hurled several pace backwards to sprawl painfully where the horses have dunged. Almost in the same breath half a dozen villagers swoop like wasps with daggers flashing to slit the Castilian's detested throat. This prompts Louis to intervene vigorously in the trooper's defence, since his gentleman's code precludes murdering a helpless adversary when he is down, except in exceptional circumstances.

Within moments the entire village has gathered in a furious debate centred round Louis and Achilles as to whether the captured trooper should be executed here and now or wrapped in chains and tortured first. Seeing no hope of reasoned justice for the fallen trooper, Louis cunningly inches the crowd around him sufficiently far for their intended victim to seize his chance by clanking to his feet behind them, throwing himself back on his original bleeding horse, and spurring it out of the village towards the east whence he had come.

As the inhabitants howl with fury, the Castilian trooper reins to a halt beyond their reach and pulls his musketoon from its saddle holster. Before spurring again to canter into the distance out of view the trooper fires a single malicious shot in a hopeful arc towards the crowd. The musket ball, too spent to kill, nevertheless arrives with sufficient force to penetrate one of the dagger-flashers' cheeks and come to rest burning on his tongue. This final humiliating injury on top of the insult of losing the fallen enemy they had so hoped to carve turns the villagers' lust for retribution against Louis himself until, discovering him to be French, they instantly take him for a government agent working in disguise under orders from Richelieu.

Louis protests his innocence in this regard, which the Catalans unanimously construe as further confirmation of their theory. For what good friendly agent would lightly disclose his agency?

As Louis persists in disclaiming any official subversive capacity, and since, to the villagers' amazement, he is manifestly genuine in his ignorance of that fact that the citizens of Lérida have *already* risen up to throw off the yoke of Castilian tyranny, they leap with absolute certainty to the conclusion that he *must* be fresh from Paris, and hence they petition him for reassurance that the flow of funds from Cardinal Richelieu, for the purchase of munitions with which to slaughter the tyrannical Spaniards, will continue unabated.

Louis responds to this with affably vague hypotheticals and then inquires what spark it was that triggered the rebellion in Lérida.

With lurid gloating the villagers depict the meet vengeance wrought on those wicked Castilians who last night slew a poor innocent Catalan hero by firing him out of a battlement cannon.

'You mean Francisco?' guesses Louis, unable not to consider with a twinge how terribly abandoned the nubile Isabella will be now, and in need of a courageous protector.

'Francisco Who?' say the villagers, who then press Louis for further news from Paris on French Central Government support for the Catalan Liberation cause.

In the end Louis only manages to extricate himself from the villager's misplaced adulation by affecting to have urgent business in Barcelona, which the villagers applaud as a further tacit admission of his official agency, causing them to beg him:

'Oh, yes. And please send us news back from Barcelona, won't you?'

Louis responds with more amiably nebulous undertakings and after another long day's travel and uncomfortable night's camping on the rocks he and Achilles find themselves trotting into Barcelona one morning bright and early through its westermost gate.

Perhaps twenty horse paces past the inner-gate guardhouse they are rushed from behind by several soldiers and Louis is hauled sprainingly from his saddle and pinned to the ground by more heavy bodies than are worth the bother of attempting to resist.

Exulting above them like a hideous eclipse of the sun, Louis sees, is the glittering visage of the escaped Castilian trooper – he whose back and pride Louis bruised before saving his throat from slitting in the cart-horse village.

'Why do you thus use me,' inquires Louis with forced mildness, 'to whom you owe your life?'

The trooper responds by harshly promising Louis too a fatal flight from the battlement cannon within two hours:

'Which would be sooner, you stinking French bastard, did not the Viceroy wish to examine you 'isself.'

'Why me?' wonders Louis.

'Our 'ighness examines *all* you stinking French bastards. And if you is not 'airless, soft, and girlish enough in the bum – and you isn't – then we kill you. Argh! Chain 'im up, lads!'

\* \* \*

Consoling himself with the hope that even if the Viceroy is homosexual he may yet have a rational soul,[3] Louis makes no protest as he is tightly bound and dragged on foot through the Barcelona streets, with Achilles Lefranc – who evidently poses so little threat that the soldiers do not even trouble to chain him – bobbing fretfully by his side. All along the streets, and leaking from dark windows like invisible toxic fumes, are the glowerings of resentful Catalans: contemplating the brash Castilian soldiers with a patience full of poison.

Round one cobbled corner Louis suddenly glimpses the sun-flooded boat-dotted blue of the Mediterranean stretching vastly to three horizons. With a groan of passion for freedom and life he strains on a reflex to be rid of his chains and is instantly rewarded with a stunning blow to the back of his head with a sword pommel, and simultaneous promises in either ear of a ball through his brains without further warning if he dares to try that sort of lark again.

At the Arsenal, Louis and Achilles are conducted through two large

---

[3] Despite no mention being made of Descartes (1596–1650) anywhere in Louis Morel's own papers, G.P.R. James has the character he bases on Morel reading Descartes, and by implication the *Meditations*, *before* his flight into Spain. Now since Descartes' *Meditations* were first published in Leyden in 1641, and since the Catalan uprising into which Louis is currently being sucked takes place in 1640, it would seem that even the so-called facts elaborated by a future historiographer royal need to be checked with a pinch of salt. This, as even the most sluggish critic of historical fiction will triumphantly point out, becomes even more anachronistically apparent when, at an earlier stage, in the vicinity of Château Morel, James has his character weaving between rhododendron bushes. But the important point here is surely not whether Louis Morel had previously read Descartes, but rather that the intellectual soil of young French heads in 1640 was already ploughed, harrowed, fertilized by Jesuits, and altogether receptive to the point of crying out, like the legendary Andalusian mares in heat, for impregnation by those uniquely silly seeds which Descartes was about to broadcast. For a trenchant critique of suchlike casuistical rationalist drivel, perhaps begin with Schopenhauer's essay on *The Fourfold Root of the Principle of Sufficient Reason*, §6.

courtyards into a stone hall and have to wait for an hour, standing all the while, being jeered at by soldiery, before the Viceroy is ready to examine them. Since Louis Morel's own account of what follows is relatively complete, let us let the next chapter let the hero himself portray his first meeting with ☞

# 17

# The Fat Viceroy

I was then [*writes Louis*] as it were caged, in the midst of four soldiers; one on either side of me; one in front, and one behind. With some attention to military form, I was led up the grand staircase towards the cabinet of the Viceroy, at the door of which I was detained, till the guard had announced my attendance.

Presently the door again opened, and I was told in a harsh tone to go in, which I instantly complied with, followed by little Achilles, while the soldiers and the Viceroy's guard remained without.

Seated in an ivory chair, somewhat resembling the curule chair of the ancient Romans, appeared a short fat man, not unlike the renowned governor of Barataria,[1] as described by Cervantes. I mean his figure; the excessive rotundity of which was such, that the paunch of Sancho himself would ill have borne the comparison. His face, though full in proportion, had no coarseness in it. His dress, I must confess, seemed redolent of the habits which, following the trooper's crude remarks, I could not but mentally attribute to him.[2] Instead of the stiff *fraise*, or raised ruff, round the neck, which at that time was still worn almost universally, by gentlemen of Catalonia,[3] he had adopted the falling collar of lace, which left his ample neck and throat in the liberty of full exposure.

His *justaucorps* of yellow silk had doubtless caused his tailor some considerable trouble, to fashion it dexterously to the protuberance of his stomach; but still many of the points of this garment were left

---

[1] *!?*

[2] As might be expected of a nineteenth-century puritan with no inkling of the *Spews of the World*'s circulation, G.P.R. James, in the version he presents in *De l'Orme*, makes no mention of the Viceroy's sexual proclivities.

[3] Another calculated V-sign at Madrid. As regards the hitherto insufficiently vaunted significance of ruffs, gird loins to be patiently mazed by Chapter 18.

open, revealing a chemise of the finest lawn beneath. His high-plumed hat, badged with a large single sapphire of immense value, lay upon a table before him. As I entered his cabinet, the Viceroy wearily raised this bonnet to his head, doubtless the more properly to represent his sovereign; but only for an instant, whereafter he laid it down again, and left his head exposed to the breath of a soft sea breeze, which fanned through the two open windows, on either side of him, as he sprawled back amid the cushions of his chair.

Immediately behind the Viceroy, between the two tall windows, stood his favourite Negro slave, an enormous specimen, splendidly dressed in oriental costume, with a turban of crimson muslin on his head, and bracelets of supple gold, like priceless manacles on his thick dark wrists. He was an abnormally tall and superlatively powerful fellow, this Nubian, and in his upright carriage, and the proud bearing of his every limb, there was something truly noble, and intangibly free, that one looked for in vain in the idle listlessness of his lord.

The Negro's distance from the cushioned chair was but a step, and a richly hilted scimitar, hinged at his waistband, proclaimed him – there being no other person in the room when we entered – personal guard to the Viceroy; as well as servant, favourite slave, and whatever other part he might be called upon to play.

I advanced a few steps into the room, followed by Achilles, and paused some two bodies' lengths from the Viceroy, obeying a slight flutter of his fingers, which intimated I had approached near enough. After contemplating my aspect in silence for fully a minute, he addressed me in tones suprisingly youthful, and even musical, considering the ungainly bulk within which his vocal cords were housed.

'I perceive, young sir,' said he, 'notwithstanding the disarray of your dress, and the dust and dirt with which you are covered, that you were originally a gentleman.'

'Your excellency is perfectly correct,' I replied, 'and the sole reason for my appearing before the Viceroy of Catalonia, in attire so deranged, is the brutal conduct of a party of your excellency's soldiery, who seized upon me as I travelled peacefully on the high road, and dragged me here in chains.'

Something hardened in the Viceroy's soft green eyes, as he leaned forward to murmur:

'What better does a former gentleman deserve than chains, young sir, when he has meanly insinuated himself into another sovereign's realm, and by the basest arts stirred up the native people, to sedition and revolt?'

'Had I done so, your excellency,' I responded, 'I should be without excuse, and the severest punishment would be no more than I merited. But I deny that I ever did so, and, indeed, how could I have?'

'How could you not have what?' the Viceroy retorted sharply.

'I mean, your excellency, that as it is barely a week since first I set foot in Spain, how could I be held responsible for inciting the inhabitants to sedition and revolt? On the contrary—'

'What contrary, pray?'

'It seems to me, if your excellency will pardon the presumption of such a perception, on the part of a humble and peaceful stranger passing through, that the immediate cause, precipitating the local folk hereabouts to riot, is your excellency's own troopers' brutality.'

The Viceroy inclined his gaze a shade to the left. Immediately the Negro slave bent forward to listen. In soft fast Spanish, which perhaps he calculated I should not follow, the Viceroy said:

'It seems you were right, Scipio. Remind me later that we must exert ourselves, else these rude *soldados* from Castile will provoke the citizens into worse excesses than even those of Lérida.' Looking up once more at me, he added in a louder voice:

'When first I heard of your apprehension, young sir, I looked upon your guilt as so evident a matter, that I did not imagine for a moment that you might have the effrontery to deny it.'

'Deny it I do, your excellency,' I affirmed gently, 'but as a matter of the meekest truth.'

'Very well. Then it is but just that you hear the full charge against you. It is that you, a subject of Louis, King of France, and thirteenth of that name, have, together with many others, wormed your way into this heartland of Catalonia, and that, as spies and saboteurs, as insurrectionists trailing the foulest lies, you have instigated the people to revolt against their liege lord and sovereign, Philip, King of Spain, the fourth of that name. Now in evidence of all this against you, a trusted Castilian trooper, of the eleventh *tercio*, deposes to have seen you – that is to say, *you personally* – with the rebels now in arms at Lérida—'

'That is not true!' I impulsively exclaimed, while little Achilles echoed beside me:

'Damned lies, damned lies!'

The Viceroy, however, with a limp flourish of his hand, bade us be silent as he continued:

'And that, moreover, you did overtake this said trusted trooper upon the high road hither, and that with other rebels, at the village of Meila, you fired on and would have slain him without mercy, had it not been for the superior swiftness of his horse. What say you in defence?'

'That the charge is malicious fabrication,' I assured him warmly, 'and if your excellency will permit, that I now relate *my* version of the events, so distorted in the trooper's report, then shall I submit with the greatest confidence, to your excellency's wisdom, in judging between the false and the true.'

'Proceed, proceed,' said the Viceroy as in loathing of an unwelcome duty, and sinking back into his cushions, seemingly exhausted by this unaccustomed exertion.

'Your excellency should perhaps first know,' I began, 'that my reason for quitting my homeland, which is Bigorre in French Navarre, is that, in defence of my own life, I had accidentally slain a fellow countryman, who, in the madness of a deluded belief, was otherwise like to have murdered me.'

'A gentleman,' demanded the Viceroy, 'or a serf?'

'A member of the *classe bourgoise*, your excellency.'

The Viceroy sniffed in a somewhat ambiguous manner, and I continued:

'To escape the immediate consequences of unfortunate circumstantial implications, and inevitable misunderstandings, I fled across the Pyrenees, guided kindly by Spanish smugglers – whose principal crimes, I may say, are against certain lunatic laws of France, and not Spain – who conducted me to a village not far from Jaca, whence I planned to proceed to Barcelona, and thence embark for Marseille. From Marseille, I intended to take the boat upstream to Lyon, thereafter ride for Paris, and there, through certain influential connexions, to negotiate a rightful and incontrovertible pardon, so that I might eventually return to my own country, and family, in security – and with my head held high.'

'Then what business', objected the Viceroy, 'could you possibly have had in Lérida?'

'I swear before God, your excellency, that never in my life have I passed through the gates of Lérida.'

The Viceroy looked sideways again and the giant Negro muttered several words in his master's ear, which alas I could not hear. Turning again to me, the Viceroy went on with the air of petulance restrained:

'So you would have us believe, young sir, that the whole tale of the soldier who accuses you is false, and that you and he never met till, for reasons miraculously opaque, he seized you this morning at the city gates, and had you brought to us?'

'Not so, your excellency,' I answered.

'Not so what, young sir? Be plain.'

'I mean, your excellency, that it is far from God's truth to say that your trooper and I had never met until this morning. On the contrary. And *I*, moreover, have the gravest charge to lay against *him*.'

'And what is that?'

'That yesterday, in the small village you call Meila, this soldier, his own horse being wounded, proceeded without a word of request or explanation, to attempt to commandeer mine.'

'To which you objected?'

'Naturally, your excellency, I opposed his brash importunacy.'

'Whereat he, perceiving you to be a gentleman, bowed instantly to your wishes, and apologized for his intrusion?'

'Rather, your excellency, did he raise his fist high to strike me, as if I were a peasant he could with impunity abuse. Thereupon, in my own defence, I plucked him up and hurled him down. Seeing him fallen, the local folk crowded round him with their knives, and I believe would have murdered him without further ado, had I not intervened on his behalf. For this good office, no sooner was he on his horse once more, making good his escape – an opportunity which for his sake I contrived – than he expressed the abundance of his gratitude by firing his carbine at my head.'

'But missed you, happily, it seems.'

'Yes, your excellency. Though the ball he shot injured one of the peasants in the face. Thus validating, in their own eyes, their hatred of, and desire to slaughter, all your excellency's troops.'

'Hmmn,' said the Viceroy reluctantly. 'Well it is for you, young sir, that you did not deny the encounter, for last night the soldier rendered to me a most detailed description of your person. Hmmn. Does your attendant understand Spanish?'

'Barely a word, your excellency.'

To my amazement the Viceroy then propositioned Achilles in Spanish to the following effect:

'If you'll pull off my boots, little man, ever so gently, I'll put you to bed tonight with three naked virgins.'

The world of uncomprehending and fearful bewilderment all over Achilles' countenance not crinkling for an instant, the Viceroy, evidently satisfied, went on to interrogate him in French, as to what had befallen us the previous day, and the Castilian trooper's conduct.

Thawed by the mild and encouraging tone in which the Viceroy questioned him, and with his penchant for bombast excited by the solemnity of the occasion, and by his unprecedented physical closeness to a genuine ambassador of royalty, Achilles now confirmed every detail of my narrative, but in such a stupendous torrent of hyperbolic eloquence, that after perhaps five minutes of the unrelenting inundation, the Viceroy, as it were in a panic of satiation, pointed up the palm of a warning hand towards Achilles, and said:

'Hold, hold. Enough. Shut up.' Then with a yawn, which now, reflecting, I suspect to have been partly deceptive, he turned back to me, and in Spanish resumed:

'You said', he said, although I most carefully had not, 'that you had been in Spain before. Where did you then reside, and to whom were you known?'

Realizing that any falsehood could prove fatal, I decided merely to be as sparing as possible with the truth, and therefore admitted:

'Last year, not least to improve my command of your excellency's language, I spent some time at Zaragoza, and there was known to the Corregidor. Also to the Chevalier of Montenero.'

'*Montenero!*' exclaimed the Viceroy, almost whistling. 'Well, well! Since we expect him here this very day, or tomorrow at the latest, then, if he give witness in favour of your character, your history shall require no further confirmation. For he is perhaps the most respected of all our foreign residents, and all Spain lauds his honour.'

'A foreigner!' I protested. 'But surely the Chevalier is a Spaniard?'

'By residence and devotion, certainly,' responded the Viceroy, 'but never by birth. Scipio . . . '

The Negro inclined his great head close again, and I heard Viceroy instruct him, in the clipped vindictive voice of a lazy man irritated into reaction:

'I will no longer be trifled with, Scipio, between these cut-throat Castilians and the factious peasantry. As to the Frenchman's accuser, see that he receive the strappado till his back be flayed red. At the same time have it broadcast that henceforth *any man* within my government who commits *any crime*, be he resident peasant or patrolling soldier, he shall learn that I too can be a Draco if need be, and write my laws in blood.'

His plump face flushed purple with the indignation of his thoughts, and the effort of such threats, the Viceroy, as he waved Achilles and myself dismissively away, added finally:

'As for you, young sir, you are safe for the present, for your story bears the air of less untruth than your accuser's. But woe to you if Señor Montenero disavow the acquaintance you have claimed. Or if he will not guarantee your honour. For then shall you die in the agony of tortures more exquisite than your vilest dreams.'

## 18

# The Tyrant Count-Duke

Original notes for this chapter direct:

*Give more background on occupation of Catalonia.*
  *Reasons for Castilian presence.*
  *Not really at all like Northern Ireland, and thank God for that.*
  *(So to speak.)*
  *Character of Olivares.*
  *Mugshot.*

**Olivares : Philip IV**
**::**
**Richelieu : Louis XIII**

*Also Parkinson's Law, which is ripped off Schumpeter's Law, which ultimately is ripped off the Second Law of Thermodynamics.*
  *Ie, in this case, vaulting ambition combined with ability and energy (ie Olivares and Richelieu, cf more heat) tends constantly to flow to the side of inherited power combined with mediocrity and lethargy (cf Philip IV of Spain and Louis XIII of France, cf less heat).*

Those were among the intentions.

The better to enact them with refreshed detail, I had planned last night to drive into Edinburgh and borrow from the University Library some two thousand pages on seventeenth-century Spain by historians less ignorant than myself.

But it is now November.

And one of the features of life in the Greenadder valley is that the road to Edinburgh, over the heights of the Lammermuirs, can be subject at not a moment's notice to winter conditions more extreme than is ever imagined by most office workers in the city – as I realized anew at about seven o'clock, when, thanks to an impenetrable freezing fog, I very nearly drove into the reservoir.

So back home through the thickening night I inched.

And here, after a reviving draught of Glenmorangie not presented by a grateful publisher, I telephoned to pick the brains of the only Senior Lecturer in Modern European History whom I have ever slept with, albeit over twenty years ago:

Dr Audrey Macpherson, now of StrathKelvin University.

After greetings too prosaic to transcribe:

'And how's Jennifer?' I continued smoothly.

'Fine.'

'Not getting any less nubile?'

'Her boyfriend doesn't think so.'

'I can imagine,' I said sadly. 'How old is she now?'

'Seventeen.'

'Yum, yum! Swoons a lot, does she? Or is she past that stage?'

'What are you getting at, Humbert? I have a great pile of essays to be marked tonight, you know. So—'

I explained Janet's aggressive contention that women don't swoon, and its relevance to Hélène Arnault in Bigorre three hundred and fifty years ago.

'Well, I wouldn't know about that, would I?' retorted Audrey. 'Not until you've allowed me to read your new novel in typescript, which I hear you're kindly proposing—'

'Who told you that?'

'Charlton Palser.'

'Oh yes?'

'Earlier this evening in McEwan's, as it happens. He and Wringhim Knox were trading conspiracy theories about Packwell . . . '

For this was some twenty-four hours after poor old General George's body was identified as having been drowned at sea.

'Don't tell me! You had a half of Guinness, Charlton was sipping an orange juice, and Wringhim was already pissed?'

'Something like that.'

'What's his angle on Packwell?'

'Whose?'

'Wringhim's?'

'"Serves the fat capitalist bastard right!" was mentioned. Also:

'"No doubt some yahoo hack formula writer is already churning out a one-dimensional monochrome gutless factoid so-called thriller in which fundemented Islamic frogmen plop like black dolphins out of the sea at five in the morning to yank the lone billionaire Australian Jew to his watery grave, and thereby destabilize all infidel convictions, by causing diarrhoea on Wall Street."'

'You historians have such good memories,' I conceded. 'What was Charlton's view?'

'Charlton declined to speak ill of the dead so soon after the dead had died.'

'There you are!' I couldn't help exclaiming. 'That's it in a nutshell.'

'What nutshell?'

'The difference between Wringhim and Charlton. Charlton, both instinctively and by virtue of cultivated sobriety, refrains, whenever possible, from giving gratuitous and obnoxious – get it? – offence. That's why he's made more money out of one and a half novels than Wringhim has out of ten.'

'I suppose so,' agreed Audrey. 'Also, Charlton doesn't parade his Scottishness all the time.'

'Very honest of him, when you remember he isn't Scottish. But you're quite right, Audrey. It's little things like that which help no end to get you reviewed in London, and on to the Gingerbread shortlist.'

'I thought Wringhim *did* get on to the Gingerbread shortlist one year.'

'So he did. However, as I'm surprised he seems never to have informed you umpteen times, that too was all a conspiracy!'

'In what way?'

'To be seen to have a token Scot on the short leet, give him a few moments patronizing attention in respect of his authentic regional voice, then award the prize as usual to either a load of claptrap set in India, where the judges have never been, or else yet again to adultery in Hampstead, which they at least know something about. It's a bigger scandal than *The Token Woman*, says Wringhim.'

'Since it's your phone bill we're talking about,' said Audrey, 'what's Wringhim's Gingerbread solution?'

'*His* solution is to refuse to allow any of his novels ever again to be entered for the prize. That way, the Decadent London Arseholes – as he styles them – at least won't have the satisfaction of knowing for sure that his latest novel wouldn't have won if it had been entered.'

'Sounds like typically rabid Calvinism to me. And yours?'

'My what?'

'Solution?'

'Oh. Well, why not establish a much more lucrative prize for fic-

tion – same catchment, ie open to all British and commonwealth novelists – but have it held in Edinburgh (or even possibly Glasgow),
administered by Scots, and judged by the same proportion of Scots to
English as the Gingerbread is by English to Scots? That should restore
the balance a bit.'

'Who would fund it?'

'Why not a big brewer, or distiller? I mean, since the connexion
between alcohol and novelists, not to mention reviewers, is so well
established.'

'Might work. Why not set it up yourself?'

'I don't think the instigators of these things should be seen to be
winning them too quickly.'

'Modest as ever, eh, Humbert?'

'"*M*odesty and *M*erit have only *M* in common."'

'Who said that?'

'I've told you before, Audrey. Twenty years ago, at least. Where's
your amazing memory now?'

'Must be Schopenhauer then. Anyway, Humbert, I am rather busy
tonight – so what can I actually *do* for you?'

'I beg your pardon?'

'You didn't really phone me up to discuss whether or not Jennifer
swoons, or whether George Packwell was or was not assassinated, so
*what is it* you're after? Is it this peculiar typescript you want me to read,
that Charlton was telling us about?'

'Not yet, thanks. But perhaps—'

'Why don't you give it to Wringhim in the meantime? He's very angry
that Charlton's read it and he hasn't.'

'Wringhim *would* have read the first instalment, if he hadn't got so
pissed as to lose all the pages. Also—' And I explained to Audrey how
Wringhim should be delighted to know I'd already written him into the
book, by including part of his poisonous letter to the *Crimes* denouncing
Mumbo Rankles. 'Perhaps you could tell him that, if you see him again
before I do.'

'As you wish, Humbert. Meanwhile Wringhim has intimated to me
that he wants you to do some typesetting for him.'

'Dear Jesus – why?'

'Some pamphlet or other, which he's decided to publish himself.'

'On what?'

'*Succeeding at Sex in London* seems to be the working title. He says
its a satire on all Britain's current ills.'

'I'll bet. Well, he knows my rates to fellow scrimshanks are . . . not extortionate. Tell him—'

'I think you'll find he's hoping you'll swap the typesetting for his feedback into your novel.'

'Hum numb bum, the devil you say. And what would *you* want, Audrey?'

'What could you possibly offer me, Humbert?'

'I could always take Jennifer off your hands come next mid-term,' I speculated nonchalantly. 'Give her some private coaching—'[1]

'I fancy, Humbert, that any daughter of mine could sail through her A levels even with your help.'

'I wouldn't let her watch satellite television on Saturday nights, of course.'

'And what am I supposed to understand by that?'

'Oh . . . nothing.'

'Then please can we get to the point?'

Immeasurably chastened, I outlined my passion to learn everything fascinating there was to be learned, within the next ten minutes, about the Tyrant Count-Duke Olivares, and the hopelessly corrupt court of Philip IV of Spain.

'You know,' I glossed, 'the Philip that looks like Herman Munster – as immortalized by Velazquez – with terminal constipation.'

'*I* wouldn't know about the constipation,' said Audrey smoothly.[2] 'But as far as Olivares is concerned, it so happens you're in luck, in that I am currently preparing a conference paper on "Spain's Great Century Of Decline". As a result of the research for which, from what you tell me, I would suggest that, for your present purposes, you could do worse than kick off with ruffs.'

'Ruffs?'

'I refer to the impossible policy, with which all the Philips – enmeshed

---

[1] If we* thought for a moment we could conceal from Audrey that we now find her daughter even more exciting, sexually speaking, than we do herself, then surely in all chivalry we would. However, since we know that she knows we can't, what's the point?

   * **'What is it with this intolerable "we"?' [J.R.]**

[2] Between certain exceptional men and women who have slept together with lifetime-peak gusto, no matter how long ago, there endures this sublime rapport.

in the delusion of their own divinity on earth – were lumbered, of saddling Spain with the defence and assertion of the Catholic faith throughout the world.'

'A bit like . . . mmmmmmmmmmmmmm, certain other foreign policies, associated with . . . ahem, certain other religious fanaticisms, that infect us still in the 1990s?'

'Very like.'

'The implication being that the doomed endeavour to uphold, restore and promulgate Catholicism, in South America, the Netherlands, the Bavarian Palatinate – even England! – had brought Spain to her knees financially?'

'Precisely so. Resulting, due to quaintly naive incomprehension of basic economics, on the part of high-handed favourite ministers such as Olivares – resulting, I say, in horrendous types and levels of taxation, which of course quickly stifled production of the goods supposed to be taxed, combined with even more bizarre and ultimately pointless prohibitions against the production, the using and wearing, and particularly against the extravagant flaunting, of a number of conspicuously useless goods, with which the indolent gentry of Madrid were totally besotted.'

'Like ruffs?'

'Emblematically so. Yet paradoxically too.'

'In what way?'

'Whilst the male, and especially the female, swaggerers of the Calle Mayor—'

'That being the King's Road of Old Madrid?'

'Indeed. Well, while the swankers paid grudging lip-service to most of the royal pragmatics against extravagance, there was one sumptuary decree enacted by Philip – which is always to say, Olivares – which, though at first it was resisted with much sulking – gave rise in due course to a whole new fashion. A fashion which was seized upon by all Spain with peacock-like crowing, and became, for the rest of the century – that is, for about seventy-five years – the single most characteristic article of Spanish male dress.'

'I have a feeling we're not talking about a new shape of cod-piece here.'

'Not directly.'

'Excuse me?'

'I mean that, like many a fraudulent codpiece, in both literal and several figurative senses, Spanish ruffs under Philip III had become ridiculously enormous, and the costly lace edging, and the elaborate devices required to keep the frills stiff, had made them possibly the most extravagant item of daily dress ever worn – in any country, at any time.'

'Gosh. That's saying something, isn't it?'

'Yes. And while attempts had been made to suppress these ludicrous ruffs, all had dismally failed. Not even Olivares was successful at first go, since the alternative collar prescribed by his pragmatics, issued in Philip's name, was either a plain linen band, or the flat Walloon collar falling on the shoulders. The plain linen was, understandably, rejected outright by persons who aspired to be well dressed, since they felt it looked mean and lacking in distinction, especially after the spreading splendour of the "lettuce frill" ruff, which had evolved to such codpiece proportions.'

'What about the Walloon collar?'

'A principal objection was that it was unstarched. So it soon got wrinkled, creased and soiled. It was also rejected on religious grounds, and with great smugness, since it had acquired odium by association with the heretic Hollanders, and even the risible Flemings. Consequently, even though the King himself – in a genuine if desperate attempt to proselytize his populace – wore the Walloon collar publicly, for some time following his first pragmatic, the clothes-conscious citizens of Madrid just could not be prevailed upon to adopt it.'

'One in the eye for the Tyrant Count-Duke?'

'Yes, but not for long. The problem was to find a new collar which should achieve the dignity of stiffness, but without the forbidden starch, "or other alchemy", as the pragmatics stipulated.'

'The project being to increase national frugality, by decreasing point-less overconsumption of starch?'

'Just so. Furthermore, the successful new ruff must maintain a becoming contrast of unsullied lightness around swarthy faces, but without resorting to the fine foreign lawns and laces which now were outlawed by royal proscription.'

'What a challenge to political genius. They didn't also have a poll tax, did they?'

'The Count-Duke's bacon was saved, on this score, by an ingenious tailor in the Calle Mayor, who, early in 1623, submitted for the King's perusal a new high-spreading collar of cardboard, covered with white or grey silk on its inner surface, and on the outside with a cloth of doublet-matching darkness.'

'Sounds even worse than a Church of Scotland minister!'

'Moreover, by means of heated iron rollers and shellac, the cardboard shape was permanently moulded into a graceful curve which bent outwards at the height of the chin, presenting, in juxtaposition with the face, the surface of light-coloured silk.'

'An instant hit?'

'Philip IV himself was pleased with the novelty, which was distinctly more "dressy" than the Walloon collar, and incurred none of the objections – such as wastage of starch – which were levelled against the ruff. So the King immediately ordered some of the new collars, which were called *golillas*—'

'Meaning?'

'*Little gorgets.* Of which Philip commanded a number to be made for himself, and some more for his brother Carlos.'

'So the smart little tailor's fortune was made?'

'Nothing so straightforward, in Madrid. Though the happy tailor danced home in transports of ecstasy to make up the King's *golillas*, he had alas forgotten that the restrictive pragmatics had forbidden *any other alchemy* to be employed in rendering the *golillas* stiff.'

'A sort of blanket ban on aphrodisiacs for collars?'

'Not only that, but the Inquisition was soon told by its spies that some secret incantations, and suspect rites involving mysterious smoking pots, and heated machines turned by handles, were being conducted by the tailor in the Calle Mayor.'

'Dark Satanic Stuff!'

'To the Inquisition it all reeked of the Evil One, and soon the unfortunate tailor and his hellish devices were hauled before the dread tribunal on suspicion of witchcraft and sorcery.'

'Is there a difference?'

'Differences were the Inquisition's speciality. Well, they couldn't work up much of a case against the poor tailor's tools, but since the *golillas* were in any case lined with silk, and because the use of silk was still in contravention of the King's own sumptuary pragmatic, the Inquisition took it upon themselves to order that the tailor's entire stock of material and all his instruments should be burned in public shame, in the street outside his front door.'

'End of story?'

'Few stories ever end in Madrid, Humbert. In this case, the tailor went crying to Olivares, who, furious that the King's collars should have been burnt, instantly summoned the president of the Inquisition Council, and rated him soundly. The president swore he hadn't had a clue that the strange silky things were for his Majesty, and argued, in defence of the Inquisition's conduct, how dangerously new the *golillas* were in shape, how mysteriously stiffened, and how blatantly they contravened the sumptuary pragmatic.'

'And when a sanctimoniously purging Inquistion confronts a Tyrant Count-Duke, face-to-face head-on, who wins?'

'Oh, Olivares. Hands down. The Count-Duke instructed the Inquisition, in no uncertain terms, that the *golillas* now had tickled his Majesty's fancy enormously, but that they were also the finest *and most economical* neckwear ever invented, as they needed no washing or starching, and would last for a year without further expense.'[3]

'*Golillas* six, Inquisition nil?'

'If you will. Philip IV, his brother Carlos, and many of the courtiers, wore the new *golilla* for the first time, at least as a matter of national solidarity in fashion, during the visit to Madrid of England's Prince of Wales, in March of 1623.'

'London's Charles the First, you mean?'

---

[3] Whereas: 'A single ruff of linen will cost six reals every time it is dressed, which at the end of the year doubles its cost.' Ie, doubled the purchase price of 200 reals, for an old-style 'lettuce frill' ruff, to 400 reals by the end of the first year of wear. (Quoted from Martin Hume. See note 5.) The real(e), quarter of a peseta or eighth of a dollar, was sometimes referred to as the 'Spanish sixpence'. 400 reals would therefore equal about 480 old sterling pence, or £2.* A staggering sum in those days, in other words, to blow per year on just one rubbish ruff.

**\* The information presented in this note should be digested in the spirit of Generous Catholic Approximism. Though it was cooked with the best of our numismatical deficiencies out of Chambers, Britannica and the Oxford English Dick, it nonetheless does not tally at all precisely with, for example, the currency equivalences suggested in R. Trevor Davies' The Golden Century of Spain (Macmillan, 1964). However, even allowing for discrepancies of 100% either way, the verdict must stand: to squander all that cash on codpiecing your neck was almost as lunatic and symptomatic of canker in government as to actively not stop grantgreed-crazed farmers from turning milk cows into cannibals.**

'So he would become.'

'What was he doing in Madrid?'

'He and the Duke of Buckingham—'

'Who fancied his chances with the Queen of France?'

'The same.'

'And did he in fact get to tup her, in the end?'

'Certainly he wanted to, right enough. All very musketeersy stuff, in those days. Anyway, Charles and Buckingham had wrung tearfully reluctant permission out of Charles's father, James the Sixth—'

'Of Scotland, First of England. If you don't mind, Audrey. Some of our readers may be English.'

'Not impossible, Humbert. Well, young Charles fancied his chances with the Infanta Maria, sister to Philip IV—'

'And presumably, visually, not quite so like Herman Munster?'

'Charles Stuart didn't think so. Indeed, so infatuated with the Spanish princess was he, that he and Buckingham had ridden across France, at breakneck speed, disguised as private gentlemen, to arrive in Madrid incognito – between five and six o'clock in the evening, on the seventh of March 1623, as it happened – all the better to woo Princess Maria himself, in person.'

'Having demonstrated the strength of his passion, by this daredevil quest through France?'

'So he fondly imagined.'

'And once in Madrid, did he too sport a *golilla*?'

'He tried everything.'

'But?'

'To no avail.'

'Why not?'

'The Count-Duke would not let the King of Spain allow his sister to marry the son of James the Sixth—'

'And First!'

'Unless James would first—'

'That's confusing!'

'Unless James would first undertake, in effect, to convert all England back to the Catholic Faith.'

'Which James wouldn't do?'

'He personally would have been delighted. But he would never have got away with it.'

'So dashing young Charles didn't win his darling Princess Maria of Spain after all?'

'No. After Olivares fobbed him off interminably, he married Henrietta Maria of France instead.'

'Sister to Louis XIII of France?'

'That's right.'

'Hence also sister to the Queen of Spain, Isabel de Bourbon, – sister-*in-law* to Philip Munster?'

'That's sort of right.'

'Both daughters of Henri Quatre?'

'Very much so.'[4]

'And just as randy with it?'

'That is an angle, Humbert, which we historians prefer to leave to you novelists.'

'Good of you to say so, Audrey. But, seriously, if Olivares was already so dominant in 1623, he must have been . . . quite suffocating in 1640?'

'Almost everyone else in Spain thought so.'

'And were they still wearing *golillas*?'

'Absolutely. Philip IV was rarely seen in any other collar, and the fashion spread like wildfire. Soon every gentleman who was anyone in Spain—'

'But not Catalonia?'

'Spanish Italy, and South America . . . they all wore *golillas* with conspicuous pride. The curve, size, and shape of the *golilla* modulated somewhat, as other fashions changed, but the principle remained the same . . . really until the pan-European triumph of the French falling-lace cravat in the eighteenth century.'

'Now look here, Audrey. I'm grateful to you for going into such detail, particularly as you've so many essays still to mark. However, some of our readers might be forgiven for wondering why, in the context of the involvement of Louis Morel in the Barcelona uprising in 1640, you feel this business, of whether or not a few indolent

---

4 And so, by way of Henrietta Maria, via her son, their Charles II, the gallant blood of Henri Quatre does not flow on in the veins of their own future Charles III, since of the Merrie Monarch's many children not one was at all legitimate.

As regards the likelihood that you, we and/or the postman may be a little ennobled by a few residual drops of the same blood, see Chapter 21, note 2.

Spanish noblemen had starch up their ruffs, is so paradigmatically vital. I wouldn't want us to be misunderstood, you see. As Somerset Maugham, for instance, quite failed to comprehend the point of the landscape gardening sequences in *Elective Affinities*. Is that not a fair comparison?'

'I doubt it, Humbert. Though I can't remember when last I had sufficient leisure to read novels by Goethe.'

'Let's stick to the ruffs, can we? You're suggesting, if I haven't misunderstood you again, that the ruffs are symbolic of a society's decline into corruption?'

'Yes.'

'The fact that so many bigwig prats could take their neckwear so seriously . . . this being the implicit confession of a deranged belief structure, not to mention a profound moral putridity?'

'I could hardly have put it better myself, Humbert.'

'And the sumptuary decrees against the earlier, more expensive, starchier ruffs: these you see as magnificently typical of absolute economic incompetence? A bit like rubbing nettle stings with nettles, because you don't know what dock leaves look like? Or letting blood in the hope of curing haemophilia? Or flushing down the drain of international shark practice some fifteen billion pounds of four nations' currency reserves, in the ostensible fond hope of somehow thereby strengthening one's economy?'

'Indeed.'

'Which, combined with other measures of like fatuousness, such as taxing enterprise and materials to the point where ever fewer goods were produced, tended constantly toward national bankruptcy?'

'That's right.'

'Is there anything I've missed?'

'You wouldn't want to forget the delusions of religious rectitude, and vicarious divinity, that caused the Count-Duke and the King to squander what little cash they had, and a lot they hadn't, on vain attempts to uphold Catholicism in the Netherlands, the Palatinate in Bavaria – even England. All over the world, in fact.'

'Goodness gracious me – if not invariably you, Audrey. But were these people really that stupid?'

'Start with rickety premises, Humbert, and you can end up with ruinous conclusions. You should know that.'

'Yes, indeed. So after another two decades, near enough, of this sort of idiocy, the Spanish government must have been very badly in hock.

Is this why the Catalans got so shirty in 1640? Because of Central Government squeezing them for funds?'

'It's not quite so simple as that, Humbert.'

'Is it ever, Audrey? But?'

'The Count-Duke's biggest failure, if you like, was his inability to grasp the fiercely local loyalties of the regions that made up Spain. Thus, we've been bandying *Spain*, close quotes, but really we've been talking about *Castile*.'

'At the heart of which is Madrid?'

'Of course. But several of the other regions had their own histories, traditions, long-standing rights, and in some cases even their own languages.'

'Like Catalonia?'

'And the Basque Country. And, perhaps the most extreme case, Portugal. Anyway, by 1640 the Catalans, who had successfully resisted many Crown attempts to milk money out of them, were in many ways much less poorly off than the Castilians—'

'Who had no option but to play ball, when the Count-Duke blew the whistle?'

'Right. So Olivares' ploys to get cash out of the Catalans grew ever more high-handed and desperate, and, not unnaturally, the Catalans waxed correspondingly more resentful and suspicious of Central Government intentions.'

'So like us Scots today – hmmmn. But what about the crunch? The spark that ignited the tinder?'

'That was the attempts by the French, under Richelieu, to invade Spain, beginning with Roussillon, which then belonged to Catalonia.'

'So the Count-Duke seized on that, did he? As an excuse to invade Catalonia himself, on pretext of defending the provincials against French aggression?'

'On the contrary, Humbert. In the first instance he was deliberately tardy about sending military support.'

'Ah. I see. To let the French knock the stuffing out of the Catalans for him?'

'Partly that. Also because his military resources were already at full stretch. And then, when at last he did send Castilian soldiers into Catalonia, his attitude, which naturally percolated down to the rank and file, was insufferable to the Catalans. His instructions to the Marquis of Santa Coloma—'

'You mean, the Fat Viceroy?'

'Certainly he was rather obese. Rather a turncoat too, in a way. Since he, a Catalan himself, was perceived as the Count-Duke's creature.'

'Aha. The Fat Viceroy as Quisling? Or a Tory Secretary of State for Scotland, with no mandate, sucking up to the Number Ten Creep?'

'All these things. Anyway, there's an intensely revealing letter from the Count-Duke to the Viceroy, which – if, being a novelist, you'd rather not go to the bother of reading it up in Spanish – you'll find translated in a professionally somewhat antiquated but nonetheless quite informative study by Martin Hume. I can't recall its exact title[5] off hand, but—'

'Well, thank you very much, Audrey. That'll certainly add up to a good few thousand words for me to hammer out tomorrow.'

'You're welcome. Now—'

'Perhaps you could just look up the Hume reference for me when you're next—'

'Get it yourself, you idle waster,' suggested Audrey affectionately. 'Now—'

'Just one last thing,' I urged her winningly.

---

[5] It is in fact *The Court of Philip IV*, Eveleigh Nash, London, 1907. We found a copy of this in Edinburgh University Library, on a fifth-floor shelf from which, since it was presented by the executors of the late Miss E. B. Lemon, in 1942, it had been borrowed zero times. Mr Hume's rendering of the Tyrant Count-Duke's letter to the Fat Viceroy goes as follows:

'Do not', wrote Olivares, 'suffer a single man who can work to absent himself from the field, nor a woman who can bear on her back food or forage . . . If the enterprise can be effected without violating the privileges of the province, well and good, but if in order to respect these the service of the King is retarded by one single hour, he who dares to uphold them at such a cost will be an enemy to his God, his King, his race, and his country . . .

'Make the Catalans understand that the general welfare of the people and of the troops must be preferred to all rights and privileges. You must take great care that the troops [ie the detested Castilians] are well lodged and have good beds; and if there are none to be had, you must not hesitate to take them from the highest people in the province; for it is better that they [Catalan citizens] should lie on the ground than that the troops should suffer.'

'What?'

'Since this is a novel . . . Well, sort of . . . Some of our readers, women like Janet—'

'Who is this Janet?'

'Will want to hear a little about the Tyrant Count-Duke's appearance. Did he have, say, dark hair?'

'Yes.'

'Matching beard and moustache?'

'Sort of.'

'Blue eyes?'

'No way.'

'Wig Billy?'

'Eh?'

'Grasping nose?'

'Typically avaricious, yes. Though in later years his personal lifestyle was deceptively saintly. In fact, Humbert, if you need more detail on what Olivares looked like, why don't you – when you've finally finished with Hume – go on to look up Velazquez?'

'Okay, okay. Now, just one last thing—'

'God, Humbert, you don't change, do you?'

'Nobody changes at bottom, Oh Love My Pussy. That's what Godfrey Blobbs doesn't realize. And it's precisely because of this deep-structure feature – limitation, if you like – of the human situation that some of our readers will be more satisfied, if possible, to learn that the Tyrant Count-Duke, after so much loathsome Tyrannizing, got the bullet in the end. What say you?'

'You're doubly in luck there, Humbert. Having over twenty years executed, humiliated or somehow offended virtually every notable personage in Spain save the King, Olivares was finally sacked by Philip in January 1643.'

'What for?'

'Failure, basically. He'd failed to prevent national bankruptcy from escalating. Failed to mollify and reintegrate the Catalans. Failed to stop the French invading Spain again. Failed – in conspiracy with Cinq Mars – to have Cardinal Richelieu assassinated. And finally, crucially, he failed to thwart the Queen's tireless efforts to turn the King against him. Parading her thirteen-year-old son in front of Philip, she tearfully exclaimed:

'"Now let *my* efforts, and my boy's innocence, serve your Majesty for eyes. For if you use those of the Count-Duke much longer, our son will be reduced to a poor king of Castile, instead of Proud King of All Spain."'

'So Philip cracked?'

'And the Count-Duke was sacked.'

'Disgraced?'

'Totally. When once he wrote from his exile in Toro, far away from the Court, to offer his services again, Philip IV replied:

'"In short, Count, *I* must reign, and my son must be crowned King of Aragon. This is difficult unless I deliver your head to my subjects, who demand it unanimously, and I cannot oppose them any longer."'

'Mighty fallen, what?'

'Further than you might guess, Humbert. For that letter from the King tipped the Count-Duke into wholesale raving madness, and he died in July 1645, less than three years after his disgrace.'

'Some of our readers will be very pleased to hear that, Audrey. Well, so the biggest failure was failure, it seems. Is that the principal difference between Olivares and Richelieu?'

'It certainly is one of them, though the Cardinal had other advantages.'

'Like what?'

'While the Count-Duke had the foresight of cunning, the Cardinal had the foresight of vision. Also, while both had a strong vindictive streak, the Cardinal's was tempered by prudence. For instance, when in 1628 he finally succeeded in besieging the Protestants of La Rochelle into submission, he instantly granted them freedom of worship, provided only that they demolished their inland fortifications and swore allegiance to the Crown. The Count-Duke, by contrast, would have delighted in brutalizing the Protestants[6] into paying lip-service to Catholicism, as a

---

6 Audrey's idea about looking up Velazquez was actually rather a good one. There are several portraits of Olivares by Velazquez, and, allowing for an understandable element of flattery, given that Velazquez owed much of his success to the Count-Duke's patronage, therein we see a face which, if stripped of its bristles, might put us instantly in mind of the sort of slimy shittiness commonly associated with 'right-wing' Members of Parliament who have also been called to many bars – too many, in the most obvious faces. Some of the contemporary English commentators also float dubieties as to whether the Count-Duke's hair was really his own.

result of which he would have had yet another revolt on his hands the moment his back was turned.'

'Interesting. Still, if the Cardinal's policies hadn't been so successful, he too might have been disgraced, by Louis XIII, and remembered by us as a failure. I mean, especially by American historians.'

'That's very profound, Humbert. Now—'

'Yes, yes. That's enormously helpful, Audrey. Thanks. I'll give you due credit, of course.'

'That's very kind, Humbert. But I'd just as soon you didn't mention me, if you don't mind.'

'As you wish. Well, I'll send you some chapters to check in a week or two. Bye for now.'

'Bye—'

'Love to Jennifer.'

'Up yours, Humbert. And goodnight.'

# 19

# Mayhem in Barcelona

Following their interview, Louis Morel cannot but feel that the fat Viceroy's Draconian resolution has erupted too late, and that the evil consequences of his languid rule have already stirred the populace to a flashpoint of no return. Meanwhile the Viceroy's giant Negro, Scipio, supervises the escort of Louis and Achilles Lefranc to close quarters, followed initially by the mendacious Castilian trooper. Shortly, though, the last laugh for the moment is on the trooper himself — since the Negro, the authority of whose lieutenancy appears limitless, orders several other lurking soldiers to seize and bind the would-be horse-thief, march him down to the courtyard, give him fifty lashes of the strappado, and then keep him in confinement pending the Viceroy's further pleasure.

'Amen, amen!' cries Achilles in French, when he realizes what's afoot, and looks down on the beating from the barred window of the third-storey room in which Louis and he are locked.

Louis derives no such pleasure from the trooper's comeuppance, since he is now plunged into helpless dangling between *joy*, at the thought that the Chevalier of Montenero will soon be here to liberate him, and *despair* — at the possibility that he will still be so dreadfully in the Chevalier's bad books that his former uncle-surrogate will disavow him utterly, thus condemning him to die in tortures more exquisite than his vilest dreams.

Memories of the Chevalier, fond and bitter, loop him round, by inevitable links, a gallery of Zaragoza sadness. The maja. Her beauty, passion, murder of the debauched prelate; her suicide. The Corregidor. His dignity, decency, paternal devotion, grief for his daughter; his death. The Chevalier. His loyal intervention on Louis's behalf, reasonable suspicions concerning Louis's nocturnal behaviour, outrage at Louis's refusal to confess; his scathing repudiation of any connexion with Louis hereafter.

Well, broods Louis, if on top of all that, the Chevalier has since heard of his shooting dead Jean-Baptiste, and subsequent guilty-like flight from Bigorre, into Spain with outlaw smugglers . . . well, why on earth should the Chevalier be expected to put in a kind word for him now?

As to Hélène, and the searing heat with which, in his mind's eye, she loathes and despises him, to the point of wishing her own wasted life at an end – it is perhaps small wonder that Louis reacts downputtingly, when Achilles generously invites him over to the window, to behold the whipped trooper's screams.

This atmosphere of tetched trepidation continues for perhaps another hour, until the Negro Scipio escorts in a flunkey bearing a tray heavy with delicious Mediterranean crustaceans and jugged Catalan wine. Once the flunkey has vamoosed, the Negro waits behind unnervingly, and looks on silently as Achilles gobbles up and Louis tentatively picks at the succulent sea-fruits on their plates. When it appears that Louis has finished eating, despite not having gorged all his prawns, the Negro politely inquires whether Señor Morel has enjoyed his meal, and would he like anything else?

'Very much. And no, thank you,' Louis replies uneasily. He has never before had to deal with an intelligent coloured person at close quarters, never mind one approximately half again as large, heavy and muscular as himself. Besides that, he is unable not to wonder exactly what, when the Negro and the Viceroy are alone together at night, each of them gets up to with the other, and who gets what out of it.

'Won't you sit down?' he now, with laboured courtesy, asks the Negro.

Scipio gracefully lowers his great weight on to a small stool by the door and, to Louis's astonishment, proceeds to petition, in subdued but fluent French, that the French agents of Richelieu – ie, Louis and Achilles – will use their influence to help rouse the Viceroy to a just and realistic sense of the oppression the Catalans have suffered under the Castilian occupation.

'We are not—'

'Be *silent*,' Louis orders the declaiming Achilles, for the intuition is mounting within him that to be mistaken for a French government agent may henceforth be not without its advantages. Simultaneously he considers the possibility that this chummy approach by the Viceroy's slave could equally well be a measure of conspiracy to entrap him. So to the Negro he replies:

'As peaceable visitors to this country, we have neither knowledge of, nor interest in, your political affairs.'

With a black scowl and reduced reserve, Scipio retorts by accusing

Louis of typically white indifference to the predicaments of the oppressed. Still cautious, Louis invites Scipio to expand on the particular problems of the oppressed in Catalonia. Scipio obliges with impassioned eloquence for several minutes. Impressed by the Negro's patent sincerity, and by the sophistication of his combining loyalty to and affection for the Viceroy with an intimate and critical knowledge of his failings, Louis – without going so far as to admit any official connexion with Paris – undertakes that, given a suitable opportunity, he will apprise the Viceroy of his own view: that only a swift and full evacuation of the hated Castilian soldiers can have any hope of averting a full-scale revolution in Catalonia.

'Thank you,' says Scipio, who then departs immediately and locks the door behind him.

Louis looks round just in time to see the last of the jugged wine trickling down Achilles throat, and in the same instant an ominous scream full of fear and hate floats through the window before being chopped short as by an axe. After a pause long enough to contain gasps of numb horror there follow sounds of soldiers rushing about in the courtyard, as if in preparation to repulse an attack. Verifying this interpretation from his window vantage, the mellowed Achilles opines:

'Jolly good. Serves them right. Let the bastards fight it out between themselves.'

'No, Achilles,' Louis admonishes him. 'Such sentiments are too facile, and will not hold. Cannot you feel?'

'Feel what?' grins Achilles blithely.

'That the undertone of nationalist resentment is indomitable? The very air pulsating with conviction: that this is the genuine uprising of a united people? Animated by lust for vengeance – regrettable, yes – but by authentic cravings for identity, and liberty too.'

More sounds of tumult attract Louis to the window, from which he hears but does not see the fat Viceroy's surprisingly musical voice giving surprisingly calm and efficient orders. When a galloping cavalry officer arrives in the arsenal with the desperate news that the rebels have burned the stables, and that hence there is no cavalry, the Viceroy from his invisible vantage commands the cavalry officer to ride back, form the horseless cavalry into foot soldiers, and either drive the rebels back or else die in the attempt. The cavalry officer wheels round and gallops off to obey but Louis sees him, the moment his horse's tail is clear of the arsenal gates, shot dead in the head and toppled out of his saddle.

Within minutes a tidal wave of Catalans is surging round every street corner Louis can see: driving a dishevelled flotsam of Castilian soldiers backwards. When the Castilians suddenly break and run, the Catalan rebels are temporarily checked by blasting cannon from the arsenal towers. In a gap between plumes of hot smoke Louis espies the tall burly form of Pere Garcés urging the Catalans ever forward: to spearhead beneath the lowest range of the arsenal cannon, and take the stronghold itself. In moments of respite caused by the cannon blasts overhead, many of the Castilians scramble back into the arsenal, while those who don't make it are shot, impaled, or beheaded by berserk hacks.

Little Achilles Lefranc, Louis notes in passing, overcome by the savagery of the carnage, and reduced to a shivering maudlin funk by the after-effects of having drunk nearly all the wine, has retreated to their cell-chamber's single bed, and is lying on his back with the bolster held tight round his ears, and tears seeping quietly from the corners of his eyes.

When Louis looks back to the fray he sees the Catalans bringing forward six small cannon which they had earlier seized from the Castilians but would have been prevented from using, had not blasting from the arsenal itself now blown off the side of a wool warehouse, thus revealing an instant supply of ready-made fascines: in the form of enormous woolpacks. Behind these the insurgents flock to regroup. Like mammoth ants heaving mountainous crusts of bread, they roll the woolpacks forward. As musket balls and grapeshot from the Castilians rake the vast sacks it is as if Birnam Wood erupts in fleeces, but for all that the Viceroy's men are unable to halt the wool-buffered Catalan advance.

Now into the arsenal courtyard with portly strides comes the Viceroy himself. Displaying an energy and courage by which Louis confesses himself astonished, the lumpy commander sprints up the steps to the cannon emplacements and eggs his troops on by fearless example. Almost simultaneously, however, the arsenal gates explode inwards thanks to pointblank fire from the six small captured cannon which the Catalans have wheeled up under cover of woolsacks. Nothing now can stop the rebels pouring in like demented lava. Despite murderous fire from the arsenal parapets they use woolpack shields to establish a strong position on the counterscarp, and Louis at his window in captivity is so engrossed in the thrilling action that he almost isn't roused by a cry of horror from Achilles just in time to whirl and dodge a deadly sword lunge aimed at his kidneys by the strappadoed horse-thief trooper, who, plumbing a new depth of treachery, has taken advantage of the hullabaloo without to pursue this private vendetta within.

Louis, unarmed, drops sideways, feints under the Castilian's sword arm, and wrestles his torso to the ground. For several minutes they roll on the floor grappling furiously, the trooper straining to snatch at a knife in his belt, while Louis pins tight his arms. All the while the Castilian gibbers and whinnies with an intensity of frenzy to murder scarcely credible to anyone unfamiliar with Spanish history, and presently his opportunity arrives when Louis relaxes a fraction in a stunned moment of reaction to having the lobe of his left ear bitten off. As with a yell of triumph the Castilian hoists his knife high for a fatal thrust he is slowed to the leisurely limpness of eye-rolling amazement, by a tremendous blow to the back of his head from the butt of a musketoon, which little Achilles Lefranc has collected from the floor of the corridor outside, where it has fallen from the custody of the soldier standing guard, whom the vendetta man has killed.

'That'll do, Achilles,' says Louis shakily, appalled by the flow of blood which a severed earlobe can turn on – for Achilles, ecstatic with pre-emptive fright, continues to hammer the musket butt down on the failed assassin's head, long after there is no chance of any life being left inside it.

'Let's tie him up,' suggests Achilles nervously, when eventually he is persuaded to stop hammering the corpse.

'He's dead, Achilles,' says Louis. 'There's no point.'

'Bloody swine,' warbles Achilles, trembling all over. 'How on earth did he get free?'

'They probably released him from his confinement,' speculates Louis, 'in order to assist in the arsenal's defence. The fact that he then elected to attempt to settle his own score first, tells us much about the self-poisoning character of all political oppression, and is emblematic of why, in the long run, all underdogs must win.'

'What about us?' worries Achilles. 'Now the door's open, what'll happen to *us*?'

Catalan witnesses of these Barcelona scenes later described with enthusiasm the patriotic ardour shown by all social classes, and: 'the courage, daring, and diligence displayed even by women and children in bringing provisions, ropes, ammunition, medicine, and all kinds of assistance to the defenders . . . Even the nuns in their convents sent biscuits and preserves, while others prayed to God for the triumph of the Catalan cause; some women dressed as soldiers and went about with swords and daggers . . . '

This surviving wealth of supplementary accounts of what took place in Barcelona during those insurrection days enables us to conclude this chapter with less qualification of the subjectivity of Louis Morel's memoirs, and hence with – in, so to speak, the spirit of nostalgic reprise – a fleeting reversion to the gloriously megalomaniacally Victorian pseudo-omniscient voice[1] depicting third (etc) persons in past tenses, the simpler the better.

Thus:

When Louis Morel had recovered his senses and staunched the bleeding from his ear sufficiently to return to the prison-room window, he saw that countless rebels had by now invaded the arsenal, and that the Viceroy with not more than a hundred Castilians was fighting a desperate rearguard with mainly swords, daggers, and other bladed weapons – as almost all firearms had been discharged and the mêlée was much too frantic to permit the leisure of reloading.

Moments later the Viceroy's overweight and unfit body collapsed in a protest of violent cramps against such unaccustomed exertions. With a mad yell of glee the insurgents pressed forward to finish him off, but perhaps a dozen loyal Castilians closed in a protective half-moon in front of their fallen leader just in time to allow the Viceroy's huge Negro the moment necessary to scoop up his master's body and remove him within the building.

Seeing the Viceroy temporarily snatched from the jaws of death, and recalling his reasonable lenity in judgement, and now his unexpected valour in action, Louis experienced mixed feelings about the upper hand being gained by the Catalans, and grave doubts as to what sort of justice might follow the victory they surely must win. So with his head full of hopeful thoughts of mediating between Pere Garcés and the Viceroy, to secure civilized capitulation terms, and minimize essential bloodshed, Louis decisively confiscated the dead assassin's sword, commanded Achilles Lefranc to follow, and sallied forth from the scene of his confinement – moments later to find the shattered Viceroy on the floor in the hall, propped against a pillar, with the faithful Scipio in anxious attendance: pressing his wheezing master to sip a cup of reviving wine.

---

[1] Or, again, Fiction as by The Top Monad. Not that we suspect Dickens of having digested a lot of Leibnitz.

'At the sound of my steps,' recalled Louis, 'the slave started up and laid his hand upon his dagger; but, seeing me, he gave a melancholy glance towards his lord, and again begged him to take some refreshment. Alas, the excessive toil to which the Viceroy had subjected his unfit person had left him no powers of any kind, and he sat with his eyes shut, his head fallen heavily forward on his chest, and seemingly unconscious of all. So it was in vain that I proposed:

'"Does your excellency wish that I endeavour to parley terms with Señor Garcés?"

'For only the most piteous groan signalled the Viceroy's awareness of my presence. Hoping then by reiteration to make him attend to the sense of my suggestion, I began to repeat it, but now came one of the Viceroy's lieutenants, running down from above, and crying out:

'"Excellency, Excellency! The galleys answer the signal. From the observatory I have seen the boats make ready. If your Excellency shall hasten, you will get to the shore in time, and be safe."

'With a great effort the Viceroy raised his head. "At all events I will try," said he. "For they cannot now say that I have abandoned my post while it was tenable. Let the soldiers take torches."

'The lieutenant flew to give the necessary directions, and taking the cup from the Negro, the Viceroy drank a small quantity of wine, after which he looked up at me. "I am glad you are free," said he in French. "My men are talking of escape, but I do not think I can effect it. However, we shall try. As for you, young French sir, they shall not injure you. Proclaim you are under orders from your great Cardinal – nay, even if in truth you are not – and they shall shower you with honours. When the time comes, and I am no more," he added with the pathos of calm dignity, "I pray you will make it known, that I did not desert my post, so long as it remained defensible at all. Will you promise?"

'Of course I undertook to report his conduct with all fairness, but also pleaded the wisdom of my accompanying him towards the boats they talked of. For though I knew not how they thought to reach the sea, surrounded as the arsenal was by the hostile populace, I felt convinced, nonetheless, that I should be in less immediate personal peril in the open streets, than shut up in the arsenal, where the first disgorgement of the enraged peasantry to break in might very likely murder me, and little Achilles too, without troubling first to inquire where our allegiances might lie.

'At the same time I fancied that in case of the Viceroy being overtaken, if Garcés was at the head of the pursuers, I should have some influence over him, in saving some blood from being spilled. While these thoughts were racing through my brain, half a dozen urgent voices, seemingly from beneath us, cried out:

'"Excellency, Excellency! The torches are lighted!"'

Then followed the escape attempt.

The Viceroy, his armpits supported by Louis Morel and the Negro at either side, led the way down the great hall, away from the double oak doors which were already shuddering under rebel battering from without, thence down a spiral staircase to a lower hall below ground level, where a dining table had been pulled aside to reveal a large oblong stone trapdoor: normally disguised as just another flagstone, but now levered aside to reveal an underground passage below, to be reached by a long wooden ladder. As Louis and the lieutenant lowered him down to the waiting Negro, the Viceroy's last faintly gasped orders to his soldiers were:

'Give us two minutes, Rodriguez. Then have all men cease their fire, repair here, and follow us down the passage. You personally I entrust with pulling the flag back over the mouth of the trap, and barring it from beneath.'

Of their exit from the secret tunnel under the arsenal, Louis records:

'The tide was out, and yet a smooth dry sand appeared to promise us a firm and easy footing to the water; but a multitude of large black rocks, strewed irregularly about the shore, obliged us to take several meandering detours, which doubled at least the real distance we were from the boats. The shouts and screams from the place of our late combat nevertheless assaulting our ears, the very moment we issued from the passage, we sped on with all possible rapidity. Seeing that he could otherwise hardly move, I took the left arm of the Viceroy over my shoulder, while his Negro supported him likewise on the right, and thus, with great effort, we endeavoured to hurry him on towards the boats.

'But now, alas, a new and far nearer chorus of rage assailed our ears, from a body of peasantry some distance south down the sands, who were racing on foot, at nearly a right angle with ourselves, to intercept our attempt to reach the shore most near the boats. The Viceroy hearing this new tumult too, and with an effort raising his head to regard the danger it foretold, he easily perceived the consequence.

'"I can go no further," said he, with the quiet dignity of resignation. "As I can die here just as well as ten paces on, I command that you good people leave me now, and hasten on with your own escape. You too, dear Scipio," he added, shrugging free of our support, and pulling pathetically at his sword.

'"Yet a little further, my lord," urged the African. "The enemy is still a ways off, and the boats are so near. Do try, dear my lord. Do try."

'The unfortunate Viceroy allowed us to lever him forward perhaps the ten paces he had unwittingly forecast. Then, as unexpectedly we all staggered on a large green rock made slippery with slime, his weariness again overcame him. His lips turned livid, his eyes closed, and he fell fainting upon the beach. As the Negro slapped his master's cheeks in despair, I myself ran ahead to the sea, there filling the shells of two large crabs with water, which I then carried back to splash revivingly on the Viceroy's face. All of this labour was in vain, however, for now I espied a second party of the insurgents, which had emerged from the dunes to our north, and circled round to the shore.'

The events which ensued were also later described by a Catalan nationalist named Ximenes Alavares – who in 1671 would become a cardinal, though that bloody afternoon in 1640 he couldn't have been any older than Louis himself – and the consensus which emerges from their two accounts is as follows.

## 20

# On the Beach

As Louis Morel and Scipio the African try bootlessly to revive the floundered fat Viceroy:

The two parties of Catalan insurgents, scenting the blood of victory over the oppressor, abandon their angles towards the galleys (which in any case are now rowing a prudent distance out to sea, there to watch what befalls ashore) and close with glee upon their prey.

Meanwhile:

Now a party of Castilian soldiers, much less numerous than the rebels, emerges from the arsenal's secret-passage exit, and is bound to join the defence leader.

Louis, the Negro and the Viceroy would thus appear to a wheeling seagull like three rock cod stranded equidistantly between three converging packs of ravenous cats.

While the yells yell ever louder and more murmurous, and the pistols begin to blast, Louis makes out the tall form of Pere Garcés:

The sprinting smuggler is catching up on the tail of the northern insurgents from the dunes.

In a longshot attempt to forestall the carnage he senses is imminent, Louis steps between the Viceroy and the dune rebels, waves his arms in a truceful manner, and shouts loud to Garcés – in French:

To *hurry-hurry forward*, to save the Viceroy from instant murder, as he personally (ie the Viceroy) had wished the Catalan people reasonably well, and was sufficiently endowed with decency and justice, for example, to have preserved Louis Morel's own life, pending testimony from the Chevalier – when many Castilians would have had him hideously tortured straight away.

This reasoned plea by Louis falls mainly on hate-crazed ears which in any case understand no French.

But Pere Garcés does indeed sprint forward in a desperate and only just successful effort to embrace and therefore save Louis Morel from the rain of thrusts, stabs and hacks that swiftly empties the Viceroy's body of life and leaves his corpse pouring blood on the sand.

185

Scipio with his scimitar flashing kills and wounds several of the attackers before he too is felled by a blade from behind and falls dying on top of his master.

The partisans now switch their attention to Louis.

There is a tense lull while Garcés, who clearly enjoys leader respect, explains urgently to his fellows that Louis, being French, and an agent working secretly for the French Premier Richelieu — hence in the Catalan cause — is not to be slain like the Viceroy.

This account appears to the rabble to be confirmed when Louis now, in terse and rapid French, accuses Pere Garcés of stooping to the most contemptible depths of anarchy:

In allowing the Viceroy to be slaughtered without a trial.

Standing back coolly from the protective embrace in which he has held Louis pinned, Pere Garcés sternly counter-accuses Louis of foolishly presuming too much on their friendship, and of the political inappropriateness of his attempting to intervene between the reborn Catalan lion and the despicable Castilian jackal.

'He may have been slothful and negligent,' persists Louis Morel, 'but the Viceroy was a not unjust man.'

'Then his crime', scoffs Garcés, 'was to have remained ignorant of the wrongs committed under his rule. Either way his execution, whether later, or sooner, was assured.'

From the mutterings and jostlings about him Louis quickly twigs that even the influence of Pere Garcés over these rebels is not unlimited.

He is also now smitten with a fresh anxiety:

That little Achilles Lefranc is nowhere to be seen.

Glancing back to where the southern horde of insurgents is in the process of finishing killing off and beginning to behead the last of the Castilian soldiers to have emerged from the escape tunnel, Louis is wracked by guilt at the realization that, in his urgency to aid the Viceroy, he has retained no perception of Achilles ever since they stumbled from the dark of the tunnel to the sunlight on the beach.

Seeing the dismemberment being inflicted on the remains of the rearguard Castilians, Louis — again in French — urges Pere Garcés in the name of decency not to let the rebels likewise mutilate the bodies of the Viceroy and the negro; since a harsh clamour to behead, castrate, disembowel and quarter these corpses is brewing up like an overheated cauldron of stew all around them.

'Why should they not gratify their anger?' objects Garcés, still in French.

'Because', explains Louis, 'the dead are dead, and can do no further harm. He who loses his respect for the bodies of the dead has already begun to despise the bodies of the living. His values are in putrefaction. Is this what you want, for your citizens of free Catalonia?'

'Very well,' agrees Garcés curtly. In Catalan he shouts:

'Comrades, hold back! Be calm, and pay heed to the ambassador of France. Over to you,' he mutters drily to Louis.

Louis takes a deep breath. Thickening his crude Catalan with what he takes to be a refined Parisian accent, he exhorts the rabble to behold his Frenchness, to remember eternal French friendship for Catalonia, and to consider the wisdom, from the freedom-fighters' point of view, of conspicuously embracing the standards of France, if they are seriously hoping for further supplies of money and weapons from Cardinal Richelieu.

'He has a point there, comrades,' interjects Pere Garcés.

'Not only must the dead not be mutilated,' continues Louis sternly. 'But even living Castilians, comrades, must be offered the opportunity to surrender. And if they accept, we must take them into custody without injury, and treat them with the consideration universally due to prisoners of war, until the time comes for them to be tried before the law.'

'When those guilty of atrocities shall without fail be executed,' Garcés adds consolingly.

'This same heroic restraint', Louis goes on, 'displayed by you good Catalan people, despite the horrendous excesses of your oppressors, you shall do well to exhibit doubly in the case of any foreign nationals you may capture in the next few days. In particular,' he adds, hoping thus to reduce the danger of the missing Achilles being summarily butchered, 'any Frenchmen taken must be brought unharmed before myself. God bless Catalonia.'

Louis Morel's oration on the beach is a huge success, from which both he and Pere Garcés emerge with their statuses much elevated. By now more droves of insurgents have raced, ambled and drifted down from Barcelona's centre, forming an adequate quorum for a legitimate mass-meeting of the Revolution. To the meeting, his stature platformed by a squat black rock thick with green slime, Garcés proposes that a Revolutionary Council of Twelve should be elected, to have supreme command of the army, and power of life and death over prisoners.

The motion is almost unanimously carried. Garcés is appointed president of the Council and commander-in-chief of the army. Various other popular and respectable citizens are elected to the Council. Louis too, to his utmost amazement, is nominated – on account of the citizens' belief in the value of French support for their cause, and the universal presumption that Louis is Richelieu's right-hand man in Spain.

Hoping to achieve some good, and to check the consequences of the rebels' high passions, Louis graciously accepts his election. Six stout porters now carry a makeshift bier bearing the bodies of the Viceroy and his slave back to Barcelona city. In the midst of this triumphal march Pere Garcés outlines to his Council members several plans for restoring order. He also sends commands ahead for no further bloodshed, and requiring the Barcelona Corregidor and other former civil officers to unite with the people to cement the liberties they have just reacquired.

Waiting for them on the cathedral steps is a confluence of notables. When all are assembled the manic hubbub subsides to a nervous hush when the Bishop of Barcelona emerges with all possible pomp. Wisely he hails the uprising and its victorious outcome as, indubitably, 'in accordance with the Will of God.' Then the Bishop slily enjoins the Catalan multitude to observe a strict penitent fast tomorrow: in recognition that some of the slain are inevitably innocent in God's eyes. With that modest proviso, absolution for all the rebels is assured.

'The populace', the Morel memoirs record, 'greeted the Bishop's speech with great roars of exultation, though privately one could not but suspect him of expediency, born of fear for his own situation.'

Next the action shifts to the Viceroy's palace, which Pere Garcés has commandeered for his headquarters. While Garcés himself goes off to bury the dead, tend the wounded and billet the men he led in from Lérida, the other members of the Council of Twelve sit till midnight deciding the fate of various Castilian villains and local traitors brought before them. At midnight the Corregidor rises and invites Louis Morel to lodge in his home, where Louis is assigned a suite of chambers fit for royalty.

After a light supper with the Corregidor, Louis, at nearly two o'clock in the morning, is just about to collapse into bed, throbbing with fatigue, too dazed by the turmoil of the day to reflect on the historical singularity of the events into whose midst he has stumbled, let alone dwell morosely on the personal unhappiness underpinning his banishment, when he hears a chirpy knock-knock-knock upon his door.

Outside it he finds Achilles Lefranc looking pleased as a well-dined Punch, and enveloped from flower-pot hat to soft brown boots in a Spanish gentleman's costume miles too big for him.

'Where on earth have you been, Achilles?' asks Louis severely.

# 21

# Achilles Reports

*Then cries the short-arsed Thespian, when Louis has pulled him into the Barcelona Corregidor's guest suite, and banged the door behind him:*

'Ah, my dearly beloved lord and master! Thank God! That when I celebrate my *februa*, in memory of my deceased friends, I shall not have to sound your name among them. How little thought I that you should escape the hands of that dreadful multitude so safely.'

I welcomed my little attendant [*writes Louis*] as his merits deserved. Congratulating him on his fine new feathers, *I* then asked *him* how *he* had contrived to evade the fury of the people, without even having been brought before the Council.

'Sooth to speak sooth, I escaped but narrowly,' replied Achilles; 'and but that my lord loves not the high tragic style, I could render my tale like Corneille – nay, like Rotrou![1] – and tell it fuller than full of horrors!'

'Get to the point, Achilles,' I instructed him.

'Yes, yes!' he enthused. 'To keep to the lowly literal, in which it is your privilege – I dare not say . . . *pleasure* – to chain my soaring spirit: when I saw that poor unhappy Viceroy faint, and a great many folks hasting along the shore with lances, muskets, knives, and other implements not never put to worse purposes than a dinner of cheese, I looked out sharpish for a nook where my meditations were less like to be disrupted by the clash of cold steel and hot bangs.'

'And what did you find?'

'Well! Seeing no such haven upon the shore, mine eye espied a patch of green turf a-slanting down from the hill to the beach, and thereto I plied my legs thrice as fast as ever upon upland before. The exercise I found very pleasant, and God knows how long I should have prolonged it, especially as some of the folks on the beach, seeing me run, pointed

---

[1]  Rotrou, Jean de; 1609–50. French tragic poet, three years younger than Corneille. Wrote innumerable plays, one of them original. Praised by Richelieu; died of the plague; now much forgotten.

189

me out with their muskets, that their friends might admire my agility, to augment which they dispatched little somethings to whistle by my head every now and then, in a most motivating manner—'

'But?'

'Exactly! Just at the brow of the turf above the beach, when my safety seemed assured: *kutchow!*'

'You encountered a problem?'

'Exactly! With never a moment to recite *Henri Quatre, c'est mon père*,[2] I found myself engulfed by a *second* crowd of brigands, twice as numerous as their cousins on the beach.'

---

[2] Henri IV (father of Louis XIII), arguably France's greatest king, was also perhaps the most indefatigably promiscuous. If you visit Henri IV's birthplace, the hilltop Château of Pau, then, as you gaze with etiolating attention through the south-facing windows to the hazy peaks of the Atlantic Pyrenees, the guide will inform your back with solemn Béarnese pride that Henri Quatre is known to have had at least fifty-five mistresses in the ranks of the higher aristocracy. If his pubic-scalp tally were to include one-night stands with ladies of lesser breeding, and fervid quickies with chambermaids, scullions and whohaveyou, Henri IV of France would almost certainly beat John F. Kennedy hands down and pecker up. Many issues to do with breeding success and genetic endowment are hereby raised, and some of them will be addressed in 'Succeeding at Sex Itself', Part IV of the present work. The point for the moment is that – contraception in France, during the half-century up to 1610, having been even more primitive, if not neglected altogether, than in the USA up to 1965 – Henri IV was not only 'father of his people' in the sense of having united and consolidated France into a frontline world power, but also biologically the male parent of many hundreds of his subjects. Hence it was that, for several decades after Henri's assassination in 1610 (see *The Counts of Mount Venus*, Chapter 28), French citizens (generally male ones) dissatisfied with the lots of their lives, including their ostensible sires, would cheer themselves up from time to time with the logical possibility that: '*Henri Quatre, c'est mon père.*' Not wholly unlike consoling yourself with the thought that you would have won the football pools, if only you had sent off the coupon.

'And how did they use you?'

'They seized me hard, and quizzed me with a thousand questions, not one of which could I answer!'

'And why was that, Achilles?'

'Because not one of them could I *comprehend*, dearest lord and master of mine!'

'And the rebels believed that, did they?'

'No doubt not, I fear. However, before the foul Spaniards could gut my throat, as I trow they much desired, here of a sudden one great fat fellow grasps hold of my shoulders, trips me down, hurls his flab-bucket self atop me, sticks his dagger point under my chin, and most suspiciously – God save him – he hisses:

'"*Diantre!*"

'"*Diantre, diantre!" I respond with great joy.*

'"*Diantre?*" echoes he, all bewildered. "Can it be? Is it true? Are you French?"

'"Yes, yes!' I assure him. "Most French, indeed. *Very* French!"

'"But no!" snarls my smothering angel. "*Mère de merde, non.*[3] Nor shall I be mocked by a rogue," and he clenches his wrist to twist his dagger up into my brain. Therefore with accentuated eloquence I distract him:

'"Wait, wait! Consider! If only your poor dear father could see you now, all set to murder me, what would he say?"

'"*Diable!*' cries he in dumbfoundment. "You *are* a Frenchman?"

'"One hundred and seventy-five per cent," I reply painfully, for several young rebels have now taken to kicking me in the ribs, beneath my interlocutor's bulk. "Albeit slightly small, and penniless besides."

'"And you know my father?" my saviour marvels, rolling off me, and pulling me to my feet.

'"Not a whit, alas," I confess. "Though dearly do I wish I did!"

'"Why is that?"

'"Because then, for his sake, my soft smooth skin you might please to preserve from the punctures these peabrains propose."'

'How did our fellow countryman take that, Achilles?'

'In a state of profound distraction, I believe. For unwittingly I had turned his mind to thoughts of his poor dear father, and who knows what familial perplexity? All that notwithstanding, he embraced me tearfully,

---

[3] 'Get away with you now.'

kissed me fraternally, and proclaimed:

'"On the honour of my father, for the virtue of my mother, and in the name of holy France I annex you." This he followed by regaling the swarthy ruffians around us with a throaty tale, full of *oses* and *anoses*, which seemed to satisfy them passing well, for instead of running me through with their divers blades, they hugged me till I was all but strangled, meanwhile chanting in grateful tones:

'"*Viva la Francia, viva la Francia!*" Or woggish words to the same effect.

'Well, after this my companion – who by the way is chief chef to the Corregidor, your host – gave me a green feather, which since has proved the finest feather ever to adorn a French tragedian's cap. For this green, you see, is the Catalonian green, and causes everyone you meet with, coming the other way, to salute you with the most lowest courteous bow. Anyhow, as I was saying, the cook and myself, having swore eternal amity on the field of battle, then, instead of proceeding down to murder the Viceroy, by which we anticipated no profit was to be got, we hied us back into the city, just in time to join in with the good local folks breaking into the palace of the general of the galleys.'

'A Castilian, you mean?'

'Not a Catalan, that's for sure! Well, there had been a little assassination, and that sort of thing, done before we came up, but the general himself had got off on his ships, and now here was the multitude taking care of all his goods and chattels what he left behind.

'I embraced their sentiments with a fellow-feeling what doubtless owed much to my joy, at being still conversational in this world, and while most of the Catalans were standing open-mouthed and drooling, before a hideous black statue in the likeness, so it seemed to my dumb Spanish friends, of Beelzebub in person, I myself slipped upstairs, where in due course I located a cunningly concealed drawer, in which were . . . *these pretty things!*' and with a flourish Achilles brandished forth from his purloined costume a string of large flawless diamonds, which were clearly of inestimable value.

'These humble stones I brought away for your lordship,' he added with a winningly appeasing smile. 'They are too splendid for a lowly soul like me – I mean, to trade for their proper value, without getting burked along the way, and I pledge your lordship shall procure an eminently more advantageous arrangement. Especially since, so everyone tells me, you are now become of most princely stature amidst these idiot rebels.'

'What else did you steal, Achilles?' I asked him mildly, as he handed the diamonds to me.

'For my own most pressing necessities,' he answered gravely, 'I satisfied myself with a small gold coin or two, what I found in a porcelain vase. And this suit of clothes which your lordship sees, plus a few lace shirts, and other articles of apparel, which your lordship is welcome to borrow.'

I had as he discoursed got myself into bed, and, though weary beyond the power of words to convey, I could not refrain from examining his diamonds, which were of a size, quality and value far in excess of any jewels I ever before had seen, or even imagined. Thinking now, sadly, how brilliantly their glittering facets would set off the lovely throat of my darling Hélène, I handed them back to their confiscator, saying:

'You must know, Achilles, that no gentleman could possibly accept of any gift so dishonestly got.'

Achilles hereupon secreted the gems once more within his voluminous attire, and riposted with considerable coolness:

'Just as you wish, dear my lordship. Then I shall take care of them personally after all. Times do change, you know, and personal moralities too. In defence of my probity, I would ask that your lordship consider this. That had the diamonds not been retrieved by me, they would even now be in the hands of some imbecile Catalan, who then would sell them on to some sharper for a pittance. Thus, not only did I liberate them with your lordship's best interests at heart, but I regard them moreover as genuinely lawful plunder, and hence shall dispose of them as property most righteously acquired. And sleep easy, besides, with no chancre of self-reproachment in my soul. Still on the same subject, for that matter—'

'Thank you, Achilles,' I said, with the dismissiveness of utmost fatigue. 'That will be all. You may wake me at one hour past dawn.'

He bowed with elaborate extravagance, and departed without a further word. I wish it were true that then I fell immediately into a deep and dreamless sleep, but the contrary is the case, and for countless long minutes I lay tensely tormented by memories: of the lush green wooded slopes behind Château Morel, the opaque green power of the Gave de Pau as mysteriously it flows through Lourdes, the exquisite young beauty of Hélène Arnault – like a soaring light receding from my view – and the innocence I had lost.

# 22

# The Council of Twelve

Barcelona, the morning following the coup, is thrumming with all manner of exciting developments. When, at about seven o'clock, Louis eventually awakens, Achilles informs him that he is invited to partake of a sumptuous breakfast with the Corregidor.[1] After various fruits and cheeses, and over a glass of sweet white wine, the Corregidor speculates fishingly as to the true views and secret determinations of 'France', by which he means 'Richelieu'. Gripped by the endemic apprehension that Louis Morel, despite his studied reticence, is indeed a French government agent, the Corregidor shows Louis a letter from the French Minister Noyers, written by express command of Richelieu, as motivation for Louis Morel to open up and divulge France's 'real intentions'.

Louis, mortified by the ingratitude of perpetuating such a deception on so generous a host, decides to take the Corregidor into his confidence, and with an abrupt blush he confesses his absolute innocence of government agency, and ignorance of French foreign policy matters.

The Barcelona Corregidor, a lifelong reader of diplomacy subtexts, interprets Louis Morel's disclaimer as profound tactical discretion, which he applauds with a rueful chuckle, meanwhile twirling his moustachioes in evident frustration.

'In any event,' he says at length, 'we would urge you to inform Premier Richelieu, by whatever channels you please, but with all the

---

[1] Some readers may be forgiven (but others not) for hoping beneath the bedclothes that the Barcelona Corregidor, symmetrically with the deceased Zaragoza Corregidor, will be endowed with a beautiful daughter. In fact, alas, the only relative of the Barcelona Corregidor's on record as being present in the city is a short fat wife with a moustache less long than her husband's, but blacker. There is, however, for such readers, a modicum of consolation coming up shortly – if you'll just bear with us.

emphasis in your power, that *the Catalan people are not to be tri-fled with.*'

'Of course not,' nods Louis.

'And that now we have drawn our swords, and drawn blood from the nose of Madrid, then if France is truly our friend, *she must make good her promises.*'

'I think you can rely on that,' nods Louis.

'Or else, for the aid we need, we Catalans[2] will *apply to another power.*'

'I'm sure that won't be necessary,' murmurs Louis, thus involuntarily embalming his uninvited status as Richelieu's emissary.

The Barcelona Corregidor, delighted with what he takes to be this laid-back pledge of support in Paris from Louis, proposes every assistance to speed his passage, beginning with a boat trip up the coast to Marseille. Since this fits in perfectly with his own plans, Louis accepts with gusto. The Corregidor writes a letter reserving Louis a berth on the next brigantine sailing north, and Achilles is dispatched to deliver the letter to the harbour-master.

Then Louis accompanies the Corregidor through city streets vibrating with sunlight, energy and optimism, to the morning's meeting, at the Viceroy's palace, of the revolutionary Council of Twelve – Citizen Pere Garcés presiding.

At the Viceroy's palace Louis learns that earlier this morning about a hundred Aragonese (ie Spanish government) cavalry have been routed and their leader taken prisoner. As Louis is going through the motions of applauding this revolutionary success, Pere Garcés takes him aside and quietly informs him that the Aragonese captain was in fact the Chevalier of Montenero, who is currently a prisoner of the Revolution in a cell at the bottom of the basement stairs.

Louis professes amazement and dismay.

Garcés warns him the Chevalier has been taken by a singularly revengeful Catalan partisan named Gil Moreno.[3] Moreover, and worse,

---

[2] If further proof be desired of Richelieu's superiority in tyranny, versus Olivares, this is surely it: the Cardinal would never have allowed the Corregidor of Barcelona to remain a native Catalan.

[3] It's been suggested to us that 'Moreno' is not a 100% Catalan name, but really is there any more contradiction in this than in Hitler not being German, or even convincingly Aryan?

the Chevalier is known to have been a friend of the Viceroy, with whom he served on more than one mission to New Spain. The bloodthirsty Gil Moreno is thus busy whipping up support to have the Chevalier taken outside forthwith and shot against the walls of the palace.

Louis protests furiously, imagining Pere Garcés, being on Moreno's side, is softening him up to accept the inevitable: the summary execution of the Chevalier. But to his surprise Garcés too privately acknowledges a great debt of protection to the Chevalier, who twice has alerted him to murderous ambushes laid by French customs officers.

'How can we save him?' demands Louis.

'You address the meeting,' says Garcés. 'Speak at length and with passion about France, the King, the Cardinal, ancient ties of comradeship, all that stuff. Never deny you are a French agent, and whatever you say, keep the subject as far away from prisoners as possible. I, meanwhile, will see what I can do.'

As soon as the meeting begins, Louis jumps up and courteously interrupts the Corregidor with an impassioned spiel about Catalan courage, dignity, history, destiny, and how delighted he is to be able to carry such favourable tidings to the Cardinal in Paris.

The Catalan revolutionaries applaud Louis Morel's praise of them but Pere Garcés has still not returned, and Louis feels his waffling stall for time is fast turning brittle and stilted. When he harps on 'history and destiny' for the third or fourth time, the Alcayde of Lérida[4] butts in to remark that the meritorious Gil Moreno will be feeling insulted at being left downstairs with the prisoner so long, and urges that the prisoner should now be brought up and tried.

Louis is obliged to yield to this, since he senses any further time-wasting rhetoric from him will turn the emotions present against him.

A minute later the squat black cast-eyed form of Gil Moreno marches in, pushing the Chevalier of Montenero in front of him. The Chevalier's wrists are bound behind his back, and the heavy-metal chain linking his ankle shackles scrapes abrasively on the floor. Despite this bondage, his back is straight, his shoulders stiff with dignity, and when he glimpses

---

[4] With profoundest apologies to home-proud Catalans everywhere (and we Scots know only too well how it feels, damn their eyes) we retain these imperialistic Castilian spellings in order to preserve as much as not impossible of the flavour of Louis Morel's original.

Louis among the Catalan Councillors a flicker of warm remembrance illumines the proud gravity of his features – though only for a moment, and unnoticed by any but Louis.

That fleeting perception sparks Louis into dredging up the background to and the morality of his own grievance – or is it a grudge? – against the Chevalier, but before he has time to engage these issues in a wholesale grapple, they are shelved again by the more public battle which now ensues; against and for the Chevalier's life.

Beginning:

*Alcayde of Lérida*
> Speak, Gil Moreno! What report have you to make, to the Supreme Council of Catalonia?

*Gil Moreno*
> A short one.

*Corregidor of Barcelona*
> Let us hear it.

*Moreno*
> On my patrol this morning, two miles from the city gate, I met with a body of Aragonese horse. I bade them stand and state their cause. When they replied in the name of our oppressor, Philip of Spain, I instantly attacked them. Dispersed some, killed many—

*Corregidor*
> You say 'I'. Do you mean 'we'?

*Moreno*
> I mean myself and three hundred loyalists.

*Corregidor*
> I see. Pray continue.

*Moreno*
> Their captain I took personally. According to the orders given out last night, I brought him here, to be tried by the Council of Twelve. Because he is a known accomplice of the tyrant Viceroy who died yesterday, and since he was taken in arms, marching against

Catalonian freedom, and is in every way an enemy to our province, I demand that he receive summary sentence now, to be turned over back to me.

*Corregidor*

What would you then do with him?

*Moreno*

March him out to the Plaza and shoot him, of course. What else does the bastard deserve?

*Alcayde*

And what reasons can the prisoner adduce, why such should not be his fate?

*Chevalier*

Very few — and even those are of such a nature that, by the looks of this self-appointed council, they are hardly worth reciting.

*Corregidor*

The Council had best judge of that.

*Chevalier*

I have in mind the universal laws of arms, the principles of common justice, the usages of all civilized nations, and the code of all men of honour.

*Louis Morel — aside ahint*

[*It may easily be supposed that such a speech was not ideally calculated to sway the Council in favour of the speaker, and I would have given much, at that moment, to stop up the Chevalier's mouth.*]

*Pere Garcés — returning*

Such reasons, sir, must remain vague and lacking relevance [*he warns grimly, prowling like a tiger round the Council table, to take his place at its head*] without you can show in detail how they validate your case.

*Louis*

The particular application of the prisoner's abstractions [*I quickly interposed*] is surely so self-evident, that it hardly requires to be pointed out.

*Corregidor*

Our eminent French comrade will forgive us [*he remarks drily*] if we invite him to explain.

*Louis*

I mean that if the Catalonians are a separate people, an individual nation, as so passionately you declare yourselves to be – at war with Philip of Spain, I need not remind you . . . indeed, you may say, with Philip of *Castille*—

*Mutters in Unison*

May the two-faced shrimp-membered bastard die in agony of the pox he deserves—

*Louis Morel*

As a proud and independent race – as a sovereign state, why, you are bound to observe the rights of all Christian nations, and to treat decently all prisoners you may take fairly from your enemies in war.

*Gil Moreno*

This foreigner is wasting our time. The prisoner is guilty as hell, and must be shot. Let us get on with it.

*Louis*

Far from wasting your time, good sir, I shall – as the voice of your largest single friendly source of aid, and funds – be saving you not only time, but also frustration, hardship, and perhaps devastation too – if only I can remind you that, as the common principles of right and justice require, **every man should be proved guilty of some specific crime before he be condemned.**

*Moreno*

The prisoner IS guilty—

*Louis*

The usage of all civilized nations, as my noble fellow Councillors needless to say need no reminding, establishes beyond debate that no man is criminal for bearing arms, *ipso facto*, except it be against the land of his birth, or the government in whose domain he resides. Now the Chevalier of Montenero, whom you so hastily endeavour to condemn—

*Moreno*

Fuck your mother's arse, Sir Fancy Frenchman![5] [*And he glared upon me with eyes the cast in which was mutated to a truly frightful squint, by the vehemence of his fury.*] Come you here to prate to us about the laws of nations? Then know that we Catalans feel full well what is due to us, and to our honour, and need no trite instruction from alien pigs like you.

*Mutters not in Unison*

Hear, hear . . .
Too much . . .
He goes too far . . .

*Moreno*

Know that we Catalans shall in any case have justice wreaked upon all our former oppressors. And if you, Sir Fancy Frenchman, do not like it, then fuck your mother's arse again. As again, of the people, of all Catalonia, **I demand the death of this prisoner**. And if this learned Council of Twelve, as they choose to call themselves, do not—

*Garcés*

WHAT? As we 'choose to call' ourselves? No, no, Comrade Moreno. As the Catalan people have elected us. And if *we*, in *their* name, do not grant you the death of this prisoner, what then?

*Moreno*

Then his life is nonetheless mine, and I will take it.

---

[5] '*Au, fugiu, fugiu, murri, franceset, desvergonyit. Fora d'açí!*'
Louis himself records this utterance in the original Catalan, but gives no translation. G.P.R. James doesn't mention it at all.

'In that same instant,' Louis goes on, 'this Moreno drew a pistol from his belt, with cool deliberation cocked back its hammer, and with leisurely arrogance was raising its muzzle up to the temple of the Chevalier, who stood firm and unblenching as a rock, confronting the Council squarely. Without the thought of a moment, which might have damped my speed, I vaulted over the Council table, and seized the Catalan's vengeful arm. It was done like lightning – almost before I knew it myself. Feeling that his captured arm could no longer shoot dead the Chevalier, the blood-thirsty villain struggled hard to turn the muzzle of his pistol upon myself.

'A good many people behind us now rushed forward, and embarrassed my movements, by striving to restrain their demented compatriot. The result was, that in his desperation to injure me, as severely as he might, before he was entirely prevented, this Moreno pulled his trigger as one might say "blind". Though the blast in my ear was deafening, the ball from his weapon did little harm to me, bar a superficial scorching, and grazing of my neck, but alas for the Alcayde of Lérida, it [Moreno's bullet] travelled on to strike that unfortunate gentleman in the midst of his throat, as a result of which he fell back against the wall behind him, choking horribly, with a ghastly wound all around his Adam's Apple, giving out so much blood, that his death in a very few moments was guaranteed.'

There are several alternative accounts of the mayhem, shouting, bleeding, scuffling, and jockeying for power that followed. Not all the narratives were certainly written by persons present, but some of them must have been, and, the general drift mostly corroborating Louis Morel's own version, we get a cameo much like this:

'By the Holy Virgin, he has killed a member of the Council!' thunders Pere Garcés. Seize him, seize him.'

As the younger and more martial Councillors rush to pinion Moreno, he strains to yell at the crowd packing the pleb end of the hall:

'Death to this self-elected council, comrades! Assist me, I beg of you. Be warned, they would make worse slaves of us than the Castilians ever did. Oh, help me, comrades. Help, help. Will no-one stand by Moreno?'

'I will! And I will!' cry the two Moreno henchmen who came in with him to guard the Chevalier.

'I will too!' vows a third faceless voice in the ruck.

But the Moreno men quickly find they have backed a very wrong horse: when every other able body present obeys Pere Garcés' command to bind Moreno, and his three supporters, and hold them pending the pleasure of the Revolution.

'Thus must we deal with those who would introduce dissension and insubordination into the new government of Catalonia,' declaims Garcés, gesticulating with the careful economy and perfect timing of a natural rhetoror. 'Members of the Council,' he continues, 'as you value whatever small services I may have been privileged to render . . . ' He invites his colleagues to join with him in considering Monsieur Morel's advice to be thoroughly sound, and that therefore, as a gesture of sovereign benevolence, potentially of incalculable value in delicate forthcoming negotiations with Paris, the Chevalier of Montenero should be spared. 'May we immediately so vote?'

The Council agree that the Chevalier's *life* should be spared, but now a vague debate brews up as to what else should be done with or to him. Louis cunningly bides his time until several of his fellow Councillors are evidently aching for their lunch, then diffidently proposes that the Chevalier of Montenero, together with any Castilian prisoners not accused of specific atrocities, should, as an act of exemplary magnanimity, be granted extraordinary amnesty – 'in celebration of the Revolution's triumph, and the spirit of Catalan compassion' – and deposited as soon as possible on the far side of the border with Spain.

With negligible dissent, the Council approves.

Louis Morel next proposes re-examination of all Castilian prisoners, with a view to the summary release of the many currently confined on grounds more frivolous than capital: so that, as ambassador, he will thus be enabled to return to Cardinal Richelieu singing even louder praises of Catalan political maturity.

After the airing of some doubtful caveats, the Council, nudged sweetly by Pere Garcés, go along with the Morel initiative, and the hogtied Gil Moreno all the while groans thwartedly and gnashes teeth of frustrated malice.

As the Chevalier is relieved of his bonds, he craves permission to address a terse word of appreciation to the Revolution.

The Revolution consents.

The Chevalier confides to the Council that his mission in these parts, whence he arrived with the Aragon cavalry, was not to subdue Catalans, but rather to advise his old friend the fat Viceroy on how to control his wayward troops.

The Council nod politely, and shuffle their feet in the sort of agitation common to most southern Europeans whose lunch-hours are at risk of erosion. This is particularly true of the Barcelona Corregidor, who is abnormally partial to his food.

Oblivious to such visceral cues, the high-principled Chevalier – to Louis's great dismay – goes on to warn the Catalans that they will not for long get away with ceding from Spain, not that he has any time for the evil Olivares but—

With the curtness of famished impatience the Corregidor shuts up the Chevalier by saying that the Catalans, rather than revert ever again to the corrupt Spanish yoke, would surrender themselves to *any other nation* willing to police by military means their current secession from Spain.

Pere Garcés now slips out briefly from the hall, to arrange transport and a safe passport for the Chevalier.

The Chevalier exploits the moments available to bow coldly to Louis Morel, and publicly thank him, with the utmost blistering frostiness, for saving his life from the bloodthirsty Moreno. 'A life especially dear to me at this juncture, on account of certain family matters approaching conclusion . . . ' the nature of which he tantalisingly does not divulge.

Louis, chagrined to the quick by this continuing hostile hauteur from the Chevalier, counters with tears in his eyes that:

'I swear by Almighty God that I do not now deserve the gentleman's esteem any less than ever I did.'

'A conscience truly clean, like a perfect human form, knows no shame,' retorts the Chevalier.

The Barcelona Corregidor breaks in to propose an urgent adjournment for lunch as Louis remarks coolly to the Chevalier that, though previously his lips were sealed by an inviolable vow, that seal has now been broken, by the tragedy of a venerable gentleman's demise. He refers, of course, to the Zaragoza Corregidor. As his thoughts associate back to the murder of the naked priest, the ravishing maja's suicide, his own flight from Zaragoza, the death of Father Francis in the snow, his own awful shooting of Jean-Baptiste, the consequent escape from his homeland in Bigorre, the loss of Hélène . . . Louis feels the mist in his eyes condense into tears which must fall. He averts his head, but not before the Chevalier has glimpsed this overpowering access of boyish emotion.

'Louis, Louis,' the Chevalier urges him warmly, ignoring the pointed scraping of chair legs, and the rising and coughing of the other Council members. 'Speak to me, Louis, why don't you? Confess, and you will feel reborn.'

Touched by the Chevalier's renewed use of his Christian name, Louis is on the verge of rushing to embrace the Chevalier, to jettison his Zaragoza secrets in a corner huddle, when Pere Garcés arrives back in the hall, emanating waves of vital purpose. Close behind him is his lissom niece Isabella, whom Louis took note of so vividly in the village called Meila. She is disguised in male attire, like a false pageboy fresh out of Shakespeare, but Louis is not fooled for a moment. Whether Isabella is the bringer of news is not evident. Either way, she follows her uncle like a devoted shadow as he rushes to squeeze the Chevalier's shoulders, inform him of a fleet horse waiting, and instruct him to speed away this instant and quit the city by the Red Rose Gate.

'Why so soon?' protests the Chevalier.

'Because,' insists Garcés, 'Gil Moreno's supporters are gathering in strength at the other end of town. If you are gone, there will be less focus for their grievance.'

'But – '

'No buts, Señor. Please go.'

The Chevalier can't tell Pere Garcés why he is so keen to stay on long enough to audience Louis Morel's exculpation, and Garcés is implacable:

'*Now*, Señor. I give you twenty horsemen, you will see, for escort to the border.'

Reluctantly the Chevalier, his gaze casting back to Louis, hastens away from the palace hall, where the Council meeting has degenerated into a disorderly jostle of factions: one desperate for lunch immediately; the other inclined to deal with the criminal Gil Moreno first.

Siding firmly with the prompt-justice lobby, Pere Garcés, stressing the need for the new Catalonia to be seen not only to respect but also to uphold law and order, calls for the Council to pass appropriate sentence on Gil Moreno: for the murder of the Alcayde of Lérida.

As Moreno screams fearful defiance . . .

'What sentence shall we deem appropriate?' is the question on many lips.

'Why, death – of course!' exclaims Garcés, apparently amazed that the matter might be queried. 'Precisely what he wished to do to Señor Montenero. It shall be done to him. With your approval, comrades?'

A few moments of hot dispute are terminated by the Barcelona Corregidor. Shirty beyond measure at this needlessly prolonged postponement of his lunch, his magisterial voice declares for:

'*Death.*'

As Louis accompanies the Corregidor back through the roasting streets, at a brisk pace bound for lunch, they hear behind them Pere Garcés commanding:

'Fire!'

A volley of shots signifies the end of the nasty Moreno, and after lunch Garcés, still accompanied by his niece in drag, turns up at the Corregidor's residence to discuss the dispatches they must write that night, to send with Louis to Paris.

'Early the following morning, as Pere Garcés rode off to supervise suppression, in the villages, of Gil Moreno's partisans, the Corregidor accompanied myself and little Achilles down to the waterside. Having, to his authority, formally resigned the seat to which I had been called on the Council of Twelve, I embarked with my effusive attendant, on board the brigantine *Tarragona*, and took my leave of Barcelona for ever.'

*Part III*

# Paris & the North

# 23

# Namechecks

'Did Louis Morel, during his last night in Barcelona, seduce the tomboy-ish Garcés niece Isabella?'

'Was she a virgin?'

'Did she enjoy it?'

'How often did they do it?'

'In what positions?'

'In which discreet corner of the Corregidor's residence?'

'And at what small hour of the morning did they prise their loins into tragic disentanglement, and enact a tearful adieu?'

Those are just a few of the questions which some readers, not unreasonably pumped up by the first footnote in the previous chapter, may now be forgiven for expecting to have lushly answered.

Alas.

Nor did we mean to imply by that 'Alas' that such readers need necessarily feel thoroughly ashamed of themselves. No more, at any rate, than such novelists as we ourselves once were – yes, yes, we do confess:

That ten years ago, even five years ago, we would have latched with growls of delight on to the presence of Isabella in the Barcelona Corregidor's house that night, inflamed the sequel with tumescence of divers erogonies, fudged up some risqué dialogue for incidental titillation in the lulls between thrusts, and enjoyed ourselves enormously in the process.

'And why not?' we might then have demanded, aggressive in defence. After all, in the words of Scotland's foremost living novelist:

The surest way of achieving adultery quickly, if you can wangle it, is to become a fictional character, as has been chronicled at length by professors of impotence. This is because the novelist requires his characters to communicate. Hence he has to bring them into contact, and one of the most commonly agreeable and fertile forms of contact is shagging one another. The same goes for drama, cinema, etc, and this explains why it is a mistake to suppose that just because serious art must *illumine* life it follows that life *should be like* art. If life weren't like art at all, then the art wouldn't be art, but it by no means follows that we can all have adultery as frequently in life as we can in novels. Allowances must be made, of course, for the novelist himself, who needs to screw around from time to time, but purely as a matter of field research, as I seem to remember Arthur Hailey saying one night on a Michael Parkinson show, though I had drunk lots of beer at the time.[1]

But what if an adulterously bent man is unable to become a fictional character?

Ten years ago we might also have been happy to quote at considerably greater length from the bloodstained thesis in respect of which StrathKelvin University still has not consented to award Wringhim Knox his Doctorate in Philosophy.

(The reader may wish to realize that the previous paragraph is indeed very true, except that ten years ago we had no inkling of Wringhim's existence. That his paragraphs today leap so lithely about our computer is thanks to Wringhim's having heard, on the Hillhead grapevine, of our involvement in text-capture techniques. Calculating that, banking on his fame as a mounting novelist, his editor must infallibly pine to publish his philosophical masterpiece too, Wringhim initiated the colleaguery between us, which we now so treasure, by telephoning one evening with the blunt suggestion that we might like to scan his typed thesis on to floppy disks which he could then groom into popular perfection on his baby Amstrad word-processor, all in kind exchange for an

---

[1] Two of our timorous tenured friends have speculated confidentially that it was Wringhim's refusal to temper umpteen sentences of this nature which decided his examiners, notwithstanding his philosophical genius, that the text he had submitted could not pass for a doctoral thesis. But for this typically reactionary rebuff from the asbestos-lined cloisters of academe, one of the most energetic creators of Scottish fiction in the twentieth century might well have been lost to the lecture hall for ever. Whether Scottish Brewers would have suffered similar losses must remain eternally debatable.

epigrammed first-edition hardback copy of Wringhim's latest novel. Having bargained fiercely for the extraordinary bonus of several pints of Guinness in McEwan's, we complied with Wringhim's wishes so efficiently that his delight must surely have transcended mortal bounds if only Tiphanie Scott-Moncrieff had not immediately declined to even read what now had become his 'major philosophical essay'. With ever fewer people buying literate books these days, never mind reading them, the publishing fraternity's zeal to immortalize Wringhim's more cerebral flights of non-fiction does not look likely to escalate in his lifetime, and for this reason we have sneaking suspicions, which even apter clichés might also describe as nasty sinking feelings, that few more moons will bite the dust before Wringhim kindly invites us to help him publish his masterpiece himself. Hence, by psychoanalytical association, the loudness of my groan when Audrey Macpherson mentioned Wringhim's having mentioned wanting to get me to typeset his forthcoming pamphlet on *Succeeding at Sex in London*.)

And now?

The best times have flown, have they not? AIDS is everywhere, so is satellite television, and therefore what is a novelist to do?

If, as Evelyn Waugh insisted, the novel is by definition something *new*, about *novel* characters, settings and situations, then where would be the novelty in us giving you the lowdown on Louis humping Isabella one hot summer's night in Barcelona in 1640, when you could just as well be watching unsmiling anal intercourse in Hamburg, on the privacy of your own television screen, in the cosily log-fired and malt-whiskily mellowed comfort of your own living room, any Saturday night in the 1990s?

And if we, the erstwhile novelists, are surfeited into such nausea, then what about you: the erstwhile readers? In general we accuse you:

(A) Of being jaded into irretrievable cynicism by today's ubiquitous overload – of glitz laminate and airwave sleaze;

(B) Of moralistic resentment that no longer can you safely regress to the promiscuous fun-sex sorties of your youth – or, even more calamitous, of your parents' youth;

(C) Of consequently aggravated dispositional hostility to the novelist who, as you see him or her, frivolously squirts in the odd episode or two of Rumpole Stiltskin, insultingly confident of thus holding your attention – which, through this facile failure of judgement, hos by the same token loses;

(D)   Of ceasing to read literate fiction altogether.

If *you* in particular are innocent, then do please forgive *me* in particular.

Certainly I need all the forgiveness I can get. In any case, moreover, my own innocence is long down the plug-hole. Since, fairly or not, I cannot but suspect you of suspecting me, I could no more at this juncture make up a zestful bout of grumpy-humpy between Louis Morel and the teenage Isabella than I could personally and in the flesh \*\*\* \*\* \*\* to pleasure young Jennifer Macpherson on the kitchen table whilst her mother looked on whisking eggs.[2] And even if this were not so, even if some bovinely divine imperviousness to the consciousness of others had so preserved until last night my spontaneous passion to portray on page the protracted impalement of a lissom maid by a prolonged cavalier, then the enterprise would still have foundered to smithereens on the reef of this morning's mail:

An invitation to speak next month, at StrathKelvin Students' Union, supported by [arguably Hillhead's foremost lady novelist] for the motion. That:

**This house believes modern writers use sex rather than talent.**

*For* the motion, would you believe?

'Then who shall be speaking against it?' I inquired on the phone after lunch.

'Oh, Wringhim Knox, if all goes well,'[3] the bright young convener replied.

'Supported by?'

'Oh . . . ' Arguably Hillhead's other foremost lady novelist.

So there it was. Innocence not only withered away by degrees, like honourable intentions all dried up, but kicked in the balls as well. The consequence for you is that, if you can't manage without a vicarious peep at Louis and Isabella playing the two-backed beastie during that

---

[2]   Conceivably as opposed to Maupassant. What do you think, Charlton? Are the brothers Goncourt to be believed?

[3]   She meant: 'on the optimistic assumption that Wringhim hasn't gone walkabout on a bender the day before.'

hot Barcelona night, you'll have to stage the show yourself. All we can pledge for sure is that:

* Louis plainly fancied Isabella so ardently that, as usual, all fond thoughts of his beloved Hélène were as absent as swallows in winter.

* Fear of Uncle Garcés would certainly not have put Louis off. If anything . . .

* We know for a fact that Isabella was present in the Corregidor's house during Louis Morel's final night in Spain.

* Louis himself records, without speculating as to causes, how unusually sleepy he was, during the first phase of his voyage from Barcelona to Marseille.

Other than that, here is a helpful little

for you to project upon.

If and whether or not that stage happens to culminate satisfactorily, we thought that — to gird us to cope with the ramifications of Paris ahead — we might usefully end this short chapter with a checklist of names named so far. Some younger readers may profit most from this exercise by jotting their own notes alongside ours, and space is therefore being made available for this purpose. The list is alphabetically by surname, except when surnames are not known. Readers should perhaps be warned that in some cases two or more names may denote (or refer to) the same individual. For example, the Fat Monk who cheats Louis at dice in the sleazy cabernet at Luz turns out later also to have been the Monsieur Saint Simon who, again in the pay of the Marquis of Roquefort, falls from an overhanging bough near Lourdes and attempts to slit our hero's throat. This is in comformity with the logical incontrovertibility that a single individual may if it likes be denoted (or referred to) by a multitude of names or descriptions.[4]

Anyway, here's our list.

*Alcayde*, of Lérida. Shot in the throat by Gil Moreno.

*Alvarez*, Ximenes. Catalan patriot, later cardinal.

*Anne of Austria*, (Mrs Louis XIII). First child (Louis XIV) born 23 years after her marriage. Was Mazarin the father?

*Arnault*, Hélène.

*Arnault*, Jean-Baptiste.

*Arnault*, Maître.

*Avecido*, Father, in Zaragoza. Naked priest, seducer of passionate maja.

*Bagnols*, Count of.

*Bourbon*, Henrietta Maria de. Daughter of Henri Quatre; wife to Charles I of England.

*Bourbon*, Isabel de. Daughter of Henri Quatre; wife to Philip IV of Spain.

*Blobbs*, Godfrey. Yuk.

*Buckingham*, Duke of – George Villiers. Notorious smartarse – did he make it with Mrs Louis XIII?

---

[4] For an exciting introduction to such issues, see (or look up) the famous slanging match between Bertrand (later Lord) Russell and (later Sir) Peter Strawson. Perhaps begin with Russell's 1905 'On Denoting' article in *Mind*, since this also is thoroughly obsessed with Charles II, 'the present King of France', and so forth. Note too how many more Oxbridge philosophers than Scottish novelists get English peerages and knighthoods.

***Carruthers***, Dr Hamish. Questioner of veracity re alcohol.

***Charles I***, King of Britain 1625–49. Got the chop from Cromwell.

***Charles II***, King of Scotland 1651–85, of England 1660–85. The 'Merrie Monarch'; umpteen children, none legitimate.

***Charles III***, King of ?? When?

***Chief Chef***, to Barcelona Corregidor.

***Cinq Mars***. Gaveston to Louis XIII – scuppered by Richelieu in 1642.

***Corregidor***, of Barcelona.

***Corregidor***, of Zaragoza.

***Customs Officer***, in Bigorre, near Morel. Brains beaten out by Pere Garcés.

***Elizabeth I***, Queen of England 1558–1603. Do you believe she was a virgin?

***Father Francis***.

***Father*** – of Louis Morel?

***Fat Monk***.

***Forrest***, Koo. Alter Other.

***Francisco***, father to Isabella.

***Garcés***, Pere.

***Garcés***, Señora. Christian name unknown.

***Golilla tailor***, Madrid.

*Henri IV*, King of France 1589–1610. See Chapter 21, footnote 2.

*Horsethief trooper*, Castilian. Also tried to murder our hero; eat his ear; what have you?

*Hume*, Martin. Old-style historian. Despite a recurring preoccupation with 'labour as a means to salvation', he could certainly teach many of his latterday academic descendents (no personal offence intended, Audrey) a thing or two about how not to construct a sentence, and also what sort of smut behind the arras is most likely to turn historical novelists and some of their readers on. Anyone just graduated from Mills & Boon, for instance, and keen to explore whether Queen Elizabeth I really was interfered with during her vulnerable pubesence (and if, so what?) might well start with Martin Hume's *The Courtships of Queen Elizabeth*.

*Hussaye*, 'Old'.

*Infanta Maria*, sister to Philip IV of Spain. Doesn't become Queen of Britain.

*Isabella*, in Barcelona. Did she, or didn't she?

*James VI & I*, King of Scotland 1587–1625, of England 1603–25. Son of Mary Queen of Scots; exceptionally unpleasant person.

*James*, George Payne Rainsford.

*Juan*, the horseman.

*Knox*, Wringhim.

*Leering alguacil*, in Zaragoza.

*Lefranc*, Achilles.

*Louis XIII*, Present King of France (1610–43).

*McMichael*, Michael and Laura. Friends in Paris.

*Macpherson*, Dr Audrey.

*Macpherson*, Ms Jennifer.

*Malicious mule*, in Pyrenees.

*Maja*, passionate in Zaragoza.

*Marie-Carmen*. Definitely did have it away with Louis Morel in the mountains.

*Miller*, in the vicinity of Morel. Smuggling sidekick to Garcés.

*Morel*, Count Roger.

*Morel*, Countess Angèlique.

*Morel*, Louis.

*Moreno*, Gil.

*Montenero*, Chevalier of.

*Moustachioed wife*, to Barcelona Corregidor.

*Olivares*, Count-Duke.

*Palser*, Charlton.

*Philip IV*, King of Spain 1621–65.

*Rankles*, Mumbo.

*Rankles*, Mrs Felicity.

*Retz*, Cardinal de. More on him soon enough.

*Richelieu*, Cardinal Armand Jean Du Plessis de. Ditto.

*Rodriguez*, Lieutenant. Castilian in Barcelona. Slaughtered behind Fat Viceroy.

*Roquefort*, Marquis of.

*Roublestein*, Janet.

*Roublestein*, beautiful daughters two.

*Santa Colona*, Viceroy of Barcelona. 'Fat'.

*Saint Simon*, Monsieur.

*Scipio*. Negro slave, etc, to Fat Viceroy.

*Scott-Moncrieff*, Tiphanie. Eminent Scottish publisher.

*Seale*, Humbert. Alter Self.

*Soissons*, Count of.

*Soissons*, Dowager Countess of.

*Stiltskin*, Rumpole.

*Thin Accomplice*. Gamester shark #2 in sleazy Luz cabernet.

*Valenais*, Chevalier of. Poisoned by Marquis of Roquefort?

*Velazquez*.

*Vergne*, Henriette de.

*Villafranca*, 5th Marquis of. Commander of Barcelona galleys; whose diamonds Achilles loots.

*Whingeing guide*, in Pyrenees.

# 24

# Whither the Cardinal?

The year following Louis Morel's departure from Barcelona is the most eventful of his life — so crammed with incident, indeed, that we shall be obliged to be both selective and terse. Thus:

When he lands at Marseille, after a safe and rapid passage, Louis prepares immediately to speed for Lyon and Paris. Back on French soil, and therefore, in language and law, that much closer to the heart of his troubles, he worries about only having enough money left to get him to Paris. And yet he cannot bear the thought of writing home to Morel for help: with all the weight of confession, ignominy, dependence and squirming that would entail.

'I felt that night', he would later record, 'that my only resource was to rush forward at pell-mell speed, having placed my trust in time and chance . . . '

After dinner in their waterfront tavern, however, Louis is stimulated into the adrenalin of horror when Achilles unpacks from a trunk the new clothes he was commissioned to procure for Louis before leaving Barcelona.

Before my astonished eyes [*writes Louis*] there first appeared a splendid Spanish riding dress of philomot cloth, laced with silver, and perfectly new. It had a black beaver and white plumes, which, together with the untanned riding boots, sword, and dagger, all handsomely mounted, must have cost, even in the most conservative estimation, not less than one hundred louis d'or.

'Where on earth, Achilles,' I began to rebuke him, but then was amazed into silence by his now dragging forth a long leathern case, containing: a rich dress suit of white silk, laced with gold; a white sword with gold hilt, a bonnet and plume that would flatter a prince, with collars of Flemish lace, gold-embroidered Brussels gloves, and exquisite Cordova shoes. If he had opened a box full of serpents I could not have gazed into it with purer horror, my purse feeling lighter by a pistole for every fold he unplied in that rich white silk.

'There, there! How's that?' cried Achilles, rubbing his hands in pride, and contemplating these costly accoutrements with delight as unqualified as my own dire consternation. 'What a peerless Alexander the Great I should make,' he went on, 'all wrapped in that heavenly silk! Never, your lordship, was such an opportunity lost, for the wardrobing of a theatre. Never, never!'

'What on earth do you mean, Achilles?' I demanded sternly. 'Where have these garments come from?'

'I mean, your lordship, that despite all the other great snips to be had, I employed great heroism of spirit, you see, to confine my purchases to only what I deemed needful – nay, most *vitally indispensable* – to your lordship's own urgent necessaries.'

'How much, Achilles?'

'How much what, your lordship?'

'Did you pay for all this regalia? How much more than I gave you did you spend?'

'Never a sou, your lordship!' swore Achilles blithely.

'What! Then they must have been stolen,' cried I.

'To be sure!'

'Then how dare you?' I fairly roared at him.

'But not by me!' he protested plaintively, raising his forearm to protect his ears, as if in fear that I should strike him.

'Then how came you by these items, Achilles?' I insisted grimly – obliging my fists, for the moment, to be calm.

That story is easily told [*explained Achilles*]. When your lordship went away with the Corregidor to the Council, after bidding me buy you a riding suit, I went out myself with Jaccomo, as they call him; the cook. Well now, as we were marching along in search of a *fripier*, we passed by the ruins of the arsenal, where your lordship and mine were confined, as you recall, and where I killed the savage soldado, him what would have stuck your lordship's guts. But that is all by the way. Well now, the arsenal in Barcelona today – or at least, the day before yesterday – is in a terrible state to report. Partly battered to pieces with balls of all those cannon, and partly blown up too from within, as it seemed to me.

Well now, just as we, that's Jaccomo and me, had decided we might as well be going in for a little look round – in case of patriots still trapped in distress, don't you know, and things of that sort – then suddenly out from a whole heap of ruins creeps this peasant fellow, with two huge mails on his back, and a heap of other things, we could tell, in a bag around his neck. At first he shrinks in terror from our warlike aspect, but after a little sweet cajoling he recovers his courage, takes breath, and tells us this long story, which Jaccomo translates for me, to the effect that, having arrived in the city too late for the famous plunder of the day before, he had yet hunted about the rooms still not collapsed in the arsenal, till he had found all the fine raiment your lordship sees before you now, and a theatre wardrobe'sworth else besides.

'Now look here, my man,' then says Jaccomo, who is marvellous well experienced in such affairs. 'This is criminal dishonest what you have done, and fiendish immortal too.' On with menacing tones and stormy frowns Jaccomo proceeds: to advise our peasant looter friend of our sad civic duty which confronts us. That is to march the likes of him straightway before the Council of Twelve, what are ordering in blanket batches the summary hanging to death by the neck of all pillagers red-hand apprehended.

'And that means you,' Jaccomo points out with great emphasis, lest our peasant be slow in his marbles.

'But why me?' protests he, with one huge rolling tear in each eye, most belike the downtrod poor wronged again. 'For all I have took was abandoned, in this building unsafe to inhabit, and is of no value no more.'

'We citizens shall be the judge of that,' says Jaccomo, who then makes the wretch exhibit before us all his booty. 'If, as you say, it is all of no value no more,' remarks Jaccomo with great dispassion, 'then you shan't be wanting nowt in payment for it. Shall you?'

Now at this the peasant fellow sees that Jaccomo and me have him hard by the yangyangs, and so – his mind sore crowded with sorry thoughts of his pregnant wife, hungry babies, sick old mother, spavined mule and rabid hound – he starts to blab like a virgin no longer. 'Why me? Why me?' he sobs.

But myself by now having rummaged his merchandise, and seeing there was goods what would suit your lordship most handsome, I instruct Jaccomo to put forward on our behalf such an offer in cash as any blubbering peasant in prospect of hanging would be thoroughly daft to decline. That was to say: all what was in my pocket. And that was to say: seven fine louis d'or, all genuine and frequently bit.

'You are a great lunatic to offer this twit so much,' objects Jaccomo, 'when these wares are now ours for the taking.'

But I knew, as Jaccomo did not, that your lordship's honour would never allow his conscience to wear such dudes without you had paid for them fairly. So I stuck by the price I had named, our captive went off in ecstasies over his gold – doubtless more than his life's wages to date – Jaccomo makes do with what no theatre's wardrobe certainly won't be seeing a stitch of now, and, to crown the many achievements of your humble servant's day, your lordship is now dressed fit for Paris, ain't you not?

Next morning – 16 June 1640 – Louis is disconcerted to learn from the Marseille harbour master that the first Lyon boat up the Rhône will not be till the next day again, and that even then it will be too slow to guarantee his being first to deliver to Richelieu in Paris the continent-shaking news from Catalonia. It being out of the question to take Achilles Lefranc all the way to Paris on horseback, at any speed, Louis resolves to gallop ahead and leave Achilles, in custody of most of the seven-louis wardrobe, to take the boat.

Achilles whimpers touchingly at the thought of being parted from his lordship, and presses Louis at least to take over guardianship of the looted Villafranca diamonds, on the ground that:

'Bludgeoned, as he would say, by my counsels of probity, little Achilles had – or at least, said he had – heroically resolved to return the diamonds to their rightful owner, if ever he found the opportunity, which quite likely he did not much anticipate; all subject, however, to the unconditional reservation, that he, being as it were the interim custodian of the gems, had the right to make use of any part of their value, in case either his own circumstances, or mine, should legitimately so require. But in the meantime he remained under the most excruciating anxiety, lest he be robbed on the way to Paris, which he did very much anticipate, and therefore did he plead with me most urgently, that:

'"Your lordship being a shade the more valiant of us two, and doubtless like to pass a shorter space of time upon the road, I *implore* that your lordship shall take charge of the packet in which I have the stones enveloped."

'I did as he wished, though I would willingly have been excused. Then, leaving him to shed his tender tear or two over this temporary separation of our ways, I mounted the post-horse that had been brought me, and galloped north on my journey to Paris.'

After only two days of what must have been uncommonly gruelling riding, particularly in view of Rhône valley temperatures in June, Louis Morel arrives in the capital and heads for an auberge in the Quartier St Eustache. In his room – it is late afternoon – he throws himself on the bed for an hour's recuperation before daring to attempt to present himself before the Cardinal. Thinking to fall instantly into refreshing sleep, he is in fact too exhausted to do so, and instead lies wrestling with a seemingly endless queue of tormenting contenders: the stark contrast between this sordid cupboard in the smelly city inn and the bucolic bliss he has left behind in Bigorre; a vision of deploring condemnation distorting with shadows the fair face of Hélène Arnault; his mother too; and his mission to brief the First Minister of France on the Catalan Revolution, but where shall Richelieu be found? And how will the unknown stranger gain an audience?

By the time he gets to being suffocated by a plethora of the Cardinal's famous cats, Louis has in fact descended deeply into dreams, and it is only the sharp consciousness of a surfeit of stale garlic breath that rouses him quickly enough to finger a rancid Gascon who is already in his room, and poised to lay hands on Louis's bags.

'What on earth do you think you are doing?' demands Louis, sitting up.

'Thank the Lord you are awake, sir,' the Gascon replies smoothly, turning away from the saddle-bags, bowing to Louis, and backing to the door in a unified pantomime of total greasiness. 'For I am commanded by our landlord to inform you, sir, that our supper is served below.'

Realizing that if he doesn't eat first he is liable to disgrace himself by fainting in the presence of Eminence, Louis curtly informs the Gascon he will follow him down to dinner. It is a round-table affair, more like a college fellows' repast than the isolated small-tables ambience of bistros in Paris today. During the second course, and as the wine carafes are replenished, some of the other diners wax expansive. One reveals himself to be 'a veritable Caesar in war'. Another warns that he is notoriously 'irresistible to women'.[1] A third quotes third-party commendations of his own 'unparalleled knowledge of international politics'.

And so on.

As the holders-forth protract their cheese, and quaff bumpers in celebration of their exploits, Louis grows impatient to be off in search of the Cardinal. To his left is a quiet shopkeeper who so far, by his own testimony, is not known to be a trojan superwarrior, or a Minotaur in bed. Quietly Louis asks the quiet shopkeeper if he can suggest a good guide to guide a stranger round Paris. As bad luck would have it, the

---

[1] 'Clearly his genes live on.' [J.R.]

quiet shopkeeper is obliged to get back to his wife and children as soon as possible, and the bumptious Caesar man, overhearing Louis's quiet question, insists there is no better guide in all Paris but himself:

'For I know the city, sir, as a Mohammedan knows his Koran!'

Anxious to lose no more time, Louis closets his misgivings about the Caesar man, runs up to collect his dispatches for Richelieu, locks his chamber door, then directs the Caesar man to lead him to the Palais Cardinal by the swiftest-possible route.

Forty minutes later Louis, become suspicious, establishes by quizzing a local greengrocer that he has been led entirely to the wrong side of town. When he turns to vent his wrath on the deceitful Caesar man, he sees nothing to be seen of him bar a last glimpse of his backside disappearing up an alley in parallel with the sunset.

'I shouldn't waste your breath, your honour,' mutters the greengrocer. 'You'll never catch him now.'

Further discourse with the greengrocer, who seems an honest fellow migrated in from the provinces (rather than Parisian bred in the bone), reveals that the Caesar man is known all over the capital for a tremendous scoundrel, and that the auberge where Louis is lodged is notoriously a major centre for petty crime.

'That is strange,' reflects Louis, 'for it was recommended to me most fervently, by my landlord in Marseille. Anyway . . .'

In respect of a little welcome cash the greengrocer assures Louis that his adolescent son Bertrand will infallibly lead any gentleman straight to the Cardinal – or at least, 'let's be candid, your honour' – straight to the Cardinal's residence.

If you were to look down on the Cour d'Honneur of the Palais Royal tomorrow – if you were the last fat magnate, say, in a low-hovering helicopter – you might imagine some intricate macro-scale board game were there being played: sundry citizens of Paris, perhaps, taking on all alien tourists. For you would see the crisp rectangle of the court, striped with some dozen bright white lines along its length, intersected with fainter stripes across its width, with neat white circles in the midst of 233 of the 234 squares thus formed, and antlike people everywhere: enacting behaviours inscrutable to you. Some sitting on the white circles for unpredictable numbers of minutes, some walking between the squares in zigzag patterns of intriguing apparent purposiveness, while a smaller number – almost like the balls in a bizarre contact sport – move at a great rate everywhere, in sporadic jerky bursts. The latter are, of course, the kids on skateboards, and rollerskates, who in the main are breathtakingly adroit at dodging the handbags old ladies swing at them.

If now, your titanic curiosity having overleaped the urgency of your meeting with bankers in Bonn, you have your pilot lower you down, you will find that the white lines are in fact chequered, and the white circles are the tops of pillars, all about the right diameter to seat two bums back to back, and with serrated sides striped black and white, like the skintight upper thighs of Billy Bunter's Sunday-best trousers. Now the contrast between this garish modernism on the courtyard floor, and the massive stone archways, balconies, balustrades, austere tall windows, lofty ornate statuary, and cool grey slate roofs all surrounding, may well make you exclaim, according to your temperament, education, and so forth:

'Goodness gracious.'

'What the fuck?'

Or even:

'Is it art?'

But when you learn that the alternative proposal to Daniel Buron's *Les deux plateaux* (as the much acclaimed and equally reviled '*travail in situ*' is named) – an alternative proposal which was advocated with a shamefully vehement want of shame by the flunkeys themselves – was to turn the Cour d'Honneur into a car park for civil servants, you are bound, are you not, to applaud the decision taken, and the blows thereby struck for respite and repose, for space and light amid concrete and darkness, and for leisure, imagination, and fun?

If you are not yet convinced, breath deeply and look around you. On a bright sunny day before lunch you will see, between the Bunter pillars, where a sub-prefect's senior administrative assistant's air-conditioned Citroën is not now stationed, a short portly gentleman in an olive-green jerkin, wearing Doctor Marten shoes, with his right arm extended high, and his fingers splayed out like fat twigs. If you picture to yourself the later Jean Gabin wearing spectacles and a cloth cap, with white eyebrows, a white moustache and a cigar stump clenched beneath it, you will know him when you see him.

But why is his arm held high?

Why his fingers splayed?

It is for all the sparrows to perch upon, as many as ever could perch on one plump hand, with a dozen others like tiny queuing jets in mid-air above, as eagerly they watch for the mix of seeds and crumbs to be produced by the other hand in his jerkin pocket. All around him pustular German teenagers grunt, American senior citizens say 'Wow!'

and 'Gee!', while microchipped Japanese cameras go whir and click, as
they never would for a penpusher's Renault.

If then a little north-east you saunter, through the Galerie Orleans to
the Jardins du Palais Royal, looked down on by the shutter-twitching
residents of some of the chiquest pied-à-terres in Europe, you will
find – behind the avenues of trees that line the lawns, and underneath
the fancy flats – you will find twin parallel arcades of fancy boutiques,
antiquarian bookshops, art galleries not yet closed by bankruptcy, toy
shops, mask shops, with fantastic reflections in the spotless window glass
of pageants of history in miniature within reaching out to meet halfway
the images of today peering in – that's you, you realize with a start: that
covetous pair of vicarious eyes – eyes such as Ernest Hemingway seems
somehow to have seen in Wyndham Lewis – eyes somehow trapped in
the trees above a scene of wiggy aristocrats decadently dancing in just
this space all around you, in the last few days before the Revolution
would explode, to cut off all their heads. Even a lone soft-porn purveyor
you may find, most pukka, called Le Guillery Du Guignol – literally,
the Cheeky Puppet's Pecker – purveying fine line drawings of female
genitalia so arabesquely floral that for a moment you do not see they
are porn at all. But then with a giveaway eureka 'Hum!', having noticed
the price tags in that same second moment, you glance at your watch as
though monitoring the healing of a wound on your wrist and generously
suggest 'Time for a coffee?' to certainly yourself and perhaps also the
essentially efficient and incidentally ravishing amanuensical person who
descended from the helicopter with you. Thinking now to save a few
vital pounds amid your millions from needlessly frittering themselves
away, you steer a sage course round from the marble-floored arcades,
south down the Rue de Valois, and on its corner shared with the Rue St
Honoré you slump outside or dive, depending on the ambient heat, and
the carbon monoxide and lead quotients in the air at the time, into the
Café du Palais Royal. Alas, even there your grand *cafés noirs*, though
indubitably delicious, will still impoverish you by many pounds sterling,
and in addition, should you follow the arrow to *messieurs* you will find,
at the base of the puke-green tiles (so ethnic is the ethos of bygone Paris
here) no trace of the comforting Shanks that most of Western Civilization
would now consider mandatory, on which to wedge your hams. But that's
all part of the fun, and, as L.P. Hartley (or at least Sir Michael Redgrave)
didn't quite say:

'Another country is like the past. They do things differently there.'

Well, whether a common currency leading to a Federated States of

Europe ever results in proper crappers getting installed in the Café du Palais remains to be seen. In the meantime that corner of Paris remains unaccountably soothing, uplifting, and intriguingly magnetic. Let us haste to add that we personally have no vested interest in telling you this, no shares in the arcade porn shop, etc, and suggest that, if you refuse to believe us for a moment, which you are welcome not to do, you may nonetheless gauge our assessment of the alluring mystique of the Palais Royal, and its precincts, to be wonderfully corroborated by the following consideration: that if you hunt assiduously in your local public library, or possibly second-hand bookshop, you will eventually discover a remotely contemporary short story to be situated thereabouts, by one of Bearsden's[2] greatest living short-story writers.

But of course it wasn't always quite as it is today. In 1640 there were no boutiquey arcades, let alone Billy Bunter pillars, and the Palais itself had not even yet become Royal, as is confirmed by the following literal quotation from the official noticeboard outside the front gates of the Cour de l'Horloge, just next to a largely eye-catching euro-symbol which informs tourists and natives alike, of all colours and tongues, that their Airedale terriers are banned:

'It was in 1624 that the Cardinal of Richelieu bought a Parisian hôtel, by the side of the Rue Saint-Honoré, in a densely populated area, close to the Louvre, and to the [fortified] enclosure, recently abandoned, which had been built by Charles V.[3] The Cardinal acquired, not without difficulty, most of the neighbouring houses, and he enlarged the garden by clearing away a part of the ancient ramparts. He entrusted to the architect Lemercier, creator of the Sorbonne Chapel, the aggrandisement of his hôtel, which work was carried out between 1628 and 1642. Lemercier also constructed there a theatre, where Molière would play from 1660. As for the Cardinal, he did not enjoy the benefits of his improvements for long, since he died in the Palais on 4 December 1642, having bequeathed his property to the Crown. In November 1643 Anne of Austria[4] abandoned her uncomfortable apartments in

---

2  Area of Greater Glasgow where most citizens eat more fresh fruit and vegetables, don't smoke roll-ups, enjoy less rickets, and tend to vote Conservative in secret.

3  Charles V of France, 1337–80. Also known as Charles the Wise, but still not popular with his taxpayers.

4  Lately become widow to Louis XIII of France.

the Louvre, to install herself in the *Palais Cardinal*, which now took
the name *Palais Royal*.'

What we have to remember then, is that what Louis Morel approaches,
this warm evening in June 1640, is very much the Palais Cardinal as it is
still in the process of becoming. Monumental grandeur already erected
stands only feet away from on-going building-site chaos in the form of
haphazard piles of masonry, heaps of sand, hastily downed tools waiting
to trip you round every corner, and everywhere the risk of fouling
your flash Spanish boots in a rubble-dusted deposit of the rank black
faeces — like the dung of a Pyrenean bear with internal bleeding — which
down the centuries have betokened the on-the-job diligence of masons
throughout France, in that they refuse to go further afield.

'Yes?' snarls the porter, whom the guards have summoned from
a snack.

'I am urgently arrived from Barcelona,' explains Louis. 'And I must
see the Cardinal now.'

'Fat chance,' sneers the porter triumphantly. 'That's what they all say.
And anyway, who are you?'

*25*

# At the Palais

'I am . . . an associate of the Marquis of Roquefort,' replied I [*writes Louis*], and I must see his Eminence *now.*'

'What is your business?' demanded the porter.

'Business of such import, my friend, that I shall stop here all the night if need be. For the Cardinal will surely thank me, when he hears my vital news.'

'Come with me,' said the porter, after much laborious cogitation. Then he led me across the *Cour* [*de l'Horloge*], wherein a carriage was standing, with horses harnessed, and torches already burning at the doors, though the summer sky was yet light. 'Monsieur Noyers[1] will be here in a moment,' continued the porter, indicating the carriage. 'You

---

[1] François Sublet, Seigneur de Noyers, and Baron de Dangu. 'He was a little man, an indefatigable worker of forty-eight when he became secretary [of state for war] on 17 February 1636. In the seven brief years next preceding the death of Richelieu, Sublet supervised the preparation of some 18,000 letters and dispatches which have survived as minutes in the Archives de la Guerre. From these and other letters one may reconstruct his bustling administration. He wrote once to an army commander:

'"Perhaps you will be astonished to see in one single day so many messengers, almost all bearers of changing orders. But the good pilot changes his sails as many times as the wind changes, without being blamed for fickleness . . . "'

From the excellent *Richelieu and the Councillors of Louis XIII*, by Orest A. Ranum, which highlights – what many English historians of 17th-century France had missed – how dependent Richelieu was (in maintaining his favour with Louis XIII) on secretaries such as Noyers, who kept him posted on variations in the King's health, mood, prejudices and affections; even down to the King's bowel movements and enema insertions.

may address your petition to him.'

'My business is with his Eminence the Cardinal alone,' I insisted, doubtless with the appearance of more dignified authority than truly I felt, 'and I warrant he will severely punish any servitor whom he discovers to have withheld from his attention the momentous tidings I bring.'

The porter looked at me, then at the carriage, then at the sky. For fully a minute he personified perfectly the torment of Buridan's Ass.[2] At length he conceded:

'If your business be truly important, you had best see someone who can judge of it. And if it turn out to be maggots, you had best not never been born.'

On that frowning note, he led me from the court, through an archway, thence into a small hall, and on to a cabinet beyond, which – entirely without windows, so far as I could see – was hung all round with rich Flemish tapestries, and lighted by a single silver lamp.

'Here sit you down,' commanded the porter. 'And wait.' With that he departed, and closed the door with an ominous slam.

Perhaps fifteen minutes later, by which time I was perspiring profusely, a light clicking noise behind one of the hangings was immediately followed by the appearance, as between the drawn curtains on a theatre stage, of a tallish and slender gentleman not yet sixty years of age, clad smartly in a suit of black cavalier's velvet, with a high plumed bonnet above. His complexion was pale, but his eyes clear and sharp, under eyebrows expressively arched. A somewhat prominent nose imposed over lips rather thin and compressed, while his moustache and beard were both sparse by nature and trim by discipline.

As I saw, on the far side of the lamp, that this gentleman had yet to remark my presence, I now cleared my throat and stood up.

---

[2] The silly donkey who fabulously expires of agonized starvation between two equidistant carrots. Supposedly described by the French philosopher Jean Buridan (d. 1366), although, according to our *Britannica*:

'The example of a dog, not an ass, dying of hunger between two equal amounts of food occurs in his commentary on Aristotle's *De Caelo*. Exploded legends made him [ie Buridan, presumably – and not the donkey, or dog] the founder of the Vienna university and the lover of a queen of France . . .'

'What, what? What is this?' he cried, starting back with a wince of alarm. In that instant of apprehension his height seemed to stoop, and a sag to embrace his shoulders, as if a history of disease had enfeebled the frame of his youth. But then, having noted no semblance of murder in my aspect, he recovered himself in a twinkling, and, growing stern, just like the porter he demanded:

'Who are you?'

'My identity, sir,' I informed him politely, 'shall be revealed to the Cardinal de Richelieu alone.'

'What is that in your hand?' the cavalier then wished to know.

'Confidential dispatches from Spain,' I replied. 'For his Eminence's eyes only.'

'Give them to me,' said the cavalier stranger, holding out a commanding hand.

'Who are you?' parried I.

'I am much in the Cardinal's confidence,' riposted he, his fingers snapping with impatience. 'Come, come.'

There was an authority in his tone that almost induced me to obey. But then, reflecting that I might be called to a severe account by the notoriously martinet minister, for any such error of judgment, I persisted:

'That I can give this intelligence to no-one but his Eminence himself – save only, perhaps, if you can produce me an express order, from his own hand, that I should entrust the papers to you.'

'Tchee!' exclaimed my interlocutor, and with a fleeting cold smile he seized writing materials from the table, where they lay by the silver lamp, and penned in a large rapid hand:

> *Deliver your packet, without delay,*
> *to the bearer of this order.*
> *Richelieu.*

Dumbfounded that the Cardinal should have presented himself disguised as a cavalier, I made a bow so low as momentarily to veil my discomfiture, and placed the letters from Barcelona in his outstretched hand. He broke the seals with the ease of long practice, and read through the papers with the devouring rapidity of genius. Meanwhile, in the grip of a nervous fascination – for I knew now I could never conceal my real identity from such a piercing intelligence as this, and what if the news of my crimes in Bigorre had come already to the Cardinal's attention? – I covertly inspected his countenance for signs, among the lines, of the despotic and even vindictive passions with which the world of rumour charged him.

But for the moment, at least, there was no malice in his gaze, and only an occasional flicker, as of a dry black humour, gave the smallest clue as to what thoughts raced round his brain.

Now like a rearing snake he stepped back and looked up.

Like a voyeur caught *in flagrante*, I broke from his challenging gaze, flushed hot, and looked down.

'You were inspecting me severely, sir,' said the Cardinal with unnerving mildness. 'Are you a diviner of countenances?'

'Never, your Eminence!' I replied. 'I was but teaching myself to know a great man — lest ever I be privileged to converse with another.'

'So diplomatic an answer, sir, would make many a courtier's fortune,' said the Cardinal, smiling lightly. 'And though it shall not of itself make yours, nor shall it harm you either. For it is well to remember that flattery is never wasted in court circles — where even the noblest prince is vain as the vainest woman. If the flattery be too thick, they may scrape some of it aside, as with excessive rouge. But they will also take infinite pains not to wipe away the base.'

To be apprehended thus, in an act of the crassest flattery, which in the instant of its utterance had seemed naught but sincerest truth, seemed then to me so degrading, that hot blood lit my cheeks with shame.

Remarking my confusion, the Cardinal, with a sardonic twitch of his lips, continued:

'Enough of philosophy for the minute. I am now required elsewhere for perhaps an hour. Thereafter I may have some questions to ask you. Meanwhile, I shall be obliged if you will await my return.'

'But of course, your Eminence.' I bowed.

'Do not stir from this room,' he went on. 'There', he pointed to a tall but narrow corner case of books bound lavishly in gold-lettered leather, 'you will find food for the mind. As to your physical needs, they shall be taken care of. Otherwise, speak to no-one.'

Left alone in that windowless chamber, I swam for several minutes against a flood of turbulent thoughts. Was this really the extraordinary minister, who thrived on the thunders of war, in the whirlwinds of political intrigue, and who at that very moment controlled the fates not only of France, but of half of Europe beyond?

At that juncture two servants brought in a small table of lapis lazuli, on which was laid a bowl of fruit, a carafe of wine, and a china cup beside a matching pot, which, by its aroma, I supposed must contain coffee – a beverage I never before had tasted, but had heard praised by poor Father Francis, who had grown to depend upon it in the East.

This waiting service was performed in profound silence, but at length one of the Cardinal's stealthy attendants in a whisper desired me, in the name of his lord, to partake of the refreshments provided. Then with a swift low reverence he followed his associate out of the cabinet, and silently closed the door behind him, all as if in fear that I should make him any answer, or require further discourse with him. And I could not help wondering, when the attendants had left me, what system of subtle terror the Cardinal must have devised, which could drill any two natives of Paris into habits of silence like that.

Thinking these thoughts, I addressed the table they had left me, and helped myself to a handful of cherries, with a glass of light wine, followed by several cups of that most exquisite refreshment called coffee. That done, still alone, and apprehensive as to what might transpire when the Cardinal should inquire into my identity, and background, I inspected the corner bookcase, hoping there to find suitable diversion. Passing over histories and tragedies, essays and memoirs, I fixed at length upon a volume of Ovid – my interest, in the curious mind and inventions of this author, having been stimulated by my conversations with the Marquis of Roquefort, and the experiences I had undergone, while a guest in his hunting pavilion.

By midnight I was adrift in an ocean of fantastic reverie, which at the time I attributed solely to the Roman's lush poesy – the mastery of his couplets, and his exuberant disregard for all moral concern – but which I later realized must also have been inspired by the quantity of coffee I had drunk, when of a sudden the Cardinal reappeared, again through his private door behind the Arras, but wearing now a dressing gown of comfortably faded silk, and accompanied by some six motley cats.

Readjusting my impressions to accord with reality, I hurriedly laid down my reading, and made to rise.

'No, no,' said the Cardinal breezily. 'Be still.'

My obedience was rendered the easier, in the same instant, by the arrival on my thighs of two of the minister's cats, which animals proceeded to behave as though the fabric of my breeches were the bark of fallen trees.

'Put them down, if you like,' said his Eminence, but with an undertone which I felt implied that he would think the less of me if I did. 'Monsieur – ?'

With great dread I confessed my name, my pedigree and home address. Happily, the Cardinal had heard no word of my disgrace – or, if he had, his powers of dissimulation were absolute.

'How is your mother these days?' was his only polite expression of any interest in my family. 'And what took you to Barcelona in the first place, Monsieur Morel?' he next wished to know.

I told him – which was not untrue – of my wish to improve my command of the Spanish tongue, to master Catalan, and to diminish my inexperience of the world.

'Yes, but – why Barcelona?'

Cautiously I dissembled without untruth:

'I was there to rendezvous with a dear old friend of my family, who is steeped in all matters Hispanic.'

'His name?'

'The Chevalier of Montenero.'

'Montenero, eh?' murmured the Cardinal, who then lightly clapped and rubbed his hands in pleasureful anticipation, as one of the silent servitors came in again, with a tray bearing a fresh pot of coffee and a plateful of small cakes, which were coated with chocolate glaze.

I waited in silence as the Cardinal delicately ate one cake – none was offered to me – and poured himself a cup of dark brown coffee, the saucer of which he then rested thoughtfully on the back of a large black cat, which was purring contentedly in his lap.

'Are you fond of Ovid, Monsieur Morel?' he then inquired, having read the spine of the volume I had chosen from his shelves.

'I—'

'He is my favourite author too, you know. No shame in that! Probably I read him more frequently than any other author.' His tone was effortlessly that of everyday conversation, such as two persons of coeval status might conduct upon any subject of no grave import, but of passing mutual interest.

Essaying an appropriate response, I replied with sincerity, but not vehemence:

'In the last year, your Eminence, Ovid has certainly become one of my favourite poets. And yet I am nervous of reading him so often as I might wish.'

'Why is that?'

'I find there is an enervating tendency in his works, repeated exposure to which might severely relax one's mind.'

'Ah! But *that* is the very reason why *I* read him!' replied the Cardinal.

'For Ovid, to me, following a long day of vexatious activity – when every thought is bound to causality, interest and consequence – then is his poesy like a bed of roses to the mind. And there, free from care, calmed by the delicate pastels of his petals, balmed by the dreamlike fragrance of his scents, one's powers delight in the feeling of freedom to idle without guilt, and thus recuperate their vigour, for the business of the following day.'

This was hardly the conversation I had anticipated. Nodding assentively, and extruding the unease in my hands, by means of stroking the cats on my thighs, I consoled myself with the thought that, surely, the Cardinal soon must pilot our discourse towards those recent tumultuous events, in the north of Spain, concerning which I felt amply equipped to portray to him a first-hand account of the background, from the Catalan point of view.

Not a bit of it, however. His Eminence continued, as he sipped with relish at his coffee, to talk of and by reflexion to Ovid. 'There is a constant struggle, you see, Monsieur Morel,' he affirmed, 'in every human frame, between – let us call them – *feeling* and *reason*. In youth – as you, being yet so young, should know – it is normal that *feeling* shall rule. Rule like a vigorous queen, one might say, with imagination her humble first minister.'

I saw, as he paused for a moment, a fleeting wry smile curl the moustache above his cup; and I could not but wonder what private images were bright in him, of his relations with our present King.[3]

'In later years,' the Cardinal went on, 'when *feeling* has achieved for a man all that *feeling* can – swept him into untold follies, wherefrom, if he die not first of the pox, or whatever, he will have gained a wife, a mistress or two, and a much depleted treasury – then *reason* succeeds to the throne, to achieve what *feeling* could not, and to remedy all she got wrong. And what follows next?'

I lifted my hands from the backs of his cats, in a minimal gesture intended to intimate that I trusted his Eminence would tell me.

'It is my speculation, Monsieur Morel,' he said, 'that as you yet inhabit the age of *feeling*, while I am long resident in *reason*, one consequence necessarily is, that in reading such a writer as Ovid, what we cull for ourselves from his genius is as different, let us say, as the wax and the honey from the same patient flower. Do you not agree?'

---

[3] Louis XIII.

How could I not?

'And while what touches you,' enthused the Cardinal, 'and alarms you a little, so you say, is the witty brilliancy of the poet's language, the lusciousness of his metaphor, not forgetting the practical cynicism of his advice on how to seduce young women, all that is but old hat to me. By contrast, that which may still inform, charm, and ennoble the reader's *reason*, throughout his sager years, is to perceive, through the radiant garb of some perfectly apt and yet hitherto unexpected allegory, newer aspects and subtler implications of some long-established truth. What, for example, could convey a truer picture, of an ambitious and daring minister, than Ixion[4] as portrayed by Ovid: in his embracement of the cloud?'

I realized with a shock, that as the Cardinal spoke he was inspecting me closely, full in the face, with a grim smile charged with melancholy meaning, to which I had no idea how to respond.

'Certainly I had never before considered Ovid in that light,' I admitted. 'Though doubtless, henceforth, I shall derive even greater pleasure from his verse, through tracing his allegories to their core – for the pleasure of which, of course, I shall have only your Eminence to thank.'

'Your thanks are not due to me,' replied the Cardinal, 'but to an English statesman, who wrote a fine book upon the subject near a century past,[5] in which, as he elucidated the wisdom of the ancients, his own acuity shone fully as bright. In England, you see, Monsieur

---

[4] Ixion. Randy murderer who dares try to tup the goddess Hera. When Hera foils him by substituting a cloud for her own fair self, the randy bugger tups the cloud anyway, and thus becomes sire of the Centaurs. Cf the quaint Hollywoodism: 'He'd fuck a log pile, if he thought there was a rattlesnake in it.' The allusively subtextual implications (Cardinal Richelieu screwing the people of France, etc) are surely too blatant to labour.

[5] This phrase, 'near a century past', would on the surface of it appear to suggest that the Cardinal does not here refer (as has been supposed) to Sir Thomas More, who was beheaded (so to speak) by Henry VIII of England (*sic*) in 1535. However, we should also consider that Louis may simply have mis-remembered the Cardinal's exact form of words, and/or equally that the Cardinal himself may have got his dates slightly out, in which case who in France would have dared put him right?

Morel, the reign of *reason* comes sooner and lasts longer than with we French – though they may be considered a younger people.'

'Does that mean your Eminence believes', I inquired, 'that the progression from *feeling* to *reason* proceeds apace, not only with the decades of men, but also with the centuries of nations?'

'Generally, yes.' The Cardinal nodded abstractedly. 'Most nations in their infancy are brash, hasty; swayed more strongly by impulse than by thought. Easily led; governed with difficulty. Gradually, however, they turn politic, cautious, wary of costly wars, conservative of the wealth and advantages they possess; latterly somewhat indolent – even decadent – till at length they subside into dotage. Just like men!' he added with an impish flash.

I applauded with a facial adjustment, and by continuing to tickle his cats.

Seriously the Cardinal continued:

'But that is all theory. In practice the world as we know it is too young to confirm such postulates on the histories of nations. All we know for certain is, that nations too have their different characters – just like men – that likewise the vigour of some will outlive others; that some will die violent deaths; others be wasted by catastrophic plagues; while many shall perish by protracted decay, and be overrun by new young blood.'

'Does your Eminence refer to the later Romans,' I supposed, 'and the brutal energy of the barbarian hordes?'

'That is an obvious instance,' he gestured with a hint of impatience. 'Well, a thousand years from now, perhaps, wise men may seriously claim to know what nations are, and catalogue their nature. For the present, it suffices merely to understand our contemporaries more comprehensively than they know us, and then to rule them through that advantage. And now, Monsieur Morel . . . '

Without conscious volition, I suddenly found myself standing, and gingerly detaching cats' claws from my breeches. As the Cardinal concluded:

'I thank you for a pleasant hour. You will, if you please, notify your lodging in Paris to the staff in my porter's lodge, and keep them advised of any change. In due course you shall hear from me again. Meanwhile, we are grateful for your news from Spain. Enjoy your sojourn in our incomparable capital – and do your best to eschew bad company. Good night, Monsieur Morel.'

# 26

# A Low-life Masque

Not surprisingly, Louis's interview with Richelieu affected him profoundly.

'What amazed me most', he reflects, 'was how the Cardinal contrived to speak not one single word on the business that had brought me before him. Indeed, Catalonia's very name was never once uttered. And yet, as we now know, the very morning following my audience with his Eminence, large bodies of men marched into Roussillon. More were despatched south from all corners of France. The French fleet in the Mediterranean sailed for Barcelona. In short, in a remarkably brief space of time, Catalonia was provided with all supplies and support necessary to sustain a long and active war against her oppressors in Madrid.'

After that audience — the adrenalin and danger of fulfilling his mission to brief the great Cardinal who might also order his execution, if once he heard of the manner of Louis's killing of Jean-Baptiste — Louis suffered the sort of desperately depressing comedown that often afflicts athletes and rock stars the mornings after their finest nights before. For a week he hardly enjoyed a single hour of sleep unbroken by hammering anxieties about the past and present, and paranoid projections into a dark, shapeless and suffocatingly hostile future.

Richelieu had promised to call upon him again. But when? Why? Would it be to employ his talents in service of the King, or to arraign him for his crimes in Bigorre? Well then, given the risk of the latter, should he not now pre-empt the Cardinal, by enlisting with the Count of Soissons, as planned before his hasty flight from home? But wait a minute. What if the Count of Soissons is already prejudiced against him, by intelligence from his mother, the dowager Countess, who is Louis's mother's own best friend from long ago, and may well have received bitter letters from her, bewailing the black sheep's deeds? If so, then truly he has no protector left to turn to, no bolt-hole to run to, and even little Achilles, it seems, has abandoned him — or been imprisoned for petty larceny in Lyon, or quite likely murdered en route.

As the full futility of remaining perched with no role in the great dishonest money-leeching smelly metropolis bears down on him, Louis's thoughts and feelings about Hélène become so intense and frantic that nothing survives of them beyond sporadic elliptical ejaculations such as:

'Unworthy.' 'Lost.' 'Hopeless.' And:

'*Doomed.*'

He can't have lain on his bed in the shady auberge non-stop all that time, wallowing in the near catatonic gloom which his memoirs conjure up, but how often he sortied forth to explore the 'incomparable capital', and how hard he essayed to enact the Cardinal's avuncular admonition to 'eschew bad company' . . . we simply cannot say – for Louis doesn't tell us, and no-one else will ever know. What we can establish is that this fallow interlude lasted several weeks. This is because the next bout of action which Louis has preserved for us takes place before breakfast 'a week to the day following Saint Bartholomew's Eve'.[1] Louis is lying in bed, toying with the costs and benefits associated with thinking of going to the bother of getting up and facing the day, and wondering yet again why Richelieu should have been togged up in such unclerical dress that night, and who it was the Cardinal could have rushed out to visit. After all, would not virtually every other citizen of France be expected to present himself at the Palais, with politic patience pending the premier's personal pleasure?

Or was it *her*self?

As his thoughts revert to sex, and the cost of getting any in Paris, either on a straight commercial basis or (and financially yet more disastrous) in terms of wining, dining and hiring carriages for ladies with more elevated aspirations, Louis is on the brink of realizing how devastatingly soon he will be literally destitute – 'but three louis d'or and the odd few sous, at the bottom of my purse' – in the sense of no longer able to pay by the week for his grimy room and greasy dinners in the shady auberge, when suddenly the owner of the room cum stewer of the dinners rushes in without knocking, to announce:

'Oh, monsieur, monsieur!' he cried, with an aspect of great terror [*writes*

---

[1] Eve / Day equals 23/24 August. Re the St Bartholomew Massacre, 1572, and its indelible fingerprint on French consciousness, see *The Counts of Mount Venus*, Ch. 6.

*Louis*]. 'If you have anything at all in your bags which you would wish to conceal, you would wish to conceal them now!'

'What on earth do you mean, Monsieur Cafarde?' I replied in irritation, as I swung my feet to the floor.

'There are officers of justice searching round the floors below,' the landlord lamented, wringing all the while his rather fat and hairy hands.

'And what is that to me?' I demanded, though now my own heart was pounding, as I thought of the Cardinal's policy, and how badly it must fare with me, if they had learned of Jean-Baptiste.

'They say, monsieur,' said the landlord, 'they are inquiring after a personage, who, from the description they recite, sounds uncommonly like yourself.'

'Nonsense, man!' I scoffed, though with confidence that was all a deceit, and in that same moment my door burst open to admit the burly forms of two armoured sergeants, closely followed by a mincing *greffier* [clerk of some court], the latter being sombrely menacing, in the robes of his black office.

'What is this?' I strenuously protested, leaping up to frown down upon them, for they were none near as tall as I. 'What business have you with me, and how dare you come upon me thus?'

'Typical,' sneered the larger sergeant, who stationed himself at the door, sword drawn, while his companion rushed to block any possible egress from the window, which only a bird or a madman might in any case attempt, on account of the cessheap beneath. Now the greffier, remaining cautiously close to the sergeant by the door, commanded me:

' . . . in the King's name to surrender.'

'I would if need be, in principle, be entirely willing to surrender my person to the custody of his Majesty's legitimate officers,' I informed this unprepossessing and somewhat musty-smelling gentleman. 'But I fear, in the present case, that there must be some mistake.'

'What they all say!' chuckled the sergeant at the window, who was appreciably younger than the other two.

'What mistake?' insists the greffier, very ominous.

'*Your* mistake,' I tell him with vigour, 'in that I have only been in the city a very short space of time — hardly long enough to engage in crime, even had that been my wish.'

'One hour is quite long enough,' frowns the sergeant at the door, in the voice of one who knows.

'Yes, yes!' chortles his younger colleague. 'Villains with the knack commits crimes like what I eats oysters!'

'You are accused, sir, of *filching*,' intoned the greffier, with horrific solemnity.

'Filching *what*, from *whom*?' I challenged him.

'That excellent good citizen, Jonas Echimillia, of the persecuted race of Abraham, avers against you, monsieur, that last night, towards ten of the clock, you entered his dwelling, wherein he gives shelter to old servants cast off by ungrateful masters, and that there, under the falsest pretences, you did abominably appropriate a white silk suit, laced with gold. To the identity of the said eloped suit Monsieur Echimillia will eternally swear, and therefore we command you now, monsieur, to open up your swallow-all, or trunk-mail, or whatever is the thing beneath your bed, in which you keep your worldly goods, and reveal to myself and the sergeants whatever it may contain.'

Now while the droning greffier proceeded thus, so sanctimonious and prolix, the intimation came upon me that here were semblances and tones somewhat hollow, and I heard a distant echo in my mind of the warning vouchsafed me by the honest grocer whose honest son had at last led me to the gates of the Palais Cardinal that night: that this Parisian auberge so vehemently recommended in Marseille, was in fact no tower of rectitude at all. Glancing suddenly at mine landlord, who all this while had affected to stand by me to one side, as if in tacit sympathy with my cause, I surprised him – though he noted me not – in the flagrantly complicit act of sending expressive facial signals to the greffier: nods, winks, grimaces, and all that sort of thing.

*Aha*, I then said to myself. *So this is how the land lies here. So this is how these varlets know of the folded presence, in the valise beneath my bed, of the white silk dress, laced with gold, so inexpensively purchased by little Achilles, in Barcelona before we left.*

Much stimulated by the audacity of their conspiracy against me, I determined to best them in their own dissimulating enterprise, and to that end I now affected the alarm of guilt *in flagrante*, and with all the ingratiation I could muster I feigned an earnest desire to bribe my visitors into relenting connivance, in respect of:

'Shall we say fifty pistoles?'

'How dare you, monsieur?' scoffed the greffier.

'Not never for a *hundred* pistoles!' the senior sergeant, he that blocked the door, exclaimed with priceless disdain.

'Nay, nay,' said the landlord, as though behind me in spirit, as he stood in his dishonest flesh. 'Worthy sergeant, be not too severe upon my young gentleman lodger. Consider his youth. His inexperience of the wicked city. Echimillia is a tender-hearted man, for all that he is of his race, and would not wish for a harsh revenge. Accept therefore, for my sake, the hundred pistoles the young gentleman has offered you, and let him go free this time.'

The sergeants and the greffier then began, as it were grudgingly at first, but with mounting generosity, to exhibit symptoms of mercy, and to express their pity for my youth and innocence of the ways of Paris, all with so much self-congratulating solemnity, that for a brief spell my woes in general were forgotten, my indignation and anger of the moment were vanquished, and I collapsed backwards on to my bed, overcome with a childish laughter so unexpected, and so near hysterical, that the tears coursed forth from my eyes.

Perceiving the fit of mirth upon me, the two bogus sergeants appeared more than a little confounded, not to say insulted; but the greffier, a little man, whose risible organs were evidently unsuited to the legal severity of the role into which he had been cast, found himself unable to resist the infectious nature of my guffawing, and broke into a sort of bass cachinnation, which he at first attempted to disguise as a cough, and then to stifle in the sleeve of his robe, but with conspicuous lack of success.

This plague of hilarity next afflicted the hirsute landlord, who, with one eyebrow raised in censure, while the other wriggled beyond all control, as his lips enacted a desperate battle not to grin, was within a minute overpowered by the ludicrous incongruity of the greffier's failure to smother his laughter, and hence erupted likewise, although rather in deafening bellows, which made the timbers of the floor vibrate beneath our feet, while the host's great fat sides shivered. By now the sham officer by the window, being of a younger and more impressionable stamp, was also overcome by giggles, which were high and near hysterical in pitch, as often is the case with younger women in a flock. But he at the door, being perhaps the principal mover in this scheme, and feeling himself most at the threshold of a loss, was quite the contrary in his reaction.

With a snarl of fury this thwarted charlatan stepped forward with his sword raised high. Whether it was to intimidate me into compliance with his will, or really to run me through, shall never now be known, for the prospect of his importunate rage so switched my own attitudes into a total reversal that ere he had taken two steps I was up upon my toes to greet him, had knocked the blade from his hand by dint of a blow to his wrist, had grappled his garments by the throat and thrust him back to the landing without, and with my right hand, which now pressed the tip of my own dagger beneath his ear, had by chance brushed off his head the helmet of his borrowed office, to reveal a telltale head beneath.

This was, in short, the very identical person of my hectoring guide on that first night in Paris, he who had bragged of his unparalleled success with women, then of his incomparable knowledge of the city, before leading me off as far as possible away from the Palais where I wished to go.

'*Eh bien*, my gallant guide,' I murmured, as I gouged my dagger a little way into the flesh of his neck. 'So it is you?' For it really was most ingenious how he had contrived to change completely the shape of his face, by cutting his immense beard into a small peak – more like a beard of gentry – shaving each of his cheeks, and leaving nothing but a light moustache on his upper lip.

'No offence, your honour,' he now squirmed in a different voice. 'We was just having a little jest on you, see. For a wager. Ain't that right, lads?' he inquired most supplicatingly of his colleagues.

'You are a most miserable scoundrel, my friend,' I informed him calmly. 'But what intrigues me most, I do admit it, is how such a wily buffoon as you, could fantasize for a moment, any hope of duping me, with a ruse so stale as this. Hmn?' And for good measure, and to encourage his confessional eloquence, I scythed a light wound in his neck.

At this he screamed most like a rabbit being got by the throat by a stoat, and I scented vermin urine, rising up from his dampened hose.

'What say you, rogue?' I pursued him, shaking his collars, as he whimpered to feel his blood ooze.

'It were because of your Flemish lace, monsieur,' explained the window man, 'what you wore in our midst at dinner.' Still giggling, at the sight of his senior's discomfiture, the younger villain now showed his core to be forged of sterner stuff, as he continued:

'But come, monsieur. You have found us out, fair do's, but now you must let Caesar go.'

'Oh, I must, must I?' Abandoning the vanquished Caesar to his blubbering, I now turned to confront the younger man, who by this time had his short sword drawn.

'We shan't not bother you no more,' the giggler promised shamelessly.

'How very right you are,' I agreed, then rushed upon him, deflected his weapon wide, broke it from his grasp, pinned his wrists behind his back, and bundled him from the window to the cessheap forty hands below. 'If ever there be another time,' I called after him, 'it shall be your *life* goes flying!'

When I turned back to treat further with the three other fraudsters, I saw naught but their heads bobbing hastily down the stairs, and though for a moment I deliberated giving chase, and pursuing them for justice, ere I could enact this impulse I was overwhelmed by a tide of unspeakable lassitude, followed swiftly by the most abject despair: at the realization, not only that my solitude in this wickedest of cities was more absolute than ever, but also that the grubby comfort of my cell in this sinful auberge could be mine no longer – as, with my last coins so nearly spent, I must seek a new lair for my woes.

'Why accord so trivial an episode such extensive coverage?' You may visualize Janet Roublestein objecting.

And if so we must reply: partly because the bogus-sergeants scam is one of the few incidents during these months which Louis himself has recorded in unbroken narrative; but mainly because both the narrative tone (which, unusually, Louis seems to have taken a certain pride in polishing) and the details themselves tell us much about his state of mind, feelings, and what R.D. Laing might have termed his ontological security – or lack of it – throughout those listless August days. Most especially revealing, even conventional psychoanalysts should agree, is Louis's explosion – at just the point where a more mature and confident adult male human of like martial prowess (not necessarily older than Louis now is, but nonetheless past the point of what veterinary surgeons discussing the aging process in your pussycat refer to as 'diminution of playfulness') might well have launched straight into retributive blows, swipes, dagger thrusts, and kicks of buttocks down stairs – into typically adolescent laughter.

Is this not conclusive proof, if corroboration were needed, of a young man's emotional instability, vulnerability, desperation to be liked, craving for company . . . really to the point where, had not the boastful Caesar sergeant's thwarted rage aborted Louis's nascent mirth, and ignited his volatility into catastrophic reaction, we might well have had an outcome wherein Louis benevolently forgave the red-handed conmen, admired their brazen audacity, engaged them as temporary henchmen, and harnessed their earning ingenuity into replenishing his own dire exchequer?

If the world of unactualized possible worlds[2] were not so infinite, or nearly infinite, or nearly nearly infinite . . . , we might seriously attempt a completely rounded moving picture in full Technicolor® of Louis's character and history via the reflexive nuances revealed by exploring to the limit all the probable consequences of things he might have been a breath away from saying, and deeds he could well have been a kiss away from doing, but didn't. Fortunately (Charlton will probably opine, though Janet may opt to differ) such absolute verisimilitude is not now and never was nearly so possible as flying to the moon on a bicycle, out of which consideration we are certainly licensed, and some may feel obliged, to follow Louis into the next few months by means of a series of hops, skips, and loops which a self-conscious perpetrator of fictions in more than one dimension might confess to under the description 'narrational helicoptering', and which blithely goggle-eyed American teenagers achieve for themselves a hundred times a night by stabbing as hens peck at the *Fast Forward* and suchlike slave controls on their video system zappers.

Like so . . .

---

[2] Cf, for starters, the fat bald man wearing Plato's beard in that doorway astride Pegasus, as floated by Willard Van Orman Quine in *From A Logical Point Of View*.

# 27

# Out & Down

Louis vacates the shady auberge within the hour.

He goes in search of and late that afternoon relocates the honest grocer whose honest son, on his first night in Paris, led him at last to the Cardinal's Palais. To the honest grocer he confesses his homeless pickle, and through his honest offices is by dinnertime installed in what we would now call digs, *chez* a lonely homely widow of an age beyond temptation (at least for Louis), who has the additional advantage of being not Parisian by birth.

His landlady is tall, skinny as a stick insect, and has faded grey hair and blue eyes. She is eminently clean, kind, much respected, and has no close friends locally. To Louis she seems like a highaway bird flying serenely in skies of a constant past, for whom touching down occasionally in the imperfect present is a duty to be cheerfully borne. To cook and serve up his dinner, for example.

For several days, perhaps a week, Louis does nothing but wallow in the comfort and security of not feeling preyed on by everyone around him, and a pleasant sense of anonymity deriving from the reflection that no-one else in the world who might possibly want to interfere with him – not even the Cardinal – could have any clue as to his whereabouts.

Or could he?

What about the secret police?

When worries about his impending absolute destitution come alight again they clone and spread to buzz round the scenario wherein the Cardinal in fact knows perfectly well where Louis is lodged, and is merely paying him out the rope of a few days' grace in which to get himself hanged if he doesn't hoof it back in time to report his change of address to the Palais porter's lodge.

Louis is thus not wholly unlike a reasonably honest but penniless citizen in Tory Britain who, having changed abodes, must weigh the devil of being pursued for an insane local government tax he cannot afford to pay – if he declares himself – against the deeply shitty sea of not being able to vote against the party he most abominates, if he[1] keeps his whereabouts secret.

Increasingly, in the evenings, after bidding Madame Beaupère goodnight, Louis examines, fondles and fantasizes over the sparkling candlelit facets of the Villafranca gems – which, since accepting custody of them from Achilles before leaving Marseille, he has carried in a pouch attached to a sash inside his clothes.

Now the Villafranca necklace of diamonds, though individually of fewer carats and less uniquely priceless than the all-time heavyweight greats – such as the *Koh-i-noor* and the Sancy – were nonetheless collectively, and as an integrated unity of exquisite jewellery, so stunning to look at, to touch, and to imagine setting off the soft smooth throat and pulsing bosom of the sweetheart who can never now be yours, that it never once, during the first month of his stay *chez* the Widow Beaupère, occurred to Louis to hock them.

For where, from whom, in the underworld of Paris, could Louis – a stranger; a gentleman thinly disguised; a queer fish like a sore thumb in the argot and ethos of theft and fencing barter . . . could he hope to obtain one thousandth part of what the diamonds must truly be worth?

And besides, what about the sternly moralistic injunctions he had laid upon Achilles?

*Bludgeoned, as he would say, by my counsels of probity, little Achilles had . . . heroically resolved to return the diamonds to their rightful owner, if ever he found the opportunity, which quite likely he did not much anticipate . . .*

But what contempt, nevertheless, must the browbeaten servant feel hereafter, if ever he should discover that his high-principled master had later stooped to flogging the booty himself, and a for a rock-bottom price at that?

Thoughts such as those are constantly at the back of Louis's mind, and make frequent pilgrimages to its forefront, in those early October days

---

[1] Alternatively: 'an insane local government tax he or she cannot afford to pay – if he or she declares himself or herself – against the deeply shitty sea of not being able to vote against the party he or she most abominates, if he or she keeps his or her whereabouts secret.' From *How to Crucify an Innocent Sentence* (Janet Roublestein, ed.) §69; Bacchante Press, forthcoming.

when, all his coins bar a few sous gone, he confesses his penury to Madame Beaupère, and is touched and embarrassed to the point of tears when that good lady's immediate response is to extend him a month's credit on his rent, and stuff a cash loan in his fist.

'Thank you, thank you,' gabbles Louis in grateful bewilderment. 'But really I can't possibly . . . '

'Of course you can, monsieur,' Madame Beaupère contradicts him, with matter-of-fact serenity. 'And you must.'

Realizing he has no option but to accept, Louis is stung into rash profusions of confidence about how the debt will be repaid: either from an influx of funds from his father back home – which is long overdue, he says – or out of wages paid him by the Cardinal, who has promised him lucrative employment.

Alone again in his room that night, Louis flushes with shame at the deceit of his promises to the widow, and with remorse at the attempted seduction of Hélène and the shooting of Jean-Baptiste which landed him in this treacly soup in the first place, and now make it impossible for him to write home for the sort of help any normal young gentleman in Paris would expect every second week, and as a matter of right.

Then comes self-hatred, on the back of self-accusation: that the root reason he has not advised the Palais of his new address is his own despicable cowardice: fear of the Cardinal's merciless justice, should he hear of the killing of Jean-Baptiste.

Furiously rejecting this charge of conscience, since a gentleman is never a gentleman if not fearless, Louis elects immediately to go for broke – or rather, the reverse – in his relationship with the Cardinal.

So he rushes out into the starlit Paris streets, and makes his way to the Palais, there to leave his details with the porter.

How in any case, he consoles himself by considering, could Richelieu enlist his services:

If (a) he believed young Monsieur Morel to be trying to hide?

Or (b) he was genuinely ignorant of his whereabouts?

'At the Palais, despite the hour, there were tonight all classes of persons of both sexes going in and coming out. Every style of dress imaginable was on display, from the princely justaucorps whose arabesqued embroidery left scarce an inch of the original material visible, to the threadbare pourpoint, whose overlong service in the ways of

the world had rendered it thinly smooth, as an old courtier's tir-
ing tongue.

'When at the porter's lodge window I explained my business, I
was invited round behind the scenes; principally, I suspect, to relieve
the plump porter and his young lieutenant from the labour of writing my details. "Right there," said the porter, having produced from
a cupboard a ponderous ledger, full of thousands of names, which
he now banged down on the table in front of me, and stabbed at
with his finger. When, in the next available boxes, I neatly inscribed
my real name, and Madame Beaupère's address, the porter, breathing heavily, leaned over me, read with effort, and said with some
impatience:

'"Should have saved yourself the trouble, my son. We got that
one weeks ago." In proof of which, he flicked back several pages
bearing hundreds of names, and referred my attention to the exact same
information, in a small but neat black hand.

'Minutes later I departed from the Palais Cardinal for the second
time; feeling, if that were possible, even more hopeless than when I
arrived.'

On his way home Louis drifts into a boisterous cabaret. There, on
Madame Beaupère's borrowed cash, he begins to drink. Soon he is
approached by a luscious strumpet, who takes him for a soft touch.
At first he chivalrously buys her a drink but declines her more carnal
advances. An hour later he adjourns to spend an hour on her in a
seamy closet nearby. After that he returns to the cabaret and, tacky
with self-reproach, gets thoroughly drunk. After being ejected from
the cabaret at shortly before dawn, Louis allows the last three or four
small coins in his care to be wheedled out of him by a legless beggar
in the Rue St Jacques. Then he realizes he is too drunk to find his way
home, so slumps down to sleep it off in the shelter of a stableyard
archway.

Thus begins a phase of several-week dereliction in Louis's life. His
borrowing from the widow gets more shameless as it grows more
shameful. His drabbing becomes ever more basic and sordid as his
alcohol dependency escalates. So far down the slippery slope does
he slide that his memory is impaired – to the point where, frequently,
he is unable to recall what he did the night before. Where? Who
with? Who to? The account he has left us of those days, though not
consciously disingenuous, is tantalizingly sketchy. 'How could I have

allowed myself', he will declaim in an isolated outburst, 'to engage in such reprehensible deeds?' Yet often that is all: the reprehensible small print is withheld.

For an eloquent objectionable correlate to Louis Morel's miserable exile in Paris that year, we can think of nothing closer than the various exiles of Byron – in London, Venice; the world. Louis was no sort of poet, and in the main his prose lags leagues behind the forthright fireworks of Byron. But on many other counts the correspondences are remarkable. Both were highborn aristocrats, physically robust, athletic and courageous. While Byron never misses a chance to slily boast of his prowess at swimming, Louis too was quietly proud of the aquatic skills he developed in his teens, after the millpool drowning from which Jean-Baptiste saved him.

On women.

Both Byron and Louis were vigorous debauchers of them. 'In the last two years,' wrote Byron to John Murray from Venice, 'I have had more women than I can count or recount . . . ' And yet, with a few pedestalled exceptions – like Louis's rose-tinted adulation of his mother, and Byron's deathly devotion to his half-sister, Augusta Leigh, whom Bertrand Russell felt strongly he (ie Byron) should never, as a true-blue English earl, have rogered[2] – they also share a somewhat condescending disdain, sometimes sated disgust, for the gender on whom they preyed. The phrase 'no high regard for the sex' recurs like a chorus throughout Lord Byron's confessions.

On drink.

'I drank more than I like,' is another Byron riff, which can just as well

---

[2] See the *History of Western Philosophy*, Book Three, Chapter XXIII. Russell, in our view, wrote this work because he needed the money. While this may be pardonable in a novelist, it is less so in a philosopher. Even Wringhim, give him his due, makes no secret of not expecting 'to make a fucking penny' out of his 'major philosophical essay'. In Russell's case one consequence was that he had not read all his authors sufficiently recently, or adequately at all. We believe this is true of his treatment of Byron (and also venture to suspect that Lord Russell might have done likewise, had he had half such a peachy half-sister as Lord Byron) and particularly of his failure to understand or fairly represent Schopenhauer (Book Three, Chapter XXIV).

characterize Louis. Then again: 'Yesterday, I dined out with a large-ish party, where were Sheridan and Colman . . . and others, of note and notoriety. Like others of the kind, it was first silent, then talky, then argumentative, then disputatious, then unintelligible, then altogethery, then inarticulate, and then drunk . . . I carried away much wine, and the wine had previously carried away my memory – so that all was hiccup and happiness for the last hour or so, and I am not impregnated with any of the conversation.'

Uncommonly prescient of Glasgow writers today, indeed,[3] when they convene round Wringhim Knox, in McEwan's, to debate the state of the nation (Scotland), the war of liberation against the oppressor (Westminster), and how their publishers are ripping them off.[4]

And the Meaning of Life?

'I have been considering,' wrote Byron in 1821, 'what can be the reason why I always wake, at a certain hour in the morning, and always in very bad spirits – I may say, in actual despair and despondency, in all respects – even of that which pleased me over night. In about an hour or two, this goes off, and I compose either to sleep again, or, at least, to quiet.'

Ah, yes. Quiet.

'If I had to live over again, I do not know what I would change in my life, unless it were *for not to have lived at all*. All history and experience, and the rest, teaches us that the good and evil are pretty equally balanced in this existence, and that what is most to be desired is any easy passage out of it.

'What can it give us but *years*? and those have little of good but their ending?'

Now though it was Byron who wrote those words (again in 1821, when he was aged thirty-three), they might just as well have been uttered by Louis Morel during his Parisian ordeal in late 1640 (when he was aged twenty-one).

Whether Louis's claustrophobic pessimism is quite so constitutionally bottomless as Byron's, or to a greater degree a secondary biproduct of his present dismal circumstances, we are happy for our readers to

---

3 Provided, for Burgundy and Claret, you substitute Export and Grouse.

4 'Those that have publishers, I think you should add.' [P.C.]

determine.[5] What we can tell you, to assist, is that when even the gentle Widow Beaupère turns creditor worm, reads her dissolute lodger a motherly[6] riot act, lends him one final louis and serenely warns him:

'No more . . . '

Then we get Louis reflecting:

' . . . that I likened the dwindling of my change from that one gold piece to the handfuls of couscous they donate in Morocco, to condemned men slowly dying, of impalement.'

Stung crimson by the implacable tranquillity of Widow Beaupère's implied rebukes, Louis summons together 'the vestiges of my will' in a resolution to abjure toping and whoring, and to spend his few remaining pennies instead in a program of self-improvement, in the sense of upping his earning potential. To this end he spends the following morning on the trail of utilitarian literature, and eventually from a barrow vendor in the Rue St Jacques he buys two teach-yourself manuals: one on the history, theory and current practice of military strategy; the other on how to make a fortune by outsmarting your competitor gamblers. From that day forth he hardly stirs from his room, so wrapt is he in reading, re-reading, memorizing and extrapolating from the formulae, recipes, shortcuts and

---

[5] Byron himself remarked: 'I have found increasing upon me (without sufficient cause at times) the depression of Spirits (with few intervals), *which I have some reason to believe constitutional or inherited.*' Our italics. However, if you are a British Medical Wowser browsing for environmental and lifestyle grist for your etiological axe, you will doubtless be delighted by Byron's further confession:

'I have got very drunk with them both; but, if I had to *choose* . . . I should say, "let me begin the evening with Sheridan, and finish it with Colman." Sheridan for dinner – Colman for Supper. Sheridan for Claret or port; but Colman for everything, from the Madeira and Champaigne at dinner – the Claret with a *layer* of *port* between the Glasses – up to the Punch of the Night, and down to the Grog or Gin and water of daybreak.'

Even Wringhim Knox, to the best of our knowledge (which is better than many), has never sunk so low as gin at daybreak. A pint or two of chilled light Carlsberg, perhaps, but only to damp his thirst.

[6] 'Why, in English, is there no feminine of "avuncular"?' [J.R.]

surefire winning gambits in the pages he has purchased. At meal times, with the widow, he is once more his civilized, courteous self – yet distant, abstracted, and he declines even table wine with his meat.[7] One consequence of this born-again abstemiousness, happily for us, is that Louis's memory of the ensuing days is undamaged, and recorded in quotable detail.

I soon began [*he would recall*] to look upon the gaming-table as the only resource which Fate held out to me; for the military matters, with which I had become conversant, could hardly repair my fortunes, until I should come in some prospect of a suitable commission, with materiel and men to command.

Therefore, with indescribable assiduity, I rehearsed every calculation in that book [entitled *Hazard, Not Chance; The Surest Way Of Winning*] a hundred times, until every possible outcome became no longer a matter of arithmetic, nor even of memory, but of instinct.

Three more weeks elapsed.

By now I felt both qualified, and as confident as ever I should, of my ability to outgame the professionals of Paris. As I had no money remaining, then, on the security of my restored composure, and sobriety, I imposed on Madame Beaupère to advance me one very last louis – acutely conscious, all the while, that here, in my hands, were that dear good lady's life's savings.

That louis I changed into crowns, and with a pounding heart, as soon as the day fell to dusk, I proceeded to a certain house, in a *quartier* nearby, where, so my honest friend the grocer had informed me, there took place every night the sort of serious gambling I required, but for the order of minor stakes which were all that I, with my pittance of crowns, could afford to venture.

A narrow passage lined with filth led me soon to a steep wooden stairway. At its bottom I could make out the drone of many voices in the building above. On a small platform at the top of the stairway, like the base of a hangman's gibbet, two men of middle years, very red in the face, were wrangling with great aggression, over the failure of some joint endeavour. As they ignored me, I squeezed past them, ducked under an oaken lintel, and arrived at the threshold of a spacious though

---

[7] Cf Byron's Jekyllish regimen: 'I have fed at times for two months together on *sheer biscuit and water* (without metaphor) . . . '

low-ceilinged room, with two wide windows at its further end. There were some twenty small tables dotted about, all square, and in most cases lined by two, three, or four intently faced citizens, with little mounds of coins at their wrists – some very little indeed – and either cards or dice on the tables between them.

'That will be one crown, please, sir,' said an ingratiating voice at my elbow.

'What on earth for?' I rejoined, turning to regard the politely serious countenance of a small man with a pale face, whose shoulders, body and legs reminded me of a black rat with no tail.

'Admission, sir,' he deferentially explained, and as I wished to play, I paid.

The odours in that place were manifold, noisome and fetid. Frowns and scowls of devouring passion, debasing vice, and sheer squalid misery were inscribed on every forehead I beheld. All the players were men, and, though I had by now a fair idea of what likely took place in the upper storeys, here the only women in view were two maids – plain of feature, thick in body, and grandmaternal in years – whose role it was to ferry fresh flasks of wine to the tables, when they espied a terse forefinger raised.

Suddenly the whole degrading scene inspired my every sense with a sickening revulsion. The slimy moistness of the constant sniffs and coughs; the sharp, hissing intakes and plosive exhalations of halitoid breath; the clipped drawling urgency of the muttered bids and responses; all was a tableau of ugliness so far from the blue skies, green trees and honest healthy faces of my home, that I would have given much to turn on my heel, there and then, and gladly flee that den of sin – save only that I had naught to give worth giving, nor any other site of hope, to betake myself to.

'A throw of the dice, sir?' the rat-like fellow, breaking in upon my reflections, proposed in tempting tones. 'Or something more – shall we say? – *scientific*?'

'If anyone felt like piquet . . . ' I suggested with a nonchalance I did not feel, for piquet, I was confident, was the one game I could not lose.

'Ah, yes. Yes, yes. The game at table seven is nearly over, I believe. For Monsieur Girème . . . will have to be leaving soon. And Monsieur Dunois, I have no doubt, will be delighted to oblige you.'

Now the detail into which Louis goes, on the vicissitudes of his gambles, particularly when he embarks on complicated arithmetical defences of the moves he chose to make, and the bids he wagered, would drastically overdraw us beyond the word budget agreed for this chapter. The nitty gist, however, goes as follows.

Monsieur Dunois seems at first reluctant, making out that his wife was expecting him home hours ago, and also that he has already lost quite enough for one night to the devilish Monsieur Girème. The Ratman then presses Monsieur Dunois, as a special favour to him, to vouchsafe the courteous newcomer (that's Louis) the pleasure of half an hour's sport. Monsieur Dunois hums, haws, finally kindly agrees; and he and Louis sit down facing each other at piquet.

'Piquet', says *Britannica*, 'is essentially a game for two players . . . The pack of 32 cards is used . . . Twelve cards are dealt to each player . . . The remaining eight cards, the stock, are spread face down. If either player holds carte blanche (a hand with no court card) he announces it and scores ten points. Nondealer (also called elder, or major) discards from one to five cards and draws an equal number from the top of the stock. If he leaves any of the first five, he may look at them and replace them without showing them to Dealer . . . ' and so on for a further nine densely rule-governed paragraphs.

Monsieur Dunois, according to Louis, plays a bold and more hazardous game, by comparison with Louis's own more cautious, systematic, and theoretically successful approach. Only 'some fortunate runs of the cards' in this game make Dunois eventually the winner, and even then Louis's loss is 'but two crowns'.

'Double or quits, for the little you have lost?' proposes Dunois cheerily, passing Louis a cup of dice.

Knowing he shouldn't, since no scientifical scheming will give him an edge with the dice, Louis accepts. Throws; loses. Throws again; loses again. 'Then we threw one final time – and I was penniless. I bore it more calmly than I would have had expected, but now had no alternative but to thank my adversary for the entertainment of his company, and withdraw into the cold wet night.'

As Louis walks away, he overhears Dunois observing in a whisper to the Ratman:

'He plays fiendish well at piquet, you know. That young gentleman. If Luck tonight had been evenly shared between us, he would surely have cleaned me out. Better watch him, in future.'

Louis is of course never so crass as not to realize that whisper was destined for his attention, but neither is he immune to its effect. What was it the Cardinal had said? *If the flattery be too thick . . . you may*

*scrape some of it aside, as with your excessive rouge. But you will also
take infinite pains, rest assured, not to wipe away the base.*

With the result that, the following morning, after a miserable three-
hour sleep, Louis is again astride the thorny puzzle of how to scrape
up enough cash with which to present himself for a second attempt in
the gambling den. The Villafranca diamonds? Again he fondles them,
debates the options, and again rejects this possibility; though this time
more on practical grounds, and less on moral. The Widow Beaupère?
No! In his rejuvenated sobriety he absolutely cannot bring himself to
touch her for one more sou. In any case, he is seriously concerned that
his former depredations have all but broken the widow's bank. Fresh
red meat, for example, has not been seen on her table for several days.
Well then?

'"Thank Heaven," I thought then, "that I still have my signet ring."
This was of purest gold – no diamonds – and, aside from the splendid
workmanship, and the evident antiquity of its pedigree, must have
seemed, to the vulgarest eye, worth a very handsome price, for the
value of its metal alone. As my mother, with her own hands, had fitted
it upon my finger, not long after my final return from Pau, and after
she had recovered from her distress, at my fracas with the Marquis of
Roquefort, it required on my part a monumental conviction of necessity,
to overcome my fond filial feelings, to the point where I could part with
that ring.

'In fetching it, from a secret flap within my valise – for since my
flight from Morel I had not worn the ring, lest its seal proclaim
my family name, or its gold my gentry stature – I encountered again,
within the same repository, that packet of papers regarding the Count
of Bagnols, about which, in recent weeks, I had completely forgotten.
Shivering alone in my room that morning – for it was recently become
December; cold and grey – as I waited for the hour to approach when
the doors of moneylenders, pawnsters, and dealers of like ilk would
be opened, I read again through the whole correspondence, between
the Count himself – then a young man such as I was now – and the
rebellious Rochellois. And vibrating as it were in harmony with every
phrase in Monsieur Bagnols' hand, I seemed to hear the uplifting music
of a fine discrimination, between right and wrong, which, so natural and
effortless as it was, I felt must constitute the essence of true chivalry of
the mind. All this to me was a vast implicit reproach: of my undeniable
hand in the maja's death; Father Francis too; then my importunate
caressing of Hélène by the stream; my shooting of poor Jean-Baptiste;

my flight from my parents with no word of farewell; and of late my over-indulgence in spiritous drink; my unfeeling rental of tired harlot loins; my inexcusable frittering of the Widow Beaupère's hard-saved nest egg; and now . . . now . . . '

In this vein he goes on for another 1653 words: upbraiding himself; bewailing the Fate that had left him so devoid of Grace – yes, and him a Catholic too, of a sort; extolling the superwomanly qualities and virtue of occasional ladies such as his mother, and of course Hélène; envying the spartan valour and relentless probity of such natural gentlemen as the Count of Bagnols and the Chevalier of Montenero; reviling himself again; and finally concluding wearily:

'But what are resolutions?'

'Akin to thin air!' you the reader may chortle, as you now learn that as soon as the pawnsters had a hope of being open, Louis hastened out without his hat, and hocked his ring in the second shop he tried: 'to a most respectable *Jew*eller, [*sic*] who bought it of me for perhaps one-fifth of its worth, and vowing all the while that he should certainly lose by this transaction.

'Six new louis, however, now swelled my purse; and, as I waited for night, and from my window watched the first snow of winter begin to fall, I glanced again and again at the subtler stratagems for piquet, in that cursèd book of games. At seven o'clock I stood again, my boots white with snow, at the foot of the stair to that establishment where I had left all my money, just twenty hours before.'

Tonight the society of gamesters strikes Louis as 'somehow even more ruffianly'. He fancies he senses 'every eye round the room turned upon me'. As Louis enters, the self-deprecating victor of the previous evening, Monsieur Dunois, is spectating on a tense four-way bout of *vingt-et-un*. Stirred by a sotto murmur in his ear from the circulating Ratman, the suave Monsieur Dunois breaks away from his onlooking, greets Louis with the warmth of long camaraderie, and regretfully supposes the young gentlemen has: 'returned tonight all primed to extract his revenge?'

'If that should please you also,' returns Louis, through teeth clamped by nerves.

'But of course. Of course. As our stakes are so modest – unlike . . . ' he gestures disapprovingly at the fraying tempers round the game of *vingt-et-un*. 'No gentleman, as you know, ever plays for the sole motive of winning a great deal of another man's money, and therefore he ought to take care – that he does not part with too much of his own. Me, I play for amusement purely, and therefore let us joust merely with crowns, as we did with such pleasure last night.'

Encouraged by this diffident moderation on the part of his opponent, Louis agrees. 'He again played boldly, and I with my same counting caution.' Strangely, though, tonight the cards seem no longer favourable to Monsieur Dunois. 'Lady Luck', he laments ruefully, 'has switched her allegiance.' Within an hour Louis has 'upward of fifty crowns in a heap by my elbow'. The *vingt-et-un* table has lost its audience, and all spectators have gravitated round the gladiators at piquet. As Louis continues to win, he hears grudging wishes in the background: wishes that such skill was less unique. Meanwhile one of the wine maids keeps a goblet by his right hand charged with really quite passable Burgundy – 'on the house,' the Ratman nods admiringly.

'Too adept for me, you are, I fear,' says Monsieur Dunois, rubbing his perspiring brow with a kerchief, for a crackling fire and all those unhealthy bodies in a low-ceilinged space have cooked up a good hot fug, in despite of the snow without. 'But though you are plainly my master at cards, you will not refuse me, I trust,' the courteous loser goes on, *his vexation commendably restrained*, as he snaps his fingers at the Ratman, 'a more equal opportunity, of mending my fortune with . . . these?'

Suddenly, as by magic, the cup of dice is back on the table, warmly greeted by a hush of gasps – for here comes a battle that every man can follow. Just like when a contest of masterclass chess gives way to heavyweight boxing. And Louis? Does he wisely bow out? Withdraw chanting grateful regrets, and so on? Well, no. As you've guessed, quite the contrary. Even, which is doubtful, had the gambling-den regulars been disposed to allow him to depart, so many crowns up, Louis is already doomed within himself:

' . . . by the evil spirit which had overcome me. I had gained so much as to wish to gain so much more. Bright hopes of buying myself out of all difficulties, of dicing my way to Triumph over Fate, began to swim before my eyes, not a little assisted by the fumes of that heady Burgundy, which in turn, all thanks to my absolute continence of late, had risen to my brain like summer larks.'

They throw.

Dunois wins.

Throw again.

Same result.

Double or quits?

Dunois cleans up for the third time in succession.

'And I watched the coin, which had adorned my side, mounding higher and higher on his. Oh, what agony of mind I experienced then; of conscience, remorse, despair . . . giving way, in my desperation, to *suspicion*. At piquet, the cards had been squarely dealt – that was plain. But what about these dice?'

Thinking back to the night when he and Old Hussaye caught the Fat Monk (who was really Monsieur Saint Simon) and his Thin Accomplice conniving at cards, in the sleazy Luz inn, Louis is overtaken by the conviction that here, now, there is some chicanery afoot with these dice. How else could they fall out so overwhelmingly in Dunois's favour? Thrice running? And at such a crucial time?

'Treble or quits?' Monsieur Dunois magnanimously offers.

Louis accepts, having determined to notice some fishy bias as the dice roll to rest: some evidence of weighting?

But no. Not only do all five dice, when tossed by Monsieur Dunois, appear to turn with random abandon, but even the winning hand (Dunois's three queens, to Louis's pair of pairs) is quite distinct from the previous round, in which Louis's two kings were trounced, to a chorus of hisses and cheers all round the table, by a fourth twirling knave from Dunois.

So what now?

Apparently observing that Louis has too few coins remaining to play again, Dunois affects to begin winding up his evening, and gathers his winnings towards him.

'Quadruple or quits?' proposes Louis grimly, his pink eyes balefully daring the winning player to back away now.

As horrified exclamations and exulting cackles circle round the room, and secondary wagers are bandied:

'But, Monsieur!' protests Dunois. 'I do not see . . . '

'I am good for it,' vows Louis. 'If *I* lose, *you* shall not.'

Whence Louis's access of confidence, given access to no further funds? It is because 'my memory was become pregnant' with swelling images of Dunois's manner of handling the dice: how the professional gambler, 'with the dexterity of a juggler' would pince up all five dice like tiny nuggets of coal between the five long white fingers of his left hand only, turn them upwards through two right-angles with a showman's flourish, as he might the steaming lid off a pot, then popping them into the cup in his right hand, shaking it with great concentration of superstition by his right ear, before bundling the little cubes down out of the cup to the baize, with an outspreading gesticulation of both hands like a breaststroker starting to swim.

So much of Dunois's pre-throw dumb show, indeed, could be geared to the swapping of dice, in and out of his long frizzy sleeves, that Louis is rapidly convinced, *not* that the villain has been slipping in *favourably* weighted dice for his own throws, but rather that the exchanges have been made more cunningly: to remove *inferior* dice loaded for *bad* hands, with which Louis has just made his throw. That would explain why his own best hand, in the three throws tonight, was the two pairs that lost to three queens.

Would it not?

Throbbing with certainty that it *must*, Louis waits till, following his own throw, again a low two pairs, Monsieur Dunois is approaching a climax of good-luck rattling by his ear. Then Louis rises up like a devil through a stage trapdoor, hurls himself over the table, pinions Dunois's slender wrists in his own powerful hands, and shouts:

'His sleeves! His sleeves! The brigand has leaded dice in his sleeves. Search him, search him!'

A predictable pandemonium ensues, of bustling and jostling, and theorizing for and against the likelihood of this outrageous accusation holding water. Louis is fawningly persuaded by the Ratman to back off, as Monsieur Dunois with crucifixional dignity agrees to remove his upper garments – in full view of all.

When none of the groping hands so eagerly lent discovers any morsel of smuggled ivory about Monsieur Dunois, the corporate animus turns exceedingly ugly against Louis.

'Lying bastard.'

'Wot's 'ee fink 'ee's abat?'

'Slit the fuckah's froat frim.'

And other hostile cries rend the air. A moment later, Monsieur Dunois, having resumed the dignity of his chemise, walks round the table to where Louis stands in his quandary, all organs clenched, and fuming.

'You have insulted me despicably, sir,' sneers Dunois, who then backhands Louis across the nose.

Louis's second nature is to pluck for his sword, but this has been anticipated by some forty hands which now pile into him, seize hold of him, belt him about the head, tear his own sleeves off him, manhandle him off the floor and over to the windows . . . as the Ratman shouts stridently to the wine maids:

'Shutters open!'

Seconds later the defenestrated body of the latest foxed dicer in Paris is frozen for an inertial instant in the cold flaky air, before it plummets like a castaway hay bale, through the snowthick city night.

# The Great Debate Begins

Thank you, Madam Chair.[1] Second of all I sincerely thank this house for asking me to speak on a matter so close to my own vital organs. Third of all I misquote from Sir David Lyndsay, as follows:

> Friends, undergraduates, Sassenachs, lend me your ears;
> For I come to bury the motion, not to praise it.
> The evil that false motions do lives after them,
> So 'tis good to strip them to their fallacious bones,
> And so we shall with this.

Like all politicians, Mark Antony is less concerned with truth than with *persuasion*. His honourable-man speech is clever because it *seems* to want one conclusion (that we're all well rid of Caesar), while the rhetoric is secretly aimed at a very different conclusion – and one which is not mentioned in the latest Pizz lager posters: that Brutus and Co are despicable murderers. But so what?

So this:

That *rhetoric is the art of persuading the plebs.*

A good rhetorical speaker, like Mark Antony, does not ram deductions into his audience's ears at the outset. He introduces his premises diffidently, gives his listeners time to draw their own conclusions, and thus encourages them to swell with pride in what they feel to be their own intellectual achievements.

Rhetoric *may* persuade the plebs of what is true. But mostly it aims to align the will of the throng with the will of the speaker.

The objective of rhetoric is hence not insight, but rather *achievement*

---

[1] 'I think a little footnote here on people – male or female – being "chairs". Frankly, *I*'d say "Madam Chair*man*", but that's not in character with Janet, who'd probably be politically correct with "Chair*fem*".' [J.R.]

*of intention.* Not *perception* of truth, but rather *control of others' beliefs.* Hence, also, control of their *behaviour.*

I began with the nature of rhetoric – and why?

Because here we are tonight, in a debating chamber, debating a motion, and because in such debating situations – particularly those broadcast from London – it is just such empty, bombastic, despicable *rhetoric* that so frequently infects even the noblest-hearted of Scots with forgivable cynicism, and drives us, trembling with the fury of thwarted self-determination, out of our flats and down to McEwan's – where, I should inform you, the Pizz is precisely twice the price of what you lucky buggers are paying at the bar here tonight. So make the most of it, kiddos.

I, by contrast – I mean by contrast with the wankers in West-minster – am very fortunate tonight, in possessing two immense advantages. That was what I had written in my notes, but I am now going to mention first an impromptu third advantage, and it is this. That, conspicuously unlike the two first speakers *for* the motion, you will notice, Madam Chair, that *I* shall not *insult* anyone – having no *need* to do so, even had I any such *desire.* Thus:

Young Mr Shambley there, or whatever his name is, who spoke first for our wrongly dishonourable enemies – Mr Shambley, I say, in his desperate tirade of barely audible slavering, has insulted my right honourable colleague Mr Humbert Seale, on the ground that even such a red-blooded able-bodied be-testicled person in the prime of his virile youth [such as Mr Shambley has the hilarious lack of perspective to represent himself as a being] is unable, he says, to stomach the level of wholly gratuitous sex and violence in Mr Seale's novels, without being quote violently sick unquote. Well:

(a) why not sexily sick?

And (b) it would seem that, curiously enough – or do I mean vicariously? – Mr Shambley must have managed to zip through a couple of Mr Seale's sickening fictions (sickening, it is true, but principally by virtue of their politically irresponsible and superficially Euro-directed A–Scottishness) in the twenty-minute interval between our prunes and ice-cream and the banging of Madam Chair's gavel. I say this because, as everyone almost now knows, if they didn't already, our young Mr Shambley there, or whatever his name is, was sick in the toilets twice in quick succession, immediately before he was called to order, and invited to unbutton his twaddle.

But perhaps, on reflection, I am being a little unkind here, and should ask you to wonder whether the real root cause of Mr Shambley's dinner returning into the world in two such multi-hued cluster-bombs – and you may take this as absolute Gospel, Madam Chair, for I was in there myself at the time, as it happened, in hopes of a peaceful wee – was the better self of his less conscious mind, shading into the possibly-not-yet-quite-annihilated wisdom of his unconscious body, coming over rightly stricken:

With *guilt*, Madam Chair . . .

At the *fundamental dishonesty*, Madam Chair . . .

Of *the incomparably puerile shit-slinging tactics*, Madam Chair, which Mr Shambley's intellectual bankruptcy was driving him to attempt, and which his heart-of-hearts knew was doomed to fail.

Are I pee, Mr Shambley.

And what next?

Ah, yes. Mr McColgate. And who, Madam Chair, does the second ranter for the motion elect to insult?

Myself.

And on what ground?

My underpants. The age, fabric, presentability in public, even the very *existence* of my underpants are called into slanderous question by poor Mr McColgate's best (because only) attempt to divert this house's attention from the primordial and indestructible *unwinnability* of the case for their catchpenny motion. I do not propose, Madam Chair, to insult this house's acumen, by rehearsing epistemological truisms – such as that, if my underpants are bereft of existence, they could hardly be expected also to possess age, fabric and public presentability – but rather to urge us all to join with me, in doing Mr McColgate the favour which his newspaper occasionally deserves, of striking from the record his unfortunate *argumentum ad Wringhim* tonight. And this because he must be forgiven for not having prepared any speech, in support of a motion which he knows fine is indefensible, especially given the weightier matters on his mind, such as what the fuck to say in the second leader in tomorrow morning's *Clarion*, on how many more bits of their anatomy the Tories are going to shoot themselves in with the Rich Fart Tax, of which as of two o'clock this afternoon Mr McColgate had not written or even thought of a single word, as he confessed to me in McEwan's.

Up yours, Jocko, and mind and pass that bottle over here the moment I subside.

Which brings me back, Madam Chair, to the first immense advantage which I rejoice in possessing tonight. It is – wait for it – being able to rely absolutely on – all ready? – the . . . *abnormal intelligence of this house.*

[THUNDEROUS APPLAUSE, CHEERS, RAAAS, AND BANGING OF BEERMUGS ON COLD HALL FLOORBOARDS.]

Second, and consequently, I have no need to stoop to rhetoric – even had I any inclination to do so – since I know that this house will take pleasure in following, agreeing with, and voting in favour of a few simple logical and common-sense considerations, all of which lead, inexorably, to the conclusion that this house does NOT believe that *modern writers use sex rather than talent.*

But what is it, actually, that this house believes it believes? Or rather, doesn't believe? It is:

*That . . . modern writers use sex rather than talent.*

MODERN WRITERS. USE SEX. **USE SEX** . . . RATHER THAN TALENT.

Surely not! For what motion could be more demeaningly fuzzy than that? Crying out for the strictest critiquing, as our fine furry cousins at Yale might say. Thus . . .

'What is a *modern* writer?' Wringhim went on to inquire, with only a dash of artless rhetoric.

A writer belonging to 'the modern age', perhaps? But what would that mean? If we took 'modern' in 'the modern age' to mean the same as 'modern' in 'modern history', as prescribed by, say, the Penguin *Dictionary of Modern History*, we would have go back to the French Revolution: to 1789. Hence Scott would be a modern writer, unequivocally, but what should we say about Burns? And if then 'with yet greater courage', we followed the curious practices of certain elder universities in England, we might find that 'modern history' began with the Roman occupation of Britain! That would make Sir David Lyndsay a 'modern' writer, and Robert Henryson too! Which would be a case of limiting ludicrousness, would it not? Since it would follow that *all* masters and mistresses of Scottish literature were *modern* masters and mistresses – which would be as minimally meaningful as the Radio Two disc jockeys who describe *all* the slop they play as 'wonderful' and 'marvellous'.

Then perhaps a 'modern writer' was a 'modernist writer'? Or should it now be a 'post-modernist writer'?

'Not being a lecturer in *English*,' boomed Wringhim, glaring disparagement at two single ladies pushing thirty who were, 'let alone a neo-post-deconstructionist, I cannot presume to suggest exactly which eras those slogans denote. I have, however, a sneaking suspicion that, for writers like myself, a marginally less inapposite description might be "*post*-post-modernist", with "*post*-post-post-modernists" warming up on the touchlines.

'My verdict, then, on the adjective "modern", as in the bare statement of our motion, is that it is incurably vague, and that this house therefore needs to groom it with a definition.'

Likewise with 'writer'. Was Godfrey Blobbs a writer? In obvious senses, yes. He wrote sentences, which his secretary typed into his word-processor, and which his wife and seventeen editors then tried to make comprehensible. He published books, which contained sequences of sentences, which, insofar as they were comprehensible, were not literally true. In this sense, again, Godfrey Blobbs *was* a writer of fiction.

'And yet, as he himself has frankly remarked – quote:

'"I'm *not* a writer. I'm a story-teller." *Rather like you, really, Seale*,' Wringhim flung aside at me, beneath his blazing breath.

Not dissimilarly with *Spews of the World* journalists. Were they 'writers'? In trivial senses, of course they were. They hammered out copy, met editors' deadlines – well, sometimes – and were members of the NUJ. 'And yet,' wailed Wringhim, his arms windmilling, 'the trivial senses are simply *too trivial* to be worth the bother of pursuing. To suggest, for example, that *This house believes that* **Spews of the World** *reporters use sex rather than talent* would be to state such a horrendous truism that no house so abnormally intelligent [CHEERS, RAAAS] as this would be persuaded to sacrifice a precious Wednesday evening in the boozer to debate it.

'My conclusion, then, with the noun "writer" is that its extension – that is the range of persons it denotes – requires meaningful restriction before this house can sensibly formulate the very motion in which it does not believe.'

We next came to the *use* of *sex*.

What on earth could it mean to say that 'modern writers *used* . . . *sex*'? Was it that some of them exploited their personal sexual allure in order to seduce vulnerable publishers with fat wallets? Might that explain how **** ******* became a financially successful novelist as well? But that would instantly revert us, wouldn't it, to the problem of what we understood by 'writer'?

Then again, perhaps the writers who 'used sex' were those – occasionally English, but mainly American – who, Miller/Hemingway-style, toured round the planet hoovering up new sexual experiences, in order later to describe them in what was presented as fiction – 'rather than risk the pain of real creation, or the exercise of genuine *talent.*'

'So my provisional conclusion regarding *sex*,' thundered Wringhim, who was really getting into his stride now, especially since Jocko McColgate, helpfully attempting to sabotage our side, had poured him a brimming paper tumblerful of Glenmorangie, 'is that how writers *use* sex is a third petitioner for careful distinctions, hand in glove with linguistic refinements.'

'SEX "RATHER THAN TALENT"!' now rattled the footlights. Rather than? But that could mean two significantly different things. It could mean *in the absence of*. Or it could mean *in preference to*. So our motion could be restated, either: *This house believes modern writers use sex* **because they haven't got any talent**. Or else: *This house believes modern writers* **prefer** *to use sex than to use talent.* Perhaps because using sex was less troublesome? Or . . .

'More lucrative, could it be?

'Therefore, I suggest, a fourth contention crying out for arbitration is what the expression "sex rather than talent" should be taken to mean.'

And on the back of those, and a few more such post-Wittgenstinging distinctions, Wringhim – by dint of several adroit conflations, and other mean rhetorical devices instantly transparent to anyone who had waded through his 'major philosophical essay' – arrived swiftly (intermittently flourishing the notes in his left hand while sucking at the diminishing Glenmorangie in his right) at the 'irrefutable conclusion' that: not only 'is it the case that no Scottish writer worth the salt on his porridge uses sex **rather than** talent', but, much more importantly, no genuine Scottish writer 'ever was, is now, nor ever shall be' who does not 'make joyous use of **both sex AND talent**'.

In final corroboration of which, Wringhim treated us all to three short verses by Burns, triumphantly followed, as his pinking eyes flashed taunts all round the hall, and he gaily ignored the increasingly agitated tinkling of Madam Chair's time-chimer, by a several-page quotation from his own work in progress: the pamphlet on *Succeeding at Sex in London*. This, in parts, was so provocatively full-frontal that even my own heart was felt to quail a little, convinced that Wringhim, before the evening was out, was going to proposition me about typesetting this ghastly document for him. And then, as with boisterous glee he recited a particularly purple patch, all to do with 'banishing bad vaj niffs from built-up areas', a half-dozen squadron of outraged feminists, including the two unmarried English Literature lecturers, rose up and stormed in a bristling body from the hall, despite the half-price white wine still available at the bar, trilling 'sick in the head', 'never could write decent prose', 'depraved old man', 'incurable alcoholism', 'clear need of psychiatric attention', and many other expressions of refined disapproval, until the rubber swing-doors flapped behind them.

'See me, McColgate?' exulted Wringhim, as, to rapturous applause from the multitude of his followers, he flopped back on to his chair and scooped up the other's whisky bottle in the same practised feint.

'Mnyuh?' replied the deputy editor of *The Clarion*.

'Just got shot of your six best votes for you!' enthused Wringhim. 'Let's see if Mr Marchmont[2] Seale can match that!'

---

[2] Marchmont being a middle-class Home Counties enclave to Edinburgh not wholly unlike Bearsden to Glasgow. To the best of our knowledge, however, no great short story writers are active or even alive in Marchmont today. Rather is it principally populated by elderly widows and spinsters, and their Scottie dogs that dote on After Eight mints, as you can tell from the pavement stools. Furthermore, and *pace* Knox's jibe, we personally have *never* resided in that quarter.

# Literate Life after Satellite Sex?

Aside from his few pints of sheepshearer lager with Jocko in McEwan's at lunchtime, Wringhim had been commendably abstemious all day, polishing his talk for the debate tonight to the point where he evidently hoped that an anglicized adaptation of it might be accepted for publication by the *The Crimes*, as an antidote to that Judas Rankles. He is notoriously capable of self-discipline, occasionally – Wringhim, I mean – and has been known to go for weeks on end with not a drop of alcohol on Mondays.

Thus it was that Scotland's premier novelist was present and fit to deliver by far the most memorable speech of the night, quite a lot of which is most faithfully transcribed in the previous chapter.

Next came Audrey,[1] third for the motion. Unfortunately we cannot copy to you such an accurate snapshot of what she said, since during her opening remarks I felt my Talkman click off in my breast pocket, and I knew from previous experience that Wringhim would kick up a fearful stink if he caught me taking it out to change over the cassette. 'Fucking toffee-nose Edinburgh Secret State . . . ' and other castigations that for the moment I could manage without.

One thing I do recall clearly about Audrey's gig, though: the way she kept returning to the point that all the historical evidence went to indicate that women's sex drives have always been every bit as strong as men's. I remember this particularly well on account of its prompting me, the third or fourth time she repeated it, to jump up without thinking and chant:

'Point of information, Madam Chair?'

'If Dr Macpherson wishes to take it, Mr Seale.'

'Keep it brief, Humbert, will you?' winced Audrey.

'I'd like to put it to Dr Macpherson, Madam Chair, whether certain

---

[1] Co-opted with reference to her principal publication to date: a 500-page monograph on *The Female Orgasm as a Politically Indecisive Factor in Sixteenth-century France*.

relatively recent episodes of twentieth-century history don't go to prove that *some* women's sex drives are appreciably – if not *disturbing-ly* – strong-*ger* than some men's?'

This treacherous ruse secured the general juvenile snigger it deserved, and I've always thought there are few sexual phenomena more stimulating than a tall broad-shouldered intellectual brunette blushing violently pink with embarrassment. But the point of any debate, at the end of the evening, is to *win*, and from that point of view my tactic was certainly successful: in dislodging Audrey even further out of whatever composure she had possessed at dinner. From then on she stuttered and ummed with a frequency that those familiar with her as an accomplished Senior Lecturer must have found scarcely credible.

The principal thrust of her argument, such as survived, was to the effect that while all *great* writers used 'sex *and* talent', in that, by definition, they *possessed* talent, and, insofar as Sex is, so to speak, inextricably bound up with Life, they naturally did not exclude Sex from their artistically dutiful coverage of Life, nevertheless it was true to the point of nauseating that many modern writers exploited Sex, utilizing little or no Talent, and this either because so to do was more immediately lucrative than anything more cerebrally taxing, or else, and quite simply, in lamentably many cases, because they – the 'writers' – were *possessed of no talent to use*. In the interests of verisimilitude we have to report that Audrey did name several names in this regard, but in the further interests of not being sued ourselves we are not going to repeat them – except to admit that two were sisters whose surname does not begin with X, and that Godfrey Blobbs wasn't mentioned at all.

'Finally,' I quote Audrey with generous hindsight, 'how we must wish it were *not* the case: that such bigoted lowbrows, and their publishers, would, for the better good of the public, and especially the public's children, *desist* from peddling such Filth without Flair, and become – oh, if only they could! – a degree or two more like Shakespeare, the ultimate literary genius, really the Mozart of drama, who – as even the odious and despicable Mr Humbert Seale, Madam Chair, has the decency to bring out, in his loathsome *Prince Hamlet, Hypostar* – who, I repeat, never prudish, observes and utilizes sex with witting candour, and who (I refer here again of course to Shakespeare, and not to Mr Seale), in his uniquely brilliant and multifaceted mirroring of Life, focuses more intensely on the paramount power of sexual motives, than leftover stereotypes from Victorian schoolrooms would prefer us to believe—'

'"With *my* tongue in *your* tale?"' The Deputy Editor of the *Clarion* leered up at her loudly.[2] '"Nay, come again!"'

This was the last straw on the back of Audrey's discomfiture, and, her time in any case being long up, she subsided in a fetching heap of Liberty-printed breast-heaving indignation.

To make way for me.

And I began with what I rightly calculated would get a cheap half laugh either way.

'How I do *agree* with Dr Macpherson!' I clapped. 'How very *generous* of her to clinch our case for us! And what do I mean by that, Madam Chair? Simply this. That yes, as Dr Macpherson so eloquently emphasizes, the principal subject of literature is what? Human life, none other. And what are the three great landmarks in our lives? They are of course: birth, copulation, and death. Now since, happily, most of us get to copulate – or, failing that, *want* to copulate – over a far longer period of time than is given us either to be born in, or to die, it is consequently not only permissible, but also artistically mandatory, that the novelist *must* allow sex to play a prominent part in the fictions he or she creates.

'In other words, Madam Chair, not only is there no contradiction between *sex* and *talent* in the achievements of creditable fiction, but quite the reverse is the case. That is to say: fiction which excludes, or attempts to exclude, sex entirely is either intended for children, or else it is utterly negligible. Or both. That in practice it is impossible to stifle the great tumescing impulse into absolute silence may be illustrated by the following quotation, from the *Guardian*'s report on a 1987 meeting of the British Association, addressing the issue of whether or not British children's books are overly Thatcherized and Whitehoused. Quote:

'"Mr Tucker, of Sussex University, read from Richmal Crompton's book, *William the Fourth*. Crompton was an unmarried classics teacher, and, Mr Tucker suggested, did not quite appreciate how riveting the description of William's Aunt Jane at the fair might be:

'"Aunt Jane had [quote] mounted [quote, quote] a giant cock. It went faster and faster. There came a gleam in her eyes, a smile of

---

[2] Quoting from *The Taming of the Shrew*. Scene & line you may unearth yourself in your CD ROM Shakespeare. Jocko is in reality more erudite than he appears most nights, and has written a seminal work on the Aretino Postures.

rapture on her lips. She seemed to find the circular motion anything but monotonous . . .

'"This [Mr Tucker] said, was the only bit of Richmal Crompton that reasonably approximated to normal playground conversation."'

All of which, I stressed, was not only:

'Indisputably correct, but also of crucial relevance to our theme . . . '

At this moment, now standing theatrically, I became aware that my declaiming gaze had fastened on the smooth clear facial features of a very attractive young woman who appeared to be gazing with wrapt-hearted dreaminess at me. This was Jennifer Macpherson, who evidently had come along tonight to bolster her unmarried mother, and perhaps to get a taste of how excitingly sordid undergraduate existence would be for her too, in less than a year from now. What a pity, I then went on to reflect, that Jennifer was not really *looking* at me at all, but merely pretending to project her attention at the any-old-footlighted-cynosure of the moment, while inwardly she wallowed in the primal physical delight of having her left breast stroked beneath her Aran sweater,[3] and its nipple mechanically needed, by the pony-tailed boyfriend beside her – a second-year zoology student, as Audrey would confess to me later.

As the back of my mind attempted to rally from this latest trauma, its middle earth realized with a jolt that the automatic pilot joysticking his mouth had by now rambled to the brink of a less trivial argument, to be shunted along these lines:

'And what precisely, Madam Chair,' I demanded of her with portentous intensity, 'are we to embrace as a *modern writer*? Hmm? Absolutely not the tetchy old men of the fifties. Certainly not the long-grey child of the sixties. No more the faded superbrats of the seventies. Then how modern, now, are the writers of the 1980s?

'And the answer, in respect of our great debate tonight, is inevitably:

'*Not nearly modern enough!*'

'And why is that?

'Partly, I put it to you ["certainly would love to," cried out my

---

[3] The Union hall was some ten degrees colder than members of parliament, bank clerks, judges and the like would dream of consenting to work in. Due, as ever, to inadequate government funding of education.

silent subtext], because the eighties are already history, albeit *modern* history, as even my right learned adversary Dr Macpherson must surely agree. But principally, I urge you to consider, because there has been such a change – if not progression – in educated attitudes and what pass for civilized tastes, over the past ten years, that, *even if* it had been true in the early nineteen-eighties that serious novelists overdid their sex, and undersexercised their talents, it would no longer be the case today.

'Now this shift is substantially, and sadly, due to the impact of AIDS on our personal habits, and our expectations of art and literature. But it is also, and more permanently, due to advances in technology which, happily, not even the Thatchers and Whitehouses could, can, or will ever be able to do much about. To illustrate this point, let us glance at my own work in progress . . . ' Here I give them a tightly potted summary of the adventures of Louis Morel right up to the confession that even we ourselves only a few years ago would have latched with growls of delight on to the presence of Isabella in the Barcelona Corregidor's house that last night in Barcelona, 'inflamed the sequel with tumsecence of divers erogonies, fudged up some risqué dialogue for incidental titillation in the lulls between thrusts, and enjoyed ourselves enormously in the process.

'"And why not?" we might then have demanded, aggressive in defence. But times, Madam Chair, have changed. AIDS is everywhere, especially, thanks to the stupidity of our police, in Edinburgh. So, now, is satellite television [ . . . ] and therefore what is a novelist to do? If, as Evelyn Waugh insisted, the novel is by definition something *new*, about *novel* characters, settings and situations, then where would be the novelty in me giving you the lowdown on Louis humping Isabella one hot summer's night in Barcelona in 1640, when you could just as well be watching unsmiling anal intercourse in Hamburg on the privacy of your own television screen, in the cosily log-fired and malt-whiskily mellowed comfort of your own living room, any Saturday night in the 1990s?

'And so, if I may be permitted to echo my most eminent predecessor, Mr Knox:

'"So what?"

'Just this, Madam Chair. That thanks to technologies such as pirate porno videos, satellite television and minority sexual tastes for all on the World Wide Wank, which are effectively impossible to censor, the reader with a thirst for lurid insights into other people's intercourse can get it much more luridly off a television screen or non-interlaced low-radiation monitor for chronic close-up droolers than out of a novelist's pages. Accordingly, discerning readers become less interested in, possibly jaded by, the sort of lingering full-frontal close-ups that might have seemed relevant to the point of liberating just a few years ago. And the novelist who hopes to survive, will – consciously or not – adapt in directions more palatable to the reader.

'"*Which* directions?" you may well ask. And I reply:

'*Even if I know, and only time will tell, I'm not letting on tonight!*

'And so, on the strength of all relevant reasons, arguments and facts, supported by the critiques, clarifications and quotations both my right honourable colleagues and I have presented, I conclude without reservation not only that *modern* writers do *not* use sex rather than talent, but rather that, in the present climate, there may be an insidious backlash danger, so far as *peopling* the world[4] is concerned – I mean, if you'll permit me, Madam Chair, in terms of giving your reader a good old fashioned hard-on to take to bed[5] and fuck his wife with, or vice versa – that modern writers do not use sex enough!

'I therefore thank this house for its liberal attention, and invite it warmly to join with me, in voting vehemently *against the motion.*'

And now, despite six garbled minutes each of specious non-arguments and fourth-hand stale jokes ripped off EBC sitcoms and recycled American soaps, from the Oxbridge debating superstars specially imported to wind up the cases, the house *did* overwhelmingly side with right – with Wringhim, ie, myself, and not forgetting Miss McKechnie.

There followed a stampede to the bar before the special half-price offer on sheepshearer lager and tepid white wine got pumpkinned, and all around me I was dazed by the frenzy of informal post-debate debate on the issues I had raised. First a semantic wrangle as to how 'unsmiling anal intercourse in Hamburg' had best be interpreted. Was it the proprietor of the anus that was unsmiling, or the lodger within it – or indeed the anus itself? If the latter, was this primarily a comment on the Germanic sense of humour, or rather fresh evidence that buggery was on the whole bad for you, at least when – as was often the cases with anuses – the

---

4 'As per the self-deception of Benedick in *Much Ado*. See? I can do it too!' [J.R.]

5 Or better: stay in it! Remember, Audrey? Those endless Sunday mornings in Grantchester? Ah . . .

buggerer was a little too huge for the buggeree to accommodate with comfort?

But all that was as nothing compared with the interrogation of the third speaker for the opposition as to how most easily to tune in to this sort of obnoxious perversion on Saturday night, and where least riskily to purchase an illegal FilmWet decoder – and for how little?

Noting in a cocktail of relief and chagrin that the only schoolgirl I had been aware of in the audience, young Jennifer Macpherson, had by now vanished, no doubt to engage in naive but repeated and increasingly prolonged missionary intercourse with her zoological partner – of the sort most congenial to her headmistress, and which some of us older folk present could still dimly remember – I quickly satisfied this clamour for clandestine information to the best of my ability, and then was called upon to umpire a scrum of conflicting views as to whether Louis Morel does or doesn't hump Isabella in Barcelona.

'If he doesn't, he's a wimp,' is one angle.

'Not a Wimpy?' quips a snotty wag.

'If they *do* do it,' opines Madam Chair seriously. 'Surely we should be allowed to know. After all, there's nothing shameful about love enacted with tenderness, is there?'

'Absolutely not!' I fervently agree, having yet to claim my expenses off her.

'But if there's any *doubt*,' objects Audrey, who by now is exhibiting symptoms of white-wine belligerence, 'it would be cop-out gratuitous to stick it in, Humbert, wouldn't it?'

For another fifteen minutes dissension rages as to how the interested parties would write and re-write our book for us. Considering that calls for my lynching might well greet any admission that so far as I am aware Louis Morel is never going to lay hands on Isabella again, and that the thwarted would-be lover has just been hurled out of a first-storey window in Paris, and is split seconds away from oblivion, I keep my tongue grimly mum until, thankfully, Wringhim stomps over to rescue me – albeit most unwittingly.

Now for anyone who for some lines has been wondering how the centre of attention at the Union bar could for so long have been myself, given the presence this evening of the more explosive Commander Knox, here is the whole truth:

When I wrote my original talk for the debate, on the assumption that

I would be speaking *for* the motion, ranged opposite Wringhim *against*,[6] I formulated also a number of incendiary dirty tricks to hold in reserve, consistently with demonstrating ostensively to the undergraduates that all forms of parliamentary behaviour have got everything to do with winning by any device you can get away with, and nothing to do with truth. And one of the dastardly ploys I thought I might try was to press upon Wringhim, just before the debate began, the two preceding chapters 'A Low-life Masque' and 'Out & Down', on the ground that I would greatly value his response to them, especially as no-one else had yet read them, not even Charlton Palser. That, strictly speaking, was not true either, but then how was Wringhim to know that? And I, meanwhile, could be confident that, provided he'd already had enough to drink, Wringhim would be so distracted by having these red-hot virgin chapters in front of him, that the purity of his rhetoric against the motion must be visibly sullied.

So much for our best-laid plans.

However, thinking ever to gently burlesque the disgraceful number of selfish-fascist-shit Conservative politicians[7] who still subscribe to the simplistic neo-Darwinism of Herbert Spencer, and hence will proudly inform you that the secrets of success in any old rat-race are *fitness* and *adaptability*, I decided on the train this afternoon, once I'd half-forgotten the coffee spilled over my knees by WhatRail? lurchomotion, to convert the original plan to sabotage Wringhim into an inverted clone to sabotage Audrey: by pressing these two chapters, which I had after all gone to

---

[6] Koo suggests we should perhaps make it clearer that this unexpected switch was thanks to a fervent plea from Madam Chair half an hour before the debate kicked off, over our vegan risoles in the Union refectory. This in turn was the result of some convoluted etiology involving the two Hillhead lady novelists refusing to perform in the same forum as Mr Knox, Dr Macpherson refusing to argue either against the motion or alongside Mr Seale, and Mr Palser having been flown during the eleventh hour to an emergency British Council convention in Helsinki on 'The Rightful Role of the Semi-colon in Queen's-English Fiction for the Twenty-first Century'.

[7] 'There are indeed few occasions in literature as in life when understatement and irony are not preferable to overstatement and fulmination.' [P.C.]

the bother of photocopying, on Wringhim still, but immediately before *Audrey* stood up to hold forth – on the ground that the blatant loss of Wringhim's attention, and the violence of his reading habits, would be very unnerving to Audrey.

Well, that too was little more successful than the Poll Tax,[8] since not only was Wringhim not yet drunk (though he had by now emptied the last quarter pint of Jocko McColgate's Glenmorangie into the paper cup in front of him), but throughout Audrey's talk he leaned back in his plastic chair, arms folded, patiently, almost respectfully silent, and beaming over his spectacles at Audrey's face and upper body in an attitude of possessively fond appraisal which I remember now I noted at the time I didn't like the look of at all.

Nevertheless, though persistence may not always pay, it is a not-negligible value. I mean by this that the moment Audrey sat down, Wringhim did indeed seize hold of my pages, as a result of which his subsequent escalation of sniffs, grunts, sneers and scowls of scorn at me were greatly disadvantageous to whatever slickness the Oxbridge superstar winding up with fatuous jokes for the other team might otherwise have displayed.

Thus it is that Wringhim sits on at the debating table while the rest of us jostle, drink, and disagree round the bar. As he ploughs through my pages, his practised left hand makes an end of that Glenmorangie. Possibly there is less of his liver left than there used to be, and in any case I have the definite impression that he gets drunker quicker these days. Certainly he has achieved the (exceedingly) *bellicose* phase of the traditional *amicose, jollicose* . . . progression by the time he slams down the final page of Chapter 27, as Louis Morel has only two split-seconds left before impact, and stumps to buttonhole me by the bar:

'You fucking devious morally bankrupt whathappensnext *wanker*, Seale – '

'Now, now, Wringhim,' I rebuke him. 'Young persons present.'

'Edinburgh-nosed twisted arsehole PRAT,' roars Wringhim. 'WHAT HAPPENS *NEXT?*'

---

8  Quote from Bryant's *Age of Chivalry?*

*30*

# Overpowering Provocation

Louis has been falling through the snowy Paris night for quite a long time now, six weeks in fact, and here we have had Christmas in between, though they in Paris then are still awaiting theirs. Wringhim and others may therefore now be relieved to learn that Louis is not killed instantly by his fall, which is broken by a collapsing bounce off a sloping pent-house roof over a vendor's stall on the street below, and then cushioned by two inches of fresh snow on the cobbles. Nevertheless – whether due to some trauma to his head, or more to the agony of a dislocated shoulder: we do not know – his consciousness is lost for some indeterminate time after the jeering gamblers close the shutters after him.

His memory will be that when he does come to it is in the greatest physical pain he has ever known: all centred on his shoulder wrench and torn muscles in his neck and down his back. In the fog of this nightmare – which we might compare to being blindly aware, yet without powers of speech, of every slice of the surgeon's knife through unsuccessfully anaesthetized nerves – sounds a babble of tongues soon overridden by the clear decisive voice, it seems, of the Chevalier of Montenero. Moments later several hands lift his battered body from the snow but the additional spasmic pain of the pressure of their ministrations on his wounds is so severe that now with a last spurt of gratitude like an abscess bursting he loses consciousness again.

When he surfaces once more it is in response to a surge of agony too deep for sleep to survive caused by the surgeon who has just relocated his shoulder. 'Drink this,' says the quack, pressing a powerful sedative potion to his lips. Minutes later the patient subsides anew, this time into a snowstorm of fragments of dreams like a room thick with pages torn up and thrown through the air. As the scraps of white settle like wearying moths they appear to form the facsimile of a taunting palimpsest through which burn runes of flame that sear the dreamer's brain with unbearable torment as they spell out this cynical trialogue:

*Cad* Never mind my uncle. That is none of your affair. Just fetch the wine, as I tell you. Then be gone.

*Fop* I say, Charles, you do have a way with servants!

*Cad* It is vital to remind them, Antoine, who is *master*.

*Lush* Hear, hear.

*Fop* And shall you, with the same authority, command this maid, whom you hope to marry?

*Cad* I do not *hope* to marry her, Antoine. I simply *shall*.

*Fop* How can you be so confident?

*Cad* She is beautiful. *I* love *her*. Therefore, *she* loves *me*.

*Fop* That does not follow!

*Cad* In *my* experience, Antoine, it does. In yours, of course, it may not. But then, just look at yourself. How less endowed by nature you are, than I. Less tall, less handsome, and less lavish in your privy proportions.

*Lush* Hear, hear. [**Eructation.**]

*Cad* For *me*, I repeat, is it is *inconceivable* that my suit should not meet with requital.

*Fop* Well, if you insist. [*To the brim, if you please. That'll do.*] But even supposing the wench herself is pliant as you imagine, and beautiful as the moon, is she really the match for you?

*Cad* What do you mean, Antoine? Pray elaborate.

*Fop* Think of her father's position. It is so lowly, is it not, that the girl herself – her education, habitudes, expectations – must surely be beneath you?

*Lush* Quite right too. Fuck them rigid, is what I . . . what I –

*Cad* Do give over, Gubgub. You can barely fuck your own right hand when you aren't plastered. As it is – look here, if you're going to be sick . . . oh, shit.

*Fop* Never mind, Charles. Now you can command your uncle's servants to clean it up. But first you must tell me more about your little Hélène.

*Cad*  What about her?

*Fop*  The educational gulf that must lie between you, say. With her father a mere country lawyer. For your sake it worries me terribly.

*Cad*  So good of you to say so, Antoine. But really you must not be distressed. My dear Hélène's learning and accomplishments shall shame the whole court, and her manners outshine a princess.

*Fop*  How can this be?

*Cad*  It is because, despite her father's lowly station, the girl herself has been reared and groomed by Countess Morel of Bigorre.

*Fop*  How very extraordinary.

*Cad*  Indeed, Antoine. And nor do I yet know why. Soon, however, I shall delve to the bottom of the matter. You may rest assured of that.

*Fop*  And is this lady, the Countess Morel: is she too come to Paris, with her ward?

*Cad*  Absolutely not, Antoine. And here's another puzzle.

*Fop*  What do you mean, Charles?

*Cad*  That I cannot for the life of me divine – as yet, I mean – why , her father should have removed her from the Countess, and fetched her here to Paris. For to do so has inevitably drawn attention to her familial relationship with *him*, who, in his squat and hideous looks, and his mean and grasping personality, is the total reverse of his daughter.

*Fop*  How extremely intriguing.

*Cad*  Yes, well. But I remain – to his face – Monsieur Arnault's most humble and very obedient servant, etcetera, etcetera, as but for this curious whimsy of his, I should never have met my Hélène, nor now be poised to wed her. Which happiness, let's toast again. Cheers.

*Fop*  Cheers, Charles. Although . . .

*Cad*  What?

*Fop* What about her *birth*? I mean, your uncle: how will he feel about her *station*? He who is so proud of your family's blood?

*Cad* Uncle will come round. He always does. And besides, this grafting father of Hélène's has been quietly amassing a considerable fortune of his own, it seems, which will doubtless go a long way towards patching over any holes in her pedigree, so far as Uncle is concerned. In any case, come what may: before another year is out I shall either have made Hélène Arnault my wife, or else have perished in the attempt.

*Fop* Hmn. Well. Sounds like good news for me too!

*Cad* Surely not. How?

*Fop* I mean that as you are about to become a happily and properly married mature gentleman, you will be looking to discharge Jeanette –

*Cad* Certainly not, Antoine. Hands off.

*Fop* Come off it, Charles!

*Cad* No, no. I'm perfectly serious. Two strings to his bow is only natural to a man, and in our family it is *de rigueur* to possess both *madame ma femme* and *mademoiselle ma bonne amie*. Even if it were not, there are satisfactions I require of Jeanette which a chaste wife must never imagine.

*Fop* Why so?

*Cad* Lest she come to imagine them with other men too, when her husband's back is turned. So there it is, Antoine. Jeanette remains my property, and you can fuck off.

*Lush* Ahu, Gud. Need . . . *dlink*.

*Cad* Shut up, Gubgub. Go back to sleep.

'The sleeping draught which I had taken,' writes Louis, 'in counteraction with the pain of my body, and compounded by this torment of my mind, soon brought me to the realization, that here was no legend on parchment, but a conversation of the greatest reality, taking place in the very next room. And as the principal young poltroon – whose uncle, it seemed, was the proprietor of this establishment wherein I lay – discoursed with such brutal nonchalance, of the adultery he already proposed to practise upon *my* Hélène, the joy of my boyhood and the love of *my* life, such a fiendish rage possessed me, to enact sweet vengeance upon him, that, disregarding my bandaged weakness, and the agony afflicting my limbs, I reared up from my bed in the darkness, swung my legs to feel for the floor, groped around me in hopes of a weapon, and then – at the end of a moment lit indelibly from within my own head, as by lightning in an August night sky, I collapsed like a poleaxed ox.'

Not only has he passed out from standing, but he must also have hit his head again during his fall. When he comes to once more there is grey day shafting through the shutters, and he realizes he has been discovered stark naked and shivering on the floor by a benevolent bystanding nun.

'A rosy-cheeked, fattish soul, formerly of a charitable sisterhood, she seemed to me one of those kind-hearted dames who attach themselves to great families, and act as a sort of almoner, attending the ailing womenfolk, and any sick servants, with somewhat more skill than an apothecary, and more attention than a physician.'

To the present patient the kindly sister suggests that if 'Monsieur' will just be sensible, and accept her assistance to pull him to his feet, and get him back into bed, and cover him up decently, then he will shortly be favoured with a visit from someone who takes a *special interest* in him. Groggily Louis goes along with this, vaguely thinking, hearing after-echoes of that voice in the snowy night, that the special someone must be the Chevalier of Montenero, appearing from nowhere to save him again. Imagine then the intensity of his flabbergastedness when, minutes later, it is Hélène herself who appears round the door, rushes to his bedside, presses her palm to his haggard brow, and passionately exclaims:

'Oh, Louis! Are you all right?'

There follows a curious interview in which Louis, even allowing for the physical hammering he has received, and his dopy mental state, plays second fiddle to Hélène, in a key that strains his range. For here is a young woman who is taller than he remembers, whose beauty is now compounded by a vitality and aura of lithe muscular strength above and beyond what lesser gentleman would covet in their sweethearts, and whose perceptions, reactions and dialogue can be incisive to the point of unnerving. If he were Clint Eastwood then Louis would doubtless report his impression of Hélène today as recalling the change that overcomes an out-of-work actress once she's been cast in a leading role: she easily expands into the authority of knowing that she owns her part, and that no-one except serious illness, death or bankruptcy of the production company is likely to take it away from her.

All this, plus the guilt of reliving in his mind in her presence the circumstances of their last parting, reduces Louis to a stammering bedbound incoherence full of very basic syntax. Having attempted to form an intention to gallantly declare to Hélène how very much he still loves her, he finds himself enmeshed instead in a potentially endless explanation of how truly innocent he is of the MURDER of Jean-Baptiste. But when Hélène gently presses him, he is obliged to concede, and with conspicuous misery, that he cannot so swear to being innocent of the KILLING of Jean-Baptiste.

'But it was an *accident.*'

'Dear Louis,' responds Hélène stroking his hair. 'That is what I have always believed myself, and what I was sure you would attest. Maître Arnault – my father – alas, with his lawyer's suspicious brain, thinks otherwise.'

'I *promise*—'

'Hush, Louis. Do not strain yourself. The time I am permitted to remain with you is short. Allow me, therefore, to communicate my father's position.'

'Oh, Hélène—'

'If you wish to see him, he says, then he will see you. But strictly provided you account for every moment of your conduct, and can demonstrate to his satisfaction that the killing of Jean-Baptiste was not your doing.'

'But it *was*. So I *can't*. Oh, *God.*'

'Be still, Louis,' insists Hélène, as she swoops to kiss his sheet-white brow. 'That you swear it was an accident is good enough for me, and *I* forgive you. As to my father, there is no doubt a leaven of malice in his proviso. But you see: it was only on condition that I would convey his cruel message, that *they* would permit me to see you.'

'Then you do not . . . '

'Not what, Louis?'

'Not hate me?'

'Hate you, Louis?' exclaims Hélène, seizing his hand, and pressing it to her lips. '*Hate*, you!'

'I mean—'

'Hark! They call me,' says Hélène, rising in some consternation from his bedside. 'I must go.'

'No, no. Don't leave me now.'

'I'm afraid I must, Louis. But—'

'When can I see you again?'

'Most assuredly,' vows Helen. 'Just as soon as *they* will let me. Yes, yes. I'm coming,' she snaps tersely at the rosy nun, who has re-entered the room to fetch her. 'Wait outside.'

As the nun obeys, Hélène leans down, embraces Louis's naked shoulders, and kisses him most encouragingly. But then she pulls free abruptly, glides away, and has closed the door behind her before Louis's good elbow can lever him up on his bolster, to call after her:

'What about this young scoundrel called Charles?'

# 31

# A Turn-up for the Book

Whether Louis was drugged again, or simply fell at length into a deep recuperative coma, we cannot say. His next recorded memory is of bursting into wakefulness at dead of night to wrestle with what Maître Arnault can possibly be up to: taking his daughter back from Countess Morel, bringing her here to Paris, and is it all a dream?

But no: it isn't, as is duly confirmed by the creeping hues of morning, which also reveal, to Louis's astonishment, that he is no longer lodged in that private hôtel belonging to the unknown uncle of the unknown Charles, but now is back in his digs with the Widow Beaupère. When his frantic shouts bring the landlady rustling to his bedside she explains with apparent unconcern how Louis was borne back by four porters during the afternoon the day before yesterday, unconscious on a litter. Since he must be very hungry now, and thirsty too, can she offer him a little beef broth?

After the broth, and some bread to dunk in it, and a glass or two of wine to wash it down, Louis is urged by Madame to remain in bed and be looked after. Blood up, however, and feeling his strength returning, he gratefully dismisses the widow, and forces himself out of bed and into his clothes – despite atrocious shoulder pains and headaches which he attributes to drug cocktails of goodness-knows-which ingredients. On checking his clothes and possessions he is further amazed to unearth in his pouch precisely one hundred louis d'or. These, he reckons, must have been secreted there for him by Hélène (who else?) but sourced from Maître Arnault. His joy at the sight of this tidy sum is thus instantly blemished by problems of morality interbreeding with pride as to whether and for what he should make use of the money.

Ethical issues concerning money put him naturally in mind of Achilles Lefranc, and accordingly he commissions Madame Beaupère to summon the friendly greengrocer's son, whom he sends with a note to the shady auberge in the Quartier Eustache, on the off-chance that the bubbly little Thespian may by now have made it up here, from whatever embroilments befell him in Lyon.

An hour later Louis is discreetly overjoyed by the arrival – puffing up the widow's stairs with tears as of jubilant salvation in his eyes, exhibiting symptoms of enormous poverty, and clad in monkish rags – of Achilles the man himself.

'What on earth have you been up to, Achilles?' demands Louis severely, to mask the dry lump in his throat.

After your lordship's departure [*replies Achilles, gratefully scoffing a large platter of bread, cheese, cold meat and garlic mayonnaise, washed down by a flagon of red table wine, all kindly provided by the Widow Beaupère*] I embarked in the boat for Lyon – just so soon, that is to say, as it thought itself fit to sail, which in your lordship's terms was most procastinarious. Well, thus began our long, slow voyage up the River Rhône, what at first was marvellous tedious – not the Rhône, I mean, what is passing spectacular in places, if you like that sort of thing.

However, boredom being the spawner of many a progeny, or however the old saying goes, it were not long before I hit upon a promising divertissement, in the form of a rather pretty young woman – a most succulent little plum, indeed, if your lordship will forgive my saying so. Now the lady's father being, she told me, a respected elder merchant of Lyon, I lost no time in paving my path to his daughter, through seeming first to present my humblest compliments – 'obedient servant' and suchlike tripe, what comes so easily to a resting tragedian, as your lordship has perhaps remarked – to her father.

'Eh? Whojasay?' he replied, a trifle deafly.

'I have the honour to introduce myself as Monsieur le Comte de Haut Grilmagnac,' I repeated. Hereupon the merchant inquired with a hint of suspicion why a lithe and nimble young blade like I should be plodding up the water in a barge. It was because, I explained, due to my literary and artistic prestidigitations, I much preferred the tranquil motions of the river to the cramped joltings of a post carriage, or the testicular hardships of the saddle, and had therefore sent all my equipage ahead by land, in the custody of my servants.

'Dah!' was all he had to say to that, whereupon I gave him up as an incorrigible duffer, and proceeded then to woo the divine Alicia with no further subterfuge, and of course with the utmost charm. Furthermore when we moored to dine that night, and old Monsieur Colas waxed grumpier than ever, I contrived, when the meal was done, to flourish from my pocket a handful of gold – as though it were there merest cupful scooped from the Rhône, though in truth it was all I possessed – and with the air of a prince to whom gold is but a burden, I asked casually what was to pay.

Now while the illicitous Alicia was plainly ravished with this glimpse of my opulence, the old merchant himself — though never for a moment did it prevent him from allowing me to pay for his dinner — grew more uneasy with every moment that they passed in my vicinity, and contrived so adroitly to always get betwixt Alicia and me, whenever the moments seemed most portentous for my ministrations to prevail — to the tune of moonlight, stars, the song of crickets, nightingales, and the like — that the presentiment swelled within me of some commerce between them, or at least intended by the merchant, over and above — if not, as it were, beneath and behind — what a good father does to his daughter, or gets her to do to him.

And this was a very painful panoply of imagery for me, as your lordship can perhaps imagine, in terms of your lordship's own experience: envisioning my darling Alicia, the most scrumptious little pusspuss in France, cast adrift in a stagnant backwater, to be debauched with neither fire nor sap, by the most withered old piece of cracked bamboo that ever knock-knocked on his dotage.

'How about it, Alicia?' I put it to her, in a stolen moment at Lyon, as he wheezed up the jetty behind us.

'About what, Monsieur le Comte?'

'You are sleeping with your father, are you not? Don't lie to me now.'

'Oh, monsieur!' and she blushed like a rose.

'It won't do, you know, Alicia. Just think if you got with child: your son would have two heads. Whereas with me . . . ' I hinted, with consummate delicacy, at the bliss she could expect to enjoy, by contrast with the humiliation and suffering of prison, trial, and abominable punishments, if their incest should be discovered. In response my fair enslaver whispered hastily — for the old wheezer was catching us up — that I should lodge in an auberge named the *Lion Rouge*, and there wait for her *billet doux*. Sure enough, the following morning comes my summons: to the Rue Lance-pierre. There, in a small but comfortable lodging, I find Alicia all distraught.

'What's the matter, my pretty?' say I.

Her face half in tears, half in hopeful smiles, like an April morning after breakfast, she tells me that now she is alone in the world, having no other friend but me.

'What about your father?' I inquire.

That cruel tyrant, she now explained, had *commanded* her, on pain of horsewhipping of her buttocks, to abandon all thoughts of me *for ever*. But this, she swore, the passion I had kindled in her would not permit. Therefore, being ever too frank, she said, to deceive anyone, let alone her carping father, she at once refused and defied him, thus sparking a fearsome quarrel – in the course of which his horsewhipping of her buttocks was partially successful, as she showed me – leading soon to his casting her off and away: penniless, and out of his house.

Now though I well perceived that with such a charmer's assistance my dearly beloved pistoles would fly like starlings all over Lyon, I resolved – as a gentleman such as your lordship would have resolved – to lull all risk of my Alicia suspecting that my affections were somewhat withering, by entertaining her with all assiduity, till better luck should furnish me with the means of some honourable retreat. Accordingly I despatched a young lackey out to a reputable *traiteur*[1] to buy in a good dinner, as the infallible means of consoling a damsel so distressed, and the entrée to true consummation.

Thus over rich ragouts and heady burgundy the hours slipped lightly by, and Alicia's sparkling eye bespoke volumes of her triumph over the conquest she had achieved – that is to say, over myself – and her anticipation of the delights impending – that is to say, beneath my loins. Oh, alas, your lordship, that mortal joy should be so transitive! And that into the midst of our burgeoning bliss, and nearly unclad limbs, there should rush trouble, gloom, and thwarting spite, in the form of four ferocious flunctionaries, who pitilessly arrested poor Phyllis – as her true name transpired to be – on the charge of having robbed her former venerable protector, and myself along with her, would your lordship believe, as her accomplice, inciter and pimp?

Now though my vixen darling protested her innocence, in terms and amid tears that must have melted the harsh heart of Minos, and bended the hard ear of Rhadamanthus – or is it the other way round? – yet, as the bulk of the purloined loot were found in the bottom of her valise, the unfeeling officers waxed cynical to a man, and marched us twain to prison forthwith, with no ceremony further than to relieve us of all our right valuables, and every last farthing we possessed. Some mornings later – three or four, perhaps, though it seemed like a year at the time – the constables came again to hurry me up to the bench

---

[1] Combined grocer, delicatessen, and general delicious smoked-, cured- and baked-food take-away.

before a fat magistrate who tells me in doom-laded tones, that the case against young Phyllis he is reserving for his private consideration later, but as for me I am proven a multiple felon, being conspirator, thief, solicitor of dupes for tarts, and arch-impersonator of Monsieur le Comte de Grilmagnac, which he makes out I plainly ain't, even supposing that gentleman to exist, which in his gall he esteems highly doubtful.

'Two months bread and water in the clink,' was the outrageous breach of justice imposed on these trumped-up counts, 'then whip him through the town, in the birthday suit he prefers, and boot him hence. *Et voila!*'

'That accounts for two months of your absence,' observes Louis. 'What happened after that?'

'Ah, your lordship!' sighs Achilles with benign resignation, wiping his lips, then draining the wine. 'The pace of life, life has taught me, is in proportion to one's means. And with no means, and especially with no clothes, a poor man travels slow.'

'No doubt. But how, in your very nakedness, did you manage to travel at all?'

'By night the first days, your lordship. And then these rags I received of two sisters in Thoissey – twin concubines to an absentee priest, who preferred (the ladies, I mean), so they kindly said, my nubile young body to his.'

'And then?'

'With the sisters I dallied, as was necessary to build up my strength, till the eve of the prelate's return. And then, with a few sous quietly lent by his alms box, I turned my nose north again, to beg my poor way up to Paris, to serve your lordship as never before.'

'And that took you all this time?'

'Dear your lordship! Since they expelled me from that accursed Lyon, where injustice and cruelty reign supreme, never a moment was avoidably wasted, until Monday of this week, when at last I reached the luxurious auberge recommended us in Marseille, and where your lordship had bade us tryst.'

'What happened there?'

'The landlord, whom I instantly did not take to, informed me most emphatically that no such personage as your lordship had ever there resided, nor been known to enter Paris.'

'But you didn't believe him?'

'How intimately your lordship knows me!'

'Kind of you to say so, Achilles. Still, that was Monday. This, so

Madame Beaupère informs me, is Friday. What happened in between?'

'Since, as your lordship knows better than I, the second law of all great success is to make our enemies work for us, I soon had this hostile *Cafarde*[2] feeding me greasy stews in his kitchen, and bedding me down in his stable, in exchange for some scullial chores during the day, plus stand-up one-liners at night, in not the best of my possible tastes, for his odious guests after dinner. Thus kept I my spirit alive in hope, and my body fuelled with lard, till there arrived today to inquire for me, in the auberge yard, that honest lad whom your lordship sent, and whose news brought me untold joy.'

'And right glad I am to see you too, Achilles,' says Louis, wincing as he shifts in bed. 'Now, since you're here . . . '

---

[2] Literally, 'cockroach'. But here also with overtones of 'slimy slug', 'crapulent toad', 'impotent mother-fucker', 'born-again child-molester', and so on.

# 32

# One More Piece

Louis has Achilles exercise his apothecary's-apprentice chirurgical skills on the mending but still painful shoulder. After this the servant presses his master to recount all that has happened to *him*, since their parting of ways at Marseille.

'I could not reasonably refuse to tell my history to my little attendant, though it occasioned less amusement to him than his had done to me. His face grew longer and longer, and his professions of outrage and sympathy on my behalf grew louder and more profuse, at every incident I detailed, till at last, passing over my unexpected and wholly mysterious interview with Hélène, I informed Achilles how, after having been conveyed home during my unconsciousness, I had found in my pouch those hundred coins.

'This news cleared his countenance as by magic. "For a hundred louis d'or, your lordship," cried he, "who in the world would *not* be thrown out of a window?"'

But then, returning to quiz his master more closely re his mother's gold ring, which he pawned to fund his gambling, Achilles becomes positively pugnacious.

'Such a price!' he laments. 'Less than one quarter of the ring's true worth. Oh dear, oh dear!' he wails, eyes rolling. 'And therefore . . . allow *me*, your eminence,' he begs portentously, 'to endeavour whether or not the ring may yet be reclaimed.'

'*Never*, Achilles,' retorts Louis, 'never, NEVER call me "eminence". There is but one Eminence in France, and that is the Cardinal. To address any other thus were tempting Fate, and risking your hide besides. However . . . '

Permission is duly granted for Achilles to attempt recovery of the ring. This he achieves the following day by devising a confidence scam worthy of one of the middle-period Simon Templar plots: benevolently bribing a lounging Archer from the Court of Aides into helping him blackmail the grafting pawnbroker on the ground that the ring in question had been stolen from the Cardinal's household by the young pseudo-gent with the pointed beard who had hocked it so cheap in a hurry – and that whereas Achilles, weapon-backed by the Archer, is empowered with governmental authority to re-buy the intrinsically priceless ring for precisely what was paid for it, the pawn-broker must otherwise resign himself to the scaffold at dawn. This naturally raises the question of how much precisely *was* paid for the ring, and since here the pawnster unwisely goes for 'fifteen louis d'or, Monsieur: not a penny less', Achilles is thus enabled to retort:

'That is a damned lie, you abominable hound. The price you paid him was *six*, as we know from the young varlet himself, whom we tortured nigh to death yesterday.' This torrential fabrication being confirmed by menacing nods from the scowling Archer, Achilles exploits his moral advantage to beat the re-purchase price down to *three* louis d'or, enabling Achilles to haste home chez Widow Beaupère with both the ring for his master and two prized coins for himself, while the Archer returns to his duties the richer by one bonus louis, and with a lifelong allegiance to Achilles.

Louis with a Capital Ell is immediately delighted by Achilles' success in reclaiming the ring, then swiftly plunged into morose memories of his parents, gloom over the contrast between heaven on earth in Bigorre and hell in France in Paris, paranoid anxiety as to why the Cardinal has never yet sent for him again, and a desperate yearning to find out *why* Maître Arnault has brought Hélène to Paris, *who* the obscene young cad can be who so cynically threatened to simultaneously wed and cuckold Hélène, and *where* in the city he can find again that private hôtel to which some saviour ferried him following his wounding fall through the snow.

Christmas comes, is celebrated modestly with Madame Beaupère, and then quickly forgotten. In early January Louis invests a cautious proportion of his anonymous windfall in a fleet new palfrey befitting a fearless cavalier expecting to be called upon to serve his state in perilous missions at any moment. During his daylight hours he rides in ever-widening circles round the city, in a protracted vain attempt to relocate that hôtel that housed Hélène, and those cackling drunken poltroons. In the evenings, to conserve funds, he stays in and reads. Having burned his manual on how to get rich quick by outsmarting the sharks, he concentrates now on military history and strategy. Perceiving with serene sensitivity a somewhat grim and time-killing side to her lodger's lucubrations, the Widow Beaupère draws him out some evenings after dinner into longer and more open-ended conversations than hitherto. In the course of one of these, Louis is intrigued to learn how once upon a time, before her own marriage, Madame Beaupère was governess to the teenage Henriette de Verge – star-crossed sweetheart of the Count of Bagnols, and victim to the Marquis of Roquefort.

'Madame was in turn not a little surprised that I too should be acquainted with so much of the history. "Concerning which it seems, Monsieur – alas, I know little more than yourself. As I was found to have been privy to the marriage, you see, I was sent away directly by my young lady's father, and denied all further communication with her." "But the murder?" I urged the good woman. "Is there anything you can tell me of that?" "Only," she replied, "that I saw with my own eyes the bloody spot where the poor count was slain, and the dents and rips in the turf, made by the combatant's feet. And what a fearful struggle it must have been too, Monsieur, for two of the Marquis of Roquefort's own men remained ill at the village for weeks afterwards, and no-one was allowed to see them but his own surgeon, and even then one of them died at the end of it all, and his confession was said to be so strange, so perplexing and disturbing, that the priest sent to Rome for instruction, if he should divulge what he had learned or no. The following year I became affianced in Paris, and I heard no more of the family, save only that someone told me, to my great and enduring grief, that my young lady had died shortly afterwards, in a convent close by Auch."'

Naturally anxious, Louis records, to pass on the La Rochelle papers which chance, in the form of the failed assassin Monsieur Saint Simon (aka Fat Monk) had thrust into his hand: to any surviving member of the family, either on Henriette de Vergne's side, or on the Count of Bagnols', he attempts with cordial vigour to jog any cobwebs in the widow's brain – but to no avail, since:

'Though tolerating my queries, and with great good humour, she remained, apart from what she had already told me, no less ignorant than myself.'

The following afternoon, his head buzzing with the renewed frustration of having failed to pinpoint the mansion harbouring Hélène, and the added aggravation of now possessing one more piece in the Bagnols jigsaw, but having no notion where to place it, Louis returns to his digs to be told by the widow that during his absence a tall dark gentleman stranger has called to speak with him, and has promised to call again.

'Well . . . *who* was he?'

'I do not know, Monsieur. The gentleman did not say.'

'Well . . . *when* will he call again?'

'"Perhaps this evening," the gentleman said. "Or else at some later date."'

# 33

# Tall, Dark & Plausible

Where reason has no clue [*reflects Louis*], to guide her through labyrinthine doubt, she pauses at the entrance, while imagination steps more boldly in, and child-like tramps the maze. Thus, while I had no cause to believe that *one* tall stranger should seek out my company, any sooner another, my fancy set to work despite my will, like a forest fire during drought.

'Maître Arnault!' was my very first thought. 'It is the father of Hélène, come to treat with terms of peace!'

Yet no! For never in anyone's eyes, not even a woman's, could the lawyer appear as tall.

Then was it the Chevalier, come to tender reconciliation, and inquire as to my health?

But no again! As my closer questioning of Madame Beaupère disclosed that *this* mysterious stranger was a *younger* man, and perhaps – to guess from the cut of his overcloak – a clergyman of some rank.

A clergyman!

Then was the Cardinal come himself, to press me into service? Encore no, for the Cardinal was already old, and looked older. Still, so I speculated, if it was not his Eminence himself, it was . . . likely some younger emissary?

But *who?*

And *why?*

And *when* would the personage return?

My disposition being ever impatient of uncertainty, and my spirits heavy with the dull failure of days past – failure again to find Hélène; failure to otherwise discover any motive to illumine my life; and failure to devise any prospects of income, once my windfall coins were spent – I was now by reaction consumed with an insupportable excitement, leavened up with a pinch of dread, as to what this visitation could bode.

Even worse, as day waned, and night waxed, and every wild conjecture lay spent with a panting exhaustion, was the mounting irritable anxiety that the cloth-seeming stranger *would not now return*, this evening . . .

And possibly not ever again.

Cursing him heartily, whoever he was, I obliged my twitching frame to settle down by my parlour fireside, with a treatise on horse-drawn artillery. My concentration revolting, in the circumstances, against the dry arithmetic of optimum elevation angles, I found myself soon drifting in a flame-gazing reverie, full of phantoms devoid of all meaning but their own florescence, and extinction in cremation, when suddenly in bursts Achilles most obtrusively to announce:

'Wake up, your lordship! Hup! The dark stranger is come again!'

> False glory and false modesty, madame, [*confess the stranger's own secret memoirs*] are the two rocks on which men who have written their own lives have generally split, but which Thuanus[1] among the moderns and Caesar among the ancients happily escaped.
>
> I doubt not you will do me the justice to believe that I do not pretend to compare myself with those great writers in any respect but sincerity, – a virtue in which we are not only permitted, but commanded, to rival the greatest heroes.
>
> I am descended from a family illustrious in France and ancient in Italy, and born upon a day remarkable for the taking of a monstrous sturgeon in a small river that runs through the country of Montmirail, in Brie, the place of my nativity.
>
> I am not so vain as to be proud of having it thought that I was ushered into the world with a prodigy or a miracle, and I should

---

[1] Ie, Jacques Auguste de Thou (1553–1617). Wrote his massive *Historia sui temporis* in Latin, in hopes of postponing flak from outraged protagonists – cf our own very next chapter, and also the subtle phallic bragging of Herman Melville's lead narrator Ishmael, in *Moby Dick*. For De Thou, though, the Latin dodge was a bit of a pee in the wind, since his enemies swiftly got their revenge by listing his work in their dissuasive *Index librorum prohibitorum*, and ensuring his political ossification.

Similarly, few of us here in Scotland would stake our lives' savings (?) on Wringhim Knox's hopes of being elected to the English House of Lords. For further fascinating details not in Latin on De Thou, his achievements and albatrosses, see *The Life of Thuanus* by J.A.M. Collinson (1807).

never have mentioned this trifling circumstance had it not been for some libels since published by my enemies, wherein they affect to make the said sturgeon a presage of the future commotions in this kingdom, and me the chief author of them.

I now beg leave, madame, to make a short reflection on the nature of the mind of man.

For I believe there never was a more honest soul in the world than my father's; I might say his temper was the very essence of virtue. For though he saw I was too much inclined to duels and gallantry ever to make a figure as an ecclesiastic, yet his great love for his eldest son – not the view of the archbishopric of Paris, which was then in his family – made him resolve to devote me to the service of the Church.

For he was so conscious of his reasons, that I could even swear he would have protested from the very bottom of his heart that he had no other motive than the apprehension of the dangers to which a contrary profession might expose my soul.

So true it is that nothing is so subject to delusion as piety: all sorts of errors creep in and hide themselves under that veil; it gives a sanction to all the turns of imagination, and the honesty of the intention is not sufficient to guard against it.

In a word, after all I have told you, I turned priest . . .

'He was tall and visibly well-made,' comments Louis, 'though his clerical dress served him a good deal in this respect, concealing a pair of legs which were somewhat clumsy, and not the straightest in the world.

'His head was one of the finest I ever saw; and his face, though with no one feature that was outstandingly handsome, nonetheless, with its full rounded chin, and the broad expanse of his forehead, enhanced the impression conveyed by the sparkle in his dark brown eyes, of great powers of mind, joined with a light and brilliant wit.'

This is of course the Abbé de Retz, whom the retentive reader will recall from our own first chapter, where we quoted his disparagement of Cardinal Richelieu's liaison with the licentious Marion de L'Orme, and mentioned his character of the Count of Soissons.

Less subjective[2] facts about the Cardinal (as he is soon to be) de Retz

---

[2] Than Louis's impressions of his visitor's legs.

are as follows:

> 'John Francis Paul de Gondi, Cardinal de Retz Sovereign of
> Commercy, Prince of Euville, second Archbishop of Paris, Abbot
> of Saint Denis in France, was born at Montmirail, in Brie, in
> October, 1614.
>
> 'His father was Philippe Emanuel de Gondi, Comte de Joigni,
> General of the Galleys of France and Knight of the King's Orders;
> and his mother was Frances Marguerite, daughter of the Comte de
> Rochepot, Knight of the King's Orders, and of Marie de Lannoy,
> sovereign of Commercy and Euville.
>
> 'His grandfather was Albert de Gondi,[3] Duc de Retz, Marquis de
> Belle Isle, a Peer of France, Marshal and General of the Galleys,
> Colonel of the French Horse, First Gentleman of the Bedchamber,
> and Great Chamberlain to the Kings Charles IX and Henri III.'

'He bowed low as he entered,' says Louis, 'and advanced towards a
seat – which hastily I begged him to take – with that certain ease
of motion which betokens the confidence of high birth. Signing that
Achilles should withdraw, and fetch refreshments, I expressed myself
most honoured by my vistor's kindness, in paying me this call.'

"If there were any kindness in doing a pleasure to one's self,"
replies de Retz, "I should willingly take the credit of it. But in the
present instance, as the gratification is my own, I cannot pretend to
any merit."

'Half-closing his eyes, as he spoke, he glanced round my small
apartment in quizzical appraisal, yet too briefly to cause offence.'

"As to *honour*," de Retz continues languidly, "you should know that
your visitor is but a lowly abbé. My name is [ . . . ], and my address, for
the moment, is care-of my Auntie, the Duchesse de Retz."

"I see," responds Louis, nonplussed, and wondering.

'For though my visitor was but a few years my senior, storms and
scandals were his element, and when, before he was yet seventeen,

----

[3] Gondi was also an infamous sexual practioner of all the Aretino
Postures. Cf *The Counts of Mount Venus*, here and there.
Charles IX and Henri III were, respectively, authorizer of and
despicable accomplice in the St Bartholomew Massacre.

he wrote his famous *Conjuration de Fiesque*,[4] he surely foreshadowed the stage, and indeed the lurid scenes, in which he himself was destined to act. Already he had acquired a most extraordinary reputation – for daring, intrigue, supreme ambition; and the metal for an adventure.

'Though less conspicuously than is the case with women,' Louis goes on, 'all men contain within themselves the most bizarre contradictions. But the Cardinal de Retz was the only person I ever knew, who, upon the most mature reflection, acted in continual contradiction with himself. Often he would set in motion the most consummate strokes of policy to gain a mere bauble, or to gratify some trivial appetite. By contrast, he was equally capable of indulging the most extravagant passions, and of wilfully committing the most egregious follies, at the expense of risking catastrophe in his own most shrewd political schemes, and minutely planned campaigns. Here, in a word, was a man on whom one could never with safety depend.'

---

4  'Conspiracy of Fiesco'. The Italian Giovanni Luigi de' Fieschi, egged on by the Pope, the King of France and others, in 1547 led a conspiracy against the Imperialist Doria faction. As the plan to seize the Genoa galleys, as a prelude to seizing the city, was succeeding, Fiesco himself, while walking a plank between the quay and one of the galleys, fell off it and was drowned.

The attempted coup thus ended in fiasco, but this (*'far fiasco'* being Italian for 'to make a bottle', in the sense of 'ruin the play by fluffing your lines, or farting during a love scene') does not appear to have any direct etymological link with 'Fiesco'. Some of the parallels between the Fiesco conspiracy and the insurgency of the Count of Soissons will become manifest in our later chapters. Until then, the Fiesco affair is probably the better known historically.

According to *Britannica*: 'The Fiesco conspiracy has been the subject of many poems and dramas, of which the most famous is *Fiesco* by Johann Schiller.' No-one, to the best of our uncertain knowledge, has yet written *The Fiesco Fiasco*, and since the dead man's young wife Eleonora was endowed not only with widowhood but also prodigious wealth and beauty, and since there is no copyright in titles, this could be your plum on a plate.

Obviously Louis has yet to have this opinion of de Retz empirically confirmed by his own flesh, and yet:

'Already I had heard his character so assessed several times, not least by the Marquis of Roquefort, during my sojourn at his pavilion in Gagnères And since the latter gentleman was then calculating, as he described Monsieur de Retz to me, that my own life should not survive the week, he could not, in that instance, have had great incentive to falsification.'

In the light of such a reputation, it requires no great effort of caution on Louis's part to suspect that the visit of De Retz is not without some goal. But what? Resolving to find out, Louis has a stab at the diplomacy-fencing game himself.

"Of course, Monsieur de Retz," he says mildly, sipping the mulled wine which Achilles has by now brought up from the Widow's kitchen, "it were needless for me to give you *my* name."

"Why is that?"

"Oh, because you were surely aware of my identity before you did me the honour of this visit."

"Not so, I swear," replies de Retz, with all aspect of earnestness. "I am perfectly ignorant both of your name, monsieur, and your rank. The truth, ever simple, is that I have been informed, by persons on whom I depend, but must not name, that a young gentleman of singularly prepossessing appearance, and exquisite manners, had taken this apartment, and was supposed to be under – shall we say? – some temporary difficulty."

'I turned very red, I believe; but . . . ' De Retz affects not to notice, proceeding:

"People *will* talk, you know, of their neighbours' affairs – most especially in Paris – and as it is their nature, such as killing mice to a cat, it were futile to berate them. Besides, if there be benefits incidentally, why should we not enjoy them?"

"Benefits?"

"Such as the irresistible impulse I felt, monsieur, when I heard of your situation – to visit you, and to render you any assistance in my power. Nor shall I regret that impulse for a moment, monsieur, even if I have been misinformed, inasmuch as the misapprehension shall, at the least, have gained me the pleasure of your acquaintance."

'I was very sure of doing Monsieur de Retz no great injustice in supposing his benevolence much tinged with other feelings.'

So Louis rejoins:

"I too should be woebegone, monsieur, that such a rumour had troubled you to come here, did I not likewise derive so much unexpected pleasure from the error. As to my identity, my name [ . . . ], and my parents too, I know, would share in my joy, that the bounty you so nobly proposed to exercise upon myself, you may now bestow elsewhere."

"Morel of Bigorre?" echoes de Retz, as if amazed. "But surely that is the name of the young cavalier whom his Highness the Count of Soissons has been expecting, to join him from Béarn. Don't tell me your first name is—"

"Louis," says Louis. "I am he."

"But this is wonderful!" cries de Retz. "A veritable miracle of good fortune, I say. On the other hand, where the devil can you have been hiding, all this while?"

'Perceiving there was some mystery underlying my movements, Monsieur de Retz now applied himself with abundant enthusiasm, and consummate art, to elicit my every secret. Nor did I take great pains to conceal most of them from him. Truly it is astonishing how gladly the gates of a downtrodden heart open wide to a promise of hope. In the course of half an hour my exuberant visitor, his eyes soft with sympathy, made himself familiar with perhaps nine tenths of my history. Only over the finer points of my relations with Hélène did I draw a decent veil. Sensitive to my reticence, and alert to the danger, from his point of view, of my retiring protectively within myself, Monsieur de Retz smoothly reined our conversation back to the subject of the Count of Soissons, whom he advised me, most strenuously, to seek out with no further delay.'

"You will find in the Count," says the Abbé, "all that is charming in human nature. In his communion with society, he had but one fault originally, which was undue hauteur. But this fault he himself recognized, and has had the strength of mind to vanquish it. As a result, you will find in the Count today perhaps the most affable man in France. So take my best advice, Monsieur Morel, and set out for Sedan tomorrow. For it is into Sedan, as of course you know, that his Highness has been driven – forcibly exiled, barred from the land whose royal blood he shares – by the tyrannizing spirit, and vindictive persecutions, of our devoutly detestable Cardinal."

Observing Louis's blink of alarm, at this sudden bound to the brink of treason, de Retz at once puts down his glass and stands to leave, on the ground that:

"But the night rushes on, and I have yet another call to pay. Breakfast with me tomorrow, Monsieur Morel, why don't you? Then I can ease your passage with some further information, a few words of friendly advice – on pecking-order protocols, who needs be bribed, and with how little, that sort of thing – and several letters to convey. My aunt's hôtel at nine. Do you agree?"

# 34a

# Tenor & Baritone Flak

Sorrows come not single pies, and the same is no less true of peers, colleagues, friends and former lovers queuing up to lambaste you under 'prat', 'swine', 'paedophile', 'liar', 'sot', and other fruitful banners in the pantheon of creative criticism.

What we have in mind is yesterday, when, instead of writing five exciting new chapters before lunch, I had Wringhim on the phone for nearly an hour, then a trenchant philippic in the post from Charlton, to protract my morning coffee, followed at one minute past six o'clock – when the telephone charges become a trifle less exorbitant – by staccato bursts from Janet in various media, and culminating in the later evening with a sustained harangue from Audrey, although she would make out I provoked it.

Abbreviated corroboration of this testimony is as follows.

### Wringhim

'Good morning, Humbert. How's things?'

'Morning, Wringhim,' I mumbled, instantly wishing I had allowed the answerphone to protect me. Wringhim has this mannerism, you see, of always only saluting his youngers, especially those he regards as his cultural inferiors, by their surname – unless he is both sober and about to ask a favour. Wherefore I added:

'What can I do for you?'

After a curt but deafening guffaw, like an explosion to extinguish an oil-well ablaze, the caller responded:

'About these pages you sent me?'

'Yes?'

'You've only sent me the first thirteen chapters.'

'Yes?'

'But at the debate, the other week, you gave me chapters twenty-three and twenty-four to read.'

'Yes?'

'Well, Humbert,' he deduced with avuncular ingratiation, 'what the fuck has happened to the intervening ten chapters?'

'Nine, actually, Wringhim.'

'Never mind that. Why haven't you sent them?'

I explained that my project had been, in compliance with his own vehement request, to send him a duplicate of the chapters he personally, some months ago, had abandoned in McEwan's. 'Also, to stimulate some gauge of how motivated you then would seem, to get your hands on the sequel.'

'So that's it,' he hissed triumphantly, then fell silent.

'Well?'

'Well what, Humbert?'

'What do you think?'

'Think of what?'

'Of my chapters, Wringhim?' *You malevolent sprite*, I did not add.

'Hymn . . . '

'Yes?'

'Story has its moments, I suppose. Not exactly *badly* written . . . '

'Thank – '

'Hardly Neil Gunn though, Humbert, is it?'

'"Thank God for that," some might say.'

'If I didn't want you to do something for me, Humbert, I'd call you a toffee-nosed prat.'

'I believe you may already, on occasion, have achieved that objective, Wringhim. However, don't worry about it.'

'There is a major failing, of course.'

'Eh? What do you mean?'

'In your plot.'

'Where?'

'This business about whether or not Louis Morel murders his father.'

'Yes?'

'Assuming, Humbert – which I grant is not wholly implausible, given France in those days – that the protagonist's nominal father is not his biological father . . . '

'Yes? Yes, yes, Wringhim? Go on.'

'I'm not convinced your narrator has a fucking earthly who the biological father really is, and hence I accuse you, Humbert Seale, of descending yet again to the sub-sewer level of the gimcrack Hollywood tease—'

'Sssssh!' I hissed triumphantly. 'I'm afraid you're wrong there, Wringhim! And even if you hadn't been, you certainly would be now.'

'Well, that's your problem. See if I care.'

'You don't want me, then, to send on these later chapters?'

'When?'

'Today, if you like. I've just had them back from Charlton, which will save me making more photocopies.'

'Well,' sniffed Wringhim grudgingly. 'Please yourself. Now, about my pamphlet – '

'I say, I say, Wringhim, do you have any idea what the time is?'

'What about the time?'

'Why, it's nearly ten ay em. Peak telephone time, don't you know? This call must be costing you an absolute bomb! Have you come into money, or something?'

'Never mind that,' he grunted with such confidence as to reassure me that the suffering bill could never be his. 'Now, about my pamphlet – '

'*What* about it?' I interposed with dissuasive aggression.

'The text is complete, Humbert,' continued Wringhim, whose back is better oiled than any duck's, 'and what I want *you* to do . . . '

### Charlton

Dear H,

I was woken up at 7.20 a few Mondays back by an irate postman banging on my door. He'd been banging for quite a while, he claimed. Into my arms he thrust a mysterious package which was much too large to be shoved through my letter-box. Imagine my feelings on ripping it open three hours later only to discover the typescript of your novel in its present state of play!

I'll return to that in a moment.

First a couple of things about computers. Rebecca now has the latest top-of-the range Compaq with all the bells and whistles. It's totally wasted on her of course but so far I haven't been able to get it off her. Some drug company gave it to her apparently though goodness knows why. Probably part of some atrocity cover-up like that sickening Halcyon affair. I'm contemplating investing in a colour portable for myself in the meantime and I'd be grateful for your advice (as soon as possible if you don't mind) as between the enclosed glossy brochures.

What I particularly need to know . . .

Now to return to Louis Morel:

As I read into your chapters I grew increasingly indignant. I took the trouble to dig out the file copy of my last letter to you and as I reread it

I was not particularly thrilled to discover that you had ignored the most invaluable advice I had given you.

Nor was I overly delighted to encounter a character called "Charlton Palser" – whose very name is most instantly evocative of a senile Welsh football-player at best. May I humbly request conversion into "Paul Chalicer" which serves just as well the purposes you are after if I read them correctly and also has more dignified and even spiritual overtones together with Joycean hints at the sort of passionately religious bibulousness I have always found rather alluring in principle if only it didn't make one feel so ill and rot your brain?

But then as I proceeded I found myself reading the very letter I'd written to you and which was now glowing blue on the screen beside me. As you can imagine my indignation boiled into rage. Instead of *acting* on my advice you'd simply incorporated it wholesale into the book thereby putting ironical little quote-marks round it and making its author look a total tit.

Now here you were, it seemed to me, asking for another witty, thoughtful letter from me for you to nick and ridicule. For several minutes I must confess I wavered dangerously between fury and admiration. What an enviable ruse you'd hit on, it occurred to me, for getting everyone else to write your novel for you.

Yes, what a brigand you are, or do I mean swine?

And I vowed that if ever I gave you any more help I would insist on a share of the royalties. My agent, I promised myself, and you, would contact yours about it immediately – provided they're still on speaking terms.

With such feelings I read on again.

Then suddenly I understood what you were up to. Of course. It was the Humbert allusion that pointed me towards Nabokov. How could it not?

And I realized that far from blundering about and ignoring my advice you'd got there before me all along the way. How could I have so completely failed to notice all that Nabokovian irony in the umpteen earlier pages?

Yes, yours was the inherited – or at least, honestly purloined – territory of John Shade and Kinbote, so I understood belatedly. Obviously then I can't offer you any advice about how to write a novel and it was arrogant of me to think I could. You know exactly what you're doing, and what looked to me at first like clumsy, pompous over-writing and skimping on characterisation, and the way the narrative jerks from detailed exposition to summaries and then long-winded conversations, all that is exquisitely deliberate and what you're out to do at bottom is deconstruct the fictionality of the realist illusion.[1] (Personally I rather like the realist illusion though I know it's very unfashionable these days.)

And all to this end and with – dare I suggest? – disquieting ease you've introduced 'The Narrator' as a monster of vanity and self-importance who likes the sound of his own voice far too much and displays an unhealthy interest in little girls. His portentous interfering footnotes too. Superbly Kinbotian.

So much for isms.

As to characters though I couldn't deny a passing acquaintance with this man 'Palser' I was at first hard put to puzzle out the original for Wringhim Knox. Then in a flash it came to me: that Wringhim is none other than ***——. A subtile portrait and chivalrously subdued in parts but *** nonetheless.

Now since in Chapter 18 I find utterly unconvincing the vignette sketched therein of Charlton Palser sipping orange-juice and refusing to speak ill of the dead I want you please to incorporate the following reconstruction:

Paul Chalicer (whom I happen to know extremely intimately) is wonderfully amusing company especially when as sociably well oiled as he invariably is by six o' clock on Fridays. He is, especially then, as malicious as he is witty but all in such a context of overriding generosity of spirit that nobody expect Mumbo Rankles has ever been known to take offence.

I therefore and hereby propose thus:

That you scrap Wringhim Knox altogether (since he can, let's face it, be embarrassingly abrasive on occasion) and instead convert Paul Chalicer into an altogether more convivial literary drunkard who is still well able to lose your manuscript in the pub, etc.

By the way, what are these "Arts Commission knees-ups" you refer to and why aren't I invited?

Incidentally, moreover, the conversation about Scottish literary politics (also in Chapter 18, though a digression here) amply confirms

---

[1] We now accept, like T.S. Eliot, that this is what we *must* have meant.

my view that you should go back to that kind of contemporary satire. On the other hand . . . since I'm currently writing my own satirical novel about the Scottish literary scene, perhaps you should ignore that advice.

Yes, you should definitely ignore it.

Keep off, in fact.

Now look here.

At the risk of getting myself set up as a Fuddy Duddy I think you may be heading for a problem or two over taste. I'm thinking for instance of the scene where you have Countess Morel bed-bathing her son and finding he has a 'stupendous erection'.[2]

Then you have your Narrator's suggestive reference to his pubescent goddaughter's physical development. Don't you feel this sort of lip-smacking yumyumery may well cause offence in these prurient and paranoid times when child-molesting is getting such a bad press?[3]

And having Morel making love with the maja fatale beside the corpse of the priest? And then later regretting her death because he won't be able to bonk her again. All of this of course is a protracted Nabokovian alienation-device, I grant you – but don't you take it just a little too far?

As to the bizarre palaver over whether German anuses do or do not smile before, during, and/or after being buggered, who in the Home Counties or throughout the American mid-west is going to lap up this?

And then there's the sex bet back in Chapter 13 when the Marquis of Roquefort's floozies pull several fast ones on the young studs who fancy their virility. My objection here is not to the episode itself but rather that your depiction of it should be more erotic – since otherwise its tastelessness stands out somewhat nakedly.

Make the reader too excited to remember to feel disgusted, is what I mean. In my next letter I will send you a well-written *and* titillating sex-scene based on this episode for either a flat fee of one thousand pounds or else a pro rata percentage of your royalties.

---

[2] It's obviously stuck in *your* mind though, hasn't it?

[3]  If all the parents in Provence were miraculously transported to Cleveland, they'd be nicked before the weekend.

How's that?[4]

Penultimately, had I not perceived that you are indeed marching in the ironico-ludical footsteps of the original brilliant butterfly of Russo-Columbian letters himself I would have presumed to suggest that you needed to make your average reader *care* a lot more about virtually all the characters you present except myself. That you needed a stronger hook, in fact.

Here's the sort of thing:

At the outset your pompous Narrator finds in G.P.R. James's novel a wonderful moving confession that he sees instantly is too vividly written, really just too damned authentic, to have been created by that pitiful incompetent. Subsequent computer-aided textual analysis proves that the confession *must* be authentic. It is moreover quite fiendishly ambiguous in the way it talks of parricide. So your Narrator determines both to track down the original documents on which James drew, and also to discover for himself, and by extension for the reader, whether Morel kills his father or no – and if, so what?

Must wind up now since I have to be at Heathrow by seven. Let you know when I'm back. Meanwhile here's a few quickies mixed in from my notes file.

| Ch. | Note |
| --- | --- |
| 9 | *The Day of the Jackal.* Is the reader *intended* to remember that famous interview in which our late-lamented (tee-hee!) Prime Minister revealed that he or she *re*-reads Freddie Forsyth? |

---

[4] Sorry, but no. Subcontracting small portions of royalties is the worst administrative nightmare. Also, the way things are going, there might not be any left for 'me'. However, in grateful acknowledgement of all third-party inputs to this history, 7%* (seven per cent) of the net profits its instigator accrues will be paid on to Amnesty International until either the book itself passes into the public domain or else Amnesty disbands of its own accord due to no more work to do – probably, alas, the former. Any character still in copyright not happy with this arrangement is hereby warned to confess as much before the final draft, at which stage hos will be written out.

 **\* 'I suspect you of only doing this to win applause for your "Seven Per Cent Solution".' [J.R.]**

9     The conversation between your pompous Narrator and Janet
      goes on too long, especially the Narrator's soliloquay on parri-
      cide.
            Who is this Janet anyway?
            She obviously isn't Scottish and many of her views are
      diametrically at loggerheads with mine. Why don't you write her
      out of it and give more space to me? That'll simplify your roy-
      alty distribution arrangements and mean I get twice as much.[5]

17    This starts well, with Louis being bright before the Viceroy of
      whom the description is commendably researched. However,
      their conversation then breaks the basic 'rule' that no character
      should tell another something that the reader already knows.
            I can just imagine you sneering here though and chanting
      'Cuff the Lures'.

18    In the ruffs exchange between the Narrator and Audrey there's
      too much raw history, colourful though some of it is.
            People would rather make-believe than know, you know.
            Or so I believe.
            And if that's correct you'll stand to sell more books with less
      history and more fiction. And if that's correct you may like to
      consider fading down Audrey (devoted to her though I too am)
      and mixing up myself.

Hope that's of some use.
Love to Koo.
Beast,
P.

---

[5] See note 4.

# *34b*

# Stereo Soprano Flak

***Janet***

'Hello?'

'Congratulations!'

'What on?'

'You answered the phone!'

'It's after six.'

'So?'

'The Vatman will have gone home by now. If not fitted-kitchen hawkers. Anyway, how can you possibly help me?'

'You know I'm no good on the phone—'

'Do I?'

'Well, now you do. I prefer the licence of silence at the best of times, and in your case I'm a little fed up having my dialogue distorted and my best lines made over to your Charlton Palser.'

'From now on, Janet, you must address him as Paul Chalicer.'

'What?'

I explained.

'Curious. Well, to insure against this sort of grafting going on behind my back again, I'm not discussing the matter with you on the phone, but rather shall send you a few considered paragraphs, of which I shall have retained a veridical hard copy.'

'When?'

'Now.'

'How?'

'You got that AuthoCom package I sent you two weeks ago?'

'Yes.'

'Good. Then shove it up your modem, and give me two minutes.'

Seventeen minutes, and several screenfuls of garbage-out later, our communications computer made British Telecom shareholders richer by the following unbuggered gobbets.

\* \* \*

NOSE.TXT

This Roublestein thing. What's in a name, you may say, but there's a name that instantly typecasts your Janet as a New York Jewish momma - and I mean Noo Yoik. If you're having Roublestein it's got to be Morrie and Vera; it's got to be gefillte fish and eating, already.

Not this London Janet with her genteel reserve. Eh?

So okay you've got a nose for the salient feature (well, well you go around thinking these things don't matter,[3] and wham, suddenly that's what a person notices foremost about you). Softly, softly; this is sensitive ground.

---

[3] I was very distraught about this, and round midnight wrote Janet a long, private, personal letter of apology for any denting of self-imagery experienced, where none whatsoever was intended. The assignment of 'Roublestein' as her surname was, I explained, an ingrowing literary bad joke of little unalterable consequence. As far as her nose was concerned, it wasn't a part of the wholeness of her personhood which I had isolated for diacritical dismemberment. Now that *she* drew *my* attention to it, I could assure her that it struck me as a perfectly presentable, personable, characterful and in its holistic context attractive nose. Neither Tristramically abrupted nor yet Cyranoically haptic.* A little more abundant and authoritative than the bland and silly 'small, pert and appealing nose' that is supposed to sell all brands of frequent-wash hair shampoo, yet only the more distinctive for that. However, if despite my grovelling eulogy she would still prefer me to deedpoll her surname into, say, Smith, or even Jones, then, just as I had so gratified Paul Chalicer, so I would be delighted to oblige Janet Brown. 'A novelist has a duty to protect her originals, after all,' I wrote, especially if they are alive, well, and can afford to employ solicitors. So there you are, Janet. Up to you.

*'Which is rather to miss the point, Humbert. We aren't talking Cyrano here, but Fagin and Shylock.' [J.R.]*

SEX.TXT

It happened like this. Our MacKinnon aunt, who lives on the Solway Firth, had invited me up for a December break. We'd been to see the Burrell Collection, then in to Glasgow for tea. Daniel wanted to see the latest Schwarzenegger, and I didn't, so I left him in a Sauchiehall Street cinema with his Auntie, and then took the Clockwork Orange over to Hillhead, quietly smirking at the thought of your face. And it WAS quite a facer to actually WITNESS you, so to speak behind your back, doing your thing in the real-flesh debate.

You'll appreciate that I couldn't stay to say hello at the end (Aunt, Daniel, bedtime, etc) but may I hereby record that the occasion I witnessed was a much more decorous affair than the ribald fantasy you painted it into?

Of course, I can see why you had to exaggerate. It was a brave attempt to create intellectual sexual titillation on a par with true-blue porn. But is this ultimately possible? Show me the reader who's prepared to pay you to make them think, and I'll . . .

What it boils down to, if I'm honest, is that what I most miss in your travesty of the debate, and equally throughout Louis Morel's solitary nadir in Paris, is a lot of honest-to-God hardcore rampant thrustingly vicariously arousing SEX. There, I've said it.

Even though I am a woman, AND passably educated, AND moderately literate, I have to admit that when I get notably less sex (the violence I can always manage without) than I think I'm paying for (in your case, paying in kind), then, quite frankly, I want a lot more of it urgently. More sex. Real sex. Romantic, but not soppy. Tender, but not limp. Vigorous, but not brutal.[4] And above all, PLOT-JUSTIFIED.

---

[4] I'm sure she was also thinking, 'Genital, but not anal.' Being a lady, though, as well as a woman, she would not say so in electronic print.

So I want you to hurry us on to where Louis Morel finally gets Hélène Arnault into bed, deflowers her lovingly, and awakens her to the protracted bliss of monogamous heterosexual intercourse. And be warned, Mr Humberto Seale: should this pass be never reached, here is one Janet who will NEVER buy a book of yours again.

Going back to the debate, I was glad to clap eyes on Audrey at last. Quite some woman, and makes one wonder what she must have seen in you – all those years ago, I mean, that you keep alluding to, with those sighs of sickening nostalgia. Can't say I spotted your Audrey's Jennifer, but that's hardly surprising, is it? I mean, do us a favour! 'Courting teen goes along to support mother on sex and writers.' I ask you! And while we're on mothers . . . [5]

---

[5] The reader must understand that what you have just read is Janet's own fiction. If she had been present at the sex / talent debate, then (a) we would have seen her, and (b) she would never have departed without making her presence felt. The actual facts are: (1) Janet was nowhere near Glasgow that night; (2) Jennifer, though she snuck off before the voting, was most certainly present, though whether that aided her mother a lot is another matter; (3) the account presented for your perusal in chapters 28 and 29 of this book is as truthful as narrative memory, notes and concealed tape-recorders can make it. Accordingly, the value of Janet's invention here must be sought not in literal veracity but rather in delicate sub-textualities such as typical feminist inability to take a male writer at his word. Now whether this is a function of aggression projected out of the biological reality that occasionally (though never always) when women do say *Don't!* they don't actually mean *Do!* (and vice) is not for us to say if we know what's good for us. On the other hand, it would probably follow that if more rapists studied harder to become feminist literary critics then the incidence of genuinely unsolicited rape in the world would decline immeasurably, to the greater good of all save diehard perverts.

***Audrey***

'Good evening, Jennifer.'

'Evening, Uncle Humbert.'

'How are you?'

'Fine.'

'Boyfriend okay?'

'Which boyfriend, Uncle Humbert?'

'Ah, yes. Touché. Silly me. Pass the revolver. Ah-hem, is your mother there, by any chance?'

'Yes.'

I allowed the ensuing pause to drag into incredulity, at my end, before courteously adding:

'Do you think I could possibly have a word with her?'

'Hang on, Uncle Humbert,' drawled Jennifer distantly.

'Yes? What do you want?' resumed Audrey, in a cool, crisp tone as of having not yet entirely forgiven my ruffling of her feathers at the Great Debate.

'I was wondering what sort of favour you would be wanting me to do you.'

'You're pissed, aren't you?'

'Certainly not on not a drop more than three cans of Stella.'

'Then what the hell are you on about?'

I explained that everyone else I had been in communication with throughout the day had been after me to *do* something for them.

'Well I'm not.'

'Lucky me!'

'Except, you could hang up.'

'In a minute. First I'd like . . . ' And I explained that, since Koo was away on a selling trip, and because we felt our readers would like some background to the exile of the Count of Soissons in Sedan, I wanted to bounce a few facts off her briefly: to check out and polish up.

'Piss off,' said Audrey, on the ground that she'd had a hard day, and wanted to catch up on the exciting pan-Euro political developments to be reported on News At Ten.

Swiftly, though, I bent her to my will by regretting in tones of jocular menace-in-jest that if after all we'd been through together she now refused to help me out in my half-hour of historical need then I would get my own back soon enough by leaking to Jennifer prime details of her mother's sexual preferences. If this seems an unforgivably abominable tactic, please consider that it isn't quite as bad as having your narrator shoot a puppy (as once subjunctively recommended by Erich Segal, author of the comparable *Love Story*) and also that (as Paul Theroux himself has suggested – though only by implication, and presumably in ignorance of Audrey) there is no telling the depths to which a desperate novelist will not stoop. Whether, in the present instance, the dividend paid was worth the moral extortion, you must judge by the following chapter.

## 35

# The Count of Soissons

*According to Audrey*

'*Why* do you want to know about the Count of Soissons?' peeved Audrey.

'Because the fate of my protagonist is about to become handcuffed to the destiny of his Highness of Soissons,' I responded affably, 'about which you know more than I.'

'What *do* you know about Soissons?'

'Let's assume that I don't.'

'Oh, very well,' sighed Audrey, who proceeded much as follows:

'You will recall that in 1515 the ancient and venerable *county* of Vendôme, in north-central France, was promoted by François Premier of France [died 1547] into a *duchy*, for the benefit of Charles de Bourbon.'

'Who was a direct descendant of Saint Louis [Louis IX, died 1270]?'

'Correct. By way of his fifth son, Robert de Clermont. Now Charles de Bourbon, thus Duke of Vendôme, left five sons, only two of whom had children. Antoine, the elder; and Louis, the younger. The first, by his marriage with Jeanne d'Albret, became King of Navarre, and left one only son, who, by default of the line of Valois,[1] succeeded to the throne of France.'

'Henri Quatre, of prodigious bedhopping fame?'

'If you must. Meanwhile, the younger brother, Louis, became Prince of Conde. From two marriages he begat two families, the first continuing as the Conde branch, while the second continued as the Soissons branch – ie, through Louis's son Charles, whose own son Louis, Count of Soissons, is the prince [ie *of the royal blood*; terribly important in French history] whom you asked me about.'

'Bloody inconsiderate of them, Audrey, being so mean with names. So many Henries, Charleses, and Louises! Bit of a novelist's nightmare.'

---

[1] Henri III, the last Valois king, was assassinated in 1589. See *The Counts of Mount Venus*, Part IV.

'Not my problem, Humbert. Anything else?'

'So our present Count of Soissons starts life with high status, royal blood, presumably a lavish income, and a rather good opinion of himself?'

'That, by all known accounts, would be a massive understatement of the case.'

'What do you mean?'

'Under the tutelage and management of a fanatically proud and at once overly indulgent mother, the Count of Soissons would appear to have matured into a teenager of the most revolting narcissism and cultivated hauteur.'

'She – the Countess, I mean – would be the lady after whom was nicknamed a mammoth carp in the Marquis of Roquefort's moat?'

'If you say so, Humbert. That doesn't sound like a detail we professional historians would lose a lot of shuteye over.'

'Quite often repulsive adolescents metamorphose into moderately tolerable adults. My aunts say the same of myself. What about you, Audrey?'

'Teenage girls, Humbert, are notoriously less disgusting than their classmates of protuberant gender. As to the Count of Soissons, by his eighteenth birthday it was a common saying, that:

'"No one save his mother may ever see the Count of Soissons twice; for if he does not dislike them, and forbid them to sully his presence ever again, then they are invariably so disgusted by him, that they spurn him ever after."'

'And this was all his mother's fault, for pandering to his bee's-knees self-image?'

'I wouldn't want us, Humbert, to get shunted into one of your phoney Nature Versus Nurture sidetracks all night. Suffice it to say that, in the view of the foremost authorities, just as the young Count of Soissons's faults were more the product of his education, than the fault of evil innate dispositions, his very excesses in due course became a force for their own correction.'

'I'm not sure I follow that.'

'I mean that as he increasingly found himself avoided by coevals who normally would have become his staunch companions, and sometimes even deserted by his servants, so in his later teens he was often much at leisure to enjoy his rank, dignity and uniqueness on his own.'

'And?'

'As he was in truth endowed with very considerable powers of mind, and qualities of character, he in due course worked out for himself where the principal cause of his loneliness lay.'

'Within himself?'

'How perceptive you are.'

'And what did he do about it?'

'How far it is possible to truly and irreversibly reform our own worst traits is a thorny issue – as you, Humbert, will appreciate more than many. But so far as observable behaviour was concerned, the reports that have come down to us suggest almost unanimously that the Count of Soissons did indeed achieve a rare reformation for the better.'

'Cut back on slagging off his peers, and suchlike?'

'How quaintly you put it. So that by the time of his exile in Sedan, not a trace of his former habitual disdain remained visible in his features, or in his reception of visitors, no matter what their rank.'

'We don't know, though, what depravities of haughtiness may still have been infecting those deepermost recesses of his heart, that not even Stella Artois can reach to?'

'That's very true, Humbert. But so what?'

'Many a man, having had to struggle to rid himself of vices born of bad mothering, would have been left with certain feelings of bitterness.'

'Resentment of his mother, do you mean?'

'Just so. I'm thinking for example, of Henri III, and how he took it all out on his Mother Medici.'

'Not so the Count of Soissons, at least so far as we know. Towards the Countess he would appear to have always remained a model of filial affection, consulting her wisdom, and acting in accordance with her wishes on all occasions when his own interests and honour did not oblige him to overrule her.'

'Are we not, here, treading back uncomfortably close to the toes of whether women are fit to govern?'

'You may be, Humbert. For me it's not an issue.'

'Hum. Let's move on, can we, to the reasons for his being outlawed in Sedan.'

'Starting when?'

'The antipathy between Soissons and Richelieu.'

'The Count's view – which some of us would consider an over-simplification, and probably a witting one – was that the Cardinal was nothing but a ruthless arriviste who had fawningly prised all the reins of government from the feeble hands that should have held them.'

'Louis XIII?'

'Of course.'

'And the rank, power, wealth, and latterly the popularity of the Count of Soissons – all must have seemed like quite a threat to the Cardinal.'

'Absolutely.'

'So?'

'Richelieu, never a man to live in fear passively, resolves either to win the Count's allegiance, or else to crush him utterly.'

'How does he try to win him?'

'He offers him – in a famous phrase – "in one Circean cup, everything that *he* fancied could tempt the ambitions, and seduce the passions of *him* he sought to gain."'

'Oh yes? How?'

'By a confidential messenger the Cardinal proposes to the Count the hand of his [Richelieu's] own favourite niece, the Duchesse d'Aquillon. Plus an immense dower settlement in ready cash. Plus the reversion of all his own enormous possessions inside France. Plus the great honour of the sword of Constable of France. Plus the power and benefits of whichever provincial government in France the Count might fancy.'

'Quite a package. Which most of us, I dare say, might find it difficult to refuse.'

'Yes. But not so the Count de Soissons, who conceived himself mightily insulted by the offer, and struck the Cardinal's messenger across the face for daring to propose the hand of the widow of a mean provincial gentleman [ie Marie de Vignerot, Richelieu's niece, who was also the Duchesse d'Aquillon], to a prince of the blood royal of France.'

'Sounds to me like hauteur bred in the bone!'

'Maybe. Unless . . . '

'A cunning set-up?'

'As you know, Humbert, I'm not such a great one for conspiracy theories as you men. However, it has been suggested that the Cardinal knew perfectly well how the Count of Soissons would react, and therefore deliberately insulted him – in his own terms – but under cover of a grandiose array of apparent pacific bounty, which any innocent bystander must judge to be sincere.'

'Is it not equally possible that the Cardinal's overtures *were* made in good faith, in this one instance, and that it was the the Count of Soissons who played the first disingenuous move: by *pretending* to be offended, and exploiting his affected royal dudgeon as an *excuse* to snub the Cardinal, and exacerbate his dander by thumping his messenger? For, as we all know, there's no surer way of enraging a lofty principal than by humiliating his trusty ambassador. We've only got to look at poor old Kent in the stocks,[2] haven't we, to remind ourselves of that?'

'None of these theses is impossible, Humbert. It's not one of the best documented phases of the Cardinal's rule.'

'What of the ensuing *facts*?'

'Behind the Cardinal's mask of slighted generosity – no doubt about this – a characteristically fierce personal resentment of the Count of Soissons weighed in with all his other motives for engineering the destruction of that prince.'

'Personal resentments, with Richelieu, being, as it were, the essence of the fuel that kept his spirit firing?'

'Very much so. Even when, latterly, his body was wasted by chronic sickness and advancing death.'

'Can we take it then, that, once the feud between the Cardinal and Soissons was out in the open, no opportunity would ever be lost of gratifying his animus against the Count?'

'Correct.'

'Did he, Richelieu, try to do the Count for Huguenot sympathies – as, whether or not spitefully beguiled by the Marquis of Roquefort, he persecuted the Count of Bagnols?'

'Be reasonable, Humbert. This is not my best period, and in any case I'm not an encyclopaedia of the French noblesse.'

'Of course not, Audrey. Besides, in these accelerating times of all the world's knowledge on seedy ROMs, why bother to even memorize your own home telephone number? I take it, then, you've never heard of Roquefort and Bagnols?'

'The names ring a distant bell, but that's all. As to Bagnols, I'm sure there are at least three small towns or villages of that name in France. So which would your Count be Count of? And what's his claim

---

2 In *King Lear*, II.2. Kent, the archetypal loyal servant, is mock-
ingly confined to the stocks by Regan and her husband Cornwall:
to spite, belittle and provoke old Lear – Regan's father. Is not this
play, multi-dimensionally superior to *Hamlet*, incontestably the
greatest tragic drama of all?

to fame?'

Briefly I told of the mad passion of the Count of Bagnols and Henriette de Vergne, with its tragic ending brought about by the malicious envy of the Marquis of Roquefort getting Bagnols framed for a Huguenot activist, then murdered fresh from his sweetheart's bedroom window, so soon after his miraculous escape from the Bastille.

Audrey sniffed eloquently, and said:

'Obviously a frivolous novelist, Humbert, would be in his element there.'

'Or hers!'

'Serious history is another matter, though. And as far as the Count of Soissons is concerned: given his status, power, wealth, and growing popularity, the Cardinal would certainly need to nobble him with something enormously more weighty than a little Huguenot hankering.'

'Like High Treason?'

'All treason, under Richelieu, was High.'

'Particularly when it came to being punished for it!'

'As you say. Still, for a long time the Cardinal was unable to pin anything on the Count. While the latter continued to reside in the midst of the court, in the society of his King and Queen, conspicuously loyal, even Richelieu found it impossible – though all of Paris was rife with intrigue – to devise any case against him.'

'But that wouldn't deter the Cardinal?'

'On the contrary. Starved of grounds for legitimate impeachment of the Count, the Cardinal exploited every ounce of his influence over Louis XIII to ensure that the Count was subjected to a ceaseless barrage of petty vexations, privations, snubs, innuendoes – even apparently authorless practical jokes of the wetter and more painful kind – until, hurt that the King had not intervened more energetically to halt this juvenile cruelty, the Count of Soissons packed his bags and set off to establish his own more harmonious court-in-exile in Italy.'

'Leaving Richelieu fizzing in Paris?'

'Hopping mad – no doubt about it. First, because the Count was now effectively outwith the Cardinal's own controls. Second, because, as the arteries of Richelieu's police state hardened, and civil liberties disappeared by the wayside nightly, popular regard within France (especially Paris) for the Count of Soissons soared.'

'What steps did the Cardinal take?'

'With his accustomed superhuman industry, he mounted a fresh offensive, this time of dissembling suasion, flattery, and invitations to reconciliation, culminating in a devilish piece of moral blackmail: Richelieu making out that only the Count of Soissons, with his incomparable military abilities, could guarantee victory for France in her current war [1635–6] with Spain and Austria.'

'So the Count was lured back by the carrot of martial glory?'

'As so often, in the history of men.'

'Did he get it?'

'What?'

'Martial glory?'

'No. Despite having superheroically checked the Imperial forces in Picardy, and that despite the Cardinal having starved him of supplies and reinforcements, the Count of Soissons was robbed of the renown he had earned by the Cardinal rushing to the scene of victory – together with Louis XIII, to secure all honours and glory for the King, and leave the Count once more eclipsed.'

'Must have felt a bit galling!'

'Historians sympathetic to Richelieu assert that it was vengeful resentment, at being cheated of his military fame, that finally tipped the Count of Soissons into full-blooded conspiracy against the Cardinal.'

'But?'

'Others maintain that when, after his exile in Italy, the Count returned to France, and found the laws of the state subverted by the state itself—'

'Meaning Richelieu?'

'Who else? And individual liberty become a tradable commodity, and the public good sacrificed everywhere to the particular interests of one insatiably ambitious man, well . . . '

'Like Brutus, the Count of Soissons conceived it a civic duty to rid the nation of the vaulting dictator?'

'That's one slant on it.'

'Where?'

'In what has come to be known as the Conspiracy of Amiens.'

'When?'

'1636. It was after the siege of Corbie, in Picardy. There, the Count of Soissons had been the prime mover in retaking the town from the invading Imperialists. But Richelieu had placed in titular command, above the Count, the King's own younger brother.'

'Gaston of Orleans?'

'Yes.'

'A prize lamebrain prune!'

'Arguably. Certainly always game for a schoolboyish conspiracy, usually against his royal brother.'

'Confident of never being seriously punished himself?'

'Exactly. Even when his co-conspirators were being imprisoned, tortured and executed all over France, Gaston – or "Monsieur", as the King's next-in-line brother was always styled – would count on getting off with a severe talking to, or a temporary banishment to Blois.'

'So how did the Conspiracy of Amiens come about?'

'Thrown into closer contact than ever before, by their co-operation at the Siege of Corbie, Gaston and the Count of Soissons had ample opportunity and time to interbreed their various grievances. According to what reasoning, specious or not, and moral conviction, self-deceptive or not, we will never know. But at the end of the day their concerted conclusion was that the Cardinal must be got rid of.'

'Assassinated?'

'That depends who you believe.'

'And who do you believe?'

Audrey then concluded our lesson by sketching two rival interpretations of the Conspiracy of Amiens:

SOISSONS AS J. CARTER   V.   *SOISSONS AS J. KENNEDY*

There was never any lack of
                    *Uniting their private grievances,*
others, besides Gaston, to take
                    *Gaston of Orleans and the Count of*
the view that the only sure means
                    *Soissons determine to have the Cardinal*
of terminating the Cardinal's
                    *murdered at Amiens. Two bravo*
supremacy was to kill him.
                    *gentlemen, by the names of Saint-Ibal*
However, as the consent of
                    *and Montrésor, are appointed to do*
the Count of Soissons could
                    *the deed, on receipt of a signal from*

never be obtained, to engage
in pre-emptive murder, it was
determined rather to arrest
the minister at the council at
Amiens, and submit his conduct
to the judgment of a legal
tribunal. The irresolution of
Gaston, Duke of Orleans,
suspended the execution of the
conspirators' purpose at the
moment most favourable for
effecting it, and before another
opportunity presented itself,
the conspiracy was discovered.
The Duke of Orleans fled to
Blois, while Monsieur le Comte
(as the Count of Soissons was
popularly known) retired across
the country to the independent
stronghold of Sedan, the gates

*Gaston. In due course an opportunity*
*presents itself. The Cardinal is alone*
*at the foot of his staircase, which*
*he has descended prior to entering*
*his carriage. All around him are the*
*conspirators and their henchmen. The*
*commissioned assassins have their*
*hands ready on their concealed*
*pistol butts. Eagerly they watch the*
*countenances of both Gaston and the*
*Count of Soissons, awaiting tensely*
*the prearranged fateful wink or nod.*
*But the moment passes. No signal*
*to kill is forthcoming, since Gaston*
*is too cowardly and the Count – for*
*whatever reason – is too irresolute*
*to give it. Richelieu, for the moment*
*unaware of the peril he has escaped,*
*drives away in his carriage. Gaston,*
*in a funk, flees to Blois. The Count of*

of which were willingly thrown

> *Soissons, as a wise precaution against*

open to him by the Duke of

> *his co-conspirator blabbing, removes*

Bouillon, who, though a vassal

> *to the security of Sedan — confident*

of France, still held that

> *that Richelieu would never dare*

important territory between

> *attempt the siege of so impregnable*

Luxembourg and Champagne, in full

> *a place, while still pressed on every*

and unlimited sovereignty — and

> *side by the other wars which he*

who nursed no lack of grudges

> *himself has sparked.*

against Richelieu.


### According to De Retz

The Count [of Soissons] was courageous in the highest degree of what is commonly called valour, and had a more than ordinary share in that boldness of mind which we call resolution. The first is common and to be frequently met with among the vulgar, but the second is rarer than can be imagined, and yet abundantly more necessary for great enterprises; and is there a greater in the world than heading a party?

The command of an army is without comparison of less intricacy, for there are wheels within wheels necessary for governing the State, but then they are not near so brittle and delicate. In a word, I am of the opinion there are greater qualities necessary to make a good head of a party than to make an emperor who is to govern the whole world, and that resolution ought to run parallel with judgement,—I say, with heroic judgement, which is able to distinguish the *extraordinary* from what we call the *impossible*.

The Count had not one grain of this discerning faculty, which is but seldom to be met with in the sublimest genius. His character was mean to a degree, and consequently susceptible of unreasonable jealousies and distrusts, which of all characters is the most opposite to that of a good partisan, who is indispensably obliged in many cases to suppress, and in all to conceal, the best-grounded suspicions.

This was the reason I could not be of the opinion of those who were for engaging the Count in a civil war [ie, against Richelieu] . . . [3]

[However] . . . for fear of being tedious I shall only tell you in one word that the Cardinal, contrary to his own interest, hurried the Count into a civil war, by such arts of chicanery as those who are fortune's favourites never fail to play upon the unfortunate.

The minds of people began now [late 1640] to be more embittered than ever. I was sent for by the Count to Sedan to tell him the state of Paris. The account I gave him could not but be very agreeable; for I told him the very truth: that he was universally beloved, honoured, and adored in that city, and his enemy dreaded and abhorred. The Duke of Bouillon, who was urgent for war, be the consequence what it would, improved upon these advantages, and made them look more plausible, but Varicarville strongly opposed him.

I thought myself too young[4] to declare my opinion; but, being pressed to do so by his Highness, I took the liberty to tell him that a Prince of the blood ought to engage himself in a civil war rather than suffer any diminution of his reputation or dignity, yet that nothing but these two cases could justly oblige him to it, because he hazards both by a commotion whenever the one or the other consideration does not make it necessary; that I thought his Highness far from being under any such necessity; that his retreat to Sedan secured him from the indignity he must have submitted to, among others, of taking the left-hand, even in the Cardinal's own house; that, in the meantime, the popular hatred of the Cardinal gained his Highness the greater share of the public favour, which is always much better secured by inaction than action, because the glory of action depends upon success,

---

3  Following the lead of G.P.R. James, that staunch pioneer campaigner for copyright law enforcement, we have lifted the present passage with great assiduity from De Retz's secret *Memoirs* – to this point faithful even to *em*ming the dash [—], where normally we would *en* [ – ]. Yours sincerely, &c. In the remainder of the passage the content of the text is equally authentic, and only the form has been lightly edited; for example, to break down several-page paragraphs into chunks fit to read on a plane.

4  The Abbé de Retz was just twenty-five at this time.

for which no one can answer; whereas inaction is sure to be commended as being founded upon the hatred which the public will always bear to the minister.

That, therefore, I should think it would be more glorious for his Highness, in the view of the world, to support himself by his own weight, that is, by the merit of his virtue, against the artifices of so powerful a minister as the Cardinal de Richelieu [ . . . ] than to kindle the fire of war, the flagrant consequences whereof no man is able to foresee; that it was true that the minister was universally cursed, but that I could not yet see that the people's minds were exasperated enough for any considerable revolution; that the Cardinal was in a declining state of health, and if he should not die this time, his Highness would have the opportunity of showing the King and the public that though, by his own personal authority and his important post at Sedan, he was in a capacity to do himself justice, he sacrificed his own resentments to the welfare and quiet of the State; and that if the Cardinal should recover his health, he would not fail, by additional acts of tyranny and oppression, to draw upon himself the redoubled execrations of the people, which would ripen their murmurings and discontents into a universal revolution.

This is the substance of what I said to the Count, and he seemed to be somewhat affected by it. But the Duke of Bouillon was enraged, and told me, by way of banter,

"Your blood is very cold for a gentleman of your age."

To which I replied in these very words:

"All the Count's servants are so much obliged to you, monsieur, that they ought to bear everything from you; but were it not for this consideration alone, I should think that your bastions would not be always strong enough to protect you."

The Duke soon came to himself, and treated me with all the civilities imaginable, such as laid a foundation for our future friendship. I stayed two days longer at Sedan, during which the Count changed his mind five different times, as I was told by M. Saint-Ibal, who said little was to be expected from a man of his humour. At last, however, the Duke of Bouillon won him over. I was charged to do all I could to convince the people of Paris, had an order to take up money and to lay it out for this purpose, and I returned from Sedan with letters more than enough to have hanged two hundred men.

The Count's remittance, of 12,000 crowns, I carried to my Aunt de Maignelai,[5] telling her that it was a restitution made by one of my dying friends, who made me trustee of it upon condition that I should distribute it among decayed families who were ashamed to make their necessities known, and that I had taken an oath to distribute it myself, pursuant to the desire of the testator, but that I was at a loss to find out fit objects for my charity; and therefore I desired her to take the care of it upon her. The good woman was perfectly transported, and said she would do it with all her heart; but because I had sworn to make the distribution myself, she insisted upon it that I must be present, not only for the sake of my promise, but to accustom myself to do acts of charity.

This was the very thing I aimed at,—an opportunity of knowing all the poor of Paris. Therefore I suffered myself to be carried every day by my Aunt into the outskirts, to visit the poor in their garrets, and I met very often in her house people who were very well clad, and many whom I once knew, that came for private charity. My good Aunt charged them always to pray to God for her nephew, who was the hand that God had been pleased to make use of for this good work. Judge you of the influence this gave me over the populace, who are without comparison the most considerable in all public disturbances. For the rich never come into such measures unless they are forced, and beggars do more harm than good, because it is known that they aim at plunder; those, therefore, who are capable of doing most service are such as are not reduced to common beggary, yet so straitened in their circumstances as to wish for nothing more than a general change of affairs in order to repair their broken fortunes. I made myself acquainted with people of this rank for the course of four months with uncommon application, so that there was hardly a child in the chimney-corner but I gratified with some small token. I called them by their familiar names. My Aunt, who always made it her business to go from house to house to relieve the poor, was a cloak for all. I also played the hypocrite, and frequented the conferences of Saint Lazarus.

---

[5] Marguerite Claude de Gondi, wife of Florimond d'Halluin, Marquis de Maignelai. Died 1650.

# *36*

# Sedan

Unaware of the systematic extent of De Retz's suborning of straitened gentlefolk all over Paris, yet sensitive to the campaigning cynicism underlying his nocturnal visitor's suave persona – put on guard, in his own terms, by 'a restless after-niggling of my conscience, like the distant banging of a stable shutter, throughout a windy night' – Louis Morel, by the time he sets off for breakfast chez De Retz's aunt, has determined to have nothing further to do with De Retz himself, or the Count of Soissons.

Or anyone else at Sedan.

Or any transaction smacking remotely of treason against the State.

There is, besides, the consideration that, should he absent himself from the capital for any prolonged period, he may never again locate Hélène before she is bullied and rushed into tragic marriage with that aspiring adulterer cad named Charles, 'whose drawling self-satisfaction, and decadent Parisian vowels, I recalled with ineffable loathing.'

At the Hôtel de Maignelai, Louis, despite himself, is awed into a psychological defensive by the sheer scale of the architecture, the numbers of fawning attendant gentleman, the servants galore in sumptuous livery, and the prodigious peripheral bustle of preparation for catering and hospitality – all of which reminds him, with pangs of debilitating longing, of his memories of how Château Morel too must have been, a century or so ago, when the family fortunes were not yet ravaged.

Having embraced Louis with easy familiarity, fed him breakfast in a small south-facing dining-room, and then dismissed all his attendants, De Retz produces from a secret inner pocket a packet of unsealed letters.

'Have a look through these,' he says causally, passing them to his guest.

Louis reads.

'Are these the papers you would have me transport to Sedan?' he asks two minutes later.

'Among others.'

'But this is downright treason.'

'The Cardinal would certainly say so,' De Retz agrees affably, as he nibbles at a sweet dried fig.

'I do not feel, monsieur,' responds Louis, selecting his words with care, 'that I myself am sufficiently partisan, either by natural inclination or acquired conviction, to have the right to accept your commission.'

'Treason, Monsieur Morel, is the fashion. It is, after all, a most noble species of treason. Treason as a prelude to *Liberation*. Now there's a fine word. And therefore: not only – in the glamour and thrills associated with it – is liberational treason *like* supererogatory sex, but it has come, in recent months, to be gauged as the shibboleth of sexual attraction *in itself*.

'The Cardinal has worked hard to deserve a lot of treason, and now every gentleman and lady worth the salt in their mingled perspirations are taking delight in giving it him. The *frisson* of danger thus generated translates vigorously to excitement in the bedchamber. If you won't partake of it, no lady in vogue will oblige you.'

'I hadn't thought of it that way,' confesses Louis. 'However, talking of ladies—'

'You will find, moreover, that though the tongue of treason come not fluently to you in the abstract, like Latin in a pastor's schoolroom, you will nonetheless pick it up with great facility in Sedan: like Spanish in a maja's boudoir.'

'I cannot afford the time,' blurts Louis flatly.

'What time, monsieur?'

'I have business of my own in Paris, you see.'

'No. I do not see. What business, pray?'

Louis finds himself blushing. De Retz's deft manipulations have succeeded in making him feel like a proverbial parochial worm: for putting his personal anxieties and projects above the great cause of overthrowing the Cardinal.

'It is . . . a private matter,' he insists with conscious lameness.

'Involving a woman?'

Louis could not deny it.

'This Hélène – I believe you said – whom you touched upon last night?'

'Well, yes.'

'What about her?'

Reluctantly Louis explains:

About Hélène's unexpected appearance in Paris, apparently transported here by her lawyer father; and the odious pledges of the faceless
Charles – to marry Hélène, and deceive her.

'*Now* I see!' beams De Retz, dabbing his figgy lips with the corner of
a rolled-up napkin. 'Now look here, Monsieur Morel . . . '

Half an hour later De Retz has persuaded Louis that the visit to Sedan
will only be brief – an interlude of initiation; that soon thereafter Louis
will be back in Paris, the better to serve the Count of Soissons in the
capital, in league with De Retz himself.

'And in the meantime, Monsieur Morel, I myself, who know this
city most infinitely better than do you, shall be all eyes and ears
for this lady you are missing, and the knave whom you say aims
to wrong her.'

In support of that platform, De Retz writes a fresh letter to the Count
of Soissons, urgently requesting the lieutenancy of Monsieur Morel back
in Paris as soon as possible.

'What more can I say?' the plausible conspirator concluded. 'Other
than: here, with my compliments, are some funds to insure your journey.'

By late morning Louis has arranged to leave Paris, paid the Widow
Beaupère a retainer to keep on his lodging, bought 'a docile jennet'
for Achilles Lefranc to ride, and after an early lunch they trot off east.
Due to Achilles' docile pace, and periodic needs to stop, it is after sunset
before they reach La Ferté Sous Jouarre,[1] but thanks to a cold clear
moonlit night Louis is still able to evince aesthetic sensibilities again
some way in advance of his age by admiring 'the abbey in all its stark
beauty, framed by the pale winter sky' – before adjourning to one of the
several waterside inns.

After staging the next night in Reims, they proceed north-east until,
late the following afternoon, they reach the left bank[2] of the Meuse
at Remilly, some three miles upstream from Sedan. Having negotiated
with a local entrepreneur, Louis elects to convey both themselves and
their horses down the last lap to Sedan by boat. This is partly not to lose

---

[1]  For more lingering detail on this quaint little riverside town, see
    *The Counts of Mount Venus*, Chapter 9.

[2]  If you imagined your nose pointing north of west: towards (as
    the crow flew) what the English called their Channel.

another night on the road, and also because the Abbé de Retz has given him so much cash to cover his journey expenses that he feels it would be a shame not to spend quite a lot of it.

'But the drawbridge is raised!' Louis complains in alarm to the boatman, as the massive fortifications of Sedan become visible round the final river bend.

'No matter, your worship,' grunts the boatman. 'Theys'll drop it down to let youze in.'

'But how do you know?'

'Theyse letting *all* folks in what come, your worship. For every man what comes this way is afire to dethrone the Cardinal, like, and bound to take the field for the Count.'

The boatman's naive prognosis proves correct at least so far as obtaining entry to the city is concerned.

Though it was not by the drawbridge [*Louis goes on*], but by the landgate they call the Luxembourg, that we were in due course permitted to enter.

Immediately we were within the city walls, my bridle was seized on either side by one of a pair of long-practised pikemen, and the same performed upon Achilles, while the four sharp points of their partners' pikes were pressed suasively to our throats.

Thus constrained, though yet a-horse, we were led onwards and upwards round cobbled wynds to a small guard-house, where we were obliged to dismount and present ourselves to the officer of the watch within; as sleepy-looking a fellow as one might imagine, and growing sleepier from his dinner.

'Whom seek you in the good town of Sedan?' demanded the officer, in the droning lilt of a barrow vendor, that bespeaks much repetition.

'I am come to seek his Highness the Count of Soissons,' replied I.

'Upon what business?'

'With despatches, from . . . his agents in Paris.'

'Proof?' yawned the officer.

I presented for inspection by lamplight the Abbé de Retz's seal, upon his letter to the Count. With this the officer seemed instantly satisfied, and detailed one of the four pairs of pikemen to chaperone us up to the Castle.

Within the citadel, Achilles having been detailed to attend to stabling, I was detained half an hour in an anteroom, until a tall and gracious page, more splendidly attired than I myself, arrived to summon me down

various corridors, up stairs, and through a second small ante-chamber
tenanted only by a youth of some seventeen years nodding studiously
over a book, to a heavily metalled door set within an arch between
two pillars – which door the page opened with an ostentatious bow, and
ushered me beyond.

The room I then entered was large and lofty in the style of François I,
hung with fine Flemish tapestries of fading hues, and furnished throughout in dark heavy wood.

Those sombre colourings, overcast by the carved oak plafond above,
would perhaps have lent a gloomy air of yester years to the scene, were
it not for a large glass-bowled lamp, containing numerous candles, which
hung by a chain from the ceiling, to illumine, immediately beneath, the
pages of a book being read by a gentleman reposed in a capacious easy
chair, who at this very moment was simultaneously turning with great
eagerness to the following page, and wiping tears of laughter from
his eyes.

Upon his hearing the door close discreetly behind me, the reader
jumped up, laid down his book, and extended to me the open arms of
welcome; though meanwhile endeavouring with difficulty to recompose
his countenance into gravity.

As I advanced, my bundle of letters ready in my hand, the Count of
Soissons – for he it was – addressed me with the frank affability of a
long-known elder cousin:

'Monsieur Louis Morel of Bigorre?' he exclaimed.

'Indeed, your Highness,' I replied.

'You catch me in an occupation which the proverb would attribute
only to fools,' chuckled he.

'What is that, your Highness?' I inquired.

'Laughing to myself!' he laughed out loud again. 'Although, with such
a companion as Sancho Panza[3] in one's mind, one may fairly claim to be
never alone. But tell me . . . '

---

[3] Gauging by the lachrymation of the Count's solitary mirth, in the
   light of his habitual sombriety, we divine that he must have been
   reading Chapter XVII of Part II of *Don Quixote*, the conclusion
   of the 'Adventure of the Lions', wherein the battle-avid knight
   hastily plops upon his head the helmet full of hot ewes'-milk
   curds, which the doughty squire Sancho has just bought off some
   shepherds hard by. But you might judge otherwise.

During the several minutes following the Count sat me down, summoned a servant to pour me wine, and emphasized several times how very welcome my arrival in Sedan was to him personally. 'For you have been a long-expected guest!' he stressed, in a tone of affectionate rebuke. 'Yet now you are arrived,' he added more seriously, 'however great the pleasure of your presence to me, it were perhaps better for yourself to have stayed away.'

'I cannot imagine', I responded, 'anything better for myself, than the honour of being attached to the Count of Soissons.'

At this − his broad, expressive countenance like an equinoxial sky − he smiled, sighed and frowned, all within the space of the drawing of one breath. 'Most kind of you to say so, Monsieur Morel,' he murmured. 'But tell me now: how is Paris? Who have you been meeting there, and what words are on their lips.'

More than a little ashamed of the ignominious solitude of my sojourn in the capital, I countered by suggesting that perhaps his Highness might prefer first to peruse the letters I had fetched him, whereafter I might essay to answer any questions remaining.

'Well bethought,' he nodded agreeably, and waved me to help myself to more of that delicious sweet white wine, as with a small silver-hilted dagger he himself broke open the seals on the various letters, prior to smoothing them out in a pile.

'Heaven only knows . . . ,' he exclaimed as he read the first.

'Aha. Oh, yes!' he interjected with bitter irony, as his eyes raced down the second − presumably from Monsieur, the King's brother. 'My good cousin of Orleans can ever be relied on!' The third communication he put aside without comment. Then, as he digested the longer epistle from the Abbé de Retz, the Count several times glanced aside at me − as though to compare the character which the Abbé's written words assigned me with such impressions as he already had formed for himself.

In some trepidation, I sat still, sipped my wine, and waited.

The Count, when he had done reading, rose up in the grip of competing reflections, walked several times across the length of his spacious saloon, stopped once to turn a log in the chimney, and in due course returned to his seat, all the while sliding his right hand up and down the bejewelled broad sword belt which hung across his breast − as another might stroke his beard.

'Monsieur de Retz, I find,' the Count resumed, 'has made you aware of some, but by no means all, of the circumstances of my present situation. And in this, as is his wont, he has done wisely: to leave such delicate and more intimate communications to myself. Now, how shall I put this?'

As the Count debated within himself, I remained attentively silent.

'In respect of the immense mutual esteem,' he continued somewhat abstractedly, again with that absent fondling of his baldric, 'between my mother and yours, I had some months ago not a moment's hesitation in saying, that if you would join me here, you should be welcome to the first vacant situation in my household that should befit your own considerable rank. Since then the post of first gentleman of my bedchamber has fallen vacant, and until this moment I have held it in reserve for you, in hope that you soon would join me – as now you have. Have some more wine, why don't you?'

As I served myself, the Count indicating with a flick of his fingers that he would not join me, he went on:

'However, we are talking here of a role which, of its nature so close to my person, would necessitate total confidence – and confidentiality – between us.'

'Absolutely, your Highness,' I nodded with some misgivings. For it seemed to me that the Count was kindly pondering whether to offer to keep me about him in Sedan, whereas my own urgent priority was to return as soon as possible to Paris, and rediscover my Hélène.

'Now the thing is,' said the Count, evidently in some embarrassment, revealing as he looked near me, but not at me, that his left eye, when excited, took on a marked independence of his right, 'that while your family name, and the reputations of your father, and his father's father, and the unimpeachable character which my mother attributes to yours . . . while all these factors in themselves would tend to bespeak you nothing but noble in your blood, and estimable in your person, there are nonetheless several apparent lacunae in your history, which would trouble me deeply, were you unable to round them out.'

'Like what, your Highness?' I rather croaked, for my throat, despite the wine, had turned very dry.

'Monsieur de Retz', the Count tapped the Abbé's letter, 'advises me that the story you have told him, regarding your departure from Bigorre, and your wanderings since, may be considered somewhat colourful – not to say blemished, in view of your relative youth – and in need of some justification. He informs me, moreover, that in effect he met with you by accident—'

'Forgive me, your Highness,' I objected, 'but it was the Abbé who sought out me.'

'That is precisely his point, Monsieur Morel,' the Count retorted warmly. 'That when he sought you out, and engaged you in conversation, he detected no evidence of any intention, on your part, to journey hither and enlist with me – as my mother informed me that your mother had informed her that you would. On the contrary, according to the Abbé. He was distinctly of the opinion that had he not pressed you to do so, and given you funds to that end, you never would have left Paris. He also insinuates, without giving details, that you were less than wholly discreet towards him, in speaking of your own affairs. For these reasons, Monsieur Morel, I must ask you now to explain yourself.'

Now Louis, predictably, feels rather as you do when you imagine you're going in for a routine chat with your nice old friendly bank manager, and suddenly it is a new, younger, different fish-kettle sort of bank manager you're dealing with – an abrasive arsehole from Huddersfield, say – who before you've hardly sat down in his overheated office stabs aggressively at his console until up on his monitor flash screenfuls of green transaction details you have no idea how he could have any idea about, and he advises you beneath his steamy pebble spectacles that he really must ask you now to explain yourself.

Though his first reaction is black vengeful rage against the Abbé de Retz, for setting him up so chummily while at the same time commissioning him to bear such a letter against himself – not wholly unlike the letters sent in the custody of Rosencrantz and Guildenstern on the ship with Hamlet, beseeching England to kill the Prince; though it is doubtful whether Louis would have been aware of this at that moment – his second thought is that: fair enough, De Retz's primary loyalty is to the Count, and yes, there are a lot of apparent warts and carbuncles all over the previous year of his life, which any self-regarding prospective employer would be insane not to wish to hear justified.

So Louis proceeds to recover his situation by apologizing to the Count of Soissons for any trace of having seemed to wish to withhold his more intimate details from the Count's attention, and urges that this ostensible reluctance be construed merely as a diffident preference not to burden his Highness's preoccupations any further, with the minutiae of problems which in the context of questions of national destiny must seem introspectively trivial.

'However,' he continues, or at least says he did, 'if your Highness should deem it vital to satisfy yourself as to the character of such a candidate for the honour of being allowed to serve so near your person,

I cannot convey the intensity of relief and recovered happiness I myself would thereby experience: in being permitted to expose my tally of misfortunes, sins and griefs before the conscience and judgement of a Prince so universally esteemed and beloved as your Highness is all over France.'

We said 'says he did' advisedly just there, because Louis's memoirs go on to claim that 'nor when I spake thus I did break faith with truth, nor flatter in any degree' – which 1990s cynics may find a little hard to stomach without a snort. Let's not forget, though, that self-deception can be immensely sincere. In Louis's case, our reading of the text, within the interpenetrating matrix of metatexts, suggests:

(a) that he really believed he meant what he said, when he said it to the Count;

And:

(b) that insofar as a leven of retroactive distortion may have crept into his description of this conversation, this was largely (some may say laudably) the product of an immediate, instinctive, and soon to mature and strengthen, bond of affection and loyalty which the Count of Soissons inspired in Louis – a mingled sentiment of spontaneous allegiance and selfless desire to serve, which, in his own words:

'Despite my inevitable respect for his authority, and admiration of his outstanding qualities, I had not felt, nor ever could feel, for the cold, dry character of the Cardinal.'

Freud might have analysed it otherwise, but he's dead, and we aren't yet, so let's press on in the meantime.

And the present upshot is that Louis, thrown on the defensive, but with his emotional partialities already engaged, makes a 95% clean breast of all his crimes, misdemeanours and angst since leaving home after shooting Jean-Baptiste. By the time he concludes, his voice having twice choked with passion during his description of the bizarre, tantalizing, and finally dispiriting brief reunion with Hélène in his sickroom in the unknown Paris hôtel, he notes with incredulous gratitude that the Count of Soissons again has tears in his eyes – tears of sympathy this time: for the mangle Louis has been wrung through, and the heartache he has suffered.

'Upon my honour I believe you,' exclaims the Count impulsively, rising up and clasping Louis to his breast. 'Monsieur de Retz was overly hasty in calling into question your discretion, and he shall be told so.'

'No, no!' protests Louis mildly, not wishing to convert the Abbé into a needless enemy.

'Yes, yes!' retorts the Count. 'But we shall thank him too, for drawing your history to our attention, and your plight to our compassion. Sympathy, however, though it may already comfort him or her who excites it, is oft more akin to an anguish to him who *feels* it. Until, that is, he is able to gratify his awakened benevolence by some suitable gift or service. In my case, to you. But first, as you are weary from your journey, and the night wears on, and I have letters to read and sign, I shall pass you over to Monsieur de Varicarville, who shall attend to your every requirement.'

The Count of Soissons then embraces Louis again, with the fondness of a protective elder brother, and wishes him goodnight.

Monsieur de Varicarville, Louis soon finds, is like a fussing uncle to the Count. *Too* kind and sincere for sustained conversation without embarrassment, de Varicarville is like Polonius as interpreted for Victorian ladies.[4] For all that, he sees that Louis is well fed and warmly bedded, and after breakfast the following morning, he summons him back for a second, brighter, and more dynamic chat with the Count.

And when they revert to his difficulties with Hélène, Louis is astounded to hear the Count of Soissons come close to derisive scoffing. Nothing insurmountable in all that, the royal prince pooh-poohs airly:

> What do you mean? asks Louis.
>
> Don't *tell* her you killed her brother! suggests the Count.
>
> But I *have* told her, wails Louis.
>
> Did you check the corpse's pulse? objects the Count. Test for breath against your blade?
>
> Well, no, concedes Louis. But—
>
> Did you see the body buried?
>
> Of course not, says Louis. He was too busy being spirited into flight by the smuggler Garcés.
>
> There you are, then! concludes the Count.
>
> Where am I?

The logical hard fact is that *you* don't *know* that you *killed* the lady's brother. Or that *you* killed him. He might still have had life within him, when you left him, and been nursed into recovery by a local leech, or alternatively killed off by the same leech's remedies.

---

4 As opposed to *Prince Hamlet, HypoStar*, Chapter 9.

Happens all the time. Either way, *you*, Monsieur Morel, did not *kill* him. Then again, even if he was killed right there on the riverbank, the final snuffing of his last breath in this world could well have been executed by a third party: creeping upon the scene when you had fled. If so, once more: the verdict 'killed the lady's brother' cannot be hung on you. For all these reasons, I urge you most cordially not to prejudice the future happiness of you both for the sake of this one flimsy scruple.

Suddenly the backstabbing dreadful thought of possibly having spent a year of his life running away from a door that never had any hellish monster snarling behind it in the first place is too much for Louis. Slumped in his chair, for several minutes he masks his face with the palms of his hands.

Not sobbing exactly, but not breathing too easily either.

Patiently the Count of Soissons waits until his younger companion looks up again.

Well? he then asks kindly.

No, replies Louis. He can *see* the muzzle of his weapon pointing straight into Jean-Baptiste's belly. He can *hear* the fatal blast; *smell* the blood as out through the victim's peppered leather jerkin it spurts as from a wineskin exploded. There simply is no way, Louis quietly concludes, that any mortal on this earth could have survived such a blast at that range.

Oh well, sighs the Count, though with something of a military commander's nonchalance. If he's dead, he's dead! But you aren't, and neither is his sister. So why make bad worse by torturing both yourself and her simply because you inadvertently killed him? If, as you say, the lady loves you at least as much as you love her, she will certainly forgive you in time – if, indeed, she hasn't already. What women most want, you know, is security, comfort, attention, sexual gratification, and children. And they're much more likely to get all that from a living cavalier with both a fortune and ample virility than they are from one dead brother.

But I do not have a fortune, objects Louis morosely. And then . . .

Yes, yes?

It's not so much Hélène that's the problem, he explains, it's her father: the lawyer Arnault.

What about him?

Briefly Louis unpacks the background, then confesses further details re the plot afoot in Paris to get Hélène summarily wed to the decadent fop named Charles.

I entirely respect your sensitivity of feeling, says the Count with a hint of impatience. However, it sounds to me as if the lady's father should be no problem − especially if . . . when − soon, you see, the political situation in France should have changed to the point where converting a bumkin attorney into a fawning lesser noble will pose you no greater problem than a two-line letter to me.

But suppose they marry her first? objects Louis, close to raving as his mind's eye beholds it.

I think it highly unlikely, the Count of Soissons counters evenly. From what you tell me I would wager a thousand crowns that the mansion wherein you were bedded, nursed and then sedated rather heavily, and where, it further seems, Mademoiselle Arnault herself was lodging, was the Paris hôtel of the Maréchal de Châtillon − whose nephew, Charles, is notoriously a harebrained youth with few brains and no spunk, and a sexual braggart besides.

How, insists Louis, can the Count be so sure the Maréchal's nephew won't get to marry Hélène before he can be prevented − by Louis, that is?

His uncle won't let him, says the Count matter-of-factly. Monsieur de Châtillon is a gentleman of high breeding, and a formidable soldier, but above all an incurable snob. The idea of any nephew of his hitching up with a country lawyer's daughter − why, the Maréchal would have a fit!

Who would then inherit? Seriously. If the Maréchal were to die?

Well, yes. The bounder Charles would then be free to do as he liked, and extremely wealthy with it.

This reflexion does nothing to quell Louis's agitation, but thoughts of Maréchal Châtillon − a stalwart Richelieu supporter − have channelled the Count of Soissons's consciousness back towards the trough of his favourite hobbyhorse: the Cardinal's malignant tyranny over France, and the need to cut it out.

May not Maître Arnault have somehow contrived to become intimate with the Maréchal himself? worries Louis. In which case—

The King himself is in poor health, you know, cuts in the Count blackly. And the Cardinal is plainly banking upon the prior death of his Majesty . . .

But why? wonders Louis.

So he can seize the reins of regency, of course.[5] The villain has nothing to lose, you see, since if Death takes him first – as already He has promised several times to do, and then reneged – well, what matters that to him? No, no. Our duty now is to pre-empt both Death and the Cardinal, by toppling the latter during his life, so he can be made to suffer during his ruin – as so many innocent others have been made to suffer by him – until the former comes to claim him.

Perceiving that the Count of Soissons is working himself into a habitual rage of indignation, Louis resigns himself to the role of nodding auditor until the storm passes.

Having rehearsed, with the fluency of a troubadour reeling off a lengthy ballad he knows by heart, an astonishing list of his grievances against the Cardinal, the Count concludes abruptly:

---

[5] The dauphin, the future Louis XIV, is at this time barely two years old, having been born in September 1638. This is because his mother, Anne of Austria, despite having been married to his father Louis XIII, in 1615, did not give birth to him (ie Louis XIV), or to anyone else, for another twenty-three years. This, you may feel, makes the eight-year married childlessness of Countess Morel, our Louis's mother, look like chickenfeed, and paves the way for a whole new order of worldly-wise speculation. Not least since the two decades of heirlessness was a rankling point between Louis XIII and his Queen, not least due to a tireless sidestream of rumours that Anne of Austria, gambling perhaps on what she took to be her proven infertility, was at various points submitting her royal person to adulterous tupping by the Duke of Buckingham, Cardinal Richelieu, Mazarin, and virtually everyone else in Paris above the rank of potboy. If you were to glance dispassionately at some of her portraits, not knowing who she was, you might think she was doing quite well to get tupped by even the potboy (and we say this not sexistically, but just as biological posit) – which may go to show what a powerful factor regality could be, in achieving sexual success against your natural odds, at least before the days of genetic fingerprinting, ratpack *Spews* reporters, and German photographers like koala bears up eucalyptus trees with their howitzer-like infra-red lenses. More on these angles in Part IV.

'And so I *will* march on him, foul incubus that he is. And I *will* unseat him, imprison him, try him fairly, and see him punished. And how shall my actions be judged by history, I wonder? Foul treason against my King, as the Cardinal would have it? Or a crusade of loving liberation, in the service of my country? What do you think, Monsieur Morel?'

Louis sidesteps any embarrassment here by reciting an apposite cliché:

'As the saying goes, your Highness:

'*Once the sword is drawn, best throw away the scabbard.*'[6]

---

[6] A common refrain down the long centuries of French insurrections. The first reader to send in a postcard correctly identifying the date of its first utterance will receive a prize bottle of our favourite Rhône rouge.

# 37

# Tilting

Twenty minutes later:

Louis is led by Monsieur de Varicarville to take his place at one of two long tables laid for fifty breakfasteers each in the citadel great hall.

An atmosphere of boisterous bonhomie like the icing on a cake of many layered aggressions prevails as the variously greatly and lessly highborn conspiring gentlemen divert themselves from thoughts of mainstream war-before-long with taunting talk of jousting sport after breakfast if the weather stays fair – as if six centuries of so-called progress in history had suddenly been stricken from the record, or never taken place at all.

'The Duke of Bouillon,' records Louis, 'who divided the interior of the citadel equally with his princely guest, had this morning made some twinge as of the gout an excuse for taking his breakfast with the Duchess, in his own apartment. As the Count did likewise habitually, there was in consequence an increased freedom of raillery and repartee about the hall, which doubled again the moment after the Duke's herald had called out that the tiltyard of the castle would be open at eight of the clock to such as chose to run at the ring; following which would be a *course des têtes*.

'Neither of these exercises had I ever beheld, and hence was not a little eager for the conclusion of the meal, though thinking only to spectate.'

However:

'After breakfast I returned to the apartments of the Count of Soissons, to attend him, with the rest of his suite, to the tilt-yard.

'In his chamber I found him already dressed for the sports, and at this moment pulling on to his right hand a glove of strong buff-leather. Regarding me with a good humour that betokened his great enthusiasm for the contests to come, he exclaimed:

'"What, Monsieur Morel! Not gloved! You will never hold your lance, you know, without this vital second skin. Choose one from the heap there, and be sure the fit is snug."

'Hastily I endeavoured to excuse myself, by informing his Highness that I was quite unused to such exercises, and could only prove an embarrassment to him.'

But:

'"Nonsense," he replied, laughing seriously. "If you are to become my gentleman, I must first inspect how you ride, ply your sword, hold your own – all these things – before I could possibly entrust to you a regiment of my cavalry.

'"Gouvion! Leave off the boots, and go order Monsieur Morel's horse to be saddled. At once!"'

Now of course:

'There being no manner of means of opposing the Count's command, without ensuring myself even greater discredit, and possible banishment from his intimacy, I was obliged to accoutre myself as he ordered, and accompany him out to the arena.

'Nor can I easily express the depth of my anxiety, at the prospect of exhibiting myself before some two hundred spectators – mainly battle-hardened veterans, at that – in the attempt to rehearse those equestrian accomplishments which I had never before so much as witnessed, let alone begun to perfect.

'I was yet supremely young in such matters, it must be said, and had vanity more than sufficient to bring on fits of timidity, where a prospect of failure risked ridicule.'

Outside, in the frosty but brightening February morning:

'The tiltyard consisted of a turfed rectangle, within the castle walls, of perhaps one hundred and twenty generous paces long, by eighty wide. Within was an inner oblong, enclosed by split-wood barriers, of some two hundred feet in length, by fifty in breadth. To here from the court before the Count's apartments in the citadel the distance was so short that he had had the horses sent on ahead, and thither proceeded himself on foot, followed by myself and a dozen other gentlemen of his suite.

'As we approached, the crowd who had assembled to witness the exercises, amongst whom were a great ruck of soldiery, hailed the oncoming Count with shouts and cheers that would have left the Cardinal in little doubt as to the loyalty and devotion here enjoyed by his principal adversary of the moment.'

As the commoner sorts peel aside for the Count:

'His Highness was greeted by a tighter knot of the more distinguished exiles who had flocked to his standard ever since the first report of his determination to take arms against the Cardinal.'

Within this knot, the first notable notable to engage Louis's attention was:

'A strong-featured gentleman of about fifty; in whose eyes, nose and chin, even before I had heard him named as the Duke of Vendôme, I fancied I could discover a striking likeness to the many portraits and busts of Henri Quatre I had seen since first reaching Paris.'[1]

Second, but no less, was:

'The Duke of Bouillon himself; and certainly never did I behold a countenance which, without being at all handsome, possessed so pre-eminently *intellectual* an expression. All mind, seemed the Duke to me. Mind quick to perceive; strong to repel; and no doubt bold to uphold. Overall the impression was more impressive than agreeable, and gave warning of impulses springing all from the brain, and none arising in the heart.'

Now it seems to us that, from whatever motive, Louis's description of the Duke of Bouillon is deliberately – even suspiciously – imprecise, euphemistic, and evasive of the stark truth that Bouillon was one of those absolute egotists who would just as soon carve the fat from under your skin to grease his boots with (in Schopenhauer's quaint

---

[1] César de Vendôme, natural son, or bastard, of Henri IV and his favourite mistress, Gabrielle d'Estrées (one of the celebrated pair of peaches in the bath), was the great King's favourite son. Also the focus, if not always the cause, of many of the most sinister discontents of the legitimate heir, Louis XIII. These themes are festooned with fascinating detail in Elizabeth Wirth Marvick's *Louis XIII: The Making of a King*. For example:

'César's sexual precocity was also likely to inspire a wish in Louis to emulate him, especially since, if Des Yveteaux is correct, César had been initiated into the "secret pleasures" of his father. When at the age of six-and-a-half Louis was reproached for showing his penis to the little daughter of his maître d'hôtel, he told Madame de Monglat that César had taught him to do this – which was possibly true, though Héroard [the young prince's physician] attributes the accusation to Louis's spiteful feelings towards César. If the king [Henri IV] – himself not above such conduct – trained his eldest son in his own ways, it would not be surprising if that child, in turn, initiated the younger one.'

Rather suggesting that even France's greatest king would certainly be done for weanie-wagging in Cleveland.

trope[2]) as pass the time of day with you; if it suited his purposes, that is, and were it not for his rationally self-interested obedience to social strictures, peer-group pressures, and fear of such legal penalties as he imagines might one day catch up with him. Consistent with, but in no way proving, this somewhat harsher view of the Duke is the photocopy currently clipped to the side of our text monitor: of a portrait of Bouillon by Baltazar Moncornet, which shows a bowl-faced slob like a fat, black, almost clean-shaven Springer spaniel with gout – with dark, armadillo-like armour to signify his personal strength and valour in combat, and a long-shot landscape of victory-in-battle in the background, to hint heavily at the subject's incomparable mastery of military strategy.

However, let's not forget that Louis was there, *sur place*, while we were not.

'After he had clasped the Count de Soissons in their matutinal embrace,' our reporter continues, 'the Duke of Bouillon's quick dark eye took in myself. The Count, perceiving his host's inquiring and manifestly hostile glance, he beckoned me to advance, and introduced me to his ally by my name, my pedigree, and my candidacy for the post of first gentleman of his bedchamber. The Duke bowed so low as to seem, to myself at least, satirical, and, with impeccable ostentation of politeness, welcomed me effusively to Sedan.[3] Hereupon the Count, with a curt smile suggesting he read clearly what was in his friend's mind, quietly murmured:

'"Have no fear, Maurice. If Monsieur Morel is not yet rock-solid for you, he is certainly no way agin you."

'"*He that is not for me*", replied the Duke of Bouillon, with that casual flaunting of scriptural expressions which was so regrettably common during these years, "*is against me*. Neutrals I despise."

'Nine tenths of the blood in my body, so I felt, must have risen to inflame my cheeks, in response to the Duke's unwarranted slur. Meanwhile the Count, observing his host to be in irritable mode, and correctly judging that mine was no disposition patiently to bear a second such taunt from any man, led me quickly on to the barriers.'

Here follows an unusually sustained wealth of detail on the antique

---

2   *On the Basis of Morality*, §14.

3   Which is, after all, in capitalistical terms, *his*. Ie, Sedan is the Duke of Bouillon's own inherited *property*.

sports now enacted. Monsieur de Riguemont, the Count of Soissons's chief *écuyer*, has been appointed *maître de camp* for the day. At a signal from him a fanfare of brass draws all eyes to the field. The *écuyer* opens a gate into the space within the barriers. After him troupes a motley of valets and *estafiers* bearing piles of lances and pasteboard blocks on which are painted fanatical gnashing heads of Cannibalistic Moors, Infidel Turks and other Eternal Enemies.

The Count of Soissons mounts up with panache. Followed by the Dukes of Bouillon, Vendôme and La Valette, the Count canters inside the barrier enclosure. From there he calls back to Monsieur Morel to catch up and keep near him. Louis leaps obediently astride his horse, which Achilles Lefranc is holding ready for him, most importantly. As he prances after the Count he is joined by several dozen other gentleman of rank eligible for the limelight. Bringing up the rear are numerous grooms, valets, and lesser bickering lackeys, among whom Achilles adroitly insinuates himself.

The barrier gates close.

Those not within to compete now clamber up the barrier poles to secure a better view.

Further off, but better vantaged for a bird's-eye, the Countess of Soissons and the Duchess of Bouillon, framed as by a colourful ruff of younger ladies beside and behind them, look down from the citadel balcony upon which they sit with sedate ennui.

Approximately two-thirds down the course from the entrance gate stands a wooden post with a strut-supported cross-bar near its top; in the form of a roadside gallows. From this bar is suspended a shallow hook on which is suspended a small wooden ring made bright by scarlet silk bound tightly round it. On a stool behind the post is perched the Count's personal page: to ascertain by sound and touch, as well as sight, whether any of those gentlemen whose lances miss the inside of the ring (thus failing to carry it away) yet graze its dangling perimeter – thus at least avoiding the shame of an absolute duck, by scoring one inferior point.[4]

The *maître de camp* now ranges the tilters in their order of attempting to tilt. Louis is glad to learn he will be preceded by five more experienced cavaliers, from whose fortunes he hopes to introject some instruction.

'His Highness himself of course took the lead, and I observed

---

[4] 'The phallocentric symbolism here is more than flagrant enough without the "scarlet".' [J.R.]

that much hidden strength of arm, combined with dexterity of practice, was necessary to couch the lance with any semblance of ease
and grace.'

After pausing for a moment with his long sharp lance erect, the Count
gently spurs his mount to a demi-volte, nods his head to the balconied
ladies, then in smooth succession drops his point to the ready, hugs his
elbow firm to his side, nudges his horse to a canter, then a gallop. All
the while he keeps the angle of his weapon steadily above the right ear
of his horse, its tip in a uniform line with his own forehead. As he passes
the post at a thunderous belt he skewers the ring dead centre and bears
it away. Tumultuous applause in the form of cheers, claps, whistles and
the odd over-zealous pistol shot into the sky greet this further evidence
of Our Leader's Invincibility, as the marker page emerges from cowering
behind the post to cry:

'*Un dedans! Point mort! Parfait!*'[5]

One of the *estafiers* now runs out to lodge a second ring on the
hook.

The Duke of Bouillon proceeds to emulate the Count. With none of
the Count's easy elegance, and albeit with less immaculate centricity, he
nonetheless carries off the ring on his prong.

Next should come the Duke of Vendôme, but to everyone's surprise he
declines. A sudden onset of rheumatics, he ruefully explains: stiffening
up his old war wounds.

So on to the Duke of La Valette. Though seeming to prance his charger
and wield his lance with consummate expertise, somehow he fails to ride
away with the ring, and a gasping hush of dismay deplores this failure
until the valiant marker page shouts back:

'*Une atteinte! Bien touché, oui-oui! Un point, alors.*'[6]

Next the Count of Soissons calls for Louis to have a stab. Dreading
the utter fiasco he fears, Louis divines that the Count, though in excellent
humour, and enjoying a flask of wine in celebration of his exemplary
success, will tolerate no No for an answer.

'And I own that I wished myself, at that moment, anywhere in the
whole wide world but Sedan. There being no remedy, I had at least
the consolation of confidence that – no matter whether I should carry
off the ring, or even touch it at all, I could manage my horse with the

---

[5] 'Our Lord's a Peerless Thruster! Bet your man can't match that!'
[6] Feel free to look up.

best of them. Alas, I had forgotten that, in every successful co-operation between a man and his horse, the two parties must concur. While the fine roan I had purchased in Paris was an excellent roadster, it now transpired that for such activities as we both were compelled to essay, in the field before the multitude, he had no enthusiasm whatever. It was, therefore, with only unimaginable difficulty that I reined him through our demi-volte, to please the ladies, before beginning the course. This accomplished, he galloped on steadily enough towards the ring; but then, just as I began to feel my lance was fairly aimed, the animal under me caught a glimpse of the marker lad behind the ring, instantly swerved sideways as from a coiling viper, and reared with his front hooves high through the onlooking grooms and *estafiers*, who dispersed like terrified sheep.'

Worse:

As the roan bucks and lunges, and Louis wrestles to rein and kick him back under control, the animal's fetlocks get caught in a pile of the pasteboarded Moors and Turks for spearing later, such that both horse and rider keel over sideways, to vee their legs at the sky.

Loud cruel guffaws from the Duke of Bouillon give licence to a general hilarity. Within moments several hundred eyes are streaming with mirth, as the sides beneath them heave hugely helpless with laughter.

'Certainly,' vows Louis, 'in the height of my wrath I could happily have murdered them all.'

Especially the Duke of Bouillon.

Fortunately, though, for the Duke, and the hooters and cacklers all around him, by the time Louis has got remounted and trotted back to base, his better senses have cooled his dander.

'"Your Highness sees," said I, as I approached before the Count, "the dismal issue of my best attempt to give you pleasure. Perhaps you could now excuse my further needless exposure to the ridicule of Monsieur de Bouillon, and his colleagues."'

But the Count of Soissons, with breezy high spirits, will hear of no such thing. Louis, he insists, managed that horse just as well as that horse could be managed. Not even the Duke could have done better. And so?

'"Anticipating the present situation, and the grief it must cause a proud young gentleman, I have sent a groom for a mare of my own, that has a mouth like finest velvet, and will obey the least squeeze of your leg. Here she comes!"'

So Louis, to oblige his host, and satisfy his prospective employer, has no option but to straddle the velvet mare, and take a second tilt at the ring.

'Now finding, by the evidence of all my senses, and an intuition of perfection between my thighs, that it was more the Count's mare who would wish to direct me, than I her, I was liberated to concentrate my every faculty upon balancing my lance — above the mare's right ear, just as had the Count himself — and aiming at the ring.'

Seconds later:

Bang.

Raa . . .

Young Monsieur Morel has speared the ring, dead centre, carried it away, caracoled round, and fetched it back for the Duke of Bouillon to admire.

While:

'The spectators outside the barriers, and even the lofty ladies on the balcony, who had jeered with the Duke at my former failure, now vied with the heavens to shout the loudest approbation of my feat.'

The Count of Soissons squints with benevolent quizzicality at the Duke of Bouillon, who pretends not to have noticed Louis's triumph, and is deep in affected debate with the Duke of Vendôme on the ideal colour and vintage of wine to set off a barbecued pig.

The pasteboard Enemy heads are now placed on the stylized Enemy bodies (ie slender wooden stakes), and:

'The Count of Soissons, who well perceived that my humiliation and anger had made further success of redoubled importance to me, beckoned me close beside him, and in a whisper bade me mark well the manoeuvres of the Crusaders preceding me; and, above all things, to be sure to neither lose my cap, nor withdraw either foot from my stirrups; since, though merely a custom of etiquette, the *course* would be forfeit thereby.'

All is now ready — the heads, ie those not trampled into pulp by Louis's roan, being staked up at regular intervals in parallel with the barriers. To culminate the *course*:

'Beyond the line of stakes, his back to the sun, a most ferocious-looking Saracen face was fixed to one horizontal arm of an iron stand, about eight feet high off the ground.' This contraption, you may know, is a quintain,[7] the idea being that if you aren't a jolly good tilter then, even if you get the Saracen on the one arm with your lance through his eye, then, if you aren't galloping fast enough, or don't duck in time, the other arm rotatating fast on its central pivot will swing round to stun the back of your head with force in proportion to the violence of your stab at the Saracen. A sort of physically poetic justice, if you like, for all persons except the heroically swift, the superhumanly nimble, and those too cowardly to risk hitting the Saracen in the first place.

And for those who survive the quintain:

'Perhaps five horse lengths beyond it, in the centre of the course, was a post on which was hung, in the manner of the sign of an inn, a target painted to resemble the head of Medusa, with a wide circle of intertwining serpents, like a halo enclosing a small round face.'

When the *maître de camp* waves his flag, a fanfare sounds, and the Count of Soissons leads off. Down the line of Moors and Turks he charges, beheading them cleanly with a sabre swung by his left arm, as his right both cradles his lance and keeps a light touch on his reins. In the split second following his successful decapitation of the fifth and final Moor or Turk the Count transfers the reins to his sword hand, swings up the lance, hits the Saracen on the quintain, ducks fast enough to avoid the quintain's revenge, though in the process loses the Saracen's head off the tip of his lance. Not to worry, though, as:

'His highness, galloping on, shouted out to an *estafier* in the corner to catch his lance, which already was spinning through the air, as the Count himself, one pistol already drawn from his saddle-bow, successfully discharged it at point-plank range through the midst of Medusa's brow.'

As if that isn't enough:

'Before the crowd could draw breath to cheer,' the Count has reined up tight, wheeled round, holstered his first pistol, drawn the second, and shot Medusa again – through the back of her head this time, so the bullet tears out her mouth.

'He then made a complete volte, during which he replaced his second pistol, drew again his sword, and, galloping in a circle back to the

---

[7] Could it be some devilish bubble-meaning such as this that Paul Chalicer had in mind when he titled his mammoth quintain *The Quintain*?*

   * *'Please scrub this note from the published text.'* [P.C.]

Saracen head, which had fallen from his lance, he thrust with his sword *en tierce*, stuck the Saracen in the forehead, and raised high his hand *en quarte*, with the head on the point of his sword.'

But the applause (more claps, shouts, whistles, calls for encores) which salutes the Count of Soissons's achievements as he canters back to the throng are as the coyest virgin's whisper compared with the prolonged deafening rapture which ensues when the realization is born, and then proliferates like fruit flies, that the trophied Saracen's saracenicity is only turban-deep, and that the features beneath − domed forehead, arched brows, sallowed eyes, long nose, pursed lips . . . yes, you've guessed − though cartooned to satanic proportions, are (in what to a thick-skinned warrior of the mid-seventeenth century, must come as the acme of allegorical subtlety) none other than Cardinal Richelieu.

# Part IV

# Succeeding at Sex Itself

## 38

# Anal Intercourse, AIDS
# & Sovereignty for Scotland

Dear Janet,

First of all many thanks for the loan of your vibrant young Charlotte and her dynamic young David last weekend, and I'm sure it's only the forgetfulness of hovering senility that prevents us from allowing you to share in our wrapt admiration for the clipped pertinancy of the comment one of them so discreetly uttered in the very split instant of alighting upon her bottom in the mud.

That was in a soggier cleft of what we know locally as the valley of the shadow of odious jet fighter-bombers roaring over to induce miscarriages in the sheep at less than half the legally permissible height above the ground. Once upon a time we fondly imagined how the next sort-of British government might clip these yahoos' wings a bit, or at least cut their petrol rations, but now we are obliged to view the total independence of England from Scotland as the only conceivable hope.

Still, few clouds of shit are without a little lining of toilet paper somewhere, and in this case I had Wringhim on the phone for an hour[1] this morning when I might very well otherwise have been composing this memo to you.

Funny thing is: he seems immensely excited about the political situation.

On the ground that – once the Scottish Labour faction and the Nationalists have got over their understandable howls of grief, buckets of tears, and inevitable mutual recriminations – there is bound soon to

---

[1] We've since discovered whose phone he's been abusing. To publish the details in book form might appear unduly disloyal, but individual inquiries will be dealt with in confidence.

swell an irresistible backlash of separatist passion even in the breasts of most traditionally and genetically conservative Scots, even if not, as Wringhim himself admitted in 'the blubbery womanish paps of *** . . . ', whose actual name had perhaps best be *** . . . ed in case the not unknown notion takes hold of his one remaining brain cell to try to sue us for telling the truth. As Otto Dix so rightly remarked, in defence of not having painted Hitler's moustache on to Hitler's face until after the war was over, and the Führer suicided:

'I didn't want to go to prison over a moustache, and anyway everyone knew it was Hitler.'

Quite right too.

As for Wringhim — well, I won't burden you London folk with the minutiae of the rest of that hour, though you may care to take note that he (ie Wringhim) does seem to be riding a winner to the extent that not only am I myself more politically aroused and itching to act than ever before but so are Graham and Maggie, our shepherd and shepherdess, Jimmie the heating-oil tanker driver, but even most English immigrants in the area (such as Nigel and Wendy who run the coffee shop, as you may remember, up at the fish farm by the sawmill) are ashamed of their association with Westminster, and clamouring to see Scotland independent. Whether it brews into full-scale liberationist insurrection such as we witnessed in Catalonia in 1640, well, most of us prefer to doubt it; on the ground that we in Scotland are far too civilized, intelligent, and (crucially) *educated* to stoop to such primitive measures. Now if you then press us – as your Charlotte indeed did, over cheese at Saturday dinner – to tell you:

'What other solution is there?'

I reply:

'Don't ask me. Ask Wringhim.'

'And what will he say?'

'If you get him when he's raving pissed – orange-eyed and breathing barley fire in McEwan's, or come through to Edinburgh for the day, to rabble-rouse around Milne's Bar – he'll tell you he can't wait for the day when the Anglo-colonized streets of the capital are bloody and rubbled as those of Belfast.'

'But he doesn't really mean it, you mean?'

'I think at the time he *does* mean it. And there, you may opine, is a cardinal difference between Wringhim and me. Fortunately, though, if you're lucky enough to catch him the morning after, especially if it's one of his better Mondays, he's more likely to advise:

'"Stop paying taxes to wankers with no mandate to collect them. Every time you get a correct demand for income tax, national insurance, VAT, or whatever, pay that sum instead into a central Independence For Scotland Fund."'

'But that would be breaking the law,' objected your Charlotte's David.

'But only peacefully,' as Charlotte remarked.

'And they can't put a million people in Barlinnie,' said Koo.

'That's right,' I agreed. 'As Wringhim so infallibly reasons:

'"If enough people do it, it'll work."

'The practical problem, as ever, is whether enough people will. If they don't, it'll be Wringhim in Barlinnie in the meantime, and the rest of us will have to work out a third solution. Now, who's for rhubarb fool and ice-cream?'

I realize that to any other ex-reader of fiction for BirdDog that might have seemed like an artistically solecistic digression, but I wanted to convey to you a brief taster of just how refreshing it was for us maturing dinks to be effortlessly entertained by your lithe nineteen-year-olds; as opposed to our actively struggling to entertain maturer dinks as usual, and increasingly gasping grumps.[2]

Also, though I mustn't promise you that I didn't let them watch satellite television (as you may recall I promised Audrey about Jennifer, since Jennifer's still technically a schoolgirl, with all that implies for my conscience), because although it wasn't an entertainment option I had actively offered, not to say mentioned at all, I nonetheless discovered them hard at it with my zappers on the study couch when I went through with a bowl of Provençal olives during a break from preparing dinner, and later when I returned from the kitchen bearing postprandial port and Glenmorangie.

However, and you'll be pleased with me here, unbeknown to the young folk I had earlier taken the mature precaution of interfering catastrophically with the dip-switch settings on the FilmWet decoder, in consequence of which you may safely assume that anal intercourse from Hamburg was neither spectated upon, discussed, or in any way emulated by consenting adults of any age in the Greenadder valley during the course of your babies' visit.

---

[2] 'Meaning?' [J.R.]

Which brings us, albeit kicking and screaming, to AIDS.

And whether we liken it to an elephant in our living-room, or a loaded revolver by our dinner guest's placemat, or a final demand from the Inland Revenue for more than we've ever possessed, we may opt to do little about it (and it is what we *do*, don't you agree, rather than what we think or desire, that defines the differences between us?) but we'll be hard put to think it away.

Now be assured, most assuredly, that the fact of our not ignoring AIDS at this moment is not for any other moment because I suspect your Charlotte of having it, or being likely to contract it, but rather because I wonder how far the ubiquitous risk has already affected our paternal, maternal, avuncular and [whatever-the-other-word-should-be] emotions and practices more radically than we easily realize.

Let me illustrate my point with an example more intimately historical than merely earnest health-programs on television showing condoms being rolled on erections:

It is 1968 and Audrey and I are visiting her mother's senior sister in Oxford. Dinner is both scrumptious and plentiful, and enhanced by patient counsel into how to savour more finer wines and less gassy cans of Tartan Special. All very refaned – until bedtime, that is. Then we swiftly discover that trying to get to grips with your own girlfriend in Audrey's auntie's house after midnight is like vaulting the Berlin Wall in your Y-Fronts.

Whereas now!

Twenty-four years on, here's us, with at least one of their mothers' explicit blessings, ushering your unmarried teenagers straight into our best en-suite guest double bed, and pampering them the following morning with tea and toast to prolong their lie-in. Now it's not that we mind, and we like to think it isn't because we're envious,[3] but we can't help wondering how far these agreeable proceedings (agreeable, unde-niably, from the pov of the tea-and-toast enjoyers) represent less of an exponentially upward curve in moral enlightenment than we might fondly imagine, and more of a new variety of reactionary manipu-lation, of the form: bond them young, reinforce their monogamous bonking – with comfortable double beds, tea and toast, etc – and their promiscuous liaisons will be fewer; ergo, likewise their risk of AIDS.

---

[3]   'Course you bloody well are!' [J.R.]

But fewer than whose?

Fewer than *ours*, you see. Furthermore, will it work? Or will they react against our benevolent interventions, and turn into playperson bunnies in their thirties, just when we were settling down? Or might they, *par contre*, get so jaded so young that by their mid-twenties tea and toast will be all that remains? Looked at another way:

> He never once did sleep with her
> Though they must have made love a thousand times

As Robin Williamson celebrated teenagency in the sixties. But may the day come – 29 April 2016, for instance – when a retiring twenty-year-old troubadour will rite along these lines:

> I never once did manage an erection
> To make love with you with
> Though we must have had tea and toast together
> Nearly every Saturday and Sunday morning
> For two years and nearly nine months?

Ultimately it's their problem, of course. The young now and hereafter, I mean. And there's no question in the meantime but that your Charlotte and David are ever so much more civilized than we were (forgive me, Audrey, but it's true) at the same age, and infinitely more stimulating company for us than I could possibly have been for Audrey's auntie. Indeed, the only regrettable consequence of their visit, at my end, is that I haven't got any whisky left. Not to worry, though. This will be remadeed by my least bruised credit card before you make it up yourself at the end of the month, and with this in mind, and before we leave the subject of anal intercourse entirely behind us, I had better perhaps warn you that there's quite a lot about it in this ghastly pamphlet Wringhim's asked me to typeset for him.

'Why should you need to warn me?' I can almost hear you murmur, 365 miles away.

Because not only does Wringhim want typesetting, but he desperately needs hands-on editing too. In fact, I'm going to refuse to do the typesetting unless he agrees to cough up for a competent editor. He can afford it too, at the moment, since he's just had a much larger bursary out of the Caledonian Arts Commission than they've ever given me. So: are you interested?

Basically his theses, in the anal intercourse passages, are that:

(a) regardless of prevailing vogues for syphilis, herpes, AIDS, or come-what-may, anal intercourse varies in direct proportion with political and cultural (morality isn't an issue for Wringhim) decay and disintegration;

(b) whether as symptom or cause, for the cultural and political health of a nation, anal intercourse (heterosexual every inch as much as homosexual: he's never a queerbasher, Wringhim) should be dialectically discouraged – though by no means legally outlawed.

And I think we'd better confess, Janet, that in the present climate we're inclined to agree with Wringhim here. Not on cultural and political grounds, though. More on mechanical and what you might call hydraulical grounds, and very much with AIDS in mind. This is because, as some of the more macho American novelists of the twentieth century, such as Miller, Hemingway and Mailer, seem (for reasons perhaps best kept to themselves) not to have noticed, it is statistically more normal for a said vagina to be too small to comfortably accommodate a given penis than it is the other way round. Miller, you would have thought, could have got an inkling of this if not from Havelock Ellis then at least from Anus Nun as he fucked her, since she specifically told him that intercourse with her husband Hugger had to be helped along with Vaseline, since Hugger's penis was so huge.[4] But it may have been that this truth was too uncongenial for Miller to assimilate, and/or that he was pissed at the time. Either way, if that's how it stands between your average penis and vagina, just think of the same willow wand in relation to your poor little junior-sphincter and less generously lubricated rectum.[5] Certainly mine is. From which the painful consequence

---

[4] "'Allegedly,' should you not perhaps drop in here?' [P.C.]

[5] Ten years ago, of course, we would never have dreamed of communicating such cogitations to a lady. And nor would we now, or would we, if the stakes had not risen up? Also, Janet did very much intimate, didn't she, in her SEX.TXT that she wanted more sex henceforth than hitherto.

is likely to be, however tough the rubber encasing the phallus, an increased risk of lesion in the sheath itself and/or the poor little rectum being buggered up, and hence a greater danger of infective enminglement between the sperm of the buggerer and the blood of the buggeree. For these reasons alone (and aesthetics entirely aside[6]) we're inclined to advise that anal intercourse is best adjourned until further notice except possibly between diehard trueblue monogamists who probably wouldn't dream of it anyway if they don't have FilmWet decoders or can't set the dip-switches correctly.

Now be all that as it mibbe, Wringhim, in support of the above sort-of platforms has dredged up a very eclectic cocktail of evidence. Some of the historical stuff he's obviously cadged off Audrey, and some of the contemporary data he claims to have gathered himself. For instance, his contention that anal intercourse is more rampant per head of population in Edinburgh than Glasgow (principally due to the influx of English yups to the New Town) – and in England than in Scotland, and in London than in Liverpool, and in Westminster and Hampstead than in Stoke Newington and Brixton – he maintains is not only upheld by local government and health-service statistics, but also by his own field trips such as expeditions to Hampstead Heath in the early evenings armed with a telescope. I'm a bit sceptical about this last point, myself, and think it more likely that Wringhim got his Hampstead dirt off locals in the Flask in Flask Walk, since I happen to know (i) that Young's Special Bitter is his favourite English ale, (ii) that the print in the corner depicting the dashing cavalier allowing the coy virgin to fondle the tip of his riding crop is one of Wringhim's favourite visual representations, and (iii) that he can't stand walking.

Nevertheless, even if some of his rabider frills are a trifle fanciful, or even fudged, to a degree that would again ensure his failure to secure a PhD in any subject, his fundamental perceptions are not to be sneered at, and his chains of reasoning are perfectly sound. *If*, as he argues, the way to succeed at sex in London, in London terms, is to be a

---

6  Or below. Consider, for instance, the revulsion of the Abbé de Brantôme, in his *Lives of Gallant Ladies*: 'How disgusting they [heterosexual sodomists, on this occasion] are, to neglect a lovely, pure, specially granted part of the body [the vagina] and take a disgusting, dirty, filthy prohibited part [the rectum], put in a prohibited direction too.'

social-climbing capitalist lickspittle who votes Conservative, gets private medical care, sends hor children to private (called public) schools, is languid, suave, insincere even when not sarcastic, lightning quick to roll over slavering to be mounted by the first casual promiser of any vague hope of advancement, and generally steeped in '*mauvaises fois*'[7] to the uppermost gills, and *if*, at the same time, the way to succeed at sex in Scotland (if not all districts of Edinburgh), in Scottish terms, is to be a committed social democrat (lower-case) who till now has voted Labour or Scottish Nationalist, vocally supports and actively uses a national health-care system, entrusts har children to state education, is candid, outspoken and sincere even when ironic, refuses to roll over for any manner of man, woman or beast, no matter how wealthy or powerful, and genuinely imbued with a sense of national history, tradition, achievement, pride in the present and aspiration for the future, *then* certainly this divergence of what constitutes sexual triumph, devoutly to be wished, is yet another stout nail (along with our different languages, the fact that the Scottish legal system is both distinct from and less blatantly feudally unjust than the English, the screaming injustice of a shotgun wedding, perpetuated by force and falsehood, during which Scotland has never voted Tory, and so forth) in the coffin of the so-called 'Union', whose burial is now inevitable, and should be effected without further delay, unilaterally if necessary, before the mouldering corpse, already putrid, is devoured by the dogs of war.[8]

I thought it necessary to tell you all this, Janet, to give you a chance to decide if editing Wringhim is a job you'd want to take on. If so, let me know, and I'll tell him to approach you. You'll probably find he'll try to beat you down to a couple of beers next time you're in Glasgow, but I should stick out for say £15 per thousand words, which should gross you about £600 for about two days' work. Hardly princely, is it, compared with bankruptcy lawyers' pay? But then we have the less-corrupt standards.[9] If there's any quibbling about your

---

[7] *Sic.* See what we mean?

[8] 'Perhaps you could suggest that purists may discover a structural template for this paraphrase in Henry James's *Princess Casamassima*?' [P.C.]

[9] 'Yes, I get it. The Ode to Joplin? We are ugly, or whatever, *but* . . . ?' [P.C.]

ethnic suitability, ie from Wringhim, you could tell him several of your great-great-grandfathers were Scottish on your distaff side. That'll shut him up.

Well now. Thousands would hardly credit it, but the original purpose of this memo was to ask if you wouldn't mind terribly looking through my own new chapters before you come up. I was going to send them to Paul Chalicer first. Nothing personal, it's just that I wanted to catch him before he went to America. However, we seem to have missed that boat for the moment, since both his answerphones are unplugged, which is always the last thing he does before going abroad. How most peculiar. Anyhow. The main difference now is that you'll be able to get in there first this time with suggesting that I write him down and you up. As for Louis, I've decided that I want him back in Paris by the time you've finished the present chunk, so after coffee I'm going to put a second file on this disk containing the gist of the three chapters following. As before, the facts themselves are non-negotiable, but do feel free as a vulture to write or rewrite as many as possible of the following sentences yourself.

XOX

H.

# 39

# The Next Three Chapters

Only the gist, mind you. So you won't feel confused back in Paris. Well, talking of Paris. In Chapter 40, which we may call 'Talking of Paris', the Count of Soissons, after the feasting after the tilting, summons Louis back to his private apartments. There he asks Louis solemnly if he is still game for a mission. The fact that the Count has considered that Louis might have changed his mind may be construed as characteristic of a character prone to sudden changes of mind himself.

'You must feel free to retract, Monsieur Morel, if . . . '

And so on.

'What mission?' asks Louis eagerly. Any excuse to get back to Paris, and Hélène, would be pounced on. But of course he can't tell the Cunt that. Sorry, I meant Count.[1]

It's like this, explains the Count. Despite all the noble efforts of the

---

[1] Dearie me. But it could have been worse, and once was. In the Sunday following my first week of being wooed by Audrey, before we had yet moved the earth together, let alone her granny's settee, I was invited to Sunday Lunch with The Parents. Gallantly suppressing their first-sight hostility (my hair was twice as long as Audrey's, etc) during pre-prandial gins-and-tonics, they visibly cracked over the roast lamb, when I dropped the hungover dope-numbed on-edge clanger of asking their daughter, in a deafening mumble, if she could please: 'Pass the red-cunt jelly?' You might have thought a clinical psychiatrist and his missus could forgive you a little slip like that, but not the Professor Macphersons, and I sometimes reflect that if my fling with Audrey had not been doomed for more up-front reasons, it would never, in the long-term, have survived her mother's malice. And I wonder: would it have made a huge difference if I'd been bonking a daughter or preferably granddaughter of Freud?

Abbé de Retz to seduce straitened gentlefolk, there is still another vital stratum of society in Paris that needs to be won over. The bravoes, swashbucklers, and in a much more honest word *criminals*, of whom there are said to be about 20,000 in Paris, with an underground network all over France.

'How?' asks Louis.

The means, the Count tells him, are his problem. Just so long as we can all be sure the criminal fraternity will rise up when the civil war breaks, and declare in favour of Soissons, and Freedom, but engineered in such a wise that the Count will not be personally overcommitted too far to dissociate himself from the hoodlums if and when need be. All of which rings a warning bell in Louis's brain and reminds him of that faraway interlude in the Marquis of Roquefort's hunting pavilion, when the Marquis too had remarked casually of the Count of Soissons that:

'Want of resolution is his greatest failing.'

Privately Louis determines to compensate for the Count's propensity to vacillate, and publicly he doesn't neglect to ask his new commander for the sort of funds necessary to win over 20,000 thieves, conmen, extortionists, thugs and murderers.

'All that you need', vows the Count, 'you shall have.'

This audience over, Louis, on quitting the Count's apartments, has his left ear hissed into by Monsieur Varicarville that:

'Your little man Achilles has been seen entering the Duke of Bouillon's chambers!'

It is a pleasant if somewhat cool late afternoon and so Louis and Monsieur Varicarville swing their arms, rub their hands, and affect to take pleasure in the bracing air as together they stroll the citadel precincts while watching to nobble Achilles when he exits from chez the Duke. Meanwhile in sotto tones they circumspectly converse themselves into a relationship of increased mutual trust. After an hour of no Achilles reappearing Monsieur de Varicarville feels able to confide in Louis his harrowing doubts as to the wisdom of the Count of Soissons leading an uprising.

'What's the problem?' asks Louis.

De Varicarville confides a personal assessment of the Count's character which is virtually identical to the one we cribbed off De Retz in Chapter 35. Concluding:

'And since his Eminence [Richelieu] possesses in high degree all those qualities the Count does not, and is amply endowed with courage besides, and lacks little but health and compassion, to rise against him were tempting fate.'

'Unless victory be assured,' suggests Louis.

'Victory, Monsieur Morel,' sighs the older man, 'is *never* assured.'

'Achilles,' calls Louis, seeing his henchman descending the Duke of Bouillon's staircase, 'come here!'

Next Achilles is severely quizzed by Louis in the presence of De Varicarville. At first the blushing short-arsed Thespian[2] responds with a scarcely credible bluster of bombast and hyperbole.

'Shut up,' snarls Louis. 'And tell us the truth.'

The truth, it emerges, is that the Duke of Bouillon has just spent forty minutes haranguing and latterly bribing Monsieur Morel's servant into working to sway his master into an unswervingly warlike stance, all the better to bolster the Count of Soissons into civil war with. I haven't quite decided yet, but this may be the moment to make it clear to everyone that the conflict between Count and Cardinal in France in 1641 and the conflict between Scotland and England now could hardly be more otherwise. What the Count and his supporters are contemplating, assuming their sundry consciences to be clean, is deposing a tyrant person *within* a nation. What we Scots require, by contrast, is the removal of our *logically distinct nation* from the spoiling clutches of *the nation tyrant England*. So our situation is instructively much closer to that of Catalonia versus Spain, both in 1640 and now.

Unfortunately, it is doubtful whether Achilles realizes this.

'How much did the Duke give you?' demands Louis.

'Only ten crowns, your lordship.'

'Give them to me.'

'Aw, your lordship, come on!'

'Give them to *me*, Achilles, and I shall give them back to *him*. I command you, moreover, never to take bribes again.'

So that's that, except that later on Achilles will seem so hangdog miserable that Louis will *give* him a second ten crowns, ostensibly by way of reward for his honesty in confessing to having taken the bribe.

And does another little moral tale hang scraggily thereby, or not? Mustn't tub-thump, though.

Having dismissed Achilles, and bid adieu to Monsieur de Varicarville

---

[2] 'Suggest a Boolean search here. See how frequently you've abused this portentous diglossic.' [J.R.]

until dinner, Louis, in reflective mode, continues his walk down into the town. As he wanders about Sedan in the fading light he concludes from all the evidence of frenzied extension of battlements, and multiplication of cannon emplacements, that the Duke of Bouillon himself doesn't anticipate peace for long.

The hour before dinner finds Louis back in his chamber, gazing meditatively from the window. Knock-knock, and in bustles the Duke of Bouillon himself. Louis stands stiffly; greets his host/guest formally, and returns the ten-crown bribe. Abruptly the Duke apologizes for his rudeness during the morning's tilting. It was, he says, because he had somehow gained the impression that Louis's mission in Sedan was to undermine the Count of Soissons's resolve to war upon Richelieu.

'I am absolutely determined, your grace,' replies Louis politely, 'to throw myself absolutely behind the Count – when once I perceive that the Count himself is absolutely and irrevocably determined to go to war against the Cardinal.'

'I take it, Monsieur Morel,' rejoins the Duke, 'that you are invited to attend tomorrow's Council?'

'Indeed, your grace.'

'Then shall you hear news from Paris which, even to a prince so redoubtably . . . cautious as his Highness, shall constitute an irresistible goad.'

This takes us to Chapter 41, which could be titled 'The Hero and his Mother'. I haven't decided yet how to do it, and in some ways would prefer not to. Certainly if we asked Wringhim he'd tell us to either scrap it altogether, or else rework it in the manner of Neil Gunn. But that would never do, and furthermore, even though I too have become more of a partisan Scot than I used to be, I still get discernibly irritated when Wringhim & Co affect to discover and reveal to the world that the likes of Hugh MacDiarmid and Neil Gunn are Great Writers of International Stature. It just isn't true, and I can't see what's to be gained by pretending it is. Burns and Scott, yes. MacDiarmid and Gunn, no. Of course I'm not saying they're devoid of merit; just that nothing worth having is to be gained from disingenuous plots to pump them up. Oh, but woe! I've just had a presentiment of Wringhim's apoplexy when he reads this. Silly thing is – and I'm not just saying this to butter him up – I actually think Wringhim himself is already a more accomplished novelist than Gunn ever was. As for those 'Scottish Literature Specialists' in the universities who boast with cackling glee that Shakespeare will be excluded from their syllabus the moment they can get away with it, no wonder words fail them.

So it's partly to spite Wringhim et al that Chapter 41, in some form, will not be omitted, and if you've any ideas on the matter, Janet, please feel free to sing out. The first problem is that, following the curt departure of the Duke of Bouillon, Louis, again at his window, gazing up at the faint daylight fading down as the stars twinkle up, really seems to have had a rather extraordinary experience.

Literally translated:

'While a host of meandering fancies crossed the back of my mind, dimly glimpsed through shadows, and distantly subdued, in sympathy with the stillness of the night, I felt a gloomy preoccupation come upon me. A dissatisfaction, it was, which I could sense in moments of weakness, whether of body or of mind, might plunge me into the profoundest depression; despair, indeed, at the sense of how extremely little my actions, so seemingly deliberate at the time, were in any way controlled by my reason, and hence attributable to myself. And yet . . . my self. Myself must take the blame.'[3]

I think what's really bothering Louis here is that, to be true to his preferred image of himself, he would have spoken to the Duke of Bouillon along the lines of:

'You're a fat loathsome never-to-be-trusted shit. Go fuck yourself.'

Whereas, when the crunch came, he was initially coldly courteous, and latterly submissively agreeable. Like a junior civil servant with some ideals, steamrollered by a bullyboy minister. For us, or me at least, this only-too-human failing is one of Louis's more likeable features, but by the same token one can sympathize with it seeming to make him think he hates himself.

But much more dramatically problematical than that:

'As in that loneliness I audienced the soft murmur of the Meuse, and a chorus of puffs and sighs as a gentle winter wind played through the embrasures of the citadel, I was put cruelly in mind of many such a starry sky smiling down on my own fair land, so far south, and long ago. And I longed with all my soul to be there again, in sight of my beloved

---

[3] Note again, despite Louis's still having no knowledge of Descartes, this further evidence of what we might call his propensity to pre-Cartesian schizophrenia. Very like the EBC Wimbledon commentary team.

Hélène, picking flowers, perhaps, as my father looked fondly down from the window of his library, and my mother . . . '

There's a break in the narrative here, followed by a short sequence of notes and phrases which Louis himself seems never to have linked together, and which we could not hope to do justice to in translation or pastiche. What seems to have happened is that, in the very moment of 'mother' following 'father' in his reverie, Louis was overwhelmed by a mystical vision in which the spirit of his mother, soaring free from her earthly body, flies over him in the aspect of a great white swan, with the burnished gold wings of an angel. For a moment she hovers over him, as if the huge swan could hover like a humming-bird, but in slow motion, and her moist dark eyes, flashing brighter than ever in the prime of her beauty, beam down on him a loving sadness so sweetly forgiving as to remind Louis with unbearable intensity of all the ways in which he has failed her, and how undeserving he is of her love. As though in punishment for these sins, he is unable to hear or in any manner divine the few words that seem to issue from her barely moving lips. Then bang. The moment is over and the hovering angel-swan disappears upwards into the sky like a vertical-take-off jet.

As the apparition vanished, it left Louis in a swoon. When he came to he was confused, and even when he wrote about it later he was plainly unsure what to make of his experience:

'I feel sure, now, as I sit and reason upon it, that my *vision* was entirely an effect of my *imagination*, to which the late hour, the darkness, and my own previous thoughts all contributed. And yet . . . the *fancy* must have been most overpoweringly strong to thus compel the very organs of my sight to so co-operate in the deceit.'

Patently there he is struggling to rationalize himself away from the miraculous-revelation interpretation to which, both emotionally and by religious conditioning, he is understandably drawn. As further evidence of this intellectual muddlement:

'I am sure that the Almighty Being who gave laws to nature, and made it so exquisitely regular, even in its irregularities, never suffers His Own Laws to be changed or interrupted . . . '

To which he can't resist adding:

' . . . except for some great and extraordinary purpose.'

The next problem, for us, is that, being vigorous atheists ourselves, we would in some ways prefer not to represent a protagonist who isn't. Yet even today we could not honestly deny, as we head for 2001, that new hardbacks by the likes of Billy Graham commonly sell in runs of 400,000, while paperbacks of Schopenhauer do not. Indeed, not even Paul Chalicer has ever yet shifted 400,000 American hardbacks of his best-selling novel(s),[4] which implies the almost equally tragic consequence that the average reader today would not only rather believe than know, but also rather believe than imagine. Consequently, what we have to watch out for is that, now the logical arguments and empirical evidence against theism are so incontrovertible, the efforts of self-deception required to reject or eject them in the first place, and keep them at bay thereafter, are so taxing, the emotional investment so costly, that the said subscribers are liable to cut up extremely ferocious in the face of open threats. In the interests of subtler sabotage, therefore, it would have been attractive to portray Louis, in delicately positive pastels, as intellectually ahead of his time, a pioneer humanist, with moral values in advance of the sky-pie bigotry all around him.

The trouble is: we can't. Louis *is* a Catholic. He *does*, however vaguely, believe in God. He *is* convinced, in some nebulous way, of the existence of a Heaven-place, where the souls of the good in heart and pure in spirit, such as his mother, will go, although he himself may not. Louis Morel is thus, in religious terms, very much the minor aristocrat of his age, and really his only substantial anticipation of more enlightened days to come is in his aesthetic regard for the sublime in nature – as documented far above. So our ongoing puzzle here, for Chapter 41, is how to depict the religious construction Louis puts on his vision of his mother, and the philosophical quagmire this plunges him into, without sounding banal, without inadvertently dropping sops of grist for the God Squad to snuffle up, and without getting up our own nose.

All that is small beer, though, beside the great heady hogshead posed by the issue of *Magic!*

Yes, I thought that might widen your eyes, and what I'm getting at is this. While I will undertake to demonstrate – almost as rigorously as Schopenhauer and Bertrand Russell, and just as rigorously as Wringhim Knox – that theism is necessarily false, I'm not nearly so persuaded that there's nothing to be said for magic. Wringhim will hate me for it,[5] I know, but what I'm getting at is this.

---

4  Recently he was outraged to discover several copies of his British first edition in a remainder store in Norwich.

5  Please see Chapter 43, 'Extended Footnote to the Last Three Chapters'.

If we were all omnipotent magicians, I can't imagine you not agreeing, we could all be perpetually happy, for everything that we willed would happen instantly and effortlessly. In that thought lies the attraction of the idea of magic. But we *could not* all be omnipotent magicians, since either our wills would conflict (two of us willing to bed the same glamorous filmstar), or we would all be willing *exactly the same thing*. But if we all willed *exactly* identically, we would all be the same 'person'. Hence we could only ever bed ourself, which might impair our eyesight.

If we then more chastely inquire whether *anyone* is a magician, of *any* potency, the *Oxford English Dictionary* gives us, as its main definition of 'magic':

'The pretended art of influencing the course of events, and of producing marvellous physical phenomena, by processes supposed to owe their efficacy to their power of compelling the intervention of spiritual beings, or of bringing into operation some occult controlling principle of nature.'

Now I know, Janet, how fond you are of the OED on your CD-ROM, but I think you'll agree that's a pretty appalling definition, even by Oxford standards. For a start, by talking of magic as a 'pretended art' the definition *assumes* that anything presented as magic *must* be bogus. Also, the phrase 'occult controlling principle of nature' either cannot refer to magic, or is a self-contradiction! If *occult* means *as yet undiscovered,* then an occult principle of nature has nothing to do with magic, and relativity theory was an occult principle of nature until 1905. But if *occult* means *magical* or *supernatural,* the self-contradiction is obvious: what on earth could be a *supernatural* principle of *nature?*

So the OED definition is left with the possibility that magic, if magic there be, is *theurgy*: control of nature through control of the gods or demons that rule nature, with all the baggage of claptrap that presupposes. Though we're now on *Sexorcist 75: The Suckabus Rides Again* for the kiddies (both in age and mind) I think we can safely say that not even moderately intelligent theists believe any longer in the *real* (objective, external . . . ) *existence* of angels, demons, goblins, fairies, ghosts and the like. But if there are no angels, demons, or other supernatural middlemen, there can be no theurgy.

Does this mean there can be no magic? Logically it by no means follows, and if you're itching to sneer here you had better have up your sleeve some ready answers to questions such as these:

Why is belief in magic so tenacious in the history of all peoples? Why did the Greeks and Romans take magic so seriously as to make it punishable by death? Were our forefathers all so stupid as to persecute absolutely impossible crimes, such as black magic and witchcraft?

The fundamental belief in non-causal (ie non-physical) influence is much more universal than culture-specific allegiance to specific deities – except perhaps among scientists, and positivistic laymen like Wringhim, who endorse the scientific worldview. Yet even many scientists seem to retain a tinge of superstition: a residual uneasy feeling that though physical explanation exhausts *nature*, it may not exhaust *reality*.

Why, oh why, Mr Knox, was Isaac Newton an alchemist?

Our own, slightly less militant view of the matter – and you, Janet, are welcome as ever to differ – goes like this. *Materialism* is the belief that physical explanation does exhaust reality. Materialism is thus physics on the throne of metaphysics. If magic is possible, materialism (as a philosophy) is mistaken. Hence, magical 'phenomena' are, philosophically, the most important facts of all experience. If there are any! And if it is anything:

Magic is the direct action at a distance of my will on your will, or of my will on a physical object. And the aim of magic is to extend the sphere of willing beyond the physical person of the willer. Hence the perceived survival value, to non-magicians, of killing off all potential hostile magicians.[6] And candidate magical phenomena will include: hypnosis, hypnotherapy, wart-charming, Christ-like 'miracle'-curing, wounding or killing by means of intentional willing alone, telekinesis (eg moving compass needles by willing alone), intentional communication of thoughts at a distance, and the apparently magical 'perception' that enables sleepwalkers like Lucy Westenra in *Dracula* to avoid injury up the Whitby cliff. Clairvoyance and precognition also count as magical if

---

[6] The primacy of the *will* of the magician, or witch, was recognized by Paracelsus [c. 1490–1541]: 'If I bear malice in my will against anyone, that malice must be carried out by some medium or *corpus*. Thus it is possible for my spirit to stab or wound another person without help from my body in using a sword, merely by my *fervent desire*. In such imagining, women outdo men . . . for they are more ardent in revenge.' Women like: Old Queen Margaret, in Shakespeare's *Richard III*; Meg Murdockson, in Scott's *Heart of Midlothian*; Madame Defarge, in Dickens' *Tale of Two Cities*; Faye Dunaway as Milady, in Richard Lester's *The Four Musketeers*; and to some extent Audrey's mother.

their information is obtained through the active, seeking *willing* of the medium.

Nature, we might say, plays snooker on the table of causality. Magic, if there is any, is able to dive underneath the surface and pop up unexpectedly, as a wrinkle that natural science cannot explain. Not yet, anyway. And even if such phenomena do ever occur, they are not very impressive. Suppose we hear a story about a baby suffocating in his cot. His mother is mixing cocktails and chatting to visitors. Suddenly her consciousness fills with an image of her child choking. She rushes upstairs to save him. His will-to-live has communicated directly, at a distance, with her will. Or has it? If so, then, as a result, the mechanism of her brain has been triggered to screen an image of his danger. Very satisfactory, in this case, but what of the thousands of unfortunate babies whom magic fails to save? Perhaps the current success story was not really a case of magic, but of statistics. Maybe that baby's mother *often* had such disaster apprehensions, 99% of them groundless. Then the present happy outcome is not magical but statistically predictable.

Magic, at any rate, is physically impossible. If a strange event occurs, a scientist *cannot* consider magic as a possible explanation. Not until he takes his scientist's hat off in the evening and reaches for his Glenmorangie. But still, if X is physically impossible, yet X happens, X must be explained somehow. So before we pooh all possibility of magic, before we legislate against it *a priori*, we must believe the world to be completely intelligible! And who does?

Another consideration:

Suppose that in 200 years there are no clockwork watches in the world. All watches are electronic. Does this mean that clockwork watches are impossible? Similarly, if magic exists, or ever existed, it must have (had) *some* selective advantage: helping the mother to save her baby; enabling the sleepwalker not to plunge over the precipice; maybe even locating game, food or water via clairvoyance. But the *potential* selective advantage of science is vastly greater than that of magic. For example, science enables us to place a video camera in Baby's bedroom. This lets us monitor his welfare more successfully than if we rely on Mummy's dire premonitions. So we would expect a see-saw relation: on any planet, as science ascends, magic will atrophy. And to hope to discover the most impressive cases of magic, we should expect to travel back in time, to before the dawn of scientific thought, or across the planet to some primitive society that so far has eluded the clutches of missionaries, 'civilization' and post-graduate anthropologists. But if we go back in time, we cannot conduct repeatable experiments. We can only read and ponder. And if we study a primitive society in Borneo, we will infect its members with at least the *doubt* that our science (helicopters, medicine, transistor radios) is more powerful than their magic. And as we study them, they will begin to lose whatever magical powers they had.

All very vexing.

For our own part, we make no claim to magical powers. Even if we thought we had any, we'd keep quiet about them, though you could expect to notice a dramatic improvement in my royalty statements. But to any magic-watcher today with the requisite funding, like well-endowed American monster-watchers all over Loch Ness in summer, we would rent the following ricketsy model:

A magical action, being an internal communication through ultimate reality (ie *the body*, of which science, due to limitations intrinsic to objective knowledge, may only ever know *the skin*) may not be restricted by such physical limits as the speed of light. Physical messages, say, to get from the front door to the back door, have to walk down to the end of Front Door Street, turn left, then walk back along Back Door Street. And they can't walk any faster than the speed of light. Whereas magical messages, if there are any, have the privilege of running straight through the house from the front door to the back. In which case, *even* if magical messages only travelled at the speed of light (or less) *through* the house, they would still *seem* to travel faster than light (given that light has to take the long route: Front Door Street . . . , etc).

This metaphor would allow magical communications to *seem* to be instantaneous even though they weren't quite. For instance, if the corridor between front door and back door were very short, while the roundabout route was very long. There, would, however be no reason to expect that magical communications could travel backwards in time to interfere with events that have already taken place. And it might just be *imaginable* that magical communications could get sidetracked on their way through the house. Perhaps even put on ice for many years. Hence it is not inconceivable that my will might be influenced, today, by a belated magical information packet from the will of a person long dead. Please note, however, that even this would not open any floodgates to earnest two-way communication with the dead!

The dead *are* dead, alas. Or maybe, for them, *tant mieux*. Spirits, qua disembodied souls, *are* a nonsense, and you might just as well spend the rest of your life watching *Ghostbusters*. Magic, though, in the weak sense adumbrated above . . . well, you'll long ago have divined from the diffidence of this divagation that your humblest Humbert is in a spot of embarrassment. The reason is that, unbeknown to Louis as yet, his mother, in faraway Bigorre, in the region of Lourdes, dies on just this very night when he has his vision of her as an angel-swan, and (though it is impossible to pinpoint precisely, since none of them are wearing Japanese quartz watches) at very close to, and arguably bang-on, the self-same instant when his hovering angel-swan mirage of her disappears upwards into the sky like a vertical-take-off jet.

What got her we'll never know for sure, but from the symptoms Louis will shortly learn of (chill, vomiting, swollen stomach leading to acute abdominal agonies) it could well have been peritonitis. Another instance, in any case, of a kind-hearted, lively, passionate and still attractive woman, who might have lived another forty years, rapidly ceasing to exist altogether. One curious aspect of the episode is that, despite the dramatic ascent upwards of the form of his mother, which in religious imagery might obviously be taken to symbolize being plucked up to Heaven, it never for a moment occurs to Louis that here may be an intimation of – in some uncanny way the privilege of sharing in – the moments immediately preceding his mother's passing. Rather does he merely brood (and with some justice, I think we're all agreed) on what a callous young swine he is, appraised in the light of his mother's radiant qualities, and her self-sacrificing generosity. Before my own mother died I might now have written:

'Picture, then, the incomparably greater misery that must have ravaged Louis, had he guessed the awful truth.'

Everyone is different, needless to say. But in some important ways many very diverse persons are more alike than everyone else. This is a function of perception, just as much as a 'fact of nature', but no less tragic for that. Nick Carraway, chronicling *The Great Gatsby*, observes, while contemplating the dismal physical condition of the cuckolded *garagiste* Wilson (who will in due course, in the grip of a paranoid delusion, murder Gatsby) that: there is no difference between two men so extreme as between a sick man and a well man. Not unlike the computer truism that there are only two kinds of hard disk: those that have crashed, and those that haven't yet. Analogously, thinking of fundamental worldview, we could say there are only two sorts of men: those whose mothers have died, and those who haven't yet. Graduating from the latter class to the former, I find, tends to rewrite the narrator thus:

'If Louis had realized his mother was on the brink of death, then died, then was dead, he would, after a brief spasm of anguish, have subsided into a state of sullen shock approaching torpor. For several days he would have been vaguely conscious of memory lapses unrelated to abuse of alcohol, and had this trauma occurred in the centre of open Edinburgh, as opposed to fortified Sedan, he would several times have come close to being run down by criminally speeding traffic, due to having paid insufficient attention to crossing busy roads. During the many ensuing months of weary adjustment, his most implacable psychological enemy would have been a rage of resentment against his mother, for the inconsiderateness of having abandoned him.'

Interestingly, Louis's own reaction, when he does learn the truth, will approximate closely to that scenario, if we remember to peep with care behind the masque of his forthcoming escapades in Paris, and allow for the inevitable abeying of gnawing distractions which takes place, when his own life comes under fire. In the meantime, Janet, if you could be so kind as to advise us how to swing it, we want the reader to share with us a *soupçon* of shame at the voyeurism implicit in knowing the protagonist no longer has a mother, while he himself does not. It's a bit like knowing Mumbo Rankles is effectively impotent, in his loins just as much as his head, because his wife hissed as much in your ear one night, while pissed in a Glasgow curry-house. And while you know, you also know that he doesn't know you know. And that gives you a certain edge of epistemological advantage over him, which your best self would as soon not possess.[7]

So much for Chapter 41.

In an ideal microcosmic novel we would now be allowed to whisk straight back to Paris, in Chapter 42, which might there be titled 'Lots of Non-anal Heterosexual Sex in Paris'. That this is not possible is thanks to some extraordinary events which take place in Sedan the following day, and naturally suggest the chapter title 'Diamonds Are For Pawning'. It all begins when Louis is informed by Achilles that the Count of Soissons's

---

[7] Narrators vary acutely in the qualities of their consciousness. Nick Carraway has much to commend him, Dr Watson is dependably middle-class, but few can have been more in advance of contemporary psychiatry than Robert Louis Stevenson's Dr Jekyll: 'Others will follow, others will outstrip me on the same lines; and I hazard the guess that man will be ultimately known for a mere polity of multifarious, incongruent and independent denizens.'

page is at hand to lead him to a General Council in the citadel Great Hall. Luminaries present include the Abbé de Retz, fresh from Paris, who embraces Louis as an invaluable longlost friend. Also ambassadors from Spain, on a mission to promise men and money to the Count of Soissons and his faction, strictly provided they waste no more time before waging ruinous civil war on the Cardinal.

When the meeting is called to order, the Duke of Bouillon kicks off with eloquent old-campaigner's rhetoric about:

'The paramount obligation to free our nation, ourselves, and indeed our King himself, from the stifling regime of the usurper tyrant Richelieu.'

Next on the rostrum is the quasi-Polonial Monsieur de Varicarville, who speaks with the moderation of caution, and rehearses several good reasons why the Count of Soissons should not declare war against the Cardinal. Then the Abbé de Retz allows himself to be begged to speak, and argues:

'As his Eminence's bodily powers are daily declining, and as the hatred of the people for him grows in proportion, so let us have peace until war is inevitable, and who knows? In the meanwhile the ogre may die of his ailments, and save us all much bloodshed.'

The Duke of Bouillon then shafts deprecating jibes at De Retz, who responds with droll speculations on the consequences for belligerence of gout. The Count of Soissons, as Master of Ceremonies, defuses the wrangle, and invites Louis Morel, as new First Gentleman of his Bedchamber, to edify the assembly with his views. Louis with the fluency of conviction echoes the wisdom of striving for peace right up to the final minute of the eleventh hour. As the Count is nodding pliantly in agreement, the Duke of Bouillon lumbers to his feet once more, waving a ribboned scroll, and cries:

'The twelfth hour, gentlemen, is already struck! If your Highness would read this?'

With the gloom of foreboding accentuating the disparity between his good and his lazy eye, the Count accepts the scroll from the Duke. First silently, and then quietly aloud to the gathering, he reads a committal proclamation from Louis XIII of France. Since we just happen to have the full text stored on a phrase key, you might as well read it now:

IN THE KING'S NAME!

Dear and well-beloved,

The fears which we entertain, that certain rumours lately spread abroad of new factions and conspiracies, whereby various of our rebellious subjects endeavour to trouble the repose of our kingdom, should inspire you with vain apprehensions, you not knowing the particulars, have determined us to make those particulars public, in order that you may render thanks to God for having permitted us to discover the plots of our enemies, in time to prevent their malice from making itself felt, to the downfall of the State.

We should never have believed, after the lenity and favour which we have on all occasions shown to our cousin the Count of Soissons, more especially in having pardoned him his share in the horrible conspiracy of 1636, that he would again have embarked on similar designs, had not the capture of various seditious emissaries, sent into our provinces for the purpose of exciting rebellion, of levying troops against our service, of debauching our armies, and of shaking the fidelity of our subjects, together with the confessions of the said emissaries, fully proved and established the criminality of our said cousin's designs.

The levies which are publicly made under commissions from our said cousin – the hostilities committed upon the bodies of our faithful soldiers, established in guard upon the frontiers of Champagne – the confession of the courier called Vausselle, who has most providentially fallen into our hands, stating that he had been sent on the part of the said Count of Soissons, the dukes of Guise and Bouillon, to our dearly beloved brother, Gaston, Duke of Orleans, for the purpose of seducing our said brother to join and aid in the treasonable plans of the said conspirators; and the further confession of the said Vausselle, stating that the Count of Soissons, together with the dukes of Guise and Bouillon, conjointly and severally, had treated and conspired with the Cardinal Infante of Spain, from whom they had received and were to receive notable sums of money, and from whom they expected the aid and abetment of various bodies of troops and warlike munition, designed to act against their native country of France, and us their born liege lord and Sovereign; these, and various other circumstances, having given us clear knowledge and cognisance of that whereof we would willingly have remained in doubt, we are now called upon, in justice to ourself and to our subjects, to declare and pronounce the said Count of Soissons, together with the dukes of Guise and Bouillon, and all who shall give them aid, assistance, counsel, or abetment, enemies to the state of France, and rebels to their lawful Sovereign; without, within the space of one month from the date hereof, they present themselves at our court, wherever it may be for the time established, and, humbly acknowledging their fault, have recourse to our royal clemency.

[Signed]

LOUIS.

That missive, effectively a declaration of war upon the Count of Soissons by Cardinal Richelieu, could not have been better calculated (as indeed it likely was) to unite the factions in Sedan behind the Count in unmitigated bellicosity.

'Since the war is now essential to the safety of the Count, and in any case ineluctable,' agrees the Abbé de Retz, 'let us all now hope our Spanish friends are come equipped to make good their earnests of funds.'

Attention now focuses on the Spanish ambassadors, whose oily responses give ground for suspicion that while Spain is happy to hurry France into civil war, she doesn't want to pay for it.

The Duke of Bouillon complains, in tones of bitter scorn, that Spain is not serious in her promises of support: the Count-Duke Olivares, as usual, is happy to spite Richelieu in so many words, but lacks the cash to make them good.

At this taunt the senior Spanish ambassador, a tall, dark aristocrat with the build of an aging bullfighter crossed with the younger Dracula, leaps to his feet and ripostes with Latin passion. He is the Duke of Villafranca, formerly Commander of the Barcelona Galleys. So sincere, he swears, is Spain, in her support of the anti-Richelieu forces, that he would gladly contribute funds to the war kitty from his own personal fortune – if only he had not suffered such crippling losses when the Catalan rebels looted his palace, during the uprising there last year.

On a wave of inspiration Louis Morel jumps in and asks the Duke if his fabulous Villafranca diamonds have ever been recovered.

Alas, no.

Louis then presumes to presume, given the Duke's warm pledge of a moment ago, that if the said diamonds could suddenly be located, their value would just as instantly be invested in the war budget?

Being suspiciously Spanish, the Duke of Villafranca smells an immediate rat, but is unable not to concur.

Monsieur Morel then excitedly excuses himself for a moment and rushes back to his turreted room to retrieve the diamonds from the moneybelt under his mattress. Achilles Lefranc, being caught opportunistically succeeding at sex with the Duchess of Bouillon's laundrymaid, reacts with wails of dismay when he sees his hard-filched diamonds about to vanish but sees sense smartly when Louis threatens him with a thrashing later in respect of ravishing juveniles on his master's bed if he doesn't shut up at once.

Back in the Great Hall, Louis flaunts the diamonds to great applause and explains to all how happily by chance he came to be in Spain at just the very moment to rescue the gems from a Barcelona looter. Eyes streaming with tears at the sight of his jewels rediscovered, and dread of losing them again so soon, the Duke of Villafranca now pleads to be allowed to keep what is rightfully his, in return for which he will do what he can to squeeze some gold out of Olivares.

But that is all too hypothetical, retorts Louis, since:

'If your sovereign were serious in our support, your grace, the money would be here with you now.'

In a desperate bid to retain potential ownership of his heirlooms, Villafranca grudgingly proposes that the diamonds be pawned in the meantime, with the pawn advance to go into the down-with-Richelieu float, and the onus on himself to arrange redemption later. Next the three principal jewellers of Sedan are summoned and instructed by the Duke of Bouillon to form an impromptu consortium with an urgent brief to value the Villafranca diamonds and offer their best possible on-the-spot hock loan against the diamonds as security.

Figures of 150,000 and 125,000 French crowns, respectively, are arrived at. The jewellers go off to orchestrate disbursement of the latter sum in cash, and the Duke of Villafranca subsides looking horribly ill.

Now the General Council elects a War Council, and the War Council, among other matters, passes a motion to the effect that young Monsieur Morel, reporting to the Abbé de Retz, shall have the honour and risk of whipping up the criminal fraternity in Paris: in support of the Soissons cause. That evening, in his apartments after dinner, the Count gives Louis a final private briefing, and a mandate to collect 10,000 crowns from the treasury before he leaves – half to be taken as six months salary in advance, and the other 5,000 as slush money, with which to butter up the underworld of Paris. Other details include the decision that for the time being Louis's Paris lodging will be in the Hôtel de Soissons with the Count of Soissons's mother: on the ground that this should be the last possible hiding-place that the enemy might consider.

So there we are, Janet.

How to get all that lot into three short chapters?

Answers on several postcards, please, or preferably an ASCII disk. Having said that, I'd be even keener to have your best speculation as to whether, when and how Louis does or doesn't move the masonry of Paris with Hélène. Feel free to draft a whole chapter, if you like. (You too, Paul, if you get these pages in time.)

Re the present three chapters, I'm sorry, in view of your earlier request, that there won't be more sex in these scenes, but I really can't see where I could responsibly stick it in. Although there is an abundance of loose sex in Sedan at this time (not all of it non-anal, sad to say; mercenary soldiers, freebooters, resident strumpets, camp-followers, all that) over and above Achilles with the obliging laundrymaid, Louis himself has literally no time for it: in his rush to get back to Paris, where we will find him again four mornings later:

Trotting on a low-end dappled mare through cobbled sunlight, disguised as a grey Cistercian monk, heading for the Hôtel de Soissons, and doing his best to imagine that the Dowager Countess may not look like a great fat carp.

# 43

## Extended Footnote
## To the Last Three Chapters

Wringhim doesn't spread it about, but his strongest academic subjects, up to the age of nineteen, were maths and physics. Before retreating to Glasgow, to become more literary, and political, he had completed with distinction the first part of his Tripos in Engineering at Cambridge. As a result, underlying all his ranting and bingeing, ageing and decaying, and his personal and professional extravagances, there survives the sceptically positivistic hardnosedness that both licenses and equips him to be rather rude about 'some of your younger English novelists' (also, let's frankly concede, some anglicized Scottish ones) when, having run out of other games to play, they affect scientific profundity.

From his *Essay*, for instance:

'I have now to record a note of disquiet at the thought of being reviled for affecting to eschew interpretative criticism *within* the world of my fiction when there is the dreaded *Heisenberg Effect* to contend with. Now the Heisenberg Principle, otherwise known as the Uncertainty Principle, was elaborated half a century ago by Werner Heisenberg (a founding father of quantum physics), partly in reaction to Einstein's conservative dictum that 'God does not play dice', and mainly in heroic recognition that, particularly in the realm of the vanishingly small, the activities of *the observer* have an intrinsic distorting effect on the behaviour of *the observed* – such that doubt can legitimately be voiced as to whether (a) *the observed* has any existence independently of *the observer*, and (b) whether the mainspring of classical physics, ie objective or Newtonian causality, is inappropriate to and must be abandoned at the subatomic level.

'There are many good popular expositions of the Uncertainty Principle and its ramifications, none more lucid than

Heisenberg's own *Physics and Philosophy*, first published in English in 1959. This makes it all the more unfortunate that some of your younger English novelists in vogue have of late – half a century late, in fact – taken to incorporating gargantuan misunderstandings of the implications of the Heisenberg Principle (and other pioneer developments of twentieth-century science and mathematics) into turgid quasi-fictions which shed no light at all on physics, biology, genetics, society – or even the steamy relations between people, which are what the novel is all about anyway – and which are not madly entertaining either.

'Paramount amid the misconceptions current among this throng of ageing English Literature graduates is the notion that since classical causality has been called into question at the quantum level, it thereby must have been discredited too with respect to our daily lives, and hence we are plunged into a terrifying and/or exhilarating chaos of existential contingency and randomness such as Sartre too got bogged down in just as fatuously decades ago.

'Bollocks.[1]

'To the novelist (as opposed to the science-fictionist, that square-circle unto himself), the quantum world has little relevance. We – people, Yorkshire terriers, even literary critics – live in *the world of middle-sized objects*. Broadly speaking, in our middle-sized Newtonian world, causes fall into three classes. *Mechanical causes* (billiard balls equally acting and reacting); *stimuli* (the rising sun causing a summer flower to open); and *motives* (rumours that Julie Andrews strips off *cause* certain persons to flock to the cinema). Those three sorts of cause correspond to: inorganic matter; organic life; intelligent life. Motives, to be effective, do not require physical contact. They require to be *known*. Knowing (forming representations) is a defining characteristic of animal (certainly mammalian) life. To act as a motive, an object (trout on the kitchen sideboard) needs only to be perceived. Until Pussy *knows* there is a trout

---

[1] *'I've discussed this (or should I say these?) with Martin Bunbury [at a reception in the Chelsea Arts Club] and he suspects you of poking fun at him over his Einstein's Lost Fermat.' [P.C.]*

in the kitchen, her behaviour will not be influenced. But nor could it be influenced if Pussy had no *will* – to eat the trout; to continue living.

'Now the ascending heterogeneousness of causes and effects (from mechanical causes, to stimuli, up to motives) does not imply decreasing necessity. A stone must be kicked, whereas a Mark Antony will be determined by his Cleopatra's dreamy murmur. But the effect necessarily follows the cause in both cases. A human, we may say, is an animal whose powers of knowledge have been multiplied by words, concepts, and rational reflection. The capacity for abstract reasoning gives us a relative freedom – it liberates us from complete determination by present perceptions – but an abstract motive is still a cause. Deliberation does not remove a person from determination by motives. Rather it exposes us to a wider range of motives by which to be determined.

'Candidate novelists kindly note.'

# 44

# Mothers and Sons

Passing by my old auberge [*writes Louis*] in the Rue des Prouvaires, I soon reached the Hôtel de Soissons. Here I delivered to a servant the Count's note of introduction, bidding the man – by means of mime, as my disguise embraced the semblance of having sworn vows of silence – to present it to the Dowager Countess, and to inform her that its bearer now awaited her pleasure.

In a few minutes the servant returned, and beckoned me to follow him to the apartments of the Countess. We mounted the grand staircase, and proceeding through a suite of splendid rooms (all windowed with stained glass, in many panes of which were visible the ciphers C.S. and C.N. interlaced [to symbolize the union of Charles of Soissons with Catherine of Navarre]), we at length reached the large and well-warmed chamber in which the Countess was comfortably seated.

She was working at an embroidery frame, while a pretty girl of about sixteen stood beside her, holding a wicker box containing the various needles and coloured threads of which the Countess was making use. On my being announced, the seated lady raised her greying head, revealing a face in whose lines the wreckage of many beauties plainly showed, and fixed her eyes somewhat sternly upon me. Having inspected the features of my visage by degrees – reading, as it were for the first time, strange hieroglyphs on a page accused by others of deceit – she then glanced slowly over the grey-robed form of my person, with a grave and dissatisfied air.

'You come here, young sir,' she at length said coldly, 'dressed up as a walking lie. But you shall go away honestly weeping.'

My regard must have strayed in apprehension toward her girl, for the Countess then added:

'You may speak freely before Mathilde, Monsieur Morel. She is privy to most of my secrets. And more discreet, I might add, than many a true monk of your order.'

'In that case,' I respectfully returned, 'I would beseech your Highness to inform me, why it is that I must weep.'

'Because, monsieur, your mother is dead.'

[*Now follow several pages of rather mawkish stuff about Louis's reaction to his mother's death. Of certain related retarded responses and psychological ramifications, not all Oedipenile, you the reader have already read, when recently in Sedan. As regards immediate actions and reactions:*]

Yet the Countess of Soissons [*Louis goes on*] spoke not out of unfeeling motives. She honestly fancied me guilty of follies that, in her eyes were major crimes, and she thought – so I later was persuaded – by the terrible blow she dealt me, its impact doubled by the coolness of her own composure, at once to reprove and reclaim me.

At first I did not comprehend. I could not – I *would* not believe that what she said was true. Observing my disbelief, in the vacancy of my expression, the Countess calmly repeated:

'Your mother, monsieur, is *dead*.'

Whatever change now overcame my countenance, it was sufficiently dreadful to precipitate the Countess into fear for the consequences of her procedure. Calling loudly to her women in an ante-chamber to 'bring water, wine, anything' to revive me, she rose up in alarm and with her girl Mathilde dragged my sagging body to the chair she had vacated. There I must have remained slumped, unresponsive to any attention, as in a waking coma, for at least the two hours following. In the next memory that remains to me, I find the Countess on a stool beside me, applying a dampened napkin to my brow, while her girl kneels on the floor by my thighs, and rubs my lolling hands between her own.

'Speak to me, Monsieur Morel,' I recall the Countess was saying. And though her words no doubt departed her lips charged highly with urgency, by the time their import touched my soul they might as well have been tired grey messenger doves; exhausted, from flying over stormy seas. The sincerity of her remorse, however, was in no dispute. There were tears in her eyes, doubtless now for my mother as well as myself, and from the stream of words she uttered, though I could not grasp their sense, I felt in my heart that even had I been her own son, she could not, in that time, have desired my recovery with greater ardour. Such, then, was the scene in that chamber, when the antechamber door was thrown open, and a tall, elderly, venerable-seeming gentleman ushered in.

\* \* \*

To the Countess of Soissons the Venerable Gentleman (aged about seventy and crowned by a stack of sleek silver hair, like the Anti-Drac Professor Van Helsing, in typical misconceptions) plays the foil of Guide, Philosopher, and Forgiving Father Confessor. His present advent is therefore her cue to collapse herself, and be escorted away to repose by Mathilde, while the Venerable Gentleman takes custody of Louis, and begins his treatment by bleeding the patient profusely, as a result of which Louis spends the next two days in bed – too weak to move.

As Louis begins to revive, his conversations with Ven Gent (who knows everything worth knowing about the Countess of Soissons, and quite a bit else) reveal that Louis's mother, from her deathbed, had dictated a letter to her old friend the Countess, confiding that despite the prevailing belief that Louis had fled from Bigorre into Spain to escape punishment for murdering Jean-Baptiste, her own fundamental conviction, and the bitterest pill of all for her to swallow in these hours of her dying, was that the root motive behind Louis's disappearance was determination to indulge his lust for the buxom daughter of a local *roturier* (no mention of Hélène Arnault by name) who also had disappeared without warning or detectable trace some time later, presumably (in the view of both Louis's mother and father) kidnapped by Louis, or (which in some ways would be even more shameful, heaping the fosterling's disobedient ingratitude on top of the prodigal son's) in lustful collusion with him.

Here, yet again is noted the vitality of lust: in almost everyone's calculations as to the volitions and behaviour of almost everyone else, not excluding your only son, when once you have uncovered reason to believe he has reached the age of stupendous erections.

His mother's deathbed letter to the Countess, Louis further learns from Ven Gent, also begged her Highness to cause search to be made in Paris, both for Louis and his jailbait wench, with a view to rescuing him: 'from the debasing connexion into which, she said, the blood of Bigorre should have held him from ever entering.'

'And it was under those circumstances', Ven Gent concludes, 'that her Highness initially addressed you, in hope that the news of your mother's passing, so abruptly broken, would occasion such remorse, as to win you at once and for ever, from the unhappy entanglement into which you have fallen.'

'That the Countess of Soissons should be mistaken,' replies Louis, 'does not surprise me, for she did not know me. But that my mother should suppose any carnal passion, no matter how colossal, could have driven me to inflict so much pain upon her, and on my father, as my unexplained absence must have done, does astonish and afflict me deeply. Will you, monsieur, have the goodness, therefore, to inform the Countess that the suspicions of my mother were entirely unfounded, and that I neither fled with any young lady, nor for the purpose of trysting with any young lady, and most certainly not with a view to abducting any young lady – as her Highness herself must infallibly deduce: from the manner of my seeking out and attaching myself to her son, Monsieur le Comte.'

'Then how, monsieur,' Ven Gent inquires gently, 'to explain your unexplained absence?'

'Purely due', Louis wearily avows, still weak from his copious bleeding, 'to my having accidentally slain the son of a local lawyer, then lacking means to prove my innocence.'

'Incomparably vexed imbroglio,' murmurs Ven Gent. 'And what a tragic pity that your poor dear mother had to die so deluded, anent the honour of her son. Ah me, but I see I wound you deeper, which compoundly confounds my best intent. How sad, how sad. How very, very sad.' Seeing his reflexions have reduced Louis to miserable noiseless tears, Ven Gent cuts short the havoc he is wreaking by saying:

'I go now with your message to the Countess, and, subject to her approval, shall shortly have sent to you a few precious lines addressed personally to you by your dying mother – provided, monsieur, you can accept, and have the strength to forgive, any undertones of negative sentiment such as must have been the consequence of her erroneous beliefs, during her struggle with terminal pain.'

Soon after Ven Gent departs the girl Mathilde comes in with a tray bearing chicken broth, fresh bread, and the letter from Louis's mother: tied in a crucifix pattern with a ribbon of black silk. While Louis samples his broth, Mathilde lingers by his bedside, officially to bear his crockery away when he has done supping, but no doubt also with a kindly view to cheering him up as much as possible, and perhaps also because she considers him enormously handsome, and admires him more intensely than she does any other man in the building. There is nothing in Louis Morel's memoirs which we can honestly claim explicitly proves he got something humpy going with Mathilde, but there are certain telltale adjectivals ascribed to Mathilde (*mameles dures*,[1] *roides comme poumettes*, and others similar) which you may say betray his sexual inclinations. We must also remember that Louis, in despite of his age and virility, has not enjoyed vaginal congress with an unpaid partner since he may or may not have come together with Pere Garcés' niece Isabella during that last night in Barcelona many months ago. As to the case for full-bodied penetralial intercourse with Mathilde, more damning clues will be popping up shortly. In the meantime, we may safely assume that soothing up-frontal bedbaths, of the sort Louis was never allowed to get from Hélène, were virtually *de rigueur* from Mathilde.

Not tonight, though, as Louis is still too weak from his bleeding, and also fraught with grief, guilt and apprehension. Grief, obviously. Guilt, since although his vow to the Countess via Ven Gent was true (that he had not eloped with, conspired to tryst with, or in any way abducted Hélène), nonetheless his prime motive in speeding back to Paris from Sedan was to locate Hélène once more, unravel the mystery surrounding her disappearance from Lourdes and materialization in Paris, and be united with her as comprehensively and speedily as feasible. Therefore apprehension: in dread of his mother's dying voice.

Which said:

> My Darling Louis,
>
> We shall never meet again, upon this earth, for I do not expect to live beyond this night. Hope and happiness for me, from my mortal life, have fled. In the moments remaining to me, I have nothing to think of in the world I am leaving, but of your happiness, inheritance, and honour; and likewise of your father, and of what you owe to him, if only you could know.
>
> I write not to reproach you, Louis, but rather to warn – nay, entreat – you never to disgrace the high nobility of your blood, by dilution in a marriage which, depend upon it, would soon be as disastrous in its progress, as degrading in its conception.
>
> Oh, Louis. Dear Louis. Of course Hélène is a lovely girl, but she absolutely *is not worthy of your lineage*. Moreover you have known her *as your sister*. Think of that. By all means *protect* her, *as you would your sister*. Feel not only free, but obliged by your duty, to settle a handsome dowry upon her. *As you would your sister*. But promise

---

[1]  Original spelling.

me, Louis, I implore you, grant your mother's final wish: that never, so long as you enjoy breath in this world, shall you marry so far beneath you, as the daughter of Maître Arnault.

In Heaven, let us dare to pray, may we meet again. Till then, dearest son,

Adieu.

My own mother, the day before she died, wrote comparably to me. The circumstances were radically different, of course. My mother had been ill for many months, we knew there was no hope for her, and all the family were gathered together under the one parental roof to be with her during those last days. Some of her note to me, written during a lull of serene lucidity, between drifts of ever-more morphine, was too personal to ever be incorporated into a book cooked up for gain. Other elements seem, now, more universally emblematic of generous motherhood, self-consciously close to death. Enclosed with my mother's note, for instance, was a cheque for £2000, which she urged me to cash immediately, so that I might have some benefit from her modest estate, before the bank could freeze the deceased's accounts for months while solicitors dawdled.

There was also the line:

'You have been, and will be, a great comfort to me.'

For my mother, like Louis's mother, and perhaps yours too, was one of the hundreds of millions of decent and morally admirable people all over this planet who would rather believe than know. The following day, in the ultimate hour of her life, my mother's last words, sightlessly murmured, but with the sense of a curious joy, were:

'I must be strong, I must be strong.'

Strong – I believe she believed, even then, before lapsing into coma for the last time – strong to cross the frontier, strong for whatever journey, and strong to do justice to the eternity of a better life, to which she had subscribed for sixty-five years. For reasons which my mother could not follow, and in any case would have rejected, the only consolation for me, in her blind faith, was the knowledge of the consolation such belief afforded her. And in that void of pain, if my mother's deathbed letter had implored me with the same intensity as Louis Morel's mother petitioned him, never ever to marry a particular blacklisted girl, for whatever reason, I believe I would have managed somehow, no matter how volcanic all impulses to the contrary, to comply with her dying request. And if that conviction could hobble a

1990s atheist who entertains neither fear of Hell to be tormented in nor dread of Heaven to be even more bored in, how much more violently must it hogtie a 1640s volatile Catholic like Louis, who sincerely and fundamentally believes both that he will be reunited with his mother in Heaven, if by some happy accident he manages to get there, and that his soul will be boiled in a cauldron of eternal oily agony, if, as he deems more likely, he ends up in The Other Place?

'Every word', writes Louis, of his mother's letter, 'found its way straight to my heart; and recalling my eerie vision, on the night previous to my departure from Sedan, the fancy gripped me now that then my mother's spirit itself had flown to me, and lingered over me, to emphasize the effect of her dying words, when in due course I should read them. And so, blown by a storm of feelings such as no poet could describe, I promised in my mind to obey my mother's letter to the utmost, and renounce Hélène for ever.'

After a further two rather flat and callow pages about 'fervency', 'vows', 'Heaven', 'duty', 'obedience', 'honour', 'etc', etc, he repeats his promise in almost the same words, pledges to lay flowers on his mother's grave as soon as possible, and to kiss the stone above her bones, then concludes:

'*Alors, maman. Adieu, j'éspère bien. Mais à toi, chère Hélène, au revoir éternellement. Au revoir, aussi, toute la joie de ma vie.*'

Now we're sorry to have to end such a chapter on so cynical a note, but our impression is that here, in the profound desolation caused by the loss of his mother, made bottomless by the coerced abjuration of Hélène, we have the germ of strong grounds for suspicion that, in the weeks following, as his strength returns, and the obligation to recruit criminals for the Count of Soissons powers him up for action, Louis comes to console himself rampantly at night with the pretty brunette Mathilde.

How else, indeed, could he *know* about her '*mameles dures*' and '*roides comme poumettes*'?

# Paris by the Stars

On the third evening following the divulgement of Louis's bereavement, the Abbé-stroke-future-Cardinal de Retz comes round to inquire why Louis hasn't yet been round again to see him, and – when he learns the reason – to chivy his younger protégé out of his maudlin stupor and back into readiness for terrorism. He also informs Louis that the silver-crowned Ven Gent is in fact the celebrated Vanoni: sage, astrologer, and known by the vulgar noblesse as 'the Countess of Soissons' Necromancer'.

Next morning, grimly resolved to waste no more time in his service of the Count of Soissons, Louis summons Achilles from his billet with the Widow Beaupère and instructs him to seek out and recruit for a further mission the flexible archer of the Court of Aides who assisted him with intuitive deadpan guile in the matter of extorting the unscrupulous broker into handing back the precious ring which Louis in his quasi-Byronic nadir had pawned for such a pittance.

When in due course the Ring Archer (whose name we never learn) arrives through the Hôtel de Soissons' *porte cochère*, Louis begins by rewarding him with a further gold crown, in respect of his invaluable contribution to the recovery of the irreplaceable ring. This coin the Ring Archer accepts in a spirit of stoical dignity, knowing full well the frying of some fatter future fish is on the brink of being proposed.

Having treated Ring Archer to several generous glasses of ruby-red refreshment, Louis proceeds to muse in general terms about the infamous criminal fraternity of Paris, swashbucklers, bravos, hitmen, etc, of whom he has heard so much by way of rumour, but encountered no trace in the flesh.

A bit like going to Sicily for your holidays, if you're lucky.

'Whereas,' he goes on wistfully, 'a man such as yourself, monsieur, Parisian by birth and profession, must know all about such matters, from . . . as it were, *within*.'

'Absolutely not,' says Ring Archer regretfully.

This causes Louis, for starters, to count a further ten gold crowns on to the table, in a column like gamblers' chips. Soon Ring Archer is waxing miraculously expansive re the criminal fraternity, which, he says, is truly the underworld of Paris, in the sense of roots beneath its soil. Some colourful individuals are anonymously glossed, including two whose fortunes have never recovered since their being:

'Ruined they say, father,' Louis having resumed his monk disguise, which Ring Archer instinctively respects, 'by transacting for the Marquis of Roquefort. Now there's a vicious gentleman, all right.'

'Fascinating,' nods Louis. 'And what about the Cardinal?'

'Begging your pardon, father?'

'I mean, must there not be some fellows in France who, having once worked for his Eminence in some covert mission or other, have either fallen into disaffection for their erstwhile paymaster, or else incurred his wrath?'

Funnily enough, yes. Now the good father comes to mention it, there is a bully brace of bravos comes to mind:

'Who used to work regular for the Palais, like, till one day they went and did something on their own account, that was agin the Cardinal's wishes.'

'And?'

As a result, Louis learns, the bully brace were obliged to go underground, literally, when the thwarted Richelieu prescribed for them:

'A dose of the big round bedstead.'[1]

'Are they still in hiding?'

'They has got to take it careful, father.'

Judging the bedstead brace to be perfect for his purpose, Louis impresses on Ring Archer the likelihood of another ten crowns awaiting him, if he can get the fallen villains to report *chez* Widow Beaupère 'at midnight sharp'.

There, in the Rue des Prêtres St Paul, over two flagons of workmanlike burgundy in the small hours of the following morning, an intriguing conversation takes place. The bedstead bravos are named as 'Combalet de Montfaucon and Jacques le Moqueur'.

The latter, Louis realizes with a jolt, after an hour of trying to pinpoint at the back of his mind where on earth he can have encountered him before, is the elder of the two bogus sergeants who attempted to

---

[1] Familiar reference to that instrument of torture generally known as the rack.

confiscate the valise containing the Spanish zootsuit from his room in the shady auberge during that first morning in Paris last year – who was in turn 'the very identical person of my hectoring guide on that first night in Paris, he who had bragged of his unparalleled success with women, then of his incomparable knowledge of the city, before leading me off as far as possible away from the Palais where I wished to go', and in his bogus-sergeant phase had been known as 'Caesar'. If in a disloyal moment you are tempted to question the probability of this multiple identity, please immediately consider:

(a) If we had been making this story up ourselves, we would have rested content with a double identity.

(b) Fact *is* stranger than fiction in the sense that often what is true in fact would be spat back with jeers of scorn if it had the temerity to masquerade as fiction. As Maupassant puts it, in possibly the most insightful short essay ever written on 'The Novel':[2]

---

[2] As preface to *Pierre et Jean* – itself, like *The Great Gatsby*, one of the most consummately crafted of all short novels. Since we are only too aware that even Wringhim Knox, in company with most of his chums who teach Scottish Literature in the universities, is woefully less versed in classic French fiction than one might wish, we take this opportunity of slipping him the following further sop from Maupassant's essay, to heave at Rankles when the time is rife:

'Now the critic who, after *Manon Lescaut, Paul et Virginie, Don Quixote, Les Liaisons dangereuses, Werther, Elective Affinities, Clarissa Harlowe, Emile, Candide, Cinq-Mars, René, The Three Musketeers, Mauprat, Le Père Goriot, La Cousine Bette, Colomba, Le Rouge et le Noir, Mademoiselle de Maupin, Notre-Dame de Paris, Salammbô, Madame Bovary, Adolphe, M. de Camors, L'Assommoir, Sappho*, etc, still dares to write: "This is a novel, that is not", seems to me endowed with a perspicacity suspiciously like incompetence.'* (Penguin translation by Leonard Tancock.)

*\* Think of this, Wringhim, as our equivalent for you of your £5-note test of whether your publisher's commissioning editor has honestly made it past page 200.*

' . . . life is made up of the most different, unforeseen, contradictory, ill-assorted things; it is brutual, arbitrary, disconnected, full of inexplicable, illogical and contradictory disasters which can only be classified under the heading of "Other news in brief."

[For example:]

'The number of people in the world who die in accidents every day is considerable. But [within the conventions of fiction:] can we drop a tile on the head of a principal character or throw him under the wheels of a bus in the middle of a story on the pretext that one must allow for accidents?'

(c) Though the history of Louis Morel has its lighter and even more romantic moments, we must never forget that there is enough brutality and political oppression about in France at this time to warrant doubling Amnesty's budget.

Thus, the ubiquity of Sergeant-Caesar-becum-Jacques in his various guises gains logic from the fact that, behind his boisterous façade he lives in continuing fear of torture and murder if he is caught by the Cardinal's assassins. Sensing this, and also that Le Moqueur has sensed that Louis has twigged where and how they met before, Louis discreetly doesn't mention the matter at all, but rather hastens on to the business in hand, which is to politely inquire whether his visitors are scouting:

'For gainful work, by any chance?'

Earnestly the bully bravos confer between themselves in argot Louis can't follow. Then Le Moqueur replies for both that they'll gladly undertake virtually anything bar highway robbery and contract murder, since they would sooner starve to death themselves than do anything mean and dishonourable.

'Most commendable,' nods Louis, and next a contract of service is drawn up, whereby the bully bravos shall serve Monsieur Morel implicitly and uniquely in respect of wages of thirty crowns per month per bully, on condition that the absolute truth must be relayed to Louis at all times, at least by Monsieur Le Moqueur, it being understood and accepted by all contracting parties that *absolute truth* is a notion beyond the apprehension of honest Monsieur de Montfaucon.

At this point Louis sends the bystanding Ring Archer away with a further gold crown to slake his thirst, and confides in a conspiratorial huddle with the contracted bravos that:

'Basically, gentlemen, what we are about amounts to no less than treasonous conspiracy.'

'Doesn't bother us,' chuckle the bravos, 'so long as it's agin the Cardinal!' And for some minutes, in the confidingness of copious burgundy, they recount their cumulus grievances.

Gradually Louis works the conversation round to asking if there's any truth in the rumour he's heard that the criminal fraternity of all Paris meet secretly after dark each night at a venue known as Swash Castle, presided over by a sort of underworld Chief Magistrate known only as King of the Huns.

Taken aback by Louis's intelligence – which he owes largely to tattle gleaned off Achilles – the bravos now come over all shifty.

Louis, stressing the contingency of the month's sixty crowns on the 'absolute truth' clause, expresses his determination to be taken to Swash Castle and introduced to the King of the Huns.

Morosely the bravos doubt the realizability of Monsieur Morel's bizarre ambition.

'The realization, gentlemen,' says Louis, with the smoothness of a well-heeled paymaster, 'is entirely your problem. But it may perhaps pave your way to represent that the purpose of the meeting I require is respectfully ambassadorial. That is to say: you may lead your leader to believe that I, as emissary shall we say of a highborn personage most adamantly opposed to the Cardinal, should be perceived merely as the mouthpiece of one prince, craving audience with another.'

Montfaucon and Moqueur exchange doubtful views rapidly in the sort of shady patois in which lowborn Paris has delighted throughout the ages. Then Moqueur, aping the etiquette of Achilles, says to Louis:

'Weasel do our best, your lordship.'

Louis, warming to the clichés of the power of his new role, replies:

'If need be, gentlemen, do better! Either way, I expect you back here with good news at dusk tomorrow.'

The bravos depart, muttering.

Louis briefs Achilles on what constitutes good behaviour in the house of a reputable widow. Then he pays his respects and some money to Madame Beaupère, and returns to the Hôtel de Soissons, still as a grey monk on a humble mare, and pleased with these first steps towards accomplishing his mission.

However, hardly has he reached his apartments in the Hôtel de

Soissons, and thrown off his monkly rags, when Louis is discreetly visited by Ven Gent Vanoni – who informs him that the Dowager Countess of Soissons has expressed displeasure at his curtly vanishing during his first fully able-bodied evening as her guest, and demands that he express his contrition by joining her later this night in the Observatory of Catherine de Medici.

'Whatever for?' protests Louis in some alarm.

'The Countess hopes there to be satisfied, by the shapes of the stars tonight, as to the future fate of her son the Count, and of all others – such as yourself, Monsieur Morel – who follow in his wake.'

'And you, Signor?' I rejoined [*writes Louis*]. 'Do you join the Countess in her evident faith: that the stars will tell the truth?'

'My own opinions', replied the old man, 'signify little. Certainly I must once have seemed to descry some truth in such a discipline, before making of it a profound study, as I have done in regard to astrology. In any case, Monsieur Morel, if you will now be so good as to accompany me, I will show you the interior of the magnificent column which Catherine de Medici constructed, for the purpose of consulting those stars which are now', he added with a brief private smile, 'growing as fast out of fashion as her Majesty's once-famous farthingale.'

I followed him accordingly, and crossing the gardens, at the end of one of the alleys, came upon that immense stone tower, in the form of a column, which may be seen to the present day, standing behind the Hôtel des Fermes. It was dead of night, but beautifully clear and starlit. Looking up, one could see the tall dark head of that immense pillar, rising like a black giant high above all the buildings around, and I felt a strong intuition in that moment, that much of the credence which astrologers and their acolytes professed, might well be ascribed to the solemn and majestic scenes in which their ceremonies were enacted; and how an ardent imagination, placed on an eminence so high, above a drowsy world below, with no matter for contemplation but the bright and beautiful stars, might dream grand dreams and easily fancy that, in the golden-lettered book above, could be read the secret tales of fate, and decrees of implacable destiny. Even I? So I ventured to wonder. If I too remained long there myself, should I become an idle dreamer too, and give rein to fabulous chymeras, as foolish as any girl's?

By now we had entered the tower by a fortified door, inside which, positioned in the manner of sentries, were two small negro pages. Each of these, clad in vivid Oriental silks, bore a silver spirit lamp, which cast a light of unearthly blue to join with the shadows all around. And I could not help smiling to myself, at the thought of what pains superstitious principals will take, to provide themselves with every accessory remotely suited, to delude and deceive themselves. Anything strange, unusual, or mysterious, is ever of great assistance to the avid imagination; and the sight of those two small negroes, with their large rolling eyes and singular dress, together with the sapphire gleam of the lamps in their little black hands, like luminous eyes in the gloomy tower, were all well calculated to heat the impressionable mind, like tallow freshly dripped, to a softness ripe for moulding.

Sensing, I believe, rather than seeing my smile with his eyes, Signor Vanoni, as we ascended the circular stairs, remarked to me over his shoulder:

'That mummery is none of mine, of course.'

'The Countess . . . '

'Her Highness is resolved not to let her imagination founder for want of aid.'

'Whereas your own credence, Signor, is . . . founded on sounder principals?'

'The one ear I lend', replied Signor Vanoni, breathing remarkably lightly for a man of his years, on such stairs, 'to the science of astrology, is grounded upon a historical certainty.'

'And what is that, signor?'

'That many of the most extraordinary predictions derived from the stars have been verified contrary to all calculable probabilities.'

'Such as what, signor?'

'Is it not, Monsieur Morel, an attested fact of history that Julius Caesar once lived at Rome?'

'As well as any,' I could hardly deny.

'*Equally* well is it established,' said my leader with a certain passion, 'that not one century ago, in this very tower, an astrologer predicted to Catherine de Medici the number of years which each of her descendants should reign.'

'Correctly?'

'Absolutely correctly, Monsieur. Unfortunately, however, and this has been a prime cause of the disrepute into which the legitimate science of astrology has fallen, not a few of its practitioners have mingled a corrupt leaven of theatrical charlatanism in with their bona fide predictions. Absolutely so, indeed.'[3]

'But whatever for, signor?'

'In the desperate attempt to drape the flesh of some visual authority over the bones of their authentic belief. An understandably but ultimately despicable resort, which at the last can do no more than discredit our métier in its entirety, including its genuine core. Thus, the astrologer I spoke of, not contented with predicting what he *knew* would happen, and leaving the rest to fate, took it further upon himself to *display* to the gullible Queen the *images* of her sons in the future: in what he represented to her as a magic glass, but in fact was a conjurer's cheat.'

'And by this juggle he diminished his own credit?'

'With every reasonable mind, he did. Though not with the credulous Queen Mother.'

'Did she really believe she saw what she seemed to see?'

Somewhat evasively, Signor Vanoni replied:

'The details of the *procès verbal* of what Catherine de Medici saw, taken down at the time, are now in the hands of the Countess of Soissons.'

---

[3] Vanoni's Latinesque absolutelyism requires a little modulation. Although 'the astrologer' (ie Nostradmus, 1503–66) had a super-ficially impressive track record, he did not by any means pick 'absolute' winners every time. For example, whereas he assured Catherine de Medici that *all* her sons would become kings, the fourth and youngest (Duke of Alençon, popularly known as 'Silly') never did. Furthermore, when you recall what a sickly brood all Catherine's boys were, and how assassination was all the rage, to stake a modest flutter on all the Queen Mother's sons becoming kings was not risking colossal odds. More like a four-horse accumulator on evens front-runners. There is also the lingering suspicion that the poison-toting Queen Mother [*d.* 1589] herself may have aided in the fulfilment of three-quarters of this particu-lar forecast by accelerating the approaching deaths of François II [*d.* 1560] and/or Charles IX [*d.* 1574], to help smooth a ride to the throne for her own clear favourite: Henri III [*d.* 1589]. For lavish detail on these and numerous other perverted jockeys for power in 16th-century France, see *The Counts of Mount Venus*, pp 1–702.

'Can we believe the *procès* is authentic?'

'Beyond all question,' the old man replied emphatically over his shoulder, leading the way into a circular hall, at the very top of the tower.

'And what did the Queen Mother see?'

Waving his arms and pointing to various points of the hall, Signor Vanoni said:

'Being placed opposite a mirror, in this very chamber, after various fantastic ceremonies unworthy of a man of real science, the astrologer called upon the genius of François II to appear, and pace as many circles round the chamber, as his reign in years should last.'

'What happened next, exactly?'

'Instantly Catherine beheld a figure, exactly resembling her firstborn son, appear in the glass before her. With a slow and mournful step, he took one turn round the chamber, then wearily he began another. But barely was the second circle half-complete when the spectre of our second King François disappeared in a blink, and a second figure succeeded him.'

'The Queen Mother's second son?'

'Charles IX just as he would reign, indeed. Or, shall we say, a perfect personification of him.'

'And he too proceeded to circle the hall?'

'Fourteen times, no less. At first with a quick though irregular step, which latterly faltered and limped.'

'After him, signor? Henri III?'

'As night follows night, monsieur. And with uncanny prophetical arithmetic, this imposting enactor of our last Valois king, to the Queen Mother's marvelling applause, completed . . . nearly fifteen circles.'

'Then he too vanished?'

'Indeed, though not alone. For suddenly another figure – supposedly the mighty Duke of Guise,[4] and certainly unusually tall – appeared before the King: like a jailor to bar his way. The Queen Mother being unable to stifle a short scream of terror, the double vision dissolved in that same moment, thus leaving the chamber void.'

'How did her Majesty interpret this development?'

'Of her own accord, we are told, with no prompting from the astrologer, she divined that what this last charade foretold was the end of her regal posterity.'

---

[4] Dumas play, ref?? Or poss not bother? Life so brutish short.

'In which hazard she was proved correct, signor?'

'Precisely, monsieur!' Signor Vanoni exclaimed in an access of professional irritation. 'And there's the nub of the shame of it all. Whereas the astrologer's predictions, as to fact, were unaccountably correct – unaccountably, that is, if one denies all efficacy to astrological science – yet, for the sake of further impressing the superstitious Queen, he must needs make life an hundredfold more troublesome for us, his sincere successors, by his resort to cheap pantomime. There stands the mirror still,' he added, pointing, and drily concluded:

'Though its powers are laid to rest.'

I approached the large ancient mirror with its carved ebony frame, and as I gazed into it by the light of the lamp Signor Vanoni held, my mind glanced back to the days of Catherine de Medici, and her gay yet vicious court; and as in a moment of reverie I seemed to trace those fine vague lines of association whose thrilling vibrations notate, as it were, the music of memory, there suddenly – as though the old magician still was conjuring his tricks – the stately form of a large lady dressed in long robes of black velvet rose up before me in the glass.

# 46

# Shapes in the Night?

The large lady in black velvet being the Dowager Countess of Soissons, who has materialized through the secret door behind the no-longer-magic mirror, Louis embarks on a train of courtly apology for having been absent this evening from his hostess's Hôtel just when she happened to want him.

'Never overrate your own importance, young man,' the Countess advises him breezily. Then she commits the putative narrative solecism[1] (though Shakespeare does it quite a bit too[2]) of telling him what we all know already: that the purpose of convening in the cockpit of Catherine de Medici's Observatory Tower tonight is:

'To discover from the stars the future fate not only of my own son, but also of you yourself, Monsieur Morel — as, thanks to the far-sighted concern of your poor dear mother, I have your background facts.'

After an hour of intense star-gazing and occasional occult muttering, Ven Gent Vanoni without conspicuous enthusiasm predicts some vague and interpretable future for the Count of Soissons, and adroitly distracts attention from this calculated imprecision by announcing for Louis Morel:

'An abundance of wealth and rank, surpassing beauty in his spouse, unparalleled happiness in his marriage, unusually long life and excellent

---

[1] If you went along with Charlton Palser, say, as he then was. Cf Paul's comment on our own Chapter 17, as reported in our Chapter 34a.

[2] Eg, light-heartedly, Puck's report to Oberon in *A Midsummer Night's Dream*, 3.1. Shakespeare, needless to say, simply seethes with this sort of thing, which only further confirms that breaking the rules not only is not incompatible with succeeding at sex but also, for humans as opposed to fruit flies, is its paramount precondition. When ever, for instance, did Baronoid Whatshit have an orgasm of either description?

health – provided, your Highness, the young gentleman contrives to outlive the horrendous pitfalls lying in wait for him, during the course of the next thirteen weeks!'

While the Dowager Countess is delighted with these rose-tinted M&B prospects for her old best friend's son, Louis himself is plunged into taciturn gloom. Wealth; here he is on a retainer salary from the Count of Soissons, equivalent to 10,000 crowns p.a., and what great good is it doing him? Rank; yes, when in the normal course of most flesh his father predeceases him, he will become Count Louis Morel of Bigorre, and so what? A beautiful wife; but what woman could be so beautiful, and otherwise endowed, as to allay his bootless longing for Hélène? Happiness in marriage; therefore not possible. Prolonged life in excellent health; merely a cruel protraction of his fundamental frustration and futility.

Well then?

*May as well run the gauntlet*, concludes Louis, *with the utmost reckless speed, of whatever self-important pitfalls dare presume to seem horrendous.*

'So sorry, your Highness?' he apologizes absently, she having led him back down the observatory stair, to the garden.

'I said, young man,' she repeats severely, 'your wing is to the left. Over there. Goodnight, Monsieur Morel.'

Weaving through the bushes in a stupor of sceptical superstition, Louis is brought to a gasping halt when a white-robed figure glides by him that strikes him for all the world as the spitting image of Jean-Baptiste Arnault. Louis calls out:

'Jean-Baptiste, Jean-Baptiste!' but the white form vanishes into pitchblack archway of topiaried yew, and fails to reappear. Pale and trembling, by his own confession, and seriously disturbed in his mind (which does believe, do not forget, in souls, spirits, and by extension ghosts), Louis returns to his room, fails to sleep, and finally summons a groom to fetch Achilles Lefranc from Madame Beaupère's.

'It *was* him,' mutters Louis.

'It was *whom*, your lordship?' inquires Achilles, arriving on a wave of importance.

'Just as . . . just exactly as he lived,' reflects Louis despondently.

'As *whom* lived, your lordship?' insists Achilles kindly.

'Why, Jean-Baptiste of course,' cries Louis despairingly. Slumped on an oaken stool, he is supporting the weight of his head with the palm of his left hand pressed to his face. His left elbow, in turn, is lodged on his right wrist, which is clamped to his thudding heart.

'Jean-Baptiste *whom*, your lordship?' continues Achilles, gently prising the cloak from Louis's shoulders, before pouring him a glass of wine.

'Arnault, of course,' moans Louis. 'Jean-Baptiste Arnault.'

'What!' exclaims Achilles. 'My brother? But that cannot be.'

'What do you mean, your brother?' reacts Louis angrily, believing Achilles is poking fun at his employer's distress. 'What do you know about it?'

'Jean-Baptiste Arnault, your lordship,' says Achilles respectfully, pleased by the signs of his master's return to dominance, 'is the youngest and most legitimate son of my poor dear mother and her husband that was.'

'Husband? Which husband?'

'Her only husband in law, your lordship. If one of her several in deeds. What a generous soul she was, to be sure.'

'There, there, Achilles,' murmurs Louis, patting the little man's arm, when he sees the tears in his eyes, and recalls the tale his henchman told, on the way to Spain, of his mother's many lovers, and her various children by them, and how she shared them around before dying. 'Don't cry.'

'I'm not crying, your lordship,' sniffs Achilles. 'It's just . . . but what about Jean-Baptiste?'

With some diffidence Louis explains how, as he returned through the loom-filled night, from the observatory, he had seemed to see, as it were, the ghost of Jean-Baptiste.

'Ghost!' cries Achilles in horror. 'But that cannot be!'

'Why not?' counters Louis wearily.

'Because, your lordship, a ghost is the ghost of a *dead* person. Whereas Jean-Baptiste is alive and well.'

'Is he, Achilles?' asks Louis sadly. 'Where?'

'Why, in Lourdes, your lordship. Where he serves as our — *his* father's prentice.'

'When did you last see him?'

Haltingly it emerges that Achilles' last brief contact with Jean-Baptiste, during one of his occasional and infallibly unsuccessful missions to touch his mother's husband, Maître Arnault, for a life-sustaining sub, was *before* the accident by the river, when Jean-Baptiste got shot.

'I see,' says Louis flatly. 'Yes. And that would explain why you came to be in the region of Lourdes in the first place. Why didn't you tell me before?'

'Your lordship did not ask me,' retorts Achilles. Then, tragically: 'Jean-Baptiste?'

'Dead, Achilles,' confirms Louis heavily. 'I'm sorry, believe me. God knows, I'm *sorry*.'

After several minutes of inconsolable weeping, not vengeful, Achilles allows himself to be partially consoled by a large glass of his master's wine. With a brave wet smile he reflects:

'Poor Jean-Baptiste! As good a boy as ever lived, he was. In his heart, if not his brain. Never cruel, often kind, invariably loyal to his kin. I shall miss him just as much as if – as if he were not only my full bloodbrother, but moreover my selfsame twin. God bless you, Jean Baptiste!' Seeing now the anguish his apostrophe is causing Louis, Achilles generously goes on:

'Be not vexed, your lordship, by this poor comedian's grief. No man could know better than I, that your lordship must be almost the last gentleman in Paris to take an innocent life without cause. As your lordship has moreover been kinder far to me than my kindred by marriage – I refer here specifically to my mother's husband in law – and as your lordship has borne with me, and not spurned me, nor even beaten me in Sedan for tumbling the wench on your lordship's bed, so should I take your lordship's word against any host of vile calumners. And as your lordship so swears, that your lordship's slaying of poor Jean-Baptiste was an unintended error caused by him, then it goes without saying that your humble servant takes your lordship's words for it hooks, lines and sinkers, and my only further problem in the case is . . . *what a good little lad he was . . .* '

There follows a second and longer bout of mourning tears that make Louis feel several times worse about the matter than ever he did before. So sick with self-loathing does he become, at the plaguing thought of the life he extinguished without intent, and the misery that has dogged him since, that the issue of supernatural visitations amid the bushes is leastmost in his mind when suddenly Achilles leaves off his sobbing, lights up like a Roman candle, and reflects:

'But his spirit lives on!'

'What do you mean, Achilles?'

'Jean-Baptiste! As your lordship saw his ghost tonight, he is not lost to us entirely. Mayhap he means to salve your lordship with his forgiveness, before flying up to Heaven!'

'I don't know, Achilles,' Louis objects regretfully. If he's honest about it, he really can no longer be sure what he saw. There is also the fact of his having been infected with a temporarily aggravated impressionability: by all that star-gazing palaver in the observatory tower, and the wonderful future prophesied for himself, if he can survive the next thirteen weeks. So:

'Perhaps, after all, my eyes were deceived – by phantoms within my own head.'

'No, no, your lordship!' protests Achilles urgently. 'It *was* the spirit of Jean-Baptiste your lordship saw. I swear it was. I *know* it was!'

'Possibly, Achilles. Possibly,' Louis pretends to agree. 'But now we must get some sleep.' As a massive lassitude overwhelms him, powered by an even more depressing thought:

If Jean-Baptiste Arnault was half-brother to Achilles Lefranc, it followed that, in terms of caste stigma, in the event that Louis had either failed to receive or chosen to ignore his mother's deathbed petition, and in the further event that he had managed to rescue Hélène from the adulterous clutches of the Maréchal of Châtillon's nephew, and whisk her to the church in time himself instead:

'I should have married my own valet's sister.'

# 47

## *Whose* Sister?

The following morning [*writes Louis*], having slept with difficulty, I rose late. While Achilles was aiding me to dress, I felt palpably, almost painfully, that there was something troubling his mind. Though reluctant to audience further woes so soon, at length I asked:

'What is it, Achilles?'

He replied:

'I would not for the world speak to your lordship, this morning, on a subject so excruciatingly painful.'

'Stop beating about the bush, Achilles,' I ordered him, 'and get to the point.'

With a studied delicacy of which I had hardly judged him capable, he went on:

'Earlier this morning something very extraordinary transpired, of which your lordship, if only less exhausted, would doubtless wish to know.'

'Never mind my exhaustion, Achilles, and get on with it. Well?'

'Seldom better, your lordship. Well, barely an hour ago, as it happened, I was standing by the stable gate of this grand Hôtel, engaged in somewhat unrewarding dialogue with an impudent young woman from her Highness's kitchens, when blow me but who should pass by?'

Upon my snapping my fingers in considerable irritation, the little fellow proceeded:

'Why, the old procureur himself!'

'What? Maître Arnault, from Lourdes?'

'The very same, your lordship!'

'Your erstwhile – mmm – stepfather?'

'Absolutely himself, your lordship!'

'What did you say to him? Or he to you?'

At this question a cloud passed over Achilles' brow, and he sighed with a wistfulness sublimely pathetic, before admitting:

'Concerning myself, your lordship, the procureur, as ever, evinced but scant concern.'

'But?'

'With regard to your lordship's condition, and recent history, my father's appetite for knowledge was ravenous. Nay, nigh insatiable!'

Experiencing grave consternation, at the thought of all Achilles could tell, I asked him with threatening frankness:

'What did he ask you? And what did you tell him?'

'Not to worry, your lordship!' replied Achilles, with forgiving fidelity. 'Concerning your lordship's mission to Sedan, and our contract to eliminate the Cardinal, I let slip not a murmur. All my efforts, on the contrary, were directed to persuade the old skinflint that, though your lordship does not for a moment deny having been – shall we say? – the *hapless instrument* of Jean-Baptiste's death, nonetheless, and most tragically, the *active plucker* of the last dying fall – if one might phrase it for the boards – was the rage-maddened victim himself. Why, by the way, was Jean-Baptiste so angry with your lordship? The procureur was most keen to know this?'

'Oh, God,' groaned I. 'Never mind, Achilles. It hardly matters now. Now that . . . I don't suppose – I mean, to change the subject for a moment – he didn't, did he – your stepfather – by any chance mention Hélène?'

'Hélène *whom*, your lordship?'

'Hélène *Arnault*, of course, you nitwit,' I confess I roared at him. 'Your *sister*.'

'Hélène, your lordship,' replied Achilles with commendable dignity, 'is *not* my sister.'

'Oh, as you like it. Your *half*-sister, then. Well?'

'Hélène Arnault, your lordship, is never my *half*-sister neither.'

'Eh? What? What are you saying, Achilles? What–are–you–*saying*?'

'Please do not strangle me, your lordship,' protested Achilles, not unreasonably. 'For what I tell – at least, what I tell your *lordship* – is, as ever, never nothing, if *not the whole truth*.'

'Excuse me, Achilles,' I apologized, releasing him. 'However, please *explain*.'

'Hélène Arnault', Achilles obliged serenely, as he patted smooth his dress, 'is the blooming fruit of neither my mother's blessed womb, nor – which is even surer – of my father's pitiful loins.'

'Then for God's sake whose child is she?'

'No-one knows, your lordship. Not even the procureur, I dare warrant. You see, after my mother died, and had summoned all her lovers, to be reconciled in the hours of her dying, my father – by which term I designate for the moment my *legal* father, Maître Arnault – not a little piqued, at being known for such a cuckold, resolved within himself that, rather than risk repeat performances of horns all over his head for the rest of his life, he would just as soon not wed again. Nor was great pleasure lost thereby, one gathers, by all the ladies to whom he declined to propose.'

'Very loyal of you to say so, Achilles,' I remarked with irate impatience. 'But how does that affect Hélène?'

'Because my father had lost the one wife he never deserved in the first place,' explained Achilles, 'and because he was too much the mean and impotent poltroon to take on a second, and because all his children by my lovely mother – which is to say even including the one child most probably of my father's own seed, which is to say Jean-Baptiste – were sons, and because already he had anxious hankerings after feminine warmth, love, care and constant nursing during the pain and misery of his dotage, to be most dependably obtained from some younger woman materially dependent upon him, he resolved to acquire him a daughter.'

'Hélène is the child of some relation, you mean?' speculated I. 'A niece, or perhaps a cousin?'

'Not a bit of it!' scoffed Achilles, setting a breakfast tray before me. 'Hélène Arnault, for all that she is a pretty wench (and wisely kept well away from myself, I might add, for reasons too offensive to state – during my occasional and invariably unsatisfactory pilgrimages home) is nothing by birth, if your lordship will pardon the expression, but a lowly bastard foundling. Whom my father purchased in a tavern one Saturday evening, following a characteristically niggardly bargain he had wrung from a desperate midwife on the run, for crimes against humane anatomy which she had inadvertently committed in Provence.'

'Oh, Achilles, this is awful,' moaned I, as I pushed my breakfast away. 'Why didn't you tell me before?'

'About *what*?' replied he, seeming hurt.

'These facts about Hélène?'

'Your lordship has never before once mentioned Hélène to me,' Achilles pointed out, and with impeccable justice. 'Besides, of what possible interest, your lordship, could such a foundling bastard flibbertigibbet be, to such a gentleman as yourself?'

## 48

# Courting the King of the Huns

Following that new hotpress bombshell from Achilles, Louis nearly faints under the weight of wild speculation that deluges his aching brain.

Hélène, he is one moment convinced, is a secret natural daughter of royalty, is she not? Thus liberating him from his mother's deathbed prohibition on their marriage? For what his mother actually wrote was:

*Never, while still you draw breath on this earth, must you* **marry so far beneath you**, *as the daughter of Maître Arnault.*

Or words to that effect.

Now how he might conceivably have married Hélène after he ceased to draw breath on this earth is not a question which it occurs to Louis to ask. Rather, in a panic of despair, does he junk the whole notion of Hélène's being a candidate bastard daughter of royalty – on the ground that, if this were the case, she would never have been left in the custody of an abortionate Provençal midwife. Either that, or, even if she were in truth the fruit of royal loins, this must be a truth *unknown even to the perpetrators* and therefore *undiscoverable even in principle.* Which was a possibility so tormenting to contemplate that he might as well better accept the more probable likelihood that Hélène was merely the unwanted daysafter leftover from the Saturday night squelchy pronging, by several drunken sailors in quickie succession, of a cutprice waterside whore.

And yet . . . if that were truly so, how could the girl have grown up so lithe and comely, compassionate and clever?

Whether or not Louis continues to console himself with the Dowager Countess's girl Mathilde during the nights of those fraught Paris days we have no way of establishing, and hence must leave the sizzling biological details to your own individual imaginations, and conscience. All Louis tells us is that were it not for his commitment to dangerous action, in service of the Count of Soissons, he might well have expired of depression, or else turned raving loony.

As it was, during the afternoon following Achilles' revelation, in a renewed attempt to resolve never to marry degradingly beneath himself, and embrace the harsh hardship of solitary bachelorhood, Louis calls on the Cardinal de Retz, to deliver a verbal progress report. At dusk that night he trysts as arranged with the bully bravos Combalet de Montfaucon and Jacques le Moqueur. 'And instantly I could tell, by the self-satisfaction of their smirking, that their mission had met with success.' The bravos' mission, if you remember, and equally if you don't, was to secure for Louis an audience with the King of the Huns – ie, the senior criminal of all Paris. This boon, the bullies confirm, is duly granted: on condition that Louis agrees to being blindfolded en route, and to being naturalized a Hun.

Keen to push on, Louis consents to both conditions, making only the pointed reservation that there will be little point in any smartarse taking advantage of his blindfold to mug him, as there will be nothing of value about his person bar the ten gold crowns he has already pledged to the King of the Huns as a token of thanks for his audience. Spluttering with goodnatured bogus indignation, the bravos assure their paymaster that nothing could be further . . . and a little before midnight the three men set out, in the manner of noble plus lackeys, into a maze of Paris streets, sidestreets, back alleys, passageways, and ever darker darkness.

Within minutes of being blindfolded, round about the back-alley stage, Louis loses any certain sense of direction. Half an hour later he is totally disoriented. Through his ears, what else, he now is hearing a blackdrop of murmurs and grunts, short sharp shouts and odd sexual moans, once a donkey braying, and occasional boisterous merriment. Finally, after a last long low-arched passage, as he can tell from their tunnelling footsteps, Louis, as his blindfold is removed from behind, hears the voice of an older woman of immeasurable crudity: cackling obscenely specific speculations, pertaining to his body. Next, in the moments of blinking his sight back into focus he is astonished and outraged to be assaulted by the saidsame old crone – nearly senile, scarlet-eyed and stinking drunk – hurling herself upon him, craning up to nibble his neck, and clawing his virility.

Louis Morel's account of his visit to the King of the Huns is one of the most sustained and vivid of his surviving writings. Upward of ten thousand words. We'd like to quote it all for you, but alas to do so would unbalance our story, and run the risk of distracting your attention from its most essential core. What we therefore propose instead is that you insert your bookmark between these two present pages, here and now, and only return to the following paragraph the moment you have in the interim finished reading Victor Hugo's *Notre Dame de Paris*, or at least the chapter devoted to the Court of Miracles, which is titled 'The Broken Jug'. Although the classic tale of Quasimodo and Esmeralda, and the vile prelate Frollo, is set nearly two centuries earlier, we can't help wondering – as regards the crawling beggars, limping cripples, blood-stained burglars, drinkblotched wenches, barbecue bonfires dotting the plaza of central villainy, and all – whether Hugo (writing in 1829, when he was only twenty-seven) may not have had access to a copy of the Morel memoirs. If he didn't, the parallels are remarkable.

Anyway, and in summary:

When in a loathing reflex Louis plucks off the gibbering harpy from his body and hurls her backwards, a short but immensely broad and patch-eyed cut-throat jumps forward shouting that the stranger toff should be throttled on the spot for daring to manhandle Mother Hachoir. Instinctively Louis draws his cloak-sheathed sword to defend himself against what seems like certain death as a plague of cut-throat cronies swarms across the plaza to encircle the fracas with weapon-brandishing vows of death to the stranger toff. Fortunately for Louis the bully bravos Montfaucon and Moqueur now take a hand by stepping in, or rather, forward, to bellow for:

'Fair play of single combat, gentlemen, please. In this duel for a lady's favours!'

There follows a sword fight in which Louis has the wit to allow his antagonist – more a bruiser than an athlete – to appear more competent than he is: before disarming him with a wrist-spraining twist, and holding him hostage with a blade to his throat. Louis declines a rabid invitation to 'kill him, kill him!' anonymously issued by several of the cut-throat's own cronies in the crowd. Instead he removes his blade from the aggressor's throat, stands back, and nods to him politely. This merciful gesture is greeted with roars of scornful approval, and even the worsted bruiser has the grace to appear to applaud without too much evident malice.

After thus passing what in retrospect he came to suspect may have been his deliberately contrived initiation shibboleth, Louis is conducted to a cavern full of Huns, with weapons and alcohol everywhere, at the back of a cellar in one of several pokey-fronted taverns around the plaza. Here, at the table's head, sits the King of the Huns, a small old man, much wizened and grey, with ineffably small and cunning grey eyes, who strokes his long but wispy grey beard as he stares at Louis and demands in general to know who has dared to cause riot and strife within his royal precincts without a licence.

This is Jacques le Moqueur's cue to step forward and explain to the King that Mother Hachoir is the one to blame, for attempting to 'do the sweet' on Louis without his permission, thus obliging him to 'buff her a swagger'.

This defence is accepted with flickering equanimity, and the Hun King orders that Louis now be naturalized:

'One of us.'

All proceeds smoothly until Louis is instructed to 'repeat after me' the Huns' irrevocable Oath of Allegiance. For the oath is so crammed with immorality, criminality, and construably libellous blasphemy, that Louis feels constrained to politely decline to swear it. With flexible equanimity born of an overriding desire to get his hands on as much as possible as soon as possible of whatever gold Louis has authority to dispense, the King of the Huns agrees that in this case it will be sufficient if the stranger toff's oath be truncated to merely a pledge of inviolable secrecy. That given, the next stage is a celebratory drink. As per the custom for newly sworn miscreants, a swimming grail is now produced for Louis's consumption: full of murky spiritous liquor, which he is pressed to drain in a oner.

Having cleared the second hurdle of persuading his hosts – despite a strident heckle to the effect that he is a 'chicken demoiselle' – to grant the extraordinary indulgence in his particular case of swapping the firewater for half-decent red wine, lest he end up too incapacitated to fulfil his vital mission, Louis is rather taken aback when the King of the Huns buts in sharply with:

'But what vital mission would that be, now?'

Acutely aware of the hundred-odd close-packed heads around the cavern, all beagling for whiffs of a scam, Louis finds himself wondering in considerable consternation how to gloss his capital purpose without at once letting all the scum of Paris in on the Count of Soissons' conspiracy.

Sensing his guest's embarrassment, the King of the Huns lets Louis off the hook by confiding in general that they, the Huns, already know a lot more than he, the stranger toff, imagines. And in particular:

'We have known for some time, you see, that you are the agent of Monsieur le Comte.'

'Oh, have you, indeed?' replies Louis, nonplussed.

The King of the Huns then catalytically advertises that the Count of Soissons is universally loved among the criminal fraternity – almost in exact proportion, in fact, to their hatred of the Cardinal.

'We are perfectly well informed', he nods, 'that the Count of Soissons is preparing for war against his Eminence.'

'Oh, you are, are you?' stalls Louis.

'There is little, monsieur, that we do not know,' the King of the Huns confirms modestly. 'So you may feel free, as our messenger to him, to inform Monsieur le Comte of our sympathy. All he need do henceforth is let us know what must be done, and what suitable monetary support he can provide.'

In the face of such overwhelming information superiority in the lowest classes, Louis goes candid and says: yes, any Huns with any history of minimal military discipline and killing accomplishments would be very welcome in the Count of Soissons' army, under Louis's own command.

'How much?' insists the King.

Louis makes a diffident first offer.

'Could you possibly excuse us for a moment, monsieur?' the King responds politely.

As the Huns go buzzbuzz in the cavern, Louis takes the air alone in the plaza of villainy.

Five minutes later he is recalled, and negotiations are swiftly concluded. In respect of a round sum of crowns considerably less than the maximum Louis had budgeted for, the King undertakes (a) that a troop of about three hundred not wholly unsuitable Hun soldiers – certainly very violent and murderous ones – will gradually accumulate to rendezvous with Louis, time and date as per his pleasure, at Vouziers[1] on the Aisne; and (b) that if and when Monsieur le Comte's forces prove victorious in the formal field, any Hun in Paris, of any age or gender, who fails to rally to the call to lynch the Cardinal and all his followers will have his or her throat slit quick as winking on the spot.

Gratified beyond expectation at the outcome of this meeting, Louis, as he makes to leave, for additional effect calls out a jovial challenge – one-to-one with swords, pistols, or bare hands and boots – to whichever lurking coward dared shout out that he was a chicken demoiselle half an hour ago because he wouldn't drain off the dish of spirits. Up jumps a hotheaded meatloaf growling hideous threats to make the stranger toff eat his words backwards by ramming them back into him in all manner of unlikely ways.

'Go it, Poigno!' shout his supporters, hot on the scent of yet another

---

[1] To the north-east of Reims, and hence en route for Sedan.

thirst-making drama. But the situation is defused by Jacques le Moqueur, who vouches for his gentleman's incontestable martial superiority to the slavering pickpocket Poigno, by rehearsing with understandable embroidery the episode in which he himself, together with his junior bogus sergeant ('real name Lumière Crache'), attempting to confiscate the valise containing the Spanish zootsuit from Louis's room during his first morning in Paris the previous year – got 'fuckin' froen aht the windah, mate, juss like we was did ratz! So do us all a favah, Poigno, lad, and back off nah – befaw you iz did meet.'

Growling and slavering still, but in a quieter key, Poigno bows to the wisdom of Moqueur's exhortation. Louis makes respectful farewell obeisances to the King of the Huns, and, as a mark of the trust now reposed in him, is allowed to be led away by his henchmen with never a blindfold in sight.

During the ten days following [*records Louis*], I received every morning some news of more men, from the ranks of the Huns, having been despatched to Vouziers; and each communication from their leader, never written, repeated the most positive reassurances of his co-operation in favour of the Count, as opposed to the Cardinal, just as soon as the news of victory in battle should be followed by our pre-arranged signal: that the capital should be overrun from within, and his Eminence overthrown.

Monsieur de Retz was enchanted with the progress I had made, and declared, unable to repress a fleeting sneer even at this perilous enterprise in which he was himself engaged, that:

'Now we possess the poor, the prisoners, and the cut-throats, our success in Paris is nigh guaranteed.' Ever the exemplar of caution, however, he admonished me never to relax my efforts, in our campaign of proselytization, right up to the final hour. And evenings later, I remember, as we dined with some ladies he knew from Port Royal, whose loyalty to him was apparently absolute, he remarked in tones of some puzzlement:

'From my own researches today, I have news of a most intriguing man. Though he is certainly poor – on the brink of having to beg for his very bread, according to my scout – he is proud as a Basque, built "like a dark-skinned Hercules", and repulsed my man's most tactful proposals of contingent financial assistance, with a peremptory promise to snap his neck like a pod of beans, if he would not be gone forthwith.'

'A man of principle,' so I commented cautiously.

'Not unknown,' replied De Retz. 'Or possibly so adroit in the ways of the world, as to expect a better offer soon – from a personage of more breeding and substance, than my scout could ever affect?'

The following morning I set out to enact this proposal by the Abbé de Retz, and with more eagerness than perhaps he divined. For I was exceedingly concerned, on grounds of effective control just as much as personal security, to recruit into my service a small core of committed lieutenants, whose honesty, and other qualities of character, might in some degree counteract, and prevail over in combat, the villains I would muster at Vouziers. Thus, once more in my guise as a monk, I proceeded on foot to a small street of little repute, on the outskirts of the *cité*. Having mounted three flights of unsteady wooden steps, I knocked upon the topmost door, as instructed by the concierge below.

'Who goes there?' cried a deep strong voice, in an accent pronouncedly southern.

'I am a man of God,' I replied.

'What do you want?'

'To help you, monsieur,' I responded not untruthfully. 'If only you will allow me.'

'Stand back,' the voice ordered. 'Let me hear you descend ten steps.'

Obediently I stamped down the stair, heavily as I dared on such worm-holed planks.

Moments later the topmost door was pulled slowly inwards. Then suddenly round its edge appeared the muzzle of a pistol, followed instantly by a large, fierce face; dark-eyed and thickly bearded.

'Dear God!' I exclaimed in amazement. 'Is this true? Is it really you?'

For here, his brow beginning to crinkle in perplexity, stood a man I had thought to leave behind me for ever in Barcelona. It was my old friend, and former saviour, the salt smuggler Pere Garcés.

## 49

# Dialogue of Reunion

'Speak to me, Pere! Well, are you all right? What brought you here? Eh? And aren't you going to ask me in?'

— Please come in, Master Louis.

'Thank you. Now, have you — is there anyone we can send out for some food and wine?'

— The concierge's daughter, Master Louis. But I have no money.

'Then perhaps you will allow me, Pere? Since it is I who have come to ask favours of you. So shall we . . . ? [ . . . ] There. That's better. Now, will you tell me your story?'

— It's a common tale, Master Louis. I have fallen just as I rose up.

'You mean, I take it, that the nobility of Catalonia, finding that you rebels were successful, and in receipt of such generous aid from France, declared for the people's party, gradually leeched back from you possession of all authority, and, to secure their position, engineered the disgrace and ruin of the most popular leaders who had preceded them?'

— That's it, Master Louis.

'Of all the people's leaders you yourself would have been the most obnoxious to the gentry, having been the most powerful while the lower classes predominated?'

— In a nutshell, Master Louis.

'Ah, Pere. Excuses for false accusation are never wanting in revolutions, you know — even against the noblest spirits. Thus, I see, it was your fate to end up forced to flee the turncoat malice of even those selfsame citizens whose liberties you had defended. Spurned by your Catalan homeland, with a price on your head in Castile, and no other language at your command but French—'

— Indeed, Master Louis. My only refuge was France.

'So, having made your way here to Paris, you set yourself up in this great, luxurious, and horrendously expensive city. And soon felt — oh, most scorching curse, I know too well — like a throbbing viper bite within your breast: *a proud heart gnawed by poverty.*'

— Just so, Master Louis.

'In that case – but what about your wife? Why, Pere, what's wrong? She isn't – ?'

– Oh, but she is, Master Louis.

'But how? Why? I mean, she was so young. So very—'

– Some sunny day in Bigorre, Master Louis, you would have plucked a fair flower from the glade where it grew. That flower in joy you would have placed in the band of the bonnet you wore through the heat of a hot summer's day. Though the sweet fragrance of that flower had hung about you like a halo throughout your busy afternoon, by dusk you had forgot her. When in the weariness of night you reached to doff that bonnet off your brow, you found no scented blossom now, but just a shrivelled sapless rag. Blame yourself, Master Louis. Blame the sun. Above all, for death blame life. My wife is dead, Master Louis. Her body is down with the worms below, and as for her soul, well . . .

'Yes, Pere? What of her soul?'

– "An angel in heaven your lady already is, Señor Garcés," so the archbishop swore. "You may depend on that."

'Why, Pere! But that's wonderful!'

– I pray it is wonderful for her, Master Louis. But it is hell on earth for me.

'Why so?'

– For that I may never join her there.

'Why not?'

– Because my soul is damned, Master Louis.

'What by?'

– If it were not damned before, it were doubly damned for sure that night I slew the customs man, at the mill, who did but ply his trade.

'Ah, yes. That. But you said at the time—'

– I know what I said, Master Louis. But I then did deceive myself – and you too, maybe, or maybe not – as my soul has risen up to tell me a thousand times, and will again till the day I die:

"For all the foul Spaniards thou hast rightfully killed, Pere Garcés, *thou didst **murder** that man at the mill*."

'Yes, well. True repentance, they say—'

– It will avail me nowt, Master Louis.

'Why ever not?'

– For that if the same man came again, in the same time, and at the same place, I should murder him anew.

'There, there, Pere. Have some more wine. We all have terrible stains upon our conscience to bear, do we not? In my own case, the killing of

Jean-Baptiste—'

– Yes, but that was an *accident*, Master Louis. The silly young gowk brought the blast upon himself.

'If I had not been molesting his sister – as he must have seen it – his death would not have occurred. Therefore, I am to blame.'

– But not *damned*, Master Louis.

'Truly I hope not, Pere. Most of all for my mother's sake.'

– What? The Countess? Surely not—

'Dead, Pere. Dead, dead. Death by disease, in her case. Death by misadventure, for Jean-Baptiste. Death by murder, for . . . many others. No matter how they die, when they're gone we feel dreadful loss. Well, in most cases. But what about Isabella?'

– What about her?

'She's well, is she? I mean, she isn't . . . ?'

– Dead? Isabella! Far from it, Master Louis. Like a rose in May when I left her, she was. Being courted by a baker's lad, and very likely now is wed. Why? What's it to you?

'Oh, nothing. Just with all this death in the air, I thought – let's finish the wine, shall we? And then I'll tell you why I've come.'

– I expect you require my assistance, Master Louis.

'What makes you think that, Pere?'

– You and his nibs De Retz, Master Louis, you are plotting to kill the Cardinal.

'Eh? What? Where on earth did you hear that?'

– All over town it must be, Master Louis, for me to have heard it, for I have no friends in Paris.

'Well it simply isn't true,, Pere. The intention is not to murder an individual, but rather to depose a tyrant. There's a world of vital difference.'

– Makes no difference in the end, Master Louis. If you depose him, you'll kill him.

'He may die in due course, that's certainly true. But he is in any case already quite old, and has never enjoyed good health. Now here's my proposition . . . '

Most of the remainder of that conversation between Louis Morel and Pere Garcés is remarkably businesslike. With Louis now possessing the same sort of sway of influence and authority over Pere which once the Spaniard exercised over him, it is not long before Garcés amicably agrees to accept from Louis the aid (ie, patronage, employment, and of course money) which previously he spurned from the lackeys of De Retz. The deal is that, Louis being in urgent need of a trusty lieutenant not in awe of cut-throats and hitmen, Pere will take on the responsibility of disciplining, training and subcommanding the troop of hardened brigands and murderers which Louis has levied with the blessing of the King of the Huns.

'Wishing you to be near me meanwhile,' says Louis, 'I shall install you in my lodgings with Madame Beaupère. Tomorrow you will recruit me six new servants — not soldiers — if possible non-Parisians, and with no previous acquaintance between one another. Horses and weapons you will acquire to equip them all. All being well, my business in Paris will be concluded tomorrow night. The following morning we shall rendezvous at Meaux,[1] then on to tryst with our soldiers of fortune at Vouziers. Now, any questions?'

And now comes the strangely human touch:

Pere Garcés, suddenly uneasy, almost shy, says:

'Not really, Master Louis. Only . . . '

'Yes? Well?'

'Your ear, Master Louis?'

---

[1] Ancient market town on the Marne, some three hours' ride east from Paris, and hence en route for Sedan. In 1567, in the so-called 'Entreprise de Meaux', the Huguenots (French Protestants) attempted but failed to seize the young Catholic King (Charles IX) and his mother, Catherine de Medici. Thus began the 'Second Religious War' and also at least some of the gangrene which in 1572 enabled Charles to authorize the Saint Bartholomew Massacre, in which so many Huguenot citizens were slaughtered by their sovereign. So if there's any one moral in all this (and probably there are at least fifty-five), it's something like: If you're going to try to seize power from someone else who wants to keep it, and maybe kill hor too if you get half a chance, you absolutely must not fail in your endeavour, if you don't want hor to be thoroughly nasty to you in return, when their time ripens. As to conspiracies against Cardinal Richelieu, all previous efforts, obviously, have failed. This makes the campaign against Richelieu which the Count of Soissons will shortly lead, and in which the fate of Louis Morel is so ensnared, in some ways the most crucial of all.

'What about my ear?'

'Looks to me like it's never right healed,'[2] remarks Pere gently.

'Oh, it's all right, Pere. Thank you. Scabs over quite nicely, but then it does tend to bleed a bit if the scab gets knocked off. No risk of poison, though. Achilles, you see, has a herbal balsam to guarantee that.'

'If you say so, Master Louis.'

And that, you might think, is an adequate end to the earlobe coda. But no. For suddenly Louis turns thoughtful, pale, fidgety; his confidence drains away like blood from the throat of a Moroccan-slaughtered lamb.

'What's the matter, Master Louis?' asks Pere Garcés in some alarm.

But Louis won't say.

Pere presses him.

Eventually, his eyes adrift on romantic emotions, Louis confesses to a panic of horror at *the implications*.

'*What* implications, Master Louis?'

Of the undeniable fact that whereas (a) Pere Garcés, a formidable battle-scarred warrior, smuggler, freedom-fighter and outlaw, long inured to the summary taking of the lives of such of his fellow men as well deserve it . . . that whereas this aforesaid callous Pere has within him such milk of human tenderness as to remark with concern on the substandard mending of Louis's chewed-up ear, nevertheless (b) when his darling Hélène came upon him so suddenly briefly, as injured, shocked, naked and helpless he lay in bed in that unidentified Paris hôtel which also housed the young scoundrel nephew called Charles who had bragged to his cronies about how he planned to wed and simultaneously cuckold Hélène . . . when she had come upon him thus – Louis stressed again, and in great agitation – for all the proper devotion she had appeared to pledge anew, and the compassionate feminine concern she had affected to express in general, with regard to his dismal smashed-up state, still, for all that:

'*She did not notice my ear at all.* Nothing. Not one word about my ear. And I cannot help but wonder, therefore—'

To which Pere Garcés gruffly responds:

'Could have been your hair, Master Louis.'

'My hair?'

---

[2] The lobe of Louis's left ear, we should remember, was bitten off during the assassination attempt by the rabid Castilian trooper, back in Chapter 19.

'Concealing your ear?' suggests Pere with soft patience.

'Ah, yes!' cries Louis. 'Yes, yes! My hair! So my darling could not *see* my ear! Oh, Pere, Pere! To what happiness you have restored me. Truly, I cannot tell you . . . '

For of course:

When the gamesters bunged Louis out of that window into the snow, for daring to brand them cheats, his hair was cavalier-long. While today, as he dodges round Paris in perpetual hiding from the Cardinal, he is tonsured as a monk.

# Absolutely Astounded

All was going well the following day [*writes Louis*], until the early evening, when Achilles arrived at the Hôtel de Soissons, fresh from our lodgings with Madame Beaupère, and bearing with him a sealed note which there had been delivered, and which said:

*Attend me, if you please, at my residence, at four o'clock tomorrow. Signed, Richelieu.*

*Tempora mutantur et nos mutamur*, God knows, so I thought, recalling the palpitating heart that once had pined in me for preferment at the Cardinal's hands. Whereas now!

In considerable consternation I instructed Achilles to arrange the immediate despatch to Meaux of the six new servants whom the good Garcés had mustered during the day. Garcés himself, together with Achilles, and the Parisians Montfaucon and Moqueur, I ordered to be ready to ride with myself at dawn, with the purpose of putting as many leagues as possible between ourselves and his Eminence the Cardinal, in the hours preceding that commanded interview at four, in which I could not possibly participate, without putting in jeopardy all the hard-wrought plans of the Count [of Soissons].

My plans, however, were disarranged by very unexpected circumstances.

On returning to my apartments at the Hôtel de Soissons I sat down for a moment to compose a brief coded message to Monsieur de Retz. Almost instantly, without so much as the courtesy of a knock, my door opened softly inwards to admit the Countess's waiting girl Mathilde [she of the *mameles dures*, etc].

'I'm very busy, Mathilde,' I informed her. 'What is it?'

Advancing into the room, and with the air of a valued fellow conspirator, she pressed a sealed note into my hands.

'From the Countess?' I inquired.

'*No*, sir!' she exclaimed, with a most coquettish giggle. Then she conjured me, for the sake of her situation, to tell the Countess not a word about the matter. So saying, with a flaunting courtsey, she departed.

So hard on the heels of the Cardinal's ominous summons, and in the light of my design to flee the capital, this mystery note aroused my curiosity to the pitch of considerable anxiety. Thus, with hands less than wholly steady, I cut it open and read as follows.

Dearest Master Louis,

I have just learned from my father, that by some strange error you have not yet heard of my recovery, and that you have been wasting your days in regret for having, as you imagined, killed me, for all that the wound you gave me was in your own defence.

Oh, Master Louis, I too have been most cruelly misled, but I will no longer be commanded, even by my father, to do violence against my conscience before God. So therefore I write you this letter, to tell you I am still in life. So guilty was I, with the crime I was commanded to do you, and the worse evil in my soul, that when at length in the Château I recovered my senses again, I told them all, though my father would never believe me, that the injury I had received, was from a fall down the bank to the stream, which caused the accidental discharge of my own gun, into my belly.

Thanks be to God, Master Louis, for preserving me, for He knows I do not deserve it. And I pray he will preserve and prosper you too, Master Louis, for you must know that I have always loved you, and would have served you with all my heart, had not my elders put wicked notions and passions into my head, and my heart, that my soul was ever agin.

Praise be to God also, Master Louis, for leading me back to righteousness, by the path of a good woman's love. So that now the mist has lifted from my eyes. My back is resolutely turned against them that bade me do you wrong, for which I will ever repent me, and I beg you, Master Louis, to forgive me. As a token of my truth in this, Master Louis, I give you the following information: that if you will this evening, in the hour before dusk, go sufficiently attended to the first crossroads on the low road to Vincennes; the first crossroads, that is to say, beyond the Porte de St Mandé; and if you there conceal yourselves among the trees, you will shortly possess the means of delivering *her you love best* from much discomfort, fear, and danger.

Your servant unto death,

Jean-Baptiste.

P.S. The chariot in which they will convey her is red, with a black top, and a golden hawk on each door panel.

Now if by misadventure you chanced to reach the passage in G.P.R. James's novel *De l'Orme* in which the character based on Louis Morel arrived at approximately this juncture, you would now be informed that:

That character 'sprang up from the table', that his aspect was 'like Ixion unbound from his wheel', that the 'load was off [his] bosom', that he 'no longer felt the curse of Cain' upon him, that his heart beat anew 'with a lightness such as we know in boyhood', that the gay blood surging along his veins seemed instantly purged 'of the curdling poison that had so long mingled with it', that it was thus, as it were by counterpoint, that he 'first fully knew how heavily, how dreadfully the burden of crime had sat' upon him, and that in this (so to speak) sudden joyous resurrection of 'my spirit', he felt 'Hope once more light her torch, and [run] on before, to illumine my path through the years to come'.

We can't tell you for sure where James got that sickening guff from, though we strongly suspect a cocktail not excluding his loathsome Church of England moralizationalism, his associated smuggery concerning never bringing a blush to even the least sensitive parts of the anatomy of his most delicately feminine readers, and possibly also a headful of early-morning snuff. Certainly he didn't get it from anything in Louis Morel, and for that very reason we have to concede that this very paragraph, albeit utterly nauseating, is one of the most original in James's novel.

In fact Louis Morel says very little about the thoughts and emotions attendant upon his reading of the letter ostensibly from Jean-Baptiste, and indeed that is very probably why James felt the need, for a change, to *make up* something credible – to fill in the gaps. Nothing reprehensible about that as a strategy of course, in formal terms, as is demonstrated by the fact that we are on the verge of doing exactly the same ourselves. But at least what we put forward shall have the double advantage of being grounded upon what Louis did actually write, be it never so scant, and also free of CofE humbuggery.

First, here's what Louis definitely wrote:

'In all the whirling turmoil of my immediate responses to that extraordinary letter, nothing could have tormented me more vividly, or more cruelly, than the picture of how bizarre my disappearance must have seemed to my family, the wounded Jean-Baptiste having concealed from them that *I* was the one who had shot him. Given my mother's disapproving suspicions as to my passion for Hélène, and then, so soon after the shooting of Jean-Baptiste and the departure of myself, the almost simultaneous intervention by Maître Arnault, to secretly abduct his own daughter away from Château Morel, why then, how could my poor mother have thought other than that Hélène's abrupt removal, and my own unadvertised flight, were twin ungrateful facets of the same clandestine elopement? But then, as with Pere Garcés, the two Parisians, and little Achilles lagging behind, I rode the road towards Vincennes, I began to be plagued by doubts.'

Suppose now, not unreasonably, you enquire:

'*What* bloody doubts, for Christ's sake?'

Then we must respond:

'Terribly sorry! Can't rightly say.'

For Louis simply doesn't, and the very next paragraph in his memoirs begins:

'Beneath the ancient oaks of the Bois de Vincennes . . . '

Louis was, of course, no novelist, nor even a columnist for the fabulous 'Scotland' section of Nuncle Rudolph's *Sunday Crimes*. There is moreover the ongoing crucial question, first noted in Chapter 3 as to whose eyes, if any, his memoirs were intended for. Fair's fair, however, and since you have nobly stayed the course with us thus far, and since I have read the Morel memoirs in their entirety,[1] whereas even Koo has not, and since I am being paid (be it never so modestly) to write these lines, whereas you are or at least certainly ought to be in

---

[1] Unless in the vaults of some proud French small-town library (of which there are commendably many) there slumbers as yet undiscovered by us some manuscript fuller than the privately printed Geneva edition of 1704. In keeping with the so-called hypothetico-deductive method, that is, we accept that all we assert today remains open to revision tomorrow. Refer, if you will, to Sir Karl Popper's *The Logic of Scientific Discovery*. Failing that, strapped for time, etc, perhaps begin with Sir Peter Medawar's *The Art of the Soluble*. Notice how many more respectable scientists than Scottish novelists get English knighthoods.

more of a paying-customer situation,[2] let us take the modest liberty of presuming you wouldn't mind at this crux if we were to lightly coach you over the jumps of what we imagine our Louis's plaguing doubts most likely were.

Like so:

*The astounding letter itself?*

Is it really from Jean-Baptiste? If it is, then presumably Jean-Baptiste himself *is* still alive. And if so, then it *could* have been the real flesh&blood Jean-Baptiste whom Louis thought he glimpsed in the Countess of Soissons's gardens – and not some ethereal ghost such as, after all the stargazing mummery in the observatory tower, he was tempted to weakly imagine.

*But what about the shooting?*

As Louis casts his mind's eye back to that ghastly instant by the deep green river near Lourdes, when his gun muzzle discharges pointblank into the stomach of Jean-Baptiste, whose lifeblood then explodes outwards like spraying wine from an elephant's trunk, can he really credit that the wound thereby inflicted could possibly not have been fatal?

*But wait a minute:*

If he feels his way back down the galleries of his recollections just three seconds further, to those moments before the blast, what must

---

2  Unless you are a book reviewer, in which case we pre-emptively forgive you. As the admirable Arnold Haberdasher, of *The Clarion*, confided to me in McEwan's last year, in minimal expiation of the Rankles practice of presuming to 'review' six new novels every week, in several English newspapers: 'There's no denying it's disgusting, Humbert. At the same time, it would be equally hard to deny that the ideal novel to alight in a hard-pressed reviewer's pigeon-hole, would be Paul Chalicer's *The Oralist*.' So nearly *not* a book, in other words, at barely 30,000 words, that Paul's publishers had to bulk it out with a muscular typeface (New Century Schoolbook, same as you're reading right now) and print it on superthick paper. The advantage to the honest reviewer, obviously, is *being paid the same* for *reading far fewer words*. So, if you are a reviewer, and you have reached this footnote, in this not particularly short or undemanding book, thank you very much, and don't neglect to attempt to exact your bottle of Vacqueyras rouge, when next we should chance to——

he now see? Harrassed, attacked, his own left arm hanging useless in agony from a combination of fishgut poison and a cracking swipe from Jean-Baptiste's club-swung gun, and seeing Jean-Baptiste about to rush him, Louis, as a matter of reflex, has no alternative but to raise his musket deterringly. Yet this danger from a loaded firearm Jean-Baptiste appears to spurn. His own spent weapon now tossed aside, he hurls himself forward as though to strangle the handicapped Louis. As the muzzle of Louis's gun swings up, hinged only by his right wrist at its stock, it is seized hold of by Jean-Baptiste. Cackling as with triumphal rage the law-yer's son handles Louis's gun barrel like a pitchfork, its haft against his midriff, to heave his quarry back, back, back to the edge of the bank.

'No, no!' cries Louis. 'Jean-Baptiste, noooo . . . ' And Louis topples backwards into the stream in the same moment that his weapon fires and Jean-Baptiste collapses on the bank with blood gushing out of his jerkin.

*And yet:*

Jean-Baptiste was not a lad known for heroism. The previous bravest venture of his life, to Louis's certain knowledge, had been his childhood rescue of Louis from drowning in the miller's pool. Commendable enough, and tremendously appreciated by the Morel family, but hardly a feat calling for Hellespont courage, if you yourself were a reasonable swimmer. So could it be that Jean-Baptiste's Trojan-like bravado at the receiving end of Louis's musket is foolishly premised on faith that surely the young toff from the Château would never dream of shooting his saviour?

Foolishly?

Yes, because accidents are always crying out to happen – everyone knows that – and Jean-Baptiste, despite the tantrum into which he seems to have worked himself, at this riverbank vision of Louis on top of Hélène, can surely now see that Louis, temporarily disabled, is not in full control of his gun. Or can't he?

*But then again:*

Was this apparently cuckoo behaviour by Jean-Baptiste quite so luna-tic after all? To wilfully clasp the muzzle of a loaded gun to his midriff? Why not his throat, or his mouth? Or clamp it between his thighs? And also all that blood? Is it normal that blood from a pointblankblasted belly should spout and spray in that exploded-wineskin manner? Would it not rather pump, gulp, even retch, in a manner much less like crimson mist, and more like clotted borsch?

*And if so:*

Might the apparent accidental slaughter of Jean-Baptiste have been in reality a set-up job? A faked death contrived with layered corsets of leather and mail, and a pouch of fresh poultry blood squashed tight beneath his jerkin?

*Implying?*

Surely a conspiracy to cause Louis himself to flee, just as indeed he did. And why? To get him away from Hélène? Then who else had designs upon her? And who – for it certainly could never be Jean-Baptiste – must have masterminded the plot? Maître Arnault? Certainly he possessed plentiful cunning, and malevolence, yet would it not have been more in his interests, in the long run, to scheme to *keep* Louis *at home*? To nurture his lowly daughter's prospects, such as he might have believed they were, of securing in marriage the heir to all Morel?

*Then what other villain . . . ?*

Well, thoughts of malignant treachery certainly associate closely with everyone's image of the Marquis of Roquefort. There are moreover in Louis's memory disquieting hints of an untoward sexual interest taken by the Marquis in Hélène. The consummate roué ease with which he had snaffled her hand, to lead her in to dinner that night in Château Morel. The gallant attention and compliments he had paid her during the meal. Then the dishonourable evidence of his depraved attitudes to women in general, as revealed during that stint in his hunting pavilion. Leading by infallible extrapolation to a most disquieting vignette, whose significance may not hitherto have been adequately acknowledged:

*On the second day of the Marquis of Roquefort's stay at Morel, the winter weather brightly fine, the izard shoot in hand, Louis, lovesong sleepless, flusters late across the hall with his gun. There he is urgently intercepted by Hélène, flushed: dishevelled, and more unbearably lovely than ever.*

*As Louis encircles her waist, etc, Hélène presses her finger to his lips, and hisses in his ear:*

*'The Marquis is **no gentleman**, but rather the **arrantest villain**.'*

A description which subsequent developments prove entirely correct, but how could Hélène *know* that then?

What had the Marquis been doing to her?

And what might he have been lobbying to do to her at greater leisure later, in Louis's carefully engineered absence?

*Conspiracy-theory floodgates now being open:*

Whether or not Jean-Baptiste may indeed have survived the riverbank shooting, is the present astounding letter, ostensibly from a penitent Jean-Baptiste, in fact authored by him at all? Admittedly, the sentiments expressed seem not inconsistent with Jean-Baptiste's fundamental moral character.

But so what?

Might not such sentiments be easily feigned?

And certainly, as a lawyer's clerk, training in his father's office, he would be sufficiently literate – give or take some hilarious spelling, though don't forget that attitudes to orthography in those days were hugely more tolerant and creative than what we have sunk to now, as is witnessed by the fact that Louis Morel's own spelling (which presumably had been to some extent already corrected in the editing of his Geneva edition) has had to be radically regularized in the preparation of this present text.[3]

But so what else? For might not his handwriting be forged?[4]

*And furthermore:*

Regardless of whether the astounding letter is or isn't penned by Jean-Baptiste, how much is its face value worth?

*In particular:*

Is it *true* that Louis can expect to be reunited with Hélène at the Vincennes crossroads circa eight o'clock tonight?

*And most crucially:*

Whether or not Hélène herself will materialize in that place and time, to what extent will she be amenable to daredevil rescue, and from whom? And how many thousands of the Cardinal's secret police will also simultaneously gallop down from Vincennes, drop out of the trees and erupt from the bushes, to surround the desperate suitor and his tiny band, and arrest them for High Treason?

---

[3] Otherwise you might be getting fed up with all the footnotes.

[4] Louis does not claim any previous familiarity with Jean-Baptiste's handwriting. In any case, that would have been long ago, and here in Paris he possesses no surviving known-to-be-genuine specimen, with which to effect a comparison. The situation is thus like suddenly having to confront a new candidate Vermeer, which could be a dastardly Van Meegeren fake, and yet having no definitely authenticated Vermeer about your person, as a touchstone to refine your perception.

# Crossroads

Of course, we do not claim that *all* of those plaguing doubts swept through Louis Morel's cantering brain in precisely those formulations, or in exactly that running order. Only that *any* of them could have, *many* of them should have, and *some* of them must have. For by the time he and Pere Garcés, together with the bully bravos Montfaucon and Moqueur (the lagging Achilles Lefranc having been dumped in a tavern on the city side of the Porte de St Mandé), are lurking in the gathering bosk beneath the ancient oaks of the lower Bois de Vincennes:

'My imagination, so it felt, was like an innocent scapegoat, convicted on a false accusation of treason, and at once rent apart towards all points of the compass, by equal chains attached to my ankles and wrists, and yoked to the shoulders of four enormous dray horses, driven crazy with fear by fire. So it was, in that eternally long half hour, before the ordained time, that in one moment I would fancy in panic that I surely had mistaken the road, or that the crossroads detailed by the writer of that letter was in error, or *again* [*our italics*] that I must have been deliberately deceived, or else – and so disturbing that the trembling of my legs must have communicated my distress, as the horse beneath me grew infected with her master's discomposure, and began to whinny and rear – or else, I say, that my darling Hélène would indeed appear as forecast, but with neither need nor desire to be rescued by me, and possibly even already trapped in wedlock, to that damnable scoundrel Charles.'

As to what happens next, in the twenty minutes surrounding eight o'clock on that heady evening in early spring, Louis Morel's original reminiscing sentences wax so long and longer, in style more and morer florid, that to render them here verisimilitudinally would surtax our powers of translation.

So let us strip to our naked essentials.

First a dim squeaking of wheels is heard, down the branch-arched avenue north.

Soon hooves and nostrils steaming.

Moments later a four-horse chariot appears in the crossroads clearing and reins up by the water troughs in its centre. The chariot is red, with a black top, and a golden hawk on each door panel. Louis and his henchmen, mounted, concealed behind four large trees a little way back from the clearing, are leaning forward to stroke their horses' twitching noses, to coach their uneasy silence.

Meanwhile the chariot driver and his musket-toting navigator remain sat still, quietly muttering. From the curtain-screened chariot no person descends; nor is any face fleetingly windowed.

Nothing happens.

Then all at once the mount of Jacques le Moqueur is frighted by a high-flapping bird; a pigeon, perhaps. In sympathetic agitation all eight horses sidle and strain, and quadraphonically snort and whinny. Smelling what would appear to be this aural rat, the musket-toter comes alive as a picture of panic, brandishes his gun at the trees, and loudly warbles:

'Ho! Goes there?'

Before he has time to draw breath for a louder reprise there comes a breakneck thrumming of hooves from the west as a lone rider arrives from Paris. On a coal-black horse, his own garb jet, with a black bandana around his mouth, and charcoal about his eyes, the newcomer vaults from his saddle, bounces once by the water troughs, and disappears within the chariot. Seconds later Louis's heart erupts into peril of being chomped by his rage-clamping molars when the cool night air is cleanly sliced by affronted feminine tones:

'No, sir! I will not! You have deceived me, and I shall not [ . . . ] let me down, sir. Let me *go!*'

The voice, of course, is Hélène's, and we cannot imagine for the lives of us what finer compression of the immediate sequel we could devise for you than is already contained in Janet Rosencrantz's programmatic critique of the previous draft of the present chapter.

The lone-ranging masked latecomer from Paris [*writes Janet*] is the braggart scoundrel Charles, who is nephew to some bigwig whom we have not yet met. That much is so obvious that I cannot believe many of your readers will not already have guessed it. As to the sequence where Louis yells out things like 'Pere, you take the drivers!' and 'Combalet, hold the horses!', while he himself, pistol cocked, charges in to the chariot to rescue Hélène, who falls close to swooning (damn you) into Louis's arms while her craven molester Charles in a diarrhoeic funk scrambles out through the chariot's other door, only to be nobbled to the ground with a dagger pressed to his jugular by Jacques le Moqueur, well, if you take my advice you'll do that in elliptical précis, else it might seem overly melodramatic to such rarely hardy breeds of reader as you have not yet succeeded in alienating.

That Hélène herself has been duped unto this crossroads by foul play is also predictable. You say she says the wool-pulling device was a forged letter from her father, instructing her to tryst with him on the way to Vincennes, but how far is this really credible? It's true that, during her sojourn at Château Morel, she has lived long apart from her father – but even allowing for that, would she not know his handwriting well enough to not be taken in by a forgery? She is, after all, now at a stage equivalent to our own intelligent sixth-formers, and you don't need me to tell you just how godawful sharp they can be. Then again, if you assure me that's what really happened, I'm prepared, at a pinch, to believe you.

What I am adamantly *not* prepared to swallow is your thoroughly loathsome and insulting depiction of how, once Hélène has recovered (miraculously swiftly, needless to say) from her latest near-swoon, the lovers embrace passionately, kiss tenderly, exchange urgent professions of eternal devotion, meanwhile caressing one another with a most mature fondness, albeit through their clothes, and all this in considerable lingering detail such as tells us at least as much about the dwelling narrator as it does about his hot young lovers, before (and this is what I particularly resent) it is *Hélène* who is first restored enough to her cool, calm and collected senses to inquire what chain of conspiracies brought Louis to the scene, and to debate the implications as to what dangers lie ahead, where and how soon, and how best to circumvent them.

If you'll allow me a moment to stand back several miles from your tale of Louis Morel, and the wimpish sidekick Hélène he idealises (and of whom I have complained throughout), I see her now as an embodiment of the courtly love ethic. She carries the banner of 'romantic love' and her troops flourish because she represents passion that can only exist in a fantasy that will not be disappointed (during the span of the novel). She is the dream woman on whom Louis can project his own unrealized aspirations. But for some chapters now – doubtless for some twisted plot reason yet to be sprung on us – you have been trying to convert her into a real person. Well, I don't believe in this new decisive Hélène. By listening to me (??) and making her progressively less swoon-prone (though never immune – that would be asking too much, wouldn't it?), you are betraying Hélène's identity as a metaphor for the concept of romantic passion. She must, in other words, be *either* a symbol (golden wisps, timorous maidenhead, swooning) *or* a character (armpits, expectant clitoris, menstruation) but *not bloody both*. Seriously, Humbert, I really don't think we can let you get away with baking your cake out of both.

Thank you, Janet, for looping us back to this moment in the chariot, when Louis, his arms wrapped in a bearhug round Hélène, as, delirious with blind delight, he kisses her mouth, her eyes, her neck, her mouth again, while she, though stimulated by his unqualified ardour, presses her palms against his chest, to push him several inches apart from her bosom, so that, in this curtained twilight gloom, he can *see* how serious she is, when she recalls their entwined attention to the future rushing up:

'Oh, Louis!'

'Nyah?'

'There's something I must tell you.'

'What's that?'

'About my – but what's wrong, Louis?'

'What with?'

'Your neck. It's bleeding. Oh, Louis, what have they *done* to you?'

'No, Hélène. It's nothing. Not my neck, I mean. It's my ear—'

'But what's *wrong* with your ear?'

Louis is obliged by Hélène's concern to recount the trauma of having his left lobe bitten off by an unsympathetic Spaniard, and to explain that in the vigour of nuzzling herself just now, pressing his cheek to her pounding heart, etc, he seems to have snagged his current scab against her brooch.

'But it's nothing, Hélène,' he repeats. 'Really it's . . . '

Tears in her eyes, she dabs with a perfumed but otherwise unsullied handkerchief at the wound whence oozes his gore, and then kisses it for good measure, with the warm and generous unguent of her hot young woman's saliva.

'Now tell me what you were going to tell me,' says Louis at length.

'About what?'

'You said:

'"About my—"'

'Oh, yes!' cries Hélène, in a fusion of exultation and despair. 'I was going to say that my—'

'*Listen!*' hisses Louis, retrieving his pistol from the chariot floor.

'Oh, God! What now?' murmurs Hélène fearfully, as she too hears the commotion surging around them, like the sudden inpouring of an ocean stung to fury, as through the chariot curtains stabs of light are seen to arc, as the chariot itself begins to rock like a sea-tossed raft, in the moment before its leftside door is wrenched open, and a broad pair of armour-plated shoulders heaves in, beneath the furrowed, scarred, and clipped-grey-bearded severity of an ageing soldier's anger.

'Take your hands off that girl!' barks the intruder at Louis, in a curt but not uncultured snarl. 'And get down from this carriage at once.'

Already Louis has lunged forward and has his pistol pressed hard to the intruder's wrinkled forehead. 'By what authority, monsieur?' he demands menacingly. 'And who, in any case, are you?'

'Oh, Louis!' wails Hélène behind him. 'It is the—'

'Maréchal de Châtillon,' nods the Cardinal's loyalest general, 'and reluctant uncle to that young idiot Charles, whom my men have just saved from your Catalan cut-throat out there, whom now they have orders to hang. As for you, Monsieur Morel, you will obey my instruction immediately, if you do not wish to hang with him.'

Inching forward, his legs coiled to leap, Louis keeps his pistol pressed to the Maréchal's head. Behind him he feels Hélène shift to follow him.

'You, mademoiselle,' commands the Maréchal, his voice like breaking slates, 'will remain where you are.'

'Do as he says, Hélène,' says Louis softly, as he senses the energy of her disobedience mounting. 'Stay there for the moment,' he insists, seeing the surrounding tide of some two hundred cavaliers, in the Maréchal's colours, that swamps the crossroads clearing, their flambeaux like fireflies fluttering.

'*It wasn't me, your lordship!*' now squeals a familiar voice.

'What wasn't you, Achilles?' asks Louis evenly, over the Maréchal's shoulder, where he sees his little valet trussed to his horse, like a chicken tied for roasting.

'*I didn't tell them where you was, your lordship!*' proclaims Achilles proudly. 'Somehow they already knew!'

'How, monsieur, did you know where we were?' demands Louis quietly, tapping the Maréchal's forehead encouragingly, with his one pistolic advantage.

'Don't try my patience, Monsieur Morel,' grunts the Maréchal. 'My nephew is an idiot—'

'I say, Uncle! That's a bit—'

'Shut your mouth, Charles!' raps the Maréchal over his shoulder. 'I'll deal with you later. You see?' he adds to Louis, almost apologetically.

'A hopeless buffoon. Yet not all bad, and in any case, for my pains, *my* nephew. *That*, Monsieur Morel, is how we knew where you would be, shall we say, about to embark on this treasonous abduction. For if I were not aware, sir, of my nephew's occasional thoughts – not to mention their ramifications – several hours before they transpired, he would soon fall foul of, and unhappily prey to, certain . . . other agencies. As for you, Monsieur Morel—'

'What about me?' stalls Louis. Behind the immediate circle of some fifty mounted cavaliers, training muskets and pistols upon him, he sees three ropes looped over a flat-hanging bough, and the three gagged figures of Montfaucon, Moqueur and Pere Garcés standing helplessly beneath three nooses hanging: tightly bound and closely guarded.

With a contemptuous sneer the Maréchal advises him:

'Put down your weapon, monsieur. You are helpless.'

## 52

# Academic Plagiarism

*the sentence*
*on the other side*
*is plagiarized*

# 52

# Academic Plagiarism

*the sentence*
*on the other side*
*is plagiarized*

# 53

# Next Fix

If like a perky young puma you've just impatiently pounced from the last word of the last chapter but one but one to the first of this, gloriously thus slinging mud in the eyes of Wringhim Knox, Mumbo Rankles, all failing Hampstead adulterers, lickspittle googa followers of fraudulent French pseudo-philosophers, and other affected eschewers of fundementedly all-too-human cliffhangery, then your next fix goes like:

'So why am I helpless?' inquires Louis mildly. 'When I hold the power to kill you as you stand?'

'Save your threats, Monsieur Morel,' replies the Maréchal disdainfully. 'I am a professional soldier, you know. And professional soldiers do not fear death. Old soldiers less so. Indeed, were you to shoot me now, you would likely save me the humiliation of a lingering death in my bed before too long. So save your threats, monsieur. Put down your gun. Besides, think of your youth, your hopes – your future. If you shoot me now, you will die in the very next instant.' He flicks a gloved thumb to indicate the circle of horsebacked muskets and pistols training in upon Louis like spokes round a hub.

'Oh, he is right, he is right, your lordship!' trills Achilles in despair. 'I pray your lordship, for all our sakes, put down your pistol, and submit.'

'Shut up, Achilles,' murmurs Louis with seeming nonchalance, though his thoughts are colliding in cartwheels. 'When I want your puerile advice, I'll ask for it, all right?'

'*Oh, Louis!*' Hélène sobs invisibly within the chariot. '*I must tell you—*'

'SILENCE, YOU UNGRATEFUL GIRL!' roars the Maréchal, the bristles of his moustache curling upward with rage. 'You'll get your chance soon enough: to explain your behaviour today. Till then, be SILENT.'

'Supposing, Maréchal,' speculates Louis reasonably, 'that I were to let you live, what would you do with Hélène?'

'She will be taken back to my Paris hôtel, monsieur, where she should never have left my wife's care.'

'And what will happen to her then?'

'She will, at his convenience, be restored to her father.'

'And what will happen to her then? I mean . . . ' Louis glares bale-fully at the bystanding nephew Charles – who, he is distantly pleased to note, is rather a runt little squirt, being barely as tall as Achilles.

'That is for her father to decide,' grunts the Maréchal irritably. 'Besides—'

'What about me?'

'What about you, monsieur?'

'If I let you live, Maréchal, then, in view of your present numerical superiority, I should in effect be surrendering myself to your mercy.'

'True, monsieur.'

'What form, I wonder, might that mercy take?'

Taking a breath so deep that for a moment it seems his chest inflates like an armour-plated bullfrog, the Maréchal de Châtillon looks up for a moment as if to Heaven but in reality at the pistol still pressed to his brow. Softly, rapidly, more as a lobbying politician than a hectoring general, he advises Louis:

'If, Monsieur Morel, I were here tonight not on my own house's account, but under direct orders from the Cardinal, those orders would infallibly be for your immediate arrest, conveyance to the Bastille, and confinement therein pending his Eminence's further pleasure. Such orders are in any case, so I have good reason to believe, highly likely to be issued tomorrow.'

'Good gracious,' responds Louis. 'But whatever for?'

'Because you are a known traitor, monsieur, and have been conspiring, on behalf of the Count of Soissons, against the Cardinal and the King.'

'Oh, have I, indeed?'

'Yes.'

'If that were the case, Maréchal, then should I not be obliged to execute you now, in cold blood, no matter what the consequence to myself might be, on the ground that no more valuable service could be rendered to his Highness of Soissons, than the elimination of the Cardinal's most able general?'

'*Touché*, monsieur.'

'As you say, Maréchal.'

'In the circumstances, Monsieur Morel, and because I prefer to imagine the brash young scion of a once noble family lying headless from defeat on the field of honourable battle, than wasting slowly to death from solitude, disease, darkness, and malnutrition in a dungeon cell, I shall give you one last chance.'

'And that is?'

'Holster your pistol at once, monsieur. Surrender to me, and I shall promise you the respite of liberty until dawn, to make your way towards Sedan.'

Louis's eyes roll like the eyes of an unbroken colt in a branding stall. In longing and dread he glimpses sideways the falcon-studded chariot door that conceals Hélène. All around him he feels the Maréchal's cavaliers inching closer by the second as their snorting horses stamp and dung. Beyond, beneath the hanging bough, his gagged Parisian bravos and Pere Garcés are ready-noosed, three ropes each held taut behind by three De Châtillon cavaliers all braced for the signal to hoist. In the forefront Achilles Lefranc sobs quietly with helpless misery, his swollen eyes like tiny starlit lakes.

Turning back to the Maréchal, Louis presses his body close to the older man, emphasizing with superior height his one frail pistol advantage.

'Two conditions, Maréchal,' he stresses.

'Conditions, monsieur?' the Maréchal almost laughs.

'First, my men come with me. All of them. Unharmed. Agreed? All four—'

'I say, Uncle! *No!* Surely not that filthy Spaniard. Why, he—'

'Hold your tongue, Charles!' raps the Maréchal furiously. 'Very well, monsieur,' he concedes to Louis, with decreasing patience. 'And the second condition?'

'The lady in the chariot—'

'Is none of your concern, monsieur,' cuts in the Maréchal quickly.

Louis counters:

'Being, in the Maréchal's own words, the scion of a noble family, and an upholder of true chivalry, I require you, before I release the lady into your custody, that you promise me, upon your honour as a soldier, that you shall not allow her to be wed to any man, except *freely of her own consent.*'

'Monsieur, you ask too much,' growls the Maréchal. 'Disposing of the girl in marriage is outwith my remit. It is a matter for her father.'

'Hélène is no longer a girl,' replies Louis. 'She is a woman. Her father,' he whispers low, 'so I have reason to believe, is less concerned with his daughter's well-being and happiness, than with his own aggrandizement. Hence my second condition, upon which I absolutely insist. If you do not agree to it, Maréchal, I shall shoot you now, come what may.'

The Maréchal de Châtillon's rough tongue brushes over the bristles of his rough moustache. Perhaps he is persuaded by Louis's urgency of tone and tension of posture that here is a young gallant so brimming with romantic passion that he seriously might enact his deadly threat — which would not trouble the fearless Maréchal himself, of course, but would be greatly vexing to Cardinal Richelieu, his master. Or possibly the Maréchal has simply grown weary of this confrontation so unprofitable to him, and, having not yet dined, and being French, is desperate for his dinner. The upshot, for whatever concatenation of causal factors to which not even a thousand of these heroically intentioned pages could ever do partial justice, is that, in the course of an oral expulsion sounding much like a blatant fart, the Maréchal de Châtillon articulates:

'Dah, very well.'

'Say it,' insists Louis.

'Hwah?'

'Repeat my second condition. Aloud, before your men. And in hearing of your nephew.'

Looking much as if already fondly fantasizing Louis lying headless on that honourable battlefield soon, the Maréchal de Châtillon obediently vows:

'I pledge, on my honour as a soldier, that the girl in the chariot shall not be wed against her will — *while yet I draw breath in liberty.*'

# 54

# Succeeding at Sex by Numbers?

A little before the mid-day following [*writes Louis*] we were safely arrived at Meaux, where my coach and new servants were awaiting. There we made a light repast, filled the coach with provisions, and watered and rested our horses, before pressing on towards Vouziers, where my troop of warriors, recruited from the Huns, was to muster.

As to our identity, some subterfuge was essential, for the sake of satisfying the eternal curiosity of the ostlers, landlords, tapsters, chambermaids, strumpets, peddlars, beggars, and the like,[1] in the various small towns and villages that bestrew our way. The necessity of inventing or simply borrowing another person's name was in those days so frequent, that on my introducing myself to my own servants as the young Baron Charles de Châtillon, nephew to the illustrious Maréchal of that name, I occasioned them no great astonishment, and it was with great facility that they habituated their fidelities, and modes of address, to suit the station of that effete young gentleman.

On the second day, riding on a little distance ahead, side by side with Pere Garcés, I endeavoured somewhat to lighten the great heaviness upon my heart, by describing to him – which I had not had time to do before – such of those recent events as had taken place in Paris, as I felt it needful for him to know. Of certain items, I was surprised to discover, Pere was already more or less aware. But when I recounted to him the news that the lawyer's son, Jean-Baptiste Arnault, had somehow managed to recover from that awful gunshot wound by the river in Bigorre, at least so far as was deducible from the letter I had received (which on balance I now inclined to believe to be genuine in its authorship, although suspect in its stated intent), my Catalan comrade was frankly amazed.

He would have vowed on his mother's grave, he said, that what he beheld before him, when he ran to my assistance that morning in the

---

[1] Any one or all of whom might be spying for Cardinal Richelieu.

park, was nothing but a bloodied heap of manure in the making, that never would speak, or think, or breathe, or ever stir a single inch again, save in tiny pieces on the backs of ants, and through the bellies of worms.

'If yet the lad recovered,' said Pere, 'it is very like a miracle, indeed.[2] And now, monsieur,[3] that you have recalled my thoughts to young Master Arnault, I confess, with him in mind, that I am afraid I may have done you some unnecessary harm – in the esteem, I mean, of the Chevalier de Montenero.'

'What, Pere?' cried I. 'What harm? How? When?'

'Do you remember that day in Barcelona,' he reflected sadly, 'when together we rescued Monsieur de Montenero from the malice of the troublemaker Moreno?'

'Till my dying day, Pere,' I assured him. 'But what of it?'

'As I hurried the Chevalier away from the Council, monsieur, impatient for him to depart by the Red Rose Gate, before the Moreno faction could rally, he seemed all the while reluctant to go. As, gently, my arm about his shoulder, I obliged him, for the sake of us all, to be gone, though he yielded in his movements, yet his mind remained distracted – agonized, even – and like a gentleman in a great perplexity of grief he muttered, more to himself than to me:

---

[2] The tradition of miracles in the region of Lourdes goes back a long way, and the fantastic commercial edifice built upon the virgin vision of Bernadette Soubirous on Thursday 11 February 1858 may be seen by the ever-so-slightly cynical as a case of practice having paid off perfectly at last. Among the precedent miracles to be built upon was a bit of funny goings-on at beautiful Bétharram, only furlongs from the posthouse where Louis Morel bested the Marquis of Roquefort while cantering home from college in Pau. 'In July 1616', writes Father Jean Oyhenart S.C.J, 'a huge cross was erected on the hilltop dominating the chapel. Two months later, it was struck by a storm. It was seen to re-erect itself enveloped in radiant light.' All that, whatever it was, took place only two years before Louis was born, and but a few miles downriver from where he was fondling Hélène, before shooting Jean-Baptiste.

[3] Pere is practising relating to Louis as to the young Baron Charles de Châtillon. Later he forgets.

'"I would give my very life itself, you know, to be assured whether Louis Morel *did* slay the wretch, or . . . not?"'

'Yes, Pere?' I pressed him, in terrible agitation now, as the presentiment grew upon me, of what must come next. 'And what did you say?'

'Why, monsieur, thinking then, as did we all, that you had killed Jean-Baptiste for sure, I said happily to Monsieur de Montenero, thinking to cheer him on his way:

'"Of course Master Louis slew the wretch, monsieur! And quite right too, since he asked for it!" Upon hearing which, Monsieur de Montenero seemed to shudder in his saddle, that he now had mounted, sighed most piteously, and without another word he galloped off south.'

'Oh, God, Pere!' groaned I. 'You definitely said "slew the wretch", did you?'

'What do you mean, Master Louis?' he responded in some puzzlement.

'I mean, there's no possibility, is there, that you said, instead:

'"Of course Master Louis slew *Jean-Baptiste* . . . "?'

'Why, no, Master Louis,' replied Pere regretfully, as he sensed my dismay. 'As the Chevalier himself said he wished to know if you "*did* slay the wretch", it was in his selfsame words, with respect, that I assured him that yes, you did. I'm sorry, Master Louis,' he added, somewhat crestfallen, as he perceived echoes in my eyes, of the torment in my soul. 'Did I do wrong?'

'*Yes*, Pere!' cried I. 'I mean: no, you *meant* no harm. Only good. But what in fact you caused, in the Chevalier's mind, was the promotion from doubt to a certainty, that *I had slain . . . someone else.*'

That someone else is – or rather, was – of course the naked priest Father Avecido, at Zaragoza, whom the randy maja had murdered for debasing her. And whose body Louis then gallantly humped and dumped in the city fosse, and whose killing has been the occasion of so much tragic misunderstanding between Louis and the Chevalier ever since.

Louis is, needless to say, too mature and civilized to punish or even scold Pere Garcés for having unwittingly reinforced the Chevalier's misapprehension. He is unable, nonetheless, not to feel disheartened, if not exactly embittered, by this new cruel twist of fate, and during the rest of that long spring day (sun shining? clouds drifting? birds singing? he does not record) he rides alone, in silence, brooding ponderously upon:

'How often in life a small accidental mistake or misunderstanding appears to bring on another, and then another, and again another, to all eternity. It is as if some confounding demon lurks in our very essence, to perpetuate, unto infinity, the chain of all our errors.'

Given this frame of mind, it is not long before Louis's trekking disconsolation bogs down again in his specifically sexual errors. Those with the maja and the lowlife Paris strumpets (during his Byronic derelict phase) are incontestable. Others – with accomplished houries in the Marquis of Roquefort's hunting pavilion, with Pere's lissom niece Isabella in Barcelona, with the Countess of Soissons' *mameles-dures* girl Mathilde, and with various casual Parisian ladyfriends of the Abbé de Retz – are highly likely, and some of them are statistically certain. If you demand to know precisely how many human vaginas Louis Morel has penetrated to date, we must confess in good faith that we cannot tell you. To the best of our knowledge he has never penetrated any non-human vaginas, nor evinced any evidence of wishing to. As to girls, women and ladies, his tally of sexual success as gauged by discrete individuals conventionally penetrated must lie between five minimum and twenty maximum.[4]

Yet would either sum seem sexual success?

Sexual *success?*

Does it really inhere, as for some moments we have been tacitly supposing, in the full-time score of distinct pubic scalps notched up? If so, the father of the present King of France[5] takes a lot of beating, and will certainly never now be overtaken by me, especially considering I am already well into my forties and at least as wary of contracting AIDS as the next man or woman. As to John F Kennedy's notorious billygoating, let us never neglect the insider wisdom of Vidal:

'Most men – homo or hetero—' according to Gore, 'given the oppor-tunity to have sex with 500 different people would do so, gladly; but most men are not going to be given the opportunity by a society that wants them safely married so that they will be docile workers and consumers. It does not suit our rulers to have the proles tom-catting around the way that our rulers do. I can assure [Midge] Decter [and anyone else who does or doesn't care] that the thirty-fifth president went to bed with

---

4  If Louis too was subjected by the Marquis of Roquefort to the Star of David trial, he may well have penetrated three or four of the Marquis's houries, before shooting his bolt, within the space of a very few minutes.

5  Father = Henri IV. Son = Louis XIII. See Chapter 21, note 2.

more than 500 women and that the well-known . . . but I must not give away the secrets of the old class or the newly-middle class will go into shock.'[6]

Possibly suggesting that sexual success, in the notched-up sense, is a function of political power. Henri IV, *King* of France; JFK, *President* of the United States. Or alternatively, or additionally, that sexual success is a function of being destined to be assassinated? Was the frenzied Ravaillac also secretly in the pay of Marie de Medici – Henri's copiously cuckolded Queen?[7] May JFK's murder have been covertly orchestrated, not by the KGB and/or the Mafia, but rather by a former husband, lover, or merely long-distance admirer, like Mormon Nailher, of Marilyn Monroe? And likewise the sexually prolific, self-indulgent and depraved Roman Emperors. Julius Caesar; assassinated. Caligula; assassinated. Nero; suicided to pre-empt execution. And therefore? May it not be, in this aspect, that sexual success, at its very acme, in the fullest explosion of its most widely-screened head-of-state orgasm, is simultaneously the wilting, bleeding humiliation of sexual failure – in that you'll go no more a-swiving, will you, with several high-velocity bullets in your brain?

---

[6] The Vidal quotation is from his essay 'Pink Triangle and Yellow Star', originally published in *The Nation*, 14 November 1981, reprinted in the collection entitled *Pink Triangle and Yellow Star*, which was first published in 'Great Britain' in 1982 by William Heinemann. And very commendably candid of Gore, is it not? Coming from someone who has himself frequently tried and failed to become one of 'our rulers'. In fact the very forthrightness of Vidal's cynicism is a severe political disqualification. For is not the best qualification for deceiving others to be deceived oneself?* And Vidal, for all his hyperbole, neither is nor pretends to be.

   * *'Yes. As politicians ascend the ladders of power and senility, THEY OFTEN BEGIN TO BELIEVE the unctuous platitudes and fawning obeisances they habitually deliver. This is why the insincerities of elder statesmen can be less insultingly blatant than those of ambitious junior ministers. The juniors have yet to achieve the requisite self-deception, autohypnosis, or whatever.' [J.R.]*

[7] For more on this conspiracy theory, and the role of the Duke of Epernon, see *The Counts of Mount Venus*, final chapter.

Please excuse the excessively plethoric rhetoric in the previous paragraph, which was essential to the topping of Gore Vidal, who always needs putting down. The basic point is that notch success is eternally fragile, since it inevitably excites sexual envy, which is a particular form of malice, expressed as desire to do, cause to be done, or merely gleefully witness, some painful harm to the offensively successful perceived rival. Consequently, and especially now we have AIDS to encourage the moderating of our notching, it may be a better long-run sexual bet to confine one's perceived sexual success to the smug enjoyment of being known (in the penthouse exclusivity of one's chosen upper-echelon clique) as a 'really great lay'.

And how, in turn, might that be achieved? Peering first through the window of ubiquitous macho neurosis: for doing what, to whom, and with which, shall we have our thanks?

To hurdle us hard-onward, in these crucial inquiries, let us quote as briefly as possible:

*55*

# From Wringhim's Ghastly Pamphlet

Here [*stresses Wringhim*] we immediately encounter the eternal difficulty that English ladies (ordinary and intellectual alike) do not always
say (or at least cannot always be *known* to say) precisely what they
mean, or what they think (in cases where a prior thought process bears a
traceable relation to the utterance). To illustrate this difficulty, let us turn
for a moment to Somerset Maugham's acutely lowbrow recollections of
H.G. Wells:

'He was fat and homely. I once asked one of his mistresses what
especially attracted her in him. I expected her to say his acute mind
and his sense of fun; not at all; she said that his body smelt of
honey.'[1]

But was it *really true* that the Wells corpus smelt of honey? If so, why
hadn't Maugham himself noticed this sweet characteristic?

And even if Wells did smell of honey, was the aroma in itself
sufficient to have attracted the lady to the man, to guzzle him as might
a greedy bee?

Could it not also be the case that, over and above any hint of his
honey bouquet, Wells (being a successful novelist, even if English) was
possessed of a long, bulbous, copious, indefatigable member? And that
it was to this that his mistress was essentially attracted?

And that her reluctance to admit the fact was due partly to commendable feminine modesty, and partly to her understandable refusal
to advertise Wells' genital magnificence to other predatory ladies, who
might then have flocked to impress their vaginas upon him?

In view of these insuperable obstacles to believing what English

---

[1] Typically, Wringhim hasn't bothered to give the reference for this
quotation, and the rest of us haven't had time to chase it up before
going to press with a bit of luck before the Millennium. We can
only hope, therefore, that it isn't too badly out, and apologize most
profusely if it is.

women *say*, it is essential for the aspirant researcher into what they *want* to concentrate on, and extrapolate from: (a) what those women *do*, sexually speaking; (b) what their menfolk (English and otherwise) do, in response to what those women do.

With those parameters in mind, it is instructive to begin with the fearless counter-Victorian anthropological empiricism of sexual explorers such as Sir Richard Francis Burton (1821–90). Witness, for example, his *Arabian Nights* footnote that:

'Debauched women prefer Negroes on account of the size of their parts. I measured one man in Somaliland who, when quiescent, numbered nearly six inches.

'This is a characteristic of the negro race and of African animals.

'Moreover, these imposing parts do not increase proportionally during erection; consequently, "the deed of kind" takes a much longer time and adds greatly to the woman's enjoyment.

'In my time no honest Hindi Moslem would take his womenfolk to Zanzibar on account of the huge attractions and enormous temptations there and thereby offered to them.'

But what is so 'debauched' about wanting to add greatly to your sexual enjoyment? No! That value-loaded 'debauched' is surely merely an intelligent sop thrown by Burton to the snarling Victorian prurigentsia, which we can safely ignore, while retaining his seminal findings.

Alas, just when Burton and his fellow brave pioneers in the wilderness of unscientific sex were beginning to make some real headway, uncovering some startling anthropological confirmations of certain longstanding folklore certainties regarding sexual physiology and behaviour, along came:

Freud, the Freudians, the post-Freudians, the neo-Freudians, the post-neo-Freudians, psychotherapists, psychodynamicists, psychorapists, counter-neo-Freudian deconstructionists, and many other prolixically pleonastically preposterous persons, not all of them English by any means.

That unfortunate progression was accompanied by a series of so-called revolutionary and liberationary research programmes which claimed to have demonstrated not only that the size of the male member was irrelevant to the woman's pleasure but also that the vaginal orgasm was a non-existent nonentity. These programmes, it need hardly be added, were sponsored and directed by white anglo-saxon protestant researchers primarily of English extraction whose members may very well have been irrelevant to the woman's pleasure, and who (in many cases for obvious reasons) were themselves incapable of experiencing the supposedly mythological orgasm in their vaginas.

Not only did this constitute (in purely scientific terms) unimportant research by unimportant researchers, but the 'research' itself was carried out on small groups of white anglo-saxon protestant research volunteers who could hardly claim to be representative of the sexual population at large.

However, the results of these research programmes were popular with the white anglo-saxon protestant academic community, and consequently many straightforward home truths (such as that many women adore big cocks[2]) have been replaced by aery-faery pseudo-scientific prejudices in the popular mind.

---

2  I'm afraid Wringhim's probably righter about this than he realizes. Certainly vis-à-vis vicarious visuals, if not the phallantum of Errol Flynn in their flesh. Recently I was speaking to the editrix of an explicitly glossy women's magazine in Broadwick Street,* and she said lots of her readers, mostly women, write in to complain about being exposed to depressingly below average flaccidity, when they would much rather drool over quivering erections of virtually any virile size, although hunky ones, please, if possible. I put it to Ms @@@@@ that surely in real life most women tend to be rather cagey about erections so long as to threaten lesions deep within them, or alternatively too thick to get into their mouths without risk of choking, or causing offence due to unwanted dental snagging on the glans. She agreed with me entirely about this, but pointed out that real life had nothing to do with her magazine, and was there any reason why her young women [*sic*] shouldn't have their wild priapic fantasies too? Absolutely not, I agreed, and therefore why didn't she oblige her readership with the full-frontal massive erect phalluses they so eagerly covet? Simply because the Government wouldn't let her, she replied. I invited her to confirm whether this was because the Government itself was spitefully bereft of quivering erections of any size, but Ms @@@@@ came over somewhat diffident on this point – almost coy, I felt – and declined to comment on the record.

   * *'Fishing for a titillating commission, eh? Apollinaire in Rohans!' [P.C.]*

Only very recently has a refreshing wave of counter-sex [*sic*] research been flooding out of particularly the dark continent as part and parcel no doubt of the third world's rejection of the economic stronghold so long imposed on it by the limp tied foreskin of decadent western capitalism.

Within the last twelve months, for example, a number of incisively revealing papers published by Professor Winston and Dr Miriam Ngoto of the University of Zanzibar have provided Sir Richard Burton's earlier findings with massively overwhelming corroboration.

Moreover it now appears that when the member of the quiescent Zanzibar male is in excess of 7.5 inches (or 19.05 centimetres) there is a definite tendency in erection for the organ not only not to expand in length but actually to contract by as much as ten per cent during intercourse itself owing to an immense sideways enlargement producing a lateral friction in conjunction with the vagina which, it is reported, on occasion can bring the woman's delectable ecstasy to the point of wall nigh [*sic*] fatal.

The controversial Ngoto findings were at first fiercely contested by the white anglo-saxon protestant academic community but the tide has now definitely turned again in the popular mind owing largely to an influential review article by ***** #### in the *New York Times*, which, in combination with the resurgent strength of the American dollar, has had the unexpected but additionally confirmatory effect of increasing by several hundred per cent the sale to American ladies in their forties of all-inclusive package holidays in Zanzibar.

English ladies of all ages would doubtless be flocking after them in droves, if only the pound were less pitiful.

This is the scientifically sexual state of play at the present time, and only last week the business news section of an English Sunday newspaper leaked a strong hint of hope yet for the pusillanimous penis due to major advances taking place daily in genetic engineering techniques. The work is of course being carried out in conditions of jealously guarded secrecy, and there may well be no truth at all in the rumour that it is being funded by the Kuka Koala Korporation.

# 56

# Succeeding at Sex in Truth!?

Wringhim's intentions, in the previous chapter, are patently satirical.

Less transparent, you may feel, is the intended writher on the point of his withering. This is not by any means you English (by which he means London) ladies about whom he is so seemingly gratuitously rude, but rather the insidious imperialistic meta-hypocrisy implicit in Sir Richard Burton's resolutely dutiful honesty with regard to the black man's white whale, and the painstaking exposure he gives it, at every opportunity.

Such strategies of self-deceived tunnel-view pseudo-empiricism, directly analogous with (and developmentally parasitic upon) the paternalistic Westminster Hawhaw sops thrown soothingly, at sedative intervals, to the Scotsman's pioneering intellect (financial acumen, heroism in battle, etc) are fundamental, in Wringhim's view, to the perpetuation of the dominance of any one superficially homogeneous nation, social class, ethnic group or sex-political party, over any other, or others. It is therefore morally incumbent upon every right-thinking intellectual (by which he means left) to tirelessly saw and chop and gnaw at the deepest roots of such cancerous strategies, from all angles simultaneously, and with every weapon in hor arsenal, not excluding obscurely symbolic puerile ridicule, until no support at all remains to the vast rotten hulk, save only its own dead weight, so that the very next breath of pure fresh air in the world, like the final straw on the old camel's back, will topple the dinosaur down.

Our own feeling is that, while Wringhim is correct in theory, and while we're right behind him in his campaign to liberate Scotland from the thrall of the wake of perhaps the least scrupulous colonizing robber-barony in history, for which we in Scotland have never voted, nevertheless he would be best advised to leave the brash pamphleteering to others with less literary kudos to lose, and concentrate himself more on more of the novels which are his major achievement, and whose merits – world-class by any criteria – fly the Scottish flag with vastly greater potential longterm profit than a few crude thrusts at the wankers in London, which thrusts in any case run the risk of alienating those many geographically English intelligences (not all of them feminine) sympathetic to the Scottish cause.

Take, for example, his characteristic jibe, in the quote above, about the precariousness of the relation between the utterances and the thought processes (if any) of English/London women. Now this, I think we can all agree, is embarrassing by any standard. It is, moreover, irrelevant to, substantially contrary to, and hence wholly detrimental to Wringhim's hot-potato concern: to lampoon the Sir Richard Burtons, etc.

Why, then, does he do it?

Well, we wish we could tell us it was just an unfortunate lapse, a hiccup of slapdasherry tossed off in a hacking hurry, but we can't. For the truth is that Wringhim, both as non-fiction proser and three-dimensional flesh/blood with male hormones, testicles, and all – *but never as an artist* – is almost as much of a male chauvinist swine as the eunuchs in the English government's cabinet. And in Wringhim's case this takes the form, not of *really believing* that London women are brainless, but rather of refusing – despite all strident feminist protestations to the contrary – to jettison the traditional labouring man's notion that, in order to be successful with women, *you must abuse them first*.

We don't mean – Heaven forefend – that Wringhim is apt to *rape* women, or spank their naked bent-over buttocks with the flat of his hornier palm, or to rough them up physically at all. But he is more prone than most would prefer to be rather gruff and curt with them, especially those with cerebral pretensions, and to exploit his intellectual advantages for the sake of scoring points which are cheap at the time, worthless tomorrow, and possibly costly later.

Witness his disgraceful remarks, at the Great Sex & Talent Debate, about techniques for 'banishing bad vaj niffs from built-up areas'. Certainly this had the immediate desired effect of removing the young feminist lecturers in English literature from the hall, and hence may have contributed to our side's triumph on the night. Yet how Pyrrhic might that victory prove, in the eventual light of the feminists' revenge?

Meanwhile no reports have reached our ears that Wringhim (assuming he wants to) has managed to sleep with the aforesaid feminist lecturers, or buy them conciliatory glasses of tepid white wine in McEwan's, or exchange the time of day with them in the College Club, or even have his latest work reviewed not unkindly in their seminar critiques. On the contrary, Parthian bitches like 'sick old man' and 'incurable brain damage' are often less like echoes fading, and more like snowballs rolling.

Similarly, never yet has he come within sniffing distance of realizing

his seldom-confessed burning ambition of being invited to be inter-
viewed by \*\*\*\*\*\* ###### on the prestigious minority-viewing London
Television Fartart Show, never mind being pressed to slink back to her
place for 'coffee afterwards'.

And more recently:

Wringhim's incorrigible testing to the limit of his churl-the-girls
theory has led to his having only himself to blame for being deprived
of the opportunity of having his *Succeeding at Sex in London* pamphlet
decently edited by Janet Rosencrantz, who politely declined 'for personal
reasons' to have anything further to do with it, and him, after browsing
through his first ten pages.[1]

There, then, are negative reasons in abundance for you, Wringhim, to
moderate your discourse in the vicinity of the fairest gender, and also to
divert your energies back away from ranting tracts, and reinvest in what
you do best, which is *The Scottish Novel Par Excellence*. You walk,
you see, in the deepsnow footsteps of Dostoevsky, and the stark divide
between the tender juicy fillets of your finest fiction and the overdone
tripe of your journalistic tirades is twice as wide as the schism twixt
Jekyll and Hyde.

To confirm all that for yourselves, ladies and gentlemen, you have

---

[1] In which Wringhim contrives to pack a condensed succession of
disgusting spoofs on Burton's obsession with traditional quack
Arab, Indian and African nostrums for contracting your own and
your neighbour's wives' elephantine vaginas down to a snugger
middle-class fit, meanwhile marginally inflating the measure
of your own most miserable member by virtue of a hot-pitch
poultice, and other urogenital metaphors too superficially third-
form for Westminster comfort. Refained Muswell Hillbillies such
as Janet may thus be excused for failing to intuit that the
flapping vortexical vagina of Wringhim's rapacious Elephant
Woman is at once the Draculean sucking by England of Scottish
hydroelectricity, North Sea oil, gas, timber, duties on whisky,
intelligence, and the spinal integrity of glottally articulate trade
union troublemakers. To an intellectual Scotswoman, *par contre*,
Wringhim's satirical symbolism is too bestially blatant to be
above contempt. His pamphlet mandala and its infelicities are
thus unexpectedly congruent with Norman Mailer's in *Why are
We in Vietnam?* – except a great deal more bloody disgusting.

only to dip and wallow for a week or two in Wringhim's mammoth *Rob Roy's Women*, where you will find subtly rounded portrayals of our best of selves every inch as tender and poignant as Maupassant's Jeanne,[2] Tolstoy's Anna and Joyce's Molly, and also the heartfelt but cunningly implicit and never biblebashed conviction that the surest way in the world of succeeding at sex is to be strongly constituted in body and mind, honest, compassionate, politically liberal with a small ell, female, and Scottish.

I put that to Wringhim in person one late evening last summer. It was after dinner at Audrey's, and he and I were sprawled on the vast settee inherited recently from her shrewish mother's shrewish mother, as that glorious Glasgow western sunscape streamed in through the tall first-floor windows of Audrey's professionally enviable flat overlooking the Botanical Gardens, just seconds away from the Headquarters of the fabulous Scotland Division of what Wringhim long ago renamed the English Broadcasting Corporation.

'In fact, Wringhim,' I put it to him tentatively, as I sipped at my second goblet of choice Montbazillac, while Wringhim swigged his third, 'if one were to make the elementary but nigh universal error of identifying your narrator with his author, one must surely crawl away ladled with suspicion that had Wringhim Knox himself been born a woman, then, for the sake of maximising his emotional and sexual enjoyment of life, he had for preference been a dike. Now why is that?'

Having had his first pint in McEwan's nearly five hours before, Wringhim was by now distinctly bellicose. His cheeks were flushed, his breathing heavier than most young wowser doctors would give you a best-rate death-benefit-policy report for, and his spectacles somewhat steamy. Peering through them at his empty glass, as though debating how to punish it, at me he sideways grunted:

'Fuck you, Seale.'

Being accustomed to this sort of code, I replied:

'Please answer the question, Wringhim.'

Ignoring me, he turned and gazed over his rims at the large roll-top desk in the corner of Audrey's large corniced living-room. At it was sat Jennifer Macpherson, in a short-sleeved and fetchingly-filled ninja T-shirt, and plying trigonometrical instruments in the manner of one intent on finishing her homework in time to still nip out and join her

---

[2] In *A Woman's Life* (as Penguin have translated *Une vie*).

undergraduate boyfriend in the pub. For a magnanimous moment I thought Wringhim was worrying that Jennifer might be distressed by the unsavoury tenor of our adult conversation. Then I realized he was merely assessing the prospects of pressganging Jennifer into saving him the trouble of a stroll back into the dining-room: to get another glass of wine.

Jennifer, however, was walled away from such dangers by personal stereo headphones flooding her head, to judge by the high peak squeaks, with Michael Jackson or Madonna. Wringhim, abandoning his hopes with a rather wet dissatisfied sniff, swivelled his visage back to face the sun, and grunted condescendingly at me:

'Women, Seale, are softer than you. Smoother. Smell nicer—'

'Now look here—'

'And many of them have nice warm and moist vaginas to comfort one.'

'Yes, but if you were—'

'They're gentler than you are, more generous, and have a lot more sexual energy.'

'How, pray, would you know?'

'So it's hardly surprising, Seale, is it, that if, in a slightly different world, I were condemned to be a woman, I would much sooner be sucked by Koo, than *fucked by swine like you?*' The interrogative he italicised with such florid aggression that I realized the time had come to yield: bound up from the settee, pluck his empty goblet by its fluted stem, and nugatorially offer:

'A spot more wine before coffee?'

Stalking the Montbazillac bottle back from the dining-room to the fridge, I discovered that concern with sexual success and its contrary had also pollinated in Audrey's kitchen that night.

'God, yes!' our hostess exclaimed passionately at her sink, from which she passed rinsed dishes to Koo.[3] 'Imagine doing anything so

---

[3] Despite her Senior Lecturer's salary, and the hardly negligible American royalties from her sixteenth-century-French-female-orgasms-and-indecision book, and my having assured her umpteen times that to use one judiciously is in the long-run both more cost-effective and environmentally friendly, and the ample space in her cavernous Victorian kitchen, Audrey persists in refusing to get herself a dishwasher. Now what can this possibly tell us that we don't already strongly suspect?

fundamentally disgusting, with someone you didn't really love.'

'Well, Audrey!' I announced myself brightly. '*You* certainly used to! Didn't you?'

Not my fault of course, but nonetheless regrettable, that I was unable to intuit from the two women's backs that some deeply emotional sharing of confidences had been taking place, in the context of which my light interjection inevitably must have come as such an exacerbating intrusion that Audrey had no alternative but to round upon me furiously, hot with tears, as she hissed:

'If you really believe that, Humbert, you're even more of a stinking shit than I imagined all along.'

'He's only winding us up,' remarked Koo pacifically, drying a casserole, 'so he can clone our hysterical responses into his novel.'

'Same as ever,' fumed Audrey, turning back to her sink. 'Just like Genet.'[4]

'What do you mean?' I objected sternly, being devoutly hetero-sexual.[5]

Audrey's explication, albeit somewhat disjointed, coming from a professional intellectual, in effect accused me very personally of the cheap treble-bluff of affecting to make myself out even more loathsome than anyone, especially my more intelligent readers, such as you, would consider credible – having on my covert agenda the entirely antithetical aim of subliminally manipulating the customer into wrongly supposing that underneath it all the narrator must be quite a nice chap really.

'You mean', Paul Chalicer politely asked Audrey an hour later, he and Rebecca having called by for a glass of port, on their way home from the theatre, 'not unlike Genet's obsession with taunting the culturally monocular and sexually insecure bourgeoisie by always introducing into his novels a character named Jean Genet, who is not merely revolting by virtue of being gay, but *multiply revolting* by virtue of being *passively gay*?'

'*Death of the fucking spirit!*' snarled Wringhim, who by that time was

---

[4] Cf eg *The Miracle of the Rose*. Whether Umberto Eco's *The Name of the Rose* borrows anything more than most of Genet's title had best be left to Rankles.

[5] To the best of my conscious knowledge. Koo agrees, although Audrey has been known to cast slurs, in the heat of some goaded moment.

roaring drunk.

An hour earlier, though, when I butlered to him the last two inches of Montbazillac, and before he started helping himself not illiberally[6] to the litre of duty-free over-strength Glenmorangie which Paul had brought back from Belgium for Audrey, Wringhim was still coherent enough to unpack with characteristic vigour his newly launched theme that women have more sexual energy than men, or certainly than I do.

It is, he said, all a function of evolution.

'We aren't flirting here, Wringhim, are we, with one of those disreputable selective-advantage arguments?'

Yes, we were. He nodded.

'What is the advantage, to the woman — or rather, to her as-yet-unborn offspring — in her having more sexual energy than me, if not you, Wringhim?'

In a simplified nutshell, for my benefit, he explained seriously, it is a matter of leaving the man so shagged out, at the end of shagging, that he is less likely to have an erection left to leap out of bed and rush off to shag another woman with — always with the attendant risk that he might then *stay* with that other woman, and father *her* children — than he is to fall asleep. And this is why — in the good old days, at least — you got less nocturnal bedhopping from your mature hard-working patriarchs than you did from younger studs: because the latter had not yet had as much of their stuffing shagged out of them.

'Hmmnnn,' I reflected. 'And yet we cannot deny, can we, that if, as sweetly I dream, you pluck out of my bed the satisfied woman — the one I have just shagged, as you put it — and replace her with another (similar age, comparably voluptuous, equally naked, not a militant-separatist-lesbian sort of feminist, and so forth) whom I have not shagged yet, and if then gently you shoogle my shoulder, to arouse me to consciousness of my windfall in the night, then miraculously you will discover that here I have a tolerable erection again, to shag this new woman with, will you not?'

Ah, yes, Wringhim replied, shaking his head in comfortable despair at my ingenuity, as his eyes lapped appreciatively all over the buxom exuberance of Jennifer, as with a decisive click she snapped the rolltop shut, slid up the volume control clipped to her belt, in the moment

---

6 'This is plagiarized from Evelyn Waugh's *The Ordeal of Gilbert Pinfold*, Chapter ??' [P.C.]

before – with nothing so taxing as a kiss blown at, word murmured to, or glance squandered on us – she bounded away to the pub. But that, said Wringhim, returning his attention grudgingly to me, only supported his point the more.

'In what way?'

My gallant new erection for the second woman was, Wringhim gave me to believe, merely the flip side of his current coin.

'In what way?'

In that the vaster the number of hapless females I contrive to squirt my sickly jissom into, then the greater the selective advantage to me, who am conceptually capable of fathering thousands of children, whereas none of all those pitiful women, whose lives I had ruined, could ever mother more than twenty.

'So *sexual* success, on either side of your current coin, equals *breeding* success?'

Certainly, Wringhim agreed, so far as my *genes* were concerned.

Not wanting to sidetrack Wringhim by rehearsing an in-any-case suspect holistic critique of sociobiological simplisticity, I continued:

'And my genes don't necessarily care hugely much about *me*, the whole Humbert?'

Once *I* had served *their* purpose, Wringhim nodded enthusiastically, my genes couldn't give a shit. That much was now beyond dispute – even if, on a merely emotional level, never mind the philosophical niceties, one couldn't help feeling Richard Dawkins was——

'And nomatter whether, personally, I end up like poor old Vesuvius, our prize Charolais bull, who had to be put out of his misery last Easter, aged barely ten, because, as Maggie put it, "his poor old penal was terribly bent"?'

Evidently Wringhim rather approved of this simile, for he chuckled a disgusting chuckle.

'*Black* coffee?' inquired Audrey pointedly, as she thrust steaming mugs in our faces.

It was last night, while the north-east blizzards from the Russian steppes blew down round our lonely country house, that the far-ago conversation of that pleasant summer's evening in Glasgow drifted back to me, like an unpublished chapter of Proust. It being Wednesday – Koo away on business, our satellite dish not yet cured of its dislodgement sustained during the recent wild gales from the west – I found myself (as I stroked the cat, temporarily unable to watch other people doing it on satellite television) again really *thinking* about this, our pivotal conundrum: what is it that really *constitutes* succeeding at sex?

We had by now, the cat and I, been through notch success, great-lay success, and breeding success – none of which, when closely examined, seemed nearly so desirable as it is puffed up to be every month, in the glossy magazines.

'What does it all amount to, Puss?' I wondered, massaging the rumbling neck of the largest black feline in the Greenadder valley, who never in his life has succeeded at sex in any sense, save avoiding it, and yet is supremely content.

And there was Wringhim.

Never, during the years of our acquaintance, have we known him to be 'with' a woman of any description. He's getting on a bit now, of course, but still has masses of energy – to succeed at sex with, if he wanted. Yet his active preference in life – as opposed to fiction – seems to be to leave the 'bonking to the wankers', as he puts it, while his own drives strive undistracted towards higher goals, such as getting his 'major philosophical essay' published before he dies, bringing to their united knees both the English government and their co-conspirators known as 'Her Majesty's Opposition', abolishing the monarchy entirely out of all Britain, and ensuring Scotland's triumphal secession from whatever is left of England.

And Audrey.

Well, she's had Jennifer, and that's breeding success of a sort, certainly in terms of biological quality. And she's had me, and that's notch success for starters, followed by several other lovers since, one of whom presumably fathered Jennifer, since dates assure us I didn't, and all of whom, we would wager, will vouch for Audrey's being such a fantastically great lay that they could not possibly countenance being nibbled, pummeled and scratched; straddled, mauled and milked, with such violence; so many times a night, every night for the rest of their lives. Thus it would appear that great-lay success, just as much as notch success, lives in constant peril of collapsing into its opposite, which may explain why Audrey too, to the best of our knowledge, has lived a very celibate life in recent years, though this may also have had something to do with not wanting her young teenage daughter to overhear the tumultuous crescendos of her mother and chum hard at it.

'All very unsatisfying, Puss,' I complained, as I poured a modest dram. 'Perhaps, then, there is *no such thing* as succeeding at sex? Eh? Perhaps, in truth, it's all really *failing at sex* – greasepainted up as its opposite, to dupe the punters for a few cheap votes, like the Prime Creep's colossal sincerity. Haar??'

Captain Claws DSC responded amiably by rolling over on his back, paws akimbo, and mischievously daring me to attempt to tickle where his pillocks might have been.

Who can tell, therefore, what carnal crimes and punishments might have ensued in those next few moments, had not my cushion-smothered cordless telephone come alive with a Taiwan burp?

# Innermost Secrets

'Yes?'

'Humbert! Paul here. How are you?'

'Well, well . . . where are you, exactly?'

'London!'

'Ah.'

'I got back from Paris' – where he had been promoting the French translation, in fifteen volumes, of his *Quintain* – 'last night, and I'm off to New York tomorrow.'

'I see.'

'So I thought I'd better ring you.'

'Charmed.'

'Are you all right, Humbert? You're not pissed are you? I realize it's getting a bit late for you country folk—'

'No, Paul. Thank you. Please don't rubbish the Archers. And no, I'm not pissed.'

'Yes? But?'

'Now you mention it – in person, like this – I recall being a bit *pissed off.*'

'That's bad. What about?'

'Well, Paul. You haven't exactly been supplying screeds of hypertext to my chapters lately, have you? And we wouldn't want Amnesty not to get my money's-worth out of you for them, now would we?'

Paul laughed pleasantly, in his inimitable charming style. 'I thought you'd say that,' he said teasingly.

'So?'

'That's why I'm phoning instead. Because I haven't got time to write.'

'To tell me . . . ?'

Reverting to a sober tone cultivated for the mild admonishment of ungrateful undergraduates, in the years before his overnight success as a novelist enabled him to jack in teaching, Paul began:

'There is, I think, a problem with what you're doing.'

'Only one?'

'I mean that by adopting what I've called your "Nabokovian" technique, you take on a huge risk. Nor, in my view, do you entirely escape the consequences of that risk.'

'The risk being?'

'That your pompous, long-winded, rambling, and self-indulgent—'

'Anything else?'

'Narrator might eventually, after several hundred pages, just manage to worm his way up one or two readers' noses.'

'Such as yours?'

'Mine', said Paul with dignity, 'is not the only nose in the literate world.'

'Perhaps not,' I riposted gently, 'but it's a nose in more of a hurry than it used to be. And I wonder how many of those magical classics – crammed with pompous, long-winded, rambling, and self-indulgent deathless prose – it has hovered over lately, that it used to savour with such love? Anyway, what medicine are you prescribing?'

'Give your bloated text an enema,' Paul advised me sternly. 'Rewrite your dialogue with all the truck drivers in Cleveland in mind, and cut your length by half.'

'It's good of you to be so frank with me, Paul,' I thanked him sincerely. 'And I agree that were one merely churning out what one hoped would be seized on as a tailormade treatment for a two-hour Hollywood movie, then your diagnosis would be correct, and your remedies appropriate. But since I know you know the present opus was never targeted at Cleveland, and since there is no abundant lack of two-hour Hollywood movies in the world, and since even the worst of those movies costs millions of dollars to produce, whereas a novel requires humbly thousands, then shouldn't we feel, you and I, a certain responsibility – almost a *moral* responsibility – ' I emphasized grandiloquently, 'to occasionally embrace those prickly risks which Hollywood, thanks to its bank managers, simply cannot afford? You know? To nourish a little the life of the fucking spirit, as Wringhim would put it, and to preserve from extinction the occasional grammatical structure – above and beyond "Come on, let's go!" – which facilitates civilized thought?'

'You would be right, certainly, Humbert,' Paul agreed, 'in an ideal world. But where is that?'

'I'm sorry to say, Paul, that *I* am going to have to be a bit critical of *you* here.'

'Oh dear.'

'Yes. Because it seems to me you're in terrible danger of becoming the sort of reader who impatiently skips and flicks through 'The Tale of Foolish Curiosity' in *Don Quixote*, and Tristram Shandy's adventures in France, and 'the Man of the Hill' in *Tom Jones*, and the landscape-gardening sequences in *Elective Affinities*, and the chapters on the structure of the sperm whale's head in *Moby Dick*, and every single word of *Middlemarch*, and that, even more alarming still, you sound every inch the epitome of an author who's recently spent a disgruntling two hours with his publisher.'

Then, as Aldous Huxley said so often:

There was a silence.

'Well?'

'It's true,' said Paul at length.

'What is?'

'I did see ***** ###### this afternoon.'

'About your trilogy?' A one-volume collection of three novellas, cunningly interwoven and a-temporally multifaceted in what some critics would call The Canadian Style.

'Yes.'

'And what did he say? Does he like it?'

'He was *ecstatic*.'

'Of course. But does he *like* it?'

'So *ecstatically*', hissed Paul, 'as to only politely wonder whether I wouldn't mind substantially rewriting it, cutting the length by thirty-five per cent, changing the title, and postponing publication for a year.'

'I think you'll find', I said sympathetically, 'that the root reason is simply that they can't afford to publish you this year.'

'What do you mean?'

'They made a heavy loss last year, paying out ridiculous advances to keep ****** #### and *** ###### on their list. It's money they'll never get back, as they now realize. So they'll be pinching pennies from even such luminaries as you, Paul, in the desperate hope of saving their own skins from their holding-company overlords' accountants. Dinosaur publishing is dead, and has been for some years. Unfortunately, the larger the dinosaur, the longer – like a mammoth headless chicken – it tends to cling on to the illusion of vitality, flailing and flapping like a blind Godzilla snatching at a King Kong who never was there, until its lifeblood drains away. Boo-hoo.'

'I suppose so,' said Paul sadly. 'But I think what got me most, you know, was that he obviously hadn't found my book at all funny. "N–no, Paul," he admitted, over his sherry trifle. "I thought it a very – how shall

I put this? – mmm, *wise* book, but I couldn't honestly swear to you that I found it remotely *funny*."'

'Clearly,' I commiserated, 'his financial anxieties have impaired his sense of humour. But at least he didn't also accuse you, or rather your narrator, of being pompous, long-winded, rambling, and self-indulgent – or did he?'

'Not exactly,' said Paul vaguely. 'Though he did have this stupid quibble about the title.'

'What title did you propose?'

'*The Three Prongs.*'

'Interesting. But ***** didn't warm to it?'

'Like polar ice.'

'Failing to perceive, I take it, the oceanic depths of implicit Neptunical metaphor, the lovingly playful parabolic allusions to culturally parallel phenomena such as *The Three Stooges*, *Three Blind Mice*, *Three Men in a Boat*, *One Supernumerary Nipple*, and so on, but rather fastening exclusively on the superficially crude and provocative reference to the waggling wig billies in the Aubrey Beardsley cartoons?'

'Exactly. Especially when I also suggested he should reproduce the said genitalia, full-frontal, on the front of my jacket.'

'You spoke in jest?'

'But of course.'

'Did he get the joke?'

'Not a bit of it.'

'Then did he reject your outrageous proposal for fear of being done for obscenity?'

'Not ostensibly. The principal commercial objection, he said, was that ******** #### must be seen to continue to market only books clad in gorgeous full-colour jackets, else the trade might suspect them of being in financial difficulties.'

'Clearly,' I deduced, 'their financial difficulties are already more dire than even I imagined, and the attendant anxieties, helped along by all that alcohol, have softened the poor chap's brains. Probably, too, his wife is more given to her own book at bedtime than she was on their honeymoon pillow.'

'He did say something about difficulties at home,' mused Paul.

Here, at last, was the juicy opening I'd been waiting for – to enlist Paul's wit, wisdom and familiarity with foreign parts, on the side of the angels: in our quest to clearly formulate for Louis *the secret of succeeding at sex*.

'Wish I knew!' exclaimed Paul mysteriously.

'Oh, come on, Paul. Be generous.'

'Well,' he said thoughtfully – he's a nightbird, Paul, and his mind continues to energize into the small hours – 'is it not true that on the phallus-adorned door of the brothel at Pompeii was inscribed:

'*Here dwells happiness!?*'

'If you say so.'

'And in the long-lost *Last Tango in Paris* Marlon Brando indicates his member and instructs the nymphette fatale:

'*This is your ha-penis* – ?'

'Yes. I remember that bit.'

'Well,' cried Paul excitedly, 'what finer twin symptoms could you ask for?'

'Of what?'

'Of Nature's Great Deception! Urging, to deafening applause from desperate consumer-society salesmen, that the peachier skin and riper melons of a Marilyn Monroe, or the heftier genitals of a Blazes Boylan, would yield us infinitely greater pleasure and happiness than the modest middle-class charms of the little boys and girls next-door! Especially – in your case, Humbert – the little girls!'

'Thanks, Paul. But seriously: are you suggesting that succeeding at *sex* is merely a special case – indeed, a rather confused, because genetically deluded case – of succeeding at *happiness*?'

'Isn't it *obvious*?' chortled Paul.

'Then how does one succeed at happiness?'

'If you go along with sensible bourgeois comedy – which is also the paradigm of optimism, and hence, despite all glaring evidence to the contrary, an enduring sideshow in the Great American Dream – you will invariably find that the curtain is dropped at, or shortly before, *the wedding!*'

'Example, please?'

Paul cleared his throat in the manner of someone taking a discreet peek at his watch, with his telephone bill much in mind. Then magnanimously he continued:

'At the close of Shakespeare's aptly titled *Much Ado About Nothing*, Benedick says:

'*Come, come, we are friends. Let's have a dance ere we are married, that we may lighten our own hearts and our wives' heels.* Something like that. *Strike up, pipers!* And so on.'

'Dance, then exeunt to humpy-grumpy in private?'

'Indeed.'

'So?'

'The audience goes home temporarily reassured that *everyone lives happily ever after!*'

'Whereas, in the profounder truth of tragedy, they don't?'

'Absolutely not!' enthused Paul. 'And why not? Because *human happiness* in the lofty sense of Lifelong Bliss *is utterly inconceivable!*'

'Why is that?'

'Because it would imply the successive unthwarted satisfaction of all our desires.'

'Which would be unbearably tedious?'

'Yes. Even if it weren't biologically impossible.'

'Why is it so impossible?'

'For the simple reason', explained Paul patiently, 'that we are so constituted, being so geared up for self-preservation, that as soon as − or very shortly after − one desire is satisfied, another two or three rear up their gorgon heads. Louder, stronger, and more difficult to satisfy than the last.'

'Our appetite for good fortune is bottomless?'

'Mine certainly is,' confessed Paul. 'Isn't yours?'

'You mean, supposing you get an advance of half a million for your *Three Prongs* today, which makes you delirious tonight, tomorrow you'll be festering again with resentment at the advances they pay \*\*\*\* \*\*\*\*\*, and itching like a schoolboy on a sunny Friday afternoon for the day your film rights break all records?'

'That's life!' said Paul, and I could hear him grinning hugely.

'So if, say, my own current favourite fantasy were suddenly to erupt into three-dimensional flesh, erogenous tissue, clouds of sexual steam, and all, like a gorgeous lusting film star bursting forth from the great flat screen, and tiptoeing naked up the aisle to worship on the altar of my personal thighs . . . *even if,* I say, my fondest filthy dream came true, it would not augment by one hard-currency sou my tiny capital sum of durable happiness in this life?'

'What is your fondest filthy dream?' asked Paul in guarded tones.

I told him.

'What? Good heavens!' he protested. '*Both* of them? In the *same* bed? At the *same* time? Really, Humbert, this is worse than any of us feared. Much worse.'

'It's really no more disgraceful than the film producer's fantasy in James Jones' *The Merry Month of May*,' I retorted. 'Well, not much.

And at the same time it's so much more inventive that, so far as I know, it's never before been done. Not even in sixteenth- or seventeenth-century France. Also, Paul,' I emphasized gently, 'it *is* only a *fantasy*. And the difference, you see, between myself and your genuine psychopath—'

'Does Koo know about this?'

'Certainly not.'

'Audrey?'

'You must be joking!'

'What'll you give me', inquired Paul with lightning menace, 'not to tell them?'

'Well, Paul,' I sighed, 'if, after all we've been through, all the creative experiences, confidences, and bitching about publishers we've shared, you now want in one careless utterance to ruin my life absolutely beyond repair, well, I suppose there's not terribly much I can do to stop you. Not, that is, until after the Judas fact, at which time I would immediately and without futher warning—'

'As you say, Humbert,' he chuckled affably, 'I must be joking. But the point is – don't you see?'

'See what?'

'That if my harmless threat experiment can catapult you into such trepidation, and nightmares of Gorbals vengeance, how much more misery, alienation and destruction must you heap upon yourself, if these wildest obscene imaginings of yours were ever to fruit in the flesh? In these terms, again, there simply is no happiness that lasts. And the correlation between such episodic peaks of joy and planes of passing content as there are, on the one hand, and frenetic sexual activity, on the other, is almost certainly negative.'

'But look here,' I objected. 'You're saying all these sad things too smugly. Whereas to look at you, and converse with you, and share a curry with you in the Taj Mahal, everyone would be hard put – since you became a successful novelist – to think of any other successful novelist they knew half as happy and sexually successful as yourself.'

'You may well be right there.' Paul sounded surprised, as though he hadn't considered the matter previously.

'And yet it's obviously not a function of looks.'

'What do you mean?' he demanded suspiciously.

'Only – no offence – that since you're obviously now plumper, greyer and more wrinkled than you were before you became a successful novelist, it can't possibly be your looks which have boosted your happiness and sexual satisfaction. Indeed, if you recall that afternoon last autumn, when the two of us were strolling down dear old shower-swept University Avenue in our raincoats, you will also remember that the gaggle of gossiping and giggling female undergraduates with high breasts and lithe thighs, who nearly trampled us into the gutter without apologizing, not only were *ignoring* our presence in the flesh but actually were *failing to perceive* our very existence as sexual entities.'

'That's true,' agreed Paul equably. 'You might as well be a lamp post.'

'So it's not the looks, and neither can it be the fact itself of being successful as a novelist – since there are other successful novelists who are obviously wretchedly unhappy and probably incapable of any sexual satisfactions undeserving of long prison sentences.'

'Right again, Humbert! Though perhaps you'd better not print the names of ***** ###### and ***** ####### in this regard.'

'Again, it can't be merely a matter of money—'

'Not merely,' interrupted Paul seriously. 'Though it would be folly to repudiate money as a miraculous emollient.'

'*Money can't buy me love!* sang the Beatles.'

'So they did. But also? *Gimme money! That's what I want!* And why? Because money, you see, Humbert, is happiness in the abstract. It can't itself be consumed, but it represents (even if it can't always purchase) all the good things a man or woman (and by extension his or her lover) *might* possess. This is why, unfortunately, a rich and famous Beatle will be loved by more people than the same Beatle unknown and destitute.'

'If not loved to death.'

'That's always a risk of bubblegum fame. Fortunately for novelists, few of them ever get to be facially famous at that very low level.'

'Except . . . '

'Ah, yes. Very sad.'

'Look, Paul,' I commanded him. 'It was frightfully good of you to phone tonight, having neglected my chapters for so long, but me and Captain Claws here is coming over pleasantly drowsy, don't you know, having been pickaxing ground-elder roots like knotted elephants' trunks all afternoon—'

'Nothing to do with malt whisky, I don't suppose?'

'And you – when do you leave for New York?'

'Eleven o'clock tomorrow morning,' replied Paul nonchalantly.

'Then I imagine you've still got a mountain of housework to catch up on – kitchen sink to excavate, Y-fronts to drip-dry, and other less mentionable matters – so I'll not keep you any longer tonight, provided only you now dictate concisely, for the benefit of all our readers, *the fundamental innermost secret of succeeding at sex.* No more coy shillyshally prevarication over jejune accoutrements such as money. What we want now is the essential lowdown inside dirt. Okay?'

'Was it not Hobbes', Paul sniffed speculatively, 'who said:

'"All the delights of the heart and every cheerful frame of mind depend on our having someone with whom we can compare ourselves and think highly of ourselves."?'

'We'll take your words for it.'

'And is this not true, for many people, even if the someone else isn't even human?'

'As in?'

'*You **cruel** cat, Captain Claws!* Or *You **hateful** hound, Huckleberry!*'

'We've never heard our goddaughter say: *You **glaikit** goldfish, Goldilocks!*'

'No, but that's because cats and dogs have four legs – twice as many as us – whereas a goldfish has no legs. Mull over that one at leisure later, Humbert. My present point . . . '

But this brings us to a rather embarrassing confession. Namely, that I am not actually at liberty to impart to you Paul's personal formula for succeeding at sex – which certainly would strike many readers very much as Darwin's theory of evolution struck Thomas Huxley,[1] and which should be at least as legally patentable as a page of DNA code. The reason for my reluctant silence? Paul's insistence – not unreasonable, from his point of view – that before he told me his secret, I must tell him mine.

'What?' I expostulated, suddenly wide awake again. '*Which* secret?'

'Of *still* being a successful novelist', said Paul grimly, 'in the year two thousand and ten.'

'Come on, Paul!' I scoffed self-deprecatingly. 'That was just a bit of late-night curry-house bravado. A joke, if you like, to needle that prat Rankles.'

'No, it wasn't,' observed Paul acutely. 'I know you think you're on to something. And even if it turns out to be twaddle, I want to know what it is.'

Well, since for common-sense tactical reasons, to do with protecting intellectual property and hopefully quite a lot of future income, I was obliged to swear Paul to Hamlet-like silence for fifteen years with regard to *my* secret, I could hardly with credible dignity have complained when

---

[1] How absurdly fucking obvious! Why didn't I think of that?

Paul reciprocated by demanding of me an identical oath with respect to *his* secret.

The upshot, from the standpoint of yourself considered as box-office, may well appear understandably exasperating, and for this we can only apologize profusely, and hope you will in time divine Paul's secret (though not mine) for yourself, if you order an integrated siege to be mounted, simultaneously by the convergent and divergent divisions of your personal intelligence service, upon the following quotations juxtaposed:

'Breeding in many animals takes place only at certain times of the year, and an annual rise in testosterone level at those times serves a dual function. It increases the male's tendency to court and copulate, and it renders him a more apt combatant in any conflict that may arise, whether with another male over a female or with the female herself over the object of his desire.'[2]

*So for an animal who can breed/copulate at **any** time of the year?*

'It would make any man cold to lose,' grumbles Cloten.[3]

'But not every patient man is after the noble temper of your lordship,' protests a flunkey lord. 'You are most hot and furious when you win.'

Cloten rages impatiently:

'Winning will put *any* man into courage. If I could get this foolish Imogen, I should have gold enough. It's almost morning, is it not?'

'Day, my lord.'

'I would this music would come: I am advised to give her music o' mornings. They say it will penetrate.'

And this crystalizes for us the supporting role of the present and the three preceding chapters — which is, obviously, to gird our spiritual loins for coping with ☞

---

[2] From *The Tangled Wing*, by Melvin Konner, Chapter 9.

[3] Shakespeare, *Cymbeline*, 2.3.

# 58

# Succeeding at Sex Not At All

In the long run we're all doomed to failure.

We'll die. Our children will die. Our achievements will be forgotten. Eventually our species will perish. The sun will expand and gobble up our planet. The universe will implode to a dimensionless point, and all trace of us will be squeezed out.

Or something equally cosmically nasty will happen, to end for ever the long string of our successes.

In the meantime:

Most of us, perhaps spurred by a dim awareness that Failure awaits us in the end, remain very keen on winning.

'Everyone's a winner, baby!' the pop song optimistically urges, recognizing the exploitation potential of the average record buyer's dread of being a loser.

Even if we deny that we personally are win-crazy, we constantly, often unthinkingly, employ a win-good vocabulary. Talking about:

- Winning a share of the market.
- In *Vanity Fair*, the Major 'swore he would be the winner of her'.
- Winner take all.
- Winning the day, field, toss; the Count of Soissons's confidence.
- Winning over the King of the Huns.
- Winning the cup final, star wars; Cardinal Richelieu's respect.
- And sexually, Valentine's advice to the Duke, in *The Two Gentlemen of Verona*: 'Win her with gifts, if she respect not words.'

Valentine's suggestion shows how often *winning* is close or identical to *possessing, owning; gaining possession*. This is particularly clear in French, where 'gagner' means both 'to win' and 'to gain'.

'Faint heart never won fair lady.'

No more true than:

'Faint heart never won a profitable slice of the market.'

Yet how much more romantically significant.

475

Winning often concerns coveting, desiring, striving for, and acquiring some desirable property. Be it a fat cheque from Littlewoods, a dream holiday for one in Zanzibar, or the longed-for hand in marriage of the beautiful Hélène Arnault.

And what could remind us more forcefully of how abjectly miserable Louis Morel must feel, during the May and June of 1641, as he trains up his criminal troops in the woods and hills surrounding the little Ardennes village of Saule where they finally bivouac, and lies awake at night too fatigued to sleep, and plagued by an endless Maypole dance of flaunting thoughts, any two of which, taken together in whatever order, as major and minor premise of nomatter what syllogism, inexorably imply the same irrefutable conclusion: that his life is the most futile of failures?

For have not even his occasional seeming successes been but minor molehills preluding great mineshaft failures following? His besting of the Marquis of Roquefort in that early duel at Lestelle? Quickly followed by his banishment to Zaragoza. The eager discarding of his virginity into the maja's unresisting body. Causally responsible, Louis has now persuaded himself, for her suicide the following day. His honourable disposal of the corpse of the lascivious priest she had murdered? Directly to blame for the bitter estrangement between Louis and the Chevalier. The impulsive insinuation of his hands beneath Hélène's dress, by the riverbank near Lourdes? Leading as day into night to his tussle with Jean-Baptiste, and hence his second flight to Spain, believing – right or wrong – that he had killed the same good-hearted lad as had earlier saved him from drowning in the pool above the mill. And all the woes cascading after that?

Desertion of his parents, alienation from them; final unforgivable failure to be reconciled with his mother before her death. Hence no hope of petitioning her to renege on her deathbed admonition:

'Dear Louis. Of course Hélène is a lovely girl, but she absolutely *is not worthy of your lineage*. Moreover you have known her *as your sister*. Think of that. By all means *protect* her, *as you would your sister*. Feel not only free, but obliged by your duty, to settle a handsome dowry upon her. *As you would your sister*. But promise me, Louis, I implore you, grant your mother's final wish: that never, so long as you enjoy breath in this world, shall you marry so far beneath you, as the daughter of Maître Arnault . . . '

And then, as it were a thunderbolt sent from a vengeful heaven to punish his seeding hopes of deceiving himself into faith that his mother would soon have come round to accepting such a marriage, if only they all could have been reunited before her death, the callous intimation from Achilles in Paris, that Hélène:

' . . . is nothing by birth, if your lordship will pardon the expression, but a lowly bastard foundling. Whom my father purchased in a tavern some Saturday evening, following a characteristically niggardly bargain he had wrung from a desperate midwife on the run, for crimes against humane anatomy which she had inadvertently committed in Provence.'

Thus, while what Louis longs for above all else in the universe, during the endless second quarter of 1641, is to *marry* Hélène Arnault, he is at the same time resolutely persuaded that this could never be, *even if* he could somehow unbind himself from the coils of his mother's dying wish – since not only is it now manifest that Hélène is 'so far beneath you, as the daughter of Maître Arnault', but further that she is so very much further beneath him, by birth, as the daughter of a Rhône-side whore and any one of a quick succession of drunken sailors on Saturday night.

For all that, he yet loves Hélène so very much that he would gladly sacrifice his reputation, if he had one, his rank, even his very inheritance, if his father has not already disowned him, just to be with her for the rest of his life – to live with her in a condition of humble and sinful yet tender concubinage, pay homage to her beauty, worship her spiritually, enjoy her sexually, and even father upon her a brood of lusty sons, and some ravishing daughters besides, who, despite the lowly distaffal denominators of their ancestry, and their ineligibility to continue the long proud tradition of the Sieurs of Morel, would nonetheless mature into the most splendid specimens physically, and morally, and would be a tremendous credit and comfort to, and loyal and fond support of, their father and mother in their twilight years.

And so on, and so forth.

Still, even this more modest dream of second-best bliss now seems precisely that. A dream. A wild fantasy, in fact. Given that, to add to all his other feelings of discontent, doubt, filial defection, remorse, massive general inadequacy, etc, he now has to live with the knowledge that:

'Most tormenting of all, amongst my myriad failings, was a scourging sense of final futility, founded upon the attempt I had made, and made unsuccessfully, to rescue my Hélène from the enemy; from the braggart young Baron Charles de Châtillon, who coveted her without love, without respect, without honour, and thus without right, and who nonetheless remained in possession of the immense advantage, over me, that physical possession of the lady's person was at the disposal of his uncle, the Maréchal, albeit that he had vowed to me, on his honour as a soldier, that Mademoiselle Arnault should not be wed against her will . . . '

There. Exactly. Not be wed *against her will*. But what was her will? How might it change? Women were incorrigibly fickle, were they not? Even before Mozart, although Louis could not know this. But he had evidently read a bit of both Rabelais (who warned that women have a passion for what is forbidden) and the more moderate Montaigne, whose moderation still counselled that:

'Women . . . are more easily led by the ears' than men.

So?

If Hélène should tire of waiting for him, should despair of ever seeing him again? Or, in the most appalling possible scenario, should develop certain sexual urgencies of her own? Was she not, too, entitled to some second-best consolation – or worse, in the case of that Charles? And then again:

The Maréchal's grim undertaking bore a rowelling rider: *while yet I draw breath in liberty*, he had said. Well. Suppose he lost his liberty. Suppose he somehow managed to alienate the Cardinal, and thence got stuck in the Bastille. What then? Or his breath. Suppose he lost that altogether, and for ever. Indeed, was not part of the purpose of Louis's own sojourn in the Ardennes geared to just such deaths? Of the Tyrant Cardinal – hence, by extension, his loyalist supporters, most notably the Maréchal de Châtillon. But if so, having inadvertently experienced, been reluctantly saddled with, and foolishly brought upon himself such a dismal catalogue of other failures in the past two years, how could Louis be sure that the campaign of the Count of Soissons against Richelieu might not end in some similar shambles: the outcome indecisive, the Cardinal still at large and dominant in Paris, and the Maréchal dead on some battlefield south of Sedan.

Following that?

Hélène would be stranded in Paris, with no gallant gentleman to intervene in the matter of her grafting father's bestowing her – for gain, and uncaringly in the teeth of her weeping remonstrations, and revulsion – upon that abominable midget nephew Charles, who by now would have fallen heir to his uncle's great wealth and estates. Louis himself, meanwhile, if not also killed – or maimed beyond conjugal feasibility – would be outlawed from France for ever.

So what was his only hope?

'It lay', reflects Louis, 'in the prospect of a clear and absolute vanquishing of the royal forces under the Maréchal, whereupon the position of the Cardinal would be undermined beyond repair, the secret armies lying in wait within Paris would rise up, depose the tyrant, throw open the gates of the Bastille, and welcome with open arms the triumphal return of the Count of Soissons to the capital . . . ' as successful deposer of the megalomaniac oppressor Richelieu, benevolent liberator of the King from his evil genie, and hence as glorious Champion of a Reunited France.

All that, and much more.

And with Louis conspicuously heroic on the side of right, and of mighty victory in decisive battle, how could he then fail to prise Hélène from the clutches of the defeated ogre's underlings, and spirit her away back south: to a lifetime of quiet harmony and happiness together in Bigorre?

'It was scattered thoughts, and occasional wild hopes, such as those,' he admits, 'that gave me strength to carry on, in those months preceding the conflict, to accustom my men to the discipline of soldiery, to moderate their nightly debauches among the camp-followers that plagued us, yet to do so without dousing their fire, and also to cheer the uncertain spirits and stoke the resolution of the Count himself, during my weekly reports to our headquarters in Sedan; all this in contradiction to, nay, in very defiance of, the deep depression within my own soul.'

Louis does not say so explicitly, but if we probe a little between his lines we see that the depth of his depression (which certainly was so deep that he gives us virtually no incidental detail on the minutiae of barracking life in those months: billet conditions, stabling, weaponry, armour, catering, latrines, inter-troop rivalries, brawls, floggings, singsongs, carousings, whorings, pox potions, blood-lettings . . . all these details and many more we must imagine for ourselves) is due not only to the profound feelings of inadequacy, failure and remorse with regard to the past noted above, but also to a powerful undercurrent of misgivings, conscience and guilt relating to the flat limbo present and most likely hellish future.

*Misgivings?*

Because Louis, in his heart of hearts, realizes full well that the Count of Soissons, though personally more amiable, does not and never will possess the leadership charisma of Richelieu. He, the Count, is mentally less astute, morally less resolute, and constitutionally less energetic – than him, the Cardinal. Thus, the Count's popularity has not been positively earned by his qualities, but rather negatively conferred:

by the ever-swelling shadow of the Cardinal's *un*popularity. And Louis, imbued with such perceptions, is unable to convince himself that such a fundamentally lesser man, made figurehead by birth and fortune – and no matter how strongly backed by battalions, cannon, and money from the King of Spain – will ever definitively topple a genius like Richelieu, whose supreme abilities and relentless application have all throughout his career seemed supplemented by the most disgusting dollops of luck. And yet, despite such gnawing disquiet, Louis *must* carry on to fight for the Count – or kiss goodbye for sure to Hélène.

*Conscience?*

Born of pricking intuitions that perhaps the course he is embarked upon is neither politically nor morally just – or approved by Him On High? For what, at bottom, is that course? If not to overthrow, bring to his knees, and so ensure the humiliation, possible torture and certain execution of the first minister of the greatest nation in Europe, hence the world? A nation whose very greatness today owes almost everything to the grand strategic statesman's vision and tireless diligence of that same minister throughout his career. And, all right, there have been a few more nasty incidents, suppressions of civil liberties, summary incarcerations in the Bastille and mysterious disappearances of troublesome individuals in the night than in an ideally constituted state one might wish – yet what other French politician stranded in history with raw materials still less than a hundred years on from the Saint Bartholomew Massacre might have served his country with such savoury soufflés, while at the same time cracking less eggs?

And so where does that leave Louis?

His situation, let us remember again, is hardly comparable to that of Pere Garcés in Catalonia, or Wringhim Knox in Scotland, where the objective is both clearcut and ethically unassailable: to win back, by peaceful means if possible, the dignity of truly autonomous self-governing statehood for a small but objectively distinct and unique nation, and to do so by hacking it free of the residual rotting tyrannical tentacles of an adjacent imperialist aggressor already well down the long, slow, spiteful slide into whingeing decadence and pan-continental nonentittyhood.

The Count of Soissons's goal, by contrast, is to rock and scupper a rival boat *within* the one great power – France – and to do so in defiance of the clearly stated will of its sovereign, Louis XIII, who may well be a constipated prune, and rather more gay (albeit in a furtive, moody and mean-spirited sort of way) than his missus might wish, but *is* nonetheless head of state, *King*, anointed, and supposedly *Divinely Right*. So is it, at the end of the day, legitimate to characterize the Soissons cause, and with it Louis Morel's own present endeavour, as a noble mission of liberationary revolution? Or more like Gross High Treason, tarted up with fine slogans, to film over the selfish motives beneath?

*Guilt?*

Well, with all that lot swilling round the bottom of your mind, and clogging up your heart, how, when you woke yet again with a jolt in the night, and realized again just where you were, and why, and how much you wished you weren't, and that all the bad dreams you'd just had were abundantly true, or about to become so, how could you deny that the shallow pools of chilling sweat in all the concavities of your shivering skin had poured, through the weakened defences of your sleep: from the source of all mortal guilt?

Turning again to the sex-life of the hero, which is what most writers, readers, ignorers, and especially reviewers of fiction are most obsessed with most of the time, whatever they pretend to the contrary:

Louis, characteristically, says nothing about it, but we would happily wager the entirety of Amnesty's earnings from this book that during those miserable military months alone amid the massing Soissons forces around Sedan he not only had no penetral contact or even casual consoling cuddles with strumpets, barmaids, widows and especially the Countess of Soissons's younger ladies in waiting, during his visits to report to the White Chief in the High Citadel, but he most likely, in the arctic-dark catacombs of his long-protracted gloom, got no ghosts of an erection at all.

But suppose a miracle occurs. And why not? For it is at least ten million times more credible than any reported at Lourdes. Like this:

The afternoon of midsummer's day in Sedan. Dry, sunny, and very hot; the climate has turned continental. The sky is so blue that the Meuse below could almost be the Rhône at Arles, or at least the Loire at Blois. Louis, in a shirt of rough ratteen beneath his light cavalry armour, is perspiring profusely as he ascends the long flat steps of the winding cobbled street up to the citadel above. In the moment of his pausing to rub his brow on the back of his sweat-circled wrist two shutters above him puff open. Framed in the window behind is the second-most beautiful girl in the world. Her hair is blonde, like Hélène's, but her eyes are dark and sultry; her cheeks plump and rosy. Tightly fringing her throat is a necklace of large scarlet stones, from which dangles a small gold crucifix. Beneath her chemise of gauze like haze she is stark naked, or certainly this is true of her full and firm and sharp-nippled breasts, which are as low down as Louis can see. He thus has no way of knowing whether she has a gangrenous withered leg below the belt, and certainly no such fear afflicts him. As, lazily, the vision of pulchritude's right hand wafts a small feathered fan to cool her eyes, Louis sees her little finger curl tight to a hook, as in the subtlest of blatant come-ons. By the time her demure but fine-fleshed lips are pushed out like a lubricating flower by the tip of her moistened tongue our hero already has accumulated an erection every millimetre as splendid as the one his mother was shocked to uncover while she bedbathed him back to recovery from his ordeal in the mountain snows.

And then, alas?

The miracle is exploded, the stupendous comeback erection flopped like the Tower of Pisa H-bombed from beneath, by this out-of-the blue salutation 'from by far the most treacherous gentleman in France':

'Monsieur Morel!' he cried [*writes Louis*], embracing my shoulders as with the warm familiarity of old comradeship. 'Why, how extraordinary! But what are you doing here? Surely – but you are tired, sir, and hot. As my lodgings are hard by, you will allow me sir, will you not, to refresh your dusty palate, with a flask of cool champagne?'

'Only the urgency of my imminent audience with his Highness', I was obliged to inform him, 'could possibly excuse the incivility of my having to decline, for the moment, the Marquis of Roquefort's most magnanimous offer.'

*And my spirits sank again.*

*Part V*

# Beyond the Ultimate Orgasm

# 59

# May Day – 199?

May Day.[1]

Dear Humbert,

Many thanks to Koo and you for a very restful and restorative weekend. Two weeks later here am I yet again returning your pages with exhortations to bring this opus to a climax. As to your proposed title, I can't help wondering if you haven't just stuck *Sex* into it with the utmost cynicism – in the same way as Koo was lining your loft with jars of jam and water, to lure the bluebottles in to drown? Thus cruising dangerously in the same flightpath as is already drastically overcrowded by:

Gyles Brandreth, Julie Burchill,
Alex Comfort, Charles Darwin,
Havelock Ellis, H.J. Eysenck,
Eva Figes, Michel Foucault,
Germaine Greer, Harriet Harman,
Christine Keeler,
Peter Mayle, Kate Millet,
Claire Rayner, Theodor Reik, William Rushton,
Roger Scruton, John Maynard Smith,
Laurence Stone, Miriam Stoppard, Thomas Szasz,
Reay Tannahill, Terence,
Kenneth Walker, Marina Warner,
Mary Whitehouse--[2]

As regards Paul Chalicer's criticisms, these are certainly plausible,

---

[1] Let no man or critic discount the alternative interpretation.
[2] Clearly Janet has a point here. However, we felt it best to cut it short before she went the length of Colin Wilson.

though not for the reasons he gives. It is rather (as with Bach and his chorales) that your audience needs to be constantly reminded of *what the tune is*. Not allowing it to drown in a stream of other harmonies. Any creative musician will have his first subject, second subject, etc – development, variation, recapitulation, coda – but we'll also get the occasional *statement*, to keep the theme 'in the ear'.

But what *is* your theme? *Are* your themes?

Or should we conclude that – like Sterne, Joyce,[3] Hegel, Marx, Sartre, Foucault, Hitler and most of our 'top politicians' today – your aim is to evade the capture of pinpointing by dint of impossible constructive plethora: *too many* themes, allusions, lies, contradictions, interpretations, sudden bareback switches in midstream from one flogged-to-dropping jade to a fresh young radically opposed superstud, and suchlike, for any one plodding-after intelligence to ever convincingly dissect? If so, you may well succeed, for there's no lack of idiots out there. But is this the sort of success you truly covet?

And if so, how deeply is it sexual?

Talking of which, I'm rather fed up with you making fun of my views on the swooningly virginal (?) Hélène, ideal romantic passion, and so forth, so I decline to say any more on that head. Louis Morel's second banner, or bowstring, it seems to me, is the ideal of gratification of the senses, and the troops mustering under this flagpole are certainly giving the book much of its seventeenth-century life. Louis's scattered amours are (in one case literally) a dance with death – flammable and fallible love that dies, as it does in the bed-chamber, because it cannot hold up for long. Yet, along this artery, his spicy flitting from scene to scene doesn't demand from him any commitment. Now the trouble with some of these set-pieces is that they are jolly good outlines, but what are they ultimately doing in the grand design?

There is a third army flying its pennant too, and that is the one engaged in a contretemps over commitment in human relationships – where sisters are not loyal to a brother's death, sons may or may not kill fathers, lovers steal a trusty friend's daughter, wives turn the sheets for . . . what else do you have, I forget?

---

[3] We in Scotland are inclined to excuse from this line-up both Sterne and the Joyce of *Ulysses*, though certainly not the Joyce of *Finnegan's Wake*.

(Actually, as chance would have it, this all chimes in rhyme with a current concern of my own.) But what I'm now hungering for most greedily, O Humbert my love, is *authorial point of view*. I'm looking for *resolution* of the mysteries in the plot (*does* Louis kill his father, and if so why?), and a deepening of my insight into the eternal comi-tragic human condition (*why* do people defy relationship?).

At the same time, and paradoxically (well, I am a woman, aren't I?) I find myself drawn, particularly as regards quality of characterization, to the present-day sections. The civilians here — the modem characters who converse and debate and journalize the concerns of the fighting cohorts from the comfort of their TV armchairs — I rather like this bunch, and the way they gently stretch the wires of the cages we all live in. Take the chapter on anal sex. Now could that have been a matter for idle social chat in any other age but this? And why? Yes! And where will it all lead? Not, I don't think (and I confess I'm not sure I followed every connexion between your [or should I say Wringhim's?] rather quaint ideas on this), to the sovereignty of Scotland.

Then to what?

More likely to more tea and toast,[4] without parental prohibition or manufactured guilt, just as soon as the hormones require it. In some ways like *Walden Two*,[5] I seem to remember, but with no rising hogwash of behaviourism to undermine its longterm foundations. What I'm getting at is that (although leaving the introduction of my Charlotte and her David until your Chapter 38 and then letting them disappear again until now is breaking the rules *very badly*, is it not?) it seems to me that your personal (by which I mean authorial rather than narrational, and in any case poorly hidden) agenda is to moralistically critique this brave new age when fondly conscientious mothers such as I slip packets of heavy-duty condoms together with *41 Ways of the Joys of Sex* into their teenage daughters' (note the plural) Christmas stockings and manfully do not swoon or even hurl a wobbly when the together fifteen-year-old [Veronica, younger sister to Charlotte, and every inch as exquisitely fetching] lets slip casually at breakfast what dear old Dr Schnickelgruber over in Golders Green

---

4  'This digression is not mine.' [H.S.]

5  By B.F. Skinner. Possibly the most believable and hence hideously depressing 'Utopia' ever written.

confided to her about the 'real risks' of ingesting AIDS off one virile heterosexual boyfriend who wouldn't dream of sharing his needle even if he used one when she went to petition him [ie Dr Schnicklgruber] yesterday for her first prescription of The Pill on the ground that at least for a few years while she was young and healthy enough she'd like to experience some at least of the forty-one ways of the joys of sex more authentically than as if she were obliged to wrap up in a flak jacket every time she took a bath.

Now isn't this parent-sanctioned child-parent frankness, you argue, insidiously tending to cream the delicious Circean tingle of guilt off the age-old gingerbread game? Why, yes. I too have views on guilt. Lots of them. Which I won't burden you with now, Humbert, thank you very much. Except:

*Freedom from guilt does not imply cosy boredom in bed.*

My theory is that it leaves you free to regard sex as part of a maturing relationship, not as some clandestinely snatched explosion, which, because of the aura surrounding it, is built up in the imagination as something that must be super-abundantly wonderful every time. That way lies the myth of romantic love (yes, I know, I called it an ideal before). I'm not saying our nineteen-year-olds aren't as romantic as any other generation – I think in some ways they are more so – but that denial of the physiologically natural leads to a *perverse pursuit of passion*. Your Louis Morel's desperate all-consuming (because unsatisfied) craving for the bimbo-wimp Hélène is a passable illustration.

Now this craving pursuit is in head-on conflict with tea-and-toast values.

And my reply to what I take to be your subtextual atavistic moralizing is that the tea/toast culture is ultimately to be preferred, and that what our sexually satisfied *and* familially unhounded nineteeners are more capable of doing than we were is *seeing each other as real people*. Bums might have ceased to be taboo twenty-five years ago, but now it's anuses too, and whatever you do or don't stick into them. Hopefully out of considerateness you'd play down the farcicality in an HIV-positive presence, but then you wouldn't go cracking Cyclops jokes in a blind asylum either.

Well, *I* wouldn't.

Either way, it's an ill wind that won't puff along at least one silver lining, and the maintenance of public good judgement and taste not only does not preclude but actually is crucially parasitic upon a constantly updated sense of private proportion which now expresses itself – certainly in our household at least once a week – in the most frankly revolting hilarity. If you fancy a graphic example you could try not splitting your sides in our kitchen overhearing my young ones rehearsing with lingering glee the utmost intimate details of the 'arsehole-boil removal' Charlotte's David underwent last week. I'll trade this for the risk of teasmade lust any day.[6]

For these reasons (I think, and not just because I'm one of them) your modem mufties seem to me to live and breathe off the page quite happily. Audrey and I now have more in common than I would have believed possible a year ago, and I'm looking forward very much to meeting her at the 'Female Textuality' conference in Oxford. Even Wringhim is undeniably colourful, although I wouldn't wish to wager in advance just how well I might get on with him in the flesh.

Paul Chalicer too.

Yes, I hope you'll introduce us personally before this book is done. I can probably find it in me to forgive him for urging you to write me out, and I'd like to talk to him about his *The Quintain*, which certainly is a colossal achievement – even if, I must confess, I didn't actually quite manage to finish it, and would certainly, in the old days, never have recommended that BirdDog buy the paperback rights. As you so rightly point out, most readers do a certain amount of judicious skipping – and your little list of skippable bits in The Greats leaves out all the war bits in *War and Peace*, not to mention the fact that one can turn over two pages stuck together in *Ode to Immortality* without appreciable loss of meaning and maybe five or six pages of *In Memorium*. It's occurred to me that Paul may have started out with some notion of making *The Quintain* the longest novel ever (in which case he's failed) and that you yourself might be trying to gazump him at this very moment.

---

6 I would have preferred 'teasemaid', and so would you if you'd ever met Charlotte, but we felt on balance that to fiddle with a lady's prose behind her back might not be wholly gentlemanly. Besides, Janet has since recanted and entirely abandoned her protractedly belligerent apologist position. Something to do with Charlotte and David (both aged nineteen) having requested a dishwasher-proof casserole for their Christmas present, which made her mother gag with long-ago-flower-power revulsion.

If so, take my advice and leave it to Whoeveritis. Probably some American.[7]

No, look. There has to be some ruthless soul-searching here. What's entertaining, story-impelling digression, and what's pure self-indulgence? What's nitty-gritty hardcore bodice-ripper, and what's incidental historical autobiography, not to mention superfluous documentary detail? A lot of your Christopher Sly stuff is pleasantly droll and a nice way of building up a new set of relationships that weave in and out of the ostensible main text (or should I say body text) like fingers in a cat's cradle. But fingers can get sticky sometimes, and I think in parts yours do. The secret with experimenting like this is to maintain the soufflé touch.

Let's not forget, after all, that while today's readers browse and skip, when they've already seen all the movies being broadcast tonight, tomorrow's readers may well not read at all.

In short, Humbert, since you ask me, I find the contemporary interruptions and intrusions (and not just the ones featuring me) to be much livelier and more authentic than even the best of the seventeenth-century dashing about, musketeerish dicing with death, lovers-poignantly-parted-again cliffhangers, and so on. In fact, I wonder how much of the autobiography of Louis Morel we really need at all. Couldn't you simply cut most of the novel proper and leave some scattered fragments of Louis as a skeletal backdrop to the footnotes and asides?

Only marked pages returned.

Luv,

J.

---

[7] 'No. Almost certainly German. Don't forget that when my *Quintain* is most expertly translated into German, it still goes to some 25% more words than it needs in English. Even worse, almost every word itself is longer, which bulks out the pages obscenely, and has the entirely unfair consequence that I personally am accused by militant German Greens of needlessly wasting trees! Seriously, though, German must surely be the ideal linguistic medium, must it not, for self-regarding pompous Krauts wishing to take the cake for interminable dilation? Has Janet attempted, for example, the *Zettel's Traum* of Arno Schmidt?' [P.C.]

'I entirely disagree with Janet,' remarked Koo over breakfast on the patio, when, in preference to our electricity bill, I had read out Janet's comments to her.

'About wanting less foreplay and more climaxes, you mean?' I conjectured.

'Certainly not.'

'Audrey always used to say all women always wanted *more* foreplay,' I reflected frankly. 'But then she would—'

'Please don't be more treacherously obscene than you have to,' murmured Koo, as she lovingly buttered up the second half of her second Marks & Spencer plastic-preserved genuine French croissant, which, like EBC radio in hissy mono, is the best you can get in these London-neglected parts of Scotland where there are thousands less people than sheep.

'Yes, but—'

'Besides which,' said Koo thoughtfully, 'I've heard there are lots of men who specialize in foreplay because they're no good at anything else.'

'Thanks awfully for your support,' I responded gratefully.

'No doubt the same is just as true of novelists,' added Koo with a knowing smile. 'But it doesn't follow that they have to spoil everyone's pleasant Saturday breakfast in the sun by telling disloyal dirty stories about what they did in bed with former lovers. So there.'

'Or had done to them,' I recalled with feeling. 'Thinking of which: did not Mrs Joyce also complain that her James had a dirty mind?'

'Are you attempting to suggest—?'

'Never for a moment! Only that I'm hardly unique, in the way my womenfolk traduce me. Look at Shakespeare too. Corny cracks – get it? – everywhere, my tongue in your tail, filth all over the place – if that's how you're determined to take it.'

'Shakespeare did it sparingly, did he not?' objected Koo. 'For dramatically essential comic relief. Whereas with you – according to Audrey, certainly – it's virtually a full-time job. More coffee?'

'Who's betraying confidences now?' I countered gleefully, to which Koo replied that there was a world of difference between a good woman chastening a bumptious male by exhuming at an opportune moment some choice encapsulation of his character defects as divulged in confidence by another good woman, on the one hand, and the same aforesaid bumptious male soiling the soul of his present good woman (whom no-one else could see how he could possibly deserve to possess, in any sense) by gloating over the haptic biological minutiae of his former nocturnal and Sunday matutinal cavortions with the second good woman (whom time had proved *too* good for him to hang on to ['in every sense?']), on the other.[8]

'Never mind all that,' I commanded Koo sternly, dunking the last of my croissant in the last of my coffee, and wondering if the sunshine would last long enough for me to be expected to attempt to start the Flymo, 'as Wringhim would say. Let's stick to the point, shall we?'

Following a pointed stream-of-consciousness aside to the effect that wasn't it amazing how the grass bordering the patio had been allowed to grow to higher than the slumbering width of Captain Claws' extremely ample shoulders, Koo obligingly retorted:

'Well? And what *is* the point?'

---

[8] 'Please record in one of your silly footnotes that what I actually said was concise and comprehensible.' [K.F.]

## 60

# July 1641

'The point is the nub. Of your entire disagreement with Janet?'

'I meant that my editing suggestions, were they invited, would be the exact opposite of hers.'

'Implying that you would incline to cut, or at least cut back, the armchair commentators – such as Janet, and to some extent even your-self – and concentrate exclusively, or at least more exclusively, on the real-life seventeenth-century saga.'

'Just so.'

'But why so?'

'I'm very fond of Janet, Audrey and Paul—'

'Not Wringhim?'

'You know how I feel about Wringhim.'

'But *even if* you were just as fond of him . . . ?'

'Since I know these people in the flesh—'

'Oh yes?'

'And since their lives and thoughts – well, some of them – are in many ways similar to mine, it really doesn't do much for me, when I sit down with a book at the end of a long hard day—'

'Or on Sunday morning with a half pint of chilled Stella, while your bumptious male prepares the lunch—'

'To read about persons, problems, intellectual fads, events, current affairs—'

'The loathsomeness of the Prime Creep, the disgusting condition of WhatRail? trains—'

'Incredible arguments for the sovereignty of Scotland, and so on, which I already know inside out.'

'You would describe yourself, then, less as an aficionado of Bert-Whistle-style confrontational music, or post-Artaud interactive drama in which naked actors with RADA accents suddenly leap off the stage to rush down the aisle and hurl themselves into your popcorn-laden lap, but rather as the sort of reader who prefers not to be molested at all by the narrator but on the contrary to be spirited clean out of herself by the novelty of the settings and scenery depicted, far away in space and/or time, the engaging individuality of the characters conflicting, the intriguing intricacy of the plot unfolding, the beckoning destinies of the gallant hero and ravishing heroine, if they have any, and above all the masterly elegant eptitude of a seamless telling, so invisible as never to nark?'

'I like a good yarn,' nodded Koo.

'In our own case, *alors*, following the dastardly resurfacing of the Marquis of Roquefort, to demolish Louis Morel's revived erection at the end of Chapter 58, you would counsel us, at the beginning of Chapter 59, to press straight ahead and inform our readers that Louis, during the next few sweltering days in Sedan, finds it impossible to totally avoid the Marquis, who seems to anticipate his every footstep like a doggy ghost, and accosts him with insulting chumminess at every turn?

'That twice in Roquefort's lodgings over an obligatory flask of cool champagne the heat-blistered Louis has to struggle to smother his urge to knock the Marquis's brains out of his skull through his ears, and rather content himself with exchanging highly charged smalltalk about the miraculous Hand Of Fate that has brought two such very diverse gentlemen together once more, to fight to the death if need be side by side in the cause of the noble Count of Soissons?

'And that during the second such unwelcome conversation Louis acquires sufficient control of himself to remark with inscrutable gravity that he personally is sure to emerge from the impending battle at least "without my throat slit from behind", since the horoscope cast for him in the Tower of Catherine de Medici by the Countess of Soissons' necromancer stated plainly that "whoever attempts to take my life *by treachery*, his own shall be forfeit first"?

'And moreover that the Marquis of Roquefort pales so violently in reflex response to this bald revelation that Louis suspects him not only of bad conscience but also of a hitherto unsuspected streak of superstitiousness at least as deep as any of our top-flight tennis players today – which turns out indeed to be the case, as the Marquis of Roquefort, with utmost seriousness, dissects the distinctions between "the wizards and the charlatans" from Nostradamus right up to Vanoni?'

'I would,' nodded Koo, gazing meaningfully up at the hazing sky, and down at our cat-high grass. 'Get on with it.'

'Yes, yes,' I mused distractedly. 'And I suppose in your school it must seem horrendifically remiss of me not to have already related how, immediately after his superstition session with the Marquis of Roquefort, Louis mounts up again to the citadel for another tetta with the Count of Soissons himself. The Count he finds supine alone in a cool saloon being played to by one Van Brox, his Flemish lute-player. So overcome by the delicate depths of emotion in the music is the Count that Louis sees he is weeping in sympathy. Perceiving Louis, however, the volatile Count leaps up to embrace him, dries his wildly asymmetric eyes, and hastens on to tell his trusted young lieutenant the latest news:

'That reinforcements are expected imminently in the form of "Lamboy, with the German veterans", whereafter: "We'll cross the bridge [ie a bridge of barges, over the Meuse] and do battle with the Maréchal de Châtillon, who has been for some days at Remilly."'

'Don't forget', cautioned Koo, 'that most readers of fiction are women, and that women aren't interested in soldiers, military strategy, insane cavalry charges, and pointless killing. If I were you I'd compress any blood-and-guts bits to virtually vanishing point, and hurry on to where Louis and Hélène are reunited—well? They are, aren't they?' she insisted with sudden stridence. 'Because if—'

'My problem here', I prevaricated uneasily, 'is that I can't entirely deprive the reader – even the most sensibly feminine one – of such vital intelligence as that:

'During their interview in that cool citadel saloon, the Count of Soissons goes on to describe and rehearse his battle plans with so manic a megalomaniac enthusiasm that Louis is at first impressed and cheered by the Count's application and conviction, then depressed when he recalls all the old question-marks about "our leader's" resolution, staying power and killer instinct. Finally Louis is extremely concerned "most of all for the sake of my men" about being ordered to serve, in effect, as a cavalry pawn in the command of the Duke of Bouillon, given that, "so the Marquis himself had informed me", the Marquis of Roquefort has already been cast as a principal lieutenant in the Duke of Bouillon's division.

'"Why such concern about that?" you might well ask, and so the Count does.

'Because, Louis admits, with some reluctance and embarrassment, he has reason to believe that the suave, plausible, wily and vindictive Marquis has already mounted attempts on his own life twice – once during the hunting expedition when he pretended to have narrowly missed the izard, but in fact had been aiming at Louis, and then again when his agent the Fat-Monk-come-Monsieur-St-Simon the notorious carp-throat-slitter launched down from an overhanging bough and attempted to stab him, ie Louis, to death – and indeed more like thrice if you considered that the Marquis would very likely have slain him with scant compunction, had the teenage Louis not pre-emptively bested him at swordplay, during that early posthouse duel at Lestelle.'

'How does the Count of Soissons respond to Louis's anxiety?' asked Koo.

'By plunging into a frenzy of impromptu battleplan revision and further refinement calculated not only to convince Louis he has nothing to fear from the Marquis but also that now he comes to think about it he, the Count, intends to interrogate the Duke of Bouillon with searching severity regarding his enlistment of the Marquis in the first place. "A *very* bad man," reflects the Count, his wild eyes rolling with stern independence as he goes on to recall that the Marquis of Roquefort "is widely, though privately, known to have had murdered the Count of Bagnols, and strongly suspected of commissioning the poisoning of poor De Valenais".

'"Should we allow him to remain in Sedan at all?" suggests Louis gently.'

'I'd be inclined to hang on to the Marquis of Roquefort for a bit,' commented Koo.

'And then punish him with poetic justice in the form of a fate worse than but also including death?'

'If you must,' agreed Koo. 'At least he isn't a goody-goody bore.'

'Well, in the short term at least,' I assured her, 'you're in luck.'

'What luck?'

'I mean that what happens next is as follows. The Count of Soissons, his blood now boiling with chivalrous anger at these revived memories of the Marquis of Roquefort's ubiquitously rumoured villainy, and steaming with tarnished honour at the thought of harbouring such a stinking rotter anywhere within the glorious army of liberation he has amassed, storms off with Louis in tow to beard the Duke of Bouillon about his error of judgement in ever enlisting such a two-faced turd in the first place.

'However, it having matured into a fine sunny evening during early July, it just so happens that, as the beetling Count and attendant Louis stomp across the citadel courtyard towards the Duke's staircase, the first person's voice they encounter is the Marquis of Roquefort's itself, as that devilish personage, besuited in colourful cool silks, is airily discoursing to a bystanding bevy of lesser gentlemen on the state of Cardinal Richelieu's health, and the likelihood that:

'"The news of our party's victory, in the impending conflict, will break his Eminence's heart, and see him to his grave."'

'One might imagine', murmured Koo, tossing croissant crumbs to our pheasants, 'that such a sentiment should be music to the Count of Soissons' ears.'

'One might. But it isn't. And in point of fact, when one of the lesser gentlemen, thinking to ingratiate himself smoothly, begs "leave of your Highness" to introduce to him the redoubtable Marquis, the Count of Soissons explodes in fury, treats the Marquis of Roquefort to a triumph of insulting snubbery, and hurries on to nobble the Duke.'

'But presumably', guessed Koo, 'the Duke of Bouillon manages to calm the Count down, and persuade him not to banish the Marquis?'

'That's right. In a typical prolapse of resolution, deeply disheartening to Louis, the Count allows himself to be persuaded by the Duke that:

'"Though the Marquis is indubitably a knave in spirit, he is nonetheless enormously rich and influential, and has pledged us invaluable supplies of both men and money . . . " So please appease and placate him, etcetera.'

'Which the Count then does?'

'No. His princely pride will not stoop so low. But he does concede that the Duke may retain the Marquis in his entourage, and exploit his promised resources. "Bearing in mind, for all our sakes," he concludes, "that the man must be kept from my sight."'

'So Louis returns to his bivouac dissatisfied?'

'Actually he spends the rest of that evening dining with the Count, then takes a walk round Sedan in search of an armourer (of whom there are dozens, happily hammering at their anvils and tinkering eleventh-hour alterations to breastplates, chainmail suits, crutch guards and the like) who can provide him with a snug-fitting fully vizored helmet.'

'Louis, after all, is a coward, you mean?' inquired Koo pragmatically.

'Certainly not,' I retorted loyally. 'It's just that he has never been fully satisfied with the open-fronted salade brought away in haste from Paris, and has a superstition that if he fails to make the effort to acquire a proper vizor, he is sure to get a stray bullet in the eye. Nothing in the Countess of Soissons' necromancer's horoscope, you see, guaranteed him any immunity against low-flying loose musket balls. Not cowardly at all, therefore. Rather the discretion of true valour.'

'And does he find such a helmet?'

'At length, yes, though it costs him an arm and a leg. Anyway, content with his purchase, he retires to his closet in the Count's tower, where

Achilles Lefranc awaits him with a small flask of brandy sent up by the Count, to smooth his way to the few hours sleep which is all he can now hope for before the battle commences.'

'Magical sunset. Red sky at night? Calm before the storm? Any other clichés?'

'Calm before the storm is closest, now you come to mention it. Though it is still very hot in Sedan, and the sky is indeed red, it is an angry deepening sort of red. As if the atmospheric pressure overhead were lessening in response to the upward-thrusting build-up of military steam below. As the hot air stills to a thundery stifle, Louis, alone with his brandy, sits by his single slit window composing a letter of appeasement to his father, to be delivered by Achilles in the event of Louis's death on the battlefield tomorrow. As he labours over phrases of explanation, justification, expiation, regret, apology, and pleas for paternal forgiveness, he is suddenly transported into a bizarre eidetic reprise of his original vision in Chapter 41 in 39 of the spirit of his mother, soaring free from her earthly body, flying over him in the aspect of a great white swan, with the burnished gold wings of an angel, and hovering over him, as a huge swan-cum-humming-bird, but in slow motion, with her moist dark eyes, flashing brighter than ever in the prime of her beauty, beaming down on him a loving sadness so sweetly forgiving as to remind Louis with unbearable intensity of all the ways in which he has failed her, and how undeserving he is of her love, until equally suddenly bang: the hovering angel-swan disappears upwards into the sky like a vertical-take-off jet – this time because Louis's brandy-oiled reverie has been scared away by a darker and more immediately threatening realization . . . '

'Okay,' said Koo reluctantly. 'This one, I grant, you win. *What* bloody realization?'

'That somehow, as it were through a secret black hole in the still and stuffy night – from below, above, sideways? Louis has no perception – he is overhearing the superstitiously hushed consternation of the Marquis of Roquefort, in dialogue with two coarse-voiced companions.

'"What they said at first was indistinct," says Louis, "from the noise of a tumbrel rolling across the court." But as the tumbrel creaking fades Louis clearly hears the agitated Marquis mutter:

'"I tell you, man, I *saw* him with my *very own eyes*. Together with Monsieur de Sourdis, in the other army, and with the aspect of seniority over him. He was paler, thinner, darker – older, to be sure – but there was every line of his person and character, just as before—"

'"Nah, nah, nah, milor!" objects a guttural heavy. "Dead as a poleaxed ox he was, of his wounds, before he hit the water. Nor could any gent have stayed under so long, and not drowned twice over, even if we supposes he were not stabbed to death before."

'"But you never recovered his body, did you?" retorts the Marquis, in tones of low cold menace. "Well, René, if it was not the Count of Bagnols himself, it was the spitting ghost of the same gentleman aged. And either way, my friend, be warned—but what is that? Who goes there?" On which note the acoustic freak dissolves, and the troubled, puzzled and somewhat inebriated Louis overhears no more.'

'Knowing you,' said Koo ominously, 'I bet you're planning to end your chapter just there.'

'Thank you as always,' I countered winningly, 'for your invaluable creative contributions.'

'Anyway, Humbert,' she went on, arising decisively from our leisurely patio breakfast, as Captain Claws sought shelter indoors, 'and fortunately for you, it just so happens that I have a number of invoices to write before lunch. So since it's beginning to rain, and you'll no doubt make out you can't possibly try to start the Flymo now, could you please load the dishwasher instead?'

'I think actually,' I crooned persuasively, thinking lovingly of Pasolini as Geoffrey Chaucer in 'The Canterbury Tales', 'I'd better just turn my computer on for half an hour first. Okay?'

'What for?' she demanded suspiciously.

'To see if I can't begin to solve my apparently insoluble problem.'

'Which one would that be?'

'How on earth to manage to satisfy you? And satisfy Janet as well?'

# Schopenhauer on History

History's a funny thing, is it not? Consider:

'History is bunk!' said Henry Ford.

Or did he? Where and when? In print or speech? Speech to whom? Who reported it? Was hos trustworthy? Or perhaps aurally challenged? In which case, might not ole Henry's actual pronouncement have been 'His story's punk', intending merely to imply predictably imperfect patience with Proust?

This is not a laughing matter, so please don't snigger. At least, not yet. What's worrying us currently is whether what Henry Ford did or did not say really is or is not history. If he genuinely did say exactly what he is perhaps most famous for having said, then that surely *is* history. Or is it? Suppose that, in fact, ole Henry's self-same utterance was indeed the Proust-critiquing 'His story's punk' but also that his aurally challenged auditor misheard him as hypothesized, misreported him accordingly, and thus won Henry great renown for a degree of post-nineteenth-century-Idealist pop-philosophical acumen that the practical pioneer of mass production first of all never possessed but also subsequently preferred not to disclaim. It would then follow, would it not, that Henry Ford would go down in history as being most famous for saying what he never said at all?

Now is that history?

Alternatively, what does the very logical possibility say about history itself? Could it tend to suggest that history is indeed bunk, whether or not Henry said it was? And does that not rather depend on whether you view history as being what actually happened, or rather what historians tell you happened? If the former, then the proposition *History is bunk!* could perhaps be explicated:

*History is meaningless chaos, evolution is like water gravitating downhill, there is no Divine Intention, Hegel and Marx were a pair of temporarily in-vogue scam artistes, and each individual destiny will be doing relatively nicely if it contrives to 'rise above' Alice Cooper's 'All of my life . . . joke, . . . smoke, and then I passed out on the floor'.*

If, however, history is merely a sort of ragbag averaged-out consensus of what historians, politicians, headmasters, chiefs of police, archbishops, barons of industry, Nuncle Rudolphs, militant-revisionist-separatist-bestselling-paperback feminists, and others with like axes to grind and positions of power to abuse *please to tell* us took place in the past, then indubitably the *History is bunk!* wisdom attributed to Henry Ford must be interpreted more along the lines of:

*History is an unfathomable fankle of partial facts, infected truths, downright deliberate lies, unconsciously motivated distortions, religiously ossified fantasies, gratuitous inventions just as mischievous as schoolboys pulling the legs off spiders (ie to deceive posterity just for the hell of it), and therefore Henry's cordial counsel to you (as a practical billionaire instructing aspirants) is:*

*'Don't believe a single fucking word of it, folks. Not till you've thoroughly checked it out with your own eyes, ears, nose – and even then . . . '*

But this surely leaves us on the horns of a fearful dilemma, as if the largest highland cow in the universe had got us both skewered up the bums, you on the needle-sharp left horn and me on the right (unless you view the tragedy in reverse), and so far apart as only to dimly intuit the isolated crescendos of each other's cries of despair, does it not? When you reflect that if *history is the essentially relentless ongoing course of events, entire unto itself and independent of all observers* (and please remember, especially all you trendy young [well . . . ] English novelists, that we are talking here about middle-sized objects *par excellence*, namely people[1]), then we are no better off in relation to history than we would be if questing after Kant's infuriating Thing-In-Itself, which might somehow be knowable by suitably endowed and morally perfect angels, but never in the slightest by us, all thanks to the intrinsic limitations imposed by the forms of our dismal knowing.

Goodness gracious. Whereas:

If history is what historians *tell* us, as regards correct interpretation of 'the facts', and even 'the facts' themselves, then why on earth, or anywhere, should we pay the slightest attention to what historians tell us, when it is plain as day, and also the WhatRail? stewardess who didn't

---

[1] The hope was, Wringhim, that if we worked this into a parenthesis here and now, it would save you the bother of insisting on a virulent footnote later. Okay?

want to sell me a large coffee in case the train's lurchings spilled it off my 'small table' — as indeed it duly did, en route for 'Sex & Talent' — that for every historian who tells you '*p*' you will very soon find at least one other, and probably a hundred, who will vigorously swear to '*not p*' — very much like economists, 'social scientists' generally, weather forecasters, politicians, Eight-pint Experts On Everything, and the loathsome fat overpaid peddlers of horoscopes in the Popular Press?

But wait a minute, or even less.

If we pursue that line too ruthlessly we are in danger, are we not, of careering over the cliff of a most insidiously solipsistic scepticism, chanting righteously to the last, as we plummet to the jammy mash of our intellectual suicides, that history not only is bunk but moreover doesn't really exist either, in any remotely objective or scientifically testable-hence-acceptable sense, and that therefore we shouldn't waste even the vanishing nanoseconds remaining of that minute on any further pratings from charlatans professoring 'History', but should instead concentrate our minds — and particularly those of our bright youngsters, who may after all be exponentially obliged hereafter to support us throughout our ever-more-protracted dotage, such is progress — on the discovery of patentable new cure-all drug molecules, and controversial islands of hitherto uncharted DNA, whose existence is at least so demonstrably objective as to massively inflate our profits; all the while entrusting 'history', however patronizingly defined, to the harmless fanciful romancings of lighter lady novelists, such as **** #####, ******** ####, and @@@@ ******* ######?

Now of course we could end this chapter on that note, having sort of done our literary duty by mixing in a few pretentiously heavy bits for lamebrains to sneeringly skip. But that might, especially to such feminine readers as prefer their foreplay protracted, appear inconsiderately abrupt, and also, and infinitely less forgivable, it might leave more literal readers complaining of puzzlement as to the point of this chapter's title. Let us essay our uttermost, therefore, to round it off in a frenzy of climactic perfection, by collaging a few populistically sensationist clips on the matter of History from the collected works of the greatest philosopher in it (Arthur Schopenhauer, 1788–1860). That Schopenhauer is the most 'compleat' and ultimately the most profound of all philosophers is of course only one view, but it is at least a quite considered view, based on, among other things, the reading of Schopenhauer from beginning to end several times.

If, on the other hand, and whether or not in McEwan's Bar, you ask

Wringhim Knox to pronounce on this issue, he will instantly assure you, his sharp red eyes well calculated to deter any squeaks of dissent:

'Why, David Hume, of course.'

But while it is true that Hume, albeit very much an Edinburgh man, as opposed to Glaswegian, is indeed a very great philosopher, invaluable to Kant, and tremendously admired by Schopenhauer himself,[2] to claim for him the Ultimate Laurel of 'The Greatest' is either to evince insufficient familiarity with other philosophers or else to arouse suspicion of some hidden agenda afoot. In Wringhim's case, his insufficient familiarity is due to undue concentration on British and especially twentieth-century positivistically biased philosophy (like most British professors of philosophy, Wringhim has never yet read a single word of Schopenhauer, whereas we here, for example, have at least read quite a few words by Hume), and his hidden agenda is exactly the same as underlies and invalidates his view that if you were to seriously debate who has been The Greatest Novelist Of The Twentieth Century, your conclusion must ineluctably be (not Blaise Cendrars, Gabriel Garcia Marquez, Marcel Proust, James Joyce, Thomas Mann, Malcolm Lowry, Alexander Solzhenitzyn, Robert Musil, Günter Grass, Jaroslav Hasek – to list just a few *not*s rather less obvious than D.H. Lawrence) but unanimously Scotland's Neil Gunn.

Now this kind of programmatically positivistic discrimination not only is dishonest (whether consciously or not), but it also serves as a corrupting role model for the young, and on top of that it isn't even fair to other Scottish novelists. Wringhim himself, inword, is arguably already a finer novelist than Gunn ever was. But the crucial objection to you here, Wringhim, is that your ploy is counter-productive, risking, as it does, the catastrophe of justified ridicule, as when humourless feminists queer their own potentially sensible pitch with derision, by insisting

---

2 Particularly with respect to Hume's definitive demolition, intellectually speaking, of what you might call Organized Theism. See Hume's *Dialogues on Natural Religion* and *Natural History of Religion*. How it is that, more than two centuries after Hume's death – in our supremely advanced, scientific, educated, civilized, intelligent and sophisticated societies – we can still have state-funded 'professors' of 'theology' must surely, to any invisibly spectating and remotely rational ET, seem hugely more marvellous than any miracle yet reported from Lourdes.

on being hired as all-things-equal lumberjacks in Alaska. So let us, Wringhim, abjure such juvenile gambits, and rather work together, by all means within all honesty, to wrest back self-government for Scotland, whereafter our literature will fully mature, our young poets will cease their callow Nashville-maudlin nostalgic dreification of good old days they never knew anyway, as no-one else did either, and our novels will aspire to heights as great as any, if by then there are novels at all.

Meanwhile, having raised our philosophical colours, let us summon our herald to bugle:

From *The World as Will and Representation*, Volume I, written during Schopenhauer's twenties, published when he was thirty:

> History proceeds in accordance with the Principle of
>     Sufficient Reason (§51).
> In history the false outweighs the true (§51).
> Modern historians, with few exceptions, generally give us
>     only 'an offal-barrel and a lumber-garret, or at best
>     a Punch-and-Judy play' (§51).[3]
> History is as well studied in the village (§51).
> History keeps quiet about saints (§68).
> History could have enlightened Kant (Appendix).

From *The World as Will and Representation*, Volume II, amassed, written and refined over many years, and published when Schopenhauer was fifty-five:

> Quotes Aristotle on the superiority of poetry to history
>     (Chapter XXXVII).
> History lacks the fundamental characteristic of science – i.e.,
>     the subordination of what is known (*ibid*).
> History must comprehend the particular directly (*ibid*).
> History's knowledge is only imperfect and partial (*ibid*).
> The 'universal' in history is a fallacy: it is subjective (*ibid*).
> As history becomes more interesting, it becomes less
>     trustworthy (*ibid*).
> Differences between history and philosophy (*ibid*).
> The essence of human life exists complete in every present (*ibid*).
> Yet history hopes to make up for depth with length and
>     breadth [i.e., of comprehension] (*ibid*).

---

[3] Quote from Goethe's *Faust*, Bayard Taylor translation.

The really essential content in history is everywhere the same (*ibid*).

The material of history is . . . human clouds in the wind.

Abuse of Hegel's view of history (*ibid*).

Constructive histories [such as Hegel's] always end in a
     comfortable fat state, but they cannot refashion citizens
     morally (*ibid*).

History relates only the long, heavy, confused dream
     of mankind (*ibid*).

Hegelians should read Plato (*ibid*).

*Technology* can never make anything essentially better
     [not even steam engines and telegraphs!] (*ibid*).

The true philosophy of history teaches that history is
     untruthful (*ibid*).

To have read Herodotus is sufficient [study of history] (*ibid*).

The true value of history: what reason is to the individual,
     history is to the human race (*ibid*).

History helps a nation to anticipate the future (*ibid*).

History is the rational self-consciousness of the human race (*ibid*).

Language is to individual reasoning as writing to racial
     reasoning (*ibid*).

The *real* purpose of pyramids (etc . . . ) was to communicate
     with future descendants (*ibid*).

History (like a kaleidoscope) in reality always shows us
     the same thing (Chapter XLI).

History is full of pederasty: Orpheus, Plato, etc (Appendix to
     Chapter XLIV, 'The Metaphysics of Sexual Love').

From the essays, many of them extremely accessible and 'popular', published in two volumes in 1851 under the title *Parerga and Paralipomena*:

Great thoughts shrink . . . when they enter the parasitic brain
     of a history-writing professor (Vol. I, §1).

What historian (of philosophy) could have *read* all the writings
     he writes of (*ibid*).

No wonder the ignorant historians of philosophy copy
     one another (*ibid*).

The potential value of an anthology of original passages (*ibid*).

History . . . is the contrary of poetry (Vol. II, §233).

History is to time as geography is to space – neither
     is a science (*ibid*).

History is the favourite study of weak and lazy minds (*ibid*).

History rescues spars from the shipwreck of the world (*ibid*).

History is the sequel to zoology – because men have
    individual characters (*ibid*).

There are two kinds of history: of the will, and of the
    intellect (*ibid*).

The newspaper is the second-hand in the clock of history
    [and] all journalists are alarmists, like little yapdogs (*ibid*).

History is essentially imperfect (*ibid*).

[Still, to the well rounded intellect] an extensive acquaintance
    with history is needful (Vol. II, §254).

Finally, to round out and off those merely icebergtippishly suggestive condensed one-liners, here is an extended quotation from *Parerga*, Vol. II, §233:

'In addition to the above-mentioned imperfections of history, there is also the fact that Clio, the muse of history, is as thoroughly infected with lies and falsehood as is a common prostitute with syphilis. It is true that the modern critical investigation of history endeavours to cure this, but with its local means it overcomes only isolated symptoms that break out here and there; moreover, much quackery[4] often creeps in which aggravates the evil. It is more or less the same as regards all history, with the exception of sacred history of course.[5] I believe that the events and persons in history resemble those that actually existed about as much as the portraits of writers on the title-pages of their books in most cases resemble the authors themselves. And so they are like them only in rough outline, so that they have a faint resemblance, often distorted entirely by one feature that is false; but sometimes there is no resemblance at all.'

Being as honest as possible here, we confess what we would have liked to mix in next: an alternative translation of the Clio passage you have just read. What we quoted was from the Clarendon Press translation by Col. E.F.J. Payne. Although the Payne version is clear, lively, enormously painstaking and probably definitively thorough, one occasionally feels that, by erring a little on the side of the too faithfully literal, it slightly dulls the brightest flashes of Schopenhauer's most

---

4  Col. Payne points out that: 'Schopenhauer uses the word *Quack-salberei* and may have had in mind a play on the word *Queck-silber* (mercury).'

5  This irony echoing Hume on Organized Theism.

draconian blasts. As corrective, therefore, and to cast perspective on our own translations from seventeenth-century French, including the bits you'll be itching to get to in the following chapter, we turned to the older Bailey Saunders translations of Schopenhauer's essays, which are renowned for straying into paraphrase, but also commended, at their best, for encapsulating the fiercest flavours of the maestro's trenchancy.

But woe, alas!

When you dip into the essay cobbled together by Bailey Saunders under the title 'On Some Forms of Literature' (sixth essay in the book presented to Victorian England as *The Art of Literature*) you will find not a whisper about Clio, prostitutes and syphilis, but rather a half-inch of white vertical space where that paragraph should be, before the virtuous translator presses on with the more palatable (quote):

'The NEWSPAPER is the second-hand in the clock of history; and it is not only made of baser metal than those which point to the minute and the hour, but it seldom goes right.'[6]

Now what can we make of that?

Did the popularizing translator and/or his snivelling publisher have genuine and justifiable editorial reasons for omitting the Clio/syphylis chunk, or were they more likely driven by G.P.R. Jamesean fear that any page might 'sully, or call the blush to, the cheek of any member of the household'? Particularly when we recall that when the Bailey Saunders volumes were first published Victorian piano-leg-draping, simultaneously with the rife syphilitic prostitution so perpetuated by the likes of morally uplifting English novelists such as Dickens and Thackeray, was hovering round the summits of its barely conceivable hypocrisy?[7]

Hang on, though. Barely conceivable?

Then and there; not here and now?

How to explain, in that case, how it is that – to take just one trivial instance – if you tune in to any unctuous EBC screening of the Sean Connery popularization of my distant cousin Eco's *Name of the Rose*, and if you focus with rising eyes-narrowed revolting excitement on the brief and in any case horrendiculously gratuitous

---

6  Col. Payne's rendering gives: 'The newspapers are the seconds-hand of history; yet this is often not only of baser metal, but is seldom right.'

7  Cf Schopenhauer on prostitution.

hot young sex scene in the middle, you will — not even in Westminster, London, where EBC television reception is miraculously more visible than here in rural Scotland — you will, we repeat for emphasis, find your sensibilities appalled by not so much as a nanosecond micron of replayable-in-slow-motion exposure of the errant young Hollywood novice's subliminally waggling willie.

And why not?

Because Dearest Old Auntie Whitehouse has already snippered it out for us.

Just as she also snipped out such relatively disturbing scenes from the Gulf War as had thus far, and with difficulty, managed to survive the Pentagon's first round of censorship by blindfold.

So it was then, is now, and when shall it ever be different? Whether or not we are passionately interested in Currant Hunk's willie is surely not the point. The point is rather that our perception is being constantly manipulated by vested interests, hence our history is systematically falsified. Sometimes thanks to strangely pure supererogatory malice. But usually by chisellers after advantage, or rats with nests at risk. In the case of Hunk's willie? Television executives terrified of crossing shrivelled Conservative ladies with influence, and hence being sacked from their sinecures.

Money, money, money.

Same motive, surely, as lay behind Bailey Saunders and/or his publisher safeguarding their book sales by falsifying (and in the process perniciously trivializing) the history of Schopenhauer's thought, by suppressing his Clio-with-syphilis metaphor. 'If you cannot bring good news, then don't bring any,' as Bob Dylan and several others have remarked, with varying degrees of irony. And if anyone is inclined to suppose otherwise, hos is invited to explain, accordingly, why the following paragraph, which immediately precedes Clio in Schopenhauer, and is faithfully retained by Col. Payne, gets nothing but elisive vertical space in Bailey Saunders:

'From one end to the other, history is a narrative of nothing but wars, and the same theme is the subject of all the most ancient works of art as of the most modern. The origin of all *war*, however, is the *desire to steal*; and so Voltaire quite rightly says: *dans toutes les guerres il ne s'agit que de voler* (in all wars it is only a question of stealing). Thus as soon as a nation feels an *excess of strength*, it falls on its neighbours and enslaves them so that, instead of living by its own labour, it may appropriate the results of theirs, whether this merely exists now or includes the future product as well. This furnishes the material for world history and its heroic deeds.'[8]

Before we audience squeals of dismay in the face of such historiological pessimism, let's scoot ahead to inquire:

- *Why did Saddam Hussein invade Kuwait?*

- *Why did Argentina invade the Falklands?*

- *Why did the Japanese bomb Pearl Harbour?*

- *Why did Hitler invade Poland?*

And why did Heyday England invade, conquer, colonize and exploit so very much of North America, Africa, India, Australia, etc?

Our theory, with which you are welcome to disagree, but only with the utmost cogency, is that Bailey Saunders and/or his snivelling publisher felt the war-as-unbridled-greed contention to be too close to the truth about Heyday England, in which they yet prospered, and that therefore it had best be snipped, lest powerful sensibilities suffer pique, and book sales be downturned. Rather like Sir Walter Scott's anxious publisher expunging his raunchy bits, thus inadvertently honing a harmlessness which only a G.P.R. James could perfect. And if it be retorted that Scott was Scottish, not English, then the reply . . . sales into England . . . publisher was . . . ??[9]

Very consistent with the above conjecture, though by no means proving it mathematically, is the fascinating fact that Bailey Saunders had no compunction about translating Schopenhauer quoting Voltaire on the matter of war as theft when it was plainly the Bumptious Krauts getting the finger pointed at them, and not Supreme Britannia, who thus could cuncur with smirks. Like so:

'Does not all history show', inquires Schopenhauer, 'that whenever a king is firmly planted on the throne, and his people reach some degree of prosperity, he uses it to lead his army, like a band of robbers, against adjoining countries? Are not almost all wars ultimately undertaken for purposes of plunder? In the most remote antiquity, and to some extent

---

[8] Unquote.
[9] ??

also in the middle Age, the conquered became slaves – in other words, they had to work for those who conquered them; and where is the difference between that and paying war-taxes, which represent the product of previous work?

'All war, says Voltaire, is a matter of robbery; and the Germans should take that as a warning.'[10]

Or in Col. Payne's reading:

'*Dans toutes les guerres il ne s'agit que de voler*, says Voltaire and the Germans should be reminded of this.'[11]

That the Germans have not in fact been reminded of this sufficiently frequently, or at least successfully, may be inferred from their invasion of France (why?) in the Franco-Prussian war which was effectively terminated by their victory in the Battle of Sedan of 1870, and their invasion of as much of the rest of the world as possible (why?) in both World War I and World War II – in which the Battle of Sedan of May 1940 began the German invasion of France (why?) – and arguably also from their typically humourless attempt to dominate hence exploit as much of the rest of Europe as possible now in the 1990s, economically and fiscally this time, since they can no longer hope to get away with it militarily.

It's a small planet, of course, and history makes it smaller, so it should come as no surprise that we'll be surging ahead with our very own Battle of Sedan (more precisely known as the Battle of La Marfée) back in July 1641 just as soon as humanly possible in the following chapter. In the meantime we should perhaps find a moment to note that despite Schopenhauer's notorious and metaphysically perfectly justified

---

[10] From Chapter III, 'Our Relation to Others' of the potboiler volume presented by Bailey Saunders as *Counsels and Maxims*. For a more faithful, truer, complete and edifying rendition, refer to the end of Volume I of *Parerga and Paralipomena* as translated by Col. Payne, where 'Counsels and Maxims' is itself Chapter V of *Aphorisms on the Wisdom of Life*, which is prefaced with a motto by one of Schopenhauer's own favourite aphorists, Nicolas Chamfort (*Le bonheur n'est pas chose aisée; il est très difficile de le trouver en nous, et impossible de le trouver ailleurs.*), which Bailey Saunders and/or his snivelling publisher also saw fit to suppress, very likely thanks to concern not to alienate the more hopeful of their readers.

[11] 'Counsels and Maxims', §(29). See note 10.

pessimism, and his concomitant mordant cautions to the effect that history is awash with total fantasies, malignant rumours, calculated frauds and blatant downright lies, and that professors of history, in particular, should be consumed with large buckets of salt, he nonetheless repeatedly evinces a refreshing confidence in the power of truth to rise up righteous in time's due course.

Witness:

From *The World as Will and Representation*, Volume I:
> For the power of truth is incredibly great and of unutterable
>> endurance (§26).

From *Essay on the Basis of Morality*:
> Quotes Goethe and Plato, re the power of truth to prevail
>> (Preface to the first edition).
> The wings of time beat slowly, but truth arrives at last (§22).

From *Essay on the Will in Nature*:
> Truth can bide its time, for it has a long life before it
>> (Introduction).
> The power of truth is irresistible, its life indestructible (*ibid*).
> If the present age does not see this [ . . . ] many following
>> ages will ('Physical Astronomy').

From *The World as Will and Representation*, Volume II:
> No truth need fear anything from other truths (Chapter IX).
> Great is the power of truth, and it will prevail (Chapter XX,
>> 'Note on what is said about Bichat').
> Anything other than pure truth is subject to destruction
>> (Chapter XLVIII).

From *Parerga and Paralipomena*, Volume I:
> Great truths are always presentimented in an evolving fog
>> ('Fragments for the History of Philosophy', §14).
> Great truths are prepared for by progress of the times (*ibid*).
> The way to truth is steep and long; and no one will cover
>> the distance with a block tied to his foot
>> ('On philosophy at the Universities').

From *Parerga and Paralipomena*, Volume II:

Truth clings as ineradicably as does the odour of musk to
everything that has once been in contact therewith (§174).
Truth alone . . . is the indestructible diamond (*ibid*).
Time will give truth a thousand tongues (§243).

If we now inquire *why* the abominable high priest of pessimism could be so stoically optimistic in his conviction that truth will triumph, the answer can either be epistemologically rigorous, elaborating the conceptual frameworks stolen wholesale by both Wittgensteins, or on Saturday night in the boozer it can just as well be pleasantly conversational:

'When any absurdity is uttered in public or company,' counsels Schopenhauer, 'or is written in literature and well received, or at any rate not refuted, we should not despair and think that that is the end of the matter. On the contrary, we should know and take comfort in the thought that afterwards the matter will gradually be scrutinized, elucidated, thought over, considered, discussed, and, in most cases, ultimately judged correctly. Thus after a time, the length of which will depend on the difficulty of the subject, almost everyone understands what a clear mind saw at once. Meanwhile, of course, we must be patient. For a man of correct insight among those who are duped and deluded resembles one whose watch is right while all the clocks in the town give the wrong time.'[12]

From another angle:

Think of Tom and Dick. Tom knows that if Dick undertakes the derring mission behind enemy lines, Dick is sure to be killed, not least because Tom has already anonymously tipped off the enemy commander, Wolfgang. Tom, however, represents to Dick that the risk is maybe 70/30 in favour of success and survival. Thus, Tom deceives Dick. Why? Because Tom believes Dick is more handsome and virile than Tom himself, as seems to be confirmed by the behaviour of Gladys, who appears oblivious to Tom's discreetly admiring overtures, but goes conspicuously googa over Dick.

So what happens?

Dick goes over the top at dead of midnight, and is promptly captured, tortured and executed by the Wolfgang gang. Gladys is distraught for days but soon cheers up and develops a passable penchant for Tom, with whom she later nuptializes and procreates. Tom keeps mum about the

---

[12] 'Counsels and Maxims', §(27). See note 10.

dastardy he wrought on Dick, but in the course of decades along troops Harry, with a PhD in Twentieth-Century History and an eagle-eyed interest in proving his merely proto-professional predecessors were all mistaken.

So what happens?

Armed with fourth-generation micro-laser sub-neutrino anonymous-letter-handwriting-analysis technology, Harry swiftly succeeds in demonstrating beyond any reasonable doubt that the effective murderer of Dick was Tom – who, happily for him, is no longer around to attempt to deny it, since he died of cirrhosis of the liver the year before last. If Tom had still been around, and if he hadn't squandered his modest fortune, inherited from Gladys's Auntie Jemima, on gin, then he might have engaged smart London lawyers at four hundred pounds an hour to persuade a court to discredit Harry's sub-neutrino evidence in the light of Technical Difficulties dredged up by a Rival Expert. But even if Tom hadn't died of cirrhosis the year before last, he would certainly have expired of old age before the present century gave out, and with him would have perished the principal motivation underlying the perpetuation of his villainous falsehood.

And so, we may conclude, Schopenhauer's surprising optimism regarding the tendency of truth to come out is not without foundation, though this is largely less because of any sky-pie tendency for human moral nature to improve, and equally more because of the rather obvious fact that while it is usually in my best interests (speaking as a person, and not a novelist) to conceal my worst failings, and to practise saccharine PR on all you other suckers, it is at least as often in your best interests to be more aware of my dark, seamy and disgraceful side than I would prefer or even imagine remotely possible. All of which is doubtless why *No man is a hero to his valet*, and *Familiarity breeds contempt*, and Scotland's greatest poet felt it necessary to lament:

> *O wad some Pow'r the giftie gie us*
> *To see oursels as ithers see us! . . .*

And so on.

Schematically:

For any one given wilful Self (and all selves are): firstly, the whole truth about me, known by other selves, tends to be disadvantageous to me; secondly, and complementarily, the whole truth about other individuals, known by me, tends to be advantageous to me. There, the individuals may be human selves, sabre-toothed tigers, magic mushrooms, asbestos fibres, gamma rays, or (eventually) other planets, galaxies, universes, etc.

In this we see that the apparent paradox between Schopenhauer's optimistically patient attendance on truth and the fundamental pessimism with which he is most commonly associated is indeed only apparent. For the pessimism is about the nature of the world, considered from the moral point of view. In this context, not only is our world not the *best* of all possible worlds (as silly old and thoroughly deceitful Leibnitz would have us believe), but it actually is the precise opposite. Thus, our world, says Schopenhauer, really is the *worst* of all possible worlds, since if it was any worse than it is, it would cease to exist altogether. As indeed, sooner or later, it will. Now whether or not that's a popular view ('If you cannot bring good news . . . ') it certainly shouldn't be trivially sneezed at by any would-be professor of philosophy who hasn't read all the works mentioned in this chapter at least once. In the meantime, the good news (!) headlines include the following:

¶ Our moral depravity and our (variable) passion for truth (about other individuals) are two sides of the same tarnished coin.

¶ Since posterity outlives particular deceitful interests, there is a tendency for the mottled body of historical knowledge to gradually accumulate and refine itself — rather like our ability to distinguish between Vermeer originals and Van Megeeren fakes.[13]

¶ For every sanctimonious Auntie Whitehouse (representing home-counties English terrestrials) trying to mask Currant Hunk's willie off your television screen in case you develop certain contrary notions of your own there will tend in due course to come a marginally less hypocritical Nuncle Rudolph (representing free competition and especially large profits for Rudolph from the skies) less unwilling in most cases to let you view your movies as their creators intended.

---

[13] Reference with a pinch of salt is hereby made to Nelson Goodman's *Languages of Art*, Part III.

¶ For every buccaneering partial translator like Bailey Saunders with no compunction about suppressing what hos fears hor readership may not wish to countenance, there will tend subsequently to come a more conscientious and thorough translator such as Col. Payne.

¶ Similarly – and what worse perversion of history than to bowdlerize great middlebrow thoughts? – for every Sir Walter Scott who apparently couldn't be bothered to ensure his snivelling publisher didn't tone down his raunchy bits so as not to risk calling blushes to the cheeks of any member of any household, there will tend in due course to emerge a bolder and more enlightened publisher, less snivelling in the sense of being more fastidiously faithful to the author's creative intentions, most of all when the opportunity presents itself to create a lucrative new copyright, and hopefully just at the right time to reap the benefits of a pan-European extension of the period of copyright protection. Glory be.

¶ Last, and most culminatingly rewarding, especially for those Rankles skimming ruthlessly for Obvious Artistic Relevance, the consideration presents itself that if – let us say most humbly – there is an ongoing (albeit patchy and hiccuping) tendency for historical bunk to get debunked (even if for the worst of reasons), and where the incisive documentary profundity of the latest professorially historiographical guru has not yet correctively penetrated, there may even be temporary scope for an inquirer so flighty as The Serial Historical Novelist to contribute for a moment: by raising the odd new question (or resuscitating smothered old ones), posing a fresh hypothesis, unearthing some titbit of testimony, synapsizing hitherto unconnected considerations, and most of all by sharing with hor reader a particular passion for place and period not often encountered in the text books, and the corresponding paradigmatically human *lust to know more* that never can be extinguished, save by death, senile dementia, state-sponsored alcoholism, barbiturate addiction, Organized Theism, Tory Party dogma, Auntie Whitehouse, and umpteen other staunch campaigners – not all of them English – for more of death in life. All of which is at least consistent, is it not, with the popular success, from time to time, of even very slight contributions, such as Josephine Tey's *The Daughter of Time* (re who really did murder the Princes in the Tower?); also more sustained enlargements of historical awareness such as may be culled from Maurice Druon (*Les Poisons de la Couronne*, etc); and finally the not sensibly contestable datum that the greatest novel ever written – despite that fact that neither Wringhim Knox nor most of his cronies in the Scottish Literature departments have read a word of it, not even in English – is *the* historical novel par excellence. We are of course talking here, Wringhim, about *War and Peace* by Leo Tolstoy, a copy of which should be obtainable from any large public library, if you're too mean to buy it in BirdDog.

Well now. What you're reading at the moment certainly isn't *War and Peace*, and for this we abjectly apologize. But there are some construable scant consolations, and one of them is that not even *War and Peace* will convey to you the slightest inkling of how, in the very moment of his monumental victory at the Battle of La Marfée, the Count of Soissons was suddenly shot stone-dead, why, by whom – and under whose orders?[14]

---

[14] 'Suggest a headnote at the beginning of this chapter inviting all your readers who cannot abide philosophy to skip it.' [J.R.]

# The Battle of La Marfée

Following all that magisterial guff about History, we thought we'd better treat this chapter to coverage somewhat more stereoscopic and multivalent than merely the unqualified subjective recollections of Louis Morel. Accordingly, and – as it were – blindfolded (for we had not checked in advance whether these particular historical 'facts', whatever they were, should add more or less exciting spice to the narrative), we reached with wavering courage for volumes 11–12, *France*, of The Historian's History of the World, a twenty-seven volume 'Comprehensive Narrative of the Rise and Development of Nations from the Earliest Times as recorded by over Two Thousand of the Great Writers of All Ages. Edited with the Assistance of a Distinguished Board of Advisers and Contributors by HENRY SMITH WILLIAMS, LL.D.' and published in London and New York by the The Encyclopaedia Britannica, Inc.; first edition 1904, fifth and our edition 1926. We got it off a retiring-for-his-health second-hand bookseller for £2 on the gloomy ground, from his point of view, that if only one of the twenty-seven volumes wasn't missing then the set would be worth £200.

What a pity.

We haven't yet worked out which unfortunate Nation's Comprehensive Rise and Development has gone astray, but it certainly isn't *France*. Hence we are joyfully enabled without further ado to quote to you verbatim, stylistic farts and all:

> The count de Soissons, on the failure of his scheme [see our Chapter 35] against the cardinal, had taken refuge with the duke de Bouillon in Sedan. All the enemies of the latter, especially the exiles, looked towards this prince of the blood as the rallying-point, the support of their cause. Richelieu employed every art to pacify the count, remove his distrust, and entice him to court. All efforts proved vain; and Richelieu was even obliged to purchase the tranquillity of Soissons, and tolerate his independent posture. It was dangerous, however, to let such an example of disobedience subsist; and the

cardinal at length sent an army, under the marshal De [*sic* . . . ] Châtillon, to reduce Sedan, and take or humble the count de Soissons. Châtillon was both valorous and skilful; but nothing could compensate for the ill humour and backwardness of the troops, who, with their officers, felt more inclined to a gallant prince of the blood than to the domineering cardinal. In an action that took place at La Marfée, near Sedan, the royal troops showed neither alacrity nor determination; and Châtillon, despite his efforts, was completely put to the rout. No obstacle seemed now to prevent the count de Soissons from marching to Paris, when the almost miraculous good fortune of Richelieu saved him from ruin. As Soissons rode over the field of battle, he pushed up his visor with his pistol; it was accidentally discharged, and the victor perished. Report did not fail to say that he was assassinated, and, of course, by the order of Richelieu; but there is no evidence to support such a rumour. Louis, who, on receiving tidings of the defeat, was preparing, with equanimity, to sacrifice the obnoxious minister, was now struck with his unvarying good fortune; and, with a superstitious feeling, bowed still lower to the cardinal's will. The court did not share the monarch's obsequiousness.*e*

Now doesn't that stink of rats to you?

First, because, as soon will be revealed, it could not be contradicted more flatly than by the account of Louis Morel. But then . . . for all that Louis was an eye-witness, he might have been lying, might he not?

Second, because, if true, the Historians' History account would gralloch all the cardinal conspiracies out of their theories, which would be bad news for the story as story. Yet what if it *were* true? Think of our duty to the reader, to Knowledge, and all that.

Third, and fishiest: if you were a prince of the blood, and leader of the Liberationary Insurrectionist Forces of France, pledged to overthrow The Tyrant, and if you had just won the most crucial victory in battle of your career, which made you in effect Protector of the Nation, to whom the King would be obliged to come crawling, and *if* you were in the habit, after winning a vital battle, of pushing up your helmet visor with your pistol muzzle – if you really, really were that foolish, just imagine – is it likely, even if it could be proved to be mechanically possible (for we're not talking about snub-nosed handbag-sized Smith & Wesson ·357 Magnums here, but rather of a much flatter-handled and longer-barreled single-shot snaphance pistol, in the fist of the wrist of an arm stiff with armour), is it likely, remotely likely, that you would, on this day of your crowning glory, push your visor up with your pistol muzzle at such an extraordinary back-sloping angle that, *even if* the weapon were to discharge accidentally, its bullet must fire straight into your skull, exploding your brain, and killing you stone-dead?

Preferring to doubt it, both on commonsensical evidential grounds and – yes, yes, we confess – due to having already made a substantial commitment to Louis's version, we determined to look up the Distinguished Historians' credentials. Seldom a bad idea, in any case, as our previous chapter may have made plain.

And what can be found there?

Well, the first stepping stone is that superscripted italicised '*e*', which is the key to the particular Great Writing by the particular Distinguished Historian from which the current passage is supposedly derived. And in the present instance, '*e*' points the finger at *The History of France*, by one Eyre Evans Crowe, of whom (let's be honest yet again) we personally had never heard – not even Audrey, as it later transpired. Not to worry, though, when there are yet great repositories of learning in the land, as I reflected the following afternoon, as I reached to hoist down from their fusty fifth-floor shelf in Edinburgh University Library the five fat volumes of Evans Crowe's *History*.

'The Author may perhaps be taxed with presumption', confesses that terribly English author in his Preface to Volume I, 'for undertaking what has already been achieved by several eminent writers of that country whose progress, character, and fate are to be depicted. But French history is in a great measure English history: both are bound up together, and opinions entertained respecting the one necessarily react upon the other. This renders it desirable to have a History of France written from an English point of view . . . Each country must be a warning and a cause of reflection, not a model, to the other. And, certainly, the most interesting and useful subject of study and contemplation in the world, to an Englishman, must be France,—and, to a Frenchman must be England.'

Now I don't know about you – not yet, anyway, though feel free to change all that – but in my own corner I find (retreating to the existential present for fear any finer-boned tense might instantly melt within five miles of my Scottish indignation) I already rather dislike Mr Eyre Evans Crowe. He is an archetypal pompous Victorian, is he not? An incorrigible English chauvinist, a dismal stylist, and a bad historian to boot, as becomes even plainer when we fastforward to peruse with loathing the first sentence of the first chapter of his first volume:

'The noblest result of ages, the greatest achievement of humanity, has been to found and produce a nation.'

'You fulsome jingo turd!' I jibber furiously – but quietly too, considerately, so's not to jerk back to drudging wakefulness the isolated slumberers slumped hopelessly over, about and beside the sun-warmed window desks. 'You sanctimonious upper-arsehole-crust English prune. Noblest nation? Greatest fucking achievement of fucking humanity? You're thinking of fucking *England* – incha, Fuckface? Gleeting fucking England, eh? Well, how dare you presume . . . how *dare* . . . ?'

And so on, and so forth, for uncounted high-arousal minutes: a mounting muddy torrent of those unbridled spontaneities of intellectual response so essential to critical progress, yet which we should shudder to see in print. By the time I heave down Volume III of Crowe (nearly a kilo and a quarter it weighs; nicely bound, though, credit where it's due, good paper too, for its 705 pages, many of them still uncut), feeling closer, ever closer, to his original version of the killing of the Count of Soissons, I am awash on such a boiling sea of hatred for this long-dead pukka English tit that already I am predisposed to convict him of virtually every academic crime: partial presentation of the evidence, suppression of the inconvenient, fallacious reasoning deliberately invoked; downright lies as well, I shouldn't wonder.

All this is frightfully bad of me, of course, and I hate myself for it, but not nearly so much as I hate that stiff-collared smuglic-cool prick called Crowe for sparking me off in the first place, and then fanning my negative flames.

'Histories of countries from first to last are, I fear, no longer popular,' he observes somewhat mournfully, in his Preface to Volume III.

'Bloody right, mate!' I chortle vengefully. 'Specially not yours, you drivelling dodo duffer, you. Which could explain, couldn't it, why not one volume of your puling great-English-nation spew has ever been borrowed out of this library in over a hundred yours? Eh? Serves you fucking—'

Flabbergasted, dumbfounded, dumbstruck, thunderstruck, 'poleaxed', and numerous other clichés attempt to encapsulate the visible physiological responses of persons whose deeply entrenched beliefs and expectations are suddenly uprooted as by a tornado of irrefutable contradiction. I don't know which cliché might best have hung on me in that library in those moments, when I alighted upon Crowe in La Marfée, but it's surely a great loss to future students of method acting everywhere that no-one was secretly recording my antics on video film (at least, I don't think they were), especially as I sank my heedless six-stone buttocks[1] between the horrified thighs of a rather pretty little Thai student, who had been so inertly asleep that my peripheral vision had failed to perceive that she wasn't in fact her chair, while, for the second incredulous time, I devoured the following passage:

> Richelieu, however, [writes Crowe, Volume III, Chapter XXIX] forced the Count of Soissons to take arms against him, by summoning him under a penalty to return to France. At Sedan were the dukes of Bouillon and Guise, the latter a prelate, who had succeeded to the title on the death of his brother, that duke who was governor of Provence. The moment the league between them for attacking the cardinal was known in France, it was approved by all – by the queen, by Monsieur, by the marshals in the Bastille, Vitry and Bassompierre, and by Cinq Mars himself. The Spanish court was ready on this, as on all other occasions, to promise succours of horse and foot against the cardinal. The latter despatched the Marshal de Chatillon with an army, which Soissons soon faced with 3000 men of his own and 7000 imperialists. Both sides expected the co-operation of the Duke of Lorraine, who, however, came to neither. An engagement took place between the armies on the 6th of June, at a place called La Marfée. It was the Marshal de Chatillon who led the royal army to the attack, but his cavalry showed at once a disinclination to combat, which was most unusual, especially with this portion of a French army. The mounted gentlemen refused to make the cardinal victorious over the Count de Soissons, the cause of the latter being their own. The royal army thus suffered a signal defeat, Chatillon himself with difficulty escaping. But in the rout which ensued a cavalier approached the Count of Soissons, and, placing his pistol close to his head, shot down the prince. The event, fortuitous or designed,

---

[1] I.e., approximately: one on each side, making one and a half hundredweight altogether.

saved Richelieu from destruction, and defeated the universal though tacit conspiracy of all the court, noblesse, and even army against him . . .

So the recapped situation now is:

1 According to Encyclopaedia Britannica Inc.'s Historians' History of the World, which cites Eyre Evans Crowe's *The History of France* as its Authority:
  'As Soissons rode over the field of battle, he pushed up his visor with his pistol; it was accidentally discharged, and the victor perished. Report did not fail to say that he was assassinated, and, of course, by the order of Richelieu; but there is no evidence to support such a rumour.'

2 According to Crowe himself, in his selfsame *History*, the Count of Soissons, in his hour of triumph, was murdered by an unnamed assassin on horseback.

Now what are we to make of that? Certainly it does not follow that Evans Crowe was a good historian after all. Because he wasn't. This can be seen, can it not, in little flourishes like 'a place called La Marfée', which tells us bugger all more than 'La Marfée', meanwhile strongly indicating that Crowe hadn't gone to the bother of establishing exactly where La Marfée was, or was near – and also the rather unfortunate fact, from Crowe's point of view, that the Battle of La Marfée wasn't fought on 6 June 1641 at all, but rather on the 6th of July?

None of that, however, can excuse the Historians' History. And we cannot help but wonder, can we, whether the anomaly noted above derives merely from some editorial error in the attribution of Authority, or more probably from the deliberately dextrous corruption of information, to accord with some Establishment Version? Concretely, if the Count of Soissons, after the battle was over and won, was then shot in the head in cold blood at point-blank range by an assailant in the pay, or at least service, of Richelieu, then this would come close, would it not, to rocking to death any fond official delusion that the pretentiously legitimate governments of major powers do not stoop to contract assassination as a means of shutting up their opponents?

*We* know that's codswallop, alas, just as we have become all too familiar with 'official history' relating to the CIA, Cuba and Castro, what the Japanese did or didn't do to Chinese women in World War II, whether England didn't or did wittingly supply arms to Iraq before the Gulf War, Spythatcher, not to mention the truth underlying the so-called Union of the Parliaments of Scotland and England in 1707. But is it not possible that HENRY SMITH WILLIAMS LL.D, cobbling his Historians' History together in the final decade of the nineteenth century, and with little inkling of the short-wave radio, movie newsreels, superzoom lenses, documentary television, satellite piracy, computer hacking, database dredging of gigabytes of old text newly captured by optical character recognition, and the like, blithely imagined he could falsify as he pleased, to gratify his paymasters' expectations, or for whatever other ignoble reasons?

Whatever the final truth of all that, one certain interim truth marches forward: that however partial is the truth of Evans Crowe's account, it is at least less untrue than the Historians' History's downright lie. As corroboration of this, please consider the following contemporary report, uncovered in its original seventeenth-century French, in Volume 49 of the Second Series of M. Petitot's *Collection des Mémoires Relatifs à l'Histoire de France*, some three poring hours after eventually over a nasty cup of library tea I persuaded the traumatised Thai girl that I did not mean to rape her really. The extract is from the *Memoires* of François de Paule de Clermont, Marquis de Montglat, 'Mestre de Camp du Régiment de Navarre, Grand Maître de la Garde-Robe du Roi, et Chevalier de ses Ordres', &c., and his story goes like this:

> The Marêchal de Châtillon waited with impatience for the Duke of Lorraine to join his army, so that together they could besiege Sedan. He sent urgent letters exhorting him [Lorraine] to hurry up, and also to communicate his news. But having not found him at a rendezvous that he had specified for a certain day, he [Chatillon] sent an express messenger to Lorraine to urge him to march. This he [Lorraine] kept putting off, for a variety of excuses, which changed from day to day. Finally, however, it became known that he [Lorraine] had met with the Abbé de Mercy, representing the Emperor [ie sympathetic to Spain and hence, in present circumstances, to the Count of Soissons also], and that thence he had joined forces with the Duke of Guise at Luxembourg, and that his forces had proceeded

to march from there, without there being any signs of hostilities in the territories controlled by the Spaniards [strongly implying shared hostility to France, Louis XIII, and Richelieu, whose general, you will remember, De Châtillon most stoutly was]. Thus the Maréchal knew that the Duke was continuing to behave as usual, that is to say: never to keep any promise, and to be constantly thoughtless, lightminded and unfaithful.

And from the moment that the Maréchal realized that the Duke of Lorraine was not going to join up with him, he saw perfectly well that he had instead joined the Spaniards. There was great surprise in France at this switch of allegiance, and great condemnation of him [Lorraine] and his faithlessness, but he replied that he had merely repaid [ironical stuff, this] what had been lent him at Nancy, when his own lands had been confiscated from him by means of deceit, and hence his objective now was simply to ensure, by similar deceptive means, the rightful recapture of his property.

Nonetheless, Lamboi, knowing of the attack on the two Torcys [villages . . . ], marched to the aid of the princes; and he crossed the Meuse at Sedan by two bridges of boats, across the river close to the town. There [west of the river], their armies coming together, they found themselves engaged in battle on a plain to this [ie the French] side of Sedan. Immediately the Maréchal de Châtillon learned of this he marched straight at him [Lamboi], and, the Spaniards standing firm, the battle commenced on the 6th of July on this plain, where the French cavalry took to its heels at the outset, having never had any intention of standing firm. The infantry being thus abandoned, they were hacked to pieces and entirely defeated, and all their cannon and equipment taken. The medics of Arnauld [NB not Arnault] and the men-at-arms of the Queen and of Monsieur [the King's brother, Gaston d'Orleans] were left to do what they could.

The Marquis of Praslin, master of the [French] camp and general of the cavalry, paid with his life by [deliberately] getting himself killed without asking for quarter. It was said that he had given his word to throw in with the Count of Soissons as soon as he declared himself [ie marched out against the forces of Richelieu and the King], as had Chambor, captain of the cavalry, and that, having failed to do so, his [Praslin's] fear of falling into his [the Count's] hands made him prefer death to prison, where he could be sure of receiving a thousand reproaches, and some exceedingly disagreeable treatment [*'un fort mauvais traitement'*].[2]

The Marquis of Senecey, named before the death of his elder brother the Count of Randan, Camp Master of the Piédmont Regiment, was taken fighting at the head of his battalion, and killed in cold blood by those [of the Soissons faction] who disputed whose captive he was. The Marquis of Roquelaure [NB not Roquefort], seeing himself abandoned by the rest of the cavalry, would under no circumstances retreat, and was captured at the head of his squadron. The Maréchal de Châtillon, seeing the battle lost, withdraw into Rethel, where he did the best he could, to salvage and rally those of his soldiers who had managed to save themselves.

After the combat, the Count of Soissons, who had been spectating from a distance upon the rout of the French, trotting into the midst of his own troops, and surrounded by his personal staff, suddenly fell stone-dead from his horse, without anyone ever knowing exactly what took place, since none of those close to him had actually seen his death as it happened. They could say only that they had heard a shot, and that they had seen a horseman passing, and their master at the same time falling head-first to the ground, with one foot caught in a stirrup; and that they found he had been shot in the forehead, that the wad [stuffing for stopping your balls from falling out of your firearms, in those days] was lodged inside his head, that his face was scorched by gunpowder, all clearly indicating that he had been shot at pointblank range.

The mystery of this death has never been cleared up, and has opened the floodgates to wild conspiracy-theorizing by a multitude of wankers [*'a donné sujet de gloser à bien du monde'*[3]], to unravel such an extraordinary affair. In any case, just as the incident caused enormous consternation to his [the Count of Soissons'] party, it simultaneously gave intense joy to the Cardinal, who saw himself at once delivered of a formidable enemy, one who had caused him many worries, and who would certainly have caused him many worse worries, had he lived to enjoy the fruits of his great victory in the battle.

---

[2] Suggesting certain murkier dimensions to the Count of Soissons' moral character than anything either revealed to or divulged by Louis Morel.

[3] 'You mean you had hoped to impart to this morsel of mistranslation an imperceptibly Glaswegian inflection?' [P.C.]

So at this point it still must seem as if the puzzle of who killed the Count of Soissons, and upon whose orders, if any, is one of those delightfully intriguing historical whodunnits, which could in principle be settled once and for all on the basis of exciting new evidence, or conscience-stricken confessions sold for vast sums to the Sunday papers – like the ongoing heated debate over who was behind the killing of John F. Kennedy, and/or was the English Princess Diana a virgin really when on her wedding night she first yielded up her lovely lithesome sovereignty to the charms of Dear Prince Charles?

Though the Marquis of Monglat was indisputably a contemporary chronicler, he does not actually claim to have been present at the Battle of La Marfée, and even if he was present, he could not have been an on-site observer of the death of the Count of Soissons, since – as an inner-circle servant of Louis XIII – he would have been on the opposing side, and most likely already fled westward with Châtillon to Rethel.

Further intensive research since the last paragraph has enabled us to assure you that there are several other first-hand accounts of the battle, including de Châtillon's own despatches, and the 'Relation de Frédéric-Maurice' (better known as the Duke of Bouillon, cf the French *Arch. Nles R2 55*). All of them contradict others in some respects, and none, to our certain knowledge, gives finer detail, or makes more sense of the puzzle, than the following:

# 63

# I Witness a Count

I cannot remember [*writes Louis*] any ride in my life more unpleasant than that to the heights of La Marfée. [*This is in the very early hours of the day of the battle. Saturday, 6 July 1641. One detail all accounts agree upon is the weather during that preceding night: rolling thunder followed by torrential rain.*]

The rain had come on more heavily than ever. Our ascent was long and difficult, being traversed by many gulleys, and by copses too dense to ride through. In places the ground was so like a mire of sponge, that our horses, made heavy by our armour, had much trouble to retrieve their feet. There was, however, some consolation in the knowledge, that the enemy too must overcome such obstacles on the western side, else the high ground must all fall to us.

Day began to break heavily as we reached La Marfée heights, with still no sign of the deluge abating. The Count, in accordance with his plan, had already detached a company of musketeers to take possession of the beech wood between ourselves and his main position. We found also waiting for us several tumbrels containing provisions for the men, and ammunition in plentiful supply. Together with these was a further commission for me, signed by the Count, to assume overall command of the infantry musketeers in the wood. This authority I used to deploy our spare time in throwing up a strong breastwork of earth and boughs before the beech wood. All our men setting to work with great eagerness, before seven o'clock we had completed a formidable defence.

Towards eight the rain eased to ragged showers, which would continue throughout the day. Earlier the air had been so dark and thick that the line of the Meuse, and even the fortress of Sedan itself, had been scarcely distinguishable. But now, as by the sudden lifting of a curtain, I could see the troops of Lamboi descending towards the bridge of boats, and passing over the river, in as fine unbroken order as if they marched but to parade.

Next came the pennons and plumes, the flashing arms and beating drums, of the Princes' own brigades as they rode to war. My gaze then turned anxiously towards Remilly [a village to the east, on the south side of the Meuse, where the main Royalist army had stopped overnight], but all appeared yet still in the camp of the enemy. Looking again to the east, I saw the two allied armies approach nearly and then unite, unopposed and seemingly unnoticed by any scouts from the other side. Winding up around and between the gulleys and trees, the army of the Princes mounted slowly towards the heights where my own force was stationed. Not until nearly nine o' clock did the report of one single cannon suggest that the Maréchal de Châtillon was become aware of the legion moving against him, and that he was minded to confront us.

[Consensus figures suggest that the armies, numerically, were evenly matched. About 11,000 men on each side. While the Princes (the Count of Soissons and the Duke of Bouillon) had only 3–4000 men directly under their command, the reinforcements under Lamboi – provided by, collectively, the House of Austria (the Emperor, and Philip IV of Spain, in hot cahoots against Richelieu) – must have numbered at least 7000.

The view from the top of La Marfée is indeed panoramic, and from Louis's account it would seem that he was positioned on the summit above where the American cemetery lies today. Probably the best vantage of all. Nevertheless, when one recalls the atrocious conditions, both overhead and underfoot, and bears in mind the increasingly confused, fragmented, wounded, fleeing and dying presence of some 22,000 combatants in the field that day, one is reminded that Louis's version of events – though it seems he was fated to witness the one most crucial incident – is inevitably partial and bitty.

To get some idea of the scale of the bittiness, we may subtract from 22,000 all the very few individuals and groups of individuals whom he describes, or barely mentions, and then imagine for ourselves where the great remainder must be at any given moment, how they are engaged, who they are shooting at, lance-charging, running away from, and so forth.

An alternative route to a similar effect might be to rush to Sedan yourself, before the next paragraph, and have a good look, in the Château Fort Museum, at the cinemascopic, almost virtually realistically vast oil painting (which itself is merely the copy of a German original ten times larger) entitled 'Le Panorama de la Bataille de Sedan', by Louis Braun. Actually it doesn't portray our Battle of La Marfée at all, but rather the similarly pointless conflict and carnage fought between the French and the Germans on 1 September 1870, by the end of which day the French Second Empire had collapsed.

However, and perhaps in order to persuade HM Inspector to swallow the tax-exempting of the cost of your research trip, you could truthfully point out that the battlefield was identical on both occasions, that very little (apart from that cute single railway track in the 1870 foreground) in the way of communications, transport and the technology of mass-murder had changed very drastically in those 230 years, that neither side in either engagement, for instance, was advantaged by helicopter gunships fondly nicknamed Puff,[1] or by Stealth bombers, or by missiles with computers in their pinpoint noses, nor were their intelligences updated every second by radio, radar and digitally enhanced spy-satellite television pictures of our enemy's every movement, and that consequently the overall disorganized impression of smoke, bangs, whistles, yells, thuds, splats, crunches, human wails, equine screams, confusion, bewilderment, blood gushing, lungs bursting, breech fouling, guts spewing, and accelerated entropy generally, which we take away from the panoramic view of 1870, could just as well, with extra helpings of cloud, rain and mud, serve to colour our peripheral understanding of what Louis tells us next.]

Regiment upon regiment now presented themselves, and defiled across the underwood to adopt their appointed positions. The blasts of trumpets, loud commands of officers, the creaking and crashing of ammunition carts, soon were followed by a steady fire of artillery from beneath the hill, giving notice that the battle was commenced upon our right [to the north-west], where the infantry of Lamboi were still ascending the slopes. Surprised, I will own, to hear the cannon so near, I mounted at once into my saddle, and rode forward alone to a vantage where, beyond the trees, could be seen what passed below.

There, beyond the puffs of cannon smoke, I descried a body of the

---

[1] *'The Magic Dragon? Then how seriously is this obscenity intended?' [P.C.]*

enemy's pikemen in the act of charging our German infantry, who
beneath this onslaught were borne back near two hundred paces, yet
still maintained their order. At every step they yielded my heart beat
faster to be there, to lead them back to the attack. Or again, if only I
might be permitted, with my men-at-arms, to charge the pikemen's flank,
we should drive them all to the devil.

[Meaning: knock them back, cut them down, slash their throats,
trample them into the bog, shoot them at arm's-length; and
basically kill as many as possible as quickly as possible. Though,
as we have noted before, Louis is engagingly ahead of his age in
his occasional prose appreciations of nature, he is markedly less
pacifically advanced in his treatment of such wartime frontline
commonplaces as the aroma of erupting entrails, or how best to
depict the facial expression of a head so freshly severed from its
body that its brain is still acutely aware of the situation? This
typically 17th-century reticence re the minutiae of battlefield
squalor is thus on a par with, say, the Victorian stance on
missionary sex with sickly prostitutes, or wrestling with your
chronic constipation.

And we're all only human, aren't we?

If something is commonplace, yet aesthetically repulsive, it
comes easily to most citizens never to mention it, and to many
not even to perceive it. We all know that, except those of
us who won't even perceive it. Traumata like AIDS can of
course toggle our sensibilities, somersaulting condoms from a
furtive tacky chore into hilarious television entertainment for
all the family, and beloved saviour of shares in the British
rubber market too. Perhaps we can see this more clearly if
we try to imagine what ghastly plague could switch toilet-
paper advertisements from lovable puppies gamboling in the
garden to practical close-ups of offically recommended methods
of bum-wiping. Does the Prime Creep remain seated for the
first wipe, or is it attempted in a standing position? Top to
bottom, or bottom to top? 'One up, one down and one for a
polisher.' Is that sound Department of Health advice, or a
conspiracy foisted by the manufacturers of underpants? Such
queries, to be sure, will be condemned as frivolous, disgusting,
psychoanalytically infantile, blah-blah, until the catastrophe
toggles.

And maybe it won't.

Certainly we can always pray.

On the other hand, never forget the three universal laws of computing: GIGO (garbage in, garbage out); and if it can go wrong, it will go wrong; and furthermore if it can't go wrong, it will go wrong. Janet and I have been arguing for years that these laws could without loss be reduced to two: *It will go wrong*; and, *Garbage*. Either way, your relationship with and attitudes to your bum are bound to be transmogrified sooner or later. If it isn't sooner then you may derive satisfaction from reflecting that in the meantime it will only be perverts and troublemakers like playwrights and novelists who stoop to giving such scato their logical.

So that while, for example, you will find no mention of any such obsessional crap in the mostly-forgotten memoirs of minor country gentlemen such as Louis Morel, if you zip back to Rabelais a hundred years earlier you will instantly discover the prescient passage in which Gargantua concludes:

' . . . that there is no arse-wiper like a well-downed goose, if you hold her head between your legs.'[2]

And since from Louis, Monglat, Châtillon, the Duke of Bouillon, and umpteen others who have left descriptions of La Marfée, and umpteen similar battles, we hear precious little about the sordid particulars of impalement, mutilation, dismemberment and decapitation so rife in battle, we could do worse than supplement our flagging imaginations with this

---

[2] *'You must take my word for it, you really must,' he continues with relish. 'You get a miraculous sensation in your arse-hole, both from the softness of the down and from the temperate heat of the goose herself; and this is easily communicated to the bum-gut and the rest of the intestines, from which it reaches the heart and the brain. Do not imagine that the felicity of the heroes and demigods in the Elysian Fields arises from their asphodel, their ambrosia, or their nectar, as those ancients say. It comes, in my opinion, from their wiping their arses with the neck of a goose, and that is the opinion of Master Duns Scotus too.' From GARGANTUA, Chapter 13, Penguin translation by J.M. Cohen.*

second vignette from Rabelais:

'Then at one blow he [the monk] sliced his [the archer's] head, cutting his skull over the temple-bone and taking off the two parietal bones and the sagittal suture, together with a great part of the frontal bone; and in doing this he cut through the two membranes and made a deep opening in the posterior lobes of his brain. So his cranium remained hanging on his shoulders by the skin of his pericranium, falling backwards like a doctor's cap, black outside and red within. And he fell to the ground stark dead.'

Or, just as well, forward three hundred years to Stendhal's *Charterhouse of Parma* portrayal of the teenage idiot Fabrizio's bumbling about the battlefield at Waterloo:

'A few minutes later Fabrizio saw, twenty paces ahead of him, a piece of tilled land that was being ploughed up in a singular fashion. The bottoms of the furrows were full of water, and the very damp soil that formed the ridges of these furrows was flying about in little black lumps flung three or four feet into the air. Fabrizio noted this curious effect as he was passing; then his mind turned to dreaming of the Marshal and his glory. He heard a sharp cry close by him; it was two hussars falling struck by shot; and when he looked round at them, they were already twenty paces behind the escort. What seemed to him horrible was a horse streaming with blood that was writhing on the ploughed land, its hooves entangled in its own entrails. It tried to follow the other horses; the blood ran down into the mire.'[3]

Just the sort of thing that is now being taken for granted all over the slopes and heights of La Marfée at this very moment, as Louis goes on:]

At that moment my eye fell upon a group of officers gathered upon a little knoll, in the front of whom was evidently the Count of Soissons, to judge by his suit of armour, which I had seen in his apartments, and accompanied by an elderly man in German uniform, whom I concluded to be Lamboi. The Count was pointing with his pistol, apparently expressing his consternation, to the retreating infantry of his left wing,

---

[3] Penguin translation by Margaret R.B. Shaw.

while his companion seemed to look upon the scene, with naught but the utmost composure. The two gentlemen then conferred, and a moment later an unarmoured equerry set off at speed from the Count's side, to convey a command that caused a company of our musketeers to wheel upon the flank of the enemy's pikemen, and drive them back under a tremendous fire, allowing our Germans to advance again, and take up their position as before . . .

Now **I have here before me**[4] [*writes Humbert*] a memo to ourselves, specifying for the narration of this chapter:

'Let Louis tell it all in his own words. No interruptions. Unadulteried Authenticity.'

Well, is it not quite a bit like virginity? Once we've inadvertently lost it once, there's less to be said for not losing it again the following night. Also, if we left it entirely to Louis, we would never lift up to our cliffhangers. He's blessed with stirring ingredients, okay, but not what it takes to bake. And so for the sake of the cake:

Louis rides back to inform his men of what he has seen. The din of battle increases and Louis frets terribly that no signal has yet been given for his own men to move. Again he rides forward to reconnoitre, and sees the enemy faring poorly. Looking up again, in great exasperation, to the Count of Soissons' knoll of command, he sees a red flag sort of semaphore that now is the moment for his own force to attack: a phalanx of enemy cavalry has emerged from behind the church in the otherwise tiny village of Chaumont, and is cantering north towards the Count. In the very moment that Louis's troop gallops trumpeting, bellowing and guaranteeing death by slitting [these, remember, are the recruits from cut-throat Paris] out of the beech wood, a much larger contingent of friendly cavalry, led by the Duke of Bouillon, appears on the brow of a hill about quarter of a mile away, on the further side of the enemy phalanx.

Louis and the Duke of Bouillon launch a simultaneous downhill pincer attack on Châtillon's cavalry. 'Confronted in the same moment by the Duke, at their head, and taken unawares by our own headlong assault

---

4 'I've a nasty feeling these five words are plagiarised from Kingsley Amis. Anyone give chapter and verse?' [P.C.]

from so unexpected a quarter, the enemy's cavalry were now borne back upon their infantry, broken, dispersed, trampled down.' Here, as discussed above, mix in wounds, blood, screams, death, etc, to taste. 'His infantry threw down their arms and fled; many of his cavalry reined about to gallop from the field; and though a minority remained, with a will to fight on, it was but with the courage of despair; for the principal force of the Maréchal de Châtillon was, by that single manoeuvre, thrown into an absolute rout.'

As the victors begin to mop up, they encounter isolated pockets of resistance from desperate enemy individuals. One opposing officer in particular appears to single Louis out for one-to-one horseback sword combat to the death. Both vizors rise, to facilitate seeing what on earth is going on, and with a gasp of thrown-together emotions Louis apprehends that his tail-end assailant is none other than the loathsome runt Charles, cad nephew to the Maréchal de Châtillon and would-be abductor, furtive wedder and bragging cuckolder of the ravishing Hélène Arnault. Reminded so unexpectedly of Hélène, and of his pathetic ignorance of her whereabouts, condition, and how many other men may have done goodness knows what to her, Louis is commendably manful in mastering his understandable impulse to behead the runt on the spot, and offering him instead ten seconds in which to come to his senses and surrender. Nine, eight, then at seven with a snarl of primal hatred the futile Charles attempts a deadly sabre slash at Louis's throat but is foiled both by his own ineptitude and also the fact that the reformed (well, sort of) Parisian bully-bravo named Combalet de Montfaucon prances in from the right and fires a pistol pointblank into his nose.

'Whereat the Maréchal's nephew rode away, dying astride his horse.'

Knowing Louis, we might now expect him to remonstrate severely with Combalet for his ungentlemanly murderous intrusion, but in fact there is no time for this before Louis's agonized attention is drawn to a further tragedy. Thanks to an unusually accurate volley of musket-fire from a lone platoon of Royalist infantry beating an unusually orderly retreat back south towards Chaumont, several of Louis's cut-throat brigade are now hit when they least expected it, and/or have their horses killed beneath them. One of the victims is the faithful smuggler-terrorist from Bigorre, cum freedom-fighter from Catalonia, now become Lieutenant Garcés. When Louis dismounts by the fallen man's side he finds him shot through the neck, his jugular nicked, and blood and life fading fast.

"'Jesús, María. Jesús, María,'"[5] moaned poor Pere, as I gazed close in his eyes, from which the light of life was fleeting away.

"'I am afraid you are badly hurt, Garcés,' cried I, more painfully affected by his situation than I could have imagined.

"'I am dying, Señor Louis!' muttered he in Catalan. "All in vain. Bound for hell. Oh, God. How I wish . . . wish I had not . . . '"

"'There, there, dear Pere,' I urged him. "Be easy now. And wish you had not what?"

"'Killed the customs man, Derville, Master Louis. At the mill. Him that did but his duty. Before . . . but now . . . it is my one remorse. Oh, but great. Very vile. And for it . . . I must . . . '"

"'No, no, Pere,' I counselled him, in the absence of any priest. "As this day you repent, be assured that God will . . . ' But now I saw the heavy cloud of death envelope his mortal form. The corporeal fire of my faithful friend Pere was extinguished, his soul, I pray, already risen up to meet his Maker, and the corpse beside me was . . . nothing.'

When Louis stirs from his grief over Pere Garcés he finds chaos all around him. Corpses, drizzle and smoke everywhere, particularly from the village of Chaumont, where every building but the church is on fire. To the south of Chaumont one entire regiment of Royalist infantry, virtually intact, is retreating in the direction of Rethel. Pursued by the Duke of Bouillon's cavalry, the retreating foot soldiers maintain a murderous defence by dint of executing, with uncommon discipline, a tactic of the form: march, two, three, fifty, turn, kneel, fire, reload, march . . . Louis, having whipped the remains of his own troop forward for a support charge on the retreaters, is given confusing pause by the sudden realization that the cavalier commanding the present enemy regiment, and preserving their deadly composure in defeat, by his omnipresent cool contempt of personal danger, warm applause for his own men's courage, and constant stream of tersely shouted orders, is none other than his own old but long estranged uncle surrogate, the Chevalier of Montenero.

Unfortunately, or perhaps very fortunately, in the very moment of Louis's calling a brief halt while he mulls over the implications of this new perception, the Duke of Bouillon gallops up in bumptious person and insults Louis gratuitously by inquiring with an insufferable sneer

---

[5] We give this to you exactly as Louis has given it to us, although in Catalan 'Maria' would be unaccented.

what's happened to all his "cavalry".

"'All who have not fallen in the battle, your grace," I informed him, "are here present with me now."

"'If that be the case, Monsieur Morel," rejoined the Duke with great sarcasm, "you had best lead them back to Sedan. For one callow youth from Lourdes, monsieur, and three score scum from Paris, are of no use at all to me."' And on that disagreeable note the Duke splats away to command the ongoing Pyrrhic horseback harassment of the Chevalier's infantry.

Reading between the lines, we can't help wondering whether some of the other scum from Paris may not already have peeled away and reverted to type by slitting fallen throats – hopefully only enemy throats – and plundering lifeless bodies. Loyally, Louis does not say so. But he does admit that, when he recovers from the blind fury caused by the Duke of Bouillon's affront:

'My remaining men, having overheard the Duke, and no longer with Garcés to control them, had moved away from me, broken ranks, and now were looting Chaumont.'

Feeling betrayed, angry, depressed, none too eager to attack the Chevalier, in any case ordered by the Duke to go home, Louis decides his next move must be to report to his commander-in-chief.

The Count of Soissons.

'Riding back towards the spot where I had before seen the Count, in conference with Lamboi, and urging my horse up the hill, I saw him [not the horse] still posted on a little eminence, with a group of his officers and attendants at the distance of about a dozen yards behind him – the Count seeming to enjoy the sight of the field he had won, and his retinue apparently discussing with some animation the events lately passed.'

Louis must now be what we would describe as about a hundred and fifty yards downhill from the Count's position.

'Happy, happy, had I been able to reach him sooner. But alas, just as I was mounting the rise, a horseman dashed across the ridge like lightning, and reined in his horse a moment before the Count. I heard the report of a firearm. The horseman galloped on, and I saw the prince fall from his saddle.'

Of course by the time Louis has spurred his horse to the scene all the retinue, in a fearful tizzy, is gathered round their leader's body and rending the sky with woe.

'As I arrived, they were just untying his casque, but in vain. All that presented itself to my gaze, as I looked down, was the cold blank face of death. Above his right eyebrow was the wound of a pistol ball, which must have gone directly into his brain. His brow and forehead were scorched and blackened with the blast and smoke of the muzzle, so close must his killer have fired.'

Louis Morel then goes on:

'Thus died Louis, Count of Soissons, hero of all France in the struggle against the Cardinal. In the hour of this crucial victory, the Count's personal triumph and the success of all our efforts were dashed to fruitless ashes by his death. For myself . . . ' And Louis continues at considerable length about the multitude of desolate emotions lapping round him in those moments. Inadequacy, futility, guilt, and abject despair at the thought of never again setting eyes, or anything else, upon Hélène. Now how many of these angsts he spontaneously experienced in those seconds by his dead leader's corpse, compared with others brewed up later during the days of solitary confinement following his own death sentence [yes, don't worry, more on this shortly] is impossible to unfankle.

What we can be sure of is that:

'My brief lapse, into miserable reverie, was cut short by one of the Count's equerries, who stepped forward with the conjecture, that his poor dear master must have shot himself, due to his regrettable practice, of pushing up his visor with his pistol.

'"No, no, not at all!" cried I. "It was murder. Most blatant murder, every horrible instant of which I witnessed myself, though from too far, I am grieved to say, to have identified the assassin. There, look, smell for yourselves. The Count's own pistols have not been fired."'

Yes, yes, now chimes a bystanding page, who till this moment has been speechless with grief. Definitely it was murder, he saw it too, and, sternly prompted by Louis, he swears the assassin, though he wore no armour, had a mask across his face.

'"Had his horse a white blaze on his shoulder?" I inquired, as a terrible conviction grew upon me.

'"Why yes, monsieur," said the boy.

'"And his bonnet? There was a single plume in his bonnet, was there not?"

'"Why yes, monsieur."

'"That plume was . . . what colour, if you please? Think carefully now," I bade him. And without a second's hesitation, the boy replied,

'"Monsieur, the plume was green."

'"Ha!" exclaimed I, between rage and a strange form of joy, "then shall he die for it by my hand."'

Convinced he now knows who killed the Count, Louis turns all action-manic once more. Shedding his helmet and outer armour, he commands the Count's attendants to likewise strip his horse, which is in fact the superfast tilting roan the Count had given him to trump the Duke. Many kilos lighter, armed only with his sabre and the Count's two unfired pistols, Louis leaps into the saddle of the liberated mare, reins her nose north-west towards the little River Bar, in which direction the villain had sped.

And:

'With a pounding heart, I gave chase.'

# 64

# Hot Pursuits

Honesty here compels us to admit that since the last sentence we have ourselves zoomed all round France again in search of vital clues, missing links, uncollected papers, good-snip supermarket red wine to fill our van up with now 'Europe' has increased the tax-paid allowances,[1] and in particular any new evidence that would render our chapters following Louis's death cell-confession even more satisfying from the point of view of narrative perfection — immaculate post-climactic fusion of strands and themes such as who gives a shit about the beauties of nature (cf holistic integration with the environment, cf duties to self and compassion for others, most of all future others); rights of small vigorous nations such as Scotland and Catalonia to sovereign independence from the mouldering mammoths smothering them; the value of ultimate orgasm as top of only the second division (or is it third?) turning the crafting of novels both

---

[1] Arguably the greatest advance yet achieved by 'Brussels'. What a pity they had to reduce the duty-free allowances at the same time. Moreover and in any case, while we're at it, hands up the ardent European who can well explain why bottles of *Scottish* malt whisky are cheaper *tax-paid* in French hypermarkets, such as Auchan, than they are *duty-free* in English airports. Of course there may be good things to be said for 'Europe', but we didn't once hear them during our whirlwind tour of France, and we certainly never hear them in rural Berwickshire. Least of all from Mr Tibbs, who brings our fish on Friday mornings, and isn't terribly thrilled about being told by Brussels that soon he will be obliged to fork out £30,000 for a new and approved purpose-built Japanese refrigerated van. We'd best not render Mr Tibbs's remarks on the matter in direct quotes, but obviously they included similes involving innocent eskimos not living in the south of Spain, coupled with oversalaried Eurocrats of extremely limited intelligence.

mature and readable into a virtual impossibility;[2] reduced alcohol rations for airline pilots and throat surgeons, to be sure, but ever a little more than adequate for practising novelists; the cardinal significance of ruffs in history, ah . . . *history* – and especially the auctioning of film rights in Cannes.

As to the France we zoomed round, well, now as then:

The French are certainly misunderstood:—but whether the fault is theirs, in not sufficiently explaining themselves, or speaking with that exact limitation and precision which one would expect on a point of such importance, and which, moreover, is so likely to be contested by us—or whether the fault may not be altogether on our side, in not understanding their language always so critically as to know 'what they would be at'—I shall not decide; but 'tis evident to me, when they affirm, '*That they who have seen Paris, have seen everything,*' they must mean to speak of those who have seen it by daylight.[3]

For their part, the French may with justice retort that the English are certainly misunderstood too, and with relentless justice, since not only are their flabby labials incapable of most French vowels, consonants, and expressively expulsive plosivities, but they, the English, are not even up to enunciating English either. This you may test, if you can be bothered, by prising any sanctimonious old fart at random out of a censorship policy meeting of the EBC Board of Governors, resorting to tempting threats of spankings only if necessary, and requiring him (almost certainly) to read aloud the following suitably simple phrase:

'More moorhens maws.'

How many vowel sounds do you hear him yap?

Now ferry your identical papyrus to Scott Mackay at Caledonian Television, and count again.

Of course it's not for us to subtly hint that this dismal emasculation of English English is in any way consequent upon, viciously causally perpetuative of, or even casually emblematic of parallel dismal emasculations – perhaps one had better also say abhorrent clitorectomies – of English broadcasting, public-life probity, economic vigour, literary and creative energy generally, and (what ought to be) universal imaginative compassion for terror-driven illiterate Iraquis being fried alive by

---

[2] Witness, if you can bare two, my own tragic hankering after Jennifer Macpherson. Not to mention—

[3] Hey, Paul! Here's one you missed! [H.S., final edit.]

immeasurably superior weaponry, Serbs and Croats locked in reciprocal suicide ('Bloody animals, the lot; let 'em get on with it'), let alone the poor Whynge-Bletheringtons across the way, whose principal home, two holiday houses, top-end BMW for him plus eight-seater Peugot estate for her, yacht and all, are now being *re*possessed ('ho-ho!') because the bottoms of the frilly-knickers and asbestosis-underwriting markets have finally fallen out.

Scoff if you will. Or better, belly-laugh. They say it's good for your sex-life. And then let's have your account of how England, Their England[4] can have voted in and back the same shower of tunnel-visioned flint-hearted sour-spirited self-seeking greasy grasping arseholes for approaching two decades on the trot. No personal or political individual is morally perfect, and Scotland isn't either. But let it be not forgot that Scotland has never voted for the greasy grasping arseholes. Repeat with feeling. *Greasy Grasping Arseholes.* Not once since the Second World War, and never before that neither. *Never.* That's one abundantly abundant reason why we deserve, and one day will secure, the right to elect our own vowels.

Meanwhile, being so honest, and moreover merely a novelist, hence profoundly past, present and future imperfect, we must confess to you a recent occasion on which the French, in the form of a trim little nineteen-year-old waitress named Marie-Pascale from the Ardèche, had to be not only forgiven, but also effusively consoled and tipped, for misunderstanding the Scots, as personified by Wringhim Knox. It was in Le Grand Bouchon restaurant in the West End of Glasgow. Wringhim, who can on occasion be Balzacchanalianly generous, when he hasn't already done with all his money what Balzac did with everybody else's, had spontaneously offered in McEwan's to treat us all to dinner. This was on the strength of having heard that afternoon of an advantageous American rights deal for his novel near completion, provisionally entitled

---

4 'Shouldn't you perhaps spell it out even more clearly that the ogre you vilify is England very much as the putrid slimy cloying remains of an Imperialist Archetype and that this is not at all inconsistent on a warmly personal level with the fact that many of your own dearest friends – and indeed most bosomest bedfellows! – have been* English by birth if not spirit?' [P.C.]

**\* *'I wouldn't rule out a more historical tense. Past pure and simple, perhaps.' [J.R.]***

*The Vampyres of Sauchiehall.*

'Curry all right?' presumed Wringhim, but Paul Chalicer, just returned from Greece, expressed the view that delicate *specialités lyonnaises* would probably provoke his temporarily treacherous tummy somewhat less than a Taj Madras.

'How about if I fund the wine?' suggested Paul, seeing Wringhim sway with doubts, on the limbs of his uppermost lavishness.

So off we all trudged to the Bouchon, we all including Audrey and Koo – who had been selling to shops in Princes Square that afternoon – Paul's Rebecca, and a couple of Wringhim's crawlier cronies from Scottish Literature, whom I decline to identify by either name or description, for reasons which will not become apparent. Our waitress for the evening, Marie-Pascale, a recently arrived daughter of the proprietor's sister's sister-in-law in Le Puy, being not yet terribly advanced in her English, and particularly her Glaswegian, Paul and Rebecca swiftly leapt to the rescue by ordering for us all in French so fluent that even I myself was unable to contribute much more than a few finnicking marginalia such as that biftec in Paul's green-chilli *tornades* was welcome to be 'exquisitely rare, by all means, but please not bleeding raw to the point of seething with uncooked Mad Cow Disease'. That achieved, and the wine too prescribed, Audrey Macpherson then confided to our waitress that she personally would be grateful to have a flask of water on the table, as she still had lots of essays to mark before morning.

Now you might object here that in a French French restaurant there is no need to request water with your dinner, since its arrival is as automatic as your pot of Chinese tea in Soho. And there you would be right. Glasgow folk, however, have somewhat different attitudes to water. Handy stuff for having a bath in, from time to time, but otherwise principally that sodding wet nuisance that falls out of the sky all the time, and so why the fuck clutter up your dinner table with jugs of it, when you could just as well fill the space with tins of brainsouper lager, or bottles of Pee Adore?

Hence Audrey's specific request for water. Not just water, note, but:

'*De l'eau minérale, mademoiselle, s'il vous plaît.*'

Unfortunately this to Wringhim was spurt blood to a fighting cock. That there should be a pan-European conspiracy to market billions of extortionately priced bottles of a commodity to which, for Wringhim, we are entitled by natural right to unlimited free access is much worse than bad enough. But that the Grasping Arseholes should have exploited and exacerbated the scam, to the graft advantage of themselves and their public school buddies in merchant banking and Lloyds, by selling off the water companies, and permitting licenced privateers with secret shares in Nestlé to render domestic tap water even less drinkable than it was before, by means of kill-bud additives such as fluorides, chlorine, and endlessly recycled sewage, thus boosting sales of plastic Evian to young mothers made artificially anxious about the state of their children's health, not to mention sick to their own pregnant stomachs by the taste and smell of London tap water, is not only patently an in-itself-sufficient paradigm argument for Scottish independence (guaranteeing unlimited, free, and also drinkable water for all Scottish citizens) but also, in the meantime, a serious threat to the pressure of Wringhim's own blood.

Now given, on the present evening, the multiplication vexation of considering that he personally might be lumbered with *paying* for Audrey's mineral water – since mineral water is by no stretch of even the Prime Creep's imagination wine, and hence should not reasonably be added to Paul's wine bill – Wringhim can perhaps be forgiven a little for the menacing reluctance (musically most akin to aggressive lechery) with which he growled after Marie-Pascale's departing derrière:

'*Con gasseuse!*'

[*Sic.*]

What he intended to convey was of course along the lines:

'If we've shitting-well got to pay for Audrey's water, let's make sure we get for our money something we can't shitting-just-as-well get out of the kitchen tap – like Perrier shitting bubbles, for example.'

Sadly, and alas, what Wringhim in fact communicated to all our table except one and a half of his Scottish Literature cronies, and most of all to Marie-Pascale, was a traumatising portmanteauing of utterances not excluding:

'Gassy cunt! She's got a gassy cunt! She *is* a gassy cunt. I love gassy cunt! And what wouldn't I give to suck her/your gassy cunt!'

Picture next the frozen moment, the devastated silence, embarrassment, feminine blushes, innocent young waitress's homesick tears, the debonair aplomb with which Paul Chalicer springs to console her, explain and apologize on behalf of the baleful affronter, the meaty tip at the dinner's end, and the half-jestful sigh of retrospective relief that Koo and I share in Lourdes, to think we've left Wringhim in Glasgow.

'I don't know . . . ' I murmured vaguely, as we lay too stewed to sleep, during that sweltering night in a baking third-floor room in Le Zaragoza, a passable two-star hotel in the Place du Champ Commun.[5]

'Don't know what?' Koo murmured back, less vaguely.

'What it is between me and Wringhim.'

---

[5] This hotel was the closest we could get to the house of Maître Arnault, which I wanted to check for two details first thing the following morning, before the narrow streets of the old town filled to choking with sightseers, nuns of every hue, civilian Godsquadders armed with Nikons, careering wheelchairs packed with hopeless optimism, and pickpockets. Though the Arnault building, immediately south of the Château Fort, is basically intact, the ground floor, where he had the office in which the child Louis first insulted him, has been knocked into a neon-lit arcade selling – on the left side – scented candles housed in night-procession wind-shields inscribed with songs of praise, plastic Bernadettes of every size, take-away Jesuses to hang in the back of your car, garish yellow fluffy ducks for those with kids too small to be conned by the rest of the crap and – on the right side – instant cheeseburgers, catsupped Frankfurters, pink ice-cream and Coca Cola for American grazers unable to wait for their next McDonald's.

Our previous visit had been in late November. Cool, wet, the town sufficiently bare of bohos to reveal sad glimpses of its pristine charm. As I'd looked round the child Hélène's tiny bedroom on the second floor it had struck me, like one of those stabbing sensations of irretrievable loss when unexpectedly you stumble upon a hitherto unearthed photo of your mother in the bloom of youth, how blissful it would be to meet the nubile Hélène in the flesh, converse with her, and establish precisely how much Louis's hands have managed to achieve beneath her dress, during the fateful scene by the river, before Jean-Baptiste bursts upon them deranged with fury.

Today, the afternoon Lourdes heat as hot as Marseille Airport car park in August, the narrow streets sardined, the air shimmering with the stench of burgers, incense, armpits and other regrettable biological indispensables, I had suddenly felt overwhelmed by nausea, compounded by the fatigue of long driving in blinding sunlight, and my lust for a litre of lager.

'In what way?'

'I mean . . . you know.'

'Know *what?*'

'When I'm not with him, or corresponding with him, or writing about him or in defence of him, or in any way remotely conscious of his existence, I sometimes suddenly – like waking with a jolt in the moment before dawn – feel myself dangerously close to him, or perhaps him to me. Him *in* me? Me? Speaking as with Wringhim's voice, rehearsing Knox-type arguments, Philippicizing the "Treaty of Union" in typically Wringhhymning tones . . . even occasionally drinking a little too much—'

'Which occasion would that be?' wondered Koo, as wearily she adjusted our superfluous single sheet.

'And yet . . . '

'And yet?'

'When I'm aware of Wringhim – typesetting his atrocious pamphlet, say, or enjoying one of his novels to the point of prayer albeit honest atheist prayer that one day a novel of mine may be nearly as good, or affecting patience during one of his piratical phone-ins, or demoted to just another surrounding face in the McEwan's crowd – when I'm with him in that sort of way, and he with me, then I feel . . . mmm, almost aggressively distinct, disapprovingly different, in some ways – manners, tact, spelling and punctuation, information-technology competence, minor matters mainly – supremely superior. But always – and this is the infuriating thing – in a rather self-consciously prim sort of way, which hampers my own freedom of expression, and frequently puts the lid on my own uninhibited enjoyment of the evening in question.

'That night in the Bouchon, for example. If Wringhim hadn't been there, I'd have got Paul to order their house Montbazillac for dessert. As it was, I didn't. And why? Because I knew that while most of the rest of us would savour one small glass each, with possibly a second for myself, bloody Wringhim would swig back half the bottle, following which, on top of all that had poured before, he would become unacceptably obnoxious.'

'*Become* unacceptably obnoxious?'

'And it's this kind of constant self-sacrifice – fuck a fluffy duck but it's hot in here, squeeze my French – Pyrrhic self-sacrifice at that, which—'

'Your thrusting son, to Wringhim's domineering father,' suggested

Koo, who once studied too much Freud for comfort, during her thesis on what Dalí stole from Vermeer, and above all Leonardo da Vinci.

'Balderdash,' I believe I might have retorted, if at that very moment our bedside telephone had not seared the scorching night.

Was it foreseen and well understood, inquired our landlady's voice (sounding as if its owner had overdozed on Largactil, as if this might make the heat bearable) that two men in the car park were attempting to move our vehicle at that precise moment, which was shortly after three in the morning?

By the time I hit the first-floor landing, naked to the waist, sandals unstrapped, pyjama-striped with sweat, I'd nearly resolved, for the sake of avoiding imprisonment, that rather than hit the car bandits over the head with my fire-extinguisher – the only weapon to hand – I'd better spray them with it first. Blind them and suffocate them, but avoid dashing out their brains.

'Not that I wouldn't love to,' I muttered revealingly, as I tensed for a single bound down the last short flight of stairs between me and the fire-escape door to the car park.

'Oh, Mr Seale!' Mrs Hathaway then exclaimed behind me. 'Whatever are you doing?'

I told her.

'No, no!' she cried urgently. 'It isn't *your* car they want to move. It's *mine!* Madame Noyer made a mistake.'

Scottishly I assured the dressing-gowned and hair-netted Mrs Hathaway that I was just as ready to blind and suffocate the malefactors on her behalf as on my own.

And it was only with not a little difficulty that she managed to assure me that such violence would not be necessary. The two men in question, it seemed, were not criminals at all (?) but rather the chef and a waiter from the seafood restaurant next door. Due to the prevalence of car crime in Lourdes, the chef had taken, illicitly, to parking his Renault in the neighbouring hotel's car park. But our barman, the hotel barman, who we now realized must be something of a troublemaker, had assured Mrs Hathaway that she might park in a manner effectively blocking the Renault, which, he had said, would not require egress till the weekend.

Consequently, when the seafood chef and his mate knocked off from the restaurant, about half an hour ago, they had been distressed to discover their Renault blockaded. Knowing themselves to be in the wrong, however, in the sense of lacking permission to park where they did, and not wishing to draw Madame Noyer's attention to their unlicensed practice, they had thought to solve the problem themselves, and silently, by means of lifting Mrs Hathaway's car off the ground between them, and transporting it several yards to one side. And what could prove more conclusively that some French chefs and waiters between them consume vast quanta of alcohol during and/or after their evening shifts, when you learn that Mrs Hathaway's car is in fact a Volvo estate?

Further evidence is in any case available, in the form of the half hour of vain heaving, straining and falling face-flat on the car-park gravel, to the accompaniment of conspiratorial silence degenerating rapidly into the escalation of grunts, wheezes, curses and howls of rage which had awoken both Madame Noyer and Mrs Hathaway – whose bedrooms faced north over the car park, while our own, at the front of the hotel, looked south to the first Pyrenees.

Now the point of this sub-story, which you haven't yet come to, revolves around Millicent Hathaway. Our already being on Mr-Seale / Mrs-Hathaway terms was thanks to a brief exchange in the hotel restaurant after dinner. The remains of our lemon sorbets were being cleared away, and I, in an amiable stew of fatigue, digesting torpor, and humid heat, explained to our waitress that while I myself, by way of digestif, could happily cope with a man-size Armagnac, my wife would love nothing so much as a terribly little glass of uncooked pig.

Of course, despite knowing the difference perfectly well in theory, I had failed on the night to distinguish between *porc* (pork, pronounced 'pawr') and *porto* (port). An eminently forgivable slip, if I say it myself, especially when you bear in mind that *marc*, the knock-out brandy distilled from pressed grapes, which I had been tempted to order instead of Armagnac, is pronounced 'mar'. Well. In some situations, such as at a busy supermarket checkout on a cold, rainy, December afternoon, such a venial conflation might have passed with no comment bar a sullen inward sneer. Tonight, in Lourdes, on the contrary, our waitress – an unusually tall, thin and sinewy-looking young southern Frenchwoman, whose nose had put me instantly in mind of Laurence Sterne – exploded into such fits of hooting mirth, such as you sometimes hear floating out of Glasgow public toilets, that if she hadn't collapsed sideways on a chair at the table next to ours, she would have dropped our sorbet crockery.

'It's easily done,' smiled Mrs Hathaway,[6] who had been dining alone at that neighbouring table, and had overheard my booboo. And she went on to explain how years ago she herself had set off similar hoots by failing to specify the carrot (*carotte*) cake she wanted, and asking for a cake made of stained-glass window panes instead (*càrreaux*). Uplifted by the levity of our confessional conviviality I succeeded in postponing by at least five minutes any hope of our convulsing stringy waitress being able to fetch our digestifs, by proceeding to recall the evening during our earliest days in Provence when Koo had tickled our Spanish immigrant neighbours no end by advising them that the reason she couldn't ever have raw onion in her cheese sandwiches was that it caused her breasts to rush up to her head.

Here the wanting nuance was between *seins* (breasts) and *sang* (blood).[7]

Immediately perceiving the ferocity of Mrs Hathaway's hot blushes, in response to Koo's breasts, I divined that enough was enough, and that Wringhim's gassy-cunt story would nip our newfound Lourdes acquaintance most viciously in the bud. Likewise the tale about a summer Sunday family lunch in a chalet up Mont Ventoux when Koo, being teased by macho-nicotined Provençals, explained with some heat that even if she were inclined to consume tobacco, it would not be in the form of guaranteeing herself lung cancer by inhaling from cheap and nasty tipped cigarettes but rather along the lines of puffing at leisure on large swan-necked women's penises. Phrases here to avoid, if in doubt, decline from:

---

[6] Since Millicent Hathaway is a real person, it would seem ungrateful to describe her in the intrusive, even prurient detail that one might fudge for a made-up character. As . . . height of Barbra Streisand; build and colouring like the mature Elizabeth Taylor; soft brown eyes reminiscent of a well trained Golden Retriever; upper lip cruelly canyoned by over-applications of depilatory creams; pierced ears dangling Golders from the Green; mole like proto-cancerous blob of melted plain chocolate in the fleshy hollow between her left shoulder and neck; and so forth – Mrs Hathaway isn't a bit like that.

[7] It's not a nuance that could easily be wanting in Paris, but we're talking here about pronunciation variations at least as massive as between Berwickshire and Westminster 'English'.

*'J'adore faire des pipes.'*[8]

Not having alienated Mrs Hathaway with inadvertent filth of that nature, and having now also helped her to placate the stotious caterers in the car park, and squeeze her Volvo out of their way, we felt it only civil, seeing her alone, to include her in our somewhat bleary seven o'clock coffee-and-croissants breakfast in the hotel bar.

'Holiday going well?' she asked politely.

Ever so slightly guarded, lest she might have Revenue connexions, and equally light-headed from lack of sleep, I assured her with fervour that our present trip was for essential research purposes only, as was amply witnessed by the fact that we weren't still fast asleep in bed.

Mrs Hathaway inquired as to the focus of our research. Was it into miracles, perhaps?

Alas – in terms of our sales projections – no, I regretted to inform her. And, gripped by self-justifying courtesy, I proceeded to sketch a thumbnail of the work in progress, followed by a précis of the kind of finale details still lacking, if indeed they existed at all. Now comes our own personal closest to the whiff of a miracle in Lourdes. Mrs Hathaway, it emerged, was a great-great-somethingorother of G.P.R. James. Hasting to appease a surge of proprietorial paranoia that here must be a rival author – a budding Amundsen to my Scott – also questing for the grail of post-death-cell Morel, I simultaneously discovered that even this miracle was hardly miraculous. Mrs Hathaway, a widow of some years standing, was here in Lourdes as companion to her wealthy Jewish mother-in-law, a widow of many years standing. Crippled by arthritis, Parkinson's disease and a uniquely 'crabby' temper, the mother-in-law was here for her miracle cures. Accompanied by a long-suffering highly paid nurse, she was staying in one of the purpose-built four-star hospital-hotels within easy wheelchairing distance of the Grotte. Mrs Hathaway, pleading nostalgia (she had honeymooned in the Zaragoza) and ('always the best argument, with my mother-in-law') economy, had arranged her own accommodation in the cheaper hotel: enabling her both to give the nurse some respite during the day, and avoid being driven demented herself at night.

---

[8] 'I say, Humbert! You may not scoop the Gingerbread with this lot but they certainly ought to give you one of those guilt-edged replicas of the Channel Tunnel signed by Sir Lenny for your contributions to Franco-Britto connectivity!' [P.C.]

As to James, Mrs Hathaway supposed he probably was her most famous ancestor. Her sister had a theory that they were all clandestinely descended from Charles the Second, but this had never been demonstrated, and Mrs Hathaway is doubtful that it ever will be. While she was aware that James had written some novels, his principal achievement, in her view, was having been appointed Historiographer Royal. Other than that her knowledge of his career was hazy, except for the unfortunate circumstance that, especially during his last years, in Rome:

'He drank a great deal more than was sensible, or seemly.'

I persuaded her that this was much more forgivable in a novelist than in, say, a historian, and that there had been, and always would be, many illustrious precedents and subsequents. Poe, Fitzgerald, Lowry, King—

Had Mrs Hathaway heard of Wringhim Knox? wondered Koo.

'The name does seem to ring a bell,' she nodded doubtfully. Then with sudden enthusiasm she asked if we had yet paid a visit to the Lourdes public library.

'Not this trip.' And I explained that what I was after was more in the way of original editions – seventeenth- or eighteenth-century – and unpublished manuscripts, than the public library was liable to house.

'I suppose so,' agreed Mrs Hathaway. 'Although . . . ' and she proceeded to tell us how much fascinating material she had managed to glean in the public library just yesterday, on the history of miracles in France, from the series entitled *Histoire de la France et des Français au Jour le Jour*, published by the Librarie Académique Perrin, under the general editorship of André Castelot and Alain Decaux. Now this is a magnificent pop-historical encyclopaedia, superbly illustrated, and it certainly ought to be acquired for the libraries of all Scottish schools teaching French and history. We had ourselves referred to it with profit during the honing of *The Counts of Mount Venus*. For the present book, however, and for no particularly good reason, we had never got around to it: too inflamed, perhaps, by our passion to exhume the truth from original texts.

But we never ignore a tip, we Seales, and so, having revisted the old Arnault house after breakfast, I nipped into the public library for half an hour while Koo sat sipping iced lemonade beneath a café parasol and writing improving postcards to our goddaughters, both of whom are now distressingly nubile. As I rather feared, there was nothing in Castelot–Decaux on the death sentence passed on Louis Morel, but I imagine you can imagine my agitation when I looked up La Marfée and found (for some strange reason under '9 juillet', rather than the 6th) the following terse précis:

'*Après le complot de 1636, le comte de Soissons s'est réfugié à Sedan et s'est tenu assez tranquille, mais, en 1641, il veut profiter du mécontentement général pour prendre de nouveau les armes contre Richelieu. Bouillon, Guise et Beaufort se joignent à lui, tandis qu'Olivarès lui envoie des troupes. Il rencontre l'armée du maréchal de Châtillon à la Marfée. Il est vainquer, mais il est mortellement blessé, sans doute par un agent de Richelieu qui se serrait glissé dans les rangs ennemis . . .* '

That last sentence again, in literally literal English:

'He [the Count of Soissons] is the victor, but he is mortally wounded, without doubt by an agent of Richelieu who had infiltrated the enemy ranks.'

That is, Richelieu's enemy's ranks. The Count's ranks. And *without doubt?* So much surer than even such other contemporary chroniclers as Montglat. That's what really worried me. How could Castelot–Decaux be so casually confident? Unless they too had access to the Morel memoirs, either in the Cabinet des Tromperies or else in some other archive unknown to me? And if so? Might not they, or their collaborators, being eminent French historians all, hence possibly not obliged to smuggle out micro-taped facsimiles in their underpants, at this very moment be polishing for publication their own scholarly edition of those same memoirs?

'*My* fucking memoirs!' as I stressed to Koo at the pavement table outside our café, having explained to her why I was trembling as well as sweating, and had need of a double pastis.

'But so what?' she soothingly objected. 'Even if that were to happen, which probably isn't likely, wouldn't it only lend the weight of their authority to your story?'

'No, no, *no!*' moaned I, my mental torment inexpressible. 'Not if they published first. That would ruin everything, don't you see? That would ruin . . . *everything.*'

'Which everything?'

'I mean, the froggy profs would get all the glory, I would get sidelined as just another parasitic novelist, and Rankles would get to jerk off asking Nuncle Rudolph's readers if it wasn't himself that first told them so. Oh, God, God, *God . . .* '

You see? No longer can it be denied, if ever it could, that serial historical novelists are vain, jealous and prone to paranoia with regard to their modest discoveries. Almost as pronely so, indeed, as real historians, archeologists, anthropologists, paleobiologists, astrophysicists, and money-grubbing would-be patenters of everyone else's gene codes.[9] Knowing one's failings, though, is no surety of being able to overcome them. And for me, from those moments in the Lourdes public library until this very vibrant pulsating present, no two waking minutes have elapsed, and very few sleeping ones besides, when I have not felt enwebbed by neurotic impatience: to flog the van ever faster up the autoroutes, to spur on the smelly slow ferry from Calais, to fly over London in a chartered wine-laden-van-transporter plane, sky-dive over Berwickshire ahead of Koo and parachute back to my computer even sooner – to inform you with even less than the least possible further delay, that though Louis Morel is now convinced he knows who the Count of Soissons' killer is, he is less sure of being able to catch him.

Despite Louis's having shed all sheddable weight, and the advantage of his superfast tilting roan, the killer nonetheless has a headstart of several minutes. Calculating furiously as he gallops, Louis elects to gamble on two factors. The first is the probability that, thanks to his several killing-time-in-Sedan wild-boar-sticking outings with the Cardinal de Retz, he knows the lie of the land more intimately than does the fled-ahead villain. The second is that, on account of the torrential rain throughout the preceding night, the river Bar, which flows northwards towards the Meuse, at right angles to the path of the assassin's flight, will have swollen to fuller and faster than its normally fordable or even in places jumpable little self.

'And so I reined my mount in a straight line for Omicourt.'

Omicourt is another tiny village, some five miles south-west of Chaumont. Today Omicourt is perhaps best known for being the point where the Bar and (on its west flank) the Canal des Ardennes virtually touch. But of course the canal isn't there then. What is there then is an ancient cattle ford, and beside it, barely the length of a long bargepole upstream, a more recent but rather rickety wooden bridge, too narrow and flimsy to accommodate more than one horse and rider at a time.

As Louis arrives within sight of the densely wooded Heights of Sapogne, on the far side of Omicourt, he sees, with a surge of wild

---

[9] More on the very perfect gentle scholar, sometimes also known as the purely disinterested academic intellect, or yeti, in Arthur Koestler's *The Case of the Midwife Toad*.

exultation, that his gamble has paid off. The murderer, having attempted to escape due west, in the direction of St Aigan, en route for Mézières, has been baulked by the swollen river, and is now thundering wetly south towards the ford and the bridge at Omicourt. By the time Louis catches up with him he is in the middle of the river, having preferred the ford, but is having difficulty controlling his horse. Louis doesn't tell us this, but we are happy to imagine an atmosphere of intense humidity, the air so damp that the drizzle seems hardly to fall, the million greens and browns of the lush Ardennes countryside all sodden today – and blurred, like the voice of an old wino who dimly remembers killing other men he never knew, in a war he never chose to be in – and maybe a couple of buzzards playing gliders overhead. Certainly there are more than enough buzzards and other birds of prey in the Heights of Sapogne to make this not deeply symbolic detail entirely credible.

Doubtless in the Hollywood version the following scene will have to be jazzed up into a protracted desperate tussle. But what actually happens is this:

Thinking to reach the west bank ahead of the assassin, Louis spurs his roan to the wooden bridge. As he reaches the middle of the bridge – which can't be more than twenty feet in length, he realizes why the fugitive has avoided it: its far end has come adrift from the bank, and is bobbing on the flood-risen river.

'Halt, villain!' Louis now calls to the rider struggling on the ford. 'Halt, or I fire!'

The other's only reply is to turn in his saddle and point a cocked pistol at Louis.

'I knew it, I knew it,' mutters Louis, as he sees with his own eyes that the killer of the Count of Soissons is indeed the Marquis of Roquefort.

In the next moment:

The Marquis's pistol fails to fire – his powder has got damp. Simultaneously, both Louis's pistols go bang, one in either hand. As he balances on his horse while the horse sways reluctantly on the unanchored bridge, it is hardly surprising if his aim is below par. One of his bullets nicks the Marquis's horse in its neck, or perhaps its ear, while the other slams into its intended target, right enough, but only in his shoulder, or possibly his upper arm. In any case the cumulative effect of the bullet impact and the hurt horse's resentful rearing is sufficient to dislodge the Marquis from his saddle.

Now he falls into the spate-brown river, and disappears from view.

Anguished by the spectre of this devil escaping – swimming away underwater, or whatever – Louis instantly swings out of his own saddle, springboards off the bridge rail, jumps into the river, and wades, against the current, towards the ford. In the very moment of his feeling the smooth old cobbles firm beneath his heels, there is a whoosing splash only feet upstream as the Marquis suddenly surfaces sobbing for breath.

'Villain, *villain*, VILLAIN!' roars Louis as he plunges toward the gasping older man, and envelops him in a grizzly hug.

I'd quite like to stick in a furious swashbuckling swordfight here, razor-sharp sabres cleaving the humid air, ringing clashes of steel upon steel and shouts of 'Die, you die!' ruffling the buzzards above, but it simply doesn't happen. What does happen is that as Louis – and let's not forget how physically powerful he is – pins the Marquis's arms (one of which is in any case disabled) to his sides and squeezes his ribcage too tight to permit the oxygen he craves to salve his lungs, he, Louis, at the same time reaches behind the Marquis's neck with his right hand. Thinking to pull his captive's hair, to force his head back, to facilitate inquisitional eye-contact, Louis is unable to suppress a gasp of horror when it seems to him for a moment that he has pulled off the Marquis's head.

In fact it is the assassin's wig (his bonnet, needless to say, has long since swirled downstream) that has come adrift. Or rather, wigs. For not only the Marquis's public wig has come away (shoulderlength, dark and curling, as if he were a youthful musketeer) but also the private wig beneath it: short, smooth and fair – as worn to bed with his concubines, and other females he might conquer or purchase. The effect on Louis is momentarily unnerving: as he sees the Marquis suddenly bald as wrinkled marble, his pate pale as turning cream, and his apparent age now increased at one snatch by at least two hundred years.

Sensing a sag in his captor's grip, the Marquis gulps for air and kicks to break free.

Louis responds by redoubling the strength of his squeeze, and by chastening the murderer with a knee in his underwater groin. 'You are a villain, monsieur,' he informs the retching Marquis. 'You are scum. You poisoned the honest Monsieur de Valenais. You ruined by calumny – and I have the proofs of his innocence right here, in a pouch about my waist – you ruined by slander, I say, and then caused to be murdered your favoured rival in love, the innocent Count of Bagnols—'

'No, no,' croaks the writhing Marquis. 'Bagnols—'

'Silence,' orders Louis, with an emphatic tightening squeeze. 'By your destruction of Monsieur de Bagnols you also directly brought about the ruin, desperation, misery, despair and premature death of the virtuous Mademoiselle de Vergne, whose love for him, by all accounts, was dearer to her than life itself. In the years between, I have no doubt, there were others, God alone knows how many, directly murdered or otherwise destroyed by your agency. Myself you have attempted to kill three times. When we fought with swords, at Lestelle, you would assuredly have taken the life, if you could, of a boy only hours out of school. During the izard hunt in the hills of my home, you attempted to shoot me, did you not?'

'I never—'

'Silence. And then, most treacherous of all, after attempting to undermine my constitution, with the luxury of your affected hospitality, you had your hired cut-throat – the so-called Monsieur Saint-Simon, ha! – fall upon me with his envenomed dagger from the trees, as I rode home. Not so? Yes, indeed. You are scum, monsieur. Pure—'

'Let me—'

'Silence. Pure *scum*, I say. And now, today, you have murdered the Saviour of France. A man who—'

'Traitor, he was. Trait—'

'*Silence*, monsieur. While you heed these further reasons.' And Louis goes on, at not a little length, to explain to the Marquis how the death of the Count signifies not only the collapse of the liberational insurrection against the Cardinal, but also the terminal extinguishment of all his own aspirations, and prospects of personal and sexual happiness, since his hopes of recuperating Hélène from the custody of the Maréchal de Châtillon, triumphant in his role as the conquering Count's First Gentleman, have been for ever scuppered. 'For these ample reasons alone, Monsieur de Roquefort, I should be delighted to kill you, as kill you I assuredly shall, with these poor hands you have wronged.' First, and perhaps in order to ensure the Marquis has plenty of leisure in which to savour his last few minutes of life, and fully comprehend the rationale underlying his approaching banishment from it, Louis proceeds to rehearse a secondary list of the vile villain's villainies, not excluding his nauseatingly chauvinist, proprietorial, condescending and exploitative treatment of women, in general, and the revoltingly unctuous presumption with which, during his visits to Château Morel, he had patronized Louis's own dear mother.

'God save her saintly soul,' mutters Louis, more to himself than to his prisoner.

But at this point, and as it were galvanized by the threat of having to leave it sooner rather than later, the Marquis comes blazing back into life in the most bizarre manner. Like an ancient evil schoolmaster – Thwackum in *Tom Jones*, say, or *Gormenghast*'s Opus Fluke – goaded beyond exasperation by some crass Candidery on the part of his young-blood pupil, the Marquis inflates his blackbirdlike chest with indignant rage, kicks his submerged boots against the river bed, and slithers a good foot upward through Louis's startled arms, like a cake of black soap through your hand in a dirty bath, and sneers down in a snakelike hiss:

'You foolish young puppy, Morel! You really fancy, do you, that *you* know what's best for France? That *you* know better than the Cardinal? That *you* know all about women? What gives them pleasure, excites them, satisfies them? That you even knew *your own mother*, eh? That she was the paragon of perfect earthly virtue, yes? Well, sir – oof!' he breaks off, as Louis's vengeful forearms strain locked wrists like a drawbridge chain snapping tight around his waist.

'Slander my mother, monsieur,' he warns hoarsely, 'and I'll break your back *now.*'

'Kill me?' jeers the Marquis, his eyes red as Wringhim's at midnight. 'Kill me *now*, eh? Well, sir, go ahead. Kill me now. Be my guest. You silly young idiot, you. Kill me *now!* And if you do sir, and if you do? You'll never know, *never* . . . who really was your father.'

# 65

# Humbert A. Mobilay

Humbert is glumb today
Glumber than yesterday
His Taiwan takeaway
Tasted like no-can-say

And he needs a holiday
Far from this workaday
With two teen tearaways
Tyros at three-can-play

Let's hope he finds a way
Else he may fade away
Balding on top of grey
Brain cells all drained away

Humbert, your knees are clay
So are your chocks away
Nor can your fingers play
The Old Road To Mandalay

So runs the world away
Faster than yesterday
Barely got time to say
> God save Prince Charles!
> *Hahahahahahah—*

'Humbert?'
'Gnaw.'
'Did you make that up?'
'Gnaw.'
'You're lying again?'
'Yarse.'
'Anyway, while you weren't listening, the telephone rang.'
'Even worse?'

'It was Janet.'

'Not Diana?'

'She says she did meet Audrey, and they had a good blether together last night.'

'Girls will!'

'Also, neither is sure that either will ever want to speak to you again. Verbally, I think she means.'

'That bad, eh? Well! This must demonstrate, must it not, the incontrovertible value to Society At Large of feminist conferences on Female Textuality in Oxford? Maidenshead revisited, what? Or was it Radclyffe Hall?'

'Sometimes, Humbert, you really can be horribly cruel.'

'Och, just a bit for effect! And seldom before anyone's front! Must be the cruel cat's influence. Besides. Worst of all?'

'She did indicate that, thanks to her return train being stuck for two hours within a mile of Paddington, she has now read your new chapters.'

'O! That I do *long* to hear! And?'

'And that, together with considerable irritation that you had interrupted the story at just that point, and indignant pique at your giving so many footnotes to "that man Chalicer", as she put it, and despite not giving a monkey's about your philosophy of history—'

'A monkey's *what*? Don't you always wonder?'

'That she would still be interested to know what happens in the next chapter.'

'Oh, she would, would she now?' mused Humbert, rising like Botticelli's Venus digitally distorted into a ruminatant novelist reaching out for his half-empty pot of once-chilled genuine Czech Budweiser. 'Aha!' he gloated before he gurgled. 'I see, I see! Ah *hahahahah*—'

'But not so much as a captivated reader, she said. "More out of psychoanalytical curiosity."'

'Yarse. She does have Freud in the family, does our Janet. Her brother, I seem to remember, is a high-flying psycho the rapist. Ah *haha*—'

'Supper's nearly ready,' said Koo. 'Also, please clean the bath before you come down. Katie can't do us tomorrow — she's taking her grandchildren to Holy Island — and I'm leaving at seven. So hurry up.'

So it came to pass that as the novelist letliverishly towelled his soapified members, and savoured the remains of his abstemious Sunday night's second preprandial lager, and slid into the reassuring comfort of a fresh pair of reliably flapped Marks & Spencer's knickers for normal-mean-variation males, within himself at first, and then quietly to Captain Claws pfurring up the landing carpet, he happily trilled:

> My eyes are dim and I cannot see
> The arsehole of your bumble bee
> Yet sometimes when I clench them tight
> Within the womb of forest night
> A little light still deigns to shine
> Like hope of rescue down a mine
> And though that light's no right, it's free
> Like sunshine for a children's tea
> So ever while it shines for me
> And screens the scenes of yet-to-be
> In glee sings me: 'I see, I *see!*'

'Pfurrrr!' enthused Captain Claws, as rhythmically he milked the pile out of the Russian helicopter gunships slaughtering the relatively innocent all round the border of the only handwoven Afghan rug for which his hands-that-feed have ever shelled out more than three bottles'worth of Glenmorangie. 'Pfurrr-wurrr-hurrrr?'

# Condemned in the Scrotum

In the end it isn't the Marquis of Roquefort's back that gets broke.

When Louis – predictably dumbfounded by this sudden shaft at his paternity, hard on the heels of the Marquis's disgusting slur on his mother's fidelity . . . when he momentarily relaxes his grip on the assassin, hardly an instant bites the dust before a white-edged six-inch stiletto appears in the Marquis's left hand just as magically as a cardsharper's die.

So while that instant tumbles ever closer to whatever dust there might have been, were the desperate close-quarters tussle not transpiring in the middle of the flood-swollen Bar, things look darkly black for Louis's unprotected throat until suddenly a peevish squeaky voice cries out from the western bank:

'Whoa! Stop right there! Stay your hand, sir, or we fire!'

Now it is the dastardly Marquis's turn to be briefly stunned.

Alas for him, because now there is no holding the deadly purpose of Louis's vengeful fury.

Not the murderer's closet dagger, not squeaky threats from unknown newcome quantities; not nothing.

Thus ere the peevish voice on the bank gets breath for a second squeak the knife is sent spinning from the Marquis's hand, his entire body is plunged beneath the surface of the river, his chin is grasped mercilessly beneath the water, and in a short twisting wrench taught to perfection by Pere Garcés during the bivouac training of the cut-throats from Paris . . .

It is the Marquis of Roquefort's neck that gets broke.

When Louis looks up from the corpse he has created, he sees he is in effect surrounded. On the west bank, mounted, are an elderly officer in old-fashioned armour, an ancient lieutenant in ancient armour, and a line of musketeers ranged up and down the bank. Though they reek of private-army motley, there are at least twenty of them, and their muskets are all trained on Louis.

'Come out, monsieur,' squeaks the elderly officer furiously. He is livid at having been defied. 'Come out at once, or we'll shoot.'

Louis glances wearily at the east bank. Hopeless, he immediately decides. Though there are no musketeers to the east, there is no horse either. Even his own swift roan has defected to the west, and surrendered her reins to the ancient lieutenant.

Wading heavily to the bank, Louis drags the Marquis's body by its armpits.

'Who are you, monsieur? And who is he?' demands the bristling old soldier.

Louis knows by his captor's colours that here are Richelieu's men. Despite his deep dejection he calculates, rightly, that the Cardinal's camp may well not yet know of the death of the Count of Soissons. Thinking, accordingly, to postpone the drastic disadvantage to the Count's supporters, of the loss of their popular hero, he divulges merely:

'This gentleman, monsieur, was the cravenest knave in France. As he tried to kill me, so I killed him. More than that I have nothing to say. Not, at any rate, to you. Take me, if you please, to your leader. Or else let me go.'

Good try, that last line.

But of course it doesn't work.

The old captain and his creaky musketeers are what you might call the last-resort Dad's Army rearguard of the Cardinal's contingent. So far behind the main forces have they dawdled that they don't even know yet that Richelieu's troops, under the Maréchal de Châtillon, have been routed. Judging Louis, by the remains of his attire, his bearing and speech, to be an enemy cavalier of some stature, they rope him to a packhorse, conduct him in triumph to Rethel, and hand their prisoner over to the field marshal himself.

At Rethel, then and still a pleasant but unremarkable town on the river Aisne, the Maréchal de Châtillon is as close as an old, grey and very fat pachydermic warrior can be to tears. This is partly due to having been hammered in the battle, more due to the shame of the knowledge that his best troops in effect deserted him, but most of all because he has just heard of the death of his cad nephew Charles, he whose head was more or less shot off by Louis's Paris bravo Combalet de Montfaucon.

Never let it be forgotten that even harsh old soldiers are capable of soft spots, and the Maréchal's – beneath his *de rigueur* disapproval, impatience and contempt – was all for the abortionate Charles.[1]

Wisely Louis withholds from the Maréchal the detail that it was his man that blew the loathsome nephew, rival, and would-be debaucher of Hélène into bloody tufts and blobs. Resignedly he points out to the Maréchal – since it can only be a matter of hours, if not minutes, before he hears as much from some panting other messenger – that though he, the Maréchal, has lost the battle of La Marfée, he has in real terms carried the day: since the Count of Soissons himself lies slain. Cunningly Louis keeps his own counsel as to the means of the Count's killing, thinking to make more milage out of this later. But then he makes the mistake of exhibiting personal weakness, in the form of most unwarriorlike streaming tears, as he begs the Maréchal for news of Hélène: where is she now? Well? Happy? Thinking about him, unwed still, thoroughly chaste, and so forth?

'Pah!' grunts the Maréchal in disgust.

'I *beg* of you, monsieur,' pleads Louis. 'Dispose of me as you must – I have no doubt you will – but tell me first of Mademoiselle Arnault? Please, monsieur? As one gentleman to another? *Please* . . . '

(All this we are given to understand is taking place in a square beneath the Church of Saint Nicholas whose new west tower, square as the Maréchal's jaw once was, will rise to a height of 150 feet when it is completed in 1650. This afternoon, in respect for the grief of military debâcle, construction work has been suspended, and the masons are most likely away getting pissed in some tavern down the road.)

'Why did you kill this gentleman?' inquires the Maréchal gruffly, and we can imagine him pointing with a grimace at the Marquis of Roquefort's body on the cobbles. 'He was the Cardinal's creature, you know.'

'Why, monsieur!' replies Louis. 'Because he . . . he . . . why, he tried to kill *me!* That's why. As these good gentlemen witnessed,' indicating the old Quixote and his ancient Panza. 'Did you not, messieurs?'

'Schah!' spits the Maréchal. 'You are withholding information, Monsieur Morel. I know not what, nor why, and personally I do not care. Nor

---

[1] In terms of round characterization, then – gruff bear with big behind masking heart of fool's gold – the Maréchal, though militarily greatly senior, reminds us immediately of Lt. Col. Jock Sinclair in James Kennaway's *Tunes of Glory*.

is it my office to torture you. Take—'

'But Hélène, Monsieur de Châtillon! *Please—*'

'Stop your blubbing, monsieur. Shut up. TAKE HIM', the Maréchal orders loudly, 'to Mézières. Treat him fair, but keep him tight secure. To await the Cardinal's pleasure. Away.'

Let us next picture a flaccid illustration in our school biology textbook. It is human reproduction today, and we are looking side-on at a smoothly stylized penis and scrotum, no pubic hair, rashed wrinkles, genital warts, or anything off-putting like that. Now the penis and scrotum rotate by a right angle, as if their proprietor had fallen backwards on a water-bed, head facing east. His testicles look a bit lumpy and hangdog – perhaps he has developed a varicocele – but his penis is in good order, swelling in defiance of gravity, and looks to be aiming for a quick triple twelve on the staff-room dartboard. (Parent-teacher association members are urged to note that our penis here is in no wise toilet-wall distorted, in relation to our scrotum, so hopefully that at least that should not be a major stumbling block, on this occasion.)

Widen, please, the outline encompassing our gonads. See it now as the rain-murked Meuse flowing west from stricken Sedan, north round our testicles' bottoms, east to complete our scrotum, north-east and west along the underside of our nascent erection, curving round our willie's circumcised tip to meander south-east in completion of our marriage-prospect profile, before sobering up at last against the harder geographical reality of our unpaunched *os pubis*, and diverting more sensibly north – bound for beery Belgium and gritty Liège; hateful Maastricht; then north again through the noddy Nedderlands, and west at last in a curious snake-tongue split, to inflate the cold and ever dirtier North Sea.

Back in the Ardennes, we may think of the scrotum as entirely containing the medieval and strategically vital town of Mézières, while tucked between the scrotum and the penis nestles the new and rectangularly planned town of Charleville – named after the fabulously rich (before he started building it) Duke Charles de Gonzague, whose brainstormchild it was. As to the darts-playing head of the penis, there stands the modest eminence they quaintly call Mount Olympus, from which panoramic memories of relative ecstasy may be taken, along with Fuji snaps. Nowadays named ensemble, as Charleville-Mézières, the two historically discrete agglomerations nonetheless remain as distinct pyschologically as architecturally. When, last trip, I popped into a

Mézières newsagent – in deference to the prevailing thick cloud, heavy rain and dismal daylight – to ask for:

'Fujicolor SuperG, 400 ISO, by any chance?'

I was informed with conviction that there was no hope of obtaining any such sophisticated consumer perishable anywhere in Mézières, 'monsieur, you'll have to go to Charleville for that.' As if this might entail a two-hour night flight into the heart of enemy territory, rather than a five-minute stroll across the Pont d'Arches and towards the Place Ducale. The differences in tradition and mentality between Mézières (south) and Charleville (north) are thus very comparable to those between Cornhill (England) and Coldstream (Scotland) on either side of the river Tweed. Though many of the buildings in Mézières are of greater antiquity, if it's light, laughter, fun, culture and Fujicolor you're after, you're better off in Charleville. There's even, in the Rue du Moulin, a quaint little taste of home in the *Pub Mac' Hintoch* (*sic*).

And above all there is Rimbaud.

Far and away Charleville's most famous son – like Duns Scotus to us here in Berwickshire, or Mungo Park to Selkirk, or indeed Alexander Selkirk to Largo – Arthur Rimbaud was born in 1854 in the Rue Napoléon (the same busy thoroughfare, leading north to the Place Ducale, where Fujicolor is now expensively available) and hence, according to the crude and revolting topography elaborated above, in the fleshy space between the scrotum and the penis, as so kindly defined by the Meuse. There he grew up, resented his domineering mother, got bored at school, excited during the Franco-Prussian war, and wrote much derivative adolescent poetry. Whether what he wrote thereafter is the florescence of precocious genius without parallel, or merely a sick effusion of decadent impotence, is the subject of ongoing debate, especially in the College Club at StrathKelvin University.

One spring lunchtime about a year ago I was sitting there, at the windows end of the conference table in the television room, quietly trying to enjoy my game pie and coleslaw, prior to a bulk purchase of cut-price laser-printer toner cartridges from Computing Services round the corner, when in wheezed Wringhim Knox and three cronies. This was by no means a miracle, as Wringhim has many such cronies and nodding associates in the Club, some of them actually entitled to be there, and is moreover uncommonly partial to cream-smothered mounds of Mrs MacGregor's Black Forest Gahtoe, often to cap his own version of a light lunch in McEwan's.

Now today, as chance would have it:

Where Wringhim and his mates humped down, at the far end of the conference table, was in overhearing distance of two plastic-armchaired and prematurely middle-aged Post-Febrile Obstructionists from French Literature, who were comparing the alchemy of Rimbaud with the satanism of Baudelaire, as viewed afresh through the latest wave of super new critical lenses freshly ground by those fuzzy French pseudo-philosophers based in Paris–France, Oxford–England, and any institution in America stupid enough to offer them lucrative sinecures.

'Rimbaud?' growled Wringhim, glowering round from his cholesterol special. 'What do you mean, Rimbaud?'

'I beg your pardon,' replied French Literature One, with a sickly smile. 'I mean *Arthur* Rimbaud. The great—'

'Piddling wanker,' nodded Wringhim fiercely. And he then proceeded to inquire of the television room at large, and loudly – for it is a spacious and high-ceilinged forum – whether anyone both civilized and sane would deny for a moment that no human individual could ever have been both a great poet and a filthy slave trader.

'No, no, no!' pleaded French Literature Two. That Rimbaud *may*, in his later years, have been briefly implicated in *gun-running* was a possibility that could not honestly be ruled out. But *not* slave trading! All the—

'Yes. Yes, *yes!*' retorted Wringhim. . . . The evidence was irrefutable. He himself had once spent two days in the University Library checking it out, and . . . he went on to cite a couple of references that eluded my game-pied attention,[2] then repeated his menacing assertion that:

'No slave trader could ever have been a poet of any worth.'

At this point a recently acquired junior lecturer in theology looked up from the *Clarion* crossword, in which he appeared to have bogged down, and nervously inquired whether Wringhim's proposition was intended to be taken as:

'Synthetic, I wonder? Or merely analytic?' Then he – very honestly, but in the circumstances rather foolishly – added a gloss to the effect that

---

[2] Also, to be fair to me, I really was rather shocked by the seriousness of Wringhim's allegation. Prior to that I had assumed that the biggest 'moral' peccadildo attributed to Rimbaud was whether he actually went the whole hog in buggering Verlaine, or was it the other way round?

currently he was boning up on Kant, all the better to cope with a couple of hostile undergraduates, who each week heaped harsher aspersions on his personal New Testament theism.

This gave Wringhim a perfect opening to retort with blistering sarcasm:

'And suppose, my dear chap, I am to tell you that my proposition, in your canting terms, is synthetic? Will you then understand that I intend you to understand that my proposition is to be taken as synthetic *a posteriori*, or rather as synthetic *a priori*? And in either case, so fucking what?'

This was too much for Junior Theology, who slid, madly blushing, back down to his undone crossword.

While Wringhim continued:

'In fact, my dear chap, the simple truth, as I indicated but a moment ago, is every inch as plain as that tomato soup on your glaikit wee Hitler moustache there:

'*No* slave trader could *ever* have been a poet of *any worth*. The converse too.' To clinch it he added Rumpolishly:

'Can you imagine, liddies and genitalmen? Robert Burns a slave trader!' And climbed on to the conference table, cake plate and fork still in hand, to sing from 'The Jolly Beggars', which one of his folk-scene drinking buddies had arranged anew for his next Edinburgh Festival show:

### Liberty's a glorious feast . . .

Wringhim's tavern tenor being fearsome as bagpipes, and also alarmingly loud, he was barely moments into the third verse when round the doorway leading to the Cafeteria peered the agitated visage of the Dean of the Faculty of Arts. To Wringhim personally this would have amounted to no intimidation. But to the various onlooking lecturers it served as prodding reminder that, the time being seven minutes past two, there would be patient and industrious undergraduates awaiting them all over the university for lectures, tutorials, and exciting practicals in every discipline.

Deprived of his audience, Wringhim subsided to do quieter justice to the remains of his gâteau, and the incident might never have been enthralled in print had not Koo drawn my attention, as we browsed in the Rimbaud Museum to the north of the Place Ducale, on the bank of the Meuse just south of the underside of the penis, to a most astonishing resemblance – in terms of bold loops, whorls and slashes – between the shape of Arthur Rimbaud's signature and that of Wringhim himself. We accordingly purchased several souvenir postcards of the Rimbaud signature, starkly black on white, like a novel for intelligent adults, and one of them I printed anonymously to Wringhim in Glasgow, inquiring in somewhat pidgin English, I confess, as to the going rate for exporting white slave virgins from Kelvinside to Charleville-Mézières:

'Feevteen year an hole?'[3]

So far as we know Wringhim still has no idea who sent him that card, which we imagine must have got his goat quite a bit, and it'll be interesting to see how he responds – if ever his attention spans to these very paragraphs, which you yourself are just surviving. In the meantime lest you wonder why we are rehearsing all this – about the scrotum, the penis and Wringhim – let me say it's because (a) you won't get any of it from Louis Morel, and (b) it eases our narrative angst just a little to feel we have imparted to you a certain minimum kinaesthetic orientation within the geography of your current imaginative whereabouts. Thus:

Although Louis has now, beyond a doubt, been transported to the scrotum of Mézières,[4] he gives us not the slightest inkling whether his incarceration takes place within the centre of the fortified town (as it were in the left testicle) or rather in some dungeon belonging to one of the dozen or so castellated towers that bulge outward from the ramparts, overseeing the encircling Meuse like boils on the scrotal sac. Our own hunch is that Louis is probably in a cell in the Tour du Roi, at the sac's western end, and we say this because that tower, built by François I in 1516, is the most massively and impenetrably walled of all, and hence

---

3 'I'm not sure you aren't here permitting yourselves to rampage promiscuously close to certain other characters in certain of your other novels. Is this intentional? And anyway, is it proper?' [P.C.]*

     * *'Don't be so bloody nosy, Chalicer. Go fuck yourself.'* [S.M.]

4 Other fortified edifices in the region include the tenth-century Château des Fées, north of the penis, and the Château de Warcq, west of the scrotum. But no other nearby castle, in 1641, can match the Royalist stronghold security of the walled citadel of Mézières. Hence our certainty on this point.

would naturally appeal to Cardinal Richelieu as the securest repository for his political enemies.

Proceeding on that reasonable assumption:

With the death of the Count of Soissons [*writes Louis*], all my dreams of future happiness died too. Nothing remained but to turn the eyes of my wretched soul upon the past, and brood despairingly over the delights of times gone by; as the spirits of the dead are sometimes said to hover, round the treasures they amassed during life; at once regretting their loss, and grieving that they had not put their talents to fruitful use.

Thus hour upon hour slipped away, each hour a slow procession of heavy, painful minutes; gloomy, desolate, like links in the chain of death. My jailer, a grim, surly fellow, was silent as a mute. For several days he passed my tray of frugal food through a hatch in the door, without the seasoning of a single word.

Nor could I read much of hope, or even consolation, in the dour lines of his scowl. At length, on the seventh morning, my jailer came with another, much like himself, but larger, and broadbacked as an ox, and with a powerful stench of bacon. This second fellow had with him a heavy mass of irons, all chained together, which, he told me, I must now submit to having locked around my ankles and my wrists.

Despite my feelings of deepest despair, and the weakening of my health already begun, by my constant close confinement, deprivation of light and exercise, and the lamentable quality of my food, of course I remonstrated, urged my rank, and asked the reason for this new proposed degradation, which I knew must reduce my body to a condition of such weakness, that no enterprise of escape could possibly be accomplished, even were such an unlikely opportunity to present itself.

'You must wear the chains,' replied my second guardian, in a tone of the grimmest satisfaction, 'because you are *condemned*.'

'Condemned,' replied I, bewildered. 'But why? To what?'

'To *death*,' he chuckled darkly. 'Sit you down now, and raise your legs to me.'

'To death?' I protested. 'But no. No, no. That cannot be.'

'Whatever is be, can be!' joked this rogue. 'And for you, monsieur, death is be soon!'

'But this is France!' cried I.

'Only just, they do say!⁵ Arms out, so please you.'

'And I have had no trial. No hearing. No judge has questioned me. Why then, how can I be condemned? No, no. It is not true.'

'You shall feel it true and a half, my friend,' the chain-bearing jailor grunted, as he turned his key in my manacles, 'when the axeman hacks your head.'

---

5 This quip may only be taken to refer to the fact that the vulnerable frontiers with Belgium and the principality of Sedan are barely a virile sperm squirt away. But it could also, on a less politically unsophisticated level, imply that France is currently so close to falling to pieces altogether that it is 'only just' still France. Rather like the 'United Kingdom' today, if you focus on the futility of the Prime Creep and the GAGAs, the redundancy of *the* 'Royal Family', the irrelevance of the Church 'of England' – to Hindus, Muslims, Welsh Humanists, Irish Catholics, Pantheist Rastafarians (not to mention us hardnosed atheist Scots too often) – and so forth. At the same time, as ever when interpreting Shakespeare,* we must simultaneously acknowledge that it would take a very senile Professor of English Literature indeed, would it not, to curtly discount the third possibility: that when the beefy chains jailer utters his 'Only just . . . ' line his mind is perhaps inflamed with some radically different content; like the gárlic goulash he covets for lunch, could it be, or mounting a hot buttered bun?

**\* Now fly to . . . ✦**

# Fatnote Following

*Take, for example, Scene 2 of Act 5 of* Hamlet.

*Hamlet and Laertes are duelling to the death, though Hamlet doesn't yet know this. Claudius, Hamlet's wicked uncle – who has conspired with Laertes to murder Hamlet – remarks insincerely:*

*'Our son shall win.'*

*Gertrude, Hamlet's mother and now also wife to Claudius (who has also murdered Hamlet's father) responds by saying:*

*'He's fat and scant of breath . . . '*

*Now that word 'fat' has lumbered earnest professors (not all of them senile by every means) with no end of gruel for waffle. In the Penguin* Hamlet, *for instance, we are told, 'There is slight evidence that it ["fat"] could mean 'sweaty', but the usual meaning was the same as today. Possibly the Queen's tone is bantering, giving expression to her motherly happiness at her now well-behaved son.' The Arden* Hamlet, *eager to preserve the Prince as a model of manliness, assures us that, 'fat must refer to Hamlet's state at the moment rather than to a permanent characteristic.'*

*And so on.*

*All very polite, obedient, and establishment.*

*But a third reading, just as legitimate and light years more elegant (see* Prince Hamlet, Hypostar, **Chapter 30**) *is that Gertrude, when she says 'He's [emphasis untranscribed] fat' refers not to Hamlet at all, but frowningly to loathsome Laertes, and is therefore loyally and innocently agreeing with Claudius that:*

*'Our son shall win.'*

*There is no proof, and almost certainly never will be, and that's what makes Shakespeare such fun to revisit.*

*Unless you are Franco Zeffirelli, perhaps, and have already solved the problem by depriving Glenn Close of the words* 'fat and' altogether, possibly on the ground that Mel Gibson's agent might threaten to sue the producers: if his molten boy were by any stretch tarred with 'bulimia'. If you also note such other minor details as the total excision of Fortinbras, you may come to feel that Zeffirelli has already achieved for Shakespeare what the French tyrant Richelieu is currently trying to do for France:

By ordering the summary excision of 'traitors' like Louis Morel.

# 68

# Elect[1] Bibliography

Arber, Agnes, 1954, *The Mind and the Eye*

Ascherson, Neal, 1988, *Games With Shadows*

Ash, Marinell, 1981, *The Strange Death of Scottish History*

Baring-Gould, William S., 1968, *The Lure of the Limerick*

Berger, John (& Co), 1972, *Ways of Seeing*

Binns, Ronald, 1986, *J.G. Farrell*

Bliss, Douglas Percy, 1934, *The Devil in Scotland*

Bradley, F. H., 1883, *The Principles of Logic*

---

[1] Yes. This bibliography is original, unique, and has never before been published. All rights – including but not limited to legal rights, intellectual rights, moral rights, immoral rights, metempsychotic and palingenetic rights, and any other rights in this or any other universe, whether now known or subsequently discovered, formulated, invented or imagined – are absolutely and unconditionally reserved by the compilers unless and until agreed otherwise in respect of lots of lovely loot. This bibliography is protected under the laws of the United States of America and other tyrannies throughout the present planet. Unauthorized duplication, database storage, bulletin-board intercourse, and any other unlicensed commercial exploitation or even mere casual tampering of a like or utterly unlike nature will render the infringer(s) liable to civil action(s) for damages and/and relentless criminal prosecution(s). Conviction(s) – official or unofficial, just or unjust – for such offences may well, in certain other tyrannies throughout the present planet, result in the ritual mutilation or removal of certain parts of your body very dear to you. So watch it.

572

Burnet, John, 1914, *Greek Philosophy*

Chambers, Robert, 1823, *Traditions of Edinburgh*

Clark, Kenneth, 1956, *The Nude*

Doyle, Sir Arthur Conan, 1893, *The Memoirs of Sherlock Holmes*

Conlon, Gerry, 1990, *Proved Innocent*

Cook, Albert, 1949, *The Dark Voyage and the Golden Mean*

Craik, Kenneth, 1943, *The Nature of Explanation*

Daiches, David, 1981, *The New Companion to Scottish Culture*

David, Elizabeth, 1960, *French Provincial Cooking*

Ehrenzweig, Anton, 1967, *The Hidden Order of Art*

Ellison, Ralph, 1952, *Invisible Man*

Farmer, Philip José, 1972, *Tarzan Alive*

Faulkner, William, 1939, *The Wild Palms*

Fiedler, Leslie A., 1972, *The Stranger in Shakespeare*

Gide, André, 1902, *The Immoralist*

Giner, Salvador, 1981, *The Social Structure of Catalonia*

Hardy, G.H., 1940, *A Mathematician's Apology*

Hogg, James, 1824, *The Private Memoirs and Confessions of a Justified Sinner:*

Homer, Humbert?, Long Ago, *The Iliad*

Humphreys, Christmas, 1951, *Buddhism*

Hunt, John, 1953, *The Ascent of Everest*

Hutton, Will, 1995, *The State We're In*

Jenkins, Robin, '1954' (!), *Fergus Lamont*

Jones, Peter, 1975, *Philosophy and the Novel*

Jones, Steve, 1993, *The Language of the Genes*

Kaufmann, Walter, 1968, *Tragedy & Philosophy*

Knox, Wringhim, 199?, *Succeeding at Sex in London*, Porridge Westerns Press (Social Criticism & Non-fiction Division), BO Pox 69, Republic of Scotland, Europe; and strictly by private subscription; punters must include documentary evidence of consenting adulthood; £125 [one hundred and twenty-five pounds sterling] per copy plus VAT [value-added tax] where applicable; post free to any address on the present planet until the end of the present millennium A.D.; also, if one dare pare a phrase from the oh-pus itself, don't say you weren't warned.

Koch, Rudolph, 1930 (English translation), *The Book of Signs*

Kornbluth, C.M., 1951, *The Marching Morons*

Leary, Timothy, 1970ish, *The Politics of Ecstasy*

Lilly, John C., 1972, *The Centre of the Cyclone*

Marcus Aurelius, 1964 (Penguin translation), *Meditations*

Nuttall, Jeff, 1968, *Bomb Culture*

Márquez, Gabriel García, 1967, *One Hundred Years of Solitude*

Masters, Edgar Lee, 1915, *Spoon River Anthology*

Mauss, Marcel, 1925, *Essai sur le don, forme archaïque de l'échange*

Mill, John Stuart, 1873, *Autobiography*

Millett, Kate, 1969, *Sexual Politics*

Milne, A.A., 1927, *Now We Are Six*

Nairn, Tom, 1988, *The Enchanted Glass*

Neville, Richard, 1970, *Play Power*

Penttilä, Risto E.J., 1991, *Finland's Search for Security through Defence, 1944–89*

Prebble, John, 1966, *Glencoe*

Read, Herbert, 1953, *Education through Art*

Richie, Donald, 1972, *Japanese Cinema*

Scaduto, Anthony, 1974, *Mick Jagger*

Scott, Peter, 1935, *Morning Flight*

Smith, Ray, 1992, *A Night at the Opera*

Schwartz, David J., 1959, *The Magic of Thinking Big*

Trench, Sally, 1968, *Bury Me In My Boots*

Walker, Alexander, 1971, *Stanley Kubrick Directs*

Wallace, Edgar, 1927, *The Avenger*

Wightman, Andy, 1996, *Who Owns Scotland*

Wiggins, David, 1967, *Identity and Spatio-Temporal Continuity*

Wind, Edgar, 1958, *Pagan Mysteries in the Renaissance*

Woolf, Virginia, 1915, *The Voyage Out*

Wright, Robert, 1994, *The Moral Animal*

Yates, Frances A., 1966, *The Art of Memory*

Youngson, A.J., 1966, *The Making of Classical Edinburgh*

# 69

# Death Countersigned

'And he [the beefy chains jailor] left me,' Louis goes on, 'confined even within my confinement, to my misery, and slammed and bolted the door of my cell, without one further word. And why, indeed, should I have cared? For had I not already given up my claims on life, having lost for ever all hope of that which had made my life dear? And yet, while moment by moment I felt my strength ebb, like evening sunlight ever weaker, as December advances, I found a certain bond with earthly being clingering[1] still, nor could I picture, without a shudder and a groan, the fond fellowship betwixt my shoulders and my head being split asunder like a log; the blessed communion between my body and my soul thus dissolved, for ever.

'For *ever*.

'Somehow that very *word* was most awful; awful beyond endurance, and the fate of all flesh, which I had never shrunk from, and which I had so often defied, in the folly of my youthful adventures, or the grip of some manhood passion, now, as helplessly I perceived its calm and soundless, yet inexorable march toward me, appeared to burgeon fresh and stranger terrors with every step, like blooms of horror on the tree of hell, as the fires of damnation roared beneath.'

There's a lot more in that vein, but mercifully we're going to spare ourselves most of it. Alternatively, we could adjourn to read Arthur Koestler's *Darkness at Noon* before our own next sentence. That Louis Morel was familiar with *Hamlet* is temporally conceivable, but practically impossible. If he had known his Shakespeare backwards, he would doubtless have mixed in here some stuff from 'To sleep, perchance to dream? To sleep? To *die*?' and reflected poignantly on the parallels between Hamlet enchained by doublebinds in the 'prison' of Denmark and Louis enchained by chains in his dungeon

---

[1] Best translation we could think of for Louis's rather unusual 'tenaçant'.

in Mézières. Perhaps also on the doomed Prince's debonair remark to Horatio:

'If it be now, 'tis not to come. If it be not to come, it will be now. If it be not now, yet it *will* come . . . '

Although a profo underscholar must prefer the pithier Edgar, in *King Lear*:

'Men must endure their going hence, even as their coming hither: ripeness is all. Come on.'[2]

In all three cases the subject is the inevitability of Death, and the puzzle is why we tend to career through most of our lives as though Death didn't exist, then get so suddenly frantic the moment His Dry Knuckles Knock. We don't regret not having been alive the year before our birth, do we? So why do we so abominate the prospect of not being alive the year following our demise? Nowadays there are plenty of trivial explanations available from neoDarwinists, sociobiologists, etc, in terms of the selective advantage of pain avoidance (cf, in human terms, avoidance where possible of the pain of having your head hacked off by dint of several leisurely chops at your neck) but for a deeper and more ultimately consoling account of the matter we could do worse (and thousands of millions of people have done and do do worse) than repair to Schopenhauer – for example, to Book Four of Volume II of *The World as Will and Representation*.

Louis Morel, though, could not possibly have been consoled by Schopenhauer (unless you also seriously believe in time travel forwards and then backwards again; of persons, as opposed to narratives), and we may feel – given his philosophical as well as vitamin deprivation – that his rather maudlin death-cell ramblings are no more maudlin, and no more rambling, than might be our own in that same hellish pickle.

So let us, in this spirit of sympathetic forgiveness, skip forward several hours to the early afternoon of that very long July day, when Louis's starving attention – he is now on hunger-strike, too, as a protest against the handless indignity of being proffered slop from the mute jailor's ladle – is distracted by the hot snorting clopping sounds of cavalry drifting in [ie, the sounds] through his vaulted window slit. These noises escalate until mid afternoon, when suddenly Louis is prised from his cell and pushed in his irons along meandering passages and sat upon a bench

---

2 'A Zeffirelli *Lear* (!) must presumably expand this to: "Come on! Let's *go!*"?' [P.C.]

in a long dark lobby, back to back and side by side with a number of other wasted-looking wretches who are similarly chained.

In a daze of weakness beyond despair (which presupposes, does it not, some spark of residual vitality?) he remains inertly slumped and oblivious to his fellow prisoners and their surroundings until suddenly (this must be about five in the afternoon) he hears as in a faraway dream the vigorous approach of strangely familiar authoritative voices including that — can it possibly be? — of his estranged old uncle surrogate the Chevalier of Montenero.

Yes, it can be. Because, as the beefy chains jailor would have it (though there is no mention of his hereabouts at this juncture) it *is* be:

The Chevalier enters the lobby in respectful but no way fawning attendance upon Richelieu.

The Cardinal, in all the sumptuous crimsons, purples and velvets of his office, looks old and frail yet at once triumphant and invincible. Only seventeen months remain before finally he will expire of all his sicklinesses. 'My Judge will soon pass sentence on me,' the dying self-deceived arrogant tyrant then will murmur in hearing only of his last-rites priest. 'I pray Him to condemn me if I have desired anything save the good of religion and the State.' But no-one thinks of that today as with urbane grace and the ring of absolute authority the Cardinal thanks the Chevalier — whom, to Louis's sluggish dumbfoundment, he is addressing as Monsieur de Bagnols — for his recent courageous rearguard exertions on behalf of the King.

If only (smiles the Cardinal, in tones of cold regret) the letters relating to the revolt of La Rochelle and the missing certificate of marriage between the Count of Bagnols and Mademoiselle de Vergne could be recovered, then . . . all else would doubtless fall into place, and His Majesty's present gratitude would be converted into an unconditional pardon, not to mention everlasting largesse. Unfortunately, until that time . . .

Like a tall thin raven the Chevalier curtly nods to acknowledge his recognition that despite his late efforts on the Royalist side, as a result of which the longstanding governmental-hitman-contract price has been removed from his head, nevertheless the original charges against him (of treason in league with the Protestant Huguenots of La Rochelle), and with them the Cardinal's malice, will never be forgotten, in the absence of documentary vindication.

Then, with a swift, polished courtier's bow — and before Louis can get his thoughts and voice together to cry out, or even croak — the Chevalier is gone: disappearing in long dignified strides back down the corridor whence he came, without having once condescended to soil his gaze upon the bench-slumped manacled traitors.

But it is to them that the Cardinal now turns, an attendant secretary and bodyguard turning behind him like large lambs behind a ewe.

When Louis's turn comes to be dealt with, the inspecting Cardinal glances down at him, icily implacable, and informs him he is a traitor, and as such already condemned.

Seeing the Cardinal about to move on, to confirm the seal of death on someone else, Louis's swollen heart just manages to power his voice for a vain protest: that universal justice demands that no man of noble birth (whether or not women of noble birth or otherwise might be different we don't know) may be condemned without the chance to speak in his own defence.

Richelieu calmly agrees that this is so, *except* where the villain has intentionally fled from the pursuit of justice, as Louis did from Paris, following his stint *chez* the Countess of Soissons.

Seeing the futility of arguing with the Cardinal, Louis begs instead for a little time to compose his soul for its Journey, and for writing materials, and the freedom of his right hand, to facilitate one last confessional letter to his father.

The Cardinal grimly nods: okay but don't ask for more time than strictly necessary, otherwise you would only be prolonging pointless misery.

Three days? pleads Louis.

Richelieu consents, then turns to countersign his death warrant, which the attendant secretary has ready on what we would call a clipboard. Having added the verbal instruction that Monsieur Morel should have his wrist irons removed, and should be allowed one visit from an absolving prelate, the Cardinal proceeds methodically down the line, dispensing condemnation all the way.

# Narrative Devices

Back in his death cell, Louis gets his manacles removed, but not his legacles. Then the mute jailor goes off, grumbling mutely, to fetch quills, ink, and reams of writing paper. As he waits for the means to externalize his bad conscience, filial guilt, and overpowering sense of failure in battle, life and 'love', the prisoner, too dazed to experience excitement, yet marvels hazily over the lately revealed amazing but apparently real identity of the Chevalier of Montenero and:

*The Count of Bagnols?*
    Was it truly possible [*writes Louis*[1]] that here, in the sombre and august personage of the Chevalier, was the dashing young lover of Mademoiselle de Vergne, whom all of us had supposed to have been assassinated, on the orders of the vengeful Marquis?
    At first, I confess, I could hardly believe this evidence, so recently and vividly impressed upon my own ears and eyes. But then, as I reflected longer, the conviction came more and more strongly upon my mind, that the identity held good, and every circumstance I then remembered spoke loudly in its support.
    Was it not he himself, I asked myself, Monsieur Bagnols in the guise of the Chevalier, who had first told me the tragic tale of his own imputed murder, and that with an abundance of fine detail such as only could have come from a chambermaid's fancy, or else a witness (indeed, a mortally concerned participant) at first hand?
    Poor, dear Chevalier. For all those years he had been doomed, his beloved sweetheart dead of sorrow, to eke out an existence in banishment; his name and title adopted in forced deceit, the remains of his fortune transmitted to Spain; and all on account of the Marquis's envy, his malice and false report, and for the want of those papers

---

[1] In part of the torrential yet patchy 'Confession' which he feels driven to make before his death.

which had gone missing so long ago, and which would have served to give the lie to the Marquis of Roquefort, to pacify the Cardinal, to restore the Chevalier to his rightful station, and to clear the good name of Bagnols.

Oh, those *papers* . . .

The next few paragraphs, concerning what we novelists sometimes call narrative devices, although those dramatists sometimes call precisely the same ruses 'staging tricks', do not constitute a digression 'proper', as Paul Chalicer might put it. However, please do feel free to return to them later if you have just been asked to fasten your seatbelt for landing, or, conceivably, if your WhatRail? to London 'service' has just at last been called through the unheated-waiting-room Tannoy.

If you aren't in that much of a panic, we invite you to consider that stories in general may usefully be divided into three broad categories: *true* (as newspaper stories ought to be); *mythic* (having a basis in fact, but enriched by the embroidery of imaginative retelling); and '*entirely invented*' (fine for children, but most often a load of twaddle [stuffed with magical swords, bewitchment and sorcery, werewolves and vampires, plus happiness ever after on earth, soon leading to eternal pie in the sky – and other physical, logical and moral impossibilities], and insulting to the intelligence, when inflicted upon educated adults).

Into which of those loose pigeon holes should the present story, or stories, be thrust? This we are proud to leave to your own juicedishus judgement. At the same time, we must ask you to doubt whether *every* story does not rely for its credibility, in a given purveyor/consumer relationship, upon what the consumer believes (or desperately wants to believe) to be true of what hos takes to be 'the real world'. Most particularly, can't we agree, as that world contains things (mineral, such as earthquakes; vegetable, such as deadly poisonous mushrooms; and animal, such as black widow spiders, tyrant cardinals, and the like) which do or could affect, interest, benefit, and most of all **threaten us?**

And is it not also undeniable that amongst the beliefs to which nearly all of us would be seen to subscribe (and that right sensibly), were we ever to be assessed by our omnisciently documented behaviour, as opposed to righteous protestations, would be these?:

*I* am less good, and less honest, than I would like others
    to think me.
If others discover how bad and dishonest I am,[2] that will be
    to my disadvantage.
If others think me better and more honest than I am, that may
    be to my advantage.
It is in my interest to continue to deceive others as regards my
    personal moral worthlessness and untruthfulness.
*You* are less good, and less honest, than you would like others
    to think you.
If others discover how bad and dishonest you are, that will
    be to your disadvantage.
If others think you better and more honest than you are,
    that may be to your advantage.
It is in your interest to continue to deceive me as regards
    your personal moral worthlessness and untruthfulness.
*We* are constantly exposed to dangers stemming from
    the cunningly concealed deceit and dastardy
    of villains all around us.
However mendacious and wicked a malefactor is ever
    proved to be, hos is probably even worse
    than that really.
The most common form of badness is grasping selfishness
    (*their* financial or sexual [etc] gain is *our* loss),
    but even worse than that, and not uncommon, is
    gratuitous spite – where their only gain
    from our loss is evil pleasure.
Our peripheral moral vision is quite right to scan constantly
    for symptoms of camouflaged scheming selfishness,
    and unalloyed malice, in the other people
    with whom we transact.

All of which may help to explain why many of the most common
and powerful narrative aids involve, introduce, or at least arouse strong

---

2  'Goodness, Humbert! If you're truly more devious and putrid
than even I've been taking you for, you must be the Devil
Him\*self!' [P.C.]
   \* *?! 'For once, fair enough.' [J.R.]*

suspicions of, deceitful and basely motivated utterances or actions. We are, so to speak, so wired that any evidence of such hankypanky engages our interest as a matter of reflex, like a tabby cat sticking her bum in the air as soon as you stroke her lumbars.

Witness a few obvious examples:

EAVESDROPPING.

Can be deliberate. Sometimes is accidental. Even if it starts accidental, it becomes deliberate if the eavesdropper persists. Sometimes the eaves-dropper is set up, but doesn't realise it. Shakespeare, as usual, is pretty good at eavesdropping. Lots of it in *Much Ado*, *Twelfth Night*, *Hamlet*; all over. Even in our own most truthful history we couldn't prevent it from cropping up from time to time – as when, in Chapter 27, the bed-bound defenestrated Louis is devastated to overhear the fop nephew Charles bragging about how he is going to debauch, marry and constantly cuckold Hélène. Indeed, in how many worthwhile plots does some form of eavesdropping not occur?

SHUFFLING IDENTITIES.

This may result from ignorance, poor perception, similarities between individuals (as when one person's telephone voice is indistinguishable from another's), or traumatic change in the same individual (aging, alcoholism, AIDS, and so on) resulting (say) in our taking a longlost old friend for a complete stranger. But the best kind of mistaken identity, from the point of view of spurring on our audience, is that resulting from deliberate deception: disguise, misinformation, and downright lies. This is because the calculating manipulation of others is seen as the most threatening case; hence, in a drama, it is the most stimulating of interest and excitement.

Of course, not all concealment or mimicry of identity is motivated by malice or humdrum graft. Think of Louis Morel seeking out the Dowager Countess of Soissons in Paris. His longterm goal (which might be called altruistic, were his passion for Hélène not so pressing a factor) is certainly to serve the Count in Sedan – and hence disadvantage the tyrant Richelieu. But Louis's immediate purpose is more respectably self-defensive: to delude and elude the Cardinal and his agents, and thus avoid the inconvenience and discomfort of imprisonment in the Bastille, and interrogation on the famous 'iron bedstead'.

And this is not to say that the wilful misrepresentation of iden-tity cannot be entirely altruistic in its aims, or at least very nearly so. Reflect. It is the country near Dover. *King Lear*, 4.6. Poor silly blind old Gloucester, resolved to snuff his miseries in self-slaughter, is trying to find a cliff to jump off. Leading him, which is to say *mis*leading him, is his own son Edgar (remember, EdGar for Good son). But Edgar (whom Gloucester himself, in his senile fog of ungrateful misapprehension [in turn engineered by his bad bastard Edmund, EdMund for Mischief] has himself reviled and banished) Edgar, we repeat, is disguised as a local yokel, both in his ragged appearance, invisible to Gloucester, and in his voice, which he peasantly hams. And all for what? To keep his daft old duffer dad from harm, induce him to fall forward off a hummock (see: even the identity of the hummock is mistaken), and persuade him that 'Thy life's a miracle', to have survived such a mighty plummet, 'So many fathom down.'

Such a scene, finely played, sets off good, sympathetic and uplifting emotions in its audience. But many of the strongest emotions, and their echoes, are less noble than that, and we may say the strongest of all are beastly bad. Even if we don't, we're still liable to sit up from our nodding, our pupils resizing, when suddenly we realize Character X is scheming to masquerade as Character Y, with arrant aim of putting one or two over on Character Z, especially if Z has already succeeded in enlisting our sympathy, or just as usefully our revulsion. Occasionally these effects can be wrought with identical twins, and Shakespeare does various adolescent things with pairs of these in *The Comedy of Errors*. John Fowles gets his perplexed protagonist in a sexual twist with voluptuous female twins in *The Magus*, and we ourselves would have loved to do something similar for you with Louis Morel, had that been congruent with Truth.[3]

Another circumstance supporting the real-life and hence narrative

---

[3] And even if it had, ringing the changes on identical twins is slightly dodgy, given their relative rarity in real life.* How would we have responded, for instance, if John Fowles had come up with another two teasing twins in *The French Lieutenant's Woman*?

  \* *'Although there's some evidence, isn't there, that the incidence of such twins, not to say triplets on occasion, is increasing? What with all those fertility drugs, and middle-class professional women having their families later and later? Perhaps, then, by the year 3000 we'll have twins in every novel!' [P.C.]*

credibility of much mistaken identity in centuries past is the infernal darkness of moonless nights in the absence of electric or even gas lighting. Sometimes combined with lamentable levels of inebriation, the unadulterated blackness of night has facilitated scores of delightful nocturnal deceptions – such as John the Clerk, in Chaucer's 'Reeve's Tale', manoeuvring the paralytic miller's well-oiled wife into his bed, by shifting the position of the cradle by which the wife feels her way back to bed in the dark, having been out to pass some ale.[4]

Deception may be practised, and identity may be mistaken by:

Characters in the story;
Readers of the story;
Narrators of the story;
The author of the story.

The present reader (that's you) may presume to object that readers of a story can hardly affect the story by deceiving characters in it, or the narrators or author of it. We agree that in the case of ninety-five novels out of a hundred (by Godfrey Blobbs, et al) your objection would sustain. But not necessarily in the final five by Paul Chalicer, Wringhim Knox, and myselves. And you? Think of yourself, for a change, as a nymphomaniac literary groupie in Hampstead . . .

For some months you have been attending the same aerobical Jane Fonda classes as Janet Rosencrantz in Muswell Hill. One evening Janet – having discovered that you too were once an underpaid breastfeeding first-hurdle reader for BirdDog, before you liberated yourself from all that male-dominated shit, by means of a substantial alimony settlement – invites you back to her place for a glass of post-Fonda plonk. As Janet absents herself to take a

---

4 Yet knew not where she was, for it was dark,
  She well and fairly crept in with the clerk,
  Then lay quite still and tried to go to sleep.
  John waited for a while, then gave a leap
  And thrust himself upon this worthy wife.
  It was the merriest fit in all her life . . .
    (*Nevill Coghill's 'translation'*)

lengthy transfer-charge call from Charlotte running out of money in Berlin, you just happen to notice and become totally entranced by the latest batch of chapters in progress by Humbert Seale, which are lying in a coffee-stained folder on Janet's kitchen table. Conceiving instant irrepressible lust for the body behind such a mind, you copy Humbert's address from the folder and the following morning you write to introduce yourself to him as a freelance photojournalist keen to main-feature him for Nuncle Rudolph on Sunday.

No less of a sucker for attention and publicity whenever he can get any than Godfrey Blobbs, Graham Greene and Franz Kafka, Humbert replies by return with an invitation to interview him at overnight length in the comfort of his Berwickshire farmhouse. As Puck would have it you pick a weekday night when Koo is away at a trade fair in the Birmingham NEC, thus creating the perfect opening for you to seduce the unsuspecting Humbert at your leisure, and perpetrate your oral specialtease upon him. A few days later, or maybe it's two years, when Humbert has recovered from your carrying off his poor old thinning pubic scalp, he immortalizes your enterprise (just as you had secretly rather hoped he would) in the form of a thinly disguised fiction squeezed into his chapter in progress — which he posts off to Janet the following day, and publishes, only lightly revised, in book form many months later. Of course I freely confess that nothing like this has ever happened to me myself since that one time with Jemima Fuddlepun, and since then she has gone on to frazzle much greater fry than mine, and has even become a novelist herself.

Thus a reader, Jemima Fuddlepun, by deceiving an author as to her identity and purposes, gets herself cast as a character, and obliges the author to gently deceive my other readers, by means of provocative decoys such as composite names, transposed details, and double-bluff truths which could just be lies.

Whether in either of her novels to date Jemima Fuddlepun has done for me as I for her I cannot yet tell you, as I haven't yet read them. Paul says they're frightfully slight.

In any case if you do do me, Jemima, we trust you'll respect the one sacrosanct rule of a good novelist's thumb: that when a real person is characterized recognizably, hos must always be represented in a supportive and sympathetic light. In the present work we hope you'll have noticed that, despite the rough ocean of crimes you have nosed your noble prow through, that one rule is strictly observed. Such that Audrey Macpherson, Koo Forrest, Janet Rosencrantz, Paul Chalicer, Wringhim Knox, and various lesser not-yet-dead souls – even Mumbo Rankles – all are painted in colours at least as warm and lovable as any of their aunties could wish for.[5]

By contrast, with the characters who've been dead for several centuries, there is no abuse of privilege involved in minutiating their nitties. Hence we need have no bad conscience about having no compunction about relating the mounting by Louis of the naked maja alongside the priest she has just corpsed. Louis confesses it himself, so why shouldn't we repeat it, so long after he's gone? Bye-bye contrast: present-day horses of the wildest wildness could never get us mounting Paul Chalicer upon the naked Janet Rosencrantz alongside the Rankles she had just corpsed, even if our very own prying eyes had yesterday witnessed through a Bond-false mirror that Paul indeed had, and Janet had too. And if we did wish to coster some such carnal cameo closely based on the loosely private fantasy lives of junior GAGA ministers, we would at the very least protect our origi-

---

5 It doesn't follow, alas to say, that we'll get any thanks from the originals themselves. Paul, for one, is so overweeningly vain that he's interpreted our best-intended efforts to stage him as an erudite, witty and chivalrous gentleman of the world as a cheap conspiracy to brand him an oily soft-touch creep, so much so that he's exacted what he takes to be his revenge by writing me into his own new novel (well, sort of*) as one 'Dumbo Griswald', a sort of grunting Scottish almost-literate Bill Sykes to Paul's own centre-of the-literary-world-stage Faginistical 'Charlemagne Plunderer'. Well, I suppose there's one honest word in all that lot, and at least it's not as good as if I'd written all of Paul's new book myself. While the important point shines undimmed: that most of our thirsts for ludicrous flattery are simply quenchless. Paul's, Janet's, Wringhim's, mine – even yours, you most intelligent and insightful of all our earthly readers.

*This is the cunningly subwoven collection of apparently totally unrelated and independently meaningless fictions which might have been entitled The Three Pongs, but which now, after nineteen bouts of ever bloodier acrimony between Paul and his publishers, has been launched upon the world as Scorpions.*

nals by disguising their identities more thoroughly. Paul, for example, we would make tall, slim, irresistibly saturnine, unbeatable at karate, and endowed with a tenth-dan penis.[6] Janet we would transform into a tall, teen, blonde and boyishly buttocked model of Parisian lingerie, given to vigorous fell-walking at weekends, and experiments with LSD.[7]

Whether we're talking about authors and narrators fooling readers (either to shield their sort-of innocent sources or to pump those readers up for the postponed orgasmic gratification of exclaiming, 'I suspected that all along, said so ages ago, didn't I? Knew it, knew it, *knew it!*') or whether, in our sort-of mirror held up to sort-of nature we're exploring the relationships between the characters themselves, and their perceptions of one another, we are advised not to relinquish awareness of the following basic logic:

That false beliefs concerning identity can be caused wittingly, or unwittingly.

And they can be caused by description, or appearance, or both. Louis Morel, for instance, all his life up till a few moments ago has believed that the Count of Bagnols was in fact the Chevalier of Montenero. This is a result of the former having successfully represented himself, by description and name, to be the latter. Compare and contrast with our Chapter 6, where the Chevalier of Bagnols (as we shall now call him, following Louis's own lead) mysteriously contrives to arrive upon the scene in which Louis and the Marquis of Roquefort are duelling to what could have been the death of Louis outside the Lestelle post-house. The Chevalier knows only too well that the Marquis is the Marquis. But the Marquis has no idea that the Chevalier is of Bagnols. This, if you remember, is because the Chevalier is naturally much older and bushier than he used to be long ago, also darkened and lined by his adventures in hot New Spain, and has furthermore taken the precaution of turning up 'with a scarlet-diamonded bandana bibbed across his face below his eyes, like a Mexican ranchero garbed against the desert dust', &c.

False beliefs concerning identity can be general, or specific. In the Lestelle scene the Chevalier succeeds in generating the general false belief in the Marquis that he, Bagnols, is *not*-Bagnols; just some

---

[6] 'And call me Charles!' [P.C.]

[7] 'And nickname me Camilla, I shouldn't wonder.' [J.R.]

saddle-smelly busybody interloper; nobody special or important. What he doesn't attempt is to trick the Marquis into the specific false belief that he, Bagnols, is in truth Mickey Mouse. Or whoever. This, in the circumstances, would be more difficult to accomplish, and anyway it isn't necessary. Thus . . . never attempt a specific deception if a general deception is adequate. The specific deception is liable to be harder to set up, and may be a nightmare to keep up.

Specific false beliefs concerning identity may be once-false, or twice-false. Take Louis again masquerading in Paris as a lowly mum-vowed monk. So far as we know this deception is merely once-false: he pretends to be someone he isn't, and that someone doesn't exist. But if he had turned up guising as a particular mute Capuchin named Domenic Francis from Toulouse, and if there really were such a person, and if Louis knew that and was deliberately appropriating Friar Francis's identity, then his deception would be twice-false: first, not-me; second, really-him. Twice-false deceptions are best avoided in real life wherever once-false deceptions will do. This is because twice-false deceptions are intrinsically more difficult to get away with, and more easily exposed – if, say, the real Domenic Francis should bumble into Paris unexpectedly. But twice-false deceptions can be jolly good fun in fiction, particularly comedies, where the audience can vicariously delight in the embarrassment of some posturing character being bearded by the righteous proprietor, and stripped of hor stolen identity.

Motivations underlying the wilful inculcation of false identity beliefs can be: benevolent, tolerable, bad, or abominable. Edgar deceives Gloucester near Dover. His benevolent purpose is to save his poor old dotard father from shameful and pointless suicide, and this we instinctively admire; the more so since Edgar himself has suffered as a direct result of the same silly papa's ingratitude. Then the Chevalier. He deceives a number of others, including Louis, as to his true identity. It seems his main concern is to carry on his life, despite the setbacks of his youth and the loss of his sweetheart, outwith the clutches of Richelieu, and in unmolested peace. Provided the Chevalier has no more deeply concealed agenda, we accept his deceptions as tolerable. They are selfish, but only in a self-defensive sense.

Thus, we ourselves are not threatened.

As regards bad and abominable motivations, what about the Big Bad Wolf? Most little girls in the audience, and even some quite statuesque ones, are inclined to tell you the Big Bad Wolf's inclinations and behaviour are utterly abominable. But really we must be careful not to let personal abhorrence and abhorror disguise themselves as morally just condemnation. Certainly it's thoroughly deceitful of the Big Bad Wolf to go transvesting as Little Red Riding Hood's grannie. But if his sole concern is to get his dinner, and if he has no prospect of getting it any other way – no cans of succulent kangaroo flesh in the cupboard, enriched with Wolf-nourishing other-mammal-bone jelly, or other goodies of that sort – then the Wolf is indeed merely Bad, and we have no right to label him Abominable. If, on the other paw, he isn't so much honestly hungry as consumed by satanic gourmet delight in Red Riding Hood's terror, and drools at the jowls as he savours with malicious glee the prospect of her screaming agony as he devours her alive, crunch-squidge and slop-gulp, then by all means call him the Big Abominable Wolf, and shoot him in the head as soon as you have hung him out in the sun for several days covered in honey and ants, and sawn off his testicles slowly.

In our own stories there is very much badness. Whether there is enough badness to be truly true to life is not for us to say. As regards the worst moral profile, which is selfishness overshadowed and sometimes downright sabotaged by supererogatory gloating spite, we are conscious of having indulged ourselves, and you too, by restricting this most ghastly of too-human traits (which festers to some degree in every breast) to a reasonable narrative minimum: not thrusting it in snoringly once every scene, like most ten o' clock movies on the Nuncle Rudolph channels, just because we couldn't think of any other way of attracting our customers' attention, and keeping it for the next thirty seconds.

Cast back.

At the mill. Pere Garcés kills the customs officer. But only as an overdone defensive measure. Not vindictively. Or at least, not purely or even primarily so. And afterwords Garcés experiences remorse. Even as he lies dying at La Marfée, that murder haunts his spirit. Then Richelieu. What a merciless monster the Cardinal must be, you may feel. To sentence our Louis to death. Countless others too. No time to recant and reform? No chance of reconciliation? Hope of forgiveness? Certainly not. Never. *Death*, by God. And soon. Now this is undeniably ruthless stuff. And all the evidence suggests that the Cardinal *was* given to grudges, and *was* prone to hurtful and sometimes homicidal retaliations. But always in harmony with, and never at the risk of queering his all-informing great purpose: the protection, preservation, consolidation and aggrandisement of The State – with whose Interests his own were so tightly entwined that when he dies he is not only fabulously rich, but utterly convinced he has never committed any unnecessary wrong, and hence is a banker for Heaven:

"'His assurance appalls me," said a bishop as he marked the perfect confidence with which the Cardinal approached death. But one of the elements of Richelieu's strength had been his conviction of the justice of his own policy; He knew that he was right; he was troubled by no weak doubts and no vacillating purposes, and when the end came the certainty that he had acted for the true interests of the Church and State enabled him to face death without fear.'

The Cardinal, in other words, dies without repenting of the evils he has committed, because he believes they were the least evils possible. Buy contrast, your arrantest ghoul will never repent of the evils hos has committed – even if hos believes they were the greatest evils possible! Why should hos? In hor cruelest lingering extremes of torturing and murdering malevolence hos is actually being sincere, authentic, true to hor innermost nature. And isn't that the most harrowing thought of all? That there really are characters like Mumbo Rankles in the world, who costume themselves in the frills and ruffs of Critical Objectivity, Counter-Post-Modernist Realism *et guffo*, and then in full and overpaid self-awareness enact their vile personal vendettas against less impotent authors: all over the Sunday heavies, for the cameras of Auntie Whitehouse, and at dinner tables all round Hampstead.

Morally, it has to be said, Rankles is no less loathsome than the Marquis of Roquefort. You might say he is even more so, given that the Marquis – right up to the moment when his two layers of wigging peel off just before Louis breaks his neck – is in some ways less dishonest and more stylish in his loathsomeness. Like Rankles, the Marquis does not trouble to disguise *who* he is, in terms of name and public biography. Rather does he scheme to disguise *what* he is, in terms of his past atrocities, his present malevolent intentions, and his relationships with other key players. So it is that for us the Marquis of Roquefort is the Big Abominable Wolf – when in our Chapter 13 he treats Louis to a luxurious and probably sexually sapping interlude at his *pavillon de chasse* at Gagnères. As he apes the perfect worldly host, apparently delighting in his young guest's company and conversation, he is all the while resolved to have Louis murdered (by the corpulent Monsieur Saint-Simon, one of whose other identities is Fat Monk at

Luz) on his ride home to Morel. And all for what? For the satisfaction of being revenged on the teenager who bested him in the swordplay duel at Lestelle.

Or can we imagine a motive viler still?

As to other shuffled identities, seventeenth-century French histories rejoice in multitudes, and the story of Louis Morel more than most. Herein lies much of its appeal to G.P.R. James, and by extension ourselves. No doubt you'll have been nursing your own score card, along with private hunches as to which feints, dodges and solar-plexus fouls cry out to be exposed in the final rounds. In particular, you may have been toying with the significance of the Marquis of Roquefort exclaiming to Louis:

'Kill me *now!* And if you do sir, and if you do? You'll never know, *never* . . . who really was your father . . . ' only moments before Louis breaks his neck. Louis himself, curiously, does not yet, in his bondage within the Mézières scrotum up till now, appear to have reflected seriously on the Marquis's penultimate provocation – perhaps he has been dismissing it as a villain's cheap ruse, or possibly the depression and vitamin deprivation of imprisonment have clipped the wings of his paranoid fancies. Either way, as the quality of his meat and drink looks up, during the last three days of life the Cardinal has allowed him, the doomed hero's tragic lust for life draws breath for a harrowing swan song, as a black hooded flock of carrion conjectures torment him. All that and more – after the break. Meanwhile we'd better press on, else even your 'service' to London might be upon you, before we get out of this chapter. So let us now speed up with:

PLOTTING MALICIOUS MISCHIEF.

The audience is outraged, yet fascinated. There is a tingle of nightmare: to feel our enemies too might be machinating thus agin us. But also the indulgence of empathy: what a thrill it would be for us to apple-pie our enemies just so. Serve them right too. And is it not thanks to this Janus within that, though we find Richard III hateful, our revulsion is not without ambivalence – as it usually is, for instance, when we tread a dog shit into the living-room carpet?

'Plots have I laid,' boasts Richard, 'inductions dangerous, by drunken prophecies, libels, and dreams, to set my brother Clarence and the King in deadly hate the one against the other; and if King Edward be as true and just as I am subtle, false, and treacherous, this day should Clarence closely be mewed up, about a prophecy which says that **G**[8] of Edward's heirs the murderer shall be . . . '

[*Potted structure of RIII.*]

Brilliant!

Also, who can help but wonder what's going to happen next?

The present work, being truthful (as Shakespeare's 'histories' are not), and less given to gutter gambits, contains less in the way of overtly and centrally malicious mischief than *Richard III*, *King Lear*, *Hamlet*, *Macbeth*, *Othello*, and so on down the list. But we have had our Marquis of Roquefort, and there is one other malicious plotter to whose snide contrivances our hero's banishment, estrangement from his parents, separation from Hélène, and eventual downfall in the Ardennes, are just as equally due. Since this is a rather lengthy sort-of novel, as opposed to a fleeting-three-hour play, we have opted, in the hope of not insulting anyone's intelligence unduly, to leave most of the malicious plotting offstage – so not papping our food for thought.

Hope that's okay.

Also, and in view of the momonumountmentenous matter to come, perhaps we'd maybe better take a teabreak, or suchlike, before the following chapter is entirely devoted to:

---

[8] **G** for George, Duke of Clarence, Richard's unsuspecting brother. (Our bold italics.)

# Gratuitous Atrocities

At the end of Chapter 34b we grudgingly allude to the comparable Erich Segal's recommendation that if we get stuck with our story we can always shoot a puppy to help it along. So far as we know Segal himself has never yet stooped to machine-gunning puppies, but presumably it works best when the puppies are newborn, helpless, innocent and adorable.

It is possible that Segal has read Maupassant, but not that Maupassant ever read Segal.

And that may be why Maupassant kills not the puppies (directly) but rather their labouring mother, and not with a machine-gun but rather with a priest's umbrella. This is in Chapter 10 of *Une Vie* (*A Woman's Life*), where a group of farm children are gathered round 'looking at something with eager curiosity and concentrated silent attention'. It is the bitch called Mirza giving birth to a litter of pups. Just when the young zealot priest arrives on the scene:

' . . . the mother in agony tensed her body and a sixth pup appeared.' Seeing this, the onlooking children shout in joy and clap their hands:

'There be another one!'

To obviate any well founded and utterly unanswerable charges of Humbertism, what follows is given in the very professional Penguin translation by H.N.P. Sloman:

'At first the Abbé stood rooted to the spot; then in a fit of wild rage he raised his great umbrella and brought it down on the heads of the children with all his force. The children scattered and ran away as fast as they could, and he suddenly found himself facing the newly made mother, who tried to get up; but he did not give her time to rise to her feet, before completely losing control he began to beat her. Being on a chain she could not escape and groaned distressingly, as she struggled under the hail of blows. His umbrella broke and with bare hands he threw himself on the dog and trampled on her madly, pounding and crushing her. This made her give birth to a last pup, which was squeezed out of her by his grip. With a furious stamp of his heel he finished off the bleeding body, which was still quivering surrounded by the new-born puppies, whimpering and blind, which were crawling about already feeling for her teats.'

And what could be more gratuitous?

Or is it?

Do we believe Maupassant, fearful of readership yawns, has elected to jolt us wider awake again with a scene which some viewers might find disturbing, if Auntie Whitehouse let them see it?

Or is he attempting some proto-Freudian statement about the misogyny of sexually frustrated fanatical Catholicism? If so, the Vatican may well pronounce his deranged canicide 'gratuitous', while militant Hindu feminists applaud his iconoclastic courage. In general, the cruellest, goriest and most erotically extreme scenes in our fictions tend to be judged 'gratuitous' if Bubo[1] Rankles (say) feels politically or sexually threatened by them, and 'culturally iconic' if it's his own favourite enemies getting their throats slit, or his own widdle pink ting that comes alive in a harmless hard-on at last.

Which is hardly surprising.

To the storyteller, however, the only atrocities which are 100% gratuitous are those that alienate your friends as well as your enemies (unless, conceivably, you *wanted* to alienate your friends), and leave you with no readers, no viewers, and no working capital to develop your next story. Every other atrocity has its potential value, and the more the teller milks it, and the less the lister sees it, the better for all concerned.

Thus, Maupassant, out of his bitch-killing, gets so much repugnance boiling against the vindictive prelate that almost everyone outside the Vatican is delighted when:

' . . . the priest suddenly felt himself gripped by the collar; a box on the ear knocked off his clerical hat and the Baron [*kindly old father to*

---

[1] Sorry about this, Mumbo. Several of my keys, including the 'm', have begun to fail, due to abnormal hammering, and the replacement keyboard is late in arriving. Another unique service courtesy of WhatRail?. However, why not look on the bright side for once? It does rather suit you – 'Bubo', I mean – and you could do worse than liken it to the limiting flaw in Cellini's block of marble. Or couldn't you?

*the heroine*] in a blazing temper dragged him to the gate of the yard and
hurled him out into the road.'

A first step towards what some of us would love to do to sanctimonious
hypocritical prelates everywhere.

More subtly, Maupassant has his atrocity still paying off many
years later:

Old Murder (the one surviving pup from the orphaned litter) has
become one of the heroine's few remaining companions. Prematurely
aged, the family fortune in ruins, her life a fading dream, her only
son a spendthrift shitty cadger, Jeanne is forced to vacate her beloved
spacious Poplars and remove to a sensible little retirement home at
Batteville. There she feels more betrayed, abandoned and lonely than
ever. Unsettled, tensely restless, above all she misses the stormy sounds
and salty tang of the sea.

And the old faithful friend ('which unconsciously she had come to love
like a human being')?

'Murder too was equally unable to settle down. On his first evening
in the house he had taken up his abode in the lower part of the
kitchen dresser and refused to budge. He lay there hardly moving,
only turning over at intervals with a low growl. But as soon as it
got dark, he staggered up and dragged himself to the garden door,
bumping against the walls. When he had been out for the few minutes
needed for his business, he came in again and sat down on his tail
in front of the still warm range, and as soon as his two mistresses
had gone up to bed, he began to howl. He went on giving tongue
all night with a plaintive, piteous howling, sometimes pausing for
an hour, only to begin again with even more heartrending moans.
They chained him up in a barrel in front of the house, but as he
was ill and had not long to live, they soon put him back in the
kitchen.

'Sleep became impossible for Jeanne, who heard the old dog moaning
and scratching all the time, unable to get his bearings in this new house,
realizing that it was not the house he knew. Nothing would keep him
quiet. After dozing all day, as if his failing sight and increased feebleness
made movement impossible when all other living creatures were alive
and active, he began to wander round ceaselessly as soon as night began
to fall, as if he dared to live and move only in the hours of darkness,
when all creatures are equally blind. One morning he was found dead,
to everyone's great relief.'

It's a sad tale, but very true, and Maupassant tells it superbly.

Shakespeare too is adept at getting maximum milage out of his atrocities.

Take Gloucester's eyes.

When in *King Lear* 3.7 Gloucester gets his first eye gouged, squeezed or gralloched out by Cornwall, and then the second put out likewise (at the pitiless insistence of Cornwall's wife Regan), 'Out, vile jelly!', our emotions, if they have not already given rise to vomit on our popcorn, are stirred to new heights of itching hostility against Cornwall and Regan, which overflow into ersatz vengeful pleasure when we learn (4.2) that Cornwall has died off-stage of a wound inflicted by the relatively humanitarian servant who attempted to prevent his plucking Gloucester's second eye (as if one were quite adequate), and when we see Regan get her what's-due in great pain (5.3), poisoned by her own sister Goneril – whose vixen motives include paranoia that her younger sister will prevail sexually with the malevolent plotter Edmund – for whom Goneril too has the hots.

Now that sort of crude tinkering with our nastier emotions would hardly of itself set Shakespeare apart from the grafting goons who produce, write, direct, distribute and broadcast most of the sickening sado drivel that pours from the skies nightly after ten, and all day too if you wish, for the cost of a bigger dish. Shakespeare's distinctive redemption, if there is any, derives from the sublimity of such scenes as the feigning Edgar tricking his thankless but pathetic and now blind (thanks to Cornwall's brutality) father into jumping off a tussock, instead of the White Cliffs of Dover; as already screened above.

Whether Shakespeare gets any more ladder-of-redemption points for the multiple atrocities (Lavinia ravished, then her tongue cut out and hands hacked off, so she can't spill the beans) and excessive revenges (having Chiron and Demetrius [the ravishers and mutilators of his daughter Lavinia] baked in a pie, Titus dispenses what he takes to be their mother Tamora's desserts by finessing her into 'Eating the flesh that she herself hath bred') in *Titus Andronicus* – or whether the original Slick Willie should for this video-nasty-topping display of unmitigated depravity be slithered thousands of points back down the snake to perdition – is an issue so fraught with literary anguish, apparently, that some Bowdling commentators have tried to solve 'the problem' by making out that Shakespeare *could not* have written this play!

And in response to such unreasoning moralistic claptrap?

Others develop gigabytes of archaic mainframe software to prove the contrary.[2]

And what is even more obscenely silly than that?

It is that these idiots[3] get paid comfortable salaries, year after year, to dispute with one another in their journals, furthering their careers by inflating their personal 'lists of publications', and in ninety-nine cases [*sic*] out of a hundred never once come close to writing a new novel, play, or even a half-page poem.

Small wonder, really, that Wringhim is sometimes so rude to them in McEwan's.[4] *Very* much ruder at times, let's be frank, than he was to the Kant-parading junior divinity peddler in the College Club. Nevertheless, though he pricks their pretentions, castigates their complacency and hounds their hypocrisies, I cannot recall ever witnessing Wringhim, verbally or in print, giving vent to gratuitous spite.[5] Certainly he can be elephantically retributive, as when dissecting Rankles in the *Clarion*. But unprovoked pleasure in cruelty and bloodshed, physical or mental, and massively excessful retaliations – which are so easy to mix in to a flagging plot, or useful to temporarily shore up a crumbling tyranny . . . these woeful deformities of humanity are less manifest in Wringhim the person than in any other novelist I know.

Think back to our dinner in Le Grand Bouchon.

If Wringhim had coldbloodedly intended that the young French waitress should understand that he was advising the rest of us that she had a gassy cunt – or that he would love to suck her gassy cunt, or conceivably even that he *had* sucked her gassy cunt, which was jolly tasty, so the rest of us should try it too, or whatever – then that would have been gratuitous, atrocious, and unforgivable. In fact, as we all now know, he intended nothing more sinister than a somewhat convolutedly implied political statement, and his hurtful gaffe was due in the main to his rather over-valuing his command of oral French, which may in

---

[2] 'Aren't you rather ungratefully forgetting that it was the *Titus Andronicus* software that got you going on Louis Morel? Ref your own first chapter.' [J.R.]

[3] 'This is too sweeping. These people aren't *all* idiots! Two of my dearest friends . . . !' [P.C.]

[4] Fawniest thing is the way they lap it up.

[5] 'Not even in his "ghastly pamphlet"? In that case, what *is* "gratuitous" spite?' [J.R.]

turn be linked to his deplorable practice of never reading classic French fiction in French, and hardly ever in English either. Of course, it cannot be denied that Wringhim was regrettably slow to admit his fault, prostrate himself on the Bouchon tiles and unconditionally petition excusement. But this is another problem: deriving from his constitutional obstinacy (which is only the flip side of tenacity, which is very essential to the sustained composition of novels), plus alcohol-not-unrelated truculence. *Not* stemming, in further words, from a gangrenous delight in others' suffering.

You'll note that if Wringhim had wanted to torment Marie-Pascale with snide remarks about her cunt, that would have been an atrocity without bloodshed, bone-snapping, entrail-dangling, genital-severing, and all the other violently entropic biological trauma which devotion to truthful duty prevents us from excluding totally from all our other novels. Such emotional atrocities (if one might so distinguish them from bodily atrocities) are lamentably frequent, particularly in novels written by women. Click on Chapter X of Emily Brontë's *Wuthering Heights*, and here we find the odious Catherine wickedly humiliating the pathetic eighteen-year-old Isabella by revealing to the repulsive Heathcliff, in Isabella's presence, the intimate confidence which Isabella just couldn't help blurting to Catherine, that:

'I [*Isabella*] love him [*Heathcliff*] more than ever you [*Catherine*] loved Edgar [*Isabella's brother, now also Catherine's husband*]; and he might love me, if you would let him!'

Catherine's paraphrase to Heathcliff the following day, as the confounded Isabella writhes:

'My poor little sister-in-law is breaking her heart by mere contemplation of your physical and moral beauty. It lies in your own power to be Edgar's brother!'

Such a betrayal of privately divulged passion could be embarrassing enough for even a Welsh international front-row forward to go down with the hot-flushing squirmies. And for a sensitive young lady in extremis, so we're told, it can occasion anguish much more searing, and lasting, than any short sharp bout of corrective masculine discipline on her bountiful bent-over bottom.[6] This aptly illustrates the point that the atrociousness of the atrocity needs to be measured both as a function

---

6   "'He is ingenious and unrelenting in seeking to gain our abhorrence!'" [J.R.]

of the hideousness of the inflicter's malice, and of the intensity of the victim's consequent excruciation. Accordingly, *Wuthering Heights*, even though not rolling in castrations, decapitations and impalements, is a much nastier story, peopled by odious shits and colourless bores, and told with less grace and compassion, than any drivelling 'shocker' by Stephen Herbert.

If you want to write a better novel than *Wuthering Heights* (which isn't actually all that difficult), and if you are determined to include atrocities in it (which isn't always illegitimate), you must make them pay their way sufficiently for most of your regular customers to accept your atrocities as not 'gratuitous'. This chapter should already have given you a jumpstart on that, and the specific exemplifications must obviously vary from customer-list to customer-list, and most crucially from you to you.

You?

Hubris springing eternal, perhaps your secret ambition is to write a novel which is not only 'best-selling' but also 'great'. If so, and if your story not only justifies but positively intrinsically *requires* that certain atrocities be portrayed, then you must further ensure audience horror at the crimes committed, and feelings of vengeful outrage against your monster, but also, and much more demandingly, an ultimate purgative sense of sad sympathy for the ogre enchained by hor own degradation, and even a final cathartic intuition of loss when the very bad baddy undergoes hor terribly earned extermination – as a footnote to your manipulated spasms of two-human relief that one more tired old serial killer, child-chewing werewolf, suburban vampire, or whatever, will prowl the world of darkest night not never no more.

Sympathies and intuitions, for example, entirely unkindled by such academically overrated narrative nasties as Camilio José Cela's *The Family of Pascual Duarte*. Now it may be that dumb animal enthusiasts are unable, even despite their protestingly adult full-awareness of having their emotions most cynically provoked, to repress a surge of mammalian compassion when Pascual shoots his dog (for looking at him in a funny way) and stabs to death the mare that threw his pregnant wife. But who in the world, other than a professor of literature perhaps, can work up more than a hoot of uncaring derision when Pascual finally gets around to slitting the throat of the smothering mother he understandably loathes, in the moment after she, in her frantic final snatching at her receding life, has bitten off her beastly babe's left nipple?

What a load of shit, in short.

And indeed, for an outstanding instance of this rare because supremely testing literary achievement – the portrait of a homicidal predator painted with none of the gilding of glitz, but imbued with the warm fellow feeling of the authentic artist, such that the beholder's emotions of pity and regret at the tragedy of this aberrant humanity are engaged with genuine sublimity, we are well advised not to repair to the early abortions of over-privileged reactionary pseudo-nihilists such as Cela, Céline and Malaparte (and their present-day inheritors by illegitimate adoption in Hampstead and Chelsea), but rather to the later novels (in terms of his oeuvre to date) of our own home-grown senior contemporary Wringhim Knox.

In particular, let us focus for an elastic moment on Wringhim's *A Cannibal Called Kilmarnock*.

Now in his *Sunday Crimes* crucifiction of Wringhim's *Cannibal*, Bubo Rankles was at great pains in the bum to expose the author's wholesale plagiarism from Thomas Harris's *The Silence of the Lambs*. Predictably, alas, the Rankles accusations are not only vindictive and puerile, but also entirely without substance.

False, in a simpler word.

This is obvious to anyone who knows that though *A Cannibal Called Kilmarnock* is Wringhim's ninth published novel, it was actually his third conceived and sixth composed.

(In fact, with the sole exception of *Rob Roy's Women*, Wringhim's order of publication is totally out of sync with his order of conception and execution. This, he never tires of admitting, is thanks to problems with London.)

It would of course be uncharitable of us to hint that Rankles, when he wrote his snide 'review', could in fact have been perfectly well aware that Wringhim's *Cannibal* text predates the publication of Harris's *Lambs* by several years. Suffice it to note that Rankles was certainly present in body, if not consciousness, at the bottom of a table in the Glasgow Taj one evening, when Wringhim was heard to lament at some length and equal vim about difficulties incurred in trying to get his *Cannibal* published. Not only was this before *Silence of the Lambs*, it was also before Wringhim and Rankles fell out so badly over Scotland v. England politics that the former placed a box ad in the following Saturday's *Clarion* to publicize, using metaphors and ironies of censor-baffling ingenuity, precisely what he intended to do to and with Rankles' risible toupé, should he ever again encounter it on the flesh.

Very unlike his stance on publishers, Wringhim's posture on his sources and influences is decidedly cagey. However, it seems not unlikely that historical nods informing his *Cannibal* include Gilles de Rais, Sawney Bean, and Issei Sagawa – the Japanese student who in 1981 shot his Dutch girlfriend in Paris, cut her up, ate some bits, refrigerated others, pretended to be loony, succeeded in getting himself shipped out of France, and since has become a free man, noted celebrity and bestselling author back home in Japan. These last details, needless to say, Wringhim could not emulate for Kilmarnock, else he could never have scaled the peaks of tragic pathos which his artistic purpose requires.

'What the fuck actually happens?' you may well ask.

And it's difficult to oblige you with satisfactory brevity, since any condensation of the plotted meat of such an extraordinary tale runs the risk of sounding a bit corny. With that between-the-tits proviso (unknown to Rankles) the bare bones hang like this:

# Wringhim's Hard-act Cannibal

Kelvin Kilmarnock is a Clydeside riveter.

One day with no notice he is made redundant when his shipyard folds following the English government's decision to place a new contract for nuclear submarines with state-subsidised undercutters in the Far East. During Kilmarnock's ensuing stint of unemployment the English government reduces the period during which he may claim earnings-related benefit. Since there are no jobs going for workers with Kilmarnock's skills he is soon reduced to the ignominy of minimal 'Income Support', which he supplements decreasingly by selling off treasures from his collection of World War II weapons built up during his twenty years of naval riveting since leaving school with no exams. Morag, his wife, has never been allowed to work, since that would have been inconsistent with Kilmarnock's role as a 'good provider'. Now, though, it is Morag who brings in a bit extra doing odd-hours cash-in-hand jobs – while Kilmarnock festers at home warming beans for their three small children, watching television junk news with great hatred, and pining for money to drink.

One night Morag comes home later than expected.

It is Thursday night (Thursday once was wages day) and Kilmarnock is surrounded by empty lager tins and two thirds down a bottle of cheap supermarket whisky: liquid consolation following the sale of a much prized Bren gun to a fellow collector in Cumbernauld. Rather than ask his wife what she has been up to, the inebriated Kilmarnock immediately pursues her with sexual advances. He has been watching a superficially titillating movie on terrestrial television; a film in which no genitals appear, but the Hollywood heroine has smooth and shapely breasts, and simulates orgasm with commendable professionalism when the tanned Hollywood hero affects to mount her in the missionary position. Morag at first, and with some alarm, repulses her husband's overtures. He is drunk, she tells him, and not so much inflamed with genuine and loving desire for her as with a juvenile craving to prove himself a stud. Predictably, this snub enrages Kilmarnock to the point where he hurls himself on

603

Morag, rips her clothes off, and realises too late that his wife was quite right: his penis is shamefully limp. Sooner than admit his impotence he goes down on her straightway and attempts to demonstrate his female-orgasm-arousing prowess by slurping oral sex – a gratification he has never bestowed on Morag before, although she has him.

And yes, unfortunately, this is the point at which he tastes another man's sperm in his wife's vagina. Morag, currently chambermaiding in the Haptic Hotel in George Square, has been seduced by a whizkid financial analyst from Surrey, who is scouting on behalf of a London-based consortium for promising-but-vulnerable Scottish companies to buy up. His name is Sebastian Blandings and his father, the Marquess of Blandings, owns (amidst numerous other assets) tens of thousands of game-shooting acres in the Scottish Highlands, and also a large chunk of International Biscuits.

Kilmarnock, as he savours this meal of his cuckolder's jissom, undergoes a short age of befuddled dumbfoundment. Then, as it were in some strange alchemical transformation catalysed by his embracement of degradation, slurping to the dregs these remnants pearls of a trespasser's minglings with the genital juices of the mother of his children, the multiple victim metamorphoses into a practitioner of deranged sexual possession, frantically tonguing all around where the interloper thrust and meanwhile dimly recalling some highbrow minority garbage on Channel 4 one Saturday night in December when the football had all been cancelled due to frost about how women in the heart of their maze of couch-grass, leafmould and warm oily pasta that horrified and humiliated you so when first you encountered it in the youth-club toilets have lurking there a little dedicated worm of pure pleasure which if you could be bothered occasionally and also if you could locate it as well might cause them to come and come and come again like Muscovy drakes in May as you lipped and licked and sucked upon it till in their convulsions of gratified debauchment they would then in growling carnal joy do anything, anything, *everything* possible to pleasure you in return with that modicum of pale-shadow spurt which was all a man was good for, could hope for, yet strove for, would die for, kill for, kill for, kill . . .

As Kilmarnock's polluted consciousness streams muddily thus he at length contrives for the first time in his life to bring the guilty Morag against her better judgement to a climax of shivers and squeals and moans which motherly she mutes as best she can so's not to wake the children in this council flat so poky small with walls so cardboard thin. Kilmarnock, himself now erect as never before, bends Morag over the bulk of their tired terrestrial television and subjects her to the anal intercourse he has never before either practised or wanted to. With Morag thus impaled against the gaudy flickerings of an ancient John Wayne movie, Kilmarnock now commands her to confess:

Who was it fucked her earlier?

Morag denies it. Protests. Complains he is hurting her. Begs him to stop. Tells him he is only crazed with drink. Deluded. Imagining things. *Begs* him to *stop*.

As Kilmarnock continues, his member stabbing deeper to her colon, his broad, strong riveter's hands encircle her neck; constrict her throat. She is lying, he informs her. Unless she now comes clean – who? where? why? – he will kill her, now, like this . . .

In fact it is only when the outraged husband, in a moment of demented inspiration, tries a different threat that the fallen wife gives in. If Morag won't tell him, he assures her, that which he demands to know, has a *right* to know, as she has a *duty* to tell him, well, in that case he is going to call the children down: to see what Mummy looks like, with Daddy's prick plunged up her arse.

'No, no, no,' sobs Morag. 'Not that, Kelvin. *Please—*'

Kilmarnock in-hisses a deep breath to shout.

Now resistance collapses. In short spasmic utterances as her husband continues to rape her rectum she tells him all he needs to know about Sebastian Blandings in his Penthouse Suite at the Haptic and how he seduced her with his plush mélange of oily public-school globetrotter's patter, champagne, oysters, and catastrophic snorts of cocaine.

The following day, Friday, Kilmarnock sends Morag and the children to stay with her mother in Lanark. In the late evening he proceeds to the Haptic in George Square. There he finds that Mr Blandings won't be back till Tuesday: he's flown down to Montpellier for a long weekend with his wife and family in the South of France, where they are restoring a sixteenth-century château. This gives Kilmarnock some vital extra hours in which to cover a number of future eventualities in his already ruined life. On Tuesday at just gone midnight he kicks his way into the Penthouse Suite in the Haptic and finds Blandings in bed with a smooth-skinned young man of twenty-two: an economics graduate in the marketing department of a company Blandings is toying with.

As his memory scars churn over the gullet tackiness of Blandings' spent seed, the viral implications of the present gay scene inflame Kilmarnock to new heats of hate. Waving the naked economist from the scene with the barrel of his Naval issue Webley service revolver, he orders the stupified Blandings to get out of bed and stand against the wall. At once fascinated and revolted by the rapid detumescence of his victim's erstwhile lust, the avenger now shoots him in the genitals. Twice. A minute later he shoots him in the stomach. In fact he pulls the trigger twice, but one of the cartridge detonators fails in this half-century-old ammunition. A second minute later, either considering the wrongdoer's atoning agony to have been sufficient, or else perhaps anxious in case some rescuing cavalry should now arrive in time to somehow save the shit from death, Kilmarnock shoots him once in the head: through his left ear as he writhes on the floor.

As Kilmarnock emerges from the lift in the Haptic foyer, hearing and then seeing police cars disgorging officers through the glass, he withdraws the Webley from his raincoat pocket, thrusts the muzzle up to the back of his mouth and pulls the trigger. But nothing happens, for the sixth round too is dud. Hence it is that Kilmarnock is overpowered by the law before he can reload and subsequently is convicted of murder and sentenced to life imprisonment.

In Barlinnie he discovers that though he had always thought of himself as a reasonably hard man, there are, for the time being, a number of others much harder. Also that passive and later active full-penetration homosexual intercourse with a heavy-duty HMPS condom is from time to time marginally preferable to no sex at all. In this climate Kilmarnock focuses his hatred on goals to be attained via development of his metal-work skills in the prison workshop, relentless body-building, and belated acquisition of some of the education denied him by his underprivileged childhood. He also has his understanding of Scottish history, culture, identity, and imperialistic colonization by England radically expanded for him in the course of stimulating creative writing classes for murderers provided weekly by one visiting Rinzeal Hyde, whomum we take to be Wringhimself.

Seven years later, when Kilmarnock is released on probation thanks to impeccable behaviour and favourable psychiatric reports, he is the coldly calculating possessor of an Open University degree in psychology. Morag has long since divorced him and migrated to New Zealand with the children, initially to stay with her sister Jean, and later to remarry a widowed sheepfarmer named McBride. This severance Kilmarnock accepts stoically as being typical of the world at large, which, he finds, is in no noticeable aspect any better than when he was removed from it, and in many ways markedly worse. The GAGA party has been returned to government by the English electorate yet again, the Marquess of Blandings has expanded his ownership of Scotland by several thousand acres, and the operational intelligence of the average citizen – especially south of the border, judging by their terrestrial television programmes – seems to Kilmarnock to have declined by at least ten points. As a qualified pyschologist he now knows his own IQ to be abnormally high, which is obviously a factor helping him to escape suspicion for several weeks following the initial blazing of a trail of grisly killings in Grampian Scotland.

Of course it is Kilmarnock who is now enacting the second act of his vendetta drama against his oppressors by having turned himself into a serial cannibal whose speciality is tearing out the throats and eating the Adam's apples of affluent English tourists and especially fishers of Scottish salmon, baggers of Scottish grouse, and telescopically unfairly-advantaged snipers of Scottish stags. Particularly horrific from the media point of view is the supersubhuman biting ferocity and power with which the predator guts the gullets of his prey. This is due to Kilmarnock's prosthetic dentures – which fit like sharp steel gloves over his front six teeth, top and bottom – that he fashioned on the sly in the Barlinnie workshop; two sets, just in case; in twice-shy memory of those dud Webley cartridges in the Haptic. It, the tabloid field day, is also admirably manured by the fanatical strength of Kilmarnock's mouth, jaw, and neck muscles, which he has had ample leisure to build up.

Curiously, the shrillness of public outcry in London and the provinces seems not to be matched in Scotland by acceptably speedy progress on the case: soon prompting vile but adroitly libel-sidestepping speculation that the Scottish police forces are insufficiently concerned about this crazy cannibal amok, so long as it's only those English buggers' Adam's apples he devours. For all that, however, it is not until the final week of September, when the internationally obnoxiously kent GAGA MP Sir Ripley Tonbridge gets thoroughly cannibalized on the north bank of the upper Tay, that the Scotfuzz Internet is pressured (reputedly by threats from the Prime Creep itself that otherwise intervention by 'Scotland Yard' will be imposed 'from above') into sending Strathclyde CID's top supersleuth to snuffle the glens of Perthshire.

This is one Detective Inspector Angus Mycroft, Scottish by mother and geographical birth, though his father hailed from Cockermouth. Now despite Kilmarnock's precautions (which needless to say are only intended to be stopgap, since he is well aware that sooner or later he will be tracked down through genetic barcoding of his spittle, or something suchlike) it only takes Mycroft two short weeks to deduce that since all the throat-munched victims to date have been (a) English and (b) cannibalized on Scottish acres belonging to the Marquess of Blandings, and given that (c) Kilmarnock's criminal record shows him arguably prone to some sort of grudge against the Blandings dynasty, plus (d) that Kilmarnock is currently to be found by day in the centre of the night cannibal's patch (he is working as a garage mechanic, in the ever bonny village of Comely), it is not unreasonable to hypothesize that grounds exist for including Kilmarnock in the short leet of primal suspects.

And Mycroft candidly puts this to Kilmarnock himself one early evening, when he finds him lingering after work in the public bar of the Comely Hotel, over his single lager shandy.

Kilmarnock replies that it would be insultingly obvious of him, wouldn't it, given his unfortunate case history, to engage in such easily solvable murders?

That same night on the Duke of Barchester's estate at Strathmungo, contiguous with a Blandings estate, a fat Austrian billionaire named Schwarzenegger gets summarily cannibalized in the gloaming while roaming home to the ranch following a tryst in the heather with a gamekeeper's daughter. Next evening in the bar Mycroft amiably accuses Kilmarnock of facile red-herringism. Kilmarnock shrugs apologetically: if only he could be of some help in this ticklish investigation. Mycroft presses Kilmarnock to accept a second lager shandy. Kilmarnock courteously accepts. During the conversation that follows, Mycroft, a gaunt and sallow man, with a mousy moustache just beginning to grey, makes it known to Kilmarnock that though he admires his intelligence, and shares many of his political sympathies, nevertheless he cannot allow this wholesale consumption of the Adam's apples of the rich English and others to continue, that he knows Kilmarnock is the cannibal, and that only hours remain before, with incontrovertible proof, he will be making his arrest.

'Is that so?' Kilmarnock appears unperturbed.

This is where Mycroft makes a dreadful error of judgement. Thinking to rattle Kilmarnock into the insecurity of awe, he piles it on about implacable forensic patience, pathological devotion to duty, never failing to get his man, etc, and cites by way of terrifying example his own current HIV-positive condition, acquired through sharing infected needles in a den of Glasgow addicts, rather than risk the blowing of his cover and the loss of a BigMan catch.

Appearing impressed, Kilmarnock nods politely, and wonders what possible category of evidence might convict an innocent man like himself.

Mycroft – perhaps his judgement is already impaired by the onset of AIDS, and the strain of concealing it from his superiors – now makes his second and last dreadful error: telling Kilmarnock how he has instructed the barman to retain Kilmarnock's first shandy glass, which he later will collect and send to the lab for saliva tests in the morning.

Kilmarnock has nothing against the barman, but at three in the morning he soundlessly prises open the snibbed window of Mycroft's first-floor bedroom in the William Wallace Hotel. Mycroft prides himself on being a light sleeper, but hardly have his fingers flexed towards the small automatic pistol beneath his pillow when the muscle-bound cannibal is already upon him. First stunning and winding his bedclothed victim with a mighty blow to his solar plexus, Kilmarnock then proceeds to eat him from life into death. As he gnaws into the policeman's craw and chews his Adam's apple like a lump of parboiled ginger, Kilmarnock also bites the tip off his own tongue, to ensure the bloody induction into his own immune system of Mycroft's HIV.

Then Kilmarnock disappears.

The police manhunt continues, needless to say, but for several weeks there are no more Adam's-apple murders.

Suddenly in the fortnight before Christmas they erupt again – only this time in London. Two eminent financiers in the City and three GAGA MPs lose their Adam's apples and their lives in traditional Kilmarnock style, one of the MPs, as chance would have it, being discovered lying throatless on top of a hypothermically unconscious homeless wino in a sexshop doorway just down the street from the Soho brothel where he was last seen sort-of alive. Despite frenetic detectival activity and harassment of vagrants no sighting of the rogue cannibal Scot is forthcoming for several months – presumably because Kilmarnock has now become a master of disguise and high-earning credit card fraud as well as of killing nauseating English adult would-be dominant males and eating symbolic parts of them, though it has to be admitted that this level of detail is never gone into by Wringhim as microscopically as Frederic Dayton might have.

In any case the next wave of Adam Apple's grisly meals (as Kilmarnock's human snacks are now known to the tabloid press, and hence to everyone else, though the Prime Creep cannot bring himself to udder the phrase 'Adam Apple' on television) takes place in opulent country mansions and their grounds throughout the south of England. All goes smoothly for Kilmarnock until one balmy evening in the bushes by the artificial lake on the walled estate surrounding Blandings Castle near Oxford. There Kilmarnock knocks unconscious a febrile young cad with his trousers down before proceeding to tear the minimally petite Adam's Apple out of the slimly pretty and nearly naked young woman whom he takes to be the Marquess of Blandings' daughter: younger sister to the snorting analist who debauched Morag.

But as it happens there has been a swapping of febrile-cad boyfriends tonight, with the result that Kilmarnock's latest victim is not Laetitia Blandings but rather her best friend from college: a commoner from Inverness whose name is Fiona, the same name Kilmarnock bestowed upon his own daughter twelve years ago. Now in a moment of rare poignancy – he has learned of his error from the following morning's tabloids – Kilmarnock acknowledges to himself that he has sunk to a state very nearly as putrid as the establishment he preys upon. For many weeks Adam Apple strikes no more as Kilmarnock struggles with remorse and self-hatred, and several times comes close to the manner of self-slaughter denied him by the dud cartridge in the Haptic foyer.

But at length the integrity of his forged-in-prison resolution returns.

Keeping an invisibly low profile (in terms of eating other people's Adam's apples), Kilmarnock bides his time patiently till the first shadow symptoms of full-blown AIDS are upon him. Then he makes various arrangements accordingly, accumulates a number of contingency props and proceeds with infinite caution to the forthcoming GAGA Party Conference at Brightpool.

Guising as a freelance political columnist for *The Scotlander*, Kilmarnock contrives, during the week, to interview a number of junior GAGA ministers, and also to have anal intercourse with three of them. The condoms he obligingly produces, to legitimize these pleasures, have been studiously repacked with tiny nicks in their teats, and with delicate sprinklings of Royal Naval blue asbestos along the rolls of their lubrication.

But the junior GAGA ministers have no awareness of this vengeful treasury – they are, indeed, pretty-pig-stupid, and have awareness of remarkably little – and one of them, besotted with Kilmarnock's affectionate virility, agrees to procure him an interview with the Prime Creep itself. This takes place with admirable pseudo-democratic informal jocularity standing at the bar in one of the lounges in the Grand Empire Hotel: the Prime Creep sipping cautiously at a half pint of Bravery bitter, Kilmarnock with a lager shandy untouched, and his Japanese pocket tape recorder whirring away smoothly on the bar counter between them until in mid-question Kilmarnock lunges so suddenly that the security men are caught napping while the Prime Creep's Adam's apple is expertly eaten out and though of course it is only seconds before they fall upon Kilmarnock like paunchy terriers upon a rat nevertheless the rat still has his prosthetic steel teeth in the Prime Creep's throat, his left arm wrapped like a G-clamp round the Prime Creep's neck, while the fingers of his right hand have already pulled the cotter pin from a grenade secreted in his trousers – an old-style Mills bomb this is, very reliable, as gloatfully detailed by Ernest Hemingway in Chapter 38 of *For Whom the Bell Tolls*.

Thus it is, with exquisite narrative balance, that the AIDS-maturing ex-con Cannibal called Kilmarnock and the Prime Creep he hates get their bloody deserts united in this fatal embrace, their stomachs blown out simultaneously.

# Contrary Criticism

Views vary viciously, one hardly need add, as to the value of Wringhim's *Cannibal*.

There are those – one might call them the Michael Quislings of Scottish letters, London-feed and covetous of English knighthoods – like Rankles, who attempt to write *Kilmarnock* off as the mere hysteria of some ungratified ambition, a cheap and nasty incitement to racial hatred (though hatred of *which* race, Mumbo? really you should be more precise), and (oh, most deadly thrust) a 'blatant plagiarism to boot'.

In fact, *pace* Rankles, if anyone has been plagiarised by Wringhim, in this instance, it is not Thomas Harris (as detailed above) but rather Humbert Seale: since the structure of Kilmarnock's career bears a more than superficial resemblance to the plot of one of my own early stories. As usual, though, it is not the working novelist who howls about such elemental creative communism, but rather the plagiarist par excellence, which is to say the impotent parasite hohself, the archetypal Rankles, the value of whose prose resides uniquely in the extended quotations studding it, and whose favourite phrase takes the form, 'as T.S. Eliot has noted,' as if somehow the perception of Eliot is hereby enshrined in validation: through the privilege of being echoed by Rankles.

Meanwhile an altogether more serious style of *Cannibal* critique has been put forward by various Auksbreech paperweights – such as Professor Sir Frankly D. Nosejobbery in the *Sunday Crimes* – who have argued, not so much that Wringhim's novel is derivative, or negligible, but rather that, despite its astonishing range of technical accomplishments, and indeed in the end to a large degree precisely on account of such flagrant ('nay, insolently flaunted') virtuosity, the author's fundamental moral authenticity must be declared suspect, to the extent that he would appear to have concocted this dismal catalogue of the most heinous atrocities less in the service of some serious and sustained political conviction (for what could be more trivial, demands Nosejobbery, than to hinge a late-twentieth-century novel round some antiquated and in any case illusory Scottish grudge against England,

Westminster and the Crown?) and more cynically in the pursuit of pecuniary gain, in the form of large advances from New York publishers, and the broilers of Hollywood tripe. Weller now:

Certainly it is true that Wringhim got a lot more dollars out of his *Kilmarnock* than from all his earlier novels put together. And undeniably this has much to do with the American market for serial cannibals being apparently insatiable. But to accuse Wringhim of exploitative catchpenny potboiling, as Nosejobbery & Co do, is to betray little other than Nosejobberyful ignorance of Wringhim the other-worldly man, and also a woefully abundant misunderstanding of the Scottish spirit, history, current total revulsion with Westminster and Whitehall, and, above all, an inviolable incapacity to comprehend the darker side of Scottish humour.[1]

Wee wonder, therefore, that for an intelligently sustained appreciation of Wringhim's achievement we must look closer to McEwan's. And there, to be sure, we find Arnold Haberdasher, who lingers lovingly in *The Clarion* on the Old Testament undertones, the Draclensteinian subtextuality of monstrosity born of slave male swallowing self-styled master-race sperm out of his own wife's vagina, and particularly the allegorical immaculacy of Wringhim's cannibalism: wherein the ponderous tyrannical predations of a large fat fish with cancer of the national gills upon a smaller but more vigorous and proudly darting neighbour is held up for cautionary scrutiny in a perfectly enantiomorphically revengeful microcosm – wherein it is not only morally just, but also profoundly artistically satisfying, not least because aesthetically inevitable, that the one Prime Creep shall suffer getting his flabby belly blown out for the many other flabby bellies equally guilty yet less figureflabbily symbolic.

Numerous English commentators, needless to say, have either written Arnold off with the odd condescending guffaw, or, more commonly, failed to notice him altogether.

Less glibly dismissible, happily, are the views of Duncan Peebles.

Armed with his unparalleled grasp of Scottish literary history and some familiarity with international substitutes, and blessed with a conscience both scholarly and uniquely honest, Duncan argues in his *Ten Great Scottish Novels* that Wringhim's atrocities in *A Cannibal Called Kilmarnock* are – 'though, to be sure, certain passages make most

---

[1] 'Which is dark enough at its brightest! Absolutely.' [P.C.]

painful reading' – ultimately justified, both artistically and politically, in that Wringhim's final chapter caps his earlier harrowing of our sensibilities with surprising tenderness, and exemplifies, subtly and with fleeting understatement, the age-old moral that occasionally some infinitely lamentable evil most be endured for a time, to pave the way for a greater good following.

By 'greater good' Duncan means that in Wringhim's finale, following the simultaneous death by Mills-bombing of both the Prime Creep and Kilmarnock, another GAGA rises to the helm as Primer Creep who soon is shown by revelations in *Private Eye* which subsequently are confirmed in *The Guardian* to be not only morally suspect but also an out-and-out Euro-securities criminal and inter-continental fraudster. This Primer Creep is in fact one of the erstwhile junior GAGAs as buggered by Kilmarnock during the Brightpool conference wearing only his doctored asbestos condom. Predictably, the Primer Creep rides out with ease the proofs of trust violation and blatant law-breaking against him. Only when in due course the pale shrinking shame of the AIDS-blown English premier can be concealed no longer from all those gerontocratic Home Counties supporters does a reactive disintegration commence which leads in the General Election following to the GAGAs being at last toppled, a liberal coalition taking power, and proportional representation being established.

And by the time Wringhim bids us farewell in his closing paragraph, procedures are under way for the abolition of the English monarchy, disestablishment of the English church, and self-governing independence for Scotland.

A better Britain, it seems, is possible after all.

Personally we have no quarrel with Duncan Peebles in his appraisal of the magnitude of Wringhim's achievement.

Where we do differ with Duncan is in the range of reference matrices that should be adopted. For instance, it's all very well to hail Wringhim as: 'probably the only Scottish novelist in the twentieth century thus far [*which doesn't leave a lot of time for the rest of us, Duncan, does it?*] to compare favourably, on a best-for-best footing, with such all-time greats as Scott, Hogg, and Stevenson.' But to be quite honest,[2] at the end of the day we have to confess a need to censure Duncan Peebles for a degree of parochialism in his focus, a parochialism which derives from dutifully

---

[2] 'Ominous pun!' [P.C.]

endeavouring to discover the gold that painfully obviously does not exist in screeds of homegrown silt, and from failing to recognise the import of Schopenhauer's counsel that 'in literature what is bad [*even if it is Scottish, Schopenhauer might well have added, if he'd ever been boozing in McEwan's*] is worse than useless [*since it distracts attention from what is valuable*]', and from consequently failing to compare Wringhim's triumphant *Cannibal* with precedent landmarks as various as Émile Zola's *Thérèse Raquin* (one thinks immediately of the masterfully macabre double-suicide finale), Leo Tolstoy's *Anna Karenin* (Anna the colonized woman, cf Kilmarnock the colonized Scot; also Anna's final moments of suiciding consciousness, cf Kilmarnock's after he pulls the Mills bomb pin ['Where am I? What am I doing? Why . . . ?']), and even a 'little classic' such as John Steinbeck's *Of Mice and Men*, in that when George shoots the simpleton Lennie in the back of the head we accept absolutely that – however distraught we may feel about it, blubbing and such – no other outcome is permissible.[3]

Now we admitted earlier that, hubris springing eternal, perhaps your own secret ambition is to write a novel which is not only 'best-selling' but also 'great'. And that if so, and if your story not only justifies but positively intrinsically *requires* that certain atrocities be portrayed, then you must further ensure audience horror at the crimes committed, and feelings of vengeful outrage against our monster, but also, and much more demandingly, an ultimate purgative sense of sad sympathy for the ogre enchained by hor own degradation, and even a final cathartic intuition of loss when the very bad baddy undergoes hor terribly earned extermination . . .

In those terms *A Cannibal Called Kilmarnock* is already not only a great Scottish novel but furthermore one of the greatest novels ever written in any language.

As if that weren't enough, Wringhim additionally contrives to bring off the almost impossible feat of compelling the reader's compassionate regret that the Prime Creep too must be wasted now for the sake of a better life for others to come. Considering the author's relentless abomination of the Prime Creep in real life, you may say the ennobling

---

[3] Wringhim, we should add, would assuredly have achieved the same pathos as Steinbeck without that sickening leaven of Last-Mohican sentimentality which is the American novelist's albatross.

sublimation (obviously much mashed in the present compressed thumb-nail) he achieves in the novel is just as uncanny a transcendence of human-stroke-moral limitation as anything in Dante, Mozart, or the finest Madonnas by Raphael. Put it another way:

Even that most hardened of all ex-readers for BirdDog, Janet Rosencrantz, has confessed to a certain mistiness enshrouding her vision, and even a hard little empathetic lump in her Adam's apple,[4] as Wringhim conducted her gently through her readerly paces, in response to Kilmarnock's dying falls.[5]

And now a yet more intimate confession.

That when I turn again, in moments of occasional leisure, to contemplation of Wringhim's gifts and the quality of his literary art – a quality attained not *because of* so much as *quite despite* his political convictions, moral failings and regrettable personal practices – I am pounded by great waves of despair. Despair akin to the feelings of hopelessness which afflicted Anthony Burgess when first he realized he could never write *Ulysses*. And here, if you like, is a hallmarking difference between myself and, say, Paul Chalicer. When *I* sing the praises of Wringhim the novelist, and when *I* make public the private hope that one day I too may be privileged to write a novel which posterity will rank not too far beneath the best of Wringhim's, then I mean what I say sincerely. But when Paul speaks the very same words, as frequently he has, I'm sorry to report that he is secretly hoping – and sometimes positively *expecting* – that you will immediately butt in to correct him, along the lines:

'Goodness, Paul! Whatever makes you say that? When you yourself are already the greatest novelist in the history of the universe! So why deny it?'[6]

In particular, when I consider the deftness of Wringhim's atrocity

---

[4] And this despite her strongly feminist aversion to Wringhim's ghastly pamphlet, and her proxy disapproval of his person.

[5] 'Yet another travesty.' [J.R.]

[6] 'You priceless slithy tove, Humbert. This really is the most diabolical inversion of the twisted truth imaginable. In the interests of moral and more importantly literary democracy I demand that you neither cut nor in any way fiddle with this footnote. If you do, rest assured I shall never again contribute to any future novel by you.' [P.C.]

depiction, the visceral vividness of his ripped-throat detail, the hallucino-genic synaesneezic sound-sensation of Kilmarnock's teeth in an English Adam's apple, the subtlety of Wringhim's footing upon the fine wire of high integrity above the netless morass of cheap exploitation, I am prey to be calmed with despondency, to anxieties that my own atrocity capacities are generically insufficient,[7] and to novice-lover dread that you the reader may scorn me – may at this very instant sneer harshly: at the blandness of my tale.

For consider.

In all the hundreds of pages you have borne with to date, where are the serial cannibals?

Where the Auschwitz, the Hiroshima, the napalm?

The ethnic cleansings and systematic genocides?

To be sure we've had a few killings, but what of that? The maja killed the evil priest. Well, why not? Didn't he doubly deserve it? And attempted killings? For all the Marquis of Roquefort's shots at Louis, it is Louis who gets him in the end. Quid pro, no? And even justice too? And okay we do have a bout of horrible butchery in Chapter 20, on the Barcelona beach, when the freedom-crazed Catalan rebels carve up the Castilian soldiers, but isn't that every hack as over-reactively forgivable as the miner mob wifies knifing off the no-tick screw-the-workers Storekeeper Maigrat's genitals in Chapter 6 of Part Five of Zola's *Germinal*?

For all these atrocious reasons and many more we realize now this chapter has inched us into a corner of thorny selves-questions. Yes, very probably we should never have written it. But a chapter once written can never be unwritten. It's just like nuclear weapons, that way. You can cut such a chapter, suppress it, bin it, pretend even to yourself you never wrote it, drink yourself the Heming way to forget it, but already that chapter has made a difference to the world, including you, and that difference can never be unmade. Similar goes for any intelligence reading that chapter. Or skimming it, skipping it, or throwing the book down on account of it. As to the effect of this chapter on you, who are we to jump that gun? It's true you are our invention in tiny part, but also more your own.

---

[7] 'You did cover the St Bartholomew Massacre fairly graphically, didn't you, in your *Counts of Mount Venus*?' [J.R.]*

*Yes, but that was live reporting. Dead easy.*

Shall you then despair of ever rivalling Wringhim's prize-scooping catalogue of atrocities in his *Cannibal*? Or will you, like us, confess to that mean competitive streak, that festering tails to the heads of resilience, that compels you now in Jacuzzi conscience to seriously consider a switch in game-plan, to summon the Cardinal back to Louis's death cell, to order for him a regime of Grand-Inquisitional tortures in the countdown to his execution, tortures both rendingly physical and exquisitely mental, commencing with the whispered news that his darling Hélène Arnault is currently being raped in the rectum, no less than Kilmarnock's near-millennial Morag, by a fine upstanding young officer of the victorious Royalist cavalry?

Assuming for these moments that she, the longlost beautiful Hélène, is not already dead?

# 74

# What the Papers Say

We could gress off narrative devices till the cows give sperm, ringing changes on *anonymous letters* (as to Brutus in *Julius Caesar*), *feigning death* (pretend X has died, make Y & Z believe it, what follows? As in *Much Ado*, *Romeo and Juliet* . . . ), and many others. But daily-mounting respect for the grim reaper is now going to confine our concentration to these last vital two:

PASSING ON THE MICROPHONE.

This lets the story be told, retold, denied, etc, from different points of view. One advantage is that the reader may thus feel flattered by promotion to the status of Detective Inspector, with a brief to establish the Real Truth to hor own satisfaction.

The microphone may be passed on between whole chapters, or large sections of chapters (as clumsily attempted in Bram Stoker's unreadable *Dracula*, in imitation of Wilkie Collins' superior dexterity in *The Moonstone*) or sometimes back and forth on a single page. For example, in our last chapter we levelled a slightly unkind but nevertheless entirely true accusation at Paul Chalicer, which he was magnanimous enough to take issue with in a trenchant footnote, engaging in the further age-old tactic of attempting to tar me with precisely the same stinking mud I had just slung at him. If we contradict one another we can't both be telling the truth, and he isn't, but we might both be lying, might we not?

So what do you think?

Another advantage of passing on the microphone from time to time is to massage the reader's ear. This is particularly important in a long narrative. Even if, say, you enjoy Des O'Conner's singing throughout a long hour of sedative terrestrial television, you might not want to listen to it all week without respite, and especially not all year.

Same goes for Bach, Willie Nelson, and the not unpleasant though musically quite conservative sound of Louis Morel's own voice.

Hence the value to the director of being able to mix in different-key contributions from the Chevalier (his 'Warning' about the Marquis, in that letter to Louis's mother, presented in our Chapter 7), Achilles Lefranc (his light-relief Barcelona 'Report' in Chapter 21), plus rousing present-day meta-perspectives from Janet Rosencrantz, Paul Chalicer, Wringhim Knox, and so on. One great narrative sadness I'm having to live with in this book is that so far I've had not a word of first-generation feedback from Audrey Macpherson, whose views I continue to value almost as highly as my own. Though I've pleaded with Audrey several times on the telephone, and even sent her bundles of photocopies on spec, the response is always the same: that she'd *love* to contribute to Amnesty's royalties, and *will* do so as soon as she can, but at the moment she's just:

'*Too impossibly busy*, Humbert. Some of us have to work for our livings, you know.'

Maybe next vacation, she'll find time, she adds.

But then she doesn't. And why? Because GAGA funding of education, particularly higher education in arts subjects, gets meaner by the month. So teachers have more classes, larger classes, and more marking; less leisure, less humanity, less originality, and worst of all less fun.

And that inevitably puts us idling novelists at risk as well. Risk of fewer consumers with the time and aptitudes to consume us. And risk of fewer characters in tomorrow's world, whom we might pass our microphones to.

BATON OBJECTS.

Like Portia's ring in *The Merchant of Venice*, and Desdemona's snotrag in *Othello*. The physical object facilitates contact, intrigue, etc, between the characters. Often it is the character currently in possession of the baton object who takes up the narrative running. Sometimes hos may be currently wielder of the microphone too.

In many old stories the baton object is a ring, sometimes with magical properties. But it can also be a living object, a stolen cultured virus (as. in some rubbishy 'science' fiction), or a crate of priceless mammals (as in Martin Cruz Smith's *Gorky Park*). The baton object may even be a person, as is the case with our own Hélène Arnault.

When we first meet Hélène in Chapter 4, 'Dutiful Thanks', she is 'the little girl, who would become the young woman, who was to wholly obsess my life'. As a *substitute* for her male brother, Jean-Baptiste, she is *physically conveyed* from Maître Arnault's residence in Lourdes to start a new life and better education in Château Morel – this being the Countess's expression of gratitude to Hélène's male father for his male son's having rescued Louis from drowning in the mill pool.

Years later in Chapter 13, 'Who Kills Whom?', Hélène has become as it were the sexual bait that Louis follows up the cool fresh stream to woo in desperation following his father's announcement, 'I have decided that you must go . . . ' to serve the Count of Soissons. Next it is the magnetism of the *physical person* of Hélène that causes Louis to reflect 'how warmly women desire a measure of kisses, caresses and pleasure, before the cardinal act' as he achieves whatever he achieves but never precisely informs us before the jealously deranged male brother Jean-Baptiste fires upon Louis then rushes to batter him with the smoking musket, causing Louis to *send* Hélène swiftly from the scene of danger and potential disgrace:

'Run, Hélène. *Run* . . . RUN,' before the tussle which ends with Louis's own gun going off in Jean-Baptiste's belly, and all the flight, exile, adventures, danger, uncertainty and often downright misery that flow from that – during which time *someone else*, male of course, arranges that Hélène be *taken* to Paris, from which she is in due course *abducted* by the cad nephew Charles, then *rescued* by Louis 'in the gathering bosk beneath the ancient oaks of lower Bois de Vincennes', this is in Chapter 51, 'Crossroads', before being *confiscated* by the cad's uncle, the Maréchal de Châtillon (Chapter 53, 'Next Fix') as a result of the Shanks-pony bargain struck between Louis and the Maréchal – that Louis will refrain from shooting the Maréchal in the head in exchange for the Maréchal's undertaking both to let Louis and his men proceed to Sedan *and* his pledging:

' . . . on my honour as a soldier, that the girl in the chariot shall not be wed against her will – *while yet I draw breath in liberty*.'

Note particularly that the Maréchal did not also guarantee that he would endeavour to ensure that Hélène *would* be wed *in accordance with* her will. This is consistently typical of Hélène's role as ravishing young woman in the mid seventeenth century. She is primarily a *passive object*. Child object, love object, sex object, and pivotal narrative baton object. Her situation is thus ultimately comparable to the would-be more militant woman (not seventeenth-century) at the close of Thomas Berger's indispensable *Regiment of Women*:

'She tried to stay on top. "You're too damned heavy!"'

'But easily he rolled her over . . .

'Also, he was the one with the protuberant organ.'

Now whether all this is obnoxious to feminists, post-feminists, pre-Raphaelite feminists and whoever-else-grabs-us is not beside the point.

Rather it is in a different universe from the point. And what is the point? Simply that *if* Hélène had been more of a Cynthia Rothrock sort of a seventeenth-century heroine, then we *might* still have had a story, but it would have been a totally different story, and not very credible either. A story in which, for instance, Hélène, oblivious to Louis's patronizing yell that she should *Run*, would already have been whistling through the fragrant Pyrenean air in a double backward somersault concluding in a flying dropkick to Jean-Baptiste's chest, knocking him to the ground, disarming him, then forcing him to see sense and revert to being a goodly subservient friend to Louis.

Then we would have had none of Louis's flight, exile and adventures, and quite apart from that, double backward somersaults and flying dropkicks are not always terribly easy, even for an unpleasantly muscular young woman, if she's got up in a bodice, long dress, petticoats, and so on in, which a lover's hands have loosened.

Thus, for us, *our* Hélène, delightful (if you're Paul Chalicer) or infuriating (if you're Janet Rosencrantz) as she may be, has been and remains to this moment very much a baton object. All her geographical transitions are caused by other players dribbling and passing her like a football, such that for Louis now, as he awaits his execution, she has become in his imagination like a grail of human gold at the end of the rainbow, except that the rainbow keeps swinging like a weathercock all round the sky, and anyway he can't see it.

Ravishing heroines like Hélène are also information packets, and sometimes quite complex ones. Other information packets can also be hinging baton objects. Possibility and credibility of information batons is a function of current technology and audience awareness of it. In one decade we might get away with a whole Hollywood story turning on the whereabouts and survival in goody hands of a unique cassette recording of a damning baddy conversation: Colombian cocaine baron discussing payoff terms with CIA rotten apple, etc. In the next decade this becomes less convincing because everyone now has twin-cassette dubbing facilities on their ghettoblasters – so even a chimpanzee would now copy the incriminating cassette several times and post sealed duplicates to various newspapers, the FBI and the Secretary General of the United Nations as a precaution against premature capture, torture, liquidation, and so on by the villains.

In early decades of the twentieth century, and certainly in all previous centuries, there were no photocopiers, facsimile transmission devices, or electronic digital scanners. This was good news for the humble sheet of scrawled-upon paper as a white-rabbit information baton of limitless narrative value. Paper is mercifully more difficult to destroy or damage beyond readability than most electronic media, but nevertheless once any uncopied original document has gone up the chimney or been buried under thousands of tons of volcanic lava, there's no hope of ever getting it back again. Thomas Carlyle must have felt this keenly if and when the truth was told about Mrs Taylor's fire being lit with the only manuscript copy of his *French Revolution*.

In the case of a long-ago book manuscript, it is possible, given reasonable memory and dogged character, to have the author start again and produce something similar to what was lost; preferably, this time, ensuring that back-up copies are amanuensically transcribed daily. The new version won't be identical to its tragic predecessor. It might be inferior, but it could also in the end be better – and there is nothing left in the world to prevent the bouncing-back author from flattering hohself to this effect.

Very different logic necessarily applies when the context is not free and creative but rather forensic and persecutive. Here the document in question is either a testament of innocence or of guilt. If it's you who's pursued, and the document proves you guilty (let's say it's a love letter to Queen Guinevere, showering mental kisses on that cute little birth mark on her upper inner thigh), then you might be inclined to destroy the document if you can. Unless, perhaps, you are George Washington. If the document proves you innocent (actually the love letter wasn't to Guinevere at all, but to Isolde, as is demonstrable by comparing the two ladies' upper inner thighs in court), you will normally want to preserve and parade it.

And in an ideally just world the Counsel for Your Prosecution should also wish to retrieve and examine any missive that shows you innocent, if you are, but where is that world? All too frequently in this world, not excluding London and the West Midlands of England, the prosecution and its lackeys (MI5, CID, 'anti-terrorist' squads, and all) are much keener to notch up brownie points securing another conviction than to assist your defence in the slightest. And where is the border between *not helping* and *deliberately hindering*?

Popperly put:

In any society that valued justice not just in lip service but also in donkey work, the prosecution would be duty-bound to help the defence make its case as strong as possible. *And then* destroy that case *provided that* it can still be irrefutably demonstrated that the defendant is guilty as rats. Whether such perfect justice prevails in any society on this planet now is doubtful. But it certainly doesn't in the France of Richelieu, no more than in England today. This is one of the reasons why, throughout our history of Louis Morel, the Chevalier of Bagnols has been so concerned to recover, and also has had so little help in recovering, those missing papers (hereinafter the Bagnols Papers) which he is convinced could demonstrate his innocence of treason all those years ago.

You'll have noticed how the Bagnols Papers have surfaced briefly between the waves of our tale, then vanished during whole tides of chapters. And you are now perfectly situated to appreciate just what a subtle cementing information baton these papers have been all along, as you peruse this terse resumé:

CHAPTER 6:

Father Francis now distraughtly confesses to the Chevalier that a certain packet of papers entrusted to him by Maître Arnault, for delivery to the Chevalier, appears to have been stolen.

The Chevalier, normally unperturbable, is greatly agitated by the disappearance of this packet, so Louis suspects its contents must somehow have been vital to the Chevalier's affairs. But in what way?

The Chevalier, ever considerate, tries to ease Father Francis's distress, but still fishes to deduce how the packet could have vanished.

Father Francis recalls that he stashed the packet at the bottom of his valise, togethered with a modest cache of saved-up alms money, at the sleazy cabernet in Luz.

The Chevalier mutters, evidently trying to console himself, that destiny seems to demand that he will *never get hold of these papers*, after searching for so many years.

Father Francis gently reproves the Chevalier's fatalism.

A warm debate ensues between the Chevalier and Father Francis on: predetermination, free will, divinity . . .

CHAPTER 13:

By the rising moonlight Louis wincingly prises the dagger from his hand, and attempts to stanch his bleeding with a kerchief wrapped round it and gripped tight. Then as he waits, and the moonlight waxes, he turns his attention to the dead assassin. It is of course the carp man from Gagnères, Monsieur Saint Simon – but lo besides. As Louis gingerly inspects the horrific wound where the left side of the carp man's face used to be, he feels an immense black wig slide loose in his hand to reveal enough tonsured head and reminiscent features to identify Monsieur Saint Simon as also the Capuchin Fat Monk who, with his Thin Accomplice, had attempted to cheat him at cards in the sleazy cabaret at Luz, and whom he kicked down the stairs for his pains.

Bewildered by secondary waves of shock, by loss of the blood which his kerchief is failing to keep in his left hand, and stunned by the accumulating evidence of the Marquis of Roquefort's intricate treachery, Louis gropingly searches Monsieur Fat Simon's garments with his right hand, and in due course locates an inner pocket containing a packet of papers in an oilskin wallet. This he stuffs into his breeches, on the ground that these are the last garment likely to be removed from his unconscious body if soon he passes out from the appalling pumping pain creeping up his left arm from his wound. Then it occurs to him that perhaps the Thin Accomplice is insufficiently far elsewhere, and with this in mind he wriggles backwards to prop his pounding head against a large knuckly root of the tree out of which his attacker dropped, and with Jean-Baptiste's pistol wedged warily between his knees he pleads with his faculties to not desert him till help arrives.

Half an hour later it does, in the form of Jean-Baptiste, several other citizens of Lourdes, and a bizarre short-arsed declamatory Thespian who introduces himself as:

'*Achilles Lefranc!*'

As might be expected, a terrific flapping fuss attends Louis's wounded arrival back home. As he is hoisted into the Château he recovers enough consciousness to note with pique that Hélène is not present. This, a streaming-eyed Countess Morel explains, is because Hélène has swooned at the news of the attack on Louis, and has had to be put to bed. In his own chamber Louis fights to remain *compos* long enough to smuggle the packet of papers from his breeches to under his mattress.

Then he passes out again.

The following morning he is delirious with fever, caused by poison in his wound. That the toxin has not already killed him is deemed to be thanks to its being less a malicious lethal potion than the residue of rancid fish guts on Monsieur Fat Simon's dagger point. In any event by lunch the patient is lucid enough to sit up in bed, send his attendant mother to lavish her ministrations on Hélène, and peruse the packet of papers from beneath the mattress.

'To my amazement these documents contained nothing relating directly to Monsieur de Roquefort. They consisted principally of a number of letters, plus the certificate of marriage, between the Count of Bagnols and his sweetheart Henriette de Vergne, whose tragic tale had been told me by the Chevalier. The letters, from citizens prominent in La Rochelle, appeared to prove that Monsieur de Bagnols, though sympathetic in a correctly passive manner, had never materially aided the Rochellois as per the denunciation by the Marquis of Roquefort, as that had been portrayed to me by the Chevalier of Montenero. There was, however, not a word in the papers to implicate the Marquis, as indicted by the Chevalier.'

Yet the Marquis had commissioned Fat Simon to kill him, and the Chevalier had once again saved his bacon. But why should the Chevalier have bothered, especially when he was still being so unreasonably hostile over Louis's honourable secrecy regarding the nasty business in Zaragoza? And why, moreover, had the Chevalier been close by when Fat Simon fell upon Louis from the oak?

## CHAPTER 15:

'Three months and a day, Master Louis,' Achilles nods vehemently. 'In the summer of twenty-five. Yet somehow he managed to write secretly to his intendant, with orders to locate certain papers—'

'What sort of papers?'

'Papers, Master Louis, what would prove the Count clean innocent of the charges against him.'

'Charges of actively aiding the Huguenots.'

'Just so, Master Louis.'

'Brought against him by the Cardinal, as incited by the Marquis of Roquefort?'

Achilles spits expressively, between his pony's ears.

'And did the intendant find these – those papers?'

'Never tried, Master Louis. So far as I know. Suited him better, I reckon, for the Count to remain in the Bastille.'

'Which he did, presumably.'

'Well, no. There's the mystery of it. On the second day of the fourth month, the Count of Bagnols disappears.'

'Murdered?'

'Not yet.'

'How do we know?'

'Why, because within a week the Count is secretly back at Bagnols, to interrogate his intendant.'

'Whom he then punishes severely?'

'On the contrary, Master Louis. Somehow the intendant persuades the Count he has done everything in his power to further his interests. In consequence, the Count takes the intendant even privier into his confidence. In consequence, knowledge of the Count's whereabouts in hiding soon reaches the Marquis of Roquefort.'

'As a result of which the unfortunate Monsieur Bagnols is assassinated?'

'Fresh from his lady-love's window,' sighs Achilles. 'Lord, what a world.'

'And Mademoiselle de Vergne? She dies some months later – in a convent, I believe.'

'In a convent, yes, Master Louis. But in childbirth, too – Lord comfort her.'

'*In childbirth!*' you expostulate. 'The Chevalier said nothing about childbirth!'

'Comes to all women, Master Louis,' says Achilles breezily. 'Well, most what are not nuns, that is, and even some what are. As to your Chevalier's discretion, well, there's the difference between a well-bred gentleman and lowly me.'

'What sex was the child?'

'No-one knows, Master Louis. Leastways, not me.'

'What happened to him or her?'

'No-one knows, Master Louis.'

'The inheritance? I mean, the Count of Bagnols' estate?'

'Would have been seized by the Cardinal, no doubt, if most of it hadn't already disappeared.'

'Where to?'

'Can't say, Master Louis. That's the sense of "disappeared", ain't it not? Then again. There was them what noticed, not long after, that the intendant had suddenly, as by a miracle, discovered himself well enough found to set up as notary – independent, like – and buy a new house in the same town as his dear old friend Monsieur Lefranc, the apothecary.'

'Look here, Achilles,' you now remark sternly. 'Ever since we passed by the water-shed you have been talking, in a very impersonal manner, about the Count of Bagnols' "intendant".'

'That's very true, Master Louis. What an acutely attentive young gentleman you be.'

'But the intendant was your father, Achilles. Is it because you disapprove so severely, of his evidently shady dealings, that you decline to describe him as your sire?'

'Not exactly, Master Louis.'

'Well?'

Here there is a break for lunch on a hillside to the north of the river Segre. As the Catalan bandits eat and drink, discuss their next contraband load, and crack black jokes about the Spanish overlords they can't wait to overthrow, and before you all begin the hot, dry, dusty descent towards Lérida, Achilles – with a gushing frankness that at first you find hard to stomach – confides details, some of them luridly intimate, of his beautiful mother's many affaires, and her several children of diverse appearance.

'But wait a minute, Achilles,' you object. 'Surely a while back you told me that, if you had been your mother – given the ugliness of your father – you would have slept with other men.'

'That I did, Master Louis.'

'But that implies that your ravishing mother in deed [*sic*] remained faithful to your hideous father, does it not? Whereas now you're telling me that, not only did she distribute her favours with commendable generosity, but that she had several children by other men besides. This is very confusing.'

'What I meant, Master Louis, was that *if I too* were as vivacious, desirable, and lavish of life as my mother, *then I too* would have slept with other men. As my mother, with untold delight, so frequently did.'

'So the nub of your drift, whose nuance eluded me at the time, is that you *do not blame* your mother, for her . . . warmly sociable nature?'

'If I did, Master Louis, I should be wishing my own life away.'

'Ah. You mean you suspect your father, or the Count of Bagnols' intendant, is *not* your father?'

Achilles, by way of explication, describes in graphic detail his mother's tragic illness, and the deathbed scene where she summons all her lovers to her bedside, obliges her husband to swear he forgives and to embrace all the neighbours, friends and relations who have cuckolded him. Then, in the final hour of her life, she allocates care of her five children to the various implicated fathers, with – curiously enough – only the youngest son being assigned to the intendant himself, while Achilles is entrusted to the care of Monsieur Lefranc, the apothecary.

For some strange reason, confected, we take it, before the apothecary becomes alienated from the intendant, over tupping his wife and siring Achilles upon her, the apothecary has custody of the lost/secret Bagnols papers – which he keeps in a drawer with his dirty syringes.

'What happened to the Bagnols papers?' you, with poorly disguised excitement, demand of Achilles Lefranc.

'Couldn't make much sense of them myself,' admits Achilles. 'Left them where they were. By now, however, my conscience – which always has been troublesome sensitive – was hurting at the horrors of my profession, and the number of innocent folk we killed. With my warm, generous and outgoing nature, and my passion for communication – and applause, I cannot deny it – I had long had a fancy to try on the buskin. Thus far, however, alas, Monsieur Lefranc had invariably walloped me round the ear whenever the topic rose up.'

'But now?'

'One day when my gaffer is away on the far side of town, to kill off an old gent with quack potions, for the sake of his much younger wife, there comes to our door an enormous fat Capuchin monk.'

'What does he want?'

'After beating about the bush with innumerable haws, and various other lies, he confesses he is sent to purchase back the Bagnols papers, for which he offers me ten coins—'

'Ten measly livres! For a package—'

'Ten *louis d'or*, Master Louis!'

'Which offer, of course, you dismiss with contempt?'

'Which offer, Master Louis, I accept with boundless gratitude, and glee, and am fled the premises before the gaffer returns, now to seek my fortune on the boards.'

'So now, having failed to locate the said fortune in France, and having – which it is commendably candid of you, Achilles, not to conceal from me – been laughed off the stage in Paris, you are here today, and riding with me, in the fond belief that your personal pot of gold may lie lurking in Barcelona?'

'I surely will be almost as happy serving you, Master Louis,' replies Achilles, with a beam of irresistible loyalty.

By now you are entering the outskirts of a village some ten miles north-west of Lérida. Excited by the perspective cast by Achilles' tale, on the recent events in your own life, your thoughts flutter constantly back to the Bagnols papers, which are still in your own possession, and the ramifications surrounding them:

Would the Count of Bagnols' life have been saved, if those papers had not been withheld by the wicked intendant and passed on to the grasping apothecary?

If so, would the Count of Bagnols and Mademoiselle de Vergne – or rather, the Countess of Bagnols, as it seems she secretly became – have lived happily ever after? Ie, instead of being assassinated at the time, and dying miserably in childbirth?

If so, who and what would Henriette de Vergne's baby have grown up to be?

Did the child in any case survive, and if so: who and where is hos?

And so on.

CHAPTER 27:

'In fetching it, from a secret flap within my valise – for since my flight from Morel I had not worn the ring, lest its seal proclaim my family name, or its gold my gentry stature – I encountered again, within the same repository, that packet of papers regarding the Count of Bagnols, about which, in recent weeks, I had completely forgotten. Shivering alone in my room that morning – for it was recently become December; cold and grey – as I waited for the hour to approach when the doors of moneylenders, pawnsters, and dealers of like ilk would be opened, I read again through the whole correspondence, between the Count himself – then a very young man, such as I was now – and the rebellious Rochellois. And vibrating as it were in harmony with every phrase in Monsieur Bagnols' hand, I seemed to hear the uplifting music of a fine discrimination, between right and wrong, which, so natural and effortless as it was, I felt must constitute the essence of true chivalry of the mind. All this to me was a vast implicit reproach: of my undeniable hand in the maja's death; Father Francis too; then my importunate caressing of Hélène by the stream; my shooting of poor Jean-Baptiste; my flight from my parents with no word of farewell; and of late my over-indulgence in spiritous drink; my unfeeling rental of tired harlot loins; my inexcusable frittering of the Widow Beaupère's hard-saved nest egg; and now . . . now . . . '

CHAPTER 32:

Naturally anxious, Louis records, to pass on the La Rochelle papers which chance, in the form of the failed assassin Monsieur Saint Simon (aka Fat Monk) had thrust into his hand: to any surviving member of the family, either on Henriette de Vergne's side, or on the Count of

Bagnols', he attempts with cordial vigour to jog any cobwebs in the widow's brain – but to no avail, since:

'Though tolerating my queries, and with great good humour, she remained, apart from what she had already told me, no less ignorant than myself.'

The following afternoon, his head buzzing with the renewed frustration of having failed to pinpoint the mansion harbouring Hélène, and the added aggravation of now possessing one more piece in the Bagnols jigsaw, but having no notion where to place it, Louis returns to his digs to be told by the widow that during his absence a tall dark gentleman stranger has called to speak with him, and has promised to call again.

'Well . . . *who* was he?'

'I do not know, Monsieur. The gentleman did not say.'

'Well . . . *when* will he call again?'

'"Perhaps this evening," the gentleman said. "Or else at some later date."'

CHAPTER 64:

Louis responds by redoubling the strength of his squeeze, and by chastening the murderer with a knee in his underwater groin. 'You are a villain, monsieur,' he informs the retching Marquis. 'You are scum. You poisoned the honest Monsieur de Valençais. You ruined by calumny – and I have the proofs of his innocence right here, in a pouch about my waist – you ruined by slander, I say, and then caused to be murdered your favoured rival in love, the innocent Count of Bagnols—'

'No, no,' croaks the writhing Marquis. 'Bagnols—'

'Silence,' orders Louis, with an emphatic tightening squeeze. 'By your destruction of Monsieur de Bagnols you also directly brought about the ruin, desperation, misery, despair and premature death of the virtuous Mademoiselle de Vergne, whose love for him, by all accounts, was dearer to her than life itself. In the years between, I have no doubt, there were others, God alone knows how many, directly murdered or otherwise destroyed by your agency. Myself you have attempted to kill three times. When we fought with swords at Lestelle, you would assuredly have taken the life, if you could, of a boy only hours out of school. During the izard hunt in the hills of my home, you attempted to shoot me, did you not?'

'I never—'

'Silence. And then, most treacherous of all, after attempting to undermine my constitution, with the luxury of your affected hospitality, you had your hired cut-throat – the so-called Monsieur Saint Simon, ha! – fall upon me with his envenomed dagger from the trees, as I rode home. Not so? Yes, indeed. You are scum, monsieur. Pure—'

'Let me—'

'Silence. Pure *scum*, I say. And now, today, you have murdered the Saviour of France. A man who—'

'Traitor, he was. Trait—'

'*Silence*, monsieur. While you heed these further reasons.' And Louis goes on, at not a little length, to explain to the Marquis how the death of the Count signifies not only the collapse of the liberational insurrection against the Cardinal, but also the terminal extinguishment of all his own aspirations, and prospects of personal and sexual happiness, since his hopes of recuperating Hélène from the custody of the Maréchal de Châtillon, triumphant in his role as the conquering Count's First Gentleman, have been for ever scuppered. 'For these ample reasons alone, Monsieur de Roquefort, I should be delighted to kill you, as kill you I assuredly shall, with these poor hands you have wronged.' First, and perhaps in order to ensure the Marquis has plenty of leisure in which to savour his last few minutes of life, and fully comprehend the rationale underlying his approaching banishment from it, Louis proceeds to rehearse a secondary list of the vile villain's villainies, not excluding his nauseatingly chauvinist, proprietorial, condescending and exploitative treatment of women, in general, and the revoltingly unctuous presumption with which, during his visits to Château Morel, he had patronized Louis's own dear mother.

'God save her saintly soul,' mutters Louis, more to himself than to his prisoner.

But at this point, and as it were galvanized by the threat of having to leave it sooner rather than later, the Marquis comes blazing back into life in the most bizarre manner. Like an ancient evil schoolmaster – Thwackum in *Tom Jones*, say, or *Gormenghast*'s Opus Fluke – goaded beyond exasperation by some crass Candidery on the part of his young-blood pupil, the Marquis inflates his blackbirdlike chest with indignant rage, kicks his submerged boots against the river bed, and slithers a good foot upward through Louis's startled arms, like a cake of black soap through your hand in a dirty bath, and sneers down in a snakelike hiss:

'You foolish young puppy, Morel! You really fancy, do you, that *you* know what's best for France? That *you* know better than the Cardinal? That *you* know all about women? What gives them pleasure, excites them, satisfies them? That you even knew *your own mother*, eh? That she was the paragon of perfect earthly virtue, yes? Well, sir — oof!' he breaks off, as Louis's vengeful forearms strain locked wrists like a drawbridge chain snapping tight around his waist.

'Slander my mother, monsieur,' he warns hoarsely, 'and I'll break your back *now.*'

'Kill me?' jeers the Marquis, his eyes red as Wringhim's at midnight. 'Kill me *now*, eh? Well, sir, go ahead. Kill me now. Be my guest. You silly young idiot, you. Kill me *now!* And if you do sir, and if you do? You'll never know, *never* . . . who really was your father . . . '

[All that just before Louis breaks his neck for him, then is captured, conveyed to Mézières, and condemned to execution.]

Curiously, as he festers in his death cell, it seems never to occur to Louis that perhaps some substance might underlie that Marquis's final bluster. That possibly the husband of his mother was indeed not his biological sire? That maybe, for instance, his real squirting-genes-in-the womb father could have been the Chevalier himself? Or . . . ? Especially when you recall those eight years during which the Countess of Morel remained childless following her marriage to Count Roger — eight years which caused us to murmur *Baldertish!* fully as early as the end of Chapter 2.

Almost on the contrary — which you may take as a measure of the generosity of his innermost seventeenth-century spirit — Louis's thoughts at this juncture are entirely directed to this opportunity now within his grasp to render the Chevalier an astonishing service. For here, in his cell, in that belted pouch round his waist, beneath his underclothes, he is still in possession of that much travelled oilskin wallet containing the Bagnols Papers. This strongly implies, though Louis doesn't spell it out, that though he may have been disarmed, frisked and deprived of his outer clothes, he has never once been strip-searched, made to bend over while his rectum was probed for heroin, and otherwise humiliated in a state of nakedness in ways that we now take for granted. The downside to this advantage is that Louis must also, on the level of personal hygiene and grooming, have deteriorated to a condition which would appear most unfortunate, unappetizing, and bloody smelly by our standards.

Almost certainly Louis is rife with lice, rashes, sores and boils, and impregnated with the omnipresence of ordure. This is, don't forget, only a few decades after James I of England, during the course of a wild morning's hunting following a breakfast of rich red meat, and rather than go to the bother of dismounting for a few minutes beside a convenient tree to squat behind, would deliberately and happily shit himself in the saddle as he galloped, secure in the comfort of knowing that lackeys and minions would be plentifully available to clean it and him up later.

Though Louis gives every indication of possessing much higher personal, moral and intellectual standards than James I of England, he is nonetheless, just like us, a prisoner of his century – as well as of Richelieu. Understanding the multifactoriality of his bondage in space and time ought surely to incline us to feelings of compassion for his overall death-pledged plight, and forgiveness for stirring up our long-buried memories of the kind of stench you once found in the portaloos, if you could find any, at the end of an open-air rock concert.

By extension, we deduce that the Bagnols Papers themselves must be somewhat soiled, being so widely travelled, folded, squashed, dunked in the River Bar as Louis did battle with the Marquis, and so forth. They are, however, still within their oilskin packet, and must certainly be composed of fabric in every way superior to the crap-acid pulp used to mass-produce the sort of eye-insulting illiterate ripoff-format paperback that we trust you aren't reading right now. In any case, they, the Bagnols Papers – whatever they say in fine detail, and this we cannot divulge, having never yet been able to locate a facsimile copy – are clearly still legible, as is evident from poor Louis's pathetic euphoria:

# The Stories Go Underground

My Dearest Chevalier (*writes Louis*), and address you as Chevalier I must, for though I know now you are indeed, and always were, the Count of Bagnols, still there is such power in the habitudes of respect we learn in youth, that to think of you, and to address you, as My Dearest Count, would be beyond my nature; would seem, indeed, an ungrateful betrayal of that loyalty and devotion which now I find, as the hours of my life on this earth toll away, I feel for you with an intensity, and a purity, surpassed by the fire of my love for only one other soul in this world; but of her I must not write, nor even dream, else the fragile chain of reason that remains to me will melt, and dishonour my death with madness.

My Dearest Chevalier, therefore I say, how foolish I feel that never, for one moment, till here in Mézières, when to my amazement I heard the Cardinal commend the courage of Monsieur de Bagnols, did I imagine that you might be he. Yes, indeed, how very wanting in deduction I have been. For did not the Viceroy, in Barcelona, make it plain to me that the Chevalier, though much honoured in Spain, was not himself a Spaniard? And did I not also overhear the wicked Marquis in Sedan, the very night before the battle, declare to his cut-throat companions that he had *seen* the Count of Bagnols, with his *very own eyes*, seen him together with Monsieur de Sourdis, in the Cardinal's army, and that, despite the shifting protestations of the cut-throats, saying that even if their victim could ever have survived his stabs, he must have drowned twice over in the river, certainly if it was not the Count of Bangols himself that he, the Marquis had seen, it was 'the spitting ghost of the same gentleman aged'?

Well, sir, foolish I have been all along, in this as in other matters, and now for my follies I must die. True, this is sad for me, and no heart could be heavier than mine today; yet in the Greater Scheme of Things, what loss is there, in the taking of my life? Scarcely will my passing be noticed, I dare say, in years to come, as I in everything have failed; lost all; lost my leader, the valiant Monsieur de Soissons; lost my battle, against the tyrant Cardinal; lost my mother, unreconciled before her death; and above all my beloved Hélène, lost in person, lost in love; lost in any hope of hope.

Hence it is, most worthy sir, that I, so hopeless and doomed, yet find a morsel of gladness, a shadow of consolation, in this: that here, in my hands, my hands set free but to write, I now knowingly possess, as for so many months I have unwittingly possessed, the means to restore the just due of perfect reputation to the much injured gentleman whom I, in the soaring ideals of my youth, have esteemed beyond all other men; but whose good opinion of me I have lost; lost in a maze of intricate misunderstandings, some inexplicable in their essence, and others by the bindings of honour.

I speak, sir, of yourself, and it is my privilege and consoling joy, before I die, to be blessed with this undeserved opportunity . . .

'Opportunity to do *what?*' inquired Janet, as I had broken off in speechless admiration of the stimulating heights of the restless shapely legs of the young West Indian lady sitting opposite us in almost no skirt at all.

Janet and I, you see, being longstanding members of SODS (the Society of Discombibulous Scribationers, and now not immodestly computer-competent, are also become immensely valued members of PISS (the Pioneering Infotechnic Scribationers' Subgroup). And it was in this capacity that we would already have been round our meeting table in sunniest Chelsea, hotly debating the latest developments in virtual pornography enjoyable on compact disk, and whether these should be suppressed as constituting a threat to the livelihoods of the more traditionally literate sorts of pornographer known as novelists − had not our Piccadilly tube got stuck between Covent Garden and Leicester Square, on account of a bomb scare at Green Park.

And so it was that Janet had suggested, not to say insisted, that I tell her our story as per the latest pages crisp within my briefcase: to fill in the unknown stationary delay ahead of us, and also with the added advantage, as Janet put it:

'Of saving me the bother of reading it.'

'Opportunity', I therefore went on, gallantly wresting my gaze away from those sleek Caribbean thighs, 'to restore posterity's memory of himself to less disfavour in the Chevalier's esteem. By sending to him the Bagnols Papers, plus a detailed account of what happened at Zaragoza—'

'Who killed the lustful priest, you mean?'

'Exactly. And why it was that Louis couldn't confess. His pledge to the maja's father. Then the further misunderstanding caused by Pere Garcés having said to the Chevalier in Barcelona:

'"Of course Master Louis slew the wretch, monsieur! And quite right too, since he asked for it!"'

'When Pere was thinking the Chevalier was thinking about Jean-Baptiste, in the tussle at Morel?'

'Indeed. Whereas the Chevalier was of course agonizing over whether Louis had deceived him over the killing of the priest in Zaragoza.'

'So this is the death-cell confession you've been floating? What Louis writes to the Chevalier?'

'Just so. Screeds of it too. Everything right up to Louis giving the Marquis what's-for in the river, then his capture, jailing in Mézières, and sentencing by the Cardinal.'

'But the Chevalier already knows about that, doesn't he? He was present—'

'That's true. But don't forget Louis is now in a state of hellish stress, impaired health, vitamin deficiency, and desperation to confess as much as possible in the hours remaining to him.'

'How does he get his confession to the Chevalier?'

'Together with the Bagnols Papers wallet, a short letter of fond though rather formal farewell to his father, a few lines of stereotyped undying love for Hélène Arnault, and a rather touching postscript to the Chevalier, begging him to seek out Hélène wherever she may be, pass on the stereotyped devotion, and protect and care for her just as if she were his own daughter. How is all this information conveyed? Louis bribes one of the jailors with the last louis d'or remaining in his waist pouch.'

'That's a bit thin, isn't it? How does he know the jailor won't just sling the Papers in the Marne, and take the bribe to the pub?'

At this point I smile indulgently at Janet's narrative ingenuity, which the West Indian girl across the way obviously takes to be me leering at her silver-knickered crutch, since she jumps up and reseats it at the far end of the carriage, out of my vision.

'Serves you bloody well right,' murmurs Janet. 'Well?'

'Of course he doesn't give the money to the messenger *with* the message,' I explain sadly. 'He *shows* the man the coin, then gives it to him when he returns some hours later with a signed receipt.'

'What does the receipt say?'

'"Papers unread but received as intended. Proof is my exit by the Red Rose Gate. Unhappy wretch, farewell. Signed, *Bagnols*."'

'That's a bit heavy isn't it? With poor Louis so close to the chop.'

'Strict codes of honour, some of these seventeenth-century chevaliers paraded. Some might say inflexible – ah!' for our train had finally jolted back into forward motion.

'What happens next?' inquired Janet, reaching in her bag for the minutes of our previous PISS meeting.

'Having been writing furiously, all through the night, Louis is totally exhausted. While attempting to shuffle his leg irons back to his mattress he collapses in some sort of faint or coma. Don't ask me which – I'm not a doctor. He isn't a teenage girl, though – Louis, I mean – so it could be a faint, couldn't it?'

'And when he wakes up?'

'He doesn't wake up. Rather is he awoken. Sorry if that sounds poetastical. It's only myself I quote.'

'Who wakes him?' asks Janet, though the stickling half of her brain is now busy correcting a minute misrepresentation of her views on electronic plagiarism. 'His executioners?'

# 76

# Consorting with Members of PISS

This is a new chapter.

Once upon a time it would have been false, but now it's becoming true. If there were such things as angels, this chapter would be primarily set in Louis Morel's cell in Mézières. Since there are no angels, not even morally perfect Kantian ones, this chapter is only secondarily set in Louis's dungeon of death, and primarily set amidst the pleasant later-afternoon bustle of Ciao Luigi's café in the Old Brompton Road, two minutes' leisurely amble from South Kensington Underground Station.

Janet and I – me chauvinistically portering her enormous shoulderbag full of purses, car keys, housekeys, minutes, agendas, and several computer software manuals thrice the weight of *War and Peace*, as well as my own fat briefcase and overnight holdall – have decided that since barely an hour of Virtual Pornography and Any Other Business remains for us in the offices of SODS, we could just as profitably spend it lingering over a delicious Luigi cappuccino with two gratis mini-macaroons, and get the dirt from our colleagues informally after the meeting, when they would adjourn to the Brompton Arms without fail.

'Meanwhile,' says Janet, skilfully sucking the froth off her coffee, 'we might as well finish your story.'

And this is where you come in. You, the perfect reader. If you don't agree that you personally have just joined us in Ciao Luigi's, then you aren't the perfect reader. At least, not yet. Possibly you have been overworking, or drinking too heavily, or watching too much junk on satellite television. If so, perhaps you should treat yourself to a mug of hot cocoa, get a good night's sleep, and try us again, your appetite for narrative adventure refreshed, tomorrow.

Or the next day.

It really doesn't matter, in fact, when you join us, or rejoin us. We'll still be here waiting for you, and I'll still be happy to briefly recap, for your special benefit, the details I've just described to Janet:

639

That no, it isn't his executioners who wake Louis today. It is the Chevalier. When Louis comes to — he has been unconscious for thirty-six hours — he finds himself hugged in the Chevalier's lean but powerful embrace. There are tears of joy in the elder gentleman's eyes, and a tremor in his voice of concern for his young protégé's health — as he thanks him again and again for turning up the means (ie the Bagnols Papers) to finally clear his name and restore him to absolute favour with the Cardinal, and also for at last divulging the evidence (in Louis's detailed confession) to prove that Louis himself is not, after all, the sort of mendacious homicidal villain that his long and obstinate silence, following his vow to the maja's Corregidor father, had obliged the Chevalier to take him for.

'Does this mean', you now ask me reasonably, for the imminence of Louis's execution has been bugging you for several chapters, 'that the Chevalier, now back in the Cardinal's good books, has obtained his grateful and compassionate pardon for Louis?'

'Absolutely not!' I retort in genial reproof. 'A let-out so soft would farcify one of the very few inviolable rules of convincing story-telling, which is that character must remain constant. It would also be totally false!'

'Then does that mean', you inevitably wonder, 'that Louis—'

'Do get on with it, Humbert,' interjects Janet on your behalf. 'Sometimes I really think you're more of a tease than my Charlotte. He's only winding you up yet again,' she kindly explains to you, 'to protract to the last possible line your doubt as to Louis's fate.'

'So he doesn't get executed after all?' you quiz me sternly, your feelings a little bit mixed.

'Of course not!' I reply smugly. 'That would have been breaking one rule too many!'

'But you said—'

'So I did. For it isn't the Chevalier who gets Louis's pardon out of the Cardinal. The Chevalier, though restored to honourable favour, has nothing to offer which is sufficiently valuable to the Cardinal to cause him to appear to be merciful.'

'Then who has?'

'Surprisingly, perhaps, it's the Duke of Bouillon.'

'But he's just been defeated, hasn't he?' you protest indignantly, as Janet begins peeling the shrink-wrapping off her latest multimedia operating-environment upgrade. 'The rebel side collapsed, did it not, when the Count of Soissons was murdered?'

'That's right. But don't forget that the Duke of Bouillon, Frédéric-Maurice, is also the Prince of Sedan, which is still an independent principality. Although one option open to Richelieu and the King is to besiege Sedan, they have to remember that its château is the most strongly fortified in Europe, and that no previous attempt to take it by siege has ever been successful. Also, the Cardinal is wary of hounding the Duke in his bolt-hole, for fear he may apply for, and obtain, renewed assistance from Spain.'

'So what happens?'

'When the Duke of Bouillon announces to Secretary Noyers that he is in principle disposed to consider an accommodation, the Cardinal – instead of telling him to fuck off, as Louis XIII would love to – initiates a sequence of delicate negotiations which culminate – this is on the fourth of August 1641 – in the signing of a treaty according to which the League of the Princes against the Crown is dissolved. The King agrees to abandon his litigation in pursuit of eternal execration of the memory of the Count of Soissons, and to allow his body to be returned to France for burial. The Duke of Bouillon is restored to favour with the King and his rank of ducality within France. *And*, to achieve the twin false effects of making the Duke of Bouillon appear a loyal and constant leader, and Louis XIII seem a compassionate and forgiving sovereign, all the recently taken political prisoners except one are more or less unconditionally pardoned.'

'Which one isn't pardoned?'

'The Duke of Guise, currently skulking in Brussels.'

'Why isn't he pardoned?'

'That, I'm afraid, I can't tell you without looking it up. What a pity Audrey isn't here.'

'But Louis Morel *is* pardoned?'

'With the sole conditions that he swears absolute and infinite love and allegiance for the King, etcetera, and that he be immediately dispatched to and confined to banishment within Bigorre for one year, there to reflect on and repent of his sins. Routine stuff.'

'What about Hélène?' you inquire impatiently.

'Louis, naturally, wants nothing more than to seek out the Maréchal de Châtillon immediately and find out what has happened to his beloved: who may have deflowered her, married her, whether in despair of ever attaining earthly happiness without him she has taken convent vows, and so forth.'

'But that would violate his parole?'

'Exactly. Since the Maréchal is said to be currently in Paris, the Chevalier persuades Louis to allow him, the Chevalier, to make appropriate inquiries about Hélène, and to forward details posthaste to Morel.'

'While Louis rides south straight away?'

'Not so fast! Don't forget how depleted he is – from the enervation of defeat, his weeks of bad diet and foul air, and close confinement in that filthy cell. No, before he can undertake a long journey, he manages a very short journey back to Sedan, where he is reunited with Achilles Lefranc, who has been delighted, during these weeks of battle, hostility and reprisals in the external world, to shelter within the most impregnable fortress in Europe, where, in the aftermath of La Marfée, there's great demand for a semi-skilled apothecary.'

'So Achilles nurses Louis back to fitness?'

'That's right. For about a week. And then they head for home.'

'Galloping all the way?'

'Not with Achilles! Surely you won't have forgotten that time when Louis, bound from Barcelona to Richelieu, had to leave Achilles behind in Marseille, on account of his lousy riding? Thus leading to his attempted romance on the riverboat, and subsequent stark-naked ejection from Lyon? Well, this time they ride together all right, but at Achilles' pace. And this is why, when they stop over in Vienne, they are surprised to bump into the Chevalier – who has overtaken them on his way south from Paris.'

'That's a bit far-fetched!' mutters Janet, as she sips at her second cappuccino.

'It may seem far-fetched to you, my dear,' I retort indignantly. 'But it's indubitably what happens. If you don't believe me, you can make your own private pilgrimage to the Cabinet des Grandes Tromperies with a tape recorder up your knickers.'

'I don't mean *your* story,' purrs Janet. 'I mean this one', she taps her fat manual, 'about total inter-platform compatibility guaranteed future-proof. My arse.'

'Yes, well,' I nod at you apologetically, 'not only is it indubitable, but to anyone who knows the Rhône valley it's virtually inevitable, given that one party travels faster than the other. Reminiscent, in fact, of the one about the young Tibetan monk's holiday.'

You indicate unexpected interest in the young Tibetan monk.

Tersely I tell you how as a reward for being top of his class, Glang Pandita is sent for about a month's vacation of solitary navel-gazing in a vow-of-silence monastery perched for that purpose on the precipitous peak of a short but very steep Himalaya. He sets off one morning at about sunrise, follows the only path to the top – steeply and narrowly spiralled. He stops for a breather and some cheese sandwiches made without rennet (he is of course a strict vegetarian) at about midday, and reaches the top about sunset. After about a month (there are no clocks in the vow-of-silence monastery, and no Japanese wristwatches equipped with electronic calendars either) of ecstatic navel-gazing, Glang Pandita reluctantly packs some fresh cheese sandwiches (almost certainly these ones are made with goats'milk cheese), and prepares to return to the cessworld of maya below. He sets off down the path at about sunrise and stops for lunch at about midday, but of course on this occasion he reaches the bottom of the mountain *about an hour before* sunset, having been travelling downhill all day rather than up. The poser is to prove with elegance that at one precise moment on both days, of ascent before the holiday and descent after it, Glang Pandita was at *exactly the same point* on the path. 'Well?'

'What's the answer?' you ask suspiciously.

'As I was saying,' I say again, 'since the Chevalier has been riding faster than Louis and Achilles, he naturally overtakes them at Vienne.'

'Which is where?'

'It's a real little gem of a Rhôneside Roman town which often gets overlooked by tourists who, overjoyed to have survived Lyon, can't wait to zoom further south. It's also, for me, where the real Provence begins.'

'I thought . . . ' objects Janet, looking up enthusiastically – she has an unusual ability to follow the juicier bits of two stories simultaneously, which probably comes of once having been a superficial reader for BirdDog, and, as you know, she also loves objecting – 'I thought it was the nougat town which boasted of being the "gateway to Provence". You know, Montélimar.'

'Ever since Peter Maylia,' I explain, 'every second town in the South of France is either the "gateway to" or the "heart of" or the "most typically Roman exemplar of" Provence. In many ways, just like the ultimate orgasm, Provence is what you define it to be. If you wanted to define it by climate, you might start Provence at Valence, by which town the grey northern skies have traditionally reliably given way to infinite flawless blue, and the lizards are leaping out of your masonry. For me, personally speaking, Provence is quintessially defined by attitudes, and those attitudes, alongside and beneath the rolling red roof tiles, begin with a bang at Vienne.'

'What sort of attitudes?' you can't help inquiring, although, like being unable to not think of a green chimpanzee with a purple bottom for the next ten seconds, you haven't quite forgotten Glang Pandita in Tibet.

Eagerly astride a favourite hobbyhorse, and mindful that our PISS colleagues won't be boozing in the Brompton Arms for at least another half hour, I tell you the little story about what happens when Koo and I, as opposed to Louis and Achilles, stop overnight in Vienne for the very first time, having got there ready to drop.

'"Now what about parking, monsieur?" inquires our landlady in the bar. "You can park overnight in our hôtel garage, if you like, for only 26 francs." Politely I explain that we're already comfortably parked, in a quiet street, and that 26 francs strikes me as a little expensive. "You should be aware, monsieur, that there's a very big market in Vienne on Saturday morning. If you leave your car in the street, it is sure to be uplifted by the authorities at four in the morning. Even if the authorities didn't get you, there is absolutely no chance that your window would not be smashed and your radio stolen. Since you are of the opinion that 26 francs is too high a price to pay for security, and since you are Scottish, we will for you reduce the garage price to 20 francs."' I pause for breath.

'Is that the end of the story?' you wonder.

'By no means. A splendid evening follows, and in the morning when I pay the bill I see "Parking, 26 francs". A gleam of mischievous triumph illumines Madame's eye, but no-one comments as I cough up. For she knows I now know, having toured the lovably louche narrow streets on foot by night, and seen the bustling market crammed with brigands by breakfast daylight, that 26 francs is perfectly fair. That's a Provençal solution, you see, and we all part friends.'

'Whereas?' drawls Janet.

'A Normandy landlady might have grimly stuck to her lowered price, and hated us mean Scots ever after. Now whether Louis and Achilles encounter the same sort of rigmarole over stabling their horses, I cannot tell you, as Louis has not told me.'

'What can you tell us?'

'That it would appear, from Louis's mention of the first-century Roman temple, the Temple d'Auguste et Livie, that they lodge in an inn in or near the Place du Palais. And it is here, as Louis dines on lightly poached trout with parsley, washed down by a choice white burgundy, in melancholy leisure during a very hot evening in late August, that he is reunited with the Chevalier – who breezes in to the inn very dry, dusty and thirsty, and requesting a room for the night.'

'What's the first thing Louis asks him?'

'As you might imagine, he begs for news of Hélène.'

'What does the Chevalier tell him?'

'Sadly, the Chevalier is in no position to impart glad tidings. In a profusion of apology, embarrassment and self-consciously inadequate condolence, bordering on the verge of free-floating guilt, the Chevalier explains to Louis that he understands from the Maréchal de Châtillon that Hélène (not merely miffed at being abandoned to the Maréchal's custody, nor solely due to miserable acceptance of the evidence that Louis has not cared for her half as much as she cared for him, but principally due to the Maréchal having informed her – thinking in his gruffly unmalicious way to cut short the agony of her uncertainty, and on the strength of a letter conveying news of the Cardinal's sentence – that Louis has *already been* executed), and having no better offer, or hope of any description, has accepted an eager proposal of marriage from a young and minor (though vigorous and no doubt adequately virile) English Earl, and accordingly been whisked away over the Channel to Shropshire, there to undergo her nuptials.'

'Seems to me', comments Janet, 'that your Chevalier is overly stilted in his sentence construction. Why not let me run him through GrammaCzech 7.1?'

Progressively ignoring Janet's softworn frivolity, you now inquire:

'How does Louis take this news?'

'Very, very badly. So badly, indeed, that the following day he is unable to travel. Confined to bed in the inn, in a state such as we might now associate with slogans such as ME, or Yuppie Flu, he refuses to speak, rejects all solid food, and consents only to occasional sips of the herbal infusions with which he is plied by the anxious Achilles.'

'Presumably that condition can't last for ever?'

'Thankfully, no. The following day the Chevalier and Achilles together get the lacklustre patient back on the long road south-west, though at a very crippled pace.'

'Wait a minute,' drawls Janet censoriously.

'Granted.'

'What's all this got to do with Scotland?'

'Not nearly so little', I riposte with compassion, 'as *Sense and Sensibility* has to do with sense. Agreed?'

'No!' cries Janet. 'You're supposed to be entertaining us with Sex and Scotland. Yet here we are' — and in this utterance, I pang to report, she is Londonly mimicking my light Scotch brogue and mellifluous metalocutions — 'plodding through Southern France with no hope, it seems, of bonking, and even less of a haggis.'

'As in particle physics, and in Real Life, hence also in Fiction Pure And Simple, *not all is as it seems*. Furthermore,' I posit hopefully, 'patience is its own reward. And even when it isn't, oh love my pussy, it's nobler than readers for BirdDog.'

Tactfully dowsing the digression apparently flaring between me and Janet, you now inquire:

'Do Louis's spirits revive?'

'Not greatly,' I have to admit. 'As they trot in easy stages through the heat, the haze, and the heart-harrowing songs of umpteen unseen crickets, the Chevalier thinks to trick his young companion's interest back into life by stopping up with candour many cavities of mystery in the strange life of secrecy and necessitous deceit he has had to live alone for so long.'

'Starting with?'

'The Chevalier apologizes over-compensatingly to Louis for thinking the worst of him over the corpse of the Zaragoza priest. But Louis — the Chevalier rebukes him affectionately — did not, by his own aggressive silence, do himself any favours in the matter. And this at a time when the Chevalier was already sick to his soul at the constant bottomlessness of human villainy, following an in-depth going-over of his Zaragoza accounts with his banker, and the uncovering of countless frauds.'

'After that?'

'The Chevalier also relates — with a frown and in tones as of Judgement Day Soon — that only now does he fully appreciate how insidiously the wicked lawyer, Maître Arnault, had for years been labouring to undermine Louis in his, the Chevalier's opinion. "Monsieur Arnault is the arrantest conniving criminal in France", whose whatever fortune in the world is entirely founded on what he has filched from the Chevalier's coffers, peculated from the misrepresentation of his affairs, and profited by the protraction of his banishment.'

'So the second-wickedest villain, after the Marquis of Roquefort, turns out to be the father of Hélène?'

'Only the titular father,' observes Janet, examining her watch. 'Recall how humble Humbert informed us — dozens of chapters ago, it seems to me — through the confessions of Achilles, that Hélène, far from being even Achilles' half-sister (as Louis briefly feared), is naught but a bastard foundling whom Maître Arnault bought cheaply one Saturday night from a midwife on the run.'

'Achilles himself', you seem to remember, 'being a son of the nasty Arnault?'

'Again only a titular and "legal" son,' I remind you. 'According to Achilles' account, his mother – the wife of Maître Arnault – was so warm of heart and lavish with her favours, while the lawyer himself was so mean in spirit and paltry in his loins, that of all *her* children it would appear that the only one to be *biologically his as well* is the unfortunate Jean-Baptiste.'

'Does that mean', you wonder, 'that poor Louis is at least not depressed to think of Hélène as having a full fifty per cent of all her genes provided by the mean and paltry lawyer?'

'Substitute "blood" for "genes",' I agree, 'and you may well be right. Louis is in any case so depressed by everything relating to Hélène that the Chevalier now hurries on to distract him with the exciting details of his escape from the Marquis of Roquefort's assassins: how thinking him dead they tossed his body in a river, where the shock of the fast-running chill revived him just enough – he must have had a pretty amazing constitution, but modestly he does not allude to this – to get his nostrils above water as he hurtles down half a mile of rapids before being landed like a spawn-spent salmon on a mudbank, there to be discovered, unconscious and very nearly dead, by his attendants several hours later.'

'And the assassins?'

'For the sake of ensuring payment as agreed they swore blind to the Marquis that the contract had been fulfilled successfully. Thus the news of the Chevalier's murder became as general as the knowledge of his disgrace. His French estates, which could not be sold, were sequestrated and granted in trust to the Marquis of Roquefort, as a reward for his having exposed the Chevalier for a traitor.

'"So then," inquires Louis, his interest successfully engaged – this must be somewhere on the Rhôneside route between Vienne and Avignon – "you departed France for Spain?"

'Not yet, explains the Chevalier, who proceeds to tell of his months of attempting to remain in France, a fugitive with a hefty price on his head. How he learned certain arts of disguise and concealment, and how from a distance he entrusted many secrets, documents and business affairs to his former steward, Arnault, little guessing how foully he was already betrayed, and would be defrauded for years to come.'

'But the Chevalier didn't stay in France for years to come?'

'Only until shortly after the last tie binding him to France was severed: with the death in her convent retreat of his beloved and clandestinely married young wife — the beautiful Henriette de Vergne, she after whom the Marquis of Roquefort had also hankered hotly.'

'Then?'

'The Chevalier relates how, having entrusted the remains of his unsequestrated affairs and assets in France to Arnault — who had not yet at that stage promoted himself to "Maître" — he removed to Spain, where he already had some capital banked in Zaragoza, assumed the identity of Montenero, and in due course enlisted as a gentleman mercenary with Philip IV of Spain — this on the strict understanding that he would never be ordered to war with his native France.'

'Who does he war with?'

'According to his account, as preserved by Louis, the Chevalier then spent many years advancing the interests of Spain in South America. Besides attaining great distinction in the service of his adopted sovereign, it would appear that, and without any hint of avarice or extortion on his part, the Chevalier succeeded in amassing an immense new fortune for himself.'

'Exterminating Peruvian Indians and stealing their gold, you mean?' suggests Janet, as she frowns at me severely.

'Louis does not say', I say, 'that the Chevalier says that.'

'Well, he wouldn't, would he?'

'Also, you must remember that this is still the seventeenth century.'

'So what?'

'And that the French have always had their own very individual multiple standards.'

'What sort of multiple standards?'

'I'm thinking particularly of Freedom. They love it for themselves, all right. Fight for it, invent slogans about it, sing songs about, and so on. Yet they've always tended to be regrettably indifferent to Freedom for anyone else — even more so than the English, indeed. And you will doubtless have remarked, in the course of your long studies in Literature, History and Life, that anyone seriously indifferent to another's fundamental freedoms is apt to lose little time in taking them away from hor, if you give hoh half a chance. And this is why, for all their dreadful failings, we must continue to support such enterprises as the Olympic Games, the World Cup, the United Nations, and even the European Community, in order to maximize those happiest of days: when the horrible half chance is not given.

'If you don't believe me in general terms,' I address this personally to you, in great gratitude for your leniency, 'I would refer you to specific French liberty paradoxes such as Figaro Beaumarchais, who on the one hand could found his own publishing company for the express purpose of issuing the collected works of Voltaire uncensored, while at the same time, and on the other, be the prime mover in a huge greedy project to exploit Louisiana, and to import African slaves there, to work the tobacco plantations.'

'That doesn't make it any better,' growls Janet.

'What doesn't?'

'The fact that, according to you, all classic French writers are slavetraders—'

'I never—'

'Well, you certainly say the same about Rimbaud.'

'I never—'

'Or at least your crony Knox does.'

At this I hoot in triumph:

'There you are!'

'What?' scowls Janet suspiciously. Where?'

'You were asking what all this has to do with Scotland! Yet here it's you, not me, that can't stop dragging Wringhim back into it, and with him by extension Robert Burns – who not only was never a slavetrader, as Wringhim rightly notes, but furthermore remains an infinitely greater poet, person, and passionate pronger of pert poupées, than that pipsqueak pimple Rimbaud.'

Stuffing her manuals back in her bag, Janet emphasizes with affected titanic patience:

'That *still* doesn't make it *any better.*'

'Doesn't make *what* any better?'

'The virtual certainty that your Chevalier, whom up till now you have attempted to portray as unconvincingly moral, gallant and steadfast, is in truth a grafting colonizer, pillager and murderer of innocent native peoples.'

For the sake of winning yet another argument I next impress upon Janet most solemnly, though my other eye is winking at you, how demonstrably it has all along been *me,* far more than her, who has insisted on the moral complexity of character, and who explicitly states in Chapter 70 such generic propositions as: *We are less good, and less honest, than we would like others to think us; If others discover how bad and dishonest we are, that will be to our disadvantage; It is in our interest to continue to deceive others as regards our personal moral worthlessness and untruthfulness; And however mendacious and wicked a malefactor is ever proved to be, hos is is probably even worse than that really* – and that therefore the intelligent reader (again I wink at you) really cannot with justice complain of not being fed sufficient nods and winks to form the view, if hos will, that relatively Goody characters such as the Chevalier may at bottom, in their innermost hearts and best concealed crimes, be morally much murkier than can be proved by available evidence.

'Anyway,' I conclude, as Janet makes a great show of rummaging in her purse in vain, 'one thing for sure is that his new immense wealth in Spain did not make the Chevalier happy. Like a Border collie in kennels he pined for France: to return in conspicuous exculpation, in the freedom of perfect respectability to renew old ties, and to serve the King and country of his birth. For these reasons, and still with no inkling of his steward's treachery, he directed the vile Arnault – now become Maître Arnault of Lourdes – to circulate discreet rumours of a vast reward in Spanish gold being offered for recovery of those innocence-proving papers. What we have come to know as the Bagnols Papers.'

'Which at that time', you seem to recall from Chapter 15, 'were in the possession of that big fat Monsieur Saint Simon, who posed as a Capuchin monk?'

'Not quite. It's true that the false Capuchin bought the Papers off Achilles, at the time when his conscience was troubling him about his identity as apprentice apothecary, and the number of innocent victims that were killed by his master's ministrations. But bear in mind also that the reason why the master apothecary, Monsieur Lefranc, had custody of the Papers – which he kept, according to Achilles, in a drawer with his dirty syringes – seems to have been a prior complicity with Arnault, which complicity was shattered when the steward (or intendant, as Arnault then was styled) was made privy, at his wife's deathbedside, to the apothecary's having tupped her lavishly, and sired Achilles upon her. Thus the apothecary's continued possession of the Papers was by default, a situation which Arnault appears to have successfully rectified by employing the mercenary Saint Simon to bribe Achilles, in his father/master's absence, to release the Papers.'

'Which Achilles happily did?'

'Ecstatically! For the ten louis d'or he got off the Fat Monk were just what he needed to fund his defection from apothecaring, "now to seek my fortune on the boards".'

'So from then on Maître Arnault has the Bagnols Papers all the time?'

'Exactly. In the full knowledge that here is the longed-for instrument of his former master's exoneration, he keeps his possession of the Papers secret for years, all the while pocketing handsome emoluments from the Chevalier, as payment for seeming-loyally factoring that gentlemen's remaining affairs in France.'

'Until the huge reward is offered?'

'Yes. We don't, unfortunately, have any record of the exact cash figure, but it is certainly so very substantial that Arnault expects to retire on it.'

'If I get this lot, Humbert,' Janet butts in severely, finally flourishing a twenty-pound note, as it were the corpse of a rat, 'it's drinks on you in the Brompton. All right?'

'Isn't it bloody absolutely always?' I protest too much.

'What follows?' you insist.

'The Chevalier explains to Louis how Maître Arnault, thinking to pocket the whole huge reward himself, sent the Papers down to the Chevalier in Spain, in the custody of poor old Father Francis, together with some plausible letter pretending a recent breakthrough discovery. "Alas, Father Francis . . . " After regretting the cruel turns of events leading to the old priest's expiring in the Pyrenean whiteout, the Chevalier recalls his woebegone confession to having lost the packet containing the Papers.'

'Which in fact were stolen by the Fat Monk at Luz?'

'Precisely. As Louis relates to the Chevalier, the villainous Monsieur Saint Simon, in his monkly mode, and following his thwarted attempts to cardsharp Louis's money off him, and possibly also motivated by pique at Louis's having kicked him down the stairs of the inn, must have stolen the Papers inadvertently during the night, in the same satchel as Father Francis's emergency funds.'

'And that's how Louis gets hold of the Papers later? Back off Fat Simon, when he fails to murder Louis?'

'By falling on him with his dagger out of a tree. Just so. Though the wicked Simon may have suspected the Papers of having some value, we can be certain he had no inkling of the Chevalier's advertised reward – else he'd have been down to Zaragoza like a shot himself. It's likely, too, that he would have been unable to read the Papers, at least with full comprehension, and also that, being paranoid as most criminals are, he couldn't quite bring himself to give sight of such an unknown value-quantity to his current paymaster, the Marquis.'

'So Louis has the Papers all the way from Morel to Barcelona, to Paris then Sedan, but never once realizes their importance?'

'That's right. Because he, like almost everyone else, believes the Count of Bagnols to be long dead.'

'Until the moment of revelation, as the Count-Chevalier converses with the Cardinal in Mézières?'

'I think, Humbert,' says Janet, sliding her groaning bag across the floor towards me, 'that it's time we—'

'But wait a minute!' you warmly exclaim. 'The story isn't finished!'

'A story is *never* finished!' counters Janet, who now possesses over five million famous quotations on review copies of compact disks from university presses, from which to plagiarize freely. 'Only abandoned!' she adds smugly.

'Very briefly,' I continue mercifully, 'what happens

# 'next goes like this:'

Although there are several loose ends still fankling, and much that Louis might reasonably be wondering about if he weren't so fundamentally miserable about Hélène being wed off – and with her own consent, worst of all – to some bumpkin jerk from Shropshire, it would nonetheless seem that the Chevalier, having fully traced out the strange migrations of the Bagnols Papers, and deplored the vileness of the worst of human nature as manifest in the Marquis of Roquefort and Maître Arnault, and having thanked Louis yet again for having been the instrument of his, the Chevalier's, restoration to respectability, rank and dignity in France, thereafter clams up dramatically.

According to Louis's memoir, which is almost certainly the sole surviving record of that hot and dusty ride southwest from Vienne to Lourdes, the only further intelligence vouchsafed him by his elder companion related to how the Chevalier, still guising in his Spanish conquistador identity, and since Richelieu was badly in need of all the help he could get, had been granted proxy permission to levy a private army, at his own expense, to fight for the King and Cardinal in what became the battle of La Marfée.

And if the Chevalier was fondly hoping his fearless heroism in that conflict would soften the Cardinal's heart to the point of unconditional forgiveness, reconciliation and galloping agape, we need hardly remind you how sadly even this very experienced gentleman of the world, and the New World, must have underestimated the selfish cynicism of successful tyrants. Anyway that's all now history, and after several days' rest on the Chevalier's old estate at Bagnols (and this, by the way is most definitely *not* – as has on occasion been suggested – Bagnols-sur-Cèze,[1]

---

[1] Punctilious as two beggar's beliefs, we urgently forewarn any reader with designs on the following page that Bagnols-sur-Cèze, sitting as it does on the *west* side of the Rhône, is strictly speaking on the *east*ern fringe of the Gard, and not in the Vaucluse at all.

near Orange in the Vaucluse, but rather Bagnols-les-Bains, near Mende in Lozère) the three travellers head west for the Pyrenees, reinforced by some trusty, stout and most likely sporadically flatulent retainers from the Chevalier's Bagnols.[2]

Doubtless that leg of the journey was not entirely bereft of verbal intercourse, but I'm afraid we must imagine it for ourselves.

The next thing we learn from Louis is some rather naff stuff about his mangled emotions upon once more beholding the majestic Pyrenees chaining the horizon in their magical vestments of misty light, &c.

'O, proud beauty of my native land!' he exclaims, before succumbing once more to sadness that for the first time in his life his mother won't be there to welcome him lovingly home, and anxiety as to how his father

---

[2] Equally well, as you Dubliners say, is our/his Bagnols not Bagnols-en-Forêt in the hills west of Cannes, and as for what now appears to have been G.P.R. James' careless assumption that 'Bagnols' as in our Count, or Chevalier, must have been a corruption of 'Bagnoles' as in Bagnoles-de-l'Orne, of prune fame in the North, that really is beneath contempt. And while we think about it we might as better confess that it's actually a great pity, from the point of view of our tax-allowable research in all honesty, that it is not the Cèze/Gard Bagnols that is *our* Bagnols, since there are far more really quite extraordinarily voluptuous schoolgirls there (than in Bagnols-les-Bains, which nowadays has little to offer save last-hope spa-water dipping for terminal walnuts), as is apparently quite common in the short term when you live bang-next (!) to a major nuclear-waste-reprocessing plant. 'Tous les effluents radioactifs liquides sont traités avant rejet dans le Rhône . . . ' the Marcoule Atomique de Marcoule proudly advertises in its leaflet for swallow-all tourists. And, 'tous less effluents gazeux traversent, avant rejet dans l'atmosphère, des séries de filtres de très haute efficacité placés à la base de cheminées.' Rather inclines you to make the most of those schoolgirls* now, don't it not? While you and they still can.

*\* 'Please, as one of the many favours still to be repaid to me by you, will you explicitly state that you do not mean to encourage or condone lewd acts or thoughts, and I mean thoughts just as much as acts, involving girls aged less than sixteen?' [J.R.]*

may receive him.

As they enter Lourdes it must be mid afternoon. Louis, deeply solemn, begs the Chevalier to take Achilles and his retainers on ahead to Morel, to alert Count Roger to his errant's son's imminent return, before proceeding to the Chevalier's own property close by. Himself he spends a wistful hour in the crypt of the Church of the Assumption, lighting Catholic candles and saying prayers by his mother's tomb.

Whether after discharging these devout respects he stops off in a tavern in the town for some reflective fortification before his local last lap we cannot tell. But certainly some additional time has been structured before finally he arrives at Morel, for by then the sun is sinking. The Château he finds curiously quiet and deserted, not a single guard patrolling the battlements, and no attendants materializing to hold his bridle and exclaim with joy as the young master dismounts.

'Hello?' he calls out shyly. 'Hello? Anyone at home?'

Then, when the surprise celebration reception commences with the long-lost Hélène rushing out from the chapel to embrace him, her eyes wetly bright with love, I have to inform us that our hero faints.

'If this is your latest ploy to wind me up, Humbert,' remarks Janet militantly, as she imprisons Luigi change in her purse, 'be advised that you're wasting your breath.'

'And why is that, pray?'

'Because I find it perfectly credible that a young man who drinks far too much in a tavern, then rides through a hot afternoon before getting home late, may faint if he gets such a shock. Now we really—'

'"Blood drained like sand from my brain," I quote my own translation from memory, "and I fell senseless to the ground."'

Seeing that Janet and I really are now leaving the café, you interject: 'But what about—?'

Courteously I explain that we cannot delay any longer our shuffle along the road to the Brompton Arms, else we – and especially I – would lack sufficient time for several leisurely pints of draught ale, before having to trudge on to the offices of SODS for some sips of tepid white wine during the evening's event. This is the inaugural presentation of:

### The Methuselah Prize
*A new annual award for the best first novel*
*By an author aged eighty or over*

'Paul Chalicer's coming down for it too,' I advise you temptingly, 'from his four-story mansion up the Arsenal. Loves convivial intercourse with other authors, does our Paul, especially those whose novels have sold far fewer copies than his has.'[3]

'But I want—'

'And I'm therefore doubly sorry', I conclude this chapter firmly, 'not to be able to invite you along tonight. Maybe another time.' But for the moment, this moment and quite a few following, it's time for:

---

[3] 'Don't imagine I won't get you for this, Humbert. You see if I don't.' [P.C.]

## 78

# Your Personal Exercise[1]

The wedding took place on the last .....day of .....mber 1641.

That the bride was not a ...... on her nuptial night was solely due to the groom's having been unable to stay out of her ....... from midnight till dawn during those blissful weeks preceding.

...ually they were perfectly matched.

She was .......ate and he was ...ile. As the first ecstatic urgency of his .....ing her repeatedly abated, she came to teach him ......ness, sexual ...ience, refinement, and respect for ........ pleasure. By all accounts this emotional and physical ....ony between Count Louis Morel and his Countess Hélène was to ...ure throughout their .... and ....gamously ..... lives together. Their greatest ....et, being good .....lics, was Hélène's ....ility, as they both saw it, to .....ive and .... children. It would, however, be many years before they gave up .... in this regard. In the meantime their .....ly attempts to start a family were undertaken with .....ous ....gy and ..., and gave rise to .....less simultaneous ....sms every inch as ....mate as any other .....ms in the history of this .....t.

When Louis regained .......usness, following that ..... on the evening of his arrival, he had found Hélène leaning over his bed in a state of great .....ty as his father and the Chevalier stood behind her, looking on with ..... .....rn. Alternately soothing Louis's ..... with a .... scarf soaked in .... water, and ....ing his ....ks and his .... as tears blurred

---

[1] For best results, and to avoid defacing this book, and especially to not risk queering the high-pitched excitement of readers coming later, we strongly recommend that experimentation and completion of this composition is undertaken on several duplicates of this chapter blown up on a Japanese photocopier.

Permission to make such copies, of this chapter only and for non-profitmaking purposes only – plus nods, winks, nudges, cuddles and friendly fricks for the fortunate few – is pre-emptively hereby granted.

her own, Hélène was also engaged in a somewhat ....jointed ....ing ......tary on her reasons for springing this wonderfully overwhelming ....rise upon him:

How she had so wanted to ....ght him, with the fact of her not having betrayed her ....nal love for him in favour of a ....matic ..ion with some bumpkin earl from Salop; and a little bit to ...ish him too, for having ....doned her so ....ly, in his .....ful flight to Spain; but above all to satisfy her ..... of .....s as to his .....mental ....tion and ......ment to her, when his astonished weary eyes first ....ld her, in that first moment of return to Morel.

In the days following, the young .....gal's ....ly health and ...tal vigour were quickly restored by good ...., clean ... and .....course of all sorts with Hélène. As his self-image, confidence and .... for life revived, Louis lost little time in locating and assembling most of the missing ...... in the real-life ...zle which for so many months had cast him all over France and northern ..... in the role of unwitting and disposable ...n. And as he conversed somewhat .....ly with his father over ...ls, compared manly notes with the Chevalier during long afternoon ....s in the steep green .....ys of Bigorre, and most of all as he ... in ... at night with Hélène, ....ing and ......ing her in the languorous ....s between .....al ..x, and exchanging ....pered ....ets as only .... ..vers can, Louis built up the following picture.

Far from being fathered by drunken sailors on a Rhôneside prostitute, the beautiful young woman who became Countess Hélène de Morel was in fact the daughter of the C.......r and the tragically fated H.......e de V...ne.

'And now', as Louis would record, 'it all began to make ...se.' Or rather, most of it did. In retrospect, given Hélène's age, physique, looks, charm, bearing, and genetically inherited grace, it may even seem somewhat .....ish of Louis not to have divined earlier how H........ de ...... would have died in .......rth in her ....... refuge – died giving life to Hélène.

Next Louis learned from the Chevalier how for years he never knew he had a child by Henriette. Not till he received the news in the post from Maître ......., safely distanced by the Chevalier being occupied with Spanish business in ...u. Arnault, who had been transacting with the ..ns on the Chevalier's behalf, rewarding them for caring for Henriette, etc, had also been perfectly situated to take the infant Hélène off their ...ds before her first birthday, when her ... nurse had ...ed up. To the Chevalier he would represent, years later, that it was only a recent death-bed ...ter from the old Abbess Cluny which had alerted Arnault himself as to the true identity of the baby girl who, out of the melting kindness of his soft lawyer's heart, he had adopted and raised as his own.

Arnault rightly calculated that further generous ....ing would be forthcoming from the Chevalier: to finance the befitting upbringing of his daughter and only child, until such time as, in come-out candour, he could be united with her. When the Chevalier's monies arrived as anticipated, Arnault immediately invested them in .....lations of his own, and the cultivation and education of Hélène was for the time being ...lected.

Thus, when the Chevalier turned up in Lourdes one day, disguised and unannounced, the .....ster lawyer was nearly caught out. Only by vehement swearing that most of the payments the Chevalier claimed to have sent via Z....... had never arrived in Lourdes did he manage to postpone the .... of his iniquitant reckoning.

But then he had his .....wave: the heroic rescue from .....ing in the .... pool of Louis by Jean-Baptiste – leading to the predictable lavish gratitude of Louis's mother, the Countess, which Maître Arnault converted with his customary finesse into a privileged position at the Château for the burgeoning Hélène, so ensuring the Chevalier's interim approval and gratitude, and postponing yet again the inevitable hour when his, the lawyer's, accounts relating to the Chevalier's affairs would be subjected to merciless ..dit.

That Louis's ..... with ..... in the .... had been entirely caused by Jean-Baptiste hitting him on the head with a ...k and then pushing him off the path, Louis did not learn until two months after his ....iage. This was one afternoon in Lourdes when he leapt off his horse to rescue a lone derelict drunk from being beaten up and robbed by a gang of teenage ...gs. As the cowardly riverside boys fled like ...ep at the sight of Louis's sword, he realized with a ...sm of extremely mixed ....ings that the penniless wreck in the mud before him was none other than Jean-Baptiste, gaunt, ....-haired, and looking a good ...teen years older than when Louis had last seen him.

From Jean-Baptiste, then, over a bowl of hot ...p and after having adamantly declined to accept the vagrant's pathetic plea to take his .... there and then, in exchange for all the wrongs done him by him, Louis learned, by piecing together the ....s of sense in a series of individually incoherent .....ssions, not only of the mill-pond rescue ruse but also of the subsequent .......acy to cause his ...grace or banishment for the ....er of Jean-Baptiste by the river. Pathetically in his own sort of defence Jean-Baptiste went on to explain how very nearly the plan ....fired when the three layers of .... waistcoat beneath his jerkin bladdered with ...'s blood proved inadequate to withstand the blast of the .... from Louis's high-powered hunting ....et. It thus emerged that, despite all cynical ....autions to the contrary, Jean-Baptiste *was* badly ....ded in the riverside encounter, and he *did* nearly die of his ...mach wound. As evidence of which, Louis would recall with a ...t of minimal irony, he began pulling open his clothes to exhibit his ...ly scars – 'until I bade him not risk a chill.'

Meanwhile, from the Chevalier, Louis had also discovered how, innocently delighted with the ingenuity of Maître Arnault having resulted in Hélène's being placed in an ideal educative situation, under the tutelage and protection of Louis's mother, the Chevalier himself, the better to .... a close but disguised paternal eye on the development, ...al and otherwise, of his new-found only daughter, had commissioned Arnault to purchase and renovate the ancient mas (or fortified farmhouse) just up the ...... from Morel. Subsequently, foreseeing the likelihood of ....er sentiments ....ting between Louis and Hélène, the Chevalier had taken it upon himself to carefully monitor and contribute all he could to the chivalrous ....ding of Louis's developing character. As to the true nature of his relation to Hélène, this he felt, being a proud French ......man, must remain concealed until such time as the ....... Papers could be recovered and his good name .....ed.

Also meanwhile, such is the nature of industrious betrayal and manipulation, the ....-eyed Maître Arnault had ...ched the apparently preposterous project of wedding his own only ...logical son Jean-Baptiste to Hélène, hoping so to ...... whatever ample ..wries the Chevalier, and possibly also Countess Morel, might heap upon her marriage – and this despite the .....ing obstacle of Louis Morel being eminently more handsome, accomplished, courageous and patently ...... than the wooden Jean-Baptiste, and also the fact that Jean-Baptiste and the young Hélène Arnault still believed themselves .....er and ....er. Then when in due course Arnault revealed as much of the truth of Hélène's real identity to Jean-Baptiste as was necessary to convince him of their non-siblingship, the impressionable ...th was soon converted to the .... that Hélène's warm ...dness for him, kisses, hugs and all the other tactile tokens of a trusting child's affection, were indeed the first manifestations of ...nal infatuation, leading to lifelong ...ual .....ssiveness, uxorial subservience, and social advancement for Jean-Baptiste.

As the wily Arnault had long been subtly .....ening Louis's character for the Chevalier's benefit, then, when the Zaragoza ......-killing
occurred, and Louis refused to ....... in the Chevalier, the latter,
reluctantly ......ced of his protégé's despicable turpitude, and himself
for the moment .... to Spain by business of great delicacy and financial
consequence, took the unforeseen plunge of charging poor old Father
....... with the mission of informing Countess Morel, and Hélène
herself, of Hélène's exalted ...th, .... identity, and rightful station in
society – assuming, of course, that her outlawed father could ever get
himself inlawed again.

'And this', we can easily imagine Louis .....ring intimately to Hélène
around midnight on Christmas Eve, as they ... in ... together following
a .... of several .....xes, he ....ling her ......s dreamily, as she ....ly
....ded his ...hood into further ....tion, 'this, of course, was what the
Father was trying to tell me, as he pressed me to leave him behind me
in the mountain snow.'

'What did the poor priest say?' Hélène would naturally inquire, as she
....lled to .... her husband's .....ity .... ......fully between her .....rs.

'"The wind, the snow, the cold . . . all hazards grow worse," the dear
soul wheezed. "Louis, you *must* go on. If you do not, *you* will perish also.
But first a message . . . for your mother. Most vital . . . "

'"What is it, Father?" I encouraged him sorrowfully. His voice being
so faint, I pressed my ear to his lips, as painfully he croaked:

'" . . . confided to me . . . but as I now cannot, *you* must tell
her . . . "

'"Tell her *what*, Father?" I urged him, as I prayed he would not
fade.'

'And how did he reply? Mmmm!'

'Though he mouthed some broken words, the howling ..... was so
dreadful that I could not hear. Thinking, in a ... moment, to carry Father
Francis to safety in my own arms, I flogged my dwindling strength to ....
his weighty body from the snow. Alas, before I had taken three ....s with
my limp and sightless burden, a blast of gale whirled us round like a ...
and threw our bodies sprawling into what must have been the .... of a
pot-hole, deeply drifted. Down, down into the dark yielding drift we ....
until our bodies must have utterly disappeared from level view, if light
there had been.'

'Oh, how ..ful,' Hélène .... have felt, her sympathetic ......ation
deeply ...aged. 'And how Heaven then must have ...led upon me, to
not have ..... you. Sssss!'

'A minute later, gasping from the ...ic of suffocation, I contrived to scrape aside the .... of snow between myself and Father Francis, of whose ...... I still had hold.

'"Father, Father?" I called as in . . . a dream, as I ...led myself beside him, thinking to cocoon our bodies together . . . aah! together, to ..... our warmth till the storm should wane, and ...light come. "Speak to me, Father. Father? What must I tell my mother?" He making no reply, I ....ed his head, but ...pond he could not. I forced my .... within – sheeee! – his robe, upon his ....., and found it had ceased to ..... *Aaaaaah!*'

Hence we comprehend how at this time Hélène continued in .....ance of her .....nity, quality and destiny. The Chevalier, having returned once more from Spain, and fearful that Hélène might have further contact with Louis Morel, whom the Chevalier now despised and reviled (following the Zaragoza assassination, perjury, etc, as he perceived it) yet unable to say as much to Louis's fond parents, the Chevalier arranged the mysterious ....ction of Hélène from Château Morel. Once in Paris, and billeted in secrecy with his old ......e-in-arms the Maréchal de Châtillon, the Chevalier made known to Hélène their relationship. She, at first defiant and .....ieving, was in ... ...... persuaded by the Chevalier's .......tible ......rity, the Maréchal's circumstantial corroborations, not a little by the attractiveness of the idea of not having started life in the lawyer's .....um, and by extension the new hope .....safed her of not having to ...ure Louis, marriage and happiness, on the ground of her .....ior birth.

Between the Chevalier and Hélène a nearly perfect father/daughter ........ship now began to ....som. He almost the ...tome of devotion, generosity, restrained concern and subliminal discipline; she a quasi paradigm of ...iful affection, feminine .....tude, and ....ience.

Only in their views of Louis did they ...fer: the Chevalier implacable in his disenchanted ......nation, Hélène immovable in her ....... to believe her beloved capable of such ... ......s as her father denounced.

('Losing' his ......... to the ...., let's not forget, would not appear to Hélène as an evil deed within the meaning of the act, but rather as a ....ute to her .....heart's ......ty, and his ...eal to women at large, hence as a transferred compliment to herself.)

All of which explains, ....less to add, the Chevalier's readiness to hand that night in Paris when his attendants found Louis lying unconscious in the ...., having been ....ed out of the .....ing-den window for failing to make good his accusation that the ....sharp cheats were cheating. And hence that agonizingly brief interview with Hélène as he ... in ... in that closet room in the Maréchal de Châtillon's hôtel, this being all the ....act between them that the Chevalier would ...... before having Louis Morel ....ged again and returned to his lodgings with the ..... Beaupère, the landlady's address having been ....ced from a local traiteur's bill found in Louis's pockets by the good old ... who had been so ....led to discover him ..ked on the floor and then had ....ed him unconscious.

Since, moreover, during that fleeting ...side contact in the Hôtel Châtillon, Hélène was already ..... of her true name and breeding, ..... of it and ...ure in the liberation of devotion and 90% obedience to her ...found aristocrat father, it is not at all .....sistent or out......s that we were able to relate in Chapter 30 that there was a young woman who was ....er than Louis remembered, whose ....ty was now compounded by a .....ity and aura of lithe ....ngth above and beyond what lesser gentleman would ..... in their sweethearts, and whose perceptions, reactions and ....ogue could be incisive to the point of unnerving. And this is why, entirely *pace* Janet Rosencrantz and all other .....ist fillybustrixes, we were not only entitled but furthermore ....-bound to observe that *if* Louis *had* been C.... E....... *then* he would doubtless have reported his impression of Hélène that day as recalling the change that overcomes an out-of-work .....ss once she's been cast in a leading role: expanding into the .....rity of knowing that she owns her part, &c, &c.

Now back in ....des the indefatigable Maître Arnault had immediately seized upon the opportunity provided by the Chevalier's abduction of Hélène to spread the ...... that the unfortunate wench, the lawyer's own only daughter, ..... of his eye, etc, had been carried off by the renegade ....erer Louis Morel. The ...... lost little time in .....ing up the valley to Château Morel, where, much ...llen with the ... of amplified .....hood, and spiked with ....cious embellishments (such as that Hélène had in any case previously graduated as a ....mpet of the ....est virtue, having long since been ...uced and repeatedly .....ched by the ....... of .........), it arrived in good time to ...son the peace and ..rrow the spirit of Countess Morel, in the weeks preceding her ...th.

Also at this time, Maître Arnault, anticipating .....bution following the .....table discovery of his peculance, if the Chevalier wasn't ....ed first, Maître Arnault set off for ..... too. Determined to ...ge a new ....ona and station for himself in the seething .....mity of the populous capital, the lawyer took with him his son and personal dog's-body, Jean-Baptiste, and all the ......erable ...ds at his disposal, both ...len and otherwise. Quickly learning that the Chevalier, through the mediation of the Maréchal, had pledged a private .... to the service of Richelieu and the King, Arnault, astutely judging the probability of ....... to lie with the Count of Soissons and the rebels, decided upon a further ....... to relieve the Chevalier of his ....ish fortune in addition to his ...... one.

This latest attempt would begin with the further .....tion of Hélène – to be achieved by inciting the ... nephew ....... to ...nap her at the first .....roads on the ... road to Vincennes, and then .....ing her from Charles' custody as soon as the ....oon had safely transported her further .... to Champigny-sur-Marne, where his uncle owned a country retreat. It would seem that, for a supply of ....morph criminals to .....itate the success of his .....p project, Maître Arnault had quickly struck up a suitable contractual relationship with the ...g of the ...s. Villains supplied by him were to be waiting at Champigny, to overpower the unfortunate Charles, and very likely .... his ...... too.

This brings us to some ...ns of ....ts which are very dramatically satisfying.

Maître Arnault, having successfully ......lated almost everyone concerned up to Paris in 1641, now made two crucial ....rs of .....ment, as all criminals must eventually, just like monkeys on typewriters, which were to ...ve his catastrophic ..doing. First, it seems never to have occurred to him that Jean-Baptiste, his rather .....trian but by no means ...normal son, might ever develop genuine .....tic ....ings and specific mad ....tal ....ions of his own. But in fact, almost as soon as he arrived in the ever titillating and ....-sodden capital, Jean-Baptiste did just that. And the object of his ......ive amour was none other than the ...ile Mathilde, young woman-in-waiting to the Dowager Countess of Soissons, and lovingly reported in Chapter 44 to be possessed of those '...*eles dures*, ...*des comme* ....*ettes*, and others similar' which caused us to feel that Louis's own mode of description gave away his ....al ......ation, not to mention the virtual certainty of her treating the temporarily invalided Louis to those soothing up-frontal .....ths such as he had never yet had from Hélène.

If, as we allowed ourselves to suspect, it was the case that Louis did at that time enjoy full-bodied ......ative ........rse with Mathilde, then this might be seen, with the relative omniscience of hindsight, as a kind of whimsically unwitting retaliation for Jean-Baptiste's having ...ked him on the .... and ....ed him into the .... pool, and so forth. In any case, Jean-Baptiste, likely knowing nothing of his erstwhile young master's privileged ....macy with ....ty Mathilde, and repenting of the

...mes that he had committed on his father's orders, and burning with altruistic ....athy such as only one frustrated gallant ...er can feel for another – provided, of course, that the ..... they ..o are discrete – then .....led against his evil-plotting father to the point of writing to Louis that helpful but not wholly ...did letter in Chapter 50, advising Louis of his chance to ...... Hélène at the first crossroads beyond the Porte de St Mandé.

Hence it was that the ...ible Charles never got Hélène transported to Champigny, and this was where Maître Arnault made his second ...at ....ake. Arguing that the hitman bravos stationed at Champigny had not ....illed their .....act, since the Maréchal's ...hew had not been burked as agreed, Arnault then attempted to ....hold – or at any rate ..lay – his ...ment accordingly. Now this kind of ....icable .....itor's ruse might have cut some ... in the ...al provinces, where the ....inal element, being in most ..... less gifted mentally, retained a certain .....ct for the ....al order, and wary ....rd for the law. But to the .....world of Paris, as ......ified by the King of the Huns, these ....ties mattered less than ...f a whit, as a result of which the .... Arnault, ......ect of so many of the woes in our tales, had his own ...... expertly .... the following evening – though only after being .....red into .....ssing where he had .....ted the very considerable quantity of .... he had transported from Lourdes to Paris.

And hence it further was that the ....aned Jean-Baptiste – left virtually .....less, not accustomed to ....ing for himself, and finally deprived of all .... of Mathilde when the Dowager Countess of Soissons, following the ....ing of her son at La Marfée, abandoned Paris to seek .....ious encloisterment in the country, and took all her ..... with her – in due course made his ....ken way back to the only sort of home he had ever known, namely Lourdes. And there it was that Louis, having rescued the ....lict from the .....side thugs, and revived him with ... .... and a glass of grog, audienced the remainder of his ....lin confession in attentive silence, then forgave him with great .....ness of heart, on the one ...... condition that Jean-Baptiste consented to ...... employment as a steward on the Morel estates, taking his .....s from Achilles Lefranc.

Accordingly, let us ...ceed to ....lge ourselves in the liberty of imagining Louis and Hélène in ... once more. It is Christmas morning now, and she has just received of him her first .... of the day, in the form of several overlapping .....ine ......s of supreme ......ity, ....inating in one united .....sion of ....ing ...ual .....x, as her ......sing ...b ...ps .....ily at his ... ....m ....ing.

Minutes later, as they ... entwined in one last .....ious ....ace before their Christmas breakfast – Louis having briefly emerged from their canopied four-poster privacy to ..... the overnight log fire back into crackles and flames – Hélène ...ly .....rs into his most adjacent ear:

'Louis?'

'Mm?'

'I'm ....ied about Jean-Baptiste.'

'Oh? Why?'

'He isn't ....y.'

'Hm.'

'Louis?'

'Really. He's very ......y.'

'Oh? Why?'

'He ..... for the girl Mathilde.'

'Ah. Well, I ....... that's only natural.'

'Louis?'

'What?'

'Couldn't we ... ... for him?'

'Eh? But she is the Countess of Soissons' woman, my love. We can't—'

'But perhaps if you emphasized your affection for her son, his for you, and also the future happiness of Mathilde herself? I'm sure the .... and ..... Countess must be much ..... by such thoughts.'

'We should also have to ..... her .......ation,' reflects Louis. 'Money to ... in and ..... up a replacement. It could be rather ......ive,' he ruminates .......ively. Now become a .......able husband, and intendingly .......ible ....er of many, he finds himself laced with strands of ......ial ...dence and .....mony hitherto .....pected by all.

'But we have ...... of money,' remarks Hélène. Perhaps she is thinking of the ...ish ....y contributed by the Chevalier, consisting of the Spanish ...... for recovery of the Bagnols Papers, ....ed up with further Z....... funds, and the title to extensive properties and ...ts in northern Spain.

'Certainly, of course,' Hélène adds persuasively, 'the girl Mathilde must also ... her way. And as we were saying only yesterday, I need a .... woman here, ideally not of this region, for ......tion in my ....ber.'

'Well, my love,' decides Louis, 'I ....... we can but try.'

And who knows? Perhaps in his decision he isn't at all influenced by the thaumatroperotical attraction of having those *m...... d....* and *r..... comme p........* so close to him once more. In any ..... we know their ....-hunting of Mathilde for Jean-Baptiste is .....ssful, thanks to the occasional ....ful references, in Louis's subsequent writings, to the many ....pring from that union.

Which lowers us gently, as it were to touchdown at Jersey Airport, to the following consideration:

That *if* this were a ....s & B... novel, and *if* we already had a ....ative contract to complete another novel exactly like it not later than ..... months hence, we might very well ....inate this one at this point. For consider: many apparently ...ken rules have now been apparently ...ded. The two most m.......s malefactors have died ....ent deaths, the French ...... Richelieu's sickly demise has been guaranteed within the year, the sad but meet end soon (1645) of the parallel but inferior Spanish ...... Olivares – driven ... by the .... of death – was pledged as long ago as Chapter 18, the miserable English ...... Charles I will get his .... ...ped before the ...ade is out (1649), and – last but incomparably best – the ....struck lovers, so long ....ged ...rt by ...ins of ....piracy, ....dent and ..te, have not only been reunited in joy, but wed, ...ded, encouraged to indulge in a great deal of highly energetic and satisfying h........... i........e, but moreover promised a ...g .... together in conditions of as much ....th, ....ort, .....cial ....rity and .....ly .....ness together as .....ls should ever expect.

What a blight on our ...k ...ance, then, is this ....rsed h.....y, that ...ves us on to the ..d of our h.....y.

# Clitoral Simulation

Thank you for these proofs of your enhanced attention.

Although this chapter's title is grandly pagiarized from numerous satellite television channels, particularly the German ones, its innermost core objective is yet more Wagnerian still: to adumbrate certain ways in which, following those early romantic excitements and adventures culminating in sexual happiness too fantastic to detail without umpteen dots, the subsequent years of Count Louis Morel appear to have been somewhat tarnished by Real Life.

There is, nearly needless to say, the almost inevitable descent into set-tled adulthood, increasingly conservative attitudes, and stuffily bourgeois (as we would say) behaviours.

So much so that if it had pleased God (as Louis does say) to bless the Morels with fecundity, then, while one might have been glad enough to embrace Hélène as one's vivacious, ever-loyal and all-forgiving mother, one might also have mustered some grave reservations about being lum-bered with the forty-something Louis as one's hands-on paterfamilias.

Indeed, in the writings relating to what we take to be the last four decades of his life — over a hundred pages of them, as preserved in the Cabinet des Grandes Tromperies Historiques — there is remarkably little to fire the autobiographized imagination, let alone quicken the stylistic pulse.

Apart from the occasional proto-maudlin glimpse of regret concerning their childlessness itself, there is really only the odd prosaic flash of that curiously precocious aesthetic appreciation of nature[1] to which we have periodically alluded,[2] and then latterly a pre-senile obsession with the selective breeding of mountain goats: 'to preserve agility and hardiness,' (in Louis's supra-Spencerian jargon) while at the same time (in our own

---

[1] Nature, for Louis, being principally the vast wooded wilds of Bigorre, and the peaks of the high Pyrenees.

[2] 'Twice too frequently.' [J.R.]

pointed précis) producing nannies with bigger tits.

Hardly enough, in short, to warrant a long saga's lengthening.

It is, then, for reasons such as those that we must confine our quest for further narrative interest, moral insight, holo-dramaturgical resolution, consumer pacification, and so forth, to the brief eighteen months (less brief, it has to be confessed, if your one and only existence is being pointlessly wasted by the Thirty Years War at the time) between Louis's multi-orgasmic Christmas with Hélène in 1641 and the turbulently hot-headed French June of 1643.

And what does our concentration upon Louis's coverage of these months unearth?

Well!

First of all it establishes, if not exactly positively who our author's intended audience might have been, nevertheless specifically negatively that:

*Hosot cannot have been his wife!*

For consider:

The two issues preoccupying Louis throughout 1642 are first of all the matter of Hélène's paternity, and relatedly, and more tormentedly, his own. We suppose it's a bit like delayed shock, or neck problems long after a car accident, or seeing in the mirror all the signs of full-blown BSE-related CJD so many moons after the specific GAGA corruptions that caused it for you: that although it is as long ago as July 1641, and Chapter 64, that the Marquis of Roquefort, in the moments before his death, jeers at Louis:

'Kill me *now!* And if you do, sir, and if you do? You'll never know, *never* . . . who really was your father . . . '

In the end it isn't until the early January of 1642 that Louis begins to take the Marquis's terminal taunting seriously, to brood upon it, and agonize interminably over the potential ramifications.

And just as the advent of post-trauma shock, as with whiplash in your neck, can be triggered by a secondary catastrophe, so it is with Louis, and the loneliness of his goading perplexities.

'Dear God,' he confides to the privacy of his journal in the first week of February, 'if only I might discuss these matters with Hélène. But alas, she is a woman, and how could a woman understand?'[3]

---

3 Strictly, '*Mais les femmes, elles ne comprennent rien.*'

In fact it's bordering on the quaint, we may feel, for Louis to bewail his wife's want of understanding in the circumstances, when we consider – having carefully read through his transcribed lines, and then back between them – that it is assuredly Hélène who devotes herself to ministering to, feeding, comforting, and bedbathing the patient, while Louis looks in occasionally: his brow contorted with solemnity, itself a veneer concealing revulsion, which is in turn both the erupting symptom and the feeding-back servo-mechanical cause of his self-torturing existential quandary.

The patient, sadly, being Louis's father – or rather, his ostensible, titular and legal father: the unremarkable, largely inoffensive, and ultimately unsuccessful husband of his mother . . .

Like so many such husbands, and novelists,[4] Count Roger would appear, particularly in his latterly years, to have been compensatorially bibulous. Following the onset of his widowerhood in 1641, the bibulosity converts to wholesale dipsomania. With the unexpected happiness caused by the reappearance of Hélène, the revelation of her lineage, the safe return and honourable reinstatement of Louis, then the hallowed union of handsome groom and radiant bride, great joy at the jingling dowry . . . the widower's dipsomania is autolicenced to riotously overextend itself in a spiralling hellebriational bender lasting many weeks, and culminating in a massive crippling apoplexy during the night before New Year's Eve.

Since in the 1640s there are no brain scans, drip feeds, rehabilitational physiotherapies, speech therapies, and medical anticoagulants patented by rat poison foundations, there is little now to be done for the speechless and inertly bedridden Count Roger except nurse him lovingly until more strokes vegetize him further, and the clincher begins by partially paralysing his gullet, resulting within days in his choking to death in the arms of Hélène, having failed yet again: in his last desperate bid to sup broth.

Thus does our hero become Count of Morel himself.

---

[4] Once upon a time a Chinese literary critic is reported to have said:
'First, a novelist likes a drink; then the drink would love another drink; then the drinks fuck the novelist.'
That's right, isn't it, Wringhim?

* * *

In the weeks following his father's funeral, Louis finds his distaste, disgust, distrust and anger – that have so fouled the long weeks past – mutating, in sickening lurches, into remorse, self-accusation, and despair. At the same time, his secret doubts as to his true paternity have already reached nigh certainty, and the only serious problem about *nigh* certainty is that it does us no good at all. Much less good, indeed, than absolute scepticism, just as being stuck in a blizzard within five hundred feet of the summit of Mount Everest is infinitely less satisfactory than having stayed at home watching Wimbledon.

Louis doesn't put it like that, of course, but his mental excruciations are nonetheless palpably extreme. Having almost convinced himself that his father *wasn't* his father – how *could* he be: that motionless, skew-eyed, face-collapsed parody of a man, incapable of aught but gargles and groans, constant vomit and shit on his sheets? – he simultaneously lacked any clear idea of who else might have been his genital male parent; and furthermore, and worse, all conjectures along these avenues led infallibly, did they not, to besmirchments of his mother's reputation, devaluation of the memory of her virtue, and irreversible ruination of the honour of the once-proud House of Morel?

At least (so he consoles himself repeatedly, in his jottings throughout 1642) his biological sire cannot have been too lowly a menial, such as a groom from the stables, a goatherd down from the hills, or a potboy jumped up from the sculleries. For had not his poor, dear mother, in that final harrowing deathbed letter, that she wrote to him C/O the Countess of Soissons in Chapter 44, implored him 'never to disgrace the high nobility of your blood', by marrying 'so far beneath you, as the daughter of Maître Arnault'?

And no matter how low one's view of the social standing of villainous boat-eyed solicitors, one could not credibly locate them that much lower, in the niffranks, than randy grooms and greasy scullions, could one?

And therefore?

It seems to Louis to follow – from his mother's dying belief that Hélène *was* the vile lawyer's daughter, and from her 'high nobility' and 'far beneath', that she believed the successful squirter of the child Louis within her womb to be a gentleman of considerable station.

Or then again, perhaps not.

For if his mother was promiscuous – and once a woman had fallen in adultery once, it was like the thin end of the wedge, was it not? or removing your flood-staunching forefinger from the disaster hole in the dyke? – who could ever tell how many flocks of grooms and scullions she may have had queuing up to service her next? And in that scenario, with a different goaty lover every night, and perhaps even several at once, how could she possibly *know* which pumping ejaculator was the depositor of the germ of Louis?

Unless?

Yes, unless the crowing cuckolders of Count Roger that crowded his mother's bed could *all* be described as 'gentlemen of considerable station'. And that would be true, wouldn't it, if they were, say, all the house guests of the Marquis of Roquefort, during one of his group-sex-wagers weekends, as per Vicomte Turenne's Star-of-David tale, in our Chapter 13?

During the autumn of 1642 the consequent conceptual possibility that even his own mother might not have known specifically who her triumphant inseminator was seems to have driven Louis nearly demented – virtually to the preference that perhaps she *did* know, and that perhaps it was the Marquis himself. In this regard Louis harks back frequently to the implications of the communications between his mother and the Marquis when the latter came to dinner at Morel in Chapter 12: the Countess's hotblooded leading of the Marquis's conversation to the topic of:

'*Love*, for instance?'

That debonair kiss the Marquis blew her in reply, so laden with what levels of subtext?

The private conversation implicit in his allusion to 'our archetypal Venus' as emerging naked 'from the *foam* of the sea'?

And so on.

But all this, if construed as corroboration that the Marquis of Roquefort was indeed his biological sire, leads Louis inexorably to the psychoanalytically unbearable conclusions that (a) his own father had several times tried to kill him, and (b) he himself, remarkably like Oedipus,[5] and in the grip of vengeful fury, had unwittingly slain

---

[5] Except, of course, that Louis at no point tups his mother. The closest we get to this, in our stories, is probably while the Countess is bedbathing Louis after his whiteout ordeal in the Pyrenees, and happens upon his stupendous erection in Chapter 12.

his father.

In the most fearful despair over ever unravelling these nightmares unaided, Louis – as a last resort, and evidently only after overcoming colossal reluctances – writes to petition elucidation from the only other person in the world whom, he feels, (i) may know the truth, and (ii) can be trusted to tell him it.[6] This is his old uncle-surrogate turned father-in-law, the Chevalier. To the best of our knowledge, Louis's letter itself does not survive, but it would appear, to judge by his journal glosses, to have been written during the last fortnight of November 1642.

By mid December he has still received no reply.

'What secrets can the Chevalier be keeping from me?' he inquires of himself at this time.

So Christmas 1642 at Château Morel must have been dismally doleful: Louis sleepless, irritable, awash with paranoid speculations hinged around the prolonged silence from the Chevalier, both with regard to Louis's plea for enlightenment and now also concerning the father's uncharacteristic failure to reply to his daughter's festivities invitation; Hélène worried too: not to have heard from her dad, fretful re Louis's aggressive self-absorption, which he exacerbates in a phase of solomasochistic alcohol consumption that reminds her painfully of the apoplectic fate of his father, and the stark contrast between those extraordinary orgasmic gratifications last Christmas and the bleak cold comfort of today.

Towards the end of January 1643 two letters arrive at Morel from Madrid.

The first is a long fatherly homily, apologizing to Hélène for the delay, explaining about the Chevalier's involvement in diplomacy manouevres between Paris and Spain, discreetly asking after her health in a hopefully grandfatherly way, and so forth. The second is a terse holding note to Louis: upbraiding him severely for so basely presuming to query his dead mother's conjugal constancy, admonishing him for evident tardiness in beginning the begetting of his (Louis's) own family, and finally relenting so far as to express the 'solemn expectation and regretful hope' that he

---

6 Logically, his other option might have been the dowager Countess of Soissons, but if *les femmes ne comprennent rien*, presumably they can't be relied upon to tell each other's bosom buddies' sons the truth about their former gallantries either.

(the Chevalier) may be 'freed by the course of history' to respond more fully to Louis's importunate demand for fuller facts 'before the present year is out'.

Three inspired guesses might bounce you near the weight on the Chevalier's mind – but not, we fancy, so close to the weird and woeful effect the father-in-law's note has on the fraught young husband. For not a further week has passed before Louis is now convinced that his own true father is not the Marquis of Roquefort, or any anonymous one of a queue of group-sex wagerers, but rather the Chevalier himself! And that the former friend and impregnator of his mother is now conspiring to manipulate Louis into spawning a race of physically and mentally exceptional SuperGauls, by fathering its founding members on his own superior half-sister, Hélène:

'As if,' argues Louis with himself, 'like the Ancient Father Cronos, he wishes me to play the part of the Great God Zeus, whose heavenly sister, Here, is at once his wife in bed.'

Why else (so his reasoning continues) has the Chevalier chided him for Hélène's not yet being pregnant? And that stuff about hoping to be 'freed by the course of history' to tell the whole truth 'before the present year is out'? Surely premised on 'his [the Chevalier's] fond ambition' that by then Hélène will already have given birth to the first godly grandchild, or at least be heavily big with it. Too late, in other words, for Louis to thwart the project.

It certainly makes bizarre reading, though perhaps not so illogical and disturbing – given the contextually backdropped incestuous proclivities of Renaissance popes, cardinals, princes and other potentates all across Europe[7] – as the evangelical fundamentalism, 'ethnic cleansing' and downright genocide that satellite television covers so faithfully for us now, as the year 2000 beckons.

And it is true, from Louis's point of view, that the Chevalier has proved himself a master of deceit. All those years he had succeeded in being known, respected and honoured as the Chevalier, when he was really the Count of Bagnols? And specifically: those fast-flowing falsehoods at Vienne, when the Chevalier had so effortlessly persuaded

---

[7] Greenadder favourites include the one about the heat-inflamed Cosmo I of Medici proving unable not to mount his voluptuously snoozing daughter Isabella, while Vasari pretends to be fast asleep up the scaffolding.

Louis of Hélène's elopement to England and marriage to a Shropshire noddy?

Whether Louis was already contemplating the eugenical improvement of his mountain goats, and their udders, and whether the conceptual apparatus implied and developed in the furtherance of this venture may somehow have got confused with and in his pitiably solipsistic projections of malevolent causality upon the Chevalier – compoundedly distorted by his simultaneous over-indulgence in alcohol, with its attendant possibilities of vitamin deficiency, delirium, psychosis, etc – we really cannot tell. It could just as well have been the other way round, in the sense that his relationship with the goats may subsequently have evolved by way of sublimation from the hatefully hostile emotions attendant upon his conspiracy theory starring the Chevalier as Cronos.

What we do know is that:

(1) his first positive response to this welter of miserable confusion takes the form of a brutally abusive and unspecifically yet deliberately alienating retort to the Chevalier; and (2) this unshakable conviction of betrayal by 'him I had most trusted', and concomitantly that his lovely wife is also unwittingly his half-sister, brings Louis right to the brink of suicide, or at least to vivid contemplation of it. If we had more time on our hands and yours we should undoubtedly at this point dilate with strong views on the important distinctions between:

(i) *effective suicide*;

(ii) so-called *attempted suicide*;

(iii) *serious obsession with and existentially irresistible attraction to suicide*;

(iv) *fangless prattle about suicide* by cocktail intellectuals who have read a couple of Schopenhauer's popular essays[8] and hence are heavily weltersmirched by 'the vanity of existence'.

In those terms, it is indubitably in the sad syrupy trough of lonely (iii) that our Louis wallows without respite during the spring and early summer of 1643. We may therefore state as datum that during these months there can hardly have been any stupendous erections for Hélène to benefit from, since no-one known to us has ever been simultaneously immersed in sincerely Hamletic (in the popular cliché) envisagement of self-slaughter (*pace* sheer show-offs like Yukio Mishima) and prone to

---

[8] Or even worse: the 'Schopenhauer' chapter in silly Bertie Russell's *History of Western Philosophy*.

this order of tumescence.[9] Certainly not the number of Scottish Borders farmers who have either shot or hanged themselves in recent years thanks to total ruination − financial, familial, moral, aspirational as well as sexual − caused by GAGA agricultural 'policies'.

And we can't think of anything more likely to convert us into some sorts of male feminist eventually than the moving picture, so haunting our dreams of late, of Hélène at this time: so steadfast, loyal and loving − despite all sullen rebuffs and affronts, all psychological withdrawals and physical retractions she has to bear; despite no child in her wifely womb to gladden its grandfather's dotage, and no hope of getting one either (not monogamously, at any rate) so long as her convoluted consort contrives to remain locked in his library all day, to peck anorexically at his meals alone, and sleep by his lonesome all night.

Seldom, we imagine with justice, can a much cluckolded First Lady have stood by Herman in the White House with greater fortitude, charity and chastity, than the undeserving Louis gets from Hélène in this first half of 1643.

As his writings wax ever more cumbersomely metaphysical, Louis demonstrates by his omissions and evident ignorances that although now he could conceivably have read Descartes' *Meditations* without anachronisms as plied by G.P.R. James, nevertheless he has not done so. This is interesting for several reasons, one being the strong implication that mid-seventeenth-century Europe was already crying out for Cartesianism well before Descartes (who also had a woman named Hélène by the way) stepped forward to propound it.

Take Louis's ruminations, for example, on the immortality of the soul.

'If my soul is to be *immortal*,' he inquires of it, as have so many before and since, 'then what properties must it possess?' Well, first you must be *imperishable*, mustn't you? But what follows from that? *Imperishable* implies *immutable*, does it not, since whatever may be changed at all may in the course of all eternity be changed by so many degrees that

---

[9] 'If one were frivolous and also subscribed to a certain style of afterlife then one might include in one's main text the suggestion: "If you have ever killed yourself and experienced a stupendous erection shortly before doing so please communicate full details in confidence to the Maudsley." Might one not?' [P.C.]

its *identity* is destroyed? But if your fundamental *essence* is *immutable*, then how can God punish it?

For if no change is effected, then what punishment has been achieved?

'That being so,' Louis concludes in perhaps the dozenth such joylessride during June/July of this year, 'it is hard for a mortal, still immured in flesh, to comprehend how, for the Cardinal Sins we commit [such as killing ourselves], the Almighty (Yea, even He) is able to make good His Promises, of Punishments throughout all Eternity. Oh, if only—'

And then it all simply stops.

# Bridge

Yes, all that solitarily confided heartache, the angst, the interminable amateur casuistry, and other proofs of marital hardship . . . suddenly they terminate as abruptly as an English bank manager's smile, and all that remains is the aforesaid rather turgid hundred or so pages on the sorrows of childlessness, the Beauty of Nature, plus plentiful detail on the milk yields of succeeding generations of Morel Estate goats.

If only, we moaned at this juncture, Hélène too had kept a journal, then how much broader, sharper and more Fujiful a picture might we now have of the next fifty years in Bigorre: the charming particularities of everyday life – life as it never again can be – in that little-known (in those days) backwoods of Southern France; entertaining minutiae of the intellectual limitations and moral frailties of her fundamentally much loved domestics; and a stereo fix, through the acute magnification of civilized feminine perception, of her ups and downs with Louis, and her sentiments regarding his goats?

But then again: perhaps she *did* keep such a journal?

And if it may not have been destroyed?

Then if only one had a lifespan of several thousand years to devour all the archives in the Bibliothèque Nationale and its outposts?

Alas.

Either Hélène didn't, or her journal has, and in any case one doesn't.

Accordingly, it would seem, we must end our coverage here – bristling with niggling incompletions, fissuring with intimations of entropy, with the mirror to nature lying in shards upon the flags, in peril of seeming to attempt to parody the endings so typical of novels that win those highbrow literary awards strong on prestige but with hardly any prize money – were it not, we rejoice to add, for the following fortuitous concatenations of events, and words.

# Provence, Carpentras & the Petrarch Library

Finishing a big book may oft be compared to taking a vital exam. In both cases it's best to commence calmly, with cleansed perceptions, fresh insights, a clear head, a rejuvenated suntan, and thus to have preceded the ordeal with a tonic break in Provence for as long as could credibly be wangled. For a long novelist there's also the hopeful advantage that if you do a bit of travel journalism on the fly, there's an outside chance of scoring a welcome pittance from the fourth estate long before you see a penny from sales of your opus, and this in turn can be worth its weight in accountants' bills: if your colour feature in the *Sunday Crimes* persuades the Taxman to swallow all your flights, car hires, restaurant meals and hotel expenses at the first attempt.

We lived there for two years in the otherwise unremarkable 1980s, Koo and I, before Tory England fell victim to Peter Maylia. So now, in this decade closer to the crematorium, we wonder how Provence has changed.

And what is it anyway, this magical place with the magical name?

If we only flicked through Mayle, we might picture a quaint little corner of the Luberon near Apt. Lady Fortescue's Provence is more coyly inscrutable: an idyllic garden apparently on the side of some 'mountain' a few miles north of Cannes.

But that, according to Michelin, is not Provence at all!

Then again, 'the region described in this guide does not exactly correspond with the historical and administrative Provence.' Commendably honest, that, and also obliges us to buy several more Green Guides if we want to cover anything like the historical Provence. This, says *Britannica*, is a province: 'in the southeast of ancient France, bounded on the north by the Dauphiné, on the east by the Alps and Italy, on the west by the Rhône and on the south by the Mediterranean Sea.'

That definition is closer to the present-day administrative *Région* which lumps together Provence, Alpes, and Côte d'Azur, and thus the six *Départements* making up the most south-eastern corner of France. And yet, if we don't let Provence travel west past the Rhône, we lose such treasures as Nîmes, the Pont du Gard, the Camargue and *Jean de Florettes*.

Thus it appears, if we aren't a stickling pedant or a government flunkey, that Provence, within generous limits, is a feast we can move to taste. Our feast is approximately a triangle between Vienne, Montpellier and Nice. That's a vast, divers and very resilient area. Most of it has hardly noticed Mayle, and the worst affected area, round about Bonnieux and Gordes, was already badly polluted, not only by ex-pats from Reigate, but also by affluent second-homing Parisians, and colonising Dutch and Germans. The latter are still particularly unpopular in Provence. So if you're tall, fair and blue-eyed, and even if you aren't, it's a good plan to emphasize how Scottish you are.

NB not English.

If you think that's mere tartan tub-thumping, you're welcome to try being English in one café and Scottish in the next. The difference can be breath-taking.

Nor is it only in hostility to Germans and disapproval of the English that Provence displays blight on its cherries. Another thing they don't rush to tell us in the Green Guide is that the more stars a tourist attraction possesses, the more surely our vehicle will be violated in the car park. For instance, when Audrey dropped down from her gite near Dijon to visit us in the summer of 1985, with her Australian colleague Brunhild, they foolishly – awe-struck by the holy serene façade of Sénanque Abbey (two stars) – left their pathetically locked Volvo full of handbags containing money, credit cards, tickets, and passports for themselves, Jennifer and Brunhild's three teenage daughters.

All gone!

And even we ourselves, so innocent then, made the mistake of parking someone else's BMW 735i in the centre of Avignon (three stars).

'It's your own stupid fault,' sneered the police, when we complained somewhat bitterly about our smithereened windscreen and missing Blaupunkt hifi. 'First of all it's a luxury car. Second, it's got a GB sticker. Third, and worst, it's German.'

All like red rags to the local thieving bulls.

'However,' the police concluded consolingly, 'good luck with your insurance claim.'

Later we learned that professional Provençals, visiting such hotbeds of loucheness as Avignon and Marseille, always go in a second car, old and battered, and leave all the doors and the boot unlocked, so the bandits can check without damage that there's nothing there worth stealing.

But let's not knock Michelin, nor even Mayle neither. There's useful information and good entertainment in both, particularly if one reads the former, at least, in 'English'. Where else is it wrote that:

'Camargue is the land of large plantations and concentrates on the rearing of black bulls and white horses living in liberty'? Or that the 'olive tree of which there are more than 60 varieties will grow up to 600m'? Or that, in pre-Roman Provence, 'an important ritual consisted of putting in the stone lintels the beheaded victims of the conquered peoples either alive or in the carved version'?

At the same time, both those oracles purvey a rather superficial Provence. The Michelin is a straightforward tourist guide. Mayle, it seems to us, has provided a different sort of tourist guide. Fine, if that's how it's packaged. Less honest if presented as an account of what it's *really* like to live in Provence. Amusing when describing the novelty *what*. Shallow, even prudish, on the *why and wherefore*.

Take, if you will, the master mason's dog.

Mayle presents it as cute that when at last his masons turn up for work, the first man out of the truck is a cocker spaniel bitch. But why? Assuredly because Provençal masons are fanatically bloodthirsty huntsmen, every huntsman hath his hound, and only the boss mason's dog gets to work with the team during the week, since otherwise there is too much fighting, copulation and defecation all over the site. We ourselves know two such master masons' spaniels personally, and throughout Provence there are probably dozens. On the downside of this same masonic bloodlust, if you go for a bracing stroll on the slopes of Mont Ventoux on Sunday after lunch, you mustn't blame us if your bum gets shot off.

Then there are the Provençal peasants.

Or are there?

Mayle translates the French 'paysan' as 'peasant'. This is so crass that it's difficult to believe the error isn't perpetrated deliberately, perhaps out of laziness. Consider. How many peasants are there in Scotland today? How many would warm to being so labelled? Yet Provence is packed with proud paysans (countrymen or farmers, suggests Collins Robert), many of whom would happily slit the throat of anyone who called them anything so insulting as 'peasant'. Certainly they have delightful qualities, as Mayle, Lady Fortescue, and many others have noted. Optimistic, cheery, generous, passionate, and so on. But they also, being all too human, have much nastier capabilities, as tends to be noticed whenever their interests are threatened. Noticed, for instance, by the Spanish drivers who had their fruit lorries torched in Carpentras by infuriated Provençal protectionists.

Nor are supererogatory greed and pure spite unknown in Provence. One of our neighbours, in the Vaucluse Plain, was a vine-growing rich widow. Her husband, a former mayor of the village, had died in mysterious circumstances. Killed by a chainsaw while pruning up a cherry tree, said some. Drowned while fishing, said others. The truth, as we eventually discovered, was that the deceased was both a fanatical poacher (despite not needing either the fish or the money) and a cordial hater of his nearest neighbour, who owned a small château across the road. Death of the mayor was in fact caused by his foolishly slipping into the château moat while electrocuting his neighbour's carp with a mains cable.

Similarly with political attitudes.

With many Provençals, otherwise bright, charming and witty, it's as well to steer clear of politics if we don't want to hear what a fine upstanding saviour of the nation is Le Con. Or deeply depressing 'solutions' to the Arab 'problem'. One blistering July Friday I treat a gang of heroically deadline-meeting tradesmen to a lunchtime pastis. 'What's the difference between an Arab and a pastis?' one of them asks me darkly. My heart already sunk, I give up. 'You mustn't drown the pastis!' chortles my tormentor, while the rest of them roar with laughter at my discomfiture.[1]

We sound notes of caution, yet we too are addicted to Provence. It's a magnificent micro-world in which to frolic, repose, explore and

---

[1] In the context of the darker side of French character, and the practice of shooting Arabs for fun whenever there's a good chance of getting away with it, we can't help recalling Maupassant's exquisitely repellent Bel-Ami:

'And he thought of his two years in Africa and of the way he used to intimidate the Arabs in the little outposts in the south. His mouth twisted into a cruel grin as he remembered one escapade which had resulted in the death of three Ouled-Alane tribesmen and had provided him and his comrades with a score of hens, two sheep and some money, as well as something to joke about for the next six months.'

Bel-Ami, Chapter I, Penguin Classics translation by Douglas Parmée.

create. Our twenty-month stint there witnessed the completion of one novel, the writing of a second and the starting a third. That might be meagre for Maigret, but for Humberts it's prolific. And yes, the balmy weather, robust red wine and abundant garlic do contribute. As to running a business, or trying to make a living within Provence, we would forget it immediately. The tape is redder than the wine, and the authorities assume as a matter of policy that all self-employed persons cheat by at least fifty per cent. This forces such persons into just such cheating, even assuming they were innocent to start with – which most of them consummately weren't, just like Maître Arnault in Lourdes. The subtleties of subterfuge and linguistic agility required to survive this administrative nightmare are beyond many natives, let alone us dabbling strangers.

Hence it was in the mid eighties that – like so many other dabbling strangers, such as H.G. Wells – we quit our fulltime occupation of Provence: for the sake of earning a half-decent living, and also (as it transpired, and much to our suprise in the first instance) to assist in the liberation of Scotland – from England and the GAGAs.

But that doesn't stop us skipping back to Provence once a book, to keep up with old friends, and to bask in the sunshine and wine we love the most. And the heart of our personal Provence may be drawn as an inner triangle between Nyons, Orange and Carpentras. The exact location of our hideaway within that patch is privileged to remain undisclosed not far from the notable town of Carpentras, famous for its mediaeval massacre – as subliminally noted in Umberto's *Name of the Rose* – and for its thriving black market in truffles.

Carpentras is indisputably one the of liveliest, most attractively situated (with the towering white-capped Mont Ventoux as its backdrop) and architecturally pleasing towns of the Vaucluse. Every Friday morning the central squares and narrow sidestreets sprawl and throng with a magnificent open-air market, where one can buy everything from tiny painted songbirds in tiny gilded cages to roast chickens hot from the spit; fresh sea urchins from Marseille; thirty-five shades and flavours of olives from Nyons; antique prints, butter croissants by the dozen, secondhand paperback pornography, live ducks and rabbits, umpteen creamy cheeses one can sample without being arrested, cut-price shotgun cartridges . . . everything.

Even when the skies open and millions of gallons of rain pour out of them, as happened on the morning of our second Friday in Carpentras this trip. Opting not to dive into a bar for pastis quite yet, it being just eleven o'clock, we slopped soggily, bulging with fresh fruit and vegetables, from the Rue Saint Mercière Siffrein, just opposite the cathedral, to the Petrarch Library in the Boulevard Albin Durand. Petrarch, who studied law in Avignon in the early fourteenth century, also had a great affection for nearby Carpentras, and the town, aided by endowments from an affluent bishop, has responded by creating a small but exquisitely stocked library in his memory.

The general reading-room differs little from any other provincial library – wall-to-wall encylopaedias, glossy magazines, etc – and typically of a later afternoon it is packed with yawning senior citizens and tittering teenagers. But beyond the reading-room, almost like ascending grades of awareness in eastern mysticism, or possibly going up the dans in judo, is a gallery of linked archives, successively dedicated to ever earlier eras of French history and literature. The Petrarch Room itself is a major resource, and attracts scholars from all over the world.

Now the difference in character between Parisians and Provençals (and this, by the way, is not a digression, as will be made plain in a moment) is both subtle and vast. For instance, if a blue-eyed Parisian assures us the job will be done *demain ou après demain*, he means us to understand (though he may of course be lying; that's always another problem in Paris), literally:

'The job will be done either tomorrow or the next day.'

By contrast, if a dark-eyed Provençal shrugs his shoulders expansively, gesticulates extravagantly, and promises *demain*, he wishes us to infer no more than:

'Not today.'

As to the dread disjunction *demain, ou après demain*, this, in Provence, can only safely be taken to mean something like:

'Don't bank on it, mate.'

However, once, after some inevitable gaffes and social bruises, one gets the hang of the local sub-text, the average Provençal turns out to be much more industrious, serious, knowledgeable and intellectually generous than might be inferred from a superficial glimpse of hor behaviour in a restaurant at Sunday lunchtime. This is particularly true of M. Ferdinand Hugues (both his mother and delightful wife are Italian), Assistant Director of the Petrarch Library, who had twice saved our bacon at crucial crossroads in the sixteenth century during *The Counts of Mount Venus*.

After the ritual exchange of greetings, handshakes, kisses and pleasantries, M. Hugues politely inquired:

'And which epoch of our culture' – I translate precisely – 'are you smutting up this time?'

'Nothing is so smutty as the truth,' I riposted. 'Also, I want it, eventually, to be broadcast on satellite television.'

'Absolutely,' nodded M. Hugues, reaching for his jacket. 'Well, let's have some lunch, shall we, and you can tell me all about it?'

So we treated ourselves to the five-course menu at Le Coq Hardi, where the wild-boar paté with garlic was never better, and conversed at three-hour length about the history of the Counts of Morel, the long harsh reign of the Tyrant Cardinal, and seventeenth-century France in general. When, over coffee, we got past the death-cell confession – to the marriage of Louis and Hélène, Louis's agonies over his paternity, the paranoid estrangement of Louis from the Chevalier, the sudden bewildering cessation of his crass suicidal orotundities, and our dread of being doomed to a prize with no money attached – M. Hugues inhaled thoughtfully (he smokes as defiantly as most Provençals, but has more teeth than most, which he puts down to fewer cakes) and came over unusually silent. When we had finished our Cognac he said:

'Bagnols, you say?'

'Yes.'

'But not Bagnols-sur-Cèze?'

'Indeed not.'

'Nor even Bagnols-en-Forêt?'

'No, no. Believe me. Incontestably Bagnols-les-Bains.'

'*Étonnant*,' murmured M. Hugues to himself. 'Are you pressed for time?' he casually added.

The rain had vanished and the sky was infinitely blue once more, so Koo went off to Vacqueyras to stock up on our favourite wines, while I accompanied M. Hugues back to the Petrarch Library. In his office he poured me a second brandy (which of course I would not have accepted, had I not been officially on holiday) and said:

'Give me ten minutes.'

An hour later he returned, bristling with subdued excitement, to dispel my post-lunch torpor with a dusty brown box full of ribbon-tied manuscripts which completed the jigsaw-puzzle that the story of Louis Morel had become. But would I be allowed to copy them?

M. Hugues replied:

'Better not flatten to Xerox, perhaps, but you have a good camera – hey, hey? *Alors!*'

'You really don't mind?' I was so nervous at this point, unable to believe my luck, that I must have been trembling perceptibly, and was sweating in my shoes.

M. Hugues smiled benignly:

'Why should I mind?'

I described the security nightmare I had encountered in the Cabinet des Grandes Tromperies.

'Poof!' he commented expressively. 'Paris!' No, no: the only condition in Carpentras was that I must make the Petrarch Library, not excluding its Assistant Director, and the town of which he is so justly proud, a little more famous than they already are. And this we sincerely trust to do, as many of us are now enabled to almost determine for ourselves whether Louis Morel killed his father after all.

# 82

# The Kissing Link

My dear Louis,

I do not reply to your last letter to me, as I know you were not yourself when you wrote it.

Of course I sympathize with your perplexity and distress, though it seems to me you have been most remiss in your treatment of your wife, and your exclusion of her from all your afflictions, and affections, if not also your confidences.

Hélène has written to me privately anent these matters, and it has been a cause of great vexation and sorrow to me that, for reasons of loyalty, diplomacy and discretion, and due to oaths sworn in consequence thereof, I have for so long been prevented from dispelling your uncertainty, satisfying your curiosity, and accordingly restoring to harmony, happiness, and fruitfulness, your marriage with my daughter.

But that time, thankfully, is past.

His Majesty, as all France must by now be aware, is dead.

[*Louis XIII died at the Château of St Germain in early May 1643, aged forty-two.*]

Though undoubtedly a great monarch in many ways, the late King was at once most unlike his incomparable father [*Henri Quatre, le Grand, father of hundreds of his people, etc*[1]].

In particular, and despite the innumerable God-given talents and splendid excellences of education and cultivation which our good

---

[1]  As per note 2 in Chapter 21.

King Louis assuredly possessed,[2] he was notoriously difficult and, viewed with the charity of hindsight, one might say, more than a little tragic in his character. He was variable in his confidence, he was given to periodic fits of rage, to sudden unprovoked spites, and, worst of all, he was prone to long spells of inexplicable physical weakness, and inconsolable gloom. His speech, a painful problem throughout his life,[3] would regularly prove an impossible embarrassment in the company of women. Infuriatingly for him, and frustratingly for her, the higher His Majesty's esteem for a favoured lady, the more insuperable his cruel impediment would become.

The one remarkable exception, according to the best of my knowl-

---

[2] These plodditory pronouncements of the Chevalier's are complete courtier's cobblers. In fact, 'One of his contemporaries says of him [the King] that he was so indifferent in his government that all the world awaited his death with impatience, even those who owed most to him.' Just like 'our' Prime Creep. In the case of Louis XIII, trawling his biography nets us precious few merits. One juvenile accomplishment appears to have been proficient marksmanship with all manner of firearms. Put another way: the then King of France delighted in shooting things, especially those that couldn't shoot back. On occasion this enthusiasm extended to bagging his own churlish peasants. In this particular Ken's Russellification of Aldous Huxley's *The Devils of Loudon* is surprisingly close to the mark.

[3] Louis XIII had an appalling stutter, which may have been physically aggravated by surgical attempts upon his tongue during his infancy and mentally exacerbated (for neo-Cartesian psychoacolytes) by exposure to phallic bragging and conspicuous hands-on exhibitionism on the part of his promiscuous father. So, again, even France's greatest king would be doomed to the nick in Cleveland. Interestingly, Louis XIII's ineffectual contemporary Charles I of England was a terrible stutterer likewise. Both were intranational racists, in that each believed fundamentalistically in absolute monarchy and the Divine Right of Kings, and what could be more fascinating than to speculate incestuously upon the vampirically catalytical role in all this of Queen Henrietta Maria, Charles I's wife, who was also Louis XIII's sister, and had slept with him too in their youth?

edge, was your own sweet mother. Perhaps it was because her exceptional beauty was matched with unusual modesty. Possibly it was owing to the humility of her rank, and the freshness of her presence in Paris and Fontainebleau that season. Whatever the cause, it was remarked with joy by all who beheld it, with the inevitable exclusion of some of the ladies, that when, in the entourage of Her Highness of Soissons, your mother was presented to His Majesty in the summer of 1617, the effect of her charm upon him was like the working of some potion of magic. His stutter, though not altogether banished by her company, was greatly eased. His manner waxed less stiff, his spirits rose, and, which was the talk of all the Court at the time, on several occasions, and these fully public, he was seen to embrace her with great warmth and to kiss her, not coldly as prescribed by form, but fully upon the mouth, as lovers kiss, as you must kiss my darling Hélène, and as I too once kissed . . . my poor beloved Henriette.

Your mother, I say, spent many hours of many days in close company with His Majesty during the summer of that year. What further issue might have come of this, had not the Cardinal in due course intervened,[4] we shall never know. Suffice it, for the moment, for you to reflect carefully upon the chronology of events thereafter,

---

[4] We're a bit puzzled as to what the Chevalier means by this, since Richelieu's pole star had not yet arisen, and in 1617, following the assassination of Concini ordered by the teenage King, he, the not-yet Cardinal, was supposedly in a trough of disfavour. But it may be that, acting then for the Queen Mother (Marie de Medici, banished by her son to Blois), Richelieu somehow contrived to apple-pie the passion of the monarch for the mother of our Louis Morel. In this regard, let's never forget those telling Palais lines translated in our Chapter 25:

'"How is your mother these days?" was his [the Cardinal's] only polite expression of any interest in my family. "And what took you to Barcelona in the first place, Monsieur Morel?" he next wished to know.'

'How is your mother *these* days?' Must not this imply some recollected interest in how the lady was in *those* days? And in that case? It's a thoroughly musketeerious conundrum, and could well take you several lifetimes in the Biblothèque Nationale to unravel.

your mother's unswerving fidelity to Count Roger,[5] and the number of siblings with which she presented you. I write today, dear Louis, in the hope of allaying your torment. You will appreciate, however, that in doing so I incur a certain risk, as we none of us can predict what will happen to our government, our nation, and to ourselves henceforth. I trust you, therefore, to guard this letter with the utmost care, and to divulge to no-one the import of its content.

No, not even to Hélène.

To her I shall write separately, with lighter news, and advising her of my intention to visit with you in September. During my stay, rest assured, we shall converse further upon the foregoing. Meanwhile, discard your woes, I pray you. Do your duty by your wife, and to God. Allow your ever-affectionate father-in-law to hope, I say, that when, soon, he greets you again, he will find his only daughter to be at last expecting his much-longed-for heir, and yours.

Begging you never again to doubt the undying constancy of your oldest friend's devotion,

BAGNOLS.

---

[5] There is of course no contradiction in this. For a lady to be impregnated by the King – especially a young King so withdrawn, generally misogynistic, and more given to the mulish gay life than to the tireless heterosexual fathering of many more of his people – would not be accounted any dishonour to her husband. Quite the reverse, indeed, just as in the roots of Christendom.

*Part VI*

# Tale-ending House-party Pudenda

# Proposals of Marriage, Character: Rape—

Now is more than ever the perfect moment to confess: that any long and moderately complex book takes longer to confect than to devour for its first gurgitation.

Or certainly it ought to.

So that many events pleasantly fresh and vivid in the guests' recent memories are already fading fast with age, nostalgia and mould in the recollections of the host. So what still may seem like yesterday to you has more the impact of three years flown from me, during which centuries have elapsed, and also South Africans have achieved the first stages in their relatively bloodless revolution (licensing lush liberals once more to savour their aggressively supermarket-priced Cape Sauvignons), the Chunnel has finally opened for elephant rides beneath the sea, but also no man nor woman neither has set a single toe upon the moon (let alone Mars), the peoples of former Yugoslavia have held themselves up as a macrochasm to us all, while 'here at home' the GAGA Moral Gleet Factor has escalated geometrically, the Young Royals have fucked themselves and others beyond a shadow of any thinking person's doubt that, upon the natural-wastage cessation of 'Our Gracious Queen' the English monarchy should be abolished altogether — even for the English themselves, and that's really saying something, isn't it?

Closer to the bones of home, our Madam Chair, say — Queen of the Great Sex and Talent Debate way back in Part III — no longer is the succulent undergraduate peach she was, but rather has become a multiskilling whizzo producer of Arts for the EBC. It's true she continues not to thank me in many of the non-verbal ways envisioned then, but since we remain in telephone touch, and so long as occasionally she deigns to give our humble projects those invaluable subliminal plugs upon the air, between the football and the snooker, why should we junk all hope?

Of all the other wonderful women in my life, those mature at our outset are now most maturer; while those then barely legal or plainly not are today become a constantly consoling constellation of visual delights, energetic intellectual joys, incomparable feminine perfumes, culinary promises, and competent muscularities to practise walking wheelchairs round the town. Recently when I submitted to Janet Rosencrantz on the telephone, having reached her via that instrument on the fifth attempt, the view that her Veronica (fresh from sweeping the A-level board) and I should get married as soon as possible, there was a lengthy pause at my expense while at the other end and with audible suspicion the Internetting mother conveyed my proposal to the favoured daughter.

Then:

'She says, "What the fuck for?"' returned Janet, with unmaskable satisfaction.

'Why!' feigned I. 'Isn't it obvious?'

'Apparently not.'

'Because then I could lead her back to the paths of righteousness,' I exulted, 'and passing on telephone messages. And when I die – and her still a woman in her prime, most eligible – she'll inherit all my computers, won't she? Not to mention my copyrights, my moral rights, my subsidiary intellectual property ass—'

'Don't sound so desperate,' said Janet. Moments later, having relayed a mischievous travesty of my passion to her daughter, she returned with:

'Veronica says, "Tell that old goat to get off the line." She wants to call her boyfriend.'

'But my proposal! . . . '

'She says she'll fink a bow tit.'

Nor have we any doubt that, being a brilliant humanities student with a fertile memory, Veronica will prove unable not to remember me from time to time – just like your purple-bottomed green chimpanzee in Chapter 76 – as her boyfriends come and wilt.

Yes, it's bad enough with Veronica – not having her, I mean, at least in this interminable short term, while some jerking junior does. But if there's one young woman above all others upon whom my longings have projected most hopelessly since that moment when in Chapter 29 we noted her in the Great Debate audience – wallowing in the primal physical delight of having her left breast stroked beneath her Aran sweater, and its nipple mechanically kneaded, by the zoology boyfriend beside her – one physical image curvaceously supreme, I confess, upon whose delectable anatomy the quintessence of my personal Humbertism may be seen to stand or fall, it's Audrey Macpherson's Jennifer.

Maybe it's a little kinkover from memories of riproariously mounting the mother in one's prime, do you think? That when one sees the daughter twice as young yet every inch as luscious as her mother used to be, and in this case two inches lusciouser, one pines to mount her too? Of course there's an enormous difference between converting the pining to the full-blooded two-backed heterosexuality of democratic intercourse on the one hand and unilateral glistening hallucination in the other.

And what makes that difference?

If not the intersex between *character* and *opportunity*?

And if for elastic nanoseconds we focus on *character pure and simple*, which it never is, then may we not enunciate one of the basest truths of all — moral, narrative, forensic, universal — which everyone more or less stampedes to deny of hohself, while holding it true of all others? And is it not this? That I learn about my character just as I learn about your character: not from privileged inner knowledge of my soul (as Louis Morel and billions of others long before and ever since have deludedly imagined) but by observing how we behave in emergent situations, learning from our mistakes, and revising our hypotheses accordingly?

Rudneigh Bletherington, for example, ex-Eton and stiff-Upper, is madly in love with priceless Priscilla Genderghastly. Thrice has he steeled himself to pop the vital question but somehow has never yet got it out. Today is Christmas Eve. Rudneigh essays a flogging of his will to the following resolve. Fortified by one final balloon of Admiral Genderghastly's Courvoisier, he will succinctly and forcefully propose marriage to Priscilla on the dot of the twelfth stroke of midnight. Either that, or he will rush to the gun room and blow out his brains with a priceless Genderghastly Purdey.

Midnight passes.

And what happens?

Nothing at all.

Well, very nearly. No proposal. No clots of peabrain round the gun-room walls. Just another two balloons of Courvoisier, a chaste 'Guhnate, duhling', and staggering up the stairs to bed alone again. What Rudneigh could have learned from this situation, if he weren't such a twit, is what Priscilla knows already — that he is a duffer and a coward, and that if, failing all better offers, she finally decides he should 'have her hand' (his formidable inheritance looming), she will be obliged to engineer that elusive proposal herself, albeit without seeming to.

On quickly to *opportunity*.

And how better to partion it than into *consent* and *propinquity*, since if a lady consents to have sex with you, or vice versa, it isn't going to do you a lot of communally orgasmic good, is it, so long as you remain tied to your poodle-sitting in Reigate, while she's still in jail in Alaska?

Consent, in any case, we are going to presuppose. This is because the lack of it implies either chastity, which we cannot abide, or else rape, which we absolutely reject as the ultimate confession of personal worthlessness and failure, and also because we'd get into an intolerable pother of browbeating if we didn't.[1]

That leaves propinquity, whose cruciality can hardly be over-emphasized. If a naked woman presents herself to you in propitious circumstances, if we may so instantiate the concept, she can be very hard − always depending upon your character proclivities − to resist. Since, as Odysseus remarks in Book XIX of his *Odyssey*, 'the very presence of a weapon provokes a man to use it,'[2] and since a propitious woman with no clothes on cries out to be similed with a loaded gun, I am bound to admit that, on the sadly rare occasions when some naked nubile has pressed herself out of the blue into bed with me, I have never yet succeeded in persuading her to hold her fire, or even in attempting to do so. This sorry state of affairs takes us straight back to character, which in my case is pathetically Humbertical, as you see yet again, with only the slight saving grace that, being a novelist to boot,[3] I have the minimal decency not to deny it entirely behind my buffering screens, and to conceal less than half of it, approximately, from you.

And since, moreover, the right kind of propitiously propinquitous nubile can, even when swathed in Aran sweaters and buttock-hugging jeans, still be brightly likened to a double-barrelled Purdey charged with buckshot in its black-leather carry-case, the gentle reader − and especially the psychotically violent one − can prettily picture my rapture on the telephone last Monday, when Audrey phoned to say not only had she changed her plans and would like to accept our house-party invitation after all, but could Jennifer please come too?

---

[1]  Even though these scruples appear not to inhibit the mallard drakes on our stretch of the Greenadder Water.

[2]  'Name and date the first American to seriously propose gun control.' Candidate question for next release of Puerile Pursuits.

[3]  As opposed to Rudneigh Bletherington, who is a complete idiot to boot.

## 84

# Our House-party Guests

Mention must at last be made of the architecture of our house. Now your traditional stone-built Berwickshire farmhouse might be represented like this:

If the reader sees hohself as gazing from the east, the sunrise advancing behind hoh, the weekdaily ear-splitting rampage of illegally lowflying fighter-bombers not yet commenced above hoh, then the tail of the en dash is the back of what in times past was the workaday and servants' part of the house, the gable pointing north into the farmyard, while the circumflex denotes the higher, posher quarters, the gable angling from east to west, with the front windows looking south to the sun.

In those terms, what is different and special about our present dwelling may be suggested so:

The additional circumflex built on to the front represents a nineteenth-century addition to an original eighteenth-century structure (an entire extra front gable, the reception rooms large and high, the sturdy picture rails indicative, the wide sitting-room bay window looking down over rolling slopes to the reputedly trout-rich Greenadder Water) no doubt funded from some cyclical boom in pan-British agricultural affluence not unconnected with London-based English imperialism and God-franchised exploitation of wherever-the-sun-never-set.

But let us never get bogged in political gripes.

And anyway the gentler point being made today is that our house is surprisingly large. Less grand and salubrious, to be sure, than Abbotsford by the Tweed. Less populous and hilarious during the week, perhaps, than Shandy Hall in its heyday. But Greenadder Farmhouse is nonetheless sufficiently imposing, spacious and architecturally complex to:

(a) **kindle onlooking impotent envy in critics** along the lines of why should two unmarried adults and a cat (albeit a very large, imposing and spacious cat – no-one dares disagree with this) either want or deserve to live in a mansion like that?

(b) **cost us a relative fortune to heat**, particularly now that the Prime Creep and the GAGAs have temporarily got away with impositioning VAT on domestic heating fuel;

And (c) **play its occasional part in the great tradition of The House Party**, without which the history of the novel – from Homer through Henry James and P.G. Wodehouse, and right into this present moment – would otherwise be quite otherwise.

Hence it was, sufficiently rich in our accommodational assets, and credit cards to take to the off-licence, that we decided some weeks ago to throw a revision party over last weekend: a kind of rolling sociable seminar-stroke-debauch during which those contributors to this book most indefatigable and still living would gather to revel in our clean cool late November air as together we hiked the heath before early dark, to guzzle with revitalized appetites our honest country fare, and to exchange views and express final recommendations regarding perfection of this work for publication. By how many hundreds of pages should the penultimate text be pruned? Which dozens of flirtatious digressions should be minimized, what score of irritating footnotes to expunge,[1] and so forth?

---

[1] 'Or better, how few to leave in?' [J.R.]*

  *   *'Surely the best thing about Humbert's footnotes is that they aren't a lot worse than Coleridge's in* Biographia Literaria*?' [P.C.]*

Our survivors from the seventeenth century (Louis and Hélène, the Chevalier and Achilles Lefranc, even Jean-Baptiste and Mathilde) would naturally be with us too, though only as memic wraiths these days, who might be counted on to enrich our intercourse with their resonance, but not to clutter the bedrooms or hog the nosh. On the somna/soma planes our principal invitees were obviously Janet Rosencrantz, Paul Chalicer, and Audrey Macpherson too – Audrey not so much for what she had already contributed (though she did do us proud with our emblematic ruffs in Spain, in Chapter 18) but because I wished to exert gentle pressure on her to actually *read* the latest laserprint of all chapters up to 82, to comment and criticise freely, to advise on historical correctness, and in particular to respond to the question whether Louis XIII may have had one or two illegitimate children other than our Louis Morel?

We know, for example, that this most dismally self-conscious and emotionally anal king had a phase of ludicrous infatuation with the teenage Mademoiselle de Hautefort, and later something similar with the less ravishingly beautiful but also less waspish and more sentimentally sympathetic Mademoiselle de La Fayette. But we also know that both these mawkish attachments were cunningly aborted by the Cardinal (now in his ascendancy, as he wasn't when, according to the Chevalier, he conspired against the young Countess Morel) *before* they ever got beyond the monarch's puerile poems and ponderous love songs and into anything so noticeable and entertaining for the court as ballooning bellies and right royal bastardy. But it does not follow, does it, that there were no other favoured ladies, perhaps less elevated than the famous Mademoiselles, upon whom the pathetic king may have gone and done the humpy-grump, even if only as an exercise to limber him up for the loathsome labour of mounting his hideous wife for the sake of France – and that in the knowledge that all the nation knew that *even if* she hadn't actually shagged the Duke of Buckingham, as so many supposed, nevertheless she certainly would have loved to?[2]

And if there were these other ladies – sexual stalking horses, one

---

[2] As to her intercourse with Mazarin, while we accept that the Sun King himself *may* not have been adulterously fathered by the Second Cardinal, we challenge anyone who has pored studiously over their likenesses to claim the same for the Sun King's brother.

might say, for the not very virile royal rider – and if any of them had babies by him, then how much abstruse evidence could Audrey adduce for me, and, above all, had I any hope of uncovering a later encounter between such an illegitimate royal daughter, preferably, and our own Count Morel of Bigorre, or else (as the last of last resorts) of credibly making it up?[3]

With all that at stake you can imagine the depths of my despair when Audrey, the first of our coveted guests to reply, phoned up to say No. She thanked me (somewhat coolly, it must be confessed, as she claimed to have had to pay a surcharge on the postage) for sending my kilos of pages but emphatically regretted that she must decline our house-party invitation due to having too many new lectures to prepare for the impending winter term. However, she would do her best to read my typescript sometime.

Our heavy hearts, especially mine, since I never cook when we have visitors, were much lightened later that week by Paul and Janet, who both accepted, and then numbed as if by kryptonite ten days thereafter when they both phoned within two hours of one another – to cancel with jubilant apologies. Paul because he had been summoned at short notice to the University of Minnesota to receive the Great Guffem Award: for the most successful plagiarism[4] of Dickens to be published in the previous calendar decade. The prize money was only $500 and no-one was paying his fare, but the prestige, Paul insisted, was incalculable. And anyway he's a sucker for that sort of razz, is our Paul, such that not even my threats of tears, or desperate promises to billet him

---

[3] If we had the qualifications of a formula writer – which is to say someone who writes the kind of book someone else could have written just as well, and often better, and then writes the same book twenty-five times – why on earth should we bother to go to the trouble of telling you all these truths, when we could much more easily press ahead with our scantily disguised autobiographical novel detailing my simultaneous adulterous liaisons with the Princess of Wales and the Duchess of York, and the crowning glory of that final night with them both in bed together, in the mews flat above the sports club sauna?

[4] Paul has since insisted, on pain of our sexcommunication, that this most cankerous of literary denigrations be sanitized to the coveted 'pastiche'.

in the same bedroom as Janet Rosencrantz, could dent his glitz-mad resolve.[5]

As to Janet, her excuse made me really angry. It was, she explained with audible nervousness – quite right too – that the *Sunday Crimes* had offered her a commission to cover the forthcoming international feminists' conference in Prague, on 'The Positive Demasculinization of Typography'. Air fares and hotel bills paid, generous subsistence, plus a fee for her piece which few other British newspapers could afford to match.

'But what a load of shitty crap,' I protested.

'Not all of it,' she objected defensively.

'Prove it?' I demanded aggressively.

So she instantly faxed me the programme, and that made me angrier still. Screeds of drivel about nothing, plus a three-day agenda stuffed with lectures and workshops on issues and motions such as:

Macho typesetters' jargon such as 'full-out right justified text' to be replaced by 'regular dextrous text flow', the 'large bullet' [●] to yield to the 'super nipple', the 'double dagger' [††] to be scrapped in favour of the 'twin tampon', and so forth. All that was bad enough. But the one that made me really tremble with rage was the final-day open debate on whether Garamond, long hailed as a masterpiece of typesetting design, should henceforth be redescribed as 'a mistresspiece of typesetting design', in view of the data recently packaged by feminists at the University of Texas that the aesthetic supremacy of 'his' typeface was not due so much to Claude Garamond himself (now said to be less of a creative artist than previously thought, and really quite cloth-eyed) but rather to the good wife behind him.

'This *is* a load of shitty crap!' I howled at Janet when I phoned her right back.

Well, yes, she eventually agreed. But it was nonetheless a jaunt she couldn't turn down. She might make useful contacts there, she valued getting a foot in the *Sunday Crimes*, she owed it to her family not to ignore the money, and she also had a number of relatives in Eastern Europe whom she had long wanted to visit – which she could do quite cheaply from Prague.

---

[5] And besides, he concluded with finality – as if such a tawdry consideration must be sure to console a Scot – his ticket was already bought.

Those were arguments I couldn't decently refute. And even if I refuted them indecently, with all the refutational indecencies at my disposal, I know from all too tragic experience when a lady is not to be swayed. Hence it was that I had slumped into a gulf of sullen acceptance of the burden of having to write the remainder of my book myself – when Audrey phoned again to delight me with the intelligence that she wished to exercise her long-established mind-changing prerogative and accept our weekend invitation after all.

The reason?

That the GAGAs had eased her workload by allocating increased civilizing funding for the employment of more junior lecturers in humanizing subjects such as history?

'You must be joking, Humbert,' said Audrey.

No, the clincher was Jennifer, whose mother felt she would benefit from a breath of fresh air out of Glasgow, to cheer her out of the trauma of having her pony-tailed zoological boyfriend 'come out' on her by revealing his recently discovered preference for a beardless[6] but like-minded first-year mathematician picked up in the University chess club. Although Jennifer's blood test had proved HIV-negative, said Audrey, the poor girl was still very shaken and subdued, and had showed no sign of outgoing sexual inclination since.

It was thus with pleasant intimations of *déjà vu, encore vu* and *vous toutes nues* that I drove out of the Lammermuirs of Lucia fame last Saturday afternoon, down potholed B roads of mashed-rabbit-and-pheasant fame – via Duns of Dunce Scotus, Jim Clark and no-traffic-lights fame, to pick them up off the train at Berwick. Now despite and because of my having been assured on the phone by a disembodied chimpanzee at Newcastle that 'all services are running normally today', how could I be amazed to learn at the station itself that the WhatRail? express – which on an exceptional day meanders from Glasgow to London via Edinburgh and Berwick with only overcrowding, sickening lurching, foul catering and overflowing toilets to regret – had today performed more normally with a two-hour delay just east of Motherwell on account of its engine failure? This gave me plenty of time for ample shivers in the platform

---

[6] Of course we do not imply that Jennifer has a beard. As to the faintest golden down upon her sultry upper lip, you are urged, if you can get your tongue round it, to synaesthesize the sweetest-skinned peach.

waiting room while digesting the *Guardian* followed by two computer magazines and indulging in a strangely warm and fantastically fulfilling reverie of the sort that wouldn't likely be believed in any novel or even if recounted while attempting to be adjudged 'unfit to stand trial' under oath in a Court of Law.

By the time the sick locomotive eventually wheezed alongside the platform like Melville's wounded monster in the early dusk I found despite the foggy chill that my armpits were moist and my neck taut with tension. Nor were the tight dynamics of my anticipatory emotions relaxed in the slightest as I perceived the two shoulderbagged Macpherson women to be shadowed by an unexpected companion: shambling along half-behind half-between them in his unbuttoned belt-loose faded grey raincoat of the sort we used to call bumfreezers.

Embracing my invited guests less in the hot passion of heterosexual welcome than stiffly with the sudden shock of horror I exclaimed:

'Wringhim!'

'Morning, Seale,' he snarled like white fire in the night, and my spirits sank to a deeper shelf as I intuited his drinking at lunchtime, drinking on the train, and drinking throughout the two-hour delay as well.

'But what are you doing here?' I protested.

'Come to sort you out about my fucking pamphlet, you cunt,' he said. 'Now where's the fucking car?'

# Home to Roast Truths?

Readers of every degree of violence must now be persuaded that my regard for Wringhim Knox is sincere and considerable. As a magnetic original (simultaneously attractive and repulsive), as a primal screamer in Scottish consciousness, and as a rarely gifted and consummately accomplished novelist, Wringhim has long-sinus secured my inalienable admiration and personal envy. But then again, and at the same time, I confess, before last Saturday it would never have occurred to me to attempt anything so drastic as to invite Wringhim into my home for any reason, never mind to intrude upon and coarsely sully that longed-for convivial weekend amid my womenfolk.

Thus it was, as we drove home from Berwick through the sleet driving down from Siberia and settling alarmingly as snow on our higher Lammermuir ground, that I was extremely angry with Wringhim, and doubly so, without shouting about it, when I realized how extremely angry he was with me (and with almost every other traitor known to him, including 'that slimy cunt Rankles', who, by the evidence of the morning's *Crimes*, was 'going for a fucking gong' by publishing lickshittlish articles supportive of Prince Charles and his right to be '*our* fucking King'. And if my sicklied-over ire was trebled by a stark presentiment of Koo's intense displeasure when soon and snowdrifts permitting she would clap eyes upon our uninvited guest, it was quadrupled again by Audrey's unapologetic revelation that as it happened she hadn't yet had time to make a start on my pages but rather had been correcting essays all the way, and had even not minded the two-hour delay outside Motherwell, as it gave her more time for marking.

Wringhim it was, in consequence, who had confiscated my chapters from their intended participant (later, during dinner, Jennifer would tell me that she too had asked to have a look, but her mother would not let her) and groused through them with ever escalating fury, during those four hours that should have been two. Wherefore such rage against me?

It was, so Wringhim duly gave me to understand – between salvos of growls, snorts and curses – on account of the many objective atrocities

I had committed, and in particular my unprovoked and unmerited trespasses against himself, which he would undoubtedly sue me for to the grave if he thought for a moment I was worth it, and if he were the sort of spiteful London Society Drone that had nothing better to do than squander his time and talents on vindictive litigation.

'Terribly relieved to hear it,' I muttered, as I steered round a fallen dead-elm limb, and Wringhim began his preliminary catalogue of my sins against him.

I had, he attested, caricatured his identity. I had libelled him with respect to his drinking habits, crassly simplisticized the current political situation and his deeply pondered and passionately embraced convictions concerning it,[1] I had frivolously cartooned his *'Cannibal . . . '* beyond any hopes of recognition outside Scotland—

'I thought', I protested here, 'that I—'

'You shut your fucking cakehole, Seale,' said Wringhim. 'And listen to me . . . '

Now I'm sorry if this is going to offend you, but frankly I decline to replicate verbatim any more of Wringhim's very direct speech last Saturday. I'm not miles above the odd eff and cee words myself – for catharsis, emphasis, minimalistic authenticity of characterization, poetic assonance, clognitive dissonance, and for certain specifically practical speech acts such as critiquing the happiest plaintiff in the household when he sharpens himself on our sofas – but I'm buggered if I'm going to have three thousand of them gratis from Wringhim diluting with defilements this vitally almost-penultimate chapter, which will already be more than adequately reprehensible. Wringhim's further onslaught of grunts, slurs, oaths, curses and more picturesquely constructed obscenities may thus be compared to the entire page of asterisks which does not appear in ?? of *The Life and Opinions of Tristram Shandy*, as we paraphrase for the purer his further contentions that:

Not only had I abused my privilege of possessing the entire raw text of his 'chief work' on my hard disk, by lifting large chunks out of it without

---

[1] If, say, I had adequately comprehended *both* the parallels *and* the differences between Catalonia–v.–Spain and Scotland–v.–England today, I could not have failed to score fabulous points with respect to language, and also to record with interest that while Catalonia has already had the Olympic Games, Scotland gets fobbed off with the Commonwealth.

his permission, and parading them out of context, and to the detriment of his reputation as not-just-creative-artist-but-serious-thinker-too – but for the sake of putting over a number of cheapo philosophical fast ones on the unsuspecting reader I had imputed to him, Wringhim, certain ontological subscriptions and premissory fragilities which were patently best attributed to myself, and I had furthermore and most fundamentally abominably violated and exploitated his misplaced trust in me by deliberately and repeatedly delaying completion of the typesetting of his satirical pamphlet. And why had I did this deed?

It was, swore Wringhim, with the sole object of pre-emptively publishing my book first, having plagiarized the best part of his title. Now I couldn't disagree that most of his accusations were not entirely without substance. And yes it was also not totally untrue that I had deliberately procrastinated a bit over typesetting his horrible pamphlet. The last time he had hounded me about it on the phone I had informed him the hitch was his own fault: he having insisted on antiquated non-ranging folio figs in his footers,[2] causing me to have to send to California for a set

---

[2] The footer folio being the number at the page's bottom, if that's where it is, as Wringhim commanded. If you are privileged to be reading a genuine first edition of the present work, you will find the page numbers at the top, to the left and right of the folio headers. This is page *706* as numbered elegantly in italic 'ranging figs'. The figs, or figures, are 'ranging' in that the numeral characters are all of equal height and ascend uniformly from the line base. None descends below the base. If, by contrast, the number of this page were rendered in *non*-ranging figs, which might give you the runs for different reasons, it might look like 694. Other non-ranging-fig pages would be 126 and and 290. The one (1) looks like a shrivelled 'I', the two (2) like a failed keyhole and the zero (0) like a small cat's anus. If you place a larger number like 983 beside a smaller number such as 102 you may feel, as we do, that non-ranging figs look pretty antediluvian and should have no place in serious twenty-first-century typesetting. Wringhim, however, maintains that the fuddy old non-ranging figs are an essential accoutrement to the classic austerity of his rhetoric, and it was hence this quibble that enabled us to get away with postponing the public advent of his pamphlet by a further seven months.

of customized soft fonts, receipt of which I was still awaiting. Now that was a downright lie, but a spotlessly white one so far as my conscience was concerned, since my sole motivation was the hope that the longer his pamphlet could be kept from the thorny one-way bourne of publication, the greater the chance that Wringhim would give up on it first, or die before he rumbled me. Lawyers did this sort of thing to each other and their clients all the time, I knew to my calculable cost, and doctors to their patients, and so why should not altruistic novelists engage in it too, who were nobler than lawyers and doctors in all honesty, and also in every other respect except income?

But I couldn't tell that to Wringhim, now could I? Because if I did, with him in his present frame of delirium, there would have been a serious risk of fisticuffs on the front seat, and hence of me crashing the van. I should perhaps explain that our runabout vehicle is a Volkswagen Transporter, which currently was transporting me behind the wheel, Audrey gazing moodily out of the passenger window at the snowflakes, Wringhim sandwiched irately between us, while Jennifer sprawled sleepily in the back, on top of piled shoulderbags, Safeways bags, cartons of books, blankets, Wellington boots, and old potato sacks for the back wheels to grip on when the very worst came again.

And so what could I tell to Wringhim?

'You must realize, Wringhim,' I tried, 'that there is no copyright in titles. And even if there were, and given that my novel looks likely to be published before your pamphlet, I would certainly be happy to grant you my kind permission to borrow the best part of my title.'

I realized before I finished that Wringhim would not be best pleased by my comment, but on that road and in those moments, with half an anxiety looking forward to the last slope of variable track up to the farmhouse, I simply could not think of anything less unpleasing to say to him. My punishment came quickly and would fill the next ten minutes with hundreds of eff words, cee words and YouKnowWho words, in between which Wringhim managed to convey that not only was I a contemptible plagiarist of text and titles, but I hadn't even the marbles to perceive (and hence to snidely purloin) the politically point-scoring value of the irony in his. His pamphlet title, that was:

*Succeeding at Sex in London.*

'Which particular irony might that be, Wringhim?' I wondered with miraculous patience.

It derived, he gave me to understand, from the consideration that no reader who read his pamphlet, understood its premises, followed its impeccable arguments and hence was convinced by its inevitable conclusions, would be left in any doubt that in no meaningful sense – according to any politically valid, socially desirable and personally fulfilling criteria – *is it possible to succeed at sex in London at all.*

And if I were a skilful and successful plagiarist—

'Like Shakespeare and T.S. Eliot, Picasso and Salvador Dali?' I couldn't refrain from interjecting.

—I would have appreciated his terrific title irony unaided.

'Talking of successful plagiarists . . . ' I murmured, changing to lowest gear for the final snow-whited slope.

This elicited a suspiciously interrogative grunt from Wringhim.

'What about your *Cannibal*?'

What about his fucking *Cannibal*?

Boosted by newly unshakable confidence that we would get back to the ranch without spending the night in a snowdrift first while the roast pork and hot apple sauce was left to Koo and Claws, I indulged myself in drawing Wringhim's attention to the plot-structural parallels between his *Cannibal* and my own earlier story in which an earlier Prime Creep is also politically assassinated, in an earlier piece of passable poetic justice and reader satisfaction.

Thus was unleashed such a torrent of obscene abuse that Audrey was roused to take an audibly deep breath, slap the abuser's knee, and say:

'Wringhim? Please. You promised.'

Chastened more than I would have imagined possible by Audrey's intervention, Wringhim left off swearing for the moment, but kept his aggressive end up, or so he thought, with some insufferably condescending remarks about certain astonishing plot-structural similarities between my own first novel and the early Kingsley Amis.

'As you will or should be aware, Wringhim,' I retorted smugly, 'there is no copyright in plot. Not, at least, until the bureaucrats in Brussels run out of worse things to do. And in any case, insofar as a modicum of honourable inspirational homage might conceivably be posititried between the early Humbert and the early Kingsley, it is certainly no greater a modicum than the great-great modicum positittiable between the early Kingsley and the early Aldous. Refer, if you will, to the irresistibly inviting plot thumbnail tabulated by Cyril Connolly in Chapter 6 of *Enemies of Promise*, with which the early Kingsley was presumably not unfamiliar, don't you think?'

Mercifully I don't talk like that all the time, though thankfully I can if needs bust. It's a philosophically backgrounded novelist's version of karate, I suppose: you should only resort to it in emergencies, or when some overweeningly vaulting twatface overreaches the tops of your nostrils. On the present occasion, I knew – since, with all the alcohol still swilling in him, Wringhim would be a bit sluggish following it, and also because he wouldn't have read Connolly, since he can't abide books *about* writers and writing, unless they happen to be *by* 'real writers' – that it would shut Wringhim up for long enough for me to scrunch the van to a halt in the farmyard, leap out, pad round to liberate Jennifer through the side door, clap my hands with bonhomie flogged in the snowflakes, and exclaim:

'Right, everyone! Made it! Now, who's not for a cheering drink?'

# Apéritifs

It's strangely true that our Saturday evening began less frightfully than it might have – with Audrey apologizing to Koo (as she had not to me) for bringing Wringhim. They had bumped into one another in the College Club during Friday lunchtime, she explained with evident embarrassment. And when Wringhim heard what was afoot, and how Janet and Paul were unable to attend, he had declared what a nice surprise it would be for me to have the benefit of his company and counsel instead.

'Not to worry,' said Koo hospitably, though I could tell by a slight subcutaneous flicker in her left eyelid that she was only partially delighted. 'There's masses of food.'

'And masses to drink?' queried Wringhim, as if he were Lowry's wounded Consul.

Nor was he entirely wide of the mark, in the sense that the various interpersonal imperfections and embarrassments, remembrances of shady things past, fallings short of absolute universal agape, etc, combined with it being the makars' Saturday night, after all, conspired quickly to reach out for and successfully seize hold of a Panurgent dimension of amelioration in high-quality alcohol, which led by diminishing degrees to the evening's being punctuated with a number of heated debates concluding just short of real rows, and framed throughout by an ever denser marginalia of regrettable scurrility.

We're not going to relive every detail now, so you can certainly heave a great sigh of relief on that score. But we do think it only fair to admit that Wringhim, once we got him into the house, was markedly less objectionable in his behaviour, more diffident and subdued in his discourse, than either Koo or I would have believed possible. Even to the point of managing from time to time to drop his aggressive surnaming, and address me less coldly as Humbert. It occurred to me that this remission might be partly thanks to the strangeness, for him, of our isolated country situation; to the scale of the architecture, the grandeur of the big front rooms ('What's a cunt like you doing living in a place

710

like this?' he demanded [as I showed our guests round the house], but in a muted mutter); very like the unexpectedly docile reaction of Captain Claws the other day, when for the first time in his long and happily neutered life with us he had to be taken down to the vet.

In the brittle flippancy of dodgy ice-breaking, I jovially remarked upon this parallel as I led the visitors back down the main staircase and towards their second and Wringhim's third apéritif. Either he didn't follow my drift, or else he allowed the shaft to pass without flak. But Jennifer said:

'Where is the cat, Uncle Humbert?'

'Not out in the snow, that's for sure. More likely under a duvet somewhere, hiding from Wringhim!'

'You mean he's not dead?'

'Certainly not.'

'So why take him to the vet, Uncle Humbert?'

'Teeth!' I told her. 'It seems he's older than we thought – got him off a flitting neighbour eight years ago, you see, and she must have been lying about his age. Anyway, some of his gnashers are ailing. Reminds me painfully of myself, I'm sorry to say. Ha-ha-ha.'

'If he's that old,' said Jennifer seriously, 'why don't you just get him put down?'

'What? When he's still so much happier than us? Delights in sunbathing, revels in slaughtering tits, throbs with passion for his dinner? No, no, no, *no!* Just got to get the antibiotics down him twice a day for a bit, and he'll be good for a few years yet. We older folk, you see, Jennifer,' I explained as I handed her mother another brimming gin-and-it – we were back in the kitchen now – 'we older folk rather see it as . . . *practice.*'

'Practice for *what*, Uncle Humbert?'

'Caring for the ashamedly elderly! Here . . . '

'But surely, Uncle Humbert, I mean . . . ' she said hesitantly, glancing at the four sort-of adults in the room, as she accepted her glass of chilled Frascati.

'Don't be coy,' said her mother.

'Well, would you not rather care for an elderly cat?'

Winking heavily at Audrey, I replied:

'Hmn! Yes, I see what you—'

'Fifteen minutes,' called Koo, from the far side of the hob.

'Right,' I nodded, now serving Wringhim his third foaming stein of live-in-the-bottle ninety-shilling ale mixed equally with my own supercharged homebrew. If I were honest I couldn't categorically deny a naughty notion to ply him with so much drink so quickly that even Wringhim could not fail to pass out prematurely while the rest of us savoured our dinner. So I took a reserve bottle of ninety-shilling upstairs with us, him and me, to my electronic dream-factory. There, during twenty-five of the fifteen minutes specified by Koo, I showed my truculent customer a few textual tricks and typographical somersaults on-screen and laser-printed him a sparkling proof of the first chapter of his dismal pamphlet just as he'd ordered: silly little non-ranging figs and all. Despite his habitual hostility in the presence of so much Japanese hardware and American software, he was unable to disagree that the results looked not unsatisfactory.

He was also alcoholically gullible enough to swallow my promise to have the whole pamphlet output to the same standard and posted to him by the end of the following week.

Hence the relative amity with which Scotland's premier novelist followed me down the staircase for the second time – until, by the landing window, as he paused to contemplate the millions of big fleshy snowflakes from Siberia that were obliterating our van in the farmyard and thickening a thick mattress of white on the flat porch roof below, he was once more put in mind of our mountain monk Glang Pandita in Chapter 76. This was where he'd got to, and stuck in, when the WhatRail? express finally wheezed into Berwick Station.

'What's your solution, Humbert?' he now inquired again, less hatefully than in the car park.

'What's yours, Wringhim?' I repeated lightly, as we returned to the kitchen to find the ladies still drinking steadily, and dinner apparently no more imminent than it had been twenty-seven minutes ago. Koo and Audrey were standing on opposing sides of the work-top, tinkering with green salads and fruit salad respectively, and deep in a confab about Brunhild's forthcoming hysterectomy – while Jennifer sat hunched over the kitchen table, in the corner by the radiator, as she pored through *Satellite Times*.

'What? Not ready?' I exclaimed, making to freshen everyone's glass yet again.

'Five minutes,' said Koo meaningfully.

'Let the height of the mountain equal—'

'Look, Wringhim,' I interrupted him. 'I'm sure I'm much too simplified to follow it mentally. Why don't you scribble it down, while I challenge Jennifer to a quick bout of ping-pong? More beer?' I offered him, as I slid the kitchen notepad and a ballpoint across the table in his direction.

No, he'd had enough beer, thank me. Time now to 'move on' to a 'large single malt with one cube of ice, please'.

Having supplied Wringhim with a vast glass, a bowl of ice, and a litre bottle of overstrength Glenmorangie left over from Paul's last visit, I rubbed my hands suggestively and said:

'Game for it, Jennifer?'

'Any time, Uncle Humbert,' she replied as she followed me down the five narrow steps to the dining room.

'Fighting fit?'

'Fitter than you, Uncle Humbert.'

'Want a handicap?'

'Why not let's play one game first, Uncle Humbert? And then see who needs the handicap?'

'That's the spirit!' I enthused, as I offered her choice of bats.

Perhaps I should explain that our dining room is one of the large Victorian rooms at the front of the house, looking south. Due to still having lots of friends and relations with small children we've kept the decor and furniture mainly functional and 'fun', which enables us to not resent too deeply the needs of all two-year-olds to flick their baked beans and bits of hard-boiled egg at the wallpaper during leisurely Sunday lunches for all the families. While the dining table points out into the window bay, the table tennis is at right angles to this, and parallel to the wall shared with the kitchen: making perfect dopily supervised entertainment for your hyperactive ten-year-olds as their elders and begetters linger endlessly over coffee and choice marijuana.

'Ready?' I called to Jennifer from the hall end.

'Readier than you, Uncle Humbert.'

'Bounce for service?'

'You start, Uncle Humbert. I'll beat you anyway.'

'We'll see about that,' I murmured darkly, and kicked off with a vicious spin serve that Jennifer could not return, due to her mother passing behind her with a platter of garlic bread.

'Play it again, ma'am?'

'No need, Uncle Humbert. That can be your handicap.'

'Hmn. Well . . . '

The last time I beat Jennifer at table tennis had been in the Vaucluse during the sweltering July of 1985, when Audrey and Brunhild had brought their broods down from Dijon. At that time she'd had so little breasts to speak of that she was able to play me wearing no more than a pair of skimpy knickers without either of us experiencing embarrassment or me point-missing distraction.

Now, I was about to discover, things were very different.

She'd obviously played a lot of ping-pong in the years between – both at school and in the StrathKelvin students' union – whereas Koo and I never play except with visitors, and also I, at the precise time of writing, have advanced to very nearly the same great age as the heavyweight boxing champion of the world. Hence it was in great alarm that I discovered that, without an ounce of lenient charity on my part, Jennifer not only fought me back from 15–10 to 15–15 with a series of devilish oriental drop shots but then, and with her own service to come, and wittingly as a stroke of manipulative feminine gamespersonship, she suddenly unveiled her secret weapons in the form of whipping off her pullover (I did have the heating institutionally high) to reveal no bra and lots besides beneath her skin-tight tee-shirt.

So double-whammammaried was I by Jennifer's dirty trick that my next two returns were netted, almost before I knew it, like so many dead minnows. That took us to 17–15 in her favour. Desperate now (I don't mind giving young ladies a head start, but I never let them beat me willingly), I tried what I'd twice seen Jean-Claude Van Damme do so successfully in *Kickboxer*, namely shutting your eyes so much the better to zenfully kick your opponent's head in with your bare feet. This, however, proved so inadequate to my own toiling exigencies in hand that it moved Jennifer to rest her bat upon the table for a moment and ask me seriously, perhaps reflecting upon the several tins of chilled Stella she had no doubt noticed me downing, if I was sure I was feeling all right.

'Fine thank you, Jennifer,' I replied with grave avuncularity. 'It's just . . . ' and then again as the solution hit me like Clint Eastwood as the Thunderbolt:

'It's just!'

'Just *what*, Uncle Humbert?'

And I told her that while I was overjoyed to note that her bosom had grown every inch as opulent as her mother's had ever been, had anyone ever told her that her east tit (taking her forehead as the north pole, with myself as reader of her anatomical map) was apt to jounce at least an inch wider than her west tit, when she sliced her backhand serve?

Such was the ruffling of commendable feminine modesty thus engendered that I was easily able to googly Jennifer's final serve in my favour to 16–19 and then coast home to 21–19 with a clean sweep of mixed spin serves that Jennifer was much too flustered to adequately counter-cut, thus resulting in a triumph for Humbert very much in pleasurable mind of the man finally coming on top where he should be at the end of any closely fought spanking battle between my two most favourite sexes.[1]

'You're a swine, Uncle Humbert,' murmured Jennifer moodily as she shrugged back into her sweater.

'All's fair in sex and ping-pong!' I retorted cheerily. 'Change ends?'

'No,' said Koo forcefully, materializing behind Jennifer bearing a tray of plated salads. 'Starter wines, please. Now.'

Back in the kitchen, as I hoisted the Tavel rosé from the drinks fridge, I heard Wringhim grunt:

'Here.'

Looking round, I espied our self-invited guest arising from the kitchen table and approaching me with two torn pages of notepad raised like teachers' flashcards, one in each fist.

'You've cracked Glang Pandita, have you, Wringhim?' I inquired with genial scepticism.

'Yes,' he asserted harshly. 'I have.'

'Let's take it to table, shall we?' I suggested, leading the way. 'Else we might get flogged by the management.'

'Well?' he demanded four minutes later, when I had poured the rosé, Koo had lit the candles, and we were all sitting comfortably in anticipation of our deep-fried goat's cheese on a bed of green *salade tiède* with a dressing of olive oil, crushed garlic and Provençal herbs. 'That's right, isn't it?'

Affecting affected professorial concentration I scanned again through his two pages of bold black characters so uncannily reminiscent of Rimbaud. 'Insofar as I can follow these funny algebraic hieroglyphs, Wringhim,' I agreed, 'they would seem to constitute *a correct solution*. But they certainly aren't the right answer.'

'Why the fuck not?' he growled, sniffing his rosé suspiciously, as if it might be cheap real wine watered down with spiders' piss.

---

[1] 'You contemptible bastard. You're even breaking the *most* fundamental rule of all which is that even if the storyteller is compelled occasionally to protrude his* *haïssable moi* he* must *never* attempt to represent himself* as more noble and lovable than he* is known to be in real life.' [P.C.*]

   **\* 'Typically offensive to women.' [J.R.]**

'Because the right answer is *the most elegant* solution. And yours isn't. This is easily deducible from the consideration that *the most elegant solution* is much more elegant than your solution. So there.'

'Don't wait for the men,' said Koo to the other ladies, and offering them the garlic bread. 'Just start.'

'What is *the* most elegant solution?' rasped Wringhim.

And then he got grumpier still when I refused to divulge it to him in person, but rather directed his attention to the hundreds of pages of Arthur Koestler's *The Act of Creation* from which, if memory had not failed entirely over an interval of twenty-five years, I had lifted the puzzle originally.

'If I tell you now, you see,' I explained appeasingly, 'you probably wouldn't repair to Koestler hereafter. And I want you to. I think you should. And I'm confident you'll thank me when you do.'

'Pretentious prick,' muttered Wringhim, who then – grudgingly, but seeing Audrey quaffing it back with evident relish opposite – began to suck at his far-from-cheap rosé.

And I think it was that fiscal aperçu – the *very* far-from-cheapness of the Tavel – that then tipped me into a prandial panic of sheer despair, of fathomless anguish at the emptiness, the futility and the supererogatory yet mindlessly Manichean cruelty of any universe that could put me to so much trouble (planning, housework, cooking for Koo, colossal expenditure on drink for me), all fondly with a view to facilitating informed and intelligent debate on the perfecting of my opus-in-hand, and only to leave me here like this: trapped in a snowbound two-day hellhole (for there certainly would be no snowploughing on the farm before Monday) with Wringhim, who had read my pages only very imperfectly, and with Audrey and Jennifer, who had read them not at all.

# Garlic on Garlic

'And it goes without saying,' said Audrey, 'that before you might consider helping a novelist to complete her or his novel, you must be clear what she or he was attempting to achieve with it.'

'Far be it . . . ' And with the passion of great sincerity I unpacked my view that the novelist is or should be the last person to affect to know what hos hopes to achieve in/with a given novel. 'Doesn't your mother remember her Wimsatt and Beardsley?' I inquired ominously of Jennifer.

'Big willies?' she replied curiously.

'However, . . . ' I hastened on, and proceeded to gloss, for the edification of our visiting Glaswegians, the cosmopolite verdict of Paul Chalicer: that what Humbert is up to is a sort of hardcopy hypertext, 'which, properly speaking, should be "hypotext"', in which the best bits are written by everybody else, most charismatically Paul himself, while Humbert scoops the royalties.[1]

'Is everyone warm enough?' asked Koo, as, from the head of our table she frowned through the unclosed centre panel of the dining-room window shutters: at the drifting white without.[2]

---

[1] 'Less our seven per cent for Amnesty, no doubt you won't mind my reminding you.' [J.R.]

[2] If you're topographically minded, and like to think of our seating plan as a **U**, then you've got Wringhim at two o' clock, Audrey at four, Koo at six, Jennifer at eight, me at ten, and the Berwickshire blizzard at twelve.*

    * *'Since, Humbert, your dining-room faces south, and given the universal map-reading convention that twelve o'clock equals north, your readers may wish to be reminded that what you have just told them is at double right angles to the truth. However, no doubt you will go on to claim that this too is key to the fiction.' [P.C.]*

'Whereas . . . ' Now I relayed the marginally less uncharitable hypothesis of Janet Rosencrantz: that what Humbert is evidently endeavouring to create might best be described as an all-enveloping fictive operating environment – analogous, in late twentieth-century computerspeak, to Unix or Windows, and possibly also to a US military body-bag – which no-one need ever leave, or at least not for a very long time.

Now Wringhim as he reached to hoist the bottle from the coaster, to pour himself the last of the second bottle of Tavel, gave grunt to his charge that what Humbert was currently attempting was nothing less fucking pretentious than a metaphor for existence itself.

'In what way?' I inquired, intrigued.

In that, he replied, having gargled a large mouthful of rosé (having once seen a programme on wine-tasting on Channel 4, when the football on STV had been cancelled due to frost[3]):

'Existence itself is the archetypal cheat, and so is your book.'

'Thanks very—'

However, he continued, he couldn't hold out much hope for me on that score.

'Why not?'

Because while existence is indubitably very shitty-cheaty (our discreet dilution of his over-blown obscenity) it is still the only existence we have, or ever will have. And so each of us is obliged to make the best of it – or the worst, depending on such factors as character, education, and whether one votes Conservative – in the knowledge that:

'It's now or never!' he croaked like a karaoke Elvis. 'But [shitty-cheaty] novels, on the other hand, you can borrow by the dozen from the public library.'

'Knowing Humbert,' nodded Audrey thoughtfully, 'as I have, and not having read his book—'

'As you haven't!' I reminded her helpfully.

'My guess is that part of his intention is a celebration of intelligent reading.'

'What do you mean, Mum?' asked Jennifer.

Audrey explained that she meant that she suspected that I hoped that even if, as she strongly suspected, billions of readers would never

---

[3] We learned this that night in Le Grand Bouchon, following the embarrassment over the waitress's *con gazeuse* (as she might have preferred it).

read my book, while many of those who began it would never be
bothered to finish it, nevertheless her impression was that many of the
dippers and perhaps also a few of the spurners might find themselves
despite themselves railroaded along the way to nip into their nearest
Waterstone's and invest in some worthwhile classics.

'Oh, Audrey!' I cried. 'Oh . . . Audrey!'

'Yes?' she replied suspiciously. 'What?'

'It's just . . . I mean . . . ' With tears close to my eyes I confessed
how nearly speechless she had made me, with the profoundly characteristic (of Audrey) and yet simultaneously unexpected generosity
of her supposition. And in that same split second it came to me,
with something of the lightning-flash clarity supposed to have been
hallucinated by St Paul on the road to Damascus, that before the present
work was concluded I must contrive to subtly work into it, together with
relinquishment of most proprietory rights in the matter (as one might
offer new computer software as *share*ware, strictly speaking, but not
totally *beer*ware), my idea for *Gulliver's Wife*.

'Oh yes?' sniffed Audrey sceptically. 'And what's that?'

As Koo, assisted by Jennifer, cleared away the salad plates and
served the soup, I recalled for the benefit of Audrey and Wringhim
the practice of Lemuel Gulliver of never learning – despite his many
hairy experiences abroad – to love staying at home with his wife and
kids. And even when, conveniently, at the end of his fourth and final
voyage he appears to resign himself to age and decay in what many
would regard as an agreeable homelife situation ('clean-smelling sheets,
and all the soft places to fall,' as Willie Nelson himself has put it) he is
unable to do so without an extremely offensive dig at women in general,
as personified by his own long-suffering Mrs.[4]

'For these reasons,' I concluded, meanwhile drawing the cork from
our first bottle of Château Fortia white, 'if I were a feminist pasticheur
or pasticheuse of any gender, I would be strongly attracted to the idea of
making a lot of money by writing Mistress Gulliver's version of events

---

4 'I began last week', confesses Gulliver, anent his return from the
'Houyhnhnms', 'to permit my wife to sit at dinner with me, at
the furthest end of a long table, and to answer (but with the
utmost brevity) the few questions I ask her. Yet the smell of
a Yahoo continuing very offensive, I always keep my nose well
stoped with rue, lavender, or tobacco leaves . . . '

in the first person, candidly including graphic coverage of my numerous affairs with potboys, grooms, gamekeepers, rakehells, Uncle Tom Cobloafers, and all, my hilarious experiences with elementary contraceptive devices, and preferably at least six steamy lesbian relationships with dominant younger women as well, to open my eyes to the sexual inadequacies of men at large, and of my husband himself in little.'

'Shite,' said Wringhim.

'Beg pardon?' I returned politely.

Tersely he opined that gender-grinding historical pastiches of the sort I limned were invariably a load of shite written by no-hopers with nothing but shite inside them.

'*You* did *Rob Roy's Women*!' I retorted lightly.

'That's different,' he answered shortly.

And certainly he had me there, since he knows I know his *Rob Roy's Women* is a masterpiece in a class of its own. I therefore got back at him by moving the goalposts a couple of feet, with:

'No-one's disputing, Wringhim, that the shite is as you say shite. My present point, inspired by Audrey's hypothesis, is simply that if some enterprising no-hoper were to score a big hit with *Gulliver's Wife*, then, as night follows day, there would be a revival of serious interest in – and possibly even actual reading of – *Gulliver's Travels* itself. The complete text, I mean, and not just some stripped-down "Lilliput" for the under-tens. And that would surely be A Good Thing, would it not? Now . . . ' By waitering round the table to pour the Château Fortia, I effectively arrested any further cloacality on the tip of Wringhim's tongue just long enough for Jennifer to inquire:

'What do you think, Koo?'

'About what?'

'What Uncle Humbert is trying to do?'

My parallel recollection is that Koo's reply was to the effect that whatever it was in cosmic terms that Uncle Humbert might imagine he was up to it was in any case high time he got it finished and sat down to hammer out something shorter and more commercial so we could start denting the overdrafts at last, but I was by this stage already involved in a further debate with Wringhim over the garlic.

Koo's fish soup, I should explain, is a delicious development of the traditional Scottish Cullen Skink. Based on the flesh of Arbroath Smokies and pulped butter beans with a larding of garlic and sprinkles of pepper, it is served in Provençal style with wafers of golden toast, cloves of garlic, and a bowl of grated cheese.

'What you do in Orange', I advised Wringhim, 'is to rub the wafers of toast with the fresh garlic, cream their uppers with a deck of delicious fresh garlic mayonnaise lightly dusted with paprika, then add half an inch of grated cheese, and finally float your wafers like little laden rafts in the sea of your soap till the cheese begins to melt, the toast turns soggy enough to cut with the side of your spoon, and another heavenly eating experience with garlic greets the gut.'

'Butter,' he muttered.

'Beg pardon?'

Butter, he repeated. Please, could he have some butter for his toast? He wasn't a fucking vampire, he stressed, and he had already consumed enough garlic this evening to last him well past the millennium. If he had of been a fucking vampire, he nodded balefully, he would already have choked to death on all that garlic. Since he hadn't choked to death, this proved, didn't it, that he absolutely was not a fucking vampire? But the fact remained that he'd had more than enough fucking garlic, and so please could we now have some fucking butter on the table?

'Please, Wringhim,' murmured Audrey, and the back of my mind was struck by a naughty image of her firmly exerting some admonitory anatomical pressure on him under the table – as I leapt up to fetch the butter from the kitchen, and floated back the singsong caution:

'Cheese minus garlic plus butter, eh? You'll die of a heart attack, Wringhim!'

'So will you,' he retorted shortly. 'So will everyone.'

'What about *you*, Jennifer?' I inquired as I returned brandishing the butter dish.

'About my heart, Uncle Humbert?'

'No, no, no! I'm sure that'll be lavishly protected for many years to come! No. I mean, what is your impression of what your poor old sort-of uncle is struggling to achieve? In his novel?'

Jennifer replied very reasonably that she thought she would need to know a bit more about the book, her mother having refused to allow her to read it (and here she moued at Audrey, in a very fourth-form manner) before she could venture a view.

I told her about as much as would cover the inside front flap of a generous hardback jacket.

Jennifer then (and the reader must now be enabled to deplore the fact that she had recently switched from Maths & Physics, for which she had an unusual aptitude, to Film, Media, Electronic Communications Studies and World Wide Wank Applications – this following her trauma with the zoological boyfriend boyfriending another lad in the chess club, and motivated largely by a new feeling that more Buddhistically holistical forms of understanding of the world were essential to her karma) displayed a natural talent for assimilating analysis of current issues within the great grey silky web of film and media metaphors, not to mention trite clichés.

Thus:

Uncle Humbert, she postulated, was, as it were, attempting, in some sense, to make a film about film-making: telling a story where the putative core story and the parasitic story about the story and the paraparasitic story about storytelling in the round themselves become characters in the metastatic story, competing for the reader's interest, sympathy, delight, disapproval, condemnation, or whatever.

'For I am the spirit of storytelling!'[5] I chanted in approving delight. 'More wine?' and I topped up her glass.

'It's a risky business,' she said in her own words, or possibly those of her History-of-the-Cinema lecturer, 'and one which no film-maker can hope to get away with more than once.'

'Like Truffaut?' I prompted her. 'In "Day For Night"?'

Jennifer then had the audacity to suggest that I must be suffering from delusions of senility to imagine for a moment that anyone would wish to compare any novel of mine to the films of an all-time genius such as François Truffaut, although she would concede that discussion of parallels with a more superficial bread-and butter kind of director such as the Brian De Palma of 'Body Double' might not be wholly irrelevant.

'If only', I confessed with candid wistfillyness, feeling the full force of four frowns upon me, 'I too could get my lecherous directorial hands on the youthful Melanie Griffith's lovely lissom naked body, I would quite happily settle for only being Brian de Palma. Or even Orson Welles!'

'You would only end up playing with yourself, Uncle Humbert.'

'The self-indulgence of director-as-star, you mean? Like Citizen Kane?'

---

[5] 'Plagiarized again. Definitely Thomas Mann. If I had to bet I'd put my pound on the last hundred pages of *Doctor Faustus*.' [P.C.]*
  *Right author, Paul, but your pound is nonetheless forfeit!*

'No,' said Jennifer. She meant like the fat old wanker sheriff in 'Touch of Evil'.

'Fax bell's ringing,' observed Koo, though how she could hear it through Bob Marley booming away through the hall speakers we'll never know because the beckoning thread of whether women have better upper-range hearing than men was lost just like their virginities when:

'Jesus, Uncle Humbert, what a size!' gasped Jennifer beside me.

'And how would you know, young lady?' rapped Wringhim with remarkable alacrity.

'You mind your mouth, Miss Macpherson,' warned her mother automatically.

'Likes his food, does he?' marvelled her daughter, whose admiration was fastened upon the advent of Captain Claws, who had marched into the dining room from the hall (very likely to complain about Bob Marley), mounted the pingpong table with a pad-padded thud, and was sphynxing our guests with the utmost unblinking severity.

And I've no idea how he wangled it, but by the time I got back from the drinks fridge with the second bottle of Château Fortia, Claws had diverted the table into a fierce debate about the relations between such ponderables as freedom from sex drive, childlessness, happiness, tragedy, fertility and (rounded up to the nearest whisker) the Very Nature of Sexual Success Itself. So, scenting the ghost of a chance to get some of my wines'worth out of the evening after all, I weighed in by wondering with gravely pursed lips whether, in order to be sexually successful, it was necessary to be politically assassinated?

'Some folk don't change much, do they?' sighed Audrey.

'What do you mean, Uncle Humbert?' asked Jennifer, whose eyes were brightly aroused.

'Let us ponder three piggies in point,' I suggested. 'Three of the billiest goaters of other men's wives, daughters, mothers, sisters and aunties in history, yes? Julius Caesar, assassinated by Brutus and colleagues. Henri Quatre of France, assassinated by Ravaillac, whether or not with the connivance of Queen Marie and the Duc d'Epernon.[6] And John Fitzgerald Kennedy, assassinated by take-your-pick. Now—'

'Marilyn,' grunted Wringhim.

'Beg pardon?'

For the next five minutes Wringhim – shlightly shlurrily, but not

---

[6] See *The Counts of Mount Venus*, final part.

incoherently – unpacked his theory that the originating issuer of the contract resulting in the killing of JFK was in fact Marilyn Monroe. Goaded by sexual jealousy, he maintained, and befuddled by costly pharmaceuticals unbeknown to evolution [hitherto], the good-hearted glamour girl had, in a rare moment of impulsive malice, set rolling a snowball she could never recall. And it was remorse over this spasm of deathly hate, and despair over the futility of her subsequent attempts to cancel the hit, that had finally enmeshed her in suicide.

'So tragic Marilyn, you would claim – despite her several failures: professional, marital, sexual, ontological – was nonetheless a morally purer person than the Duchessa Sanseverina?'

'What?'

Briefly I reminded everyone how, in *The Charterhouse of Parma*, when the ravishing Duchessa learns of the petty Prince's plan to have her darling nephew Fabrizio quietly snuffed in his citadel prison, she not only puts out a pre-emptive contract on the Prince, but also – finally mastering certain stirrings of conscience, of which, as a blueblooded vengeful Italian, she is ashamed – *she refuses to recall the contract* once the [present] threat to Fabrizio has passed!

'Does the Duchessa have any children?' asked Audrey grudgingly, unkeen to reveal that so many decades had elapsed since her reading of Stendhal that she couldn't remember the story at all.

'No!' I crowed. 'And there, if you like, is *her* tragedy. In terms of genetic programming, hormoanal promptings and sexual hots, what she wants most in all the world is to have babies by Fabrizio. Her sister's son! But he's a wee drip who wants only to roger the Prison Governor's frumpy daughter Clelia, which he finally manages to do back up the tower, before he gets religion and the Duchessa has to settle for childless marriage to Count Mosca.'

'How does it end?' wondered Jennifer seriously, as if contemplating the bankability of a Hollywood remake.

'Terribly!' I cheered. 'Little Sandrino, the lovechild of Fabrizio and Clelia, only a few months after Clelia pretends he has died—'

'Why does she do that?' asked Jennifer.

'To smuggle the boy away from her husband, his ostensible father. This is because Fabrizio can't bear the thought of his son growing up to love another man as his father. Anyway, only a few months after they abduct him away from his unwitting non-father, the boy *really* dies! Clelia, heartbroken and tortured by remorse, survives him by only a few months more. Fabrizio, retired to his Charterhouse, lasts about another year. And the Duchessa not much longer. The final line isn't quite, but could nearly be:

'"And they all died miserably shortly thereafter."

'It's wonderful. In fact,' I nodded at Wringhim, 'it's one of the most remarkable novels ever written. You should read it some time.'

'Frothy—'

'When did Stendle die?' asked Jennifer.

'Oh, I doubt if even silly old Europe will ever get the copyright period back that far, so you needn't worry about buying up the film rights. However, since the original is in French, you will have to commission a fresh translation before your blockbuster can be produced. My rates—'

'Frothy French shite,' insisted Wringhim.

'*Please*, Wringhim,' said Audrey.

'Now in my own novel . . . ' I slipped in, and rushed on to explain how the subject of childlessness [ . . . 7] comes up – or rather, to the fore, at the end in conjunction with Louis Morel's long retirement obsession with the selective breeding of his Pyrenean—

'Goats?' echoed Wringhim incredulously.

'First above all, it's the *truth*,' I retorted defiantly. 'Secondarily, it's a *symbol*—'

'Goats!' he repeated pityingly. Pushing his soup plate forward, he at once sat back a little from the table, crossed his Terylened knees, peered at me with pink compassion over his gold-rimmed half-frames, and expanded thus:

'You seriously mean to tell us that you end your story – your fucking enormously long story, some may say – with the hero breeding goats?'

'Their mammaries—'

'Jesus wept,' said Wringhim, whose attention was then distracted yet again by the apparently mysterious emptiness of his wine glass.

'Besides,' Audrey was saying, ' . . . ,' and I realized that the three ladies or was it women by way of reaction to the wistful childlessness of

---

7 This ellipsis signifies a fierce digression on 'subject' versus 'theme'. Wringhim says my childlessness is not a *subject* but a *theme*. But this is simply wrong. Subjects are dollops of material, best denoted by verbless words, like 'Corruption of the GAGAs'. Themes, by contrast, are propositional, hence verbful. Like, 'All GAGAs take bribes.' Since the issue is so clear-cut, the digression is suppressed.

Louis and Hélène Morel had raced ahead to what was rapidly emerging as one of the central subjects of this book, namely overpopulation of the planet and what on earth can be done about it? This led infallibly to discussion of recent high-level and very costly international conferences advocating don't waste your transistor radios but rather improve the level of education everywhere, especially the education and hence emancipation of women and hence the ineluctable demasculinization of political power structures everywhere.

'And at the limit', I nodded, 'you might take the frequently observed high education of heads of arts subjects in private schools for girls often resulting in no breeding at all. Nor am I only thinking here of such classic historical spinsters as Richmal Crompton.'

If we considered our friends, suggested Koo, we would see that the voluntarily embraced childlessness (as opposed to the frustratingly obligatory infertility of the Morels) of well educated adults was already common, and probably on the increase. 'There's Paul and Rebecca,' she enumerated. 'No kids, and their choice. Us. Audrey's got Jennifer, but that's only one. Wringhim—'

'Don't forget', I reminded her, 'that in that list you've got three novelists. And novelists, as is well known, do not make good parents. For example,' and I went on to cite some contemporary cases which the laws of this land and various others oblige me not to print here. I also made the bad mistake of then reciting from memory certain remarks by Somerset Maugham[8] on the tragical inadequacy of a number of more canonical novelists in relating to their children. A bad mistake, I say, to the extent that it roused Wringhim to denounce me as pseudo-pinko Campbell Janus for daring to smirch the dinner-table air with quotes from bottombrow English farts like Maugham.

'There are of course others,' admitted Koo, 'like Janet—'

'Janet's certainly *been* a good breeder,' I agreed. 'But that was *before* she became a feminist. Now whether young Veronica and Daniel—'

'Isn't the British birth rate declining anyway?' asked Jennifer.

---

[8] 'Talking reluctantly of Maugham, Humbert, aren't you rather overdoing Wringhim as a sort of Scottish Driffield?* Better bite the Wringhim bullets head-on, I say, and be Frank!' [P.C.]

  **\* Paul refers to** *Cakes and Ale.* **Uncertain commontutters believe the senior novelist character,** *Ted Driffield,* **may or may not be a lenient caricature of Thomas Hardy.**

'The birth rate in *Scotland*', observed Wringhim, in tones of emphatic rebuke, 'is lower than it should be.' But it will begin to rise again quite sharply, he asserted, as soon as we obtain our political independence, and with it the unalloyed sense of national identity, dignity and pride which began to be insidiously sapped in 1603 and then was crippled wholesale in 1707. And such a renewal of the demographic curve upward, he stressed, is a trend the autonomous Scottish economy of the twenty-first century will be happy to live with until – the level of education then being supremely high too – the Scottish population will become naturally self-limiting. And it was even conceivable, he allowed, that the birth rate may one day rise similarly again *in England too* – after abolition of the monarchy, the established Church, the GAGAs,[9] and following the adoption of proportional representation and the right mix of national pride and international humility befitting a small, poor and globally unimportant country.

That being a charitable paraphrase of what Wringhim wished to convey on this matter at that point, you get some idea of how it would have sounded on the night, if we'd rendered it for you in perfectly pickled direct speech and left in all his *fucking*s and *cunt*s.

'Talking of fucking,' said Koo, regarding Wringhim with enveenode bellicosity, 'let's not forget . . . ' And she reminded him that, while certainly no normal healthy mother would ever wish away the life of her child, once born, it by no means followed that you weren't a normal healthy woman (despite your own mother's soliloquies to the contrary) if, having carefully considered the matter, you elected not to reproduce yourself.

---

9  NB, this is Wringhim's only footnote. The one where he suggests that since I have styled the sleazy creeps at England's helm as 'greasy grasping arseholes', I might as well expand them to 'greasy *and* grasping arseholes'. Partly to get more emphatic milage out of the consideration that an arsehole who actively grasps* is hugely more graphically odious than an arsehole merely passively greasy. But predominantly, we do not scruple to not deny, for the patter aptness of the acronym.

  **\* 'Like privatizing a public service while you're a minister, then making a fortune joining the board six months later? Is this what you mean by "an arsehole who actively grasps"? If so, why not spell it out?' [J.R.]**

'Humbert says,' she confided treacherously, 'that all men are wired with urges to kill other men, and that he personally has urges to kill [ . . . quite a list here, in addition to Rankles and the Prime Creep]. 'Well, I would say . . . ' And she suggested that while most if not all women were wired with urges to have babies, there was no cosmogorical imperative to give in to those urges, or to feel guilty about not giving in to them, just as there was no intrinsic shame in Humbert overcoming his urges to kill the likes of Rankles.

'How very true,' I chimed sonorously, as I toured the table with yet more wine. 'Your genes want to give you cancer too, don't they? And there's no shame in thwarting them there. Yet more tea, vicar?' I trilled in Wringhim's right ear.

'Not only that,' and here Koo glanced at Audrey as if for sororietal solidarity, 'but . . . ' Effectively, that no kids implies – quite apart from more foreign travel and less damage to your wealth if you have any – that other things being equal the same woman can for obvious reasons expect to experience a lot more sexual pleasure during her remaining sexually active if not exciting years, can she not?

'Even if your partner weren't immensely virile,' added Audrey, in what seemed to me a drastically overdone hint of multiblack irony which I nonetheless found myself hoping Jennifer might not notice. Yet in the same moment I experienced a spasm of guilt at possibly having conveyed an impression of Audrey in the present work as somewhat lacking in belly laughs. This is historically very unfair, and yet it can hardly be denied that in recent years she has been long on overworked seriousness and short on gregarious giggles, let alone her own darting wit. And this is something for which I blame the GAGAs above all else: they have in large measure taken Audrey's sense of humour away from me. Funding of education is ever more meanly capped, lecture loads are insupportable, Finals tutorials are packed to bursting at their asbestos seams, and there is more marking to skate over in a term than could be thoroughly ploughed in a year.

Yet Audrey is too conscientious not to attempt it all, and this has dulled her sensitivity to an irony self-evident to any underfunded student: that humourless academics make the worst of all educators. And when I think back to how it used to be – during our salad days in Grantchester, say – I am goaded to the brink of tears. One episode in particular reared up again in my mind now, as I reached across the table to top the ladies' glasses with our delicious Château Fortia (1985). It was in a state of drowsy slumber, after a night in the Green Man and several vigorous bouts in the first hours of bed, that I found myself lifting her nightie again. She's a powerful sleeper, Audrey, and always had a curious passion for never falling asleep not in her nightie, no matter what she's been doing or how much she hasn't been wearing it during the hours preceding. So now in a state of as it were instinct here am I teasing up her nightie's frilly hem and caressing Audrey's buttocks and a little beyond[10] in the most tender, respectful and gentlemanly of manners.

'What? Are you doing, Philip?' (Her last long-standing young sort of man but one before me.) 'Please don't,' murmured Audrey.

'It isn't fucking Philip,' I pointed out pleasantly. 'It's fucking Humbert. And I thought' — as with a well oiled manoeuvre I did so — 'I might just introduce myself.'

This elicited a protracted throaty chuckle from my rousing partner, as she accommodated herself to my initiative. I'd better take care to whom I said such things, she said, as they might be misconstrued.

'Not Mrs Construed?' I retorted with a thrust.

Of course when spelled out like that twenty-five years on it's not at all funny. But in that context, that bed, and in Audrey's vagina at just that intersecting moment, it stimulated such explosions of convulsive mirth intertwined with escalating orgasm that the next twenty-three minutes must surely go down as the most sexually ecstatic of my life. So ecstatic, I may say, that for several days following I thought I might have to go to the doctor about it.

'And now?' I pondered aloud.

'And now what?' demanded Audrey suspiciously, for she had caught me glancing across the table at her, in a retrospective way.

'I was merely mulling over the metaphysical nature of *wistfulness*, I informed her. As logically distinct from *regret*.'

'What do you regret, Uncle Humbert?' asked Jennifer with considerable interest.

'Two things, mainly,' I nodded sadly, as Koo politely inquired whether Wringhim wanted more fish soup.

'First, I wish—'

'Don't tell us,' said Audrey belligerently. 'Because we don't want

---

[10] 'I do hope, Humbert, that you're not hoping we're going to wonder if this characteristic filth is somehow symbolic of the author-reader relationship. Well? Are you?' [J.R.]

to hear.'

'Don't want to hear what?' I protested, somewhat alarmed at her evident dander.

'Christ, you men are all the same.'

'How you amaze me, Audrey. But *in what way*, pray?'

'Wishing your willies were half an inch longer,' fumed Audrey disgustedly.

At this point Wringhim was heard to snicker in a particularly unpleasant manner, like a sex-starved donkey winding up for a full-blast bray.

Patiently I shook my head:

'No, Audrey!'

'Whadja mean, "No, Audrey!"?'

'I mean that, on the contrary, my two regretful wishes — insofar as it makes sense at all to claim to regret what could not possibly have been otherwise — are simply that, above all, I wish my mother had not died so young, and secondly, and secondarily, that in my youth I had not eschewed piano lessons as being the preserve of poofter cissies. And this not merely — indeed, very scantily, because in the universe of those very different events my career in the entertainment business would already have been immeasurably more successful, along lines in many ways parallel to those of Elton John, Russ Conway and Mrs Mills—'

'Shite,' said Wringhim.

'No, no. Not a bit of it, Audrey. Not even the tastiest bit. Not only, I say, not only do I not wish my willie was half an inch longer, but—'

'I agree with Uncle Humbert!' exclaimed Jennifer suddenly.

'And what is that supposed to mean?' demanded her mother suspiciously.

'Well,' explained Jennifer, 'suppose you want more tea than you're getting, right?'

'Yes?' said Audrey warningly.

'Well, you don't expect to get it from another teapot just because the second teapot has a longer spout. Not necessarily, anyway. Do you?'

I applauded Jennifer's biological acumen here, adding that for breathtaking albeit shortspouted virility I would back our Blackface rams against Audrey's Thoroughbred stud stallion any day. Then I asked Jennifer if she had wrested her tea-spout simile straight, as it were, from the living flesh of life?

'Not really,' she confessed with admirable frankness. She had got it off Miss McCorkindale, her Religious Instruction mistress in third-year at St Mungo's.[11]

'Anyway, quite right,' I agreed. 'And indeed, Audrey, and for the straightness of everyone's record, not only do I no longer wish my willie was no longer not longer than half an inch no longer, but rather, ever since I got the lowdown on supreme success with women off Paul Chalicer[12] in an earlier chapter, have I frequently been tempted – most often in one highly specialized configuration of the system, it probably should not be confessed – to wish my willie was eleven sixteenths of an inch[13] shorter. Ask Koo if you don't believe me.'

'Does anyone not like crackling?' inquired Koo, rising up to clear the

---

[11] Whether or not Miss McCorkindale was personally familiar with the phallantomtom of Errol Flynn, we may never learn. Instructively, though:

'His penis was indeed unremarkable. It was, if not short, certainly not longer than that, and rather stout, I thought. That's all there was, there wasn't any more, except a terribly full, bulging scrotum.'* (From *Errol Flynn* by Earl Conrad.)

* *'So here you are, girls! In the absence of myself (or at a desperate pinch Humbert) turn your backs on mere overgrown cucumbers and stick out for pumpkin testicles!' [P.C.]*

[12] Naively I had assumed that this wisdom was acquired through Paul's hewing it, as it were, out of the living flesh – like Titian, you might say, in the midst of his lovely voluptuous young nudes of every perfume. Sadly, Paul has since confessed that he in turn got it purely cognitively: over a glass of tepid white wine from the well known popular (*sic*) botologist Dr David Desmond, during a Big Book Signing at Foyle's in the Charing Cross Road. 'But Goodness Gracious!' Paul recalls exclaiming. 'If that's really the secret why ever is it not in your books?' Nodding serenely over Paul's left shoulder, to someone much more famous and important, Dr Desmond appears to have murmured a terse parable about what a trite betrayal of Selective Advantage it would be to go publicizing such wisdom in cheep pepperbucks for the mush murkit. Paul did not entirely understand the full ramifications of this admission at the time, but I have since explained them to him.

[13] 17.4625 millimetres.

soup plates away.

'My glass is empty,' said Wringhim urgently.

'More white?' I asked him hospitably. 'Move on to a young and fruity but sublimely robust Vacqueyras rouge? Or would you rather the remains of that litre of Glenmorangie between courses? Now I wonder, Audrey . . . ' but before I could complete my preamble leading up to the crucial issue of whether Louis Morel may have had a long-unknown illegitimate half-sister of parallel blueblooded beauty, and if so [ . . . ], the goalposts were yet again displaced by Jennifer returning from helping with the roast pork in the kitchen, and looking at me in a seriously funny way.

'Koo says you'll want to see these,' she said, as she handed me the following three:

## 88

# Faxes from Minneapolis

Dear Humbert & Koo,

Just to wish you well for your house-party. Regards to whoever makes it. I take it from the news that you must have snow too. Jolly cold here but after the ceremony I was introduced to the most charming drum majorette from Quebec. She's been giving me a lot of help with my Canadian French. So glad to see that Humbert's book is so nearly finished. This should enable the rest of us to get on with our own books for a bit. Actually having said that I did have an idea on the plane for a much better ending for you, Humbert. (Left the last of your pages in a rubbish bin at Heathrow to reduce weight by the way. You did mean them to be disposable, didn't you?) Anyway your new and much improved ending goes like this.

Louis and Hélène Morel are not entirely childless after all. She conceives and gets several months into her pregnancy. One day she hears 'noises' in the library. It is Louis bonking Mathilde, the maid from Paris with the juicy fruits. She is bent over, chest down upon Louis's desk and heaving with orgasmic ecstasy. He, rampant and purple as any American president behind closed doors, has her skirts up and is taking her from the rear. Hélène collapses in horror and has a miscarriage. Louis is beside himself with remorse and repentance. Hélène forgives him until she discovers that she is no longer capable of childbearing and also Mathilde is pregnant by Louis. Furthermore she suspects and in due course discovers evidence that Louis despite his protestations to the contrary is cavorting with other women on his travels. Far from being a bumpkin breeder of goats with big tits, as you would have it, Louis is now a secret agent travelling Europe on missions commissioned by Mazarin, the replacement evil Cardinal running France. One day when Louis is in Madrid with a brief to destabilize the government of Spain Hélène concludes an unusual bargain with the leading brothel madam in Lourdes. In return for free whoring twice a week Hélène gets to deliberately infect herself with syphilis by servicing mendicant friars. When Louis returns she infects him in turn. This leads to Mathilde too getting syphilis since Louis is still bonking her as well despite his protestations to the contrary.

When Louis discovers his chancres and realizes what's up it never occurs to him to blame his wife. Rather he presumes he's got what Gott intended him to get from all his promiscuity round the capitals of Europe. Spurred by the spectre of death he becomes both celibate and frenetically creative. Very like Maupassant (in the creativity at least) he turns his hand to prolific sci-fi fabulism which in many ways prefigures Voltaire. Among the forthcoming historical events which his deceptively simple fables presage with uncanny chronological exactitude are the French Revolution, the violent disestablishment of the French monarchy, world wars in the twentieth century, the advent of AIDS, and the subsequent disestablishment in passive shame of what you would call the English royal family.

Hélène dies first since her secret syphilis gets multiplied by internal female complications. On her deathbed she confesses her hideous crime to Louis, pleads for his forgiveness and beseeches him to marry Mathilde and during the short time remaining to them to lovingly care for the only child the three of them between them have produced (probably a beautiful daughter, knowing you) who also has the great advantage of having been born before the rest of them contracted their syphilis. I will admit this leaves you with the slight problem of the feckless Jean-Baptiste who needs to be got out of the way first. Anyway that's just a detail. Thereafter in your finale Louis Morel and his second wife Mathilde, both slowly dying of syphilis, attain a level of ascetic beatitude which cries out for comparison with Lancelot and Guinevere towards the close of *La Mort le Roi Artu*. Their deaths within hours of one another are events of great poetic power and beauty. Sublimely sad yet not at all dismal so that the reader puts down your book with feelings of personal enrichment and spiritual purification, having accepted without question your final line:

'And here we end, for that is the whole truth, and any addition would be falsehood.'

Pretty good, eh? Slapped it out on the plane on my new Toshiba and despite my window-seat neighbour's protestations to the contrary. Of course if this superior denouement is to come off it will call for high degrees of narrative skill and literary delicacy which I shouldn't think for a moment you are capable of, Humbert. However, as ever, let me know if you need any more help and we can talk about percentages later.

Well, must stop now. Time for Canadian French!
Love to Koo,
Yrs,
Paul.

Then:

*Dearest—*

Yes, that really is how Paul's second fax begins. Decent citizens may be forgiven for expecting the second word to be 'Rebecca'. In fact the communication is directed to the attractive young woman we have referred to as 'Madam Chair', she who is now increasingly important in the EBC. The intended fax destination was Madam Chair's home address in the West End of Glasgow, and the twelve sentences following are so intensely and embarrassingly personal, so explicitly allusive to certain shared experiences apparently past, and mawkishly hopeful of their re-enactment at the earliest opportunity, that I have with the greatest reluctance decided – even despite all the beastly things Paul has said and implied about me in his egregious *Scorpions* – that I cannot in good (or even customarily shabby) conscience publish them here. It does not of course follow that I will not threaten to copy them to Rebecca the next time his elbows need wrenching.

And third:

Dear Janet,
Tried to telephone you in London but got Charlotte who gave me this fax number for your hotel in Prague. So I do hope this reaches you. It's about Humbert. Following our previous conversation I've had my accountants run a credit check on him and it appears he's even more worthless than any of us feared. So I'm afraid doing him for libel simply isn't on. Even if we totally bankrupted him it would cost us a fortune for the privilege. But I take it we're still agreed he must be stopped? Quite apart from the defamation dimension if we don't put a halt to him soon there will be a serious risk of his *Sex* outstripping my *Quintain*. So I wonder how you would feel about going halfers on taking out a contract on his life? Seriously, it's very fashionable here in the States and I have a friend in New York who has a friend in Chicago who says he knows all about it. I'm uneasy though about

the credibility of American hoodlums in dark glasses bumbling about Berwickshire with sawn-off shotguns and there is again the problem of cost. These contracts don't come cheaply so I understand and we would also have to pay return air fares. So I wonder especially in view of the present exchange rates if this is something you might check out in Prague? Perhaps a couple of desperate postgraduates still young enough to get student rail cards?

Well, let me know what you think.

And regards to the Witch!

Yours ever,

Paul.

# And Sew to Beds

Through roast pork, roast potatoes, apple sauce, cheeseboard featuring a ripe Vignotte, mature port-fed Stilton, creamy Cambozola, and our own local Camembert-like Bonchester, then zabaglione with fruit salad served with ice-cream and topped with whipped cream laced with Madeira, aided down by a bottle of Château des Coulinats 1986,[1] followed by coffee and Turkish delight closely followed by too many nightcaps without number, something like a cross between the following conversation and a way-over-the-limit seesaw took place.

'I know what's happened,' said Audrey.

'What has happened?' wondered Humbert.

'He's given his faxes in to the hotel fax room,' she explained. 'Terrible mistake. And they've sent the three faxes as three pages of one fax. Terribly embarrassing. Same thing happened to me in Florence last Easter. Terribly embarrassing.'

'Hmn,' said Humbert.

'Whadja mean, "Hmn"?' snarled Audrey.

'I wonder—'

'Wonder *what*?'

'Did you ever tell Paul? About your embarrassment in Florence?'

'Dunno. May have done. Anyway, who gives—'

'Yes, you did, Mum,' said Jennifer. 'It was when he came to dinner with [Madam Chair] in the first week of term. Don't you remember?'

'*No*,' hissed Audrey, with furious maternal honesty. 'I do not bloody remember.'

'In that case,' I advised them ominously, 'I don't think we can rule out the probability that Paul has done this deliberately.'

'Ssshite,' said Wringhim.

'Done what deliberately?' asked Koo.

---

[1] Perfect nursery-slope nectar for novices in the Fellowship of Dessert-wine Culture, such as Wringhim.

'Plagiarized from Audrey's true-life experiences in Florence, with a view to tricking me into plagiarizing from his false-life experiences in Minneapolis,[2] thus accumulating spurious credibility in advance for the claims he will certainly make to have written vastly more of my book than I would have dreamt of letting him. You see, Jennifer,' I informed her sadly, 'that sort of subterfuge, if successful, is as close as most novelists and film-makers will ever get to immortality.'

Mention of immortality inevitably subdued our thoughts for a moment, by reminding us of its opposite. Then, *mortality* associating comfortably with *murder*, it was Jennifer who inaugurated a brief discussion as to whether Paul was serious: in that, even if as I alleged he had in fact deliberately contrived that the second and third faxes be transmitted to Greenadder Farmhouse in seeming error – (a) to intimate without seeming to swank that he had been successful with Madam Chair where I had not yet (which could conceivably be true, but could just as well be a braggart lie), and (b) in the hope of yet again creating some ersatz fleeting fact which might aspire to the afterlife of fiction – it still by no means followed that he wasn't earnest in floating the notion that Humbert must be stopped, albeit not at any great cost to Paul.

'But I really don't think', I said, in altruistic defence of our absent friend, 'that paying to have me physically killed – in the sense of my heart stilled, my brain exploded, and my consciousness extinguished – would be in accord with his love of liberty, let alone his Christian principles.' It was much more likely, I imagined, that the assassination devised for me by an intelligence so prickly and prudent as Paul's would be pre-eminently literary – extending to protracted decapitation, as it were, the gratuitous beatings and stabbings already inflicted in his *Scorpions*.

And I went on to describe how bitterly disappointed in Paul we'd been, Koo and I, to discover how treacherously he'd changed his title on the brink of publication (from *The Three Prongs*) and how irresponsibly he'd gone on to swell the ranks of his enemies, with so many downright libellous cartoons. 'As for me,' I admitted bravely, 'my dorsals are canardial, my agape in spasms canters. No doubt in time it will contrive to embrace even Chardonnay Pilferer to its bosom again. However . . . ' My particular irritation here found vent at having my

---

2 We do not necessarily imply that none of Paul's experiences was experienced.

own monicker so maladroitly mutated. 'Dumbo', was obvious enough, certainly in its adolescent offensiveness, but also in its psychopathic derivation: it has the 'umb' string in common with 'Humbert', as even a *Crimes* crossword junkie might deduce.

'But "Griswald"!' I groaned. 'It's so pointless, and so . . . so unforgivably *fucking ugly.*'

'Please, Humbert,' said Koo.

'Has it not got to do with National Lampooning?' suggested Jennifer.

'I agree with Humbert,' muttered Audrey.

'Surely not!' I professed wide amazement.

'I mean,' said Audrey testily, 'that, in my opinion, if Paul doesn't get back to what he's best at soon,[3] he'll be courting professional suicide.'

That dread *suicide* took us straight back down the big slippery snake to *death*, hence *killing*, embracing *murder*, thence plunging us, in the twinkling of a candlelit wine glass, deep into trenchant discussion of the first of the top three moral con drums in history. Namely, in what conditions, if any, does one man, or group of men (since it usually is men, thanking your ladyships), have the right to take another person's life?[4]

'Never,' said Jennifer confidently.

'But suppose you're my doctor,' I objected, 'and I am terminally ill, in great pain, and I beg you to help me exit?'

'As usual, Humbert,' remarked Audrey, 'you're taking advantage of the innocence and intellectual inexperience of the young.'

'Cherish the thought! But in what way, oh prithee my dove?'

Audrey maintained (and seldom is she more fetching, than when belligerently flushed with fine wines, and passion for-and-against me) that the case of consciously solicited euthanasia was a red herring in the current context.

'Not jelly?' wondered Humbert.

'Why is that, Mum?' wondered Jennifer.

---

[3] Audrey means blockbusting narratives that keep you up reading all night to find out what happens next, and weigh over three pounds avoirdupois when you plonk them on the kitchen scales – presumably as opposed to silly little experimental fictions that only wankers give a toss about.

[4] The third, at the time of typesetting, is: in what conditions does a man have the right to consciously create another person's life? However, this may take second place soon.

'Because,' the good-hearted humanistical historian explained, 'it is not murder, but rather a form of suicide.'

'I think what your mother's trying to say,' I added, 'is where you're my doctor and I beg you to kill me, you-the-doctor can be considered not so much as another autonomous person – if you can envision such a beast – but rather as an extension of the practical means available to me-the-poor-patient. Think of yourself as a fully loaded Smith & Wesson by the patient's bedside, she might say. A less philosophically vulnerable explication of your mother's position, should she wish one, might be in terms of absence of conflict – don't you think, Audrey? In that, if I-the-patient really want out, and the doctor knows there is no hope for me, and helps me out – and providing hos isn't expecting to benefit from my will, marry my wife, or whatever – then there is no violent or sinister imposition of your will, Jennifer, upon and against my will. **Isn't that right, Wringhim?**' I shouted suddenly at our snuftering passenger.

'Glurrr!'

'Leave him be,' murmured Audrey.

'Why should I? He hasn't touched his zabaglione, he's accused me of trying to poison him with this delicious and hardly dirt-cheap Château des Coulinats, and for the last ten minutes he's been snoring like a nearly-dead chewwahwah. If we let him sleep on now, then, when he does wake voluntarily, close quotes, he'll sit up all night drinking my whisky. **Isn't that right, Wringhim?**'

'Fuck . . . you . . . Seale,' he growled, rubbing red eyes behind his spectacles, and breathing in a manner which young wowser doctors might describe as 'life-threateningly laborious'.

'Besides,' I smiled sweetly, 'who better qualified to pronounce upon the following . . . ?' And I outlined for them, as a paradigm to morally cogitate, the killing of the Count of Sedan by the Marquis of Roquefort, on the orders of Cardinal Richelieu, in the immediate aftermath of the Battle of La Marfée.

'If the Marquis was already in Sedan before the battle,' mused Jennifer. 'Then . . . '

'Yes, yes? Do go on.'

'Well, why didn't he kill the Count before the battle began? And avoid all that bloodshed?'

'Oh, because that would never suit a wily old fox like the Cardinal.'

'Why not?' asked Audrey, coiling to pounce on my slightest historical shortcoming.

'To have killed the leader-hero *before* the battle would only have redoubled buoyant hostility against the Cardinal and the King,' I explained. 'It would also have resulted in the Count of Soissons being replaced by a new and perhaps more capable leader-hero. Less indecisive. This could have been the Duke of Bouillon. It might have been the Duke of Guise. Then, if Richelieu lost the battle, he would not only be a loser, but an accountable assassin to boot. But as it was: either he won the battle, which he didn't, or else he lost the battle but had the leader-hero assassinated immediately thereafter. This way, the morale of the leaderless victors is destroyed by the feeling that even when they are most successful, nonetheless they fail. In their terms (most of them), they conclude that the Will of God is against them. Ergo, according to the popular psychology of defeat, the Cardinal and the King must thus be Endorsed By God – as His spiritual minister in France and temporal minister respectively. A load of tosh, in logic, but the Cardinal was a vir-tuoso manipulator of ignorance and superstition. Creator of them, too.'

'But that doesn't make the killing of the Count of Soissons . . . *right*,' objected Jennifer.

'Depending—'

'But you also said . . . '

'Yaas?'

'Well, Uncle Humbert, you also said your Louis Watchisname—'

'Morel.'

'That he goes on to kill the murderer?'

'Absolutely!' I enthused, then recited a brisk epitome of the deadly struggle in the rain-swollen river Bar, which ends with the homicidal Marquis being crucially distracted by the newcome peevish voice on the west bank, which gives Louis the vital moment necessary to knock the card-sharped dagger from Roquefort's hand, bearhug his body and head beneath the water, switch grips to his head and chin, and in the short twisting wrench taught him by Pere Garcés to snap the villain's neck.

'But that's horrible,' said Jennifer with a sideways frown.

'In what way?'

'From what you say, Uncle Humbert, it's just a cheap vengeance killing. He's killed my buddy, so I'll kill him. Isn't it?'

'Quite right, Jennifer,' said her mother, glowering at me between the candles. 'No trial, no verdict, no justice. No rule of law. Typical irresponsibility of the penny-dreadful novelist.'

'Mine is a true story,' I rebuked her with dignity.

'Possibly,' said Audrey sceptically. 'But it's you who choose to tell it.'

'Just like a Hollywood Nasty,' said Jennifer sadly.

Now before I was able to reassure the Macpherson women that not only has the Marquis of Roquefort recently assassinated the Count of Soissons but also that he has several times in the course of the novel attempted to kill Louis himself out of sheer personal delighting spite, and that therefore considerations of pre-emptive self-defence might reasonably be adduced in my favour as opposed to Hollywood's, all our attentions were violently distracted by Wringhim loudly pronouncing something that sounded to me like:

'Pearly shit.'

'Beg pardon?' I therefore responded.

Upon his clearing his throat in such a manner as certainly to destroy a small frog, and probably a medium-size alligator, I reaffirmed with feeling:

'Terribly sorry?'

Wringhim filled his wine glass from the water jug, gargled, swallowed, and knocked back the rest of the glass. Then he said clearly:

'It — is — perfectly — *legitimate*.'

'What is?'

'Killing people,' he meant. Before the democratic process has been established, and thereafter when it is abused and imperilled by those elected to administer it, the selective assassination of ambitious key players, and sometimes unfortunate figureheads, is not only legitimate, but is always to be preferred to alternative solutions which involve widerspread violence which invariably leads to the needless suffering and killing of the innocent.

'Coffee in the sitting-room,' called Koo from the kitchen.

'The history of France in the seventeenth century,' continued Wringhim, was not his forte, certainly. But he could nonetheless assure us with confidence that there was no democracy in it, and no possibility of it either. Hence, even if the Cardinal had failed, and the Count of Soissons had not only not been killed but enjoyed the fruits of his triumph in battle, *and* become First Minister of France, or whatever, there would still have been no democracy in France until at least 1789, and perhaps later still. 'It simply wasn't possible,' he maintained, because various vital developments in agriculture and industry, distribution of population and information, and so forth, had not yet taken place.

'Likewise the American War of Independence and Tom Paine,' remarked Audrey.

'That's right,' nodded Wringhim. And it was therefore inevitable that various political objectives in seventeenth-century France should be attempted and in some cases achieved by means of selective assassination of individuals. 'In our own day,' he went on, as we settled round the sitting-room fire with our coffee and Turkish delight, we had a situation where the due process of democracy in Scotland was being flagrantly perverted by the corrupt government of another nation. 'Consequently,' he asserted, if the present Prime Creep of England were to persist in his attempts to thwart the desire of the Scottish people for autonomy, it would be entirely legitimate, both politically and morally, to subject that individual – first, and preferably – with the serious *threat* of assassination—

'Possibly a severed horse's head in his bed?' I suggested.

And thereafter (Wringhim continued regardless), if necessary, with his spectacular termination in a skilfully stage-managed public situation not injurious to bystanding citizens. 'And if they didn't get the message . . . ' following the elimination thus of the current Prime Creep, it would be in order to proceed to the next. And so on until untrammelled democracy for Scotland was secured.

'Come off it, Wringhim,' murmured Audrey, as she held her coffee cup up for a refill. 'You'd never be saying that if you hadn't been drinking all day.'

'Oh, yes,' he disagreed. He would, and he did. And the only reason Audrey was denying it was because she preferred to deceive herself into not seeing the force of his arguments.

'Would you kill him yourself?' asked Koo politely.

'No,' Wringhim admitted. He personally was too soft-hearted and in any case too long in the tooth. His eyesight was no longer up to political assassinations and anyway he'd never been much good with weapons. Even as a pressganged pimply private in the militaristic Combined Cadet Force, he'd rarely hit those 'snarling wee yellow-fellow' targets with his Lee Enfield ·303 and consequently, if he were now to be let loose in London with a high-velocity sniper's rifle, he would constitute an unacceptable threat to the English general public. 'Many of whom now join with us', in believing that Scotland should be free to be Scottish. 'However,' he added ominously, 'it should not be inferred,' not by any means, from his inability to kill the enemy himself, that he could not be serious in his belief that it might be in the Scottish national interest for the enemy to be killed. 'And if the need arises,' he promised, 'as it very nearly has, then I shall pledge funds to the cause.'

'Does the team not think', I asked him a little provocatively, as with resignation vergering upon trepidation I rose up to pour the first nightcaps – being bumpers of port for the ladies, small neat nips for me, and cut-crystal half-pints of Glenmorangie and water for Wringhim—

'Think . . . ' murmured Audrey.

'Think that, the way things are going, we should now be on course for a Scottish parliament of some sort, sooner or later, and that after that it's only a matter of time?'

'Enough time', said Wringhim fiercely, had already been lost. 'Stolen wholesale, in fact.' Accordingly, if the Prime Creep and the GAGAs did not learn to abide by the rules of basic democracy soon, the night of the dumdum bullet might be upon them before they would never know nothing no more.

As further nightcaps chinked and gurgled, and the larch logs crackled and spat, the consciousness of the company engaged in ever bloodier battle with the pettily workaday strictures of the Principle of Sufficient Reason and all its Howmanyfold Roots. Thus:

Jennifer taking issue with Wringhim over the legitimacy of political assassination, insisted that the wilful terminating of life could *never* be justified. Immediately I exhumed her disgraceful suggestion earlier that we might have Captain Claws put to sleep as a matter of convenience. That was different, said Jennifer. No, it wasn't – said Wringhim. Yes, it was – said Audrey. In what way? – asked Koo. 'My glass is empty,' remarked Wringhim.

Then, the offending receptacle being temporarily full once more, he embarked on a sauce-for-the-gander history of the typically hypocritical English obsession with 'terrorist violence' as an enemy to be 'stamped out' flipsided with a thousand years of insufferable complacency over their own state-licenced murders. Among those mentioned and not instantly forgotten by your on-the-spot reporter were William Wallace, Mary Queen of Scots, Admiral Byng, Roger Casement, and more recently 'those pathetic Irish Republican people in Gibraltar'. If we needed a perfect personification of this English double-substandardness, nodded Wringhim, it was instantly available to us in the 'licensed-to-kill' preoccupation with 'that glaikit gowk James Bond'.

'But seriously,' said Audrey, who had begun to fankle in premonitions of age and decay, misery and pain, and was for the moment less exercised about GAGA two-facedness regarding political murder than she was appalled by the general reality, and her own personal prospect, of being deprived of the option of choosing the manner and moment of one's own death – hence often condemned to a protraction of misery and pain many times more atrocious than anything actually suffered 'or possibly sufferable' by lambs being lorried to France.

'Scottish Borders farmers', I assured her tragicomically, 'especially those ruined by GAGA "policies", bank usuries, and absentee English landlord exploitations, quite frequently choose the manner and moment of their own deaths!'

'Not everyone', retorted Audrey, in her trust-Humbert-to-say-something-so-childishly-tasteless voice, 'has a double-barrelled twelve-bore in their gun cupboard.'

'Everyone . . . ? In their . . . ?'

'Particularly those who are very old and ill.'

'You can borrow ours if you're desperate,' I murmured kindly sotto – Audrey being sat beside me on the fawn velvet sofa facing the fire, Koo and Jennifer on the white-silk sofa to the right of the fire, with Wringhim enthroned in the brown leather armchair to the left of the fire: perfect complement to his scuffed old brogues.

'I agree with Audrey,' said Koo. Meaning that she failed to discern either logic or humanity in a system which, while it conspired to thwart and torture the dying wishes of the eldest and most pitifully ill, just when they needed help most, at the same time actively encouraged adult male novelists such as Wringhim and myself – otherwise in reasonable control, much of the time, of their faculties and activities – to contrive their own suicides in a more leisurely and (initially, at least) enjoyable fashion, by dint of the vast quantities of overtaxed alcohol we consume.

Now Wringhim, you may already be sure, was no more able not to bite on that one than a mackerel on a rainbow spinner. There consequently followed the sort of 'lively debate' on the subject of alcohol consumption so typical of dinner parties where supposedly intelligent and educated adults drink far more alcohol than could possibly be sensible by any standard – Jennifer, for example, complaining hotly about the medical conspiracy to limit her weekly units to not more than two thirds of her boyfriend's units, assuming she had one, despite the fact that every boyfriend she'd had up till now she'd been able to drink under the table with ease and still be up first to make the breakfast the following morning.

'So like your mother,' I reflected softly, in preference to advertising that I personally would never have drunk half so much tonight were it not to numb resentment, and lubricate my handling, of our uninvited guest.

'And if *I* were a brain surgeon,' he was saying, and if Dr Knox's alcohol consumption was as high as seventy units a week [ribald hoots from the ladies here] then the last thing he would do would be to admit it in a medical-profession questionnaire, even a supposedly anonymous one, which might be secretly maliciously designed to catch you out and lay you off. And so it followed, did it not, that in all probability those respondents really consuming seventy units were deceitfully reporting thirty units. 'And what follows from that?'

'What does follow from that, Wringhim?' I asked him eagerly, as I took custody of his brandished tumbler for a refill, and scented the blood of some text to be filched.

The implication was, grunted Wringhim, that the real health problems, if any, earned at great expense by seventy units, would come to be statistically associated with thirty units. This in turn must lead infallibly to snivelling do-gooders with no imagination concluding that thirty units is a dangerously high level of consumption, hence we'd better fix the limit at twenty-one, had we not? 'Thank you, Humbert,' he nodded approvingly, as with both hands he accepted his brimming whisky.

'Don't mention Wringhim, it,' I croaked privately, as I toured the ladies with the port.

'The whole matter', he continued behind me, was a hive of the most despicable deceit: deliberate institutional wool-pulling, programmatic misinterpretation of statistics, calculated falsification of statistics in the first place, peripherally conscious hypocrisy, all the way up to 'wholesale Church-of-Scotland-style' self-deception on a mammoth scale. 'In fact,' he protruded his lips apocalyptically, 'lying about incake [yes, how could I forget this one?] of alcohol' was probably at least as rife as [its close blood relation] lying about the meaninglessness of life, and almost as unpleasant to behold as [ultimate horror] young English novelists lying about their sexual prowess.

'As for Humbert,' he pronounced, leering at me beadily as I sank back on the couch beside Audrey and sipped at my last titchy nip . . . I was to be commended for confessing to lying about my drinking habits [in Chapter 10], but he [that's Wringhim] was absolutely at a loss to understand (and hence to muster apposite forgiveness) why, throughout my novel, as though my literary spirit were putrefied with an incurable grudge against him, 'you have so exaggerated mine. Eh?'

Perhaps it was the total put-upon Eyorish sincerity of Wringhim's indignation that caused the three ladies to burst out together in roars and snorts of derisive mirth so uncontrollably bosomically infectious that even I myself was hard put to conceal the quivering of my lips behind a lowering of my moustache. Anyway it went on for at least two minutes – *haa-haa, hoo-hoo, hee-hee* . . . feeding upon itself as sides ached and tears streamed (as the darkest shades of compressed thunder towered higher up the brow of their butt) in an orgy of silly hilarity that in younger schoolgirls might have gone on all night, except that:

'You know, Humbert,' Wringhim announced at this point, 'the great problem with women', aside to me, but loudly, ' . . . with all women, even Scottish women — is the cunt.' Buttocks might be stimulating from a distance, he conceded. Breasts could be good for a fondle — if not too hairy or lumpy. But the cunt . . . the cunt was a whole different kettle of fish. Like the pot of gold at the end of the rainbow, except that there was no gold in the pot except what you thought you saw there from a distance or what you put into it yourself close up. Thus, as it were a mechanical governor on all human endeavour, the sticking point was the cunt. This was a simple and obvious truth which no honest person could deny and yet which all persons did deny much of the time, most persons most of the time, and many persons all of the time. Consequently we had wars, crusades, pilgrimages, pogroms; pontiffs, poofters, pyramids, prime creeps; other child abusers, English public schools, *Hello!* magazine, *The Daily Telegraph* and the English Broadcasting Conspiracy; trips to the moon, nincompoops walking to the north pole, the south pole, climbing up mountains and falling down off them — all for the sake of a temporary breather from their black-hole beaver nightmares of the cunt.

The human cunt, he maintained, could therefore be said to be a limiting frontier of the conditions of human experience — in many ways comparable to absolute zero temperature and the speed of light — and 'mibbe also' of the very possibility of consciousness as we know it. To this extent the tragic or Greek view of life was further corroborated, and the optimistic or American view was yet again falsified: the cunt was the fundamental sticking point, and men were intrinsically stuck with it. Now certainly it was also true, Wringhim gallantly allowed, that the cunt was not a crime for which women should be punished, since they were stuck with it too — just as much as men, indeed, and in some ways more so. But it should also never be forgotten that 'men, properly speaking' were ipso facto denied many of the salves in their metaphysical wounds which made women's lives less unbearable. Salves such as men, children, religion, and the consoling company and constant conversation of their sister women.

All the while Wringhim was haltingly but doggedly exhaling these vile dysogynistical Callumies, like toads from a high gutter gargoyle, I have to confess that I myself was gripped like a rabbit fascinated into doomed immobility by a snake, in the traditional cliché, or more latterly like so many hundreds of millions of couch-potato minds around the globe held captive by O.J. Simpson. But the moment he desisted, of course, my mangled attention roved fearfully back towards the women, to gauge the extents of their outrage, and to parry their talons of vengeance. But Jennifer, strange to say, had disappeared,[5] while Koo and Audrey — I was most astonished to perceive — were rapt in dialogue about the optimum climatic conditions in which to deadhead winter pansies. I knew from that certain subliminal flickering of Koo's left eyelid that few moons would wane before she gave me some sort of hard time over not having managed to keep Wringhim's trap shut, and yet Audrey — in so many ways the archetypal aggressive feminist academic — seemed really not to have registered Wringhim's deplorable cunt rant at all, as though it were no more to her than the radio farming news in some other distant room.

Inspired by the unbelievable good fortune of this reprieve from what had seemed an inevitably nasty row, I rolled to my feet smothering Huge Thespian Yawns, and declaimed:

'Well, everybody! I don't know about you, but myself I feel suddenly so terribly — you know? — tired and emotional that I think, don't you . . . ?'

And on that note[6] we all went to bed.

---

[5] I assumed at the time that disgust with Wringhim must have taken her off to bed, but in fact — I was to find in the course of my final tottering prowl to batten all hatches against the snow, and confine Captain Claws to his vigil in the kitchen — Jennifer had taken up a position on the sofa in the study, where, fortified by a half bottle of white Châteauneuf left over from dinner, she was ambivalently glued, with Claws pulsing sonorously between her thighs, to a FilmWet special I had thought to tape unobtrusively in the background.

[6] Koo has suggested that perhaps what is really meant by this note is a similar but more muffled note some forty minutes later, following a flashflood of unprintable havers to the accompaniment of what Wringhim described as 'one for the stairs', rounded off with a very last 'one for the top landing'.

# 90

# Koda

We come at last to Humbert's Second Law of Dwelling Dynamics, whose most general form states that:

*No matter how large a house two self-employed persons and a cat inhabit, they already need a bigger house.*[1]

Out of particular cases:

*No matter how many rooms are theoretically available in such a house for the accommodation of guests, not one of them ever contains sufficient uncluttered space in which to swing a sex-kitten more than fifteen minutes before the said guests ring the doorbell.*

This is due to:

*The constant and inexorable conspiracy* of boxes of unshelved books (if you used to be an intellectual), unsold books (if you've since become a publisher), unreclaimed sample goods from past business ventures which didn't quite work out, piles of unfiled wallet folders fat with details to pacify the VATman, computers, laser printers, computer peripherals, boxes for computer peripherals, review copies of computer software containing more megabytes of printer drivers than your hard disk's maximum capacity in the first place . . .

Plus unhung pictures, unlaid carpets, unstrummed guitars, rubbish bags full of old clothes not yet sorted for the charity shops, etc, *to fill those bedrooms to bursting,* and more bursting still in a month when you are also helping your father to move to a smaller house for his retirement and hence in addition have your own house temporarily (??) colonized

---

[1] This is by no means fourth-hand by way of Schumpeter and Parkinson, Earnest Engine, but rather derives directly from Boltzmann, Gibbs and *The Fundamental Frustrations of Inconvenient Existence.* As to Humbert's First Law of Dwelling Dynamics, it is perhaps more intuitively transparent, stating simply:

*If you can afford to buy the house you would most love to live in, you are already voting for the wrong political party.*

by canteens of family silver to be cleaned and valued, tea chests of fine bone china ditto, crates of curtains Georgian-Edinburgh tall, second sets of early editions of *Encyclopaedia Britannica*, twenty-seven lamps wired so dangerously that miracles would seem to have happened after all throughout the past thirty-eight years . . .

And so on.

And on and on and up past window height.

Now as it was only Audrey and Jennifer we were expecting for Saturday night, the two bedrooms excavated fit for a sex-kitten at minimum notice were the main guest suite and the dump. The former consists of what used to be the master bedroom – before the building on to the house of the extra/Victorian front gable – and what used to be an adjoining dressing room but is now the *en suite* bathroom. And the dump is a small bedroom, once upon a time a maid's billet, at the top of the back staircase at the north extremity of the building, where we dump visiting teenagers and other versatile young adults who don't particularly mind being wakened wider in the morning by agronomical hands leering in through the window at them from the cabs of very huge tractors.

Our sleeping plan, in terms of the typographical farmhouse profile devised in Chapter 84, was thus:

h+k     a        j

With the unbilled advent of Wringhim, however, how on earth could we possibly cope?

My initial inclination – to whisk him back to Berwick in time for the last train to Glasgow – had been doomed by the snow, and my second-best suggestion (to kit him up with a sleeping bag on the dining table) was apparently not considered amusing. Koo's proposal – that Humbert should spend forty minutes clearing the bunk bedroom (of all the suitcases, lampshades, forty-something-year-old teddy bears, wobbly painting easels and camera tripods, etc, and other white elephants crowding it) then hoover the floor, make up the top bunk and otherwise render it fit for Jennifer – was not received with enthusiasm by me, but it might well have been converted into coercified grumbles and fewer apéritifs for Humbert save for Audrey's unexpected insistence that she wouldn't hear of us (meaning Koo) going to that amount of bother over bedding and that Jennifer could jolly well sleep with her in the guest room, freeing the dump for the housing of Wringhim.

I have to say that struck me as a little mite kinky at the time, but evidently it's quite the norm for liberated mothers and daughters on modest holiday budgets wanting to keep down costs of overnight hotel stops during motoring holidays in Tuscany.

Anyway and without further ado that's how it came about that we went to bed as follows:

h+k    a+j        w

And this brings us to my terrible dream that night.

Though I first dreamt it then it haunts me still, in after-visuals like echo flashes from eight miles high, and I have a feeling it always will. With no image it begins. Only a sensation of being pulled, sucked, spirally drained. As the vertigo mounts so the spin takes shape like bright colours on a gyro top. Rotating clockwise, the wheel must be two metres in diameter.

Maybe a little more.

Strapped across its centre, limbs akimbo, is my body. Like the beautiful gypsy girl in that paste-spangled skimpy dress between whose dark-tighted legs her swarthy man hurls infallible knives.

I, however, am naked.

As my entrapment in panic, derangement and despair increase so does the volume of bangs and whishes, whistles and jeers from the markspersons sniping at me. In queuing lines of two teams my characters stand with their weapons ready to fire. Into gaudy Cowboys and Indians they have been transformed by the malice of Rankles, yet where is he? Heading the Cowboys are Wringhim Knox as Wild Bill Hickok and Paul Chalicer in his Lone Ranger's mask. Supporting them are Janet Rosencrantz, Audrey, Jennifer and Koo as the frontier heroines behind the stockade loading muskets for their menfolk, yanking arrows from bloodless wounds, and blasting the occasional screaming tomahawker in his mid-air leap as the need arises.

Except now they are all shooting me, and my blood is real.

Heading the Indian file beside them are Louis Morel as Hiawatha with Hélène as Little Running Bear beside him. In defiance of my wishes and the needs of the planet she has five or six pre-adolescent children fingering small bows and arrows beside her, a swaddled papoose strapped across her back, and her belly is big with the next. Now for reasons that vie with *The Grapes of Tantalus* to elude me comes Louis XIII of France got up as Arthur Upfield's Aboriginal detective Napoleon Bonaparte. Then Achilles Lefranc as Little Plum and Jean-Baptiste as Tonto, closely followed by Cardinal Richelieu, the Count of Soissons and the Chevalier of Montenero. I think they are guised as Sitting Bull, Geronimo and Cochise but I cannot be sure which is which or at all since these headdressed chiefs are so heavily warpainted and also because I was indoctrinated in my childhood by Hollywood and the English Broadcasting Conspiracy into perceiving the Indians as interchangeable bad guys you could slaughter by the score without ever going to the bother of meeting them face-to-face.

And this now adds to my shame.

I say 'adds to' my shame for despite the fact that my genitals have expanded enormously in response to the centripetal force of the targe-wheel spin still all my efforts to achieve an erection, as the American pulpers put it, to impress them are in vain. So my scrotum swings and flops like two decomposing turnips in a Safebury bag while my penis flails in empty space and flaps like a flood-wet draught-excluder snake against my gasping mouth.

And oh how they jibe and jest and sneer, these creatures of mine, at my pinioned mental torture and physical agony as they bang their bullets and shaft their barbs in relentless grouping at the base of my gonads till at last the pumping wound they enlarge overtakes the elephantiasis of my flaccid phallic futility, my erectile flesh and plasticized scrotal sack fall away and out of the gushing chasm between my legs an abortion is born with no arms and no legs but only a dumpy torso like a Chinese doll made of bloody sponge but with three heads which are the heads of Mumbo Rankles, the Prime Creep and the corpse of the Marquis of Roquefort turned in on one another affecting mutual admiration and respect yet exuding cruel hate as the lips of their straining deceit fail to meet but their coated tongues with no arse to lick intertwine in the middle as pathetically preferable to no sex at all while their limbless bondage squirts out away then tumbles down down down to their nothingness of hell below leaving me in spin to bleed bleed bleed my life away in my somethingmess of hell now and here.

And in this hell I feel then see my characters have ceased to shaft and laugh at me and turn instead to grapple with one another in battle in strife in hunger in sex they assimilate they penetrate they devour until suddenly multilateral agreement is reached that all the outstanding differences between them will be settled by means of all my credit cards. In the Doppler whine of this further betrayal they meltmelt down to a colourless pool of blinding light like the shield of Perseus held the better the Medusa to behead. Yet in this pool the only gorgon to behold is myself alone and in the haemorrhaging of my fecundity now I see that all the drops of blood that squish and seep are dry as sand and now become the cells of my wasting brain pouring forth between my crusted legs away.

And mirror mirror in the void now shows the wheel on which my nailed wrists span from Old Aberdeen to the Wide Western Isles of course is Scotland from above. And every cell of the brain that spurts in bursts then dribbles and drips away below my central belt is a non-renewable treasure of this small sick world surrounding. Carboniferous fuels by the tanker blaze, expiring species by the hundred thousand, rain-forest trees by the million, clean air by the billion lungful, then beauty, integrity, honour, compassion, all good cells spray away to die till only one remains my consciousness of me.

Yet from my instant slithering birth of death in this my nethermost primal nightmare now somehow like self-ejection from a smoking test plane ripe to crash with a moan I pluck me free.

And all around is black and still, and inky silence feigns supreme.

Or so it seems until between its dark plush folds in grateful joy I hear the sweet soft sound of Koo sleeping steady beside me. And the time? By the greenly ghost of the radio alarm I register half past five. Sunday morning in the farmhouse and all is not well, yet all is not all ill is all. Now roars the distant fire of the boiler in the laundry beneath the dump. Now to our bathroom I groggily totter to make much ritual water in the dark and towel off the pints of my dream.

What else?

Who tell?

And the hours till others rouse?

To the kitchen next I voyage, quietly aftertrauma trembly. There to make tea and a little conversation with Captain Claws, whom I congratulate on his colossal continence. His emergency litter continues virgin-spurned, as he prefers to wait for breakfast-making me to shovel him a wide-whiskers highway from the kitchen door to the shrubbery facing.

'Good lad,' I say. 'Keep it up.'

Outside the snow has ceased to fall. The sky is clear and colder now above a sparkling winter wonderland twelve level inches deep. As the tea infuses I platter together thin strips of hot buttered toast and confer with Claws about the vexation of being stuck with Wringhim till tomorrow at least since there's no hope of snowploughs today.

'Just have to make the best of it,' we agree as we usually do.

And as I mount the stairs in postprandial ecstasy still there is a tingle of anticipation athwart my hams. Though Koo will want her straight eight hours plus leisurely lie-in to avoid meeting Wringhim at breakfast – and hence no interruptive tea at six – the same need be less true of Audrey. Always a great one for tea and a nice bit of hot buttered toast in the early hours, why should my buxom paramour of Grantchester have changed? Seriously I tell myself what better opportunity to pin her down on whether Louis XIII of France had other illegitimate children, apart from our Louis Morel, and especially a beautiful daughter? And if so how should story tell this bead to climax more apocalyptic still than the gaunt syphilitic Arthuriana faxed so helpfully from Minneapolis by Paul?

Thus it is upon the handsome historian and her beautiful daughter that Humbert in his conscience preys with this tray of three mugs of steaming Lapsang Souchong tea and a mound of strips of toast.

Knock-knock, he ever-so-quietly knocks.

Nor is he unduly amazed or dismayed when he receives no invite to enter, and nor am I. This is because Audrey was ever a heavy sleeper and as for Jennifer when she visited us in the Vaucluse in 1985 one morning she managed to sleep through an early-morning mason's drill powering through her bedroom wall.

Add in the fact that I happen to know both generations of Macpherson women were so thoroughly plastered when they went to bed that they could hardly get up the stairs and what more justification could I possibly need for turning the door handle to our communal advantage?

Our guest bedroom I surely should explain is sometimes referred to as the Jane Austen room by those visitors versed in Regency. It is spaciously square without being Victorianly high and comfortably houses a wardrobe, chest of drawers, sofa, various book cases, a large desk bearing a computer with a LaserJet on a trolley beside it, and of course a double bed appreciably larger than anything Louis and Hélène might disport upon in seventeenth-century France. Although as practised proprietor I am amply able to reach the bed blindfold, with no stubbing of toes and slopping of tea, I realize now, as my right knee nudges the door, that there is no current call for such skills. This is because of a blue-orange light lowly cast by the booster Calor Gas heater by the bathroom door. The temperature within the room is hotter by some ten degrees than us country folk think healthy, and the atmosphere that greets my nose you could describe as finely poised between muskily exciting and overpoweringly mature. Furthermore I see, as my buttocks retreat to press the hall door shut behind me, that the twelve-watt reading lamp on the right bedside table is on, albeit redly veiled by a pair of some lady's panties. My astonishment at this, however, is eclipsed in a twinkling by outrage greatly greater – as my eyes espy from left to right the duveted sardine forms of Jennifer, Audrey, and:

'Wringhim,' I hiss. 'What the fuck are you doing here?'

'I might ask the same of you, Humbert,' he answers back benignly. There are two pillows behind his head. His cheeks look red in the scarlet light but his eyes seem surprisingly clear behind his obsolete National-Health-frame spectacles. On the table by the lamp beside him is a tumbler of water only faintly engoldened by Glenmorangie. The forearms holding up the crumpled pages over which he peers at me now are pyjama-striped green and cream. 'Well?' he adds encouragingly.

'This is my house, Wringhim,' I assure him distractedly, as I note that Jennifer's left arm and shoulder – which appear, by pinning the duvet to her body, to be all that is preventing her from rolling out of bed – were never more temptingly nude. 'I live here.'

'Yes,' agrees Wringhim. 'But this isn't your bedroom.'

'It isn't your fucking bedroom either, for Christ's sake. We put you in the dump.'

'There's no need for foul language, Humbert,' says Wringhim critically. 'Especially so late in the day.'

'But what are *you* doing *here*?'

Wringhim sniffs thoughtfully. Then he says:

'I sleep better, Humbert, when I'm with my family.'

'What?'

'Yes. It eases my loneliness.'

'I see.'

'There's no reason for you to look so distraught, Humbert.'

'I'm not distraught.'

'And anyway,' says Wringhim reprovingly, 'if you younger novelists spent less time staring at machines, and more time looking at the world—'

'Boozing in McEwan's, you mean?'

'That too,' he nods accommodatingly. 'Then there'd probably be less that you'd miss.'

'I see,' I say forlornly. 'But . . . Jennifer . . . '

'What about her?'

'Well . . . she's . . . '

'Naked?' chuckles Wringhim. 'No, not quite. She is wearing her knickers, you see. So bad luck, Humbert. What's that you've got there?' he inquires with sudden suspicion.

'Tea and toast,' I confess sadly, as I look at it cooling just as fast as any other universe.

'How repulsive,' he grimaces, and reaches for a sip of his lightly gold water.

'But look here,' I say more aggressively.

'Yes, Humbert?'

'You say you sleep better when you're with your family.'

'That's right.'

'But you aren't sleeping.'

'That's right, Humbert. But I have been, a little, and I will be again soon. Meanwhile, as you see, I'm not lonely.' Here he gently fingers the nightie frills on Audrey's shoulder, with a tenderness that might seem touching, to observers less dismal than mine.

'Well,' bravely I attempt to recover, 'what *are* you doing?' I nod at his clutch of creased pages.

'Why, Humbert,' he appears surprised at my question, 'I've been reading your final chapters.'

'What? Why?'

'You said at dinner—'

'You remember dinner, do you?'

'Please, Humbert,' says Wringhim forgivingly. 'Let's be friends before we die, shall we not? And actually, as it happens, I do remember dinner. And you being narked at Audrey for not reading your novel, and not helping you to finish it. Well, now I have read it. And who better to help you than me?' he smiles modestly.

'I see. Well?'

'Well what, Humbert?'

'What do you think? Of it?'

'It isn't actually . . . ' here his brows, nose and lips do battle in a self-warring rictus like Weir of Hermiston imposing less than the death penalty by 'an act of sheer will', 'it's not quite as dire as Paul Chalicer told us.'

'Thank—'

'Rankles'll pan you, of course.'

'See if I give—'

'But much worse than that . . . ' purrs Wringhim, with a hint of savoury mischief.

'How much worse?'

'Duncan Peebles won't like it!'

'He might not execrate all of it,' I object hopefully.

'Possibly,' says Wringhim doubtfully. 'Anyway—'

Now comes an unexpected commotion as Jennifer falls out of bed in a moaning roll. As she struggles upright she bangs her head on a projecting corner of the bookcase adjacent. 'Oh, shit,' she mutters hopelessly. Then in blinking bafflement, like a roe doe with large trembling breasts, she takes in the scene of dialogue between Wringhim and myself. Is it a groan of violate modesty that rends the room as she darts for the loo, or is it her hangover wakening?

The bathroom door bangs shut.

Long moments of glowering ensue between me and him.

Then I remark calmly:

'She isn't wearing her knickers, Wringhim.'

'No.'

Looking round the room I note piled bags and clothes on the sofa. Draped over the screen of the monitor on the desk is Audrey's style of bra. Then it comes to me that the scarlet panties dimming the reading lamp are what Jennifer isn't wearing.

'So you were lying about that,' I accuse him.

A short bar of that ghastly donkey snicker escapes him. Then he says:

'I didn't want to upset you, Humbert. I thought you might drop your tray.'

'I see.'

'Why don't you drink your tea?'

'It's cold.'

'Why don't you make some more?'

'In a minute,' I prevaricate as I hear the flush gush.

'Bloody hell, Uncle Humbert,' complains Jennifer as she reappears from the loo. I had thought she might have swaddled herself in a bath towel, but no. She is proud of her body, and rightly. In fleeting retaliation she flaunts herself, and I am smitten. So purely naked within the reach of a long-armed paw she stands – the most perfect, most beautiful, most adorable vital form in all the known universe, with a bush like the Bermuda Triangle. This reminds me intensely of my long-standing grievance that nobody thinks to agitate when painters pay young women to take their clothes off whereas novelists aren't allowed to. Perhaps if I just—

'Bloody hell,' mutters Jennifer again, as she dives to disappear beneath the duvet once more beside her mother, who protests in a distant-dream whinny.

'Seale, you revolt me,' snarls Wringhim with corrective ferocity.

'What? Why?'

'You've got an erection,' notes Wringhim, peering grimly at the midst of Koo's dressing gown.

'If it weren't for erections, Wringhim,' I defend myself shyly, 'there wouldn't be any novelists.'

'Never mind that,' he counters sternly. 'It sounds like Theory. Getting back to your practice in hand—'

'What about it?'

'It seems to me,' he nods magisterially, 'that you are agonizing too much over the ending. And that's typical of you younger novelists.'

'Younger . . . nov – Wringhim, I'm forty-something years old.'

'That might be old for an athlete,' he says contemptuously, 'or a songwriter. But for a novelist it's still pretty juvenile. And the trouble with you juveniles is you worry too much what wankers think of you. So you spend far too long clicking away on your fancy machines, making tiny changes which really aren't worth the bother.'

'Should one not be perfectionist in one's craft?'

'Absolutely,' says Wringhim, to my considerable surprise. 'But not like that.'

'Like what, then?'

'All this flapping about revision, and trying to get the ending perfect, that's just escapism.'

'Oh? And what from?'

'Fear.'

'Fear of what?'

'Fear of having nothing to write next,' nods Wringhim judicially. 'And that's because you don't spend enough time *in the world*. Live more, you should. Write *more* books, and write *more fluently*. That's how you approach perfection. Like Scott—'

'Or Trollope, I suppose?'

'Fuck Trollope,' growls Wringhim predictably.

'Shakespeare, then? Sorry. Mozart, I mean.'

'Mozart's a good example,' he allows. 'A great body of work, that's the thing. Some of it's cacky, that's inevitable. But at its best it's brilliant. That's the way.'

'I see. Okay. Well, what about my present ending? Got to get that over with haven't I? Before leaping straight into my next string quartet?'

'What had you in mind?' stalls Wringhim cagily.

'It occurred to me, as I made the tea, that I might use some of Paul's fax.'

'No, no, *no*,' says my mentor dismissively.

'Oh? Why not?'

Teasing the greying curls that sprout werewolfishly from his striped pyjama-top V, Wringhim says:

'Paul's a clever boy. He may write a great novel yet.'

'I'm sure Paul—'

'But he'll have to get a lot less clever first,' insists Wringhim.

'Endless boozing in McEwan's, you mean? And hubnubbing with tartan lamebrains.'

'That's all part of it,' he admits. 'Anyway, forget Paul for the moment. You don't need him.'

'Why not?'

'Because your ending is already written.'

'By whom?'

'By you, Humbert.'

'Oh? Where?'

'Here,' says Wringhim. For a few seconds he shuffles the crumpled A4 pages on the duvet beneath his nose. Then he reads from the Chevalier's reconciliation letter to Louis:

'"During my stay, rest assured, we shall converse further upon the foregoing. Meanwhile, discard your woes, I pray you. Do your duty by your wife, and to God. Allow your ever-affectionate father-in-law to hope, I say, that when, soon, he greets you again, he will find his only daughter to be at last expecting his much-longed-for heir, and yours.

'"Begging you never again to doubt the undying constancy of your oldest friend's devotion,

'"BAGNOLS."

'That's quite nice,' sniffs Wringhim. 'Not perfect, but no ending is, or should try to be. You've got the hero and heroine through their wild adventures. At last they are united, have intercourse, and that should be satisfying to readers. It is also not untrue to life. Not always. Also true to life is their dearly wanting what they cannot have. In their case it's children, whereas today it might be not dying of AIDS. They have their consolations, your married Morels – long life, each other, and so on – and that's enough. End of story. Time for another.'

'Just there, though? *BAGNOLS.* No more be said?'

With a weary sigh Wringhim drops my pages to the floor. He removes his spectacles, places them on the bedside table, and takes a sip of goldered water. Looking several years older, but not uncontented, he settles back on his two pillows, his head five inches from Audrey's, and says:

'You may then allow yourself a short dying fall, if you must.'

'Like what?'

'I don't know,' yawns Wringhim. 'Anything you like, so long as it doesn't alienate your readers too much. And so, for example, if I were you, Humbert, I would go easy on those goats. Also, nothing too gory or unpleasant. Not in a dying fall. For a novelist of your peculiar persuasions, Humbert, you see, the readers who stay with you to the end, and mibbe even think of buying your next book too, they are the best friends you'll ever have. You can put them through their paces along the way, if you've the skill, and knock them about quite a bit. But in the dying fall you must never forget that you are the pilot bringing them in to land, and so you must touch down smoothly now, and part on friendly terms.'

'Like women and sexual pleasure, you mean? Or Prospero licking all the audience's arse at the end of *The Tempest*?'

'Really, Humbert,' says Wringhim with a sleepy wee yawn, 'there is no need to be so vulgar, especially so late in the day.'

'You're right,' I confess. 'Must still be a little tired and emotional from all that dinner. I apologize.'

'Don't mention it, Humbert.' As Wringhim's eyelids droop, his head rolls closer to Audrey's.

'Well, would you like some tea, if I make some fresh?'

'No, thank you, Humbert. You make tea . . . for yourself and Koo. We'll wait for breakfast. Thank you.'

'Well, goodnight.'

'Night-night, Humbert,' murmurs Wringhim dreamily. 'Hope the bed . . . bugs . . . '

And you, best friends.

*Salut.*

# Readers' Notes[1]

---

[1] *Notes to Readers' Notes:*

    Readers should please note that this book is not entitled *Steal This Book* and nor (*sic*) is it entitled *Deface This Book*. The four pages following are kindly provided as bulletin-board space for all those exceptionally intelligent, diligent and/or infuriated readers who may wish to constructively and objectively enrich the total reading experience and understanding of subsequent readers by uniquely particularizing the present volume with pertinent annotations, criticisms and sundry reflections in holograph. Any reader who runs out of space on page 767 for further postings of insight and wit is urged in all decency to either buy a fresh copy of the book for hohself or at least to request it from a local public library.

    Personal problems requiring the venting of subjective spleen against the instigators should please not be paraded as Readers' Notes but rather referred privately to the publishers c/o our PO Box address. You may alternatively wish to fax or e-mail, especially if you're cunning enough to winkle out our numbers.

    Finally, readers with strong reviews for which the *Sunday Crimes* is not prepared to cough up cash may wish to publish them for free under this book's Internet Bookshop listing. Visit the Internet Bookshop at:

**www.bookshop.co.uk**